Saving Nickels

written by

TEDDY FOX

Disclaimer:

The views expressed in this publication are those of the author and do not necessarily reflect the official policy or position of the Department of Defense or the U.S. government. The public release clearance of this publication by the Department of Defense does not imply the Department of Defense endorsement or factual accuracy of the material.

Contents

To the Conclave of Charitable Chippies, a Contingent of the Indomitable Dambusters

Introduction

Alright, first off, I'll focus on keeping this 'faster, funnier' — as so many Patch wearers erroneously promise — because there are a *lot* of words ahead in the *actual* book…

     Saving Nickels began as a fun chapter-by-chapter release that I wrote for the Chippies while I stood the worst possible duty known to mankind — Boat SDO — as A) Something to help *me* kill time, and B) Something for the *squadron* to look forward to when I sat the desk — because god knows my tactical fades weren't great, my sole playlist could be called 'millennial on ecstasy,' and my roll 'ems were *constantly* behind timeline (and always ended up being the same clichéd action movies, likely referenced in this novel). In fact, the only true consistency of my watch, aside from getting random writing projects done, was the eventual playing of Doja Cat's 'Juicy' and MGK's 'Bloody Valentine' music videos. I would crank out (low quality) chapters during the 12-to-16-hour duty days (amongst the responsibilities I was *supposed* to be doing), give 'em a way-too-rushed 'once-over' for spelling errors, and print/hand out stapled copies to those who were following the book.

     Yet as I wrote more and more, the book turned from a 'fun SDO thing,' to a 'side project,' to a 'pretty hefty time suck' — and eventually morphed into a full-time *obsession*. I started to realize this book was something I *needed* to finish… then planned on making a copy of it all consolidated… and then finally figured, "What the hell — why not publish it?" After looking back on the countless hours spent writing, musing, and editing — during Shinkansen train rides, hikes across Japan, and sleepless early mornings in the Chippy 4-man — time spent determining the exact way Phase 2 of the Admin Olympics would unfold, how to further emasculate Dr. Suabedissen's identity, which cringey impersonation Nickels would botch next, the utopian setup of CP's Flat Earth Fitness, or where I could throw in yet *another* reference to 28-3… I can't believe I ever considered *not* putting this story out for publication.

     A 2-year project — coincidentally aligned entirely with my tour in the Chippies — it feels *so* damn good getting this book out for the world to critique, judge, and — *hopefully* — enjoy. Yes, it's an aviation-heavy book full of military jargon and industry jokes, and it would be far-fetched of me to imagine the ordinary reader tracking *all* of them. But that's perfectly fine — because this book wasn't written to be an ordinary, cookie-cutter story that everybody would unanimously say, "Oh, yeah, it was decent." No—to quote the great Ronald "Mac" McDonald, portraying the Nightman: "I'm not going for [only] laughs—I'm going for *gasps*." In my career, I've often said that, as a tactical aviator (especially when it comes to behind-the-boat carrier landings), I'm not going to impress anybody, but I'm not going to scare anyone, either. A pretty vanilla pilot—or, as Paddles would say, a 'Fair ball-flyer.'

Well, that sure as hell isn't my aim with this book.

Yes, some people will be appalled at some of the things this book says about naval aviation, life at sea, gym culture, beta nation, videogame nerds, sci-fi fanatics, a certain quarterback, random retired coaches, numerous Hollywood celebrities... and of course, the fucking Cyber Security Awareness Challenge.

But, on that same note, some are going to be *beyond* entertained with the litany of subtle nods, outrageous references, melodramatic scenes, and above all... a damn hearty chunk of inspirational prose enveloped by humor. And to those readers, I am *so* excited for you to get your eyes on this content, and uncover an 'open kimono' 'peek behind the curtain' in the life of carrier-deployed aviators in the tac-air community. Yes, the events in this book are 100% fiction—well, 99% fiction; you can ask WYFMIFM about his cornea damage—but the emotions are 100% *authentic*. The highs, the lows, and everything in between—that is *real*. If you don't believe me? I encourage you to do some social media searching (it's easy to find personalities these days) and ask literally any other pilot or WSO from the fighter community (hell, anybody who's spent time on a carrier, *period*) to see if I'm full of shit—or if I'm speaking truths *about* the shit.

The *Top Gun* movies can feed you the images and the bravado. TOPGUN graduate books and podcasts can walk you through some of the most demanding requirements this job asks of its aviators. Countless documentaries everywhere can show you the churched-up, made-for-TV, 'lipstick on the pig' version of naval aviation.

I will show you the *pig*. And like a five-wet F/A-18 tanker, this job can be one hell of a pig. And yet, as much as we may say we hate it, can't wait to leave it, and rue the day we bought this pig... something keeps us coming back to the joy, suffering, and memories of the steel farm afloat...

And one last note—on the topic of suffering. In *The Subtle Art of Not Giving a Fuck*, Mark Manson believed: "We suffer for the simple reason that suffering is biologically useful. It is nature's preferred agent for inspiring change." Rafael Nadal—part of the GOAT conversation—claimed: "I learned during my career to *love* suffering." Steven Pressfield said that, in writing countless best-selling books, the number one skill that he attributes to his success is "the ability to suffer." You get the picture—suffering is a reality, and embracing it is a catalyst toward accomplishing incredible feats in life. If you want to turn something—a book, a skill, even a physique—from good, to great, to *epic*... the answer is almost always *more suffering*.

Alain de Botton, a British Philosopher, once said, "Of many books, one thinks this could have been truly great — if *only* the author was willing to *suffer more...*"

I've suffered a hell of a lot for this book — and while a final product is *never* going to be perfect, I tried to get it damn close; I hope I suffered enough. Either way, if it puts a smile on your face, inspires a shift in your outlook, or even just helps you kill some time (especially if *you* happen to be an active-duty aviator on SDO), then the pain was worth it.

So, without further ado, I am thrilled to present to you:

Saving Nickels

1

The Deal

Gooooooood evening, Team Noddik! Skipper here, checking in with all you motiva-tors on yet another *beautiful* evening aboard this *fine* vessel, before I head to the seaside gym for spin class, cool off with a water-conserving 30-second shower, and then head to my rack to call it a night, eager to wake up and get back to work again tomorrow! Geeze, can you believe we get *paid* to do this?!

So, a few announcements for you guys—first off, on the topic of cardio: you know what type of collaborative NEAT would make this magnificent warship *shine* like the best dang lethal piece of machinery in the universe? That's right, folks, I'm talking about *cleaning stations* – tomorrow, 0730. And I'm gonna need *full* participation from *every* set of hands on this ship—yes, that means you, *too*, air wing! Oh, I know those flights keep you busy, but you can't *possibly* be too exhausted to throw in a little elbow grease and wax those knee knockers for the Gipper! After all—this ship has a reputation to uphold as the *cleanest* in the galaxy! We've got a big game being talked by our compatriots who believe they can outshine us—and gosh darn it, I'm certainly *not* ok with that—and *you* shouldn't be, either!

By the way, speaking of things I am *not* ok with: warfighters, remember—self-serve laundry is a *privilege*, *not* an entitlement. If I keep finding uniform items in those washers, it's going to be banned for *everyone*—and that includes me! I'm certainly not afraid to walk around this ship in unwashed PT gear—which, might I remind you, are the *only* articles allowed to be cleaned in the self-serve stations! No sheets, no uniforms, no undershirts, et cetera—guys, we have a *wonderful* group of sailors *happy* to wash those through ship's laundry! So, let's not bend the rules for ourselves and ruin it for everyone, ok? The next person I catch washing their own pillowcase is coming to *my* office to explain exactly why *they* believe they warrant an exception to policy!

A couple more things: *Trash*! Listen—we have a sorting and disposing system that's worked for decades—and let me remind you that *nowhere* in the *flawless* method does it involve—I can't believe I'm saying this—*people throwing trash overboard*! Folks, this is unacceptable. Yesterday, there were reports of not one, not two, but *three* bags of coffee grounds, soda cans, and ZYN containers being tossed off the ship's fantail! One sailor even reported seeing a *suitcase* abandoned afloat! This is *completely unacceptable*! Not only does this put the carrier in danger of missing flight ops—but geeze louise, do you have *any* idea what this does to the environment? We're out here to make the atmosphere a better place, *not* pollute it with our presence! So cut that out *now*, Team Noddik.

And lastly, to the meat of the matter—General Quarters this morning. Whooo boy… not sure what was going on, but the energy level was *flatlining*. I can't make this clear enough—'Condition: Zebra' means 'Condition: Zebra,' and 'flash gear at all times' means 'flash gear at *all times*'—*no* exceptions! If we can't follow these simple procedures in a controlled and simulated environment, then how can we *possibly* expect to execute when the stakes are real, the pressure's high, and the consequences for failing are *fatal*?! And for goodness' sake, air wing, please—stay out of the p-ways and show some courtesy to the training we're conducting. This ship is *your* home, too, and I certainly hope *you'd* want the ship's company prepared to 'Protect this Bow,' just as you do in your little DCA games. So, with that all being said, expect another GQ next week—and guys? Let's bring the *heat* this time! If we don't? Well, I'm certainly not against keeping my happy butt on this ship for an extra day, week, or even *month* until we nail it! No room for laziness—we need to work as a team and get it done *one* way: and that's the *right* way! Remember that we are *the* most lethal warfighters in the galaxy, and we need to take *pride* in that identity! If you find yourself lacking any of that pride? Come by my office, and we can talk about why.

Alright, that's all I have for tonight—continue to make it matter out there, team, and I'll see *you* out on the deck plates! Captain out."

Captain Sam Rowland set his microphone down and took a huge swig of his bourbon, exhausted from another night of spouting off asinine, mind-numbing platitudes of bullshit. He dropped his head into his hands and rustled his hair, lamenting his doomed reality, adamant that no amount of money was worth letting this career continue consuming his soul—which was a moot point, since he so willingly and ignorantly sold it long ago for blood money. Waiting for the alcohol to hit and help him endure today's iteration of the Groundhog Day from hell, Sam shook his head and groaned. "This job fucking sucks…"

He looked to his left and caught a glimpse of himself in the mirror. To call his eyes 'tired' would be an immense upgrade. His pigment was eggshell white, as if he hadn't seen the sun in years—which he *hadn't*. The wrinkles on his skin made him look ten years more experienced. Stress lines were everywhere on his face—bar above his mouth; he hadn't smiled in what felt like months. This wasn't what he wanted; he couldn't have imagined *this* was what would've happened...

He looked around his room at the various awards and accolades on the walls: 'Pilot of the Year.' 'Instructor of the Year.' 'Naval Athleticism Prowess.' 'CVW-5 Softball League MVP.' 'Nobel Peace Prize.' But one towered in importance above the rest: the 'Good Dude Award,' presented by the VFA-195 Dambusters, addressed to LT Sam "Nickels" Rowland—when he went by such a name—awarded for being a relentless worker, an inspirational leader, and—most of all—a great friend.

Next to the Good Dude Award, Sam's eye caught one of the few things that still could bring him to smile: a polaroid picture of him and his friends from the Dambusters—the 'Chippies.' It was taken during a sunset on The Porch—a scenic lookout area on the catwalk of a United States aircraft carrier, just twenty feet below the flight deck, where an F/A-18E was parked. Sam instantly recognized the paint job from side number 400—a Chippy jet. This picture—and the memories it encompassed—was the last time he remembered being truly happy in life. A time *before* the changes that came when he accepted 'The Deal,' as it was infamously known throughout the fighter community; a deal that took place just a few months after the photo was taken. *I wouldn't have ever agreed to it if I'd known that* this *would become my new reality…* He thought back to life before The Deal, just as he had whenever he was drinking—which was multiple times a day, as of late. *What I'd give to get a chance to do it all over…*

Sam went to his clothes drawer, digging into his undershirt compartment. *Still some grey ones in here... haven't needed these in ages...* He took out the photo album he kept hidden in the depths beneath his old Chippy shirts—it was filled with pictures of him and his old squadronmates; old coworkers... old *friends*.

The first page he turned to was a picture of LT Andrew "CP" Preul, picking up an astounding amount of weight—in a flight suit. It was the ship's deadlifting competition; Sam vividly remembered CP returning home from a combat flight, immediately doffing his gear and sprinting down to the hangar bay in an effort to get his chance at the trophy. "I'm doing it, Nickels," he said as he glided down the ladderwells with no regard for safety, "I'm *going for it* tonight." The on-duty Air Wing Safety Duty Officer tried to stop him, saying it was too dangerous without a warm-up set—but the pilot kept piling every plate he could find onto the bar. The ship's Fit Boss attempted to restrain Andrew, insisting that there was no time left, and they'd already handed out the grand prize of 24 hours special liberty; but Preul shook him off, too. And when a random, morbidly obese senior chief in the hangar bay chastised him for disrespecting his uniform by exerting effort in it? CP simply scoffed, got into position, chalked up his hands, crouched down to a dead stop—and *lifted*. As a result, the ship had its new champion, and a record *never* to be broken...

CP... he'd been through rough times after undergoing a very messy divorce from his days of being married to Dua Lipa. *Had a whole album written about him, too, once the split with Taylor Swift went public.* Sam had almost forgotten about CP's brief stint with Ana de Armas—before a quick breakup, when he then found his way into the life of his current wife—Doja Cat. *Damn, that guy knows how to bounce back...*

Sam hadn't spoken to CP since The Deal, but from what he'd heard? Preul had opened his own incredibly successful gym franchise: Flat Earth Fitness. The gyms were known for having one or two—if *any*—cardio machines, while being rife with squat racks, barbells, and dumbbells—equipment that *actually* contributed to an impressive physique. He even kept a 'Khaki Hour' type policy—known as 'Baddie Hour'—where, every day between 1:00 and 2:00 pm, the gym was reserved for members who were below specific body fat percentages, with a few requisite strength-level minimums. It was harsh. It was restrictive. It was exclusionary—but *damn*, was it effective. People found new levels of motivation in efforts to become part of Baddie Hour, basking in the glory of their own vanity. *The amount of smokeshows in that place must be insane...*

I wonder if he's happy? Shit... far-removed from this?! *No doubt that guy's living the life, surrounded by motivated and beautiful people every single day...*

Sam turned the page and found a picture of him and a tall man—LCDR Tom "FISTY" Flynn— high-fiving on the flight deck, celebrating in what was an impeccably-timed snapshot, surrounded by deck crews cheering, champagne popping, and fireworks exploding. *FISTY...* Sam didn't need a picture to recapture one of the most incredible days of his naval career...

He and FISTY had been sent out on a simple PGM day flight to practice some good-deal simulated JDAM and GBU-12 employments. He remembered the gigantic ordeal and spool-fest that occurred because both of their jets were mistakenly left uploaded with bullets. The Air Boss would've downed them both in a heartbeat—*if* FISTY hadn't taken charge and briefed the entire Air-to-Surface Training Rule document and firebreak procedure over the tower's button 1 radio frequency—from *memory*. It left the entire ship's Pri-Fly space in *awe*. FISTY and Sam became the only two jets to launch, after all the catapults subsequently went down because of some GQ drill the ship was running in the middle of the day. And as it turned out? It was *quite* fortunate those rounds remained in the jet... Because one minute, Sidious 11 and 12 were simulated 'IN ZONE'—and the next? They were fielding a transmission to intercept a hot, hostile, and *very* volatile enemy aircraft. The aircraft, shouting foreign obscenities over GUARD, was pointed directly at the ship with a mach number that left no time for caution. From 20 nautical miles, FISTY recognized the adversary airplane—and, more importantly, recce'd the AS-131 KILLSHIP Air-to-Surface missile on its pylon. He reminded Sam of the maximum distance launch window, or Rmax, of the KILLSHIP — and after some quick mental math, 'Sidious flight' realized they had one pass at taking down this In-Credible Threat — before that bomb was in range... and the ship was in deep shit.

Sam remembered FISTY's words so clearly: "Recommend you shoot this guy; shoot this guy, now." Sam armed up, recalling all the snapshot drill training from years' past, preparing for his one shot, one opportunity. He gained a tally at 2nm and attempted to steel himself. His arms hadn't shaken this much since his first forms flight in the T6 trainer plane, where some P8 guy taught him the basics of flying in Blue Angel-parade position. He steadied his eyes on the target. 1 mile. Closer, closer... the adversary rolled inverted. Sam pushed the stick to move his gun pipper, and followed with the appropriate lead distance. Every variable seemingly solved... he pulled the trigger. *Snap.* The adversary started departing from controlled flight... yet was still tracking toward the ship. Before the threat nose-dived down to his death, the KILLSHIP separated from the aircraft, accelerating toward the carrier, as Sam gasped in horror. *He'd reached the confines of Rmax... the ship was going to be destroyed...*

"FISTY! He got the missile off!" Sam transmitted, panicked. "It's gonna hit Mom!"

"Tally one! Stand by... almost there... *aaaand...* trigger down... snap!"

Lined up behind Sam, FISTY took a snapshot gunshot of his own — and the missile exploded, disintegrating into a million pieces of defeated employment. FISTY — *already* a living legend — had un-fucking-fathomably shot down an A/S missile.

"FISTY!" Sam shouted with euphoria, "You did it!"

"No, no, my young Padawan," he responded calmly, "*We* did it. *We* fucking did it."

FISTY... *Admiral* Flynn, now... Sam hadn't heard from him, either, since The Deal. As far as he knew, FISTY was still developing new tactics at 'The Crystal Palace' — his favorite name for his beloved TOPGUN headquarters. The former Chippy Training O ended up being the ultimate mentor to Sam — they studied the TOPGUN manual most days from dawn until dusk, as FISTY attempted to groom Sam into a lethal tactician. And when they weren't at work? There was no time off. At completely random and inappropriate venues, FISTY would quiz Sam about timelines, tactical boldface, and rote-memorized ROTs. Whether they were in the urinals together at the O-Club, enjoying beers at Porky's in Guam, or even Sam's own wedding — Flynn *had* to make sure Sam was ready at *all* times. At the latter, FISTY even talked Sam into knocking out an impromptu Defensive Basic Fighter Maneuvering briefing lab before the aisle walk-down. *That was the most 'In the Zone' I've ever been in a BFM brief... Not a single 'um.' No 'zipples.' The models' distance depiction perfectly to scale the entire time...*

thank god *I brought them with me on the big day.* Any moment was fair game for training—well, unless FISTY's own inspirational hero was playing football on a Sunday, which was essentially the *only* time Flynn would take a brief intermission from tactics...

Since The Deal, though? Sam *never* had a chance to study tactics the way he did when training under FISTY's tutelage. And honestly, he didn't really need to, with the skill these new pilots were engineered with. Sam wasn't even *close* to their level of tactical prowess. They were… well… built *differently*—giving Sam the ability to be metaphorically and tactically fat, dumb, and happy—which was part of the reason FISTY was so disappointed in the career move. *I get why he was upset*—FISTY *was never a believer in the thought of throttling back the tactical effort... but come on*—*he would've done the same thing if he'd had* this *option! This* fleet was full of tactical masterminds—pilots with virtually every algorithm and Rule of Thumb engrained into their DNA. Part of Sam wondered if even *FISTY* would be to take these guys down in BFM. *Hah… I can't imagine he'd be shooting down* their *missiles*—*but he'd at least put up pretty good fight...* He took another drink of bourbon, shook his head, and continued through the album.

The next picture was taken during the recovery from the BFM derby finals, where the freshly-minted champion Sam led the runner-up jet back for the shit hot break—a near-supersonic arrival at the carrier. He knew exactly who the pilot in the second jet was, based on the pinpoint-perfect parade position flown by his -2: LT Kyle "Low T" Camilli. Low T was the Chippy's most talented tactical pilot, the Navy's ideal junior officer, and Sam's best friend. In fact, he was the *only* person Rowland had attempted to contact since The Deal.

Of course, he never heard back from Low T; *nobody* had. Camilli had been missing from existence for roughly four years—not too long after The Deal that started so much friction in the Dambusters—with no sign of life anywhere. Sam hadn't been privy to the entire incident report, but from what he'd found while lurking on naval aviation Reddits, Low T launched on a routine DCA one night... and never returned. Nothing was found nor heard—no plane, no ELT, no distress signals or calls on GUARD. Whatever happened, it was a mystery… but Sam *did* have one lingering suspicion of Low T's existence, in the form of an anonymous email sent to him about a year ago. He kept it saved, and occasionally pulled it up to analyze the one line of text: "Had good tone today, and nearly squeezed the trigger—but I'm not taking you down without a fight first, Rowland." Sam would go back and forth—it seemed too far-fetched... it could've been *anyone* from his old fleet who found him in the global email database, or maybe Dr. Suabedissen playing some stupid prank. But the shit-talking nature of the email, combined with its mysterious anonymity *and* the fact that it was on the anniversary of Low T's disappearance… it all seemed too coincidental. Unfortunately, it was sent from one of those annoying 'DO NOT REPLY' domains, sending Sam a non-delivery report when he attempted to reply—leaving his inbox closer to max storage capacity, his heart rife with anxiety, and Kyle's status still enshrouded in mystery...

Which only added to his frustration, because for Sam, the most regretful thing about striking The Deal was abandoning his friendship with Low T. They'd gone through all of flight school together, served as "combat" wingmen for one another in the Seventh Fleet AOR, and formed a lifelong brotherhood in their collective suffering through many deployments in the Chippies. Unlike the rest, Low T actually showed sympathy toward Sam after The Deal—he wasn't overly upset, and promised that work politics wouldn't affect their friendship. And yet, Camilli's sudden faded assessment left plenty of uncertainty about his mental state... *He couldn't have just run away — I refuse to believe it. Low T wouldn't have done that; he had everything going for him. I wonder if he ever got accepted into TOPGUN...*

CAPT Rowland continued turning pages, flipping through various memory-laden pictures of his old squadron compadres—The Lorax, who got out and launched a successful rap career before taking a hiatus from society; presumably now just surfing, biking, and glailing. *I wonder if he grew his dreads back out...* There was >SADCLAM<, who Sam couldn't *imagine* left the Navy—not with his unmatched foundation of effort and dedication to the job—yet was mysteriously absent from every O-4 selection board on PERS' placement website. *The man had intensity like that world had never seen. Did he lose himself along the way? There's no way he's done pushing himself...* WYFMIFM turned into one of the biggest business tycoons of all time, with various successful ventures from Shmarkers, to directing the award-winning short horror film "FRANKENWEZ," and he even opened his own party yacht company: 'Fat Chucky's Cruise Ships.' *Hah... I wonder if any of the celebrities WYFMIFM invited ever showed up to his boat...* Sam turned the page and continued on, where he saw a picture of his old buddy JABA, who now owned and managed the most successful amusement park in history—and that wasn't just some exaggerated FITREP 'fact.' *Hah... looks like he was smart to get out and decline the O-4 promotion, after all...*

And as he admired the pictures of his past, he couldn't help but feel sentimental, knowing that those days were gone forever. He looked at his right shoulder—the place where a certain patch once lived. A patch that had encapsulated everything he and his former friends were about. A patch that carried so many memories in Sam's mind, pride in his soul, and reverence in his heart: *That Patch...*

Instead of brandishing his most treasured memento from his Chippy days, his right shoulder now wore a blank slate of Velcro—just as it had *every* day for the past five years. When he left the United States Navy, Sam took That Patch off and left it behind. He couldn't bear to wear it anymore—and even deeper down, knew he didn't *deserve* to wear it. He'd never don That Patch again unless he somehow *earned* the right—a damn near inconceivable fate, given the current state of his life...

Abandoning this symbol was supposed to signify a new start—that's what Sam told himself, anyway. He insisted that this was the only way to fully eradicate those memories of past... the only way he'd be able to replace them with new ones from the greener grass he vowed to find... the only way he'd be able to move on from being 'Nickels'...

"'For life' means 'for *life*,' Nickels!" Low T told Sam when he left, pointing to That Patch, insisting 'Nickels' would always exist; would always be one of them. Captain Rowland shook his head solemnly, knowing that such a belief was a complete delusion. *I'm not that guy anymore...* he told himself as he grabbed his whisky and drank another gulp, by now far immune to the 101-proof sting. *But that's alright...*

Sam looked outside his window—one of the few windows on the entire ship. Outside, he saw nothing but the black abyss of space. Sure, there were stars here and there, a random cruiser ship far in the distance, and his own 'friendly' Noddik tanker jets holding overhead—but not a true *friend* in sight. Sam took another chug of his bottle. *How in the hell did this happen... what has my life become?* He put the photo album down and walked up to the window. He looked outside and saw a small mass of green and blue—the planet he used to call 'home.' The place he'd do anything to return to. Sometimes, he thought about pulling a Low T—just completely disappearing... Docking on some random station, an asteroid, anything—*anywhere* to get away from the life he created by signing a deal with the devil. *Could I do it? Could I just leave?* He *did* have a flight in three hours, after all... *Maybe tonight could be the night...*

"THIS IS A DRILL, THIS IS A DRILL!" a man's voice called from the 1MC, followed by ten seconds of obnoxious bell ringing.

Sam's shoulders slumped as he sighed. "Oh my fucking *god*..." He downed the last few gulps of the bottle.

The loudspeaker continued, "MAN OVERBOARD, MAN OVERBOARD, ROOM 03-145-2-L. AWAY THE SNOOPIE TEAM."

Sam smacked his forehead. "No... no... *no*! That's *not* the correct noise to play! And this drill wasn't supposed to happen until after my workout! *And* it can't *possibly* take place in a specific room! And why the hell would you need to call the SNOOPIE team for this?! *And...*" he stopped himself, grabbed his head, and screamed to himself. "*Dude*... these guys fucking *suck*!"

Sam had been hired to teach 'these guys' something far beyond combat tactical execution. He knew their tactics were already rock solid—they were AI bots, after all; an entire fleet of AI pilots, maintainers, and ship's company robots. They were programmed to have flawless execution of every tactic known to man—better than that, in fact. They had an inherent server updating their processing systems faster than 'man' could create tactics. Every enemy WEZ and friendly LAR employment envelope was programmed into each and every worker. Anyone from the new guy pilot, to CAG

OPSO, to arresting gear worker could flawlessly name any threat range of any defense system from any country. These guys weren't competitors of the United States, however. These robots belonged to their own planet, far outside the galaxy of Sam's home globe: this fleet belonged to the Noddik Empire. And while they hadn't been interested in challenging planet Earth—not *yet*, anyway—Sam had become increasingly suspicious as the years went by...

Which made him feel more than a bit anxious. He couldn't help but feel *guilty*, abandoning his country for a potential adversary. Sure, he hadn't divulged any information beyond the 'Unclassified' level... but he also hadn't *needed* to—they already knew everything. Rather, it was a *different* area they were lacking in: Admin. Sam had signed his $500 million deal was to teach these bots the basics of Administrative procedures in managing a ship. They sought Sam out, knowing his boat operations knowledge was airtight—and picked him as the spearhead to help them learn simple things like how to conduct laundry procedures, how to react in the event of a robot falling overboard into space, or to how to properly keep the vessel the cleanest in the galaxy. Sam was breaking no military laws when he left the United States to help these droids, who'd insisted they were simply trying to become safely self-sufficient in the extra-terrestrial atmosphere. It was aviation's version of the LIV Tour; complete with a stunning secession. And with that secession, just as it did in the world of golf, came floods of disappointment and dismay directed toward Sam.

It's not like there was anything wrong with doing this. I didn't teach them anything secret... didn't violate any securities... and come on — 500 mil?! I had to do it! A trip to space... a chance to see outside the known world... it was every pilot's dream! Yet despite his internal attempts to convince himself... there was no doubt he felt a lingering sting of culpability. *Was I wrong? Is it my fault that these bots are becoming a larger, looming threat to the world back home? Did I abandon the closest friends in my life in order to strategize their eventual downfall?*

Shit... listen to me — I'm drunk — and now that my spin session is fucking canceled, I guess I'll get ready for this flight...

"TIME, PLUS 3. THE FOLLOWING PERSONNEL REPORT TO THE DECK HOUSE IN HANGAR BAY 3: FROM: SHIP'S COMPANY, CAPTAIN ROWLAND."

"*No!*" Sam was irate. *You don't start calling names yet! Jesus Christ... the uselessness of these bots... this place seriously makes the* US Navy *look competent...*

Before Sam had a chance to call the mustering office, his J-dial started ringing. He checked the caller ID. *CAG?* "Hello?" Rowland answered as he picked up the old-school corded phone.

"Hello, sir," the voice emanated with artificially-programmed vocals. "The final preparations have been made on our large force strike, and we are ready to undergo briefing."

What? Sam hadn't heard anything about this. "What are you talking about?"

"The strike against the United States of America on planet Earth, sir," the high-ranking robot responded.

Sam's stomach sunk as he responded to the Commander of the Air Group, "... Come to my office, now."

"Heading that way, sir," the bot obliged with zero emotion.

Shit! Sam threw his album back in his drawer and tossed his whisky bottle away in the 'sinkables' garbage bag—not that these robots had any idea how to sort trash, anyway. *Shit!* The day Sam had been fearing for years was finally here, and far too soon: The Noddik Empire was challenging the United States Navy to an Administrative Olympics.

2

The Admin King

When he first stepped foot on the Noddik Intergalactic Raid/Defense spaceship, Captain Rowland couldn't believe his eyes nor ears. The AI had a literal red carpet laid out for him, with some badass Noddik national anthem blaring through the parade-rest bots' external speakers.

As for the ship? It was spotless — not a spec of grease, dirt, or weird bodily fluid of any sort. It was remarkably clean to the point where Sam could imagine eating a ship quesadilla off the floor. I wonder what kind of foods these guys eat, anyway, he pondered. The walls were decorated with beautiful original art — all made from Microsoft Paint software, but brilliantly so. There were reincarnations of famous Earth-created paintings, yet Adobe photoshopped and airbrushed to make them look better. Damn, Sam thought, looking at an AI-enhanced, Kardashian-esque Da Vinci remake, now that Mona Lisa actually looks hot!

The flooring was akin to a corporate office carpet base, given that there was no need for skin-ripping non-skid; the station had the ability to electromagnetically stop and hold any aircraft to the deck when needed. The ship deck level transiting was done via an escalator and elevator system instead of dangerous ladderwells. The doors were automatic — programmed to open for the appropriate security clearance registered on the badge carried. They even installed human bathrooms for Sam's arrival, which made Million Air FBOs look ghetto. There were golden toilets with massage capabilities, three different flavors of mouthwash, Japanese-style bidets, and even a towel bot!

And the random sounds Sam had been used to on his boat of old? Nonexistent. He'd been expecting the typical ship noises — random ambient exhaust blowing, engines turning, chains dragging, alarms blaring... but there was nothing. Nothing, aside from background atmospherical Hans Zimmer music, playing up its space environment.

Bots were smiling, laughing with each other (a choppy, Kawhi Leonard-esque laughter), and generally seemed to be having a good time. It was bizarre... bizarre, but beautiful. The bots

16

themselves looked incredibly lifelike. Sure, their speech and mannerisms were rigid, but the AI appearance itself was uncanny to humans. He even saw one who was clearly designed to look like Megan Fox. Damn, *she's* hot, too… he remarked to himself.

As he reached the end of the red carpet entry, a short-haired, medium-height bot with a charismatic smile saluted him and shook his hand. *"Good afternoon, Captain Rowland. Welcome to the NIRD Jesse Katsopolis! We are very excited to have you aboard as our skipper. I am CAG; I will be fulfilling CAG duties just like in your Earthborn tactical chain of command. If you need anything, please preface the statement with 'Command;' if you have any questions, please preface with 'Interrogative,' and I or anyone else will gladly assist."*

Sam returned his smile. Seems like a nice guy — err… bot, I guess? But… 'Jesse Katsopolis?' What the hell? *"A pleasure to meet you, CAG. Do you have an actual name?"*

"Unable to compute. Captain Rowland, if you have a quest —"

"Sorry," he said, shaking his head and chuckling, *"Interrogative: Is there a name I can call you?"*

"Ah, yes, sir! Charlie Alpha Golf, or 'CAG,' is my programmed name."

Sam laughed as if it was a joke — before realizing the blank-expressioned bot was serious. *"Oh, ok… well, nice to meet you, CAG! You can call me Sam! And Katsopolis, huh? Interesting title… Interrogative: How was this ship named?"*

The CAG-bot beamed and said, *"Sam, we are big fans of you earthlings and your prowess with administrative recreational things like music, exercise, and hairstyling! We found no better way to pay homage to your planet than by naming our most powerful ship after one of the most harmonically talented, physically fit, well-coiffed humans in the history of your fine land!"*

As CAG explained the strange origins of their ship's name, Sam couldn't help but shake his head, continuing his chuckling. Well… it *is* a nice thought, I suppose… This is great. I can work with this. I will turn these guys into administrative *champions*. *"Fantastic, CAG. That is a great honor to a great man back on Earth. I look forward to training the crew of the Katsopolis into the most efficient ship this galaxy has ever seen!"*

From the moment he'd landed his F/A-18E in the airlock — via the ship's automatic landing system that descended the jet from a hover — Sam was quickly losing any sense of guilt, regret, or reconsideration. Watching jets take off via the rise-and-fly sequence, he wondered if he'd miss the catapult shots from his former carrier; wondered if he'd miss flying anything other than a 90-degree glideslope for landing; wondered if he'd miss his friends… It's going to be ok, he insisted. I'm on to bigger and better things… This is going to be revolutionary, *he* continued in his self-pep talk.

Sam took a long look around and soaked it all in.

This is fucking legit!

~

Captain Rowland throttled up. The engines rumbled to sound-deafening levels. He wiped out his controls with authority... *aft, forward, left, right, left rudder, right rudder... free and clear.* He clicked into full afterburner—unfathomably *louder*—and scanned his instruments—*Good engines, nozzles, HYDs, FCS...* the ditties he learned from the RAG still fresh in his mind all these years later. With everything checking green and a full GO status, he gave his launching shooter bot a crisp salute to signify 'ready for launch.' With everything tensed and his brain mentally ready, he braced himself, took a deep breath... and looked at his New York Times Friday crossword once again, focusing as hard as he could in his slightly buzzed state, asking himself internally: *What the hell is a 7-letter word to describe Benedict Arnold?*

He took a sip of his 5-hour Energy—which he snuck a bit of vodka into, not wanting to go through withdrawals mid-flight—and sat irate. *How does* anyone *finish these Friday crosswords?! These are not even* close *to reasonable...* He'd contemplated writing a letter to the ombudsman to get this 'Will Shortz' troll canned from crossword duties, but he remembered when CP had done that long ago and gotten the Chippies in a bit of hot water with the NY Times... *Hah. In hindsight, I suppose he could've done without including the obscenities and verbal attacks on Shortz' family. Oh, CP... that man wasn't afraid to throw out 4-letter words at a 5-letter word when he saw one...*

Amidst this internal monologue, the NIRD Katsopolis had launched Sam in the ultra-uneventful, benign takeoff sequence he'd grown accustomed to. The technology was so advanced and smooth that the automatic hover-and-fly-outbound evolution was less exhilarating than driving a Prius. Sam *detested* these weak takeoffs, and being drunk was the only way he could bear them these days. *Oh, sure, it'll be like Arnold Schwarzenegger in* True Lies, *powering up the Harrier,* he'd once thought. He even initially thought about ripping his sleeves off and letting his shirt flow in the wind to complete the vibe—but this takeoff was more Arnold Schwarzenegger in 'Junior,' as the only thing close to 'flowing' was the estrogen throughout Sam's body. As the jet accelerated on the exit path to 600 kts, the process was so transparent to the man in the box that it felt like he was still pounding liquor in his at-space-cabin; only now, Rowland was downing his homemade four loco at the speed of sound.

As he transited outbound to drill ozone holes for a 1.5-hour cycle, he internally replayed what'd just transpired in his stateroom, where CAG arrived as ordered, but did not come alone. Joining them for the meeting was the space station scientist—and fellow human—Special Operations Engineer Dr. Karl Suabedissen.

Over the years after The Deal, Sam started to realize how infuriatingly inadequate the ship was, compared to the USS Ship he'd spent time on in his days as a US Navy pilot. Eventually, he admitted that he needed a coding expert to help write new features into these bots' software, such as being able to talk like normal humans and not necessitate prefacing conversations with commands. Sam also needed code rewritten for the NIRD Katsopolis itself, after realizing how ill-suited the ship was for carrying out the most basic administrative processes. As a result, he did some research on the top scientists from Earth and came across Dr. Suabedissen—a Rutgers and MIT grad who had been living in the greater New York area, currently working on the latest virtual reality Dungeons and Dragons game.

Back when they met, Dr. Suabedissen had raved on and on about how amped he was for this pet project, "Because it was going to incorporate an optional Power Sword you could buy and level up, as well as downloadable trading cards that you could collect and use to unlock the seven holy stones that would enable you to gain access to the magical kingdom of Kalmann, where the evil troll Rutowski hides in the Forest of Illusion, and…"

Sam quickly grew weary of this story and the doctor's frenzied excitement. *Dude… this guy is* such *a dweeb… And where the hell is that name from? Swah-beh-diss-en? That's really annoying to read, say, and write...* But he politely nodded his head and said, "Oh, very nice, doctor. That sounds… cool." Back in negotiations, Rowland worked with the Noddik Empire to get a $50 million per year deal inked for Dr. Suabedissen, who took quite a bit of convincing, as well as contractually-bound assurances that he'd get to bring his VR rig and have at least 20 mandatory gaming hours a week. Sam really didn't care and obliged with an eye roll. He remembers the slightly disappointed look that Dr. Suabedissen had as he pushed his thick-rimmed glasses up with his finger and said, "Well… I hate to leave the fate of Rubelia and Princess Kelia in the hands of my underling programmers… but this is the opportunity of a lifetime! What the hell—I'm in, Mr. Rowland!"

"Excellent! You won't regret it, doctor!"

"Heh, just promise you won't pay me in Orc Silver; that currency went offline like three patches ago!" He couldn't keep himself from snorting while laughing at his own joke.

Sam took a long look and forced a chuckle out, saying, "Hah, ok, you got it, doctor…" *Jesus Christ, dude…*

And here they were, many years later, the code-genius doctor explaining to Sam, alongside CAG, the evidence behind the current AI software being up to snuff enough to take on the US Navy in the Admin Olympics showdown.

Throughout the entire conversation, Sam's stomach was churning with the nausea of anxiety. Maybe it was because he had a flight to do… or perhaps it was that that he was drunk? But no; those two always went hand-in-hand... Maybe it was because he'd been having a sentimental moment thinking about the past? *No, that's crazy—I don't get affected by that stuff… they're good memories and old friends, that's all.*

Nothing more to it… Sometimes, Sam tried to pretend he was just as robotic as his sailors — but it was a hard role to play when he was wasted.

Back in the moment, he continued flying around space to burn the time — a time that he genuinely enjoyed — despite doing absolutely nothing — because he could escape the miseries he felt at the Katsopolis. Every flight was a solid hour and a half where he could forget about the friends he left behind, forget about the mistakes he made, and forget that he sold it all for a bigger paycheck and 'greener' pastures. Sometimes, he even put his hands on the controls and pretended he was still flying a United States-variant F/A-18, without the technology to automatically take off, land, troubleshoot, fly tactics… Sometimes, he pretended he was still a *pilot* — and not an order-dishing, button-mashing, paper-pushing alcoholic. Sam often dreamed about the days of doing traditional meld mech… he longed to feel the vitamin G of flying an out… he yearned to get one last crank in…

… No! He'd then tell himself. *I don't need that stuff anymore… everything here is excellent!* Just for fun, Sam decided to practice some conduct by hitting the 'AIR-TO-AIR TACTICS' button. It was quite intuitive — you just typed in the SPINS, and everything was done for you, perfectly and automatically, as you got to sit down with your hands on your lap and take notes on the A/A fight. *This is fun,* he muttered internally as he subconsciously reached for his 5-hour Vodka.

All the alcohol in the galaxy couldn't help him take his mind off the Large Administrative Assault Fight, or LAAF, that CAG and Dr. Suabedissen had briefed him on. The doctor forecasted that official challenge would be declared in a little under 72 hours, after final testing and mission planning for next 48. *The doctor has no clue what he's getting himself into…* Unfortunately, Sam hadn't gotten a chance to chat after the meeting — human-to-human — before walking for his flight. *He's going to be considered a traitor to his home planet, and his friends will disown him — I need to talk to him…*

Granted, Sam wasn't worried about his *own* reputation back in America; he still believed he did nothing wrong, and was simply ostracized for being the *first* brave pioneer to expand his horizons and plant his flag in a new territory. *Who cares what anyone back home thinks, anyway?! I couldn't give less of a shit about my 'legacy' back there.* But the doctor… he seemed like a good person at heart; he didn't deserve to face the same wrath. Sam couldn't let the Noddiks' domination of the United States ruin everything for this poor guy…

But… was it really that? Deep down, Sam knew something was uneasy in his heart… something that he couldn't bring himself to admit out loud, nor even in his head…

"Rowland; Noddik 2, up your TAC. Looks like you're working hard out there. All those circles — that's *really* gonna help green up our T&R…"

Sam rolled his eyes and audibly groaned, recognizing the voice. *Oh great... just who I wanted to hear from... Juice...* Sam sighed and responded, "What do you want, Bobby..."

LT Robert John "Juice" Ward—or Bobby—was, in fact, another one of those 'pioneers' who departed the US Navy after Sam started the trend. However, due to reasons Sam felt entirely unjustified, the naval aviation reaction to Juice was night and day compared to him. Perhaps it was because he served a full 20-year career and would soon retire anyway? Perhaps it was because he was a hero amongst Navy JOPA for refusing to take his O-4 promotion, instead just rounding out his career as a Lieutenant? Perhaps it was simply because he wasn't the *first* to secede? *He wouldn't have had the balls like I did...* Whatever the reason, Sam couldn't put his finger on it.

But one thing was certain—and Sam *hated* to admit it: Juice was God's gift to naval aviation admin. When he joined the Noddik Empire as another human on the boat—roughly one year after Sam—it was astounding how proficient he was. His check-ins? Standard, every single time. His groundspeed on taxiways? *Exactly* the same pace as a man can trot. His switch positioning? Pristine; his position lights would come on *precisely* 30 minutes prior to sunset. He didn't believe in just "HAIL-R", "FTR-D", or "SAPDART"; he had entire *essays* of checklist acronyms he'd adhere to religiously on every flight. And the other infuriating thing about Juice: he *knew* how good he was at admin, and wasn't afraid to flex that prowess on Sam—be it the ready room, marshal, or even the middle of a flight...

"You haven't FENCE'd in yet by chance, have you?" Juice sneered.

Sam groaned again and responded, "No, Bobby, I haven't." *God, I hate this guy.*

"Well then," he responded smugly, "How about a quick hack?"

"Bobby, come on... not now..."

His tone changed to mock confusion as he said, "Oh, I'm sorry, I thought you were interested in perfecting the administrative phase of flight? I guess you must want to waste your time with tactics instead?"

"Ugh, shut up, Juice..." Sam grumbled, "I'm not even current, and I didn't brief this..."

Juice quickly fired back with, "Well then, allow me—Underrun procedure for the F/A-18 is: Lower, level, idle, boards."

Dammit. Sam was now legally current again.

Juice continued, "Hard altitudes, limited maneuvering, full crossunder, 29.92."

Left without an escape option, Sam sighed and rogered up, "Hard altitudes, limited maneuvering, full crossunder, 29.92."

"I'm at your right 3 o'clock, 1 mile," Ward talked him on to set up the fight.

"Visual," Sam begrudgingly called.

Juice began the countdown: "3... 2... 1... Fight's on; break left!"

Sam responded, "Fights on; breaking left!" and immediately pulled a hard turn left—before slowing to 250 kts and easing to a gentle 30-degree angle of bank.

Ok, dipshit, let's see if you can handle a little AUP... 'Admin Under Pressure' was a concept Sam constantly stressed at the NIRD Katsopolis, after years of building the foundational skill at VFA-195. *Anyone could handle simple administrative procedures on an emergency-free, clear-and-a-million, good-deal day—but only the truest of admin champions reached that next level when* shit went down *in AUP scenarios.* Admittedly, Sam hadn't felt the thrill of AUP, or tested his fortitude with *any* confidence-building stakes, since settling into The Deal. *That's alright... those days are behind me—life is so much better with-out adversity.*

As he reached steady parameters in his turn, Sam set the autopilot functions and turned to watch his notional adversary appear in the distance over his left shoulder. *Right on bearing, in control... but expeditiously approaching. Of* course. *As* always... ugh...

This wasn't the first time Juice and Sam had gone mano-a-mano in the art of admin. Far from it, in fact. Back in their US careers, the two had been a couple of the top pilots in the fleet, in nearly every aspect of the field—but it wasn't always that way. When Juice showed up to the Chippies as a new guy, Captain Rowland—a Lieutenant at the time—made sure to show Juice that being a Level 1-complete RAG-finisher meant *nothing* in terms of fleet-quality standards, *especially* when it came to administrative phases of flight. Sam would routinely call him out during AOMs to ask him simple things like, "Hey, new guy, if a jet were traveling at 143 kts indicated, flying slightly fast at 7.7 units, and attempted to land on a carrier going 14 kts, how many degrees would the TEFs be digging down at that moment in time, and what would his speed be if he gave one-quarter inch of aft stick deflection?"; and subsequently berate Juice when his answer was off by a couple degrees and knots. He'd challenge Juice to taxi-line drag races, disqualifying the FNG any time throttles went above 75%—or smoking him when Juice was too conservative. Sam even once talked Juice into filing a DRAFT report with ATC *and* giving a PTAPTP position update—in a *radar* environment. The audio recording was legendary amongst the Dambusters, enshrined for eternity on their Chippernet QNAP.

Simply put, Rowland hazed Bobby worse than any other new guy out there. Sam loved it. The squadron tolerated it. Juice *loathed* it...

But the misery shaped Juice—shaped him into a fucking administrative stallion. Juice was motivated like none other before him, dedicating his life to mastering this craft. IFR Supplement? Memorized. AP/1B? Juice's database of CHUM'd charts was a safer, more thorough reference. NATOPS? Juice had written entire IC updates by *himself.* And his in-flight admin?

"Holy shit…" Sam said under his breath. Juice's 'Breakup and Rendezvous' was going phenomenally. There was no stagnation, no deviation, and no sign of internal trepidation. Sam *wished* he could say he felt uncomfortable with the closure, but it was completely professional. He was tempted to fly off parameters a bit to complicate Juice's range, angles, and closure problem — but B&R Duels were gentleman's battles, and that would not be fair. As Juice came in close, at a tight-but-safe distance, he executed a smooth crossunder… and by the time Sam looked over his other shoulder to regain sight, Juice was propped up in an immaculate VMC turn away parade position.

Shit… that was good… Sam sighed and said, "Noddik 1, terminate…"

Juice roger'd up, "Noddik 2, terminate," and followed with, "God, I can't *wait* to see how you fuck this one away…" he executed a crossunder back to the left and called, "Noddik 2, set."

"Noddik 1, set," Sam echoed, too focused to respond to Juice's taunts.

"Breaking left!" Juice sped up and broke to the left, setting up Sam's chance to match — or beat — his B&R. *Shit, how in the hell am I supposed to do better than* that?!

Sam waited for the appropriate duration, then turned to get on bearing line and commence the join. As he picked up initial closure on Juice, he gave himself a pep talk: *Ok, Sam, this is easy. AUP is where you* thrive, *and you've been a join-up pro since you got an above-MIF on your first forms flight. Remember your ABCs, and control your airspeed. You've got this…* It started out fine enough as Sam approached the 0.4 distance marker on the A/A TACAN. To this point, he had been angle-for-angle matching Juice's prowess. But as he came in closer, beads of sweat streaming down his head, he noticed the jet at his canopy bow oscillating slightly around the horizon. *What?! No way! Is that me? Or him?* He kept it coming… but it started getting worse. Sam continued making micro-adjustments, smaller and quicker as he got closer. 0.4… 0.3… 0.2… and finally, it was stationary again. *Thank god — I wonder if he noticed…*

"Rowland, watch your closure!"

Huh?! Sam checked his airspeed — 280. *FUCK!* It had fallen entirely out of his scan while fixing his altitude. He tried whipping back the throttles and deploying the speed brake — but it was too late…

"*Underrun!*" Juice's voice called out, with more than a hint of excitement.

Dammit! Sam punched the nose down as his jet slid back, extending out to the perch position; his jet full of excess energy, and his heart full of shame.

"Knock it off, knock it off; Noddik 2, knock it off."

Ugh… "Noddik 1, knock it off…" The slurs from the vodka were present, Sam was sure. He didn't care. *Dammit! Was he moving his jet? How did my scan break down so badly?*

"Great hack — really impressive stuff out there. See you back on deck, Captain." With that, Juice flashed burner in front of him and peeled off.

Sam didn't respond to him. *What a fucking douche canoe. Shit… shit!* Sam was furious at being embarrassed by the man whom he'd once dominated in the admin arena. And it wasn't just this time… Juice had attempted to surpass him even back at the Chippies. In truth, Sam had been relieved to leave the US Navy because it meant escaping the hungry aviator breathing down his neck for the top admin spot. But when Juice followed suit a year later? The hunt was back on—and it didn't take too long before Juice's presence was known, Noddik-wide. His desire—combined with Sam's regression as a result of time-consuming Captain duties—led to LT Ward becoming the clear-cut top admin dog of the air wing, to the point where he was known amongst the Noddik fleet as "The Admin King." His christened nickname was certainly not without warrant, though—and that drove Sam craziest of all.

It's not my fault, he continually tried to tell himself. *I've got other tasks to worry about: Green sheets… Sailor of the Day announcements… ensuring the troops make 'Jesse' shine every morning…* He tried to validate these excuses to himself—but deep down, Sam knew something was missing. This wasn't the journey he'd imagined for himself…

Sam shook his head, cracked open a spare beer he'd brought in his flight bag, and started heading home for recovery.

Captain Rowland emerged from his F/A-18, stumbling out of the canopy and down the ladder, blowing right past the Plane Captain bot without saluting or shaking hands. *I need to get some food and then get to sleep… I feel terrible…*

He stopped by the wardroom on the way back, where plenty of AI bots were enjoying an artificial midrats meal. They were programmed to pretend to eat things, but really were just using binary, jerky motions to bring a fork to their mouths with no food, periodically cut the low-quality processed meat on their plate, and pretend to drink the warm chocolate milk in their glasses. They were also coded to discuss typical 'human' things, like, "Say, did you see the sports score from last night? The New England Patriots defeated the Atlanta Falcons 37-31!" or "Wow, the weather looks great today! A scattered layer at 10 thousand, and winds out of 240 magnetic for 14 knots!" It was not always accurate… Sam once heard them say, "I was watching a YouTube last night; dang, *Big Bang Theory* is so clever and objectively funny!" Tonight, Sam stepped in on two bot DH's discussing, "Isn't it unpredictable how much the economy has varied?" "Yes, the market will surely soon be changing again!"

He rolled his eyes and grabbed the human food that the ship had out tonight: 'Quesadillas,' as the bots called them—yet it was really just two slices of stale white bread with cottage cheese in between. *Fuck this shit,* Sam thought with frustration, instead just grabbing a bottle of canola oil from the cabinet, as he sat at a table alone to enjoy his poison.

As he sulked—buzzed and hungry—downing his oil and perusing the stock newsletter prepared by the bots, he heard a voice call out next to him, "Skipper, mind if I join you?"

Dr. Suabedissen, holding a tray with his 'quesadilla' and Capri Sun, waited patiently for Sam, who simply grunted. The doctor was wearing his usual uniform of a white lab coat with thick, black-rimmed glasses.

As the doctor took a seat, Sam stared at the boring ship-produced article, which discussed some anniversary of some random event he didn't give a shit about, as he continued to saturate his body with toxins. After roughly a five-minute silence, the canola oil penetrating his bloodlines, he asked Dr. Suabedissen, "Doctor... what are we doing? What are we trying to prove by taking on the United States?"

Suabedissen put down his juice box and said, "Sir... isn't this what it's all been about? Isn't this why you brought me aboard? In order to prove that we've become the most efficient and powerful fleet in the galaxy, we need to show that we've become a better administrative boat operation than the USS Ship. Captain, I've run my algorithm over and over—we have the capabilities to do it! This should be one of the most exciting times in your life—I haven't been this invigorated since the release of the Marshes of Magnar Expansion Pack for D&D Online! You know, the one where you unlock the Lightning Bolt seraph and morph it with the Hammer of Justice in order to defeat the Dream World guardian Arlix and save the Priestess Esmeranda—"

"Karl, enough!" Sam cut him off. He shook his head. "I just... I don't think this is a great idea." He looked up at the nerd and asked, "Aren't you worried about your reputation? Worried about what your friends will think? About being labeled a traitor, and your legacy back home?

Suabedissen took an inquisitive look at Sam, pushed his glasses up, and said, "Captain... this *is* the place where I care about my reputation. Living with AI? *These* are my friends now. Traitor?! I'll be a *hero*—we *all* will be! Captain... this *is* my home now!" The doctor looked down at his feet and quietly said, "I almost hesitate to ask, but... sir... are you *confident* in this operation? Are you sure you're not just... well... nervous about your capacity to lead the Noddiks to victory over your old comrades? Should *you* really be leading this exercise, Captain? I sense... I sense something is going on; a disturbance within you..."

His blood boiling from being questioned—and from the government-promoted trans fats in his bottle of genetically modified rapeseed cultivars—Sam jumped up and grabbed the beanpole doctor by the collar and yelled, "How fucking *dare* you, doctor?! Do you know what I've done to turn this place around?! Do you know how much work I've put into this? Do you know what I've sacrificed in terms of family, friends, and *life* to be able to live on this station and serve the Noddik Empire?! And you think I'm not *confident* in my abilities to take down my former air wing?! Stay out of my business, you pathetic little man." He released Suabedissen's collar, downed the rest of his oil, and started walking out of the wardroom. He turned around and finished with, "And for the record? I am *completely* fine with leading this LAAF, and I don't need you psychoanalyzing me every step of the way!"

As Sam turned back, the doctor called out, "Hey, Captain! The algorithm — the only thing that went wrong in statistical testing? It was the simulations with *you* as the flight lead. The probability of administrative advantage, or Paa, was 32% more likely with *Juice* in the lead jet. Is *that* what you're unsure about?" he asked, with an attempt at passive-aggressive hostility.

Sam's fists tightened, but he refused to acknowledge the doctor as he continued out. He returned to his room, cracked open one more beer for a nightcap, and — too weary to get into bed — laid down on the floor — the *non-skid* floor, a ship-wide installation he was regrettably forced to arrange, with the carpeted flooring causing bots to explode from static charge buildup. He looked around his room… much of the art on the walls was gone due to the ship's cease-and-desist orders from artists and museums around the galaxy. The only Microsoft Paint art that remained were shitty Noddik originals, which were all vandalized by disgruntled bot sailors who needed to be patched and updated to be happy again — a task that nobody had any time for, given the state of the ship's infrastructure. It was filthy. Janky. Shit broken, left and right. Every escalator had been broken for years and was now just regular stairs, albeit in more limited numbers due to the presence of elevators at most corners — elevators that were *also* broken, and now just used as storage rooms for dollies, empty tri-walls, and robotic hookups. Sam tried to ignore the noises of flight deck foghorns, the ringing tests of the ship's alarm system from every deckhouse across the vessel, and the incessant 0300 hammer banging by the most motivated construction bot on the galaxy's peskiest nail. The epic Hans Zimmer soundtrack music? It was no longer present, as the ship had not re-hacked nor paid its Spotify account in ages.

Sam took a long look around and soaked it all in.

This is fucking whack...

As Captain Rowland struggled to finally fall asleep, the last thoughts in his brain were ones that had agonized his soul for far too long: Dr. Suabedissen was right — Sam *was* nervous about this LAAF. He did *not* think this attack would go well, and was *terrified* at what that would mean for his self-worth. Thinking of the United States Navy thriving in his absence, and how pointless everything would feel if he couldn't achieve this one victory... it made him physically *ill*.

And yet, he was equally uneasy at the thought of going head-to-head with the fleet he abandoned... and *winning*. He had already scorched his reputation and legacy enough back home — to add *this* to his list of treacherous crimes against society? He would forever be known as not just a traitor... but an admin terrorist. He wouldn't just be hated... he'd be *vilified*; etched as a global nemesis in history books for eternity.

It was a winless situation, a nightmare. Rowland groaned in agony as he laid on the floor, waiting for the inebriation to shut down his brain, restless over the *other* concern weighing on him: Juice.

Sam had money, possessed rank, and held perceived authoritative power. But every man knows deep in his heart that such traits are trivial. No; what truly mattered was the *respect* of one's community — and as he'd heard since day one in flight school, there was no better way to earn that in naval aviation than *solid admin procedures*. And while he may not be the administrative aviator he used to be... Sam needed to prove he was still *good enough*.

If Juice thinks he can take my *crown? Then he's gonna find out who the fuck Sam Rowland truly is...* The Noddik Captain was damn determined to show this world — this *galaxy* — that there could only be one "Admin King" — and it sure as hell wasn't Bobby Ward.

3

BADASS

*T*o the Lords of the LA, the Kings of the Carrier, the Gods of Glideslope, and the flat-out coolest dudes you will ever meet – to the LSOs!" Captain Rowland shouted, his charged glass of champagne raised in the air.

"The LSOs!" the bots echoed in perfect synchronization.

Standing behind his podium, Captain Rowland began clapping emphatically as the entire air wing in the hangar bay cheered uproariously for the four robots on the stage. The robots – programmed slightly differently than the rest of the AI bots – sure knew how to work a crowd, as they raised their fists in triumph and clamored for more. These four… they were more human than the rest. Not as rigid, dialogue more advanced, and with actual style in how they dressed. They appeared, for lack of a better word, cooler than the rest of the bots. The rad look began with their shit-hot accessories: each wore a pair of oversized aviator sunglasses, a backward flat-brimmed New Era Katsopolis-emblem hat, and a gold chain with a diamond-plated '_OK_' hanging from the bottom. They wore loose, baggy jeans, and each had on a matching team NFL jersey of some retro player, which was a touch that Sam figured would help them pay homage to the athletic nature of LSOs. Today's team theme was the New York Jets – fitting, given the aviation milestone celebration at hand. And to finish the look, Rowland ensured they were each ordered multiple different pairs of Air Jordans to coordinate with their diverse outfits. All of this was implemented flawlessly, thanks to the algorithm written by none other than Dr. Suabedissen.

Sam couldn't help but smile. Another stroke of pure genius in his administrative revolution of the NIRD Katsopolis. When he first arrived? Sure, aircraft were landing just fine – the automatic landing system of the space station worked exceedingly well. But it was just too… vanilla. It was so boring. Admin can and should be fun, he believed. And with these changes, landing would become cool again. Taking a page from his roots in the US Navy, Sam worked with Dr. Suabedissen to develop and code a Landing Signal Officer program for a select few of the bots in this space station – and thus, created a standard for flashy administrative excellence. It was guaranteed to become a morale-booster, and give people a fun, relevant distraction from the trivial parts of carrier aviation.

Dr. Suabedissen approached Sam. "Skipper, sir – congratulations! A year of Padroids on the Katsopolis – and zero recovery mishaps! Your program has been a breakthrough like none other!"

Sam grinned. "My program?! Doctor, your code is the one to thank for all this! Incredible work, you goddamn genius!"

Growing bashful, Suabedissen couldn't help but beam and say, "Ah, sir, it was nothing! It was no tougher than coding the Calamity Clan in the D&D Quest for the Ferngully expansion pack! You know, the one where you fight the troll family under the Bridge of Boron, and then you take the raft down to the Aquatic City of Ambience, where the villager reveals himself as the Wizard of Chaos – "

"Ok, ok, calm down, doctor," Sam said with a chuckle, "But really – fantastic work, Karl."

Suabedissen smiled uncontrollably, breathing heavily, and awkwardly raised his hand for a high five.

Sam, unsure of what exactly was happening, gave a sympathetic hand up and made light contact, saying, "Ok, see you later..." and walked away to escape the conversation. Man, that guy is weird, he thought as he approached the men of the hour – the four LSOs. "Padroids, incredible work, gents! You've kept us safer than I could've ever imagined during AUP situations! And hats off to you, especially, CAG Padroids – you've led a team of some pretty certified badass dudes."

"You fucking KNOW it, Cap!" the head LSO responded enthusiastically. "We didn't just keep you safe, bro – we kept you cool!"

Sam chuckled. He didn't care that the young officer didn't show the proper respect to the rank of 'Captain' or that he called him "bro" – they'd intentionally programmed them this way. The air wing needed some fun, some spice, some swag. "Haha. Well, I sure do feel cool every time I land with you at the pickle, NEODD SWEVEN!"

NEODD SWEVEN, the head LSO, was the most intricately developed of the Paddles Androids, or 'Padroids.' His commands to a landing aircraft would override any of the other threes' commentary. His code was the most complex; the most dope formulas written into his wiring. The other Padroids were good, but NEODD was the gold standard of _BADASS_. Everybody else aspired to be him – and he'd be the first to let you know it.

In what Sam considered yet another innovative move to bring presence to administrative importance, he and Dr. Suabedissen named the four Padroids after important admin acronyms: there was NEODD SWEVEN, of course – the CAG Padroids – whose programmed wisdom made him the obvious choice for overall safety of flight inputs. His right-hand man was TTTTTT, for Time-Turn-Time-Transition-Twist-Talk, known as "T6" for short. His job was transcribing passes to the pilots in a form their inferior AI could comprehend. The technical specialist of the group was IROK, who was written to be very confident in his abilities – almost overconfident. As a result, he could give tips to pilot AIs for how he would've flown that pass, and what they could do better. Lastly, there was <MCSALAD>, who unfortunately had a bit of a programming defect... he rarely added extraneous inputs to the landings, preferred not to spout off random gouge techniques, and didn't give patronizing fist bumps to pilots when they were given less-than-perfect grades. All he did was carry the portable Padroids speaker for their entrance fanfare, and occasionally mimicked the others' motions and reactions. Dr. Suabedissen had been working diligently to fix this specimen, but it seemed to be futile. In fact, even now, as Sam watched the four Padroids celebrating – IROK doing the worm, T6 giving the 'raise the roof' motion, and NEODD SWEVEN beckoning everyone to "Make some noise!" – <MCSALAD> was resigned to simply smiling and clapping. He just seemed to be cut from a different cloth than the rest.

Sam approached <MCSALAD> and clasped his shoulder, saying, "Hey <MCSALAD>, congrats, bud – can you believe it's been a year already? You guys have done a great job making this air wing pretty damn righteous, and I think you should all be proud of yourselves."

<MCSALAD>, in his Zach Wilson Jets jersey, looked at Captain Rowland emotion-lessly behind the lens of his aviators and responded, "Thanks, sir. That means a lot." But before Sam could continue the conversation, the LSO walked away, doffing his backward "NIRD" cap and retiring to his recharge station for the evening.

Sam shook his head. The doctor really needs to fix that guy... He looked back at the other three Padroids, who were having a blast – NEODD SWEVEN was crowd surfing, while IROK and T6 started a mosh pit as a remix of 'Levels' by Avicii – with random quotes from some Supreme Court Justice – reverberated in the background.

Now, these guys – these guys know how it's done! These guys know how to be administratively boss! He grinned as he praised himself internally: What a sick addition to the fleet... these guys fucking rock!

~

"Knock, knock! Wake up, bitch! Padroids in the hizzzzz-house!"

Captain Rowland came to with a jolt, woken by the combination of the obnox-iously loud knocking and the blaring airhorn that starts in Drake's 'Forever' collabora-tion with Kanye, Lil Wayne, and Eminem—today's apparent 'walk-in music.' Each day, the Padroids picked a song to be played as they entered ready rooms to read passes. Sam could hear the lyrics starting—which, upon further review, he decided not to internally monologue about to keep himself out of hot water with copyright issues.

Ugh... these guys are such tools... how long was I passed out? He looked at his watch... it's 0930? Jesus. I feel like shit... I need another drink, and quickly...

"Open up, big guy! We know you're in there!"

NEODD SWEVEN's artificial-but-humanistic voice exacerbated Sam's pounding headache. "Hang on a minute, god!" He picked himself up off the non-skid and stumbled over to the door. As he opened it, the speaker held by <MCSALAD> boomed even louder in his ears, and Drake's verse kicked off.

Outside the door was NEODD SWEVEN, sporting a Matt Cassell New England Patriots jersey, along with a shit-eating grin as he sneered at Sam's state and asked, "Long night, Captain?" The rest of the Padroids started snickering in concert.

Damn… I probably look like shit… The entire quartet had Pats jerseys on, albeit with some strange players—T6 had on Lawrence Maroney, IROK donning a Reggie Wayne jersey, and <MCSALAD> was wearing the namesake of Stephen Gostkowski. *What the hell is going on with these random players? None of these guys were even good on the Pats! Except for Gostkowski… but the kicker? What the fuck?! Suabedissen, you idiot—you know absolutely nothing about sports!* The three crony Padroids were parading behind NEODD SWEVEN, with T6 holding their mystical blue Padroids passbook. Rowland shrugged and lied, "I wasn't sleeping… but yes, I've been busy all evening and morning with… uhh… Skipper stuff." He glanced at his empty desktop... then turned back. "And, of course, you guys know that I *love* when you stop by to interrupt me," he said sarcastically. "So, go ahead—read me my pass."

IROK appeared stunned. "Woah! No clapping? Where's the love, bro?" He looked to his other Padroids, then suggested, "Guys, maybe we should re-convene about this grade…"

Sam rolled his eyes and gave a little golf clap, and with zero enthusiasm monotoned, "Padroids, woo-hoo," as Kanye's lyrics were mid-verse.

"That's more like it!" T6 said with a grin. "Alrighty… El Capitan, we had you in side 401 for one hover descent." He looked up at Sam and said, "Starting off, we have a 'Cha-ching' for having your gloves on *and* visor down at the start."

IROK shook his head in disappointment.

"A little too much eye contact in the middle…" his tone raised as he emphasized, "*too* dim of lights with a 'Turn it up' call…" He paused and looked around at the other Padroids, before turning back to Sam and finishing with, "… and *underlined* looking-totally-uncool as you got out of the jet; for the Tight 2."

Sam was floored. "… Are you *kidding* me? You guys are Tight-ing me out? That's not even *close* to what I saw, Padroids. That pass was a 'Sick' at worst! You guys *cannot* be serious…"

In the process of revamping the Padroids system for the Noddik fleet, Sam had always felt that his homeplanet LSOs were a little too negative. As a result, he changed the grading system to—in order from best to worst—'Badass,' 'Sick,' and 'Tight.' There was also the rare but unfortunate reality of a cut pass, labeled a 'Neat'—reserved for those who did something so utterly uncool that it was detrimental to one's reputation. Throughout the years, the Noddik Fleet had FNAEB'd more than a couple of aviators for doing something egregiously dorky, like coming in with no lights, tripping down the ladder upon jet departure, or just flat-out sounding like way too much of a dweeb on the ball call—a ball that was a fixed light on the center source position, essentially there for decoration, since the jet literally descended straight down onto the LA. And, of course, there was the '_OK_' pass, or a 'Fucking Gnar,' which required something excessively cool be done to earn it. These were ultra-rare, however—for anyone *other* than the four Padroids, who were automatically awarded that grade on every single pass, giving them all 5.0-line periods without fail.

IROK raised his hands defensively, "Woah, broseph, calm down. You're not in serious trouble or anything—a Tight is technically still a cool landing, just with some pretty grossly uncool deviations. And yo, what's rule number 7? *Padroids are always right*! So, back the fuck off and take your grade like a man."

Sam felt his body temperature rising as he stared at the quartet. He and Karl had also given the fleet new 'Rules to Live By':

1. Nobody is cooler than Padroids.
2. Call the ball like a champion.
3. PPE is *not* cool.
4. No prolonged eye contact with Padroids; you are not at their level.
5. Try to look cool.
6. Don't try *too* hard, because that is *not* cool.
7. Padroids are always right.
8. Leave the jet the way you got in: as an alpha male.
9. Safety first*, fly a center ball, and don't get low.
10. Amendment to Rule 9: Don't worry about safety so much that you appear like a beta.

IROK continued, "Hey man, so here's what I would've done: First off, you don't need gloves on, *ever*. It makes it look like you're, like, worried about your hands or something—like you're *scared* in there, almost. We can see that in your eyes—well, we *should've* been able to, but your visor was down at first. Not cool. Speaking of which, once you raised it? *Dude…* do *not* spend more than *half a second* looking at us! Remember—that eye contact is established *purely* so that we know you see us—and subsequently, for you to back down by looking away, indicating that you recognize that *we* are the alphas. If you look at us for too long, it makes us uncomfortable on the platform, giving the impression that you don't realize who the top dogs are around here, ok?"

He patronizingly nodded and kept going with, "And dude, the lights! I *know* sometimes you guys think it's a contest to see who can be the darkest and most tactical fighter, hiding in the shadows like some kind of caped crusader or whatever—but trust me, darkness is *not* cool. You know what *is* cool? A fucking *rave*, bro! Padroids want a light show out there—so have those things turned *alllll* the way up, even if it affects your night vision. Trust me dude, it looks *sick* when a jet comes in and has the LA looking like EDC Katsopolis. Think of it this way: what's a better date with a girl—some kind of bullshit dimly lit intimate bar where you guys talk and get to know each other? Or a fist-pumping club where you nearly get a *seizure* from all the light stimulation, and you can just crush drinks and speak with body language before you start a fight with her beta-ass boyfriend?!"

Growing further irate, Sam remained silent—although it took every ounce of his remaining patience to do so.

"Exactly, bro," IROK affirmed. "Now, finally… that descent from the jet? Woof. It looked like you were drunk—which, granted, *would* have been cool. But instead, you just sort of seemed unathletic and weak—it was *not* a good look. Kind of a tweener, but we talked in the LSO shack and decided to give you the Tight. That was *seriously* dorky, man. Any chick sees that? She doesn't think, 'Badass fighter pilot alpha male'—she thinks, 'Get this beta another anchor.' But hey—you can take these lessons on board, work hard to correct these mistakes—"

"But not *too* hard," T6 chimed in.

IROK nodded in agreement. "Yup, that would definitely come across as insecure. Just remember that looking cool at the end is hands-down the most important part of the flight, so please give us your *full* effort and focus since we're doing that same for you, and I'm sure you'll look a lot better next time, ok, Cap?" IROK held out his hand for a fist bump, while Lil Wayne's voice now resonated in the background.

Captain Rowland continued to glare at the Padroids, infuriated. His mind was ready to explode. Debating whether or not to raise his fist and consummate the fist bump submission of inferiority, he finally lifted his hand—but instead of a fist, put his palm up. "Guys…" he paused for a few seconds. "What in the *fuck* are you talking about. Seriously. What the *fuck*. Let me see the pass," he demanded, pointing to the fabled LSO book. "Let me see it right now."

Shocked and appalled, IROK looked over at T6, who looked at CAG Padroids. NEODD SWEVEN reluctantly nodded his head, and T6 handed the book to Sam. The open page, next to the name 'Rowland,' had a straight vertical line on it—depicting the pass' glideslope—and the Padroids' notes that were previously read to him.

Sam pointed to the pass illustration. "Ok, this is *exactly* what I'm talking about, you fucking idiots." He was done being quiet. "This is a *straight… fucking… line*! There are *zero* deviations! It's a 90-degree glideslope! What in the fuck are you guys getting on my case about? The ball on the lens *does not move*! This is *pointless!*" Sam closed his eyes and rubbed his temples in frustration, then threw his arms up and continued ranting. "This is insanity! You guys do *nothing* to help our air wing! It's an automatic fucking landing! How in the hell can you *seriously* think you're making a difference?! Please, NEODD SWEVEN," he now offered his arms in mock appeal, "Please—tell my me rate of descent was too fast; tell me my pass was borderline unsafe; tell me I nearly *killed* myself out there—but *don't* fucking lecture me about how it wasn't 'cool' enough!" He looked over at T6. "A 'Tight 2?!' Do you even know what the '2' is in reference to?"

T6, taken aback, looked around at his other Padroids. Before he had a chance to take a guess, NEODD SWEVEN snatched the book back and suspiciously accused, "Dude, I'm starting to get the feeling that you see us as a joke..."

Rowland opened his arms further in exaggeration and, with wide eyes, sarcastically said, "No shit!"

NEODD SWEVEN continued, "I don't think you fully appreciate how much cooler we've made this air wing—and no offense, Cap, but you're starting to get a reputation as one of the bottom ball-flyers. I don't know what's up with you lately, but you need to check yourself, broseph. Maybe we should assign you a chalk talk with someone who knows how to fly like a stud. A real alpha male, like—"

"*Eh-hem,*" came a sound from outside Rowland's door. The five of them looked, and in walked LT Bobby "Juice" Ward.

NEODD SWEVEN lit up. "Ahhh, Juice-man!"

Looking at Sam, IROK declared, "Now *this* guy," pointing to Juice, "knows how to fly *Badass* passes! Speaking of which... I assume you're here to have yours read?"

Juice nodded while smirking at Sam and said, "Affirm, and I certainly hope it's not as embarrassing as the one we just heard."

NEODD SWEVEN snickered, handed the LSO book to T6, and cued, "Hit it, brotha."

T6 glanced at the open page, then looked back up at Ward and said, "Ok, Juicy-Juice, we had you in side 403, for one." Looking back down, he continued with the pass. "We had you... a little extended eye contact... underlined *full bright* light show for Padroids with the taxi light flash—"

"Nice!" IROK chimed in the background.

"And a jump descent from the canopy with a *little* stutter step on touchdown..." T6 looked up the Juice and smiled, "For the Badass 3!"

"Yeaaaaaahhhh!" the Padroids all cheered in unison.

IROK went with his part now, explaining, "Dude, fucking *nice* pass; looked great coming in, nothing uncool at all. *Awesome* lights out there!" He tilted his neck and winced his eyes a bit, "*Yeah*, the eye contact, we're gonna hit you on that—but nothing egregious! Just watch that. And to be fair, you're *way* closer to our level than anyone else in this air wing—so if anyone can pull it off, it's you. Great job, and welcome back, bro."

The Padroids fist bumped Juice, who then turned to look at Captain Rowland, as Eminem's verse played.

Still livid from the entire exchange, Sam marched up to Ward. He got right in his face and, as restrained and calmly as he could, stated, "I bet you think you're pretty fucking cool, don't you?"

Their faces a mere three inches apart, Juice responded, "I *know* I'm fucking cool, kemosabe." The four Padroids watched the two men's stare-off.

Sam's jaw clenched as he narrowed his eyes and said, "You know, you wouldn't have had the *guts* to come here if I didn't lead the way."

Juice's eyes matching in narrowness, he remarked, "Oh, really? What—you think you're some kind of brave, revolutionary hero for being the first to quit?!'"

His eyelids even slimmer, Sam jabbed with, "Leaving my home planet—and the comforts of the *known*—to take a path toward something bigger and bolder? Yeah, I think I'd call myself a trailblazer."

His eyes practically closed, Juice retorted, "Trailblazer?" After a perfectly timed pause, his lip curled up, and he landed the punch line *perfectly:* "I hardly even *know* her!"

The Padroids started bursting out laughing, unable to contain themselves after Juice's joke.

Even Sam was a bit shaken by the flawless comedic timing, his eyes now wide open in shock. *Fuck… that was good… even his administrative joke-telling is top-notch.* Sam couldn't bear to let him get the only laugh, though, as he thought quickly and spit out, "Yeah… well… great joke..." He paused for *way* too long—looking around in an attempt to build anticipation—before overdramatically yelling, "*…NOT!*"

The room was silent.

"Oh, Sam…" IROK cringed, his voice full of dismay. The Padroids and Juice glanced at each other, disgusted, and <MCSALAD> even covered his eyes.

Shit…

Juice shook his head. "Sam… the last time I heard a 'Not' joke, I laughed so hard I fell off my non-HOL 25X F/A-18C…"

The Padroids were cracking up; T6 even wiped artificial tears from his eyes.

Refusing to go down quietly, Sam doubled down on his joke. "Wow, an aircraft software reference… that was so clever *NOT,*" this time with no pause in the middle of the quip.

The Padroids groaned.

Juice looked around incredulously, sneering, and rhetorically asked, "Guys, is this dude *for real*?!" His eyes shot back to the captain, and he chastised, "Sam, this is pathetic... quit while you're behind, and salvage some dignity... Unless, you know, you already lost it all on that last pass?"

"Ooooohhhhhhh," the Padroids clamored in the background.

Rowland, desperate and scrambling to escape this fight without a clean sweep, stuck with his impersonation bit as he appealed to the Padroids and shouted out, "Dignity?! *Verrryyyyy niiiice!*" He looked around; no laughs. "*I liiiiike!*" Still nothing. Frantically seeking just *one* chuckle, he threw his hail mary with, "*My name-a Borat!*"

All five others were now literally shielding their eyes from this comedic catastrophe, and NEODD SWEVEN was coded so well that he exhibited physical pain from this scene.

Another verse began in the Drake song—this one Sam had never heard before. *Huh? I thought the song usually ended after Em'?* But within seconds, Sam instantly recognized the rapper that had added his piece to this remix...

Tapes on, Fight's on; Lorax bout to drop a bomb
IN with Heading, GBU-54
Cleared-so-motherfuckin-hot you'd think my name was Demi Moore
Air-to-air supremacy; you're gonna call 'Blind, sun'
I'm the fucking fighter SME, suck this AIM-9, son!
Psub-we of 1.0; fuck what the sheet says
Jammin' out rhymes like I'm motherfuckin' FrankenWEZ
Deployed at sea, memories, greatest friends you'll ever meet
Fight with honor, fight with pride, fight with brothers by your side
Shout out to my bro JABA; Skipper/XO were fuckin' lava
Hollar at ya' Clown Penis, FNGs you all da cleanest
Check in PRI, FISTY; Lorax up, and damn, I miss thee
Deuce to you, Juice; Admin God, a fuckin Zeus
WIFYMIFM? Hell yeah, I'd do it; please don't forget 'bout Staton Pruitt
Where you at CLAM? Kept us safe on every flight
Think about you every day, hope to god you're still alright
Finally, without this bro; don't know where the hell I'd be
Greatest pilot ever lived; rest in peace to you, Low T
But sometimes life gets fuckin real, a best bud takes a traitor's deal
Sold his soul for dolla bills, just to teach some admin drills
Squadron bonds should last for life, unless some mofo takes a knife
Stabs you cold right in the back, c'mon man that shit is whack
No excuse, can't believe it
That you'd fuckin launch and leave us

So, back to you Drake… I just call the shit the way it go
Chippy pride, Chippy style, Chippy-fuckin-ho, yo!

Sam was aghast at what he was hearing. There was no question in his mind about who the verse was referencing. *Did The Lorax really feel that way? Was I that fucked up by leaving them? How in the hell did he get these rappers to collab with him? And when did The Lorax pick up such vulgar language?*

The 1MC blared, breaking Sam's internal thoughts. "THIS IS NOT A DRILL, THIS IS NOT A DRILL!" A bunch of obnoxiously loud chimes filled the next ten seconds. "WHITE SMOKE, WHITE SMOKE, ROOM 3-230-1-L. ALL HANDS NOT INVOLVED STAY CLEAR."

Sam looked at the 1MC in anticipation, but nothing else came. *Uhhh… hello!? How am I going to have properly heard the message if you don't say it* twice? *God… this ship… I swear.* I think *they said 3-230 – probably laundry… fucking* awesome…"

Juice smirked. "Looks like your phenomenal stand-up has been saved by the bell, Captain Cringe. I'll leave you to your admin duties; you'll undoubtedly find a way to fuck them up like everything else you've done since you left the Chippies." He turned around and headed toward the door.

The Padroids disappointingly shook their heads as NEODD SWEVEN pointed at Sam and warned, "Bro, you make weak jokes like *those* while landing? Your ass will be grounded indefinitely." All four turned, as Sam heard IROK muttering something along the lines of "… *So* uncool…"

As the others left the stateroom, <MCSALAD> seemed frozen in his footsteps. The look on his face… Sam wasn't sure what was going on. *Did his software crash? I swear, Suabedissen, this guy's coding* sucks! But yet, <MCSALAD>'s eyes were still open, moving, and conscious… he just seemed distracted… almost lost. *Maybe he needs a soft reset?*

SWEVEN stopped at the door and looked back, asking, "<MCSALAD>, dog — you alright?"

Hearing his name must have triggered something in his circuitry, as he became alert once again and replied, "Affirm… just had a weird feeling for a second. I think I'm due for a recharge…"

The CAG Padroids gave a nod and grunt of approval.

Something inside Sam's conscience said he should stop here, say no more, and take his loss. The old Sam *would* have had such tact… But as a fighter raging white after this verbal onslaught? With his emotions stirring, the Sam of *now* couldn't stop himself. He yelled out at Juice, "Listen up, bastard — I *made* you. Without me, you'd still be that whiney little limfac of a new guy with no skill, no friends, and *no hope* in this career. It doesn't matter how 'shit hot' the Padroids or anybody else on this ship may *think* you are—because deep down, you know that you are absolutely *nothing* in Noddik aviation without me…"

Juice gave a long look at the captain, remaining stoic. He took a deep breath and asked, "Is that what you think? Sam… you just don't get it. I'm done. I'm fucking *done* playing this game, Rowland. One day, when this whole thing's over, you're going to realize what you've given up to get where you are… and you will have no one to blame but yourself." Still serious, almost *remorseful*, Juice finished with, "It's a lot lonelier at the top when you abandon your friends to get there," and left the room.

The Padroids followed right behind him—NEODD still shaking his head in disappointment, IROK muttering about Sam getting off easy, <MCSALAD> trying to regain his whereabouts, and T6's human conversation logic randomly generating, "Hey, speaking of Saved by the Bell, you know who was really hot? Kelly Kapowski, of course—but *also* that girl from the summer beach episodes Zack dated for a season. I think she was also in King of—"

The door shut, and Sam was left in silence. Finally, with some privacy, Sam rushed to his mini fridge and grabbed a cold beer, which he used to chase down a mini-bottle of Jameson from his flight bag. *What the hell did Juice mean by that? What would he know about friends, anyway… everyone knew that guy sucked at the Chippies! And Jesus Christ… another fire in laundry?! I swear to god, if there is a flight suit in that dryer…* He walked over to his computer to check his email before leaving to address the fire—and saw one unread that caught his eye, with a random lat/long in the subject line.

The email body simply said: "Nickels—Today, 1200—See you at the merge."

What?! No way… could it be…? Once again, there was no addressed email domain, so Sam had no way of responding or looking the user up. He looked at the date—it was the 4-year anniversary of Low T's disappearance. *It has to be… nobody calls me 'Nickels' anymore… nor should they…* Sam had given up his identity as 'Nickels' when he left the US Fleet. He figured it was a necessary change to help leave his old world—and his old friends—behind. *If that's actually him… I need to go. I need to find out what happened to him. But does it even matter? That life… those friends… BFM practice… it's all irrelevant now. I've got a LAAF to lead to get this empire the admin W.*

He looked at his Chippy 'Good Dude Award.' The verse from The Lorax was still playing in his head… and Juice's words reverberated there, too. His anger from earlier had quickly transformed into depression. *Shit… what's going on with me? I shouldn't feel emotion like this… I'm one of the Noddiks, now—a sophisticated admin machine sent from Earth to save the future of this empire. An exoskeleton of procedures and policies. There's no room for emotion in this job!*

Yet he couldn't shake those Lorax lyrics. Couldn't shake the curiosity of encountering Low T. Couldn't shake the feelings of... *was it guilt? Regret? I couldn't possibly... Fuck it.* He downed another shot and decided he'd do it. *I have to – plus, adding a sortie to the schedule shouldn't be too hard.*

Sam called Bravo Romeo and opened with, "Hello, this is Captain Rowland, aka Katsopolis Actual – I'd like to request an air plan change."

After the simple process of calling Bravo Romeo – who said they'd add it to a spreadsheet and call another person, who would then call another person, who would then QA the change and ask higher leadership for the verdict – the request was in the books. *Brave little watchstanders,* Sam lamented. *Slaving away in their cold, dark rooms, thinking their efforts are actually making a difference...*

Lonely at the top? Please... I'm not lonely. I have all the money I could ever need. I'm long gone from that bullshit of the past. I have respect and authority here... plus, Dr. Suabedissen! He's a great friend! Maybe I'll ask if I can join one of his LARPing games. That might be fun? Or I could join his book club – I think he was saying something about Harry Potter and the Half-Blood Prince? I heard that's a good one. The doctor said there was a very steamy kiss scene – I could get down with that.

Within minutes, a robot called Sam back to inform him his flight addition had been approved. Rowland took a swig of whiskey, finished his beer, grabbed his jacket and flight bag, and took a stroll through the ship to check out the fire before he walked for his flight.

~

Dr. Suabedissen, intensely focused and sweating, took a long look at the scene in front of him. Everything had been building to this moment – It was a long shot... but he'd run the probabilities in his head enough to be sure it was the valid decision to make. He lifted his head, inhaled, and exhaled dramatically – before raising his clasped hands, shaking them, and thrusting them down to the table – where a 16-sided die emerged, bouncing multiple times... before finally landing on... 11.

Everyone observing in the aft mess decks gasped with awe.

The doctor looked up at the Game Operations Director – a senior chief overseeing the board – and asked, "Dungeon Master – the necromancer casts a level 3 fireball into the single boss – will that fireball guide and fuze?"

The game master, wearing a crown and fingerless gloves, looked at a sheet of paper in front of him and announced, "It will."

"Huzzah!" The doctor rose to his feet and raised his arms triumphantly, his cape flowing behind him. He grinned and proudly declared, "Ladies and gentlemen, that is an attack worth 11 hit points, defeating the Warty Toad King and clearing the entrance to the lair where Splinter's Scroll lies in the treasure chest! I'll move to that space, open the chest, acquire the scroll, aaaaaand..." He looked his opponent dead in the eyes, "thus concludes my turn!"

The crowd cheered wildly as the doctor completed the trial by defeating his opponent—a random E-3 bot from ship's company—and taking the scroll, which would bolster his main character's intelligence points and teach a new magic spell for his next quest.

Suabedissen shook the young sailor's hand, and then packed up his board, cards, and character tokens. He brushed off his cape, adjusted his broach, and pushed his glasses up as he gave one last bow to the cheering bots. After soaking in the applause for a few moments, he finally began heading to his room for the evening, where he planned to re-organize his deck, apply some power-up points to his character, and potentially research his next raid—which was scheduled to be a storming of some E-5's Crystal Castle a couple of days later.

When he entered his stateroom, his phone was already ringing. Suabedissen picked up the J-dial and answered, "Level 146 Necrom—err, Dr. Suabedissen here. How can I help you?"

He listened intently before smiling and saying, "Wow, that is fantastic news, Mr. Ward! This is perfect—my algorithms have been saying that this was the ideal game plan all along, so now we should *surely* be able to find success in this LAAF!" After a few seconds, the doctor smiled and said, "Oh, don't you worry about that— we'll take care of Captain Rowland. CAG has already arranged a special contingency assignment for him, *just* in case this had happened..." He allowed Juice to talk, then affirmed, "Yes, sir—I'll let him know." ... "Yes, sir. Good morning, sir," and hung up.

He clicked the phone piece down, lifted his finger, and dialed a few numbers. When it went through, he began, "CAG, sir, this is Dr. Suabedissen. Mr. Ward just called me... he has changed his mind and accepted the offer!" ... "Yes, sir, I agree, that is the best COA to take." As he listened, Suabedissen looked up at the ADMACS display, then answered, "Yes sir, he just launched—I'll let the Padroids know the plan." ... "No, sir, Mr. Ward does not know of *OPERATION: PIGPEN*; absolutely not." ... "Yes, sir, I will be going down there shortly; I was just..." he looked over at his D&D game set, "... Taking care of some important business this morning..." He beamed as he admired his new Splinter's Scroll card. "Yes, sir, *very* close to complete with subject 14-3. He is nearly broken down... the sessions are working; you must trust me. Soon, we will have all the information we need. I just need your permission to escalate to the next level of methodology." ... "Yes, sir, understood! Good day, CAG, sir."

Dr. Suabedissen hung up the phone, donned his hood over his head, and grinned. He'd gained the Admin LAAF lead he needed, received CAG's approval to unleash the critical means of completing his latest project, *and* he'd earned one of the three Scrolls of Destiny. Today had been a *great* day.

~

<MCSALAD> sat in his recharge station, adjacent to the other Padroids who were restoring their energy for the upcoming busy day of waving. Like usual, though, he was unable to do... well, whatever those other LSOs were doing—he had no clue. He'd always just felt... *different* than them. In addition, he couldn't help but keep replaying that Drake song quietly to himself, again and again, as he struggled to understand why the song seemed to unsettle him so much. It just made him feel... a sense of yearning. Like something was missing from his life; something he'd forgotten; something he just couldn't place his finger on...

He looked at himself in the mirror through his aviators. He stared at his ridiculous mustache—a mandatory Padroids item—and his backward cap. He took it off— his hair... so much volume and coif potential, held flat and full of dead skin due to the constant hat-wearing. He looked behind him at his jerseys—there was a Neil Rackers Arizona Cardinals jersey, a Nick Folk Jets one, a Shane Lechler Raiders top, and plenty of others. He'd always considered himself a fan of American Football as long as he could remember—still, he didn't recognize *any* of these players. And his Air Jordans... he picked a shoe up and looked at the sole—he hadn't noticed before, but these weren't even FOD-free. What was going on?

<MCSALAD> tried to figure out why he felt so odd; why he couldn't get this feeling out of his heart and mind... then The Lorax's lyrics came on once more. It sounds like this guy had so many close friends from his past—and from the emotional draw to his words, <MCSALAD> almost felt like *he* knew The Lorax. And yet... *nobody* in the Noddik Empire was close with <MCSALAD> like this. Nobody really *got* close, either—it was almost as if these other Padroids and sailors didn't care about friends, squadron bonds, or other concepts of brotherhood that appeared like foreign concepts to him—yet also carried a substantial weight of importance. Something was clearly wrong, and <MCSALAD> just couldn't shake the constant feeling of anxiety...

He finally fell asleep, and the last thought in his brain was his own voice calling some name, over and over again, "CLARA... CLARA... CLARA..."

4

Dimes

*S*o, you really took the deal, huh?" Low T asked, with a disappointed tone. As he took a bite from his bowl of Grape-Nuts, he added, "Money can't buy happiness, you know…" And after swirling the cereal around for a bit, he put his spoon down and asked, "How are you going to enjoy life without Navy admin boat stuff: Non-stop pointless drills, laundry shutting down every other week, slow-as-molasses internet – when it actually works – and the noises! Nickels, how are you going to get any sleep without someone hammering away at your ceiling all night?!"

Sam looked up from his nearly-packed suitcase – his last of many – and saw Low T was now grinning. He laughed and said, "Geeze, you're right… I may need to ensure they throw some pointless chaos in my contract to make sure I don't become too homesick while I'm gone!"

Laughing as well, Low T remarked, "Ahh, man. I can't believe it… and leaving so soon, on a VIP jet flown remotely here just for you! Gonna be a hell of a time – I know you're gonna kill it out there, bro." He looked down for a second and tried to casually ask, "So, uhh… how's the rest of the squadron taking it?"

Sam shook his head and sighed with a disheartened chuckle. "C'mon, Kyle. You know just as well as I do – probably better – that they're furious. I asked CP if he wanted to get one last section lift in, and he said he was, quote, 'taking a rest day'…" Sam rolled his eyes. "At least make up something believable, you know? Skipper and XO said I can skip my checkout. I heard Lorax swear for the first time ever when he called me a 'spineless, backstabbing bitch.'"

"Wow, that's pretty harsh," Kyle said.

"No kidding. The FNGs were too busy studying for their coordinated singles 10D1 'Night PGM' to even care, and FISTY…" Sam stopped and shook his head sadly, lamenting, "He refused to even acknowledge me."

Low T frowned. "Well, Nickels… can you blame him? You were his protégé… his chosen one. He loved training and molding you into a tactical champion more than anything. The look in his eyes when you won the BFM derby last year… he was like the proudest dad I've ever seen."

Sam scoffed with a smile. "Ok, first of all, I was only his 'chosen one,'" Sam raised his hands to make air quotes, "Because you were already so damn good that you didn't need a Jedi master to teach you!" Kyle smiled sheepishly as Sam continued with, "And second… I did win that derby, didn't I?" He grinned. "Remind me, again — who did I beat in the finals?"

Low T started laughing. "Get outta here, dog! I told you — I shouldn't have even flown that day!" He spoke with amused conviction. "I didn't have any low-fat cottage cheese that morning, my legs were completely shot from the previous week's 95-lb squat session, and I was exhausted from the night before — I didn't get to bed til 9 pm!" Still grinning, he raised his finger and insisted, "Might I remind you — I only flew that day because I wasn't gonna let my boy down; because I didn't want you getting that trophy off some lame ORM forfeit!"

Laughing and rolling his eyes, Sam said, "Ahhh, whatever, you old man! Sometimes, I'm surprised your body held up through Level 3 BFM!"

"BFM's a lot easier on your joints and bones when you spend the entire sortie in the control zone," Low T boasted with a playful tone.

The two continued cracking up, while Sam continued packing up the last of his things. As the laughing died down a bit, he asked, "Do you think FISTY will ever forgive me? Do you think the squadron will? >SADCLAM< was on duty and started playing some of the angstiest scream-o ballads I've ever heard. He just kept looking at me, shaking his head, saying, 'I can't believe you're deserting us, bro. You're leaving a championship-caliber team…'"

"Hah, that's just CLAM, man. Of course he's gonna give you shit — because he cares! We all do — because, in reality, we're gonna miss a dude like you. We want you to do well, sure. But yeah — it kinda sucks how it's all going down." Kyle gave a half-smile, half-shrug.

Sam said nothing for a bit, thinking about the unspoken truths of what Low T was saying. Finally, he admitted, "Yeah… I mean, I guess I'm lucky you're still cool with me. I suppose FISTY isn't wrong to be so mad… or any of those guys, really. WYFMIFM, for the first time ever, had no interest in shooting the shit about random business ideas with me — he didn't even want to talk Shmarkers. I felt kind of… kind of sad. Felt like I was losing a great friend — him and everyone else… Kinda like I was losing my family…" Sam stopped packing and closed his eyes.

Low T clasped him on the shoulder and said, "Well, bro, you made your choice. You're an experienced dude in this biz; I and everyone else will just have to trust that you put all the proper thought into this decision. You'll be alright, man."

Still looking glum, Sam shrugged and said, "Yeah… I guess." After pausing for a moment, he asked, "CP, man… he wrote up 'Dimes' under my name on the FNG callsign board — what's that all about?"

Kyle looked away. "Uhhh… I don't know… couldn't tell you…"

Sam folded his arms. "Come on, bro. Be real with me… I'm leaving anyway. Just tell me."

Shaking his head and sighing, Kyle admitted, "Fine. Well... dimes are double the worth of nickels at half the size... and with your net worth more than doubling, well..."

"They're saying I'm only half the man..."

Low T said nothing at first. After a bit of silence, Sam tried to ignore the hurt he wore on his face by searching the room for any last things to pack. "Look, we'll always be best bros for life, dude, you know *that," Kyle started, "But if you don't mind answering: Why, Sam? Why are you doing this? I know the money is good and all... but there's gotta be* some *other reason?"*

Sam took a long look — not at anything in particular, more so of staring a thousand yards in the distance while his brain searched for the proper answer. Why *am* I doing this? I certainly don't need all that money... I mean, there's outer space involved, so that's pretty cool. Cool enough to leave my best friends behind? You could argue they are the 'known comforts' of life, and I need to pull myself away to explore the unknown depths. And this boat... these deployments... ugh... this place really, just totally sucks. It almost makes me want to have a drink after work sometimes — which is *so* not me! It's just so... *infuriating*... Sure, some of the greatest memories of my life have been on this ship — but imagine how much *better* life would be if I were living on a *competent* ship! These guys will see it, too — how could they *not* see it? *Still monologuing to himself, he surmised:* I guess... I guess I'm just tired of the shit here. Tired of getting yelled at for washing a sweaty flight suit in laundry. Tired of Paddles getting on my case for flying marginally deviating passes. Tired of waking up every day to the sound of sporadically firing catapults, test alarms, a stateroom phone ringing, or the never-ending sound of rushing water, exhaust, or random bangs here and there. Tired of these motherfuckers running GQ at 7 am. Tired of showers being shut off for hours every morning. Tired of... *everything* to do with this damn boat and this goddamn lifestyle...

Almost as if reading his thoughts, Kyle prodded for an answer by asking, "I get it — the boat isn't a world-class cruise... but I mean, is that all you want? Are you just looking for an escape from life's struggles?"

"What? No." Sam replied, somewhat annoyed. How could he say that? *"Escape? Kyle, I'm not looking to 'escape' anything... I'm not running away. I'm seeking a greater opportunity. It's the next big challenge in life. And look what I can accomplish if all goes well — I'll be a trailblazer for the Noddik Empire! Who knows? Some people may even follow once they see how great it is!"*

Low T frowned, "I didn't mean to accuse you of abandoning us — "

"I never said anything about abandoning." Sam snapped.

A silent tension grew in the room... until Kyle asked, "Hey... I'm sorry to ask, but... are you sure this has nothing to do with those?" *He pointed to the corner of the room, where there were a few unpacked awards of Sam's — the most recent awards he'd won. They were labeled 'Best Clean and Dry Checks,' 'Administrative Excellence Achievement,' 'Join-Up of the*

Year,' 'Most Valuable Flight Lead,' and, of course, the most coveted: his 'Good Dude Award.' These *awards*, however, were all 2nd place *trophies...*

Sam was now full-on perturbed. "Kyle... are you serious right now?"

"Look, dude, it's no secret that Juice has skyrocketed in the air wing in every facet of the job. His FITREP even stated that he was an average Coffee Mess Officer — and that was signed by Skipper!"

Sam scoffed. That had to be a bold-faced lie. Such a feat was impossible; the CMO ground job was a failure-producing factory. "Ok, and what metrics did they even — " Sam stopped himself and shook his head. "No, it doesn't matter. Listen, Kyle — yeah, I get that Juice has been doing ok. But fuck that guy. He's not good! I mean... I know I'm better than him. People just had voter fatigue, like Jordan's lost MVPs in the 90s. I'd take myself over Juice, 1-on-1, any day, any phase of flight. I'm not afraid of him... and I'll tell you what," Sam widened his eyes and clenched his jaw, wagering, "You sure as hell wouldn't see him doing something as bold as this," he emphasized, pointing to his packed bags. He said it somewhat convincingly; he almost believed himself...

Sighing, Low T said, "Yeah... I dunno, man. You give that guy too much shit. He's not a bad dude."

Sam rolled his eyes and shook his head. "Forget Juice, man. That's not what this is about. This is about my time to reinvent myself in a new environment. To improve upon all the dumb shit that we deal with here. To help the Noddik Empire achieve greatness in the administrative field of boat and flight operations!"

Shrugging, Kyle said, "Sure, I get that, dude. Just a bummer... seeing the boys torn apart — hate to see it. 'The Disease of Me' strikes again..."

"The what?"

Kyle shook his head. "Nevermind. Just promise me one thing, man — don't quit being Nickels. You got the reputation, the respect, the success, and, most of all, the friends you have because of who you are. Don't forget that and turn into some self-entitled, jaded asshole. Continue to be Nickels, and I have no doubt you'll find plenty of success with this new fleet," he finished, smiling.

Sam nodded and assured him, "Dude, I could never. Nickels will live on, but for a new wave of aviators. This flying... the people in this biz... the cool parts of the job... I'm gonna show another world just how badass this stuff can be. I have no doubt it's gonna be great — and to be honest, I think it's going to make me the happiest I could possibly be in life. And thanks, man. You've been my best bud here, and you've become the best pilot in the air wing. You're gonna do great here without me; all of you guys — just promise me you won't ever let Juice get the first shot on you!"

Kyle laughed. "Likewise, bro. And I won't — no one's getting the first shot on me ever again," he grinned, continuing, "Because when I see you at the merge next time?! Expect me to get my revenge for that tourney — and this time, I'll make sure I had my afternoon nap and a good yoga session to prepare!" he joked.

Snickering along with him, Sam said, "When that fight comes? Your geezer-ass is going down!"

The two embraced in a bro-hug, and Sam grabbed his luggage and left the stateroom to head to his jet for departure, unsure if he'd actually ever see his best friend again — but it was nice to know that Low T still saw him as 'Nickels, the Good Dude,' and not 'Dimes, the spineless, backstabbing bitch.'

~

Captain Rowland continued CAPing at a tactical airspeed, looking around his canopy with a diligent TOPGUN scan—the same one FISTY made him chairfly for 3 hours each night during his early Level 3 training. Yet even with his flawless lookout doctrine, he still saw nobody. *Where is he? Was this a setup or something?*

Rowland had been drilling circles in space at the lat/long from the mysterious email for the past ten minutes, as the TISM clock now hit 1205. *Maybe the time is inaccurate?* He nearly requested a mickey over GUARD, before remembering that a frog should not ask a scorpion to scratch his back.

He took a sip of the whiskey in his vest flask—but only a sip. Sam wanted to be sharp today; if he *did* encounter Low T, he wanted to show that he still has 'it' in the tactical realm. In fact, Sam made the decision as soon as he started the jet: he was going to go 'manual' on this hack. *Shit man... I haven't done manual BFM in years—I haven't* needed *to.* Dr. Suabedissen had somehow managed to code these jets with Patch-wearing levels of combat effectiveness. As to *how* the tactics were so expertly implemented into the software, Sam wasn't quite sure. The doctor was very secretive about all his algorithms, keeping them locked under multiple different passwords and firewalls on his personal desktop rig. This, however, was *nothing* compared to the vault that held his D&D playing tokens and VR gear—which required retinal, voice, and fingerprint recognition, amongst numerous authentication trivia questions involving a bunch of nerdy sci-fi franchises. And, of course, as the doctor loved to remind everyone, "Even if—even *if!*—somebody managed to hack in and answer all of the questions successfully? There is one final naval aviation riddle needed to enter the safe—and it's nearly unsolvable!" he would say with a giggle. *God, that guy is such a loser... and to think, he seriously claims he has a girlfriend who is a 'model,' bringing her VR setup during photoshoot traveling so that she can play D&D with him online? Psh... give me a fucking break, doctor... A) There's no way this girl actually exists, and B) Even* if *she did? She would be like a zero, and C) Even* if *she was hot? She'd find somebody cooler* literally *anywhere if she just opened her eyes for a fucking second, and D) —*

"Holy shit!" Sam couldn't stop himself from gasping audibly as a jet's cans lit directly in front of his canopy; the afterburner heat turning his cockpit into a hotbox of exhaust. *No way... Low T?!* In the time he took to react, the adversary jet had already reoriented itself and gotten an offensive bite on him, nearing toward his tail with its nose. Sam regained his whereabouts and intuitively pulled, relying on his old 'tactical feel' to come right back to him. The vitamin G on his body felt like a deep-tissue massage from the aviation gods. As he tensed to withstand the onset, his muscles nearly cramped after not being activated for so long—but *damn*, that pain felt good. Vascularity burst from his forearm as he remembered what it was like to be an athlete in the jet. He couldn't help but grin uncontrollably under his mask—his first smile in months. *What a rush! God, I've missed this!* As he kept the G and pull on, so came the feelings of nostalgia and thrill. He felt a sensory euphoria that reminded him of his youthful career innocence, before his life became a series of do-loops of announcements that nobody gave a shit about.

To Sam, there was *nothing* quite like mano-a-mano F/A-18 BFM. It was the ultimate sport of fighter aviation—equal conditions, similar aircraft performance, with an identical playbook of knowledge. *Everyone* saw the training videos. *Everyone* knew the numbers. *Everyone* recognized the sight pictures. It was simply a matter of the man in the box. Who would be able to endure the G? Who would be able to nail their parameters and get the extra degrees of turn? Who was savvy enough to pull for the kill shot at the right time? And most of all... *who* had the ultimate will to fight for the longest? *"It doesn't matter if it's BFM, accomplishing your dreams, or a brutal summer cut — Life is ultimately a war of resilience; the greatest of victories will be achieved by he who is simply the last one to give up."* FISTY had told Sam this long ago... and it stuck with him forever. As he kept the pull coming, the thought crossed his mind: *So... did I give up on the Chippies...?*

Lost in his train of thought while trying to stay padlocked at his 8 o'clock, Sam noticed that the attacking aircraft began drifting closer to his 7:30... 7... 6:30... He gave a quick scan forward to check his airspeed—80 knots. *Shit!* He had pulled well beyond his limit, and was now basically just a floundering RAG student with his guard down, waiting to be knocked out. *Damn... what a fucking rookie mistake...* Completely ignoring FISTY's adage about resilience, Sam began rocking his wings, signifying his admission of defeat...

... So he was understandably shocked to see the smoke in the air that came spiraling toward him. *What the fuck?!* With a live missile just seconds away from hitting him, Sam panicked, frantically trying to remember the boldface to defend against such a threat. *Uhhh... something about the flaps...?* He pulled up his most useful display these days—the Checklist page—to see if there was anything there for defenses. Nothing. *Shit! What was it again...?*

Finally, he remembered the most useful boldface of all: he hit the 'BFM' button on the jet, and the aircraft automatically maneuvered itself to get out of the way of direct impact. Despite the miss, the missile still exploded, and part of the frag hit Sam's jet. As he felt the slight vibration from contact, a bone-chilling tone went off in Sam's ear. *That sound... so familiar... what* is *that?* He scanned his cockpit and saw a yellow 'MASTER CAUTION' light illuminated. *Holy shit... a 'Deedle deedle?!'* The Noddik jets were so impressively programmed that they hadn't had a recorded caution in almost two years—when one of the bots malfunctioned and powered up with a safe'd seat. Sam cycled to his FCS page to check the damage—one of his ailerons had fully failed from the explosion.

Lost in the chaos of the moment was the BFM unfolding in real time—where Sam was now staring straight through his HUD at the enemy aircraft's tail. *No way...* Despite having a complete positional disadvantage, the Suabedissen software had calculated the perfect aerobatic steps to gain the edge on the other aircraft. Despite having no left aileron functionality, the software had reprogrammed every other flight control to get the same performance in the BFM arena, gaining degrees and utilizing energy like nothing was wrong. And *despite* thinking he was coming here to have a good deal BFM hack with his old best friend—finding a bloodthirsty adversary instead, and nearly *dying* as a result of his shitty manual jet-maneuvering—Sam was now in a position to kill this motherfucker and earn the first air-to-air shootdown in Noddik history.

Sam took a deep breath, unboxed SIM, armed the MASTER ARM switch, selected the 9X—*good tone*—and turned his VOX and ICS knobs up to full. Just before squeezing the trigger, he harnessed yet another accent he loved impersonating—Austrian, this time—and butchered a classic *True Lies* line, as he uttered: *"I'm going to fire you..."* *This is going to sound so badass on tapes!* All of this was, of course, notional—the software had already solved procedural ROE to declare this attacker hostile, and shot a missile a few seconds before Sam went through the motions to try and dramatize the moment.

The missile rocketed toward the adversary, and despite his best efforts to avoid the frag, the explosion clipped the jet. With its canopy and a leading-edge flap damaged, the jet fell into missile-induced oscillations, struggling to remain straight and level, as it turned and limped in an attempt to bug out of the fight.

Sam de-selected the BFM button, hit the 'JOIN' feature, and utilized the 'PARADE' option on the submenu. The beautiful thing about space in this narrative—and the lack of scientific research by the author—was that since it was silent out in the atmosphere, Sam would be able to pull right up to his defeated accoster and talk some mad shit to him before gunning him down. *What should I say? Maybe 'Hasta la vista, baby...'? Hmm... he might not speak Spanish. Oh, wait! How about 'Get to the Choppah!'? Sort of insinuating that this guy should've selected helos out of primary! Ehh... maybe a bit too meta... he might not fully comprehend the slam before he dies. Oh, shit... Oh, shit! I've got it! If this guy's name happens to be Dillon, then this line is going to land* perfectly...

Meanwhile, Sam's jet was flawlessly gliding its way into parade, using closure and bearing that—Sam hated to admit—looked a lot like one of Juice's manual joins. As the jet got to within 0.1nm, Sam could make out that the pilot's helmet was shattered during the explosion, and the man's bloodied face was now exposed. *Hah! Let's see this fucking jabroni...*

As he pulled into the port parade position, Sam opened his canopy—the jet automatically accounting for the increase in drag, thanks to Open-Canopy-Interconnect—and yelled out, "Dillon! You son of a—" *Huh?!*

The face of the man glaring back at him was unmistakable. Sam knew for a fact who it was, yet he couldn't believe his eyes. "… Low T...?!"

The pilot wore a vicious look of resentment, saying nothing as he looked back and forth between Sam and his displays, trying to salvage the jet and his life.

It has *to be him…* it'd been over five years, but the resemblance was uncanny—strangely, it looked like he not only hadn't aged, but actually appeared *younger*. He had a much more chiseled jaw and was healthily tanned, as if he had been soaking in mass amounts of sun. His hair had incredible flow, exposed strands curling out from his helmet where it was destroyed. And yet, his mustache remained exactly as it had always been in the Chippies—full, and bordering on out-of-regs. The 'old man Low T' looked like a young, vigorous JO.

Sam disengaged the FORM button and manually pulled further acute and closer in—well beyond the checkpoints of parade—in an effort to elicit a response from the young man who surely had to be his old friend. He took off his helmet and yelled again, "Low T!" Their wingtips were beyond overlapped, every oscillation of the damaged jet coming within inches of impacting Sam's.

With vengeful eyes, the assailant finally responded, barking back, "Low T is dead! *You* killed him, Dimes! Now, what are you waiting for? Gun me down already!"

What?! Dimes… "Low T, what the hell are you talking about?! I know it's you! Where are you going? There's no way you can stay airborne much longer! Join me, and we'll RTB to the Katsopolis—we'll get there in 20 minutes!" *What am I doing? This guy tried to kill me!*

"*Join* you?!" Low T recoiled in disgust. "Yeah, *right,* bitch!" He scanned his instruments, before glaring at Sam. "Are you going to kill me or not? Shoot me down, just like all your other wingmen!"

Kill him?! I can't kill him… he was my best friend… "Low T, please—just follow me, and we'll get on deck safely!"

With fire in his eyes, Low T stared at Sam for a prolonged few seconds... before deflecting his jet's left aileron into Rowland's right wing.

"Jesus Christ, Low T, what are you d—" Sam reactively pulled away as the once-again blaring MASTER CAUTION tone cut him off. He closed his canopy and put his helmet back on, pushing through submenus to his FCS page, where he hit the 'SURFACE COMPENSATION' button, once again re-shifting his controls to attain safe flight, despite two fully destroyed ailerons. He turned back toward Low T—who was still scrambling to stay afloat and escape—and selected the gun, with Low T's jet dead-locked in his crosshairs. Sam held steady and prepared to 'come into the trigger' vice 'pulling the trigger,' as his faithful RAG instructors had taught him long ago. Every factor for this glorious gun shot was solved; one of those employments a pilot couldn't *wait* to validate frame-by-frame in a debrief using a pencil-crafted micrometer on a val sheet. Sam focused, sweat dripping down his forehead, and prepared to take the shot… waiting for the right moment… and waiting… and *waiting*…

He couldn't do it. With frustration and despair, and intuitively drawing from another classic surfer-action roll 'em, he pulled to bullseye nose-high and screamed, "AHHHHHHHH!!!" as he shot off all 300 rounds into the abyss, his killer instinct over-powered by the eternal bonds of squadron brotherhood.

~

Approaching for landing, Sam's heart was still pounding; his mind still racing. *What the hell just happened? I need to talk to — well… shit. I guess there's nobody on this entire fucking ship who will understand. I need to speak with someone, man — even Juice? Fuck that… I'm not talking to that guy. God dammit… Low T… he's gotta be dead by now… there's no way he made it back to Earth in that jet.* Thinking more about the emotion of it all, Sam asked himself: *Why did he want to kill me? And what did he mean, 'Low T is* dead?' *Dimes… shit, I haven't heard that one in a while… still kind of hurts…*

The RTB was uneventful, despite the two failed ailerons. Well into his CV-1 arrival, Sam had already flawlessly solved the timing problem by inputting his time and DME into the 'marshal page,' as the jet flew itself perfectly to his approach point. As he penetrated down to the altitude of the Katsopolis' entrance, he heard the Pa-droids' radio check initiated.

"CATCC, Padroids, radio check on Bravo," IROK's voice called out.

"Padroids, CATCC has you loud and clear on Bravo."

"CAG Padroids, NEODD SWEVEN here, loud and clear! Working 0 over 0! Alright, everyone, it's dark out there, but we're gonna get you aboard safely—and more importantly, get you aboard with some *swag*! Let's have a nice chill recovery; Badasses only. We'll see you on the platform, baybeeeee!"

Sam rolled his eyes and input the ship speed, then keyed the mic to talk to the LSOs. "Padroids, 403."

"403, go for Padroids."

Sam spoke clearly and calmly, explaining, "403, I'll be coming in with dual aileron failures. The surface compensation feature is working fine, just wanted to give you guys a heads—"

"Woah, woah, *woah*!" NEODD SWEVEN cut him off. "Dude... ok, take a *deep breath*, 403. No offense, but you are sounding like a complete goon *already*—and you haven't even gotten to the hard part of the approach! Do me a favor, ok? *Think* about what you're going to say, *rehearse* it, and *then* key the mic. And, dude, your lights— turn those bad boys *up*, full bright! And Jesus... 'surface compensation?' 'Feature?' 'Dual?!' Am I helping talk down a *fighter pilot*, or am I discussing quantum mechanics with a *virgin*? Use cool, *fresh* terms, and stop sounding like such a geek. Ok?"

Rowland had no patience for this. "NEODD... what the fuck are you talking about? No—you know what? I don't have time for your shit. Again, just letting you *know* that both my ailerons are failed and non-functional—but I can handle this landing just fine," he explained, irritated, noting that the 'LAND' button was not X'd out.

"Your *what?* Drop the *Good Will Hunting* act and tell me what's broken. Are you talking about your intakes?"

"My fucking *wings*, you idiot! My wings are inop!"

There was a pause before the response, but Sam could clearly hear NEODD and IROK snickering about his usage of the term 'inop,' as NEODD transmitted back, "Roger the 'inop' wings, Captain. Ok, so here's what we're gonna need you do to— first off, confirm your internal lights are full bright?"

Sighing, Sam responded, "Affirm."

"Ok, great. Now, adjust your mirrors so that they're showing the inside of the cockpit. Call 'contact' when you see your vertical fin things in the reflection."

Not sure where this was going, Sam did as requested and responded, "Contact the stabilators."

NEODD's transmission began with an audible groan of disgust, before continuing, "Ok, great. Tilt the mirror down a bit... your helmet should also be in the reflection. Got it?"

Growing further annoyed and confused, Sam moved his mirror and acknowledged, "Yup."

"Ok, perfect—go ahead and lift your visor up, look yourself dead in the eyes, and tell that beta to *quit* being such a *bitch*, *start* being a fucking *pilot*, and *land* this thing like a motherfuckin' G—comprende, bromigo?"

You've gotta be fucking kidding me...

"Confirm you can quit being a bitch, Captain?"

Dude... FUCK these guys... Unwilling to lash out while on final approach, Sam simply double-clicked the mic. He guided the smooth-handling jet all the way to the air station, and got it in position to hover descend down to the non-skid.

"Padroids contact!" NEODD radio'd out. "Keep it coming, baby—you're 15-18 seconds away from bringing it home..."

Why are these idiots giving me a talk-down? I don't fucking need this; I just need to hit the— " He looked at his checklist page again—'LAND' was now X'd out. *What?! That wasn't supposed to happen in these jets! Shit... I'm gonna have to go manual... again...*

"Call the ball when you see it."

Flustered, Sam responded, "Uhhh... ball." Not *centered; the first time he'd* ever *seen it uncentered in his entire time on this spaceship.*

"Rooooooger ball..." NEODD said in a hushed whisper.

The jet was descending—but nowhere *near* controlled. Sam's lack of manual flying in years was readily apparent, and it had nothing to do with the ailerons.

To the Padroids, though? They noticed nothing, instead focused on other portions of his landing. "Liiiiiiitle brighter..." the same whispering voice called out.

Sam rolled his external lights to full brightness, while continuing to oscillate back and forth on the 90-degree glideslope descent.

"You're ooooon glideslope... ooooon centerline..."

He was on neither.

A separate voice spoke up—it sounded like T6, and was much firmer. "Easy with the eye contact."

Oh my god, for fuck's sake, I'm actually flying the fucking ball! And the *way* he was flying the ball? Looking away for even a *second* meant a quick death.

"Easy with it..."

Sam struggled to remember how to fly this way, trying to recall the lessons he learned in T-45s—decades ago. *Was it four, or five-point power corrections? Wasn't there something called a 'natural' power point? Ok, so... nose for altitude... err... power for...*

"Easy with it...!"

No, wait, that's it—power for glideslope. And... oh shit... I think I'm supposed to be trimmed for on-speed. What the fuck is on-speed again? Like 17 units or something?

"EASY! WITH! IT!!!!!!!!!!" NEODD's voice was now booming on the mic.

Well, whatever, I think I'm over the landing area—I'm pretty sure I remember what do to at this part: Sam pulled both throttles to idle.

"WAVEOFF, WAVEOFF, WAVEOFF!!!!!" NEODD screamed with furious urgency.

It was too late. Sam came crashing down—and while his adrenaline kept his back pain-free, the jet was not so lucky, as it triggered a hard landing 903 MSP code. *Oops. Oh well—this jet's due for a 728-day inspection soon, anyway.*

"Eye contact on deck."

Realizing he was still staring at the ball—and Padroids—Sam quickly looked away, now noticing his jet sat well right of centerline. He rolled his eyes. *Whatever... go ahead and fucking Tight me out again, Padroids...*

Sam shut the jet off, disembarked normally from the ladder (*No need to try something fancy and piss these guys off even more*), and walked to maintenance, where the revolutionary quick-download OOMA/FAME system he'd promised the fleet had degraded into a three-hour process...

~

As Rowland stood at maintenance, typing in the password of the jet's data recording system for the 10th time to log into the 12th necessary portion of the process, the Padroids train came steaming toward him, still wearing their Patriots jerseys from earlier. This time, however, their walk-in music was Simple Plan's 'Untitled.'

Rolling his eyes at the melodramatic theme chosen to preface his pass, Sam turned from his OOMA computer and gave a mocking round of applause, monotoning, "Padroids... hooray... alright guys, lay it on me." As they approached Captain Rowland, NEODD SWEVEN and T6 had grim looks on their faces. At the same time, IROK appeared to be holding back titillating glee as he avoided eye contact with Sam. And <MCSALAD>... he was holding his head—as if in pain—and clearly aloof from the rest of the group. He was without the standard-issue Padroids aviator sunglasses on, and looked like he wanted nothing to do with this crew—or life—at the moment. In fact, he'd even strayed from the pack and shaved his douchey mustache. For the first time, Sam noticed something odd about <MCSALAD>—and it wasn't the look of angst on the young LSO bot, either. Rather... it was as if he looked *familiar*. *I swear I've seen that face before...*

NEODD gave a slight neck kink, pursed his lips to the side, and said, "Captain... we need to talk to you for a minute..."

Rowland chuckled humorlessly. "Ok, guys. Yeah, I know, too much eye contact. *My bad*, I'll tighten it up for next time—sorry if I offended your 'alpha status.'" He added the last part in air quotes, which seemed to really fire T6 up, as his robot hands tightened into fists. "Now, if you'll excuse me, I need to finish this shit up and talk to the doctor about some flight control stuff—"

"Captain!" NEODD interrupted him. "'Too much eye contact?' Dude... what you did out there was *egregious!* You ignored *multiple* calls from Padroids, continued to stare, and by the time the deviation of eye contact was attempted to be solved? It was too late! Dude—that was *so, so, SO* fucking uncool! Can you imagine if that shit happened in the Admin Olympics? And not to mention, you sounded like a *total bozo* on the radio! God, dude... I seriously felt like I was talking to Albus Dumbledork out there."

Sam rolled his eyes. "You know, when you say the character's *first* name, it really just highlights *you* as the dork..."

NEODD's robotic eyes narrowed, as the tension in the air became even heavier.

Sam pointed to the blue book. "Read me my fucking pass."

NEODD glared at Sam, and—without moving his eyes—uttered, "Read the pass, T6..."

T6 looked around at his fellow LSOs, then brought his eyes down and read off, "Ok, we had you in 403—for one—with a Padroids talk-down: Too dim of lights with a 'little brighter' call..." He looked up at Sam with wide eyes and emphasized, "*Severely* underlined *prolonged* eye contact on the come back in the start to at the ramp—on multiple 'easy with it' calls—"

"Stop." Sam interrupted him.

The Padroids audibly and dramatically *gasped* at the act of a mere mortal interrupting them. NEODD SWEVEN's jaw dropped, and IROK's ears had literal white smoke emerging from them. <MCSALAD> was staring inquisitively at Sam while holding the LSO speaker, seemingly captivated by the emitted emo anthem—which had started playing again from the beginning; a one-song playlist, in typical Padroids fashion.

Sam asked, firmly and sharply, "How was my flight path?"

T6, taken aback, said, "Uhhh... it was fine, nerd. I already told you—we talked you down. You're welcome. Now, if you'll let me finish..."

"Let me see the pass," Sam demanded.

T6 looked around, and NEODD shrugged. He fumbled through some papers he had in his clipboard and handed the pass printout depiction to Sam.

Sam looked at the paper and shook his head. "You fucking dipshits... look at this." He showed them the paper—a perfectly straight line. "You guys have no fucking clue what's going on. I flew *manual*, and at almost *no* point was I on glideslope *or* centerline. You're making shit up. You aren't keeping me or anyone else safe; you guys are *worthless*. NEODD, you're focused on raising an air wing of 'badasses,' yet you're wearing a fucking backup QB jersey. Matt Cassell? Bro, that guy inherited Brady's 16-0 team and didn't even *make the playoffs* the next year. T6, you're named after holding instructions—and you're calling *me* the loser? IROK—hypothetical question for you: what would you fix first—the low or the slow?"

IROK, still teeming, said, "I don't need to defend myself to you... but... trick question—that's right where you want to be."

Sam laughed coldly and said, "Thanks, idiot—that's exactly what I'm talking about. And <MCSALAD>, I—"

Then Sam noticed it: <MCSALAD>'s jersey… he'd changed from Gostkowski to some other random Patriot. But Sam recognized the number from his film study sessions with FISTY — #15 — and more importantly, he remembered the athlete's exploits. While the player made little noise in 99% of his games, he had some key catches in the legendary 28-3 comeback against Atlanta. A former lacrosse player converted to NFL wide receiver: it was Chris Hogan. *Chris Hogan… is it pronounced, 'Hoo-gen?' No… although that would've been very convenient for this narrative… but why does that still sound slightly familiar? Where have I heard that name — or one very similar to it – before?* Sam stared at the Padroid, perplexed, as the reader sat equally confused as to where the hell this 'Hooben' pronunciation came from — not realizing it was a *far* reach of a plot-advancement device, implemented to facilitate a connection yet to come — a reach *almost* as far-fetched as the thought of the Patriots *winning* that Super Bowl against Atlanta…

<MCSALAD> said nothing in response, oblivious that he was being analyzed. He appeared to be high on some type of sedative — if such a thing was possible for a bot.

Continuing back to his rant, Sam said, "You guys were supposed to be programmed to make this air wing a better, cooler place — but also to make sure we stayed administratively *safe*. It's become clearer and clearer to me that you don't give a shit about safety. No, worse — you don't even know *how* to give a shit about safety."

NEODD, after a prolonged pause, asked, "Captain… answer me this: do you hate us because you truly think we're worthless… or do you hate us because you just can't handle the truth — the truth that you *just aren't that good at landing*?"

Sam turned back to his OOMA computer and didn't respond.

"Because *Juice* seems to have no problem with the way we've been handling grades here…" NEODD added.

Sam stopped typing and looked back at him. "Fuck you, NEODD… *Fuck you.* Now, seriously — just give me my Tight and get the fuck out of here."

"A *Tight?!*" NEODD asked with incredulity. "Captain… this is what we needed to talk to you about: a gross deviation of coolness inside the wave-off window? Bro, you just earned yourself a Neat, i.e., a cut pass."

Sam stared at him, stunned, as the looped Simple Plan song again hit its emo crescendo. *A cut pass?! Are you kidding?!*

"CAG is already aware — your FNAEB board will be later this week. Until then, you're grounded indefinitely."

Dude… dude! "No! What about the Admin Olympics?! The LAAF!" Rowland asked, hysterical.

IROK shrugged and smirked, "Guess we're gonna have to go with Juice-man after all!"

Un-fucking-believable… this is what they wanted all along…" I… I don't even know what to say to you. This is… wow, guys — *fuck* you *all..."*

"Well, where you'll be staying, you'll have *plenty* of time to think about it," T6 said sternly.

"And where's that?" Sam asked, his jaw clenched.

"You're headed to the Katsopolis brig, homeboy," T6 announced with glee. "Hope you like prison food…"

IROK jumped in and shouted, "And p —"

Sam heard nothing else as he felt an injection into his neck — instantly incapacitating him, as he collapsed to the floor…

~

Dr. Suabedissen donned his hood, pushed his glasses up, and let his long, flowing black cape drape behind him as he walked up to his test subject in the 7th deck laboratory. He steepled his fingertips together to display the body language of confidence — something he'd once read in a book about cultivating charisma. He clasped his hands, leaving his pointer fingers out and putting them to his lips, as he said slowly but forcefully, "I'm going to ask this one more time, subject 14-3 — and if you don't play along? Things are going to get… *painful..."* He took a deep breath and expounded, "I *know* you're aware of tactics at the S3 level… and I need you to explain them right here, *right now.* As you know, our bots are highly advanced machines capable of incorporating any global tactic to flawless levels of efficiency. However, in order to maintain our advantage, we need to input *current* recommendations into their software. So, you cretin, we can do this the *easy* way…" he smiled and took a green notepad out of his lab coat pocket protector — then shifted to a scowl and warned, "*Or,* we can do this the *hard* way…" He pointed to the center of the room, where a spotlight illuminated a red cruise box — a long, steel rectangular deployment container known for inconvenience, painful carriage, and busted knuckles.

The test subject — physically beaten and mentally battered from the torturing — said nothing. His hands and legs were tied down to an operating table — a reprieve from being forced to stand, where he undoubtedly would have collapsed from the suffering. He'd withstood plenty of abuse and slander so far — but sadly, he knew the worst was yet to come… And yet, he'd protected the Super-Secret-Sensitive information for weeks, and he sure as hell wasn't about to give it up to this prick now.

Frowning, Dr. Suabedissen translated the prisoner's silence as a decline. "No? Well then… so be it…" He walked up to the cruise box and opened the lid — reaching in and removing two objects.

The prisoner's body immediately tensed as he recognized what the doctor had grabbed: Two Squadron Toys-brand F/A-18E models in pristine condition, with long metal-rod handle attachments.

The doctor snarled as he saw the prisoner's reaction. He took a model in each hand, holding them like swords, and slowly wavered them back and forth, bringing the wings closer and closer each time. He prodded further, "So… would you like to talk to me about pursuit curves? Debrief arrows? The 12-step CAS process?"

The inmate mumbled something.

"What's that?" Suabedissen asked, ceasing model movement. "Do you have something to say after all?"

"Yeah, I do..." The tied-down man paused, cleared his throat, and said, "If you think you're getting any S3 information from me... then you're fucking *Flynnsane*. Do you *really* expect me to talk, doctor?"

Suabedissen shook his head in disappointment and said, "No, Admiral Flynn — I expect you to *cry*…" The doctor tsk'd and continued, "That is a shame… because the way these models are flying *awfully* close together… I think they just... might…"

The prisoner's eyes widened in fear.

"… touch…" The doctor moved them even closer, "… tips..." — and gave the models the slightest bit of contact.

"NOOOOO!!" the prisoner screamed, his agony reverberating in the lab.

The doctor left the models contacting each other for no less than five seconds; the anguished yells present the entire time.

When Dr. Suabedissen finally gave some safe separation between the two toy planes, the inmate's screaming was replaced by heavy breathing and sobbing. Suabedissen shook his head in disdain and announced, "Minus point — man crying. I expected much more from you, FISTY. But that's ok — you'll have plenty of chances for redemption, as this session has *just* begun. We're merely in Phase 1 of OPERATION: PIGPEN! Let's see if these models can fly a little better form this time, still on the *same* squawk..." he returned the two jets to a close-aboard position before yelling, "Uh oh!" and contacting them together yet again — the prisoner's ear-splitting wails returning.

The sound of the man's raw, painful emotion brought joy to the doctor's heart, as Suabedissen stood with an exaggerated chest-out posture and his elbows flared out — peacocking body language tips he'd also read — and thought to himself, 'This is even more delightful than the sound of slaughtering the Demi-Goblins in the Forest of Frenzy...'

Dr. Suabedissen continued to clink the models together, laughing maniacally as he watched Admiral Flynn writhe in agony at the sight of two toys being handled with abhorrent unprofessionalism...

5

The Good Dude Feud

*S*till in his flight gear, LT Rowland stormed into the ready room and ripped his helmet off, shouting, "That fucking new guy is the worst!"

The SDO – the squadron Intel O – quickly stood up and asked, "Nickels! Do you mind logging your SHARP? And how were your comms? Did you take or give or dump any – "

"I'll deal with that shit later," Rowland barked at the watchstander, who gasped at Sam's crude language.

Skipper got up from his computer – a top-of-the-line 'CAG' Laptop – and said, "Woah, Nickels – what's going on? What happened?"

Sam shook his head. "The FNG, sir. Bobby – or whatever his name is – he can't do anything right, and I just reflew my Level 4 checkride thanks to that moron!"

With a de-escalatory nature, Skipper put a hand on Sam's shoulder and said, "Nickels, hey… calm down. Take a deep breath – let's get you a white Monster." He looked to another junior officer and asked, "JABA, do you mind grabbing one?"

"Sure thing, sir," JABA responded as he ran over and opened the squadron mini fridge – full of Monsters and Celsii – and tossed a can of legal amphetamines to Skipper.

As he handed the Monster to Sam, Skipper chuckled and said, "You crazy millennials. Back in my day, coffee got the job done just fine – and now you kids can't go longer than a 1.5 cycle without this chemical junk!" Invoking a slight smile from Sam, he continued, "Talk to me, Nickels – tell me what's going on."

Nickels cracked open his liquefied cocaine and said, "Sir… I don't even know where to begin…"

Sam told him about LT Ward's extreme struggles as a wingman on this flight – about how he forgot his recording device RMM in the ready room, leading to a late start and missed check-in. About his embarrassing secure comm when attempting to call 'airborne' – on a case 1 departure – causing a crushing wave of mickeys to be sent his way. How he had to underrun on his initial join to tac-wing – to the wrong flight lead. That he took twenty minutes to tank because he spent the first fifteen trying to figure out how to extend his probe.

And it got worse – Sam discussed how Ward G-warmed in the incorrect direction. How he made AUX calls on PRI, and PRI calls on the ECM switch. His battle damage checks nearly turned into battle damage. And to top it all off, his boat recovery was brutal. He managed to have such an overshooting start that he ended up on the right side of the tower – fortunately, he had forgotten to descend. After the wave off, he gave himself a one-minute groove length that Paddles mercifully accepted since he was the final aircraft to recover. His pass? Woof. If the game plan pass was to lens-check the datums from red ball to full tall? Ward nailed it. Why Paddles took him aboard, Sam couldn't fathom. He eventually crashed down before the 1-wire and 903'd the jet. And to add insult to injury, he left his RMM in the jet this time, and had to go back and retrieve it before obtaining any shot data – not that it mattered, since his invalid performance had trainwrecked the entire mission portion of the flight.

After hearing the whole ordeal, Skipper took a long pause and said, "Ok... I get it. It wasn't one for his personal highlight reel. Frankly, it sounds pretty horrendous... but what are you going to do, just give up on teaching him? Nickels, you know what FNG stands for, right?" he asked with a smile.

"Yes, sir..."

"So you've got to put that into perspective – he's a brand fuckin' new guy; he has immeasurable amounts yet to learn. Don't forget what it was like when you were a Chippy new guy!"

"Well, come on, sir, I never did anything this stupid..." Sam said in defense.

Skipper grinned. "Oh, I seem to remember somebody trying to rendezvous, and then blowing right past me with 100 knots of airspeed advantage overhead the ship – at my altitude – before he finally gained visual..."

Sam looked bashful and said, "Yeah... I mean... but that was my first flight in the Chippies! Not even a week in!"

Laughing, Skipper continued, "How about a pilot who oversped the gear on a Case 3 departure a couple of months later?"

Twisting his lips a bit, Sam muttered, "Yeah... I mean... I guess I wasn't exactly a shit hot new guy..."

"But look at you now, Nickels," Skipper smiled. "You're not only one of my most talented JOPA pilots, but one of my best pilots, period. Your admin is second to none on this entire ship. Your tactical prowess? Sure, you may have reflown today – but you're gonna get another crack in a few days. And if it's canceled, or doesn't go well? Another after that. Hell, we'll keep trying forever if needed. We would never give up on you, because I know you would never give up on us," he said with a smile, before adding with a wink, "But I have a feeling you'll be a full-fledged division lead pretty quickly."

Sam smiled bashfully and shrugged.

"But, most important of all…" Skipper continued, "your good dudesmanship. Nickels, you've become one of the best dudes I've ever seen in almost twenty years in the community. You have an incredibly bright future in this biz if you continue on this path." He paused and looked a bit more serious as he added, "But let me warn you: There will be distractors. Frustrations. Moments that make you want to quit and give up on everything – and most dangerous of all? The Disease of Me. Don't fall for any of it, Sam. To brave the toughest moments of this job is to discover the greatest satisfaction, memories, and friendships that life has to offer. Remember that." He clasped Sam on the shoulder and finished with, "And go easy on Bobby, ok? Remember the tasking I gave you, Sam: Let the development of his abilities – and your patience in grooming those abilities – be a direct reflection of your aptitude to lead; the next step in your storied career."

Sam took a deep breath. "Thanks, Skipper, I appreciate it. That means a lot, and I won't forget it."

Skipper smiled. "Anytime, Nickels. Now, it's time for me to return to important Skipper duties…" He opened up his CAG Laptop and got to work doing what O-5s do.

Nickels exited the room with his Monster in hand, and walked back toward the PR shop to doff his flight gear. On the way there, he saw FNG Ward walking back, who looked excited as he said, "Nickels! Dude, I know I messed up a lot out there, but damn – that was so much fun! Your flight management was great, and you seemed so far ahead of me and the jet – I can't wait to be there one day! How are you feeling about the debrief?"

Sam wanted so badly to do as Skipper said – to be patient and understanding – but he just couldn't. He disagreed with it. Skipper is wrong… this is a life-and-death business… there's no room for these kinds of mistakes, foolish errors, or 'fun' on a flight like that. I need to toughen this limfac up now—otherwise, how will he learn? He took a deep breath – and double-knife-handed the young FNG. "Fun? Fun?! Bobby, what part of that was fun to you?! You should be professionally embarrassed about what just happened. You made every fucking mistake in the book – mistakes that the author hadn't even thought of! You're saying you 'can't wait' to be where I am in the jet?! Dude, no offense, but you fucking suck. You need to turn that shit around right now, or else you aren't gonna survive in this biz, let alone get anywhere close to where I am."

Juice, full of remorse, tried to apologize. "Nickels… I'm really sorry… I know there's been some growing pains, but I promise you: I'm going to work my ass off to get to where you are! We can look at my tapes, and with your help, I – "

Furiously shaking his head and still dicing invisible veggies in the air with his hands, Sam cut him off with, "Ugh! Dude! Message to Garcia! This isn't the RAG, bro – you gotta learn this stuff on your own! I don't have time to be teaching you this shit! I don't even want to look at your tapes… because Jesus – what I saw from my jet was so bad, I can't even imagine what it looks like on your displays – and I don't think I can handle any more cringing. So, let me warn you right now: this is not going to be a fun debrief for you, and it's one you will never forget – but it's the only way you're going to change. And I certainly hope you look back on this *flight often — because making it a lasting scar in your mind is the* least *I can do for you as a leader," he emphasized.*

"Bobby — you are not *good, and I don't want to fly with you anymore. You're going to be nothing more than an average JO in this job, and that's if you get your shit together. I know you've looked up to me, but you need to find a new idol, because — again, no offense — my level is way out of your league. Someday, you* might *be good enough to fly a dash-four spare off a large force attack that I'm* leading, *but even* that's *going to take a lot of work. You will never be a package commander, strike lead, or even a div lead — but you at least need to get good enough that you don't fucking die — or worse, embarrass our squadron. Got it?"*

The life had left the FNG's eyes. Sam couldn't tell for sure, but it looked like a tear may have even dropped from the silver-haired FNG's duct. With two knives of phalanges pointing at him, he held a prolonged silence before finally whispering, "Ok, Nickels..."

He turned and walked away as Sam unequipped his hand weapons and held his forehead, exhaling after the outburst, but feeling slightly better. He'll thank me one day... if he's still around... *Sam strolled toward the PR shop to take his gear off, and was so amped from the outburst that he failed to notice his observer:* Skipper, *watching from the arresting gear room, arms folded across his chest, and shaking his head in disappointment...*

~

"Congratulations, LT Ward!" CAG stated happily, "I can't think of any man I'd rather have in charge of this operation than the most administratively sound pilot in the universe: The Admin King himself!"

Juice shook CAG's hand and said, "Thank you, sir. To be leading this LAAF... and against my former coworkers... it's the greatest challenge I could ever hope for, and a true honor to be selected. My whole professional career, I've been doubted — people thought I couldn't learn to safely join in parade, let alone win first-place in 'Join-Up of the Year.' They said I couldn't find on-speed, let alone hold the record for longest manual 8.1 alpha. They told me I couldn't even make a fucking *kneeboard card*, let alone have a framed SFWT checkride KBC enshrined in the aviation hall of fame — and now to be doing this?" Juice smiled confidently, expressing, "I think a lot of people would be shocked to see this moment."

CAG smiled. "You are a true Noddik underdog story for the nation to look up to! And not to mention, I have some more good news: The line periods were just finalized, and..." he gestured to the three Padroids who were attending the LAAF in-brief.

NEODD SWEVEN, wearing a Jacksonville Jaguars Blaine Gabbert jersey, started rubbing his hands together — creating sparks between his steel palms — and chuckled, "*Well*, sir, if we're going to ruin the surprise..." before announcing, "... Ladies and gents, we've got the Noddik fleet's first ever non-LSO 4.0-line period!" The trio of

Padroids cheered wildly, taking turns fist bumping Juice and slapping him on the shoulder.

Elated, Juice said, "Ahhh, guys, no way... This is unreal! I owe it all to you dudes—you kept me fresh as hell out there, and I wouldn't have *half* the swag without you guys keeping my lights bright, my ball comms tight, and my cockpit descents fucking cool as a kite."

IROK, in his Matt Jones jersey, pumped both fists and said, "Bro, that's awesome! Kites are fucking *dope!*"

T6, sporting Josh Scobee's name, nodded enthusiastically and exclaimed, "Bro, a hot chick sees you flying a kite at a park? *Game over*, bro!" He and IROK high-fived and made obscene gestures.

Juice nodded. "Game over, indeed." He looked around and asked, "Hey, where is <MCSALAD>?"

CAG gave a slightly sad look and said, "He's in a SWAGGI-D with Dr. Suabedissen..."

"Hmmph," Juice grunted. "A Session With A General Goal of Intensifying Dopeness? I didn't realize he had been lacking on the coolness factor lately... is he alright?"

NEODD took this one and said, "Affirm, broski. Don't worry—he'll be good to go for the Admin Olympics—the doc just needs to give him a few lessons from the 'School of Cool' to get him back to SwagCon-Alpha."

"Well, if there's anyone suited to teach someone about being a badass, it's definitely Doctor Suabedissen," Juice acknowledged.

"I know, right!" T6 exclaimed. "Have you heard about his girlfriend? A fucking *supermodel*, bro!"

IROK chimed in, "Dude, that guy is a total *panty-dropper!*"

Robotic CAG clasped his hands and said, "Gents, as much as I love talking about normal human things like kites and attractive female specimen and dropping trou', we must get to the meat of the matter: the Admin Olympics in-brief!"

Juice and the Padroids nodded, listening intently as the air wing commander opened his PowerPoint and began the brief, TOPGUN-style.

CAG cleared his throat. "3... 2... 1... HACK. The year was 2026. The Noddik Empire had undergone approximately 1000 days aboard the NIRD Katsopolis, encountering exactly 365 mishaps of various categories, from catastrophic airplane landings, to apocalyptic laundry machine fires, to cataclysmic fatalities of many high-ranking chiefs and officers due to heart attacks caused by witnessing a lack of shine in the hallways. While the threat nation of planet Earth was thriving from successful technological advancements such as General Quarters—a form of live-action-role-playing *so* intensive and realistic that they become oblivious to real-life schedules and tasks; Landing airplanes safely with Landing Signal Officers and the Improved Fresnel Lens Optical Landing System—formerly the Fresnel Lens Optical Landing System; And a robust 1MC system used to give all-hands exciting hype announcements from the Big Executive Officer—things like brass shining opportunities, ship-sponsored-gambling bingo ticket sales, and Magic: The Gathering tournaments..." CAG took a deep breath after his long run-on sentence, then attempted to continue, "It came to the Noddik's attention that we were severely deficient in the art of administrative executing... uhh..." He took another brief pause as he got lost in his train of thought, his arms looking extra robotic, sitting stiffly at his side as if he had a temporary glitch or framerate crash in his lecture RAM data. To fix the glitch, he repeated his last sentence to trigger his lecture sequence and regain his cadence: "It came to the Noddik's attention that we were severely deficient... in the art of administrative *execution* as a nation. As a result, we hired a series of highly proficient, carrier-experienced United States Navy pilots to teach us the abilities needed to achieve excellence in the Admin phase of Operations."

Juice listened as CAG droned on about the utilization of essential admin things like cleaning stations, air plan cartoons, an entire type/model/series system of trash sorting, etc. He started to zone out when CAG delved into the pros and cons of different types of MatCons, NetCons, and EMCONs. He finally dozed off when CAG began explaining the importance behind creating a highly skilled army-of-one 'Tactical Actions Officer' to command the SNOOPIE Team, and the necessity of a Low Visibility Detail to squint extra hard through bad weather to avoid collisions.

Eventually, after ten minutes of napping, Juice's attention was recaptured when CAG said, "And so, given the tactical and political reasons I just explained, it is imminently important for us to challenge the United States Navy and *win* in the official Admin Olympics. As a reminder, the Olympics will consist of three evolutions, and the first to win two of them will be declared the champion—and hold Administrative Superiority in the galaxy.

"The first evolution will be Phase 1: Standard Admin. This phase will test our respective ships' abilities to handle a simple day with no external problems. As you can imagine, this *should* be a relatively uneventful competition, given the beautiful monotony and procedural compliance of our team of highly sophisticated bots. Are there any questions on the first evolution?"

As the crowd silently shook their heads, Juice hoped this vanilla phase would not be covered too heavily in the event that a documentation was ever written about these Olympics—he felt confident that something more exciting could surely be focused on instead.

CAG continued, "The second evolution will be Phase 2: Admin Recoveries. This will detail a competition between the two air wings, *specifically* geared toward earning the top landing grades. Each nation will select three pilots to each complete six landings, which will all be tallied up and averaged to calculate the teams' Grade Point Averages—the higher score determining victory. Are there any questions on the second evolution?"

NEODD SWEVEN stood up and introduced himself before asking, "Yes sir— NEODD SWEVEN, callsign NEODD SWEVEN; CAG Padroids—Sir, how will grades be determined?"

Smiling, CAG said, "Good question, SWEVEN. Both sets of LSOs will collaborate to ensure fair grading of all six participants. However, as the challenger nation, we will agree to abide by the challengee's landing system; thus, we will compete with the US Navy's means of carrier approach and grading criteria. Fortunately, I can't imagine either are much different than ours. Does that answer your question?"

"Big rog—yes, it does, sir! Should be no problem for us to win that phase!" NEODD said confidently.

CAG nodded, then went back to his slides. "The final evolution, if required, is Phase 3: Admin Adaptation. It will be two simultaneous General Quarters scenarios, with rival nations creating Red game plans for each other. If we end up in this deciding bout, the first to solve the issue and stop the clock whilst stopping the problem will be declared the Olympics winner. Are there any questions on the third, if necessary, evolution?"

When nobody stood up, CAG clicked to a random black and white airplane wrap-up slide on his PowerPoint, his voice sounding even more scripted and robotic as he concluded with, "Let me warn you, gentlemen—these Olympics will not be for the faint of heart. This is bigger than conduct—this is *Admin*. We must select our most war-hardened, standardized members, because ignorance, negligence, or non-standardance will mean a certain downfall for our nation." He clicked to a black slide and looked to the crowd, asking, "Are there any questions on the third, if necessary, evolution?" Silence. "Are there any questions on anything I covered here today?"

CAG looked at his wrist—there was no watch, but he referenced his internal GPS time sync. "I'm coming up on time 5-3—let's meet again at time 0-0 for Dr. Suabedissen's lecture on 'Seducing women into showing you their private parts.' Thank you for your time today; please give me five for critiques." As he walked off, a tactical fade-in of 'Call Me Maybe' by Carly Rae Jepson started playing in the background— the result of Suabedissen's tasking to help the briefers develop an epic soundtrack to accompany serious briefs.

The Padroids came up to Juice during the break, where IROK hyped him up with, "You totally got this, bro! I am *so* pumped for Phase 2! If those goons are anything like weak-ass Captain Rowland, this is going to be a *joke*! Those guys know *nothing* about being cool!" In jest of what he'd heard about Earth Paddles, he raised his hands exaggeratedly and said with a mock nerdy tone, "Uhhh... Paddles here... uhh roger? Uhh yeah... err... we got you high... err... coming down... uhh roger ball, easy with it, come right for bolter?!" He laughed at his own joke and elbowed Juice to elicit a response.

Juice slightly chuckled, as IROK proudly looked around to see if anybody noticed his superior laughing at his joke. Ward then added, "Yeah, I'm feeling good about it. But just realize this, guys: they aren't *complete* idiots back on Earth. We'll be playing by their rules, so it's probably worth looking at VSI gouge, proper abeam distances, and the game plan pass..."

In concerned shock, the Padroids looked at each other—and then, after a few seconds of silence, started busting up laughing. "Nice one, Juice!" NEODD cried out. "God, could you *imagine*? Memorizing numbers to fly for the entire pass... Jesus Christ, how fucking nerdy would that be!"

IROK chimed in, "I know, right!" Pretending to use his nerdy human LSO voice, he imitated again, "Uhhh... Paddles here... roger ball... uhhh I'm flying an approximate five-point-oh abeam for 40 billion VSI... err... uhh... what does VSI stand for? Uhh... er... 'Virgin Status Indication'... Ok... game plan pass here... err... my game plan is to land... roger that, Paddles? Errr... wait... *I'm* Paddles... uhhh..." until he couldn't go anymore, too busy cracking up.

T6 scoffed. "Bro, the game plan pass? What game plan *is* there aside from looking like a dope-ass baller as you touch down?!"

Juice smiled softly and said, "Hah, yeah, I guess. Hey guys, I'm gonna go use the head real fast."

As he walked away, the Padroids continued with their impersonations, "Uhh roger head usage... uhh... make sure you use proper interval... and err... appropriate groove length... errr... CLARA... roger NESA..."

Juice closed the door, drowning out the Padroids' laughter. He grabbed his head and rubbed his temples. "Dude—these guys... what the *fuck*, man..."

Juice had been 'playing the game' with the Padroids ever since he arrived at the NIRD Katsopolis. He wasn't stupid—he knew whose shoulders to rub to get in the good graces of the air wing. He knew how much it would help his career to be the Padroids' 'Yes Man,' and to hype them up every time they entered a room. And he *knew* that these 'angels' chugged the kool aid of their own cult and pushed their religion on others like it was an obligatory pilot pilgrimage to one day arrive at the Padroids Promised Land... But it didn't matter. It was all worth it to reach this moment: the opportunity to lead this LAAF and earn the most important victory of his life.

But proving Admin superiority for the Noddiks wasn't what Juice cared about, nor was he concerned with any resulting fame or fortunes. What he *truly* wanted was to professionally humiliate Captain Rowland on the grandest stage possible.

Everything in Juice's career revolved around Sam. His whole life, he'd dreamed of being a jet pilot and flying alongside others with that same aviation passion. When he finished the RAG and joined the Chippies, he felt like he was living his dream, earning the best-case scenario for what he'd wanted in flight school—a single-seat fighter aircraft located at the tip of the tactical spear, and the opportunity to serve alongside living *legends*—more specifically, *a* living legend: LT Sam "Nickels" Rowland. Rowland was a modern-day folk hero, with stories of his various exploits spread amongst VT and RAG students: the adversary/missile simo shootdown with FISTY, the record-setting 69 valid JDAM employed on a combat deployment (made even more impressive by the fact that he *intentionally* invalidated a potential 70th for numbers' sake, knowing that he'd still meet the ground commander's intent), and of course, the countless stories of his good dudesmanship. He was the ultimate fighter pilot and Good Dude—selfless, positive, and interested in the team's well-being—in a world so easily plagued by the Disease of Me.

So, naturally, Juice's world was rocked when he was treated like absolute *shit* by Sam, who appeared nothing like the RAG urban legend. Sam was the senior JOPA, nearing the end of his unprecedented JO tour and deciding where to take his talents—with seemingly every detailing opportunity on the table. But when Juice arrived? Sam had no patience for the boat, no tolerance for the lifestyle, and *certainly* no acceptance of FNG Ward. He was constantly complaining about anything and everything at sea; he demanded to be scheduled for specific events, left off others, and took every 'good deal' he possibly could, saving no food for the young. And with Juice? Sam made it a personal mission to make Ward's life a living hell.

Juice was the last 'new guy' Sam would hold JOPA leadership over, and he seemed dedicated to making sure that 'the standard was upheld,' as he'd always claimed—but Juice didn't see it that way at all. He saw that Sam had become nothing less than a diva of aviation—and a complete asshole of a diva, at that. Sam berated him relentlessly for admin mistakes, taunting him publicly for every little error and insisting that Juice wasn't possibly going to make it through his JO tour. He hazed him practically every day—reporting Juice to the Big XO for washing his flight suit in self-serve laundry, pulling circuit breakers to turn off Juice's stateroom air conditioning, and even printing out *fake* schedules—slipping them under Juice's door—so that he'd show up late to briefs and embarrass himself.

Most memorable to Juice—for all the wrong reasons—was Rowland's Level 4 checkride. Admittedly, it hadn't been Juice's best flight ever... and the senior JO certainly let him know that. The way Sam so aggressively lashed out at him in the hallway, and subsequently made multiple snide comments in the debrief... Juice could never forget it. "Showtime 14, can you explain to the room why you found it necessary to shoot this comm-air, ten thousand feet above the fight—and why you did it invalidly?"

or "Showtime 14, just *where* did you find those extra two missiles? Well, clearly, those guys wouldn't have attrited… Logical conclusion? This FNG would get shot down, and the air wing lethality result would be addition by subtraction," and even, "Bandits, you're more than welcome to stay for the comm review—and if you don't, would you mind taking Showtime 14 with you?" Everybody was cracking up the entire time; the red air actually *did* stay for the debrief, just to witness the ongoing roast of Showtime 14.

And that's the other thing that frustrated Juice: the air wing-wide tolerance. With Sam legendarily respected by his peers already, they seemed to ignore his antics. They were brainless lemmings to his juvenile jokes and new quirks, encouraging his dickish behavior and turning a blind eye to—as The Lorax once put it—the 'spineless, backstabbing bitch' that Sam had become. It was a reality that nobody wanted to accept—until Rowland had made it blatantly obvious by betraying his friends and country for millions of dollars.

At the tail end of his time as a Chippy, Sam's ego had become further inflated, and he even changed his Outlook profile job description to "VFA-195 Admin SME." He *loved* his 'standard' admin debriefs. It made Juice sick to see the cocky smile on Sam's face when he'd ask people if they had anything for admin, and they responded in awe, "Nope!" Juice wanted to take this strange flex away from him; he wanted to rob Sam of the single account he'd invested all of his pride into.

And so, Juice became a madman of admin obsession. He read through the entire F/A-18 NATOPS every single week and dug through old flight school FTIs to enhance his understanding of the basics. He made friends with the yellow shirts and gained permission to practice taxiing around the carrier deck during the early AM hours. He trained his instinctual senses by seeing how long he could keep his eyes closed during admin evolutions; at first, he was terrified to keep them shut for more than a second during a carrier launch. But within months? He was joining, battle-damage-checking, and working from the break to the 180—*all* with his eyes closed for the entire duration. He believed he could one day even fly the ball 'deadeye.' Admin had become one with his body; his stick and throttle movements an extension of his inner understandings of 'standard procedures.'

And now, here he was—with career milestones of obsessive revenge under his belt and relentless efforts leading to this moment—he stood poised, ready, and *confident*. Confident that he would lead the Noddik squad to victory in this LAAF. Confident that those doubted him when he was an inexperienced new guy would be proven wrong. But, most important to him, *confident* that finally—*finally*—he would be able to show Sam that Juice was the better pilot, the worthy Admin King, and the undisputed Goodest Dude…

~

Dr. Suabedissen pushed his glasses up and took a long look at <MCSALAD>, biting his lip and shaking his head, clearly displeased with what he was hearing. "Mr. <MCSALAD>, tell me again about these strange thoughts?" He paced around nervously, holding his left elbow with his right hand, slumping over with a meek, submissive posture. Crossing his legs as he stood, making himself appear as small and fragile as possible, Suabedissen was unable to remember *any* of the confidence-building tips he'd learned from his dating books at the moment, as he was *far* too concerned with the way this SWAGGI-D was going...

<MCSALAD> took a deep breath and slowly explained, "So, it's just these random numbers that keep appearing over and over again in my subconscious RAM thoughts: I hear 'power, pause, turn' and then instantly think '27-30 degrees.' Next, I'll see these numbers—200-300... then it transitions to 300-500... and then they get even higher..." He shrugged, wincing his eyes, and expressed, "It's so... *strange*. And two of the other numbers—500 and 90—something about those two... it's as if the numbers were paired together in my processing system..."

"Uhh... processing system..." the doctor said as he started scratching his forearm nervously, "Yes... because... you certainly don't have a brain, being a coded robot and all... hehe..." he gulped after his anxious laughter.

<MCSALAD>, sitting on the couch in Suabedissen's O-3 level office, replied, "Yes, doctor, I know." Then he paused, gave what he felt to be a human expression of uncertainty, and added, "But sometimes... sometimes, I feel like my processing system has a mind of its own. Like... I have thoughts and feelings that the other Padroids don't. For instance, I heard this song in a ready room the other day—I think it was called 'Welcome to the Black Parade.' Regardless, the other dudes didn't notice at all, but man... I just felt like *raging*. Like... do you ever feel that, doctor? Do you ever have the urge to compose a melodic piece about the deepest pent-up emotions within you, and scream the lyrics to anyone listening? Feel like writing a ballad about your heart being fucking torn out of your stomach and sliced into a million pieces by some girl? Or about how nobody understands you in this tortured life of consumerism and media-obsessed society of conformists?"

Suabedissen walked to his desk and picked up his trusty 16-sided die, rubbing it in his hands feverishly to try and calm himself down. He knew that this was *not* good.

"And when we bring these guys aboard, doctor," <MCSALAD> continued, "I don't say much—why *should* I? All the landings look the same. But sometimes I'll dream of jets coming in on a *non*-90-degree glideslope—and there are actually *deviations*. Mostly minor or average, and still safe—but man... this approach... I've never processed anything like it." He looked up and to the right, contemplating how to best describe it, before reestablishing eye contact and explaining, "It's roughly a three-and-a-half-degree descent *angle...* but somehow more like an *effective* three-degree glidepath? I don't know..." Remembering another detail, his eyes lit up as he raised his hands, "And I swear—it was almost like the landing area was slowly moving *away* from the aircraft!"

Dr. Suabedissen tried to feign astonishment. "Whaaat? For real? That's crazy..."

"I know! But doctor, you know what the craziest part was?" <MCSALAD> coded up an expression of sheepism and admitted, "... It was *way* more satisfying. Me and the guys out there—they weren't the Padroids. We weren't wearing NFL jerseys or backward hats—and maybe we didn't look as cool, doctor, but you know what? We were actually *making a difference!* I couldn't make out what the other guys were saying on the radio, but the plane was moving *in response* to their words! They landed with these... these *hook*-like things... it was insanity. And once, when a jet came to a stop on this moving LA, I could see its side number..." <MCSALAD> smiled, his eyes again lighting up in awe as he said, "It was 411... and I could almost make out the name painted on..."

"Enough!" The doctor yelled, slamming the table (and wincing as he hurt his fist). "Enough of this dream talk! <MCSALAD>, these are *not* good thoughts you are having—you need to cease this line of thinking!" He paused, pushed his glasses up, and gave a stern, suspicious look toward the Padroids as he probed, "... Have you been taking your fighter candy, <MCSALAD>?"

<MCSALAD> hesitated, looked away, and then lied, "Yes... of course I have, doctor..."

Dr. Suabedissen lifted his head to look down through his lenses like a librarian. "I'd like to observe you taking them." When he sensed his subject's uncertainty, he insisted, "Trust me, <MCSALAD>—these are key contributors toward any naval aviator's success..." He reached into his pocket protector and pulled out an unmarked can, opening the lid. "Go ahead—put one in your lip, and see how it changes your entire world..."

<MCSALAD> took the can and looked at it nervously. His strange night visions had started when he stopped taking his prescription of these Xtra Alpha Nectars, or 'XANs' as Dr. Suabedissen called them. Sure, he knew he could make all his strange thoughts go away if he went back on the drugs... but he wasn't ready to abandon this spiritual journey of self-realization. "Doctor, if it's alright with you, I'd rather not take one right now..."

Dr. Suabedissen raised the hood on his dark black cloak and stated, "I don't think you understand, <MCSALAD>; I am *ordering* you to pop a XAN right now…" as he extended his hand outward, grinning evilly as he did.

Feeling uneasy, <MCSALAD> nervously reached out and grabbed one. The visions were mystifying, yet so vivid—the enigmatic 'meatball, lineup, AOA' chant was still burning in his head. He had to think of *something* to buy himself more time to remember… "Say, doctor," he said inquisitively, attempting to generate a concerned look on his face. "I was curious—a friend of mine on the ship wanted me to help him with a raid on one of those underwater towns, and suggested I bring a fire sword—is that a good idea?"

The doctor's grin immediately turned into a scowl. "Are you talking about The Fabled Underwater City of Atlantica?!"

Still holding the XAN, <MCSALAD> replied, "Uhh… yeah…"

His hands wildly flailing, he shouted, "*Oh* my god! A *fire* sword in a water-based environment?! That is *preposterous!* I mean, even if it was the Mythical Broadsword of Lucifer's Flames, it would be no better than a simple *pixie dagger* down there, with the elemental disadvantage factored in!" He scoffed and forcefully stated, "No, <MCSALAD>, I would *not* do that at all. That raid will be a disaster! Have you done *any* research?! The path to that city is rife with monsoon monsters, piranha-centaurs, and even demi-sharks with *flame-freezing capabilities!*" Repulsion worn on his face, he continued ranting, "This… I can't even… what's this guy's name? Who was this *idiot sailor* who asked you to bring such a sword? Probably not even level 10 yet… ROFL. This noob has *no* business trying to become a Raid Lead qual yet… SMH…" he shook his head, verbalizing all these text acronyms as if they were actual words. His eyes widening a bit, he informed <MCSALAD>, "Now, what you'd *want* to do is bring more of a plasma-based weapon, *but then*, you're going to need to go to the Savage Village of Dalaarn and get the blacksmith Pitoli to forge it for water protection." He turned to grab a pen and paper from his desk, "Here, I'll write down directions to the town from the spawn point in Metulia." He scribbled down while muttering things in frustration like "flame sword, Jesus…", "would get yourself freaking PWNED," and "going to meet with the boat's guild leadership about this sailor…"

He finally finished his note and turned back while saying, "Ok, so, you'll need to buy, *or catch*, a horse—which is *far* easier said than done, might I add—and then—"

But when he looked for <MCSALAD>, there was no Padroids to be found. Realizing what had happened, the doctor threw his notepad across the room and exclaimed, "God… *dammit!"*

The Noddik Empire had a runner on their hands. "Everybody runs, Chris…" he said to himself, shaking his head. "Everybody runs." He looked at his watch and hacked the clock. "But you can't run forever…"

~

Captain Rowland rolled over and grabbed his neck, pain emanating from it. He was lying on the ground, his cheek pressed against the cold stone floor. *Where am I?* After opening his eyes and rubbing them briefly, he realized the room was pitch-black. He felt around with his hands, trying to discern his surroundings—and found himself enclosed by walls of steel bars. *Am I in jail?* The last thing he could remember was BFMing... *Low T... he tried to kill me. But* was *it actually Low T?* Then he landed, flew manual, and... *NEODD SWEVEN... my cut pass... dammit!* His dreams of leading the Admin Olympics LAAF were over... another failed chance to prove himself. And instead? All the glory would be going to... *Juice. God damn him. He planned this all along! No surprise... Juice has been looking to end my career from the moment he arrived at the Chippies...*

Sam had been onto Juice's devious plot from the day he patched; Juice was *not* a good new guy. He was way too cocky for somebody who knew *nothing* about the fleet, leveraging off things he learned in the RAG and VTs. "Well, at the boat in the Advanced CQ, you weren't supposed to trust the ball at the 90 because of the roll angle," he'd say. "I feel like BFM was *harder* in the T-45 because you had to worry about pitch buck," he'd remind everyone. "Back at 122, we would set our bingo bug to 9.0 for internal checks; it makes much more sense that way," he insisted. It was horrendous.

And it was far too commonplace to find him cracking jokes *way* too soon with the other JOs, despite having earned zero credibility in the squadron yet. Sam would never forget the day when CP served him up the sweetest alley-oop of a joke at an Air Wing Fallon mass brief, when he asked, with a smile on his face, "Nickels, what can you tell me about the SLAM-ER?" And just as a sly grin appeared on Sam's face and he got ready to slam dunk it? Fucking *new guy Juice* interrupted and yelled, "Slam 'er? I hardly even know her!" The crowd went wild with laughter, and the Overall Instructor was so impressed that he awarded CP the Mission Commander qual right then and there, and handed everyone else frosty cold beers.

Yet the greatest irritant of all: Juice so *obviously* wanted to supplant Sam as the squadron Good Dude. He made it clear from day one that his goal was to be the greatest Navy pilot of all time—a complete joke, considering how awful he was upon showing up. He would ask Sam so many questions, constantly trying to pick his brain and get insider tips for how he could surpass him, turning Sam's legacy into that of just another forgotten pilot. Juice volunteered for *every* bad deal, from covering people's port duties with no strings attached, to turning random jets, picking up overnight Alert

15s, and even taking out the ready room trash. *He took out... the motherfucking... ready room... trash! God, he was such a* try-hard!

And the worst part was: the other JOs fell for it. They *loved* him. They thought he was a genuinely Good Dude, and couldn't see that he was simply trying to push Sam out of the squadron and take his place as the #1 bro. It was sickening and mind-blowing that nobody else saw through the act of this 'BIG TRY' — the callsign that Sam had so badly wanted to bestow upon him.

This was all made even more infuriating by the fact that Skipper had tasked Sam to mentor the young kid in the art of administration, as a form of his leadership training. Rowland hadn't minded taking on the task initially, but when he saw how awful Ward was at simple admin, completely incompetent to do the simplest of flight duties? Sam couldn't take it. And yet, Skipper *insisted* he remain patient with the boy...

Too much of Rowland's time as senior JOPA was spent tutoring this idiot instead of advancing his own skills. *Skipper, why the hell would you do this to me? Look what it's led to — motherfucking Juice is the LAAF lead, and I'm here in this cell. Congratulations, Juice, you fucking bastard... you've won...* "That two-faced, son of a jackal!" Sam yelled out loud.

"Ugggghhhh..."

What was that? A groan came from across the room; it sounded like Sam had a cellmate. "Hello?" he called out, "Is someone there...?"

"Uggggghhhh... who are you?" a man's voice responded.

Sam wasn't sure if he should be honest... TOPGUN recommended using an alter ego when dealing with an ambiguous contact. "My... my name is..." he racked his brain for something cool-sounding but believable. *Bingo.* "My name is Hayden Christensen. Who are you? And where are we?"

The cellmate paused as well, then responded, "My name is Ewan McGregor. We're in the NIRD Katsopolis brig... ughhhhh..."

Ewan McGregor? It sounded pretty plausible... especially given how confidently the man said it. I suppose he's telling the truth... "Mr. McGregor, what are you doing here? And are you ok?"

"I feel terrible, Hayden. I don't know how much longer I can take this..."

"Are... are they torturing you?" Sam asked.

"Hot affirm..." the man responded, wheezing and coughing.

Oh no... I must be next... Sam had once heard wild rumors that the Noddik Empire hired Latina female interrogation experts for torturing criminals, but had no SA to their tactics. "What are they doing? Starving you? Beating you?"

"Starving my heart and assaulting my soul..." The man bemoaned. "*Obscene* and *appalling* things: unzipping my zippers... exposing themselves by rolling up certain parts of their uniform… demonstrating things with their hands and fingers… making the models touch each other… And worst of all — they didn't allow us to talk about things or share learning points for hours after we finished our conduct…"

Uhhh… what? Curious to dig further into Ewan's background, Sam asked, "Sir, Mr. McGregor… might I ask what you did to end up in the brig?"

The man was silent at first, aside from some minor moans of pain, before he answered, "I came here to save one of the 'Goodest Dudes' I ever knew, before he sold his soul and became a complete spineless, backstabbing bitch. But I know there's still good in him… I can sense it…"

Sam gasped. *Wait a second… could it be?!* He took a deep breath and hesitantly began the authentication code of aviators: "Sidious, check in, AUX. Sidious 11."

The man responded, "Sidious 12."

Hmmm… Still unsure if he could trust the man, he pushed the process further. "Sidious, SECURE, AUX." He put his hand over his mouth and said, "Sidious 11."

"Sidious 12."

No way… I need to be sure though… With his hand still over his mouth, he said, "Sidious, squawk 1234; Alpha check, Rock, one two three, sixty-nine."

The man responded with silence.

Excitement rising in his voice, Sam called out, "Sidious, check in, voice alpha 95," he made a 'bloop' noise and then said, "Sidious 11."

"Bloop, Sidious 12."

There was only one final step to finish the secret authentication sequence… "Sidious, TAC, AUX! Sidious 11!"

The cellmate excitedly called out, "Sidious 12!"

"FISTY, it's you!"

"Nickels Rowland!" Admiral Flynn responded, matching Sam's glee, "It's *great* to hear your voice!"

Shaking his head sadly in the darkness, Sam lamented, "I'm sorry, FISTY, but Nickels no longer exists… he's long gone…"

"That's where you're wrong, my young Padawan," FISTY declared with a confident look of determination that radiated through the darkness, "Because — god dammit — I'm here to *save* Nickels." And with a cool, calm huskiness to his voice, he proudly announced, "Point, titular line."

6

The GOAT

*T*he focus went toward the erupting sideline — a sea of raucous red, celebrating moments
after Tevin Coleman ran the ball into the endzone. As the extra point found the uprights,
the jumbotron refreshed to display the slaughterfest occurring on this miserable Sunday night
in Houston. The Atlanta Falcons led the New England Patriots, 28-3, with the third quarter
already halfway over in Super Bowl LI.

"Stop tape." FISTY paused the footage as the camera panned to the score, pointing to
the image with his four-colored pen. He looked at LT Rowland and asked, "Nickels — in this
situation, late in the game, with a four-score deficit... would you say the Patriots are offensive,
neutral, or defensive?"

Rowland confidently responded, "The Patriots are in a defensive position."

Calmly nodding as Sam answered, FISTY affirmed, "Nice, man, you got it. The Patriots are very much defensive here. Now, this is, of course, far beyond the classic 'defensive sight
picture' that a team is accustomed to seeing while trailing, because the Falcons are well inside
their control zone. However, the defensive game plan still very much applies. It is at this point
in an engagement where we differentiate a 'good' aviator," FISTY paused for dramatic effect
before adding with a touch of voice inflection, "from a world-class champion."

Sam jotted down notes with his multi-colored pen on his folded piece of white paper and
ID card straight-edge, attempting to soak in every bit of knowledge he could from his tactics
tutor. Ever since FISTY joined their squadron as the Training Officer, Sam's life had become
filled with these intense tape reviews, chalk talks, briefing labs, and other forms of instruction.
FISTY was a fleet-renowned TOPGUN grad, considered one of the best in the business for his
ability to explain complex concepts and definitions into practical application using his revolutionary teaching method: NFL game film.

"Let's go 10x speed." FISTY fast-forwarded the tape during the ensuing Patriots drive
for a brief duration before directing, "Stop tape." The clock read 02:07. "Here, we have the last

clocked moment of the Patriots' 25-point deficit. There are just over 17 minutes remaining in regulation. The 'box' has proven itself to be in a very, very disadvantageous spot. But what about the man in the box? What about Tom Brady?"

Nodding, Sam gave a look of understanding. He was not surprised one bit that today's lesson involved Tom Brady. They always did with FISTY – he was a TB12 superfan. Regardless of whether the brief was covering BFM, JDAM employment, or radar theory, there was a high likelihood that FISTY was going to incorporate the NFL's GOAT into his lecture.

"I want you to look here, Nickels," he said as he pointed to a freeze frame of Tom Brady's face. FISTY spoke with restraint – almost as if he was robotic, showing no emotion. But Sam knew what was to come at the end of this session – at some point in every lesson involving TB12, FISTY simply could not contain his enthusiasm… "This is the face of a man who is frustrated and fed up, but nowhere near dispirited nor ready to give up. Any mere mortal would've said, 'There's a dude at my 6, I'm about to bust the deck, and I've got no energy left – this one's over.' But Tom Brady isn't your average quarterback. He's the aviator you need to strive to be, Nickels. Tom Brady found himself at the merge, highly defensive – but refused to go down quietly. He followed the defensive game plan, complicated the attacker's kill shot, and kept fighting no matter how futile it seemed. Fast-forward."

The two continued watching in sped-up motion as a fire lit within Brady, and he began the early steps of a furious comeback. For the time being, FISTY remained his stoic self, commenting on the various strategic errors the Falcons would make to compromise their ability to hold the offensive advantage. "Quarterbacking error," FISTY remarked as Matt Ryan took a sack on third down in field goal range. "In-close overshoot; reverse," he stated as the Falcons fumbled the ball in Patriots territory. They watched Brady throw a ball that was batted by a Falcons defender, then unfathomably bobbled and caught by Julian Edelman. "Stop tape," FISTY instructed. "Nickels, walk me through a validation of this play."

Sam pointed to the screen with his pen and said, "Legalities – Edelman is an eligible wide receiver, and you can see here that the ball was thrown with the quarterback behind the line of scrimmage with no previous forward passes thrown on the play; valid for Legalities."

FISTY nodded slowly as Sam continued, "Kinematics – stable spiral thrown by Brady, within one wingspan of the intended target; valid for Kinematics. Deconfliction – not a clear lane of pass, as there is at least one defender able to make pre-catch contact with the ball. Unassessable for deconfliction. Possession – the ball was caught and controlled prior to ground or out-of-bounds contact, with possession maintained throughout time of fall plus two seconds; valid for Possession. Overall, it will be Unassessable for Deconfliction."

"Good, Nickels – but would you call this a Good or Poor pass? And does it meet Catch criteria?" FISTY paused as his student contemplated the question.

Nickels analyzed the catch, frame-by-frame again, and eventually concluded, "I would call it a Poor pass, given the group of defenders present and the risk of a game-ending interception – but it meets Catch criteria."

"I concur," FISTY maintained. "Play tape."

As they watched the remainder of the Super Bowl at normal 1x speed, Sam knew that FISTY's moment was coming soon. He could see the slightest bit of sweat forming on the Training O's brow. The two continued to watch as the Patriots tied the game — sending it to overtime — where FISTY announced, "This is it, Nickels. The point in time where Brady was finally able to neutralize the fight and expeditiously transition to offensive quarterbacking. By now, the kneeboard card is well-past thrown out the canopy, as Brady is working off pure stem-cell instincts from his previous time spent studying. I want you to take note of his shot opportunity awareness and employment efficiency. Play tape."

FISTY became silent in this final portion of the tapes, but was unable to restrain himself from rubbing his hands on his temples, shaking his head in astonishment and admiration at Brady's clinical offensive advantage utilization. The only noises coming from him were subdued gasps. Sam even saw tears forming in FISTY's eyes as his mentor soundlessly mouthed Joe Buck's final call of the game, '… Aaaaaand… it's a touchdown! Patriots win the Super Bowl!' FISTY jumped in the air, vigorously fist-pumped, and yelled, "LET'S FUCKING GO!!!!!"

Eager to enjoy the moment with his instructor, Sam stood and gave a standing ovation — but he knew he had no chance to match the intensity filling the room. FISTY continued to literally jump around the STBR, going wild with screams, waving his arms, and shouting obscenities directed toward the adversary Falcons. He was so jacked up, so impassioned, so fanatical; he couldn't control himself as the F-bombs and vulgarities were now free-flowing. "That's what the warrior's spirit is fucking about*, Nickels! FUCK yeah! Holy fucking SHIT! 25 points! 25 POINTS! 28-3; FUCK you, Atlanta! Shove it up your ass, Mohammad Sanu — talking shit about my guy TB12! Suck it, Matty Ice; your regular season MVP doesn't mean SHIT! Get your dancing old ass outta here, Arthur Blank; this is OUR TROPHY, baby!"*

Nickels shook his head and couldn't help but chuckle at FISTY's trash-talking toward the Falcons' 75-year-old owner. The Chippy Training O was a stoic slate of serenity 99% of the time — but for the moments after any Brady victory, or *the words "We'll call it a Mission Success" in a debrief, FISTY went absolutely apeshit no matter where he was — be it a bar, his living room, or the NAWDC Corsair amphitheater. He once actually had to be escorted out of an Air Wing Fallon debrief after an especially ferocious celebration when — in tape review — it was found that he got a 'guns kill' on a striker just two seconds before the carrier would've been employed upon. Sometimes, Sam couldn't tell if FISTY loved Tom Brady or tactics more… but his insatiable passion for both — and his intense fervor for teaching the merits of each — made him one of the most beloved TOPGUN grads amongst the entire Navy. In short, he was nearly unanimously considered the GOAT of tactical mentors.*

Still jumping up and down, flexing, pumping fists, and shouting plenty of "FUCK YEAH!"s, FISTY pointed with his pen to Brady's smiling face, as the QB hugged his family and teammates, and he shouted, "THIS IS IT, NICKELS! THIS IS THE REWARD FOR RESILIENCE IN THE FACE OF ADVERSITY! FUCK yeah!"

Finally calming down a bit, he crouched down with his hands on his knees, breathing heavily, sweat dripping down his red face, and told Sam, "I want you to remember something,

Nickels: Life is ultimately a war of resilience; the greatest of victories will be achieved by he who is simply the last one to give up. Tom Brady refused to give up — even when things seemed all but hopeless — and as a result, he clinched not just another championship, but the greatest come-back ever. There are going to be days in your life when it feels like you've given everything you can, you're exhausted, and it's all over — and on these days, you have an opportunity, Nickels." FISTY *looked him straight in the eye and said, "The opportunity to be just another pilot... or to become one of the greatest aviators of all time..."*

The two watched in silence as the tape played its last recorded moments — Brady atop the podium, hoisting the Lombardi trophy in the air, tears of joy streaming from his eyes — as FISTY *mirrored the same emotion, proudly beaming at his hero...*

~

Sam couldn't hold in his laughter as he continued, "Oh yeah! And Spatch's RTB in side 303 — oh my god... what a disaster! His marshal readback? He called time 'fifty' instead of time 'five-zero!' God, that kind of shit is *so* unprofessional! And *then* he flew his CV-1 at 251 knots! Jesus, he was lucky he didn't have a midair in the descent! And to top it all off — his pass..."

FISTY chuckled, exhaustion prevalent in his voice, and asked, "Ah yes... what happened again? He flew a Fair, right?"

Shaking his head, despite neither man being able to see anything in the pitch-black brig, Sam said, "No, it was actually a 'little high all the way' OK. *But...* he stated his fuel on the ball call as a 6.9! And Master, I checked his tapes — that little scoundrel's fuel was *clearly* at a 7.0 — *hardly* even mippling with 6.9. I was so embarrassed for the air wing."

"Classic," FISTY responded calmly.

"But you know, aside from that rough night?" Sam shrugged to himself. "Those cruises went pretty smoothly, admin-wise. I mean, for god's sake — the Air Boss and Mini were *so* confident in our safe and efficient flight ops that they would let the Sailor of the Day manage the tower for a recovery or two!"

Chuckling, FISTY remarked, "We really *were* quite the administratively sound carrier strike group. Well, until..." As his voice trailed off, an awkward silence filled the dark room.

Sam said nothing in response — the quiet spoke volumes enough.

"So..." FISTY asked casually, "How's it going over here, anyway? You must have turned this boat into quite the admin war machine...?"

"It's uhh... it's going well, yeah!" Sam responded with a raised pitch, as he insisted, "It's uhh... a really good group of guys!" his tone again raising artificially.

"Nice…" FISTY said with zero excitement. "How about their tactical execution? Have you had a chance to, you know, mess around in the WVR arena or lead any DCAs at all?"

"Yeah. It's uhhh… it's good! The BFM button… A/A button… A/S button—they work as advertised! Cool technology… really neat stuff." Sam shrugged with folded arms as he tried to convince himself.

"Cool…" FISTY responded—again with little emotion. He paused momentarily, before asking with a touch of sentiment: "Nickels—do you miss it? Do you miss the feeling of actually flying the jet? Do you miss your life back home? Do you miss… *your friends?*"

"I… uhh…" he stammered in shock, unprepared for such a hard-hitting question. He took a moment to compose himself, and then responded, "No, I don't. FISTY—this was my choice: to start a new legacy of aviation on a foreign planet, and leave that old world behind. It's not about friends, nostalgia, or the past. It's about chasing new goals, achieving *more* in life—the US Navy was never where my story was going to end."

FISTY said nothing for a few seconds—before catching Sam off-balance by pointedly commenting, "I didn't realize the Navy was holding you and your ambition hostage—glad to see you're doing well now, thriving in the brig of your own ship."

Taken aback and slightly angered, Sam responded, "FISTY… please. Don't try to Patch-ronize me right now—you're not my master anymore. Some shit is going down, and I'm working through it, ok?! And besides, what do *you* care how I'm doing? What do *any* of you care? All of you guys completely shunned me when I left—and let me tell you: that *sucked*. You claim we were all such 'great friends,'" Sam said as he threw up air quotes in the darkness, "Well, what kind of 'great friends' cut ties *simply* because their brother has *courage*—courage to answer the call, and take on a new challenge for *personal growth*?! Isn't this what you always preached, FISTY: pushing yourself to new limits?!"

Still stoic, but with a bit more edge to his tone, FISTY shot back with, "I preached pushing yourself for the betterment of the *team*; not giving up and abandoning everyone to advance your own personal program, simply because *you* couldn't withstand the grind anymore."

"Oh, yeah!?" Sam grew more frustrated, "Well, what about Tom Brady? Didn't TB12 *himself* abandon his team to pursue personal goals?"

"Excuse me?!" FISTY's voice was rife with disgust.

"Yeah, that's right—you're lecturing *me* about giving up on the team, when your hero went and did the *exact* same thing. Brady saw the Bills on the rise and the competitive nature of the AFC on the horizon. He pulled chocks on the team that had kept faith in him during all those years—and he did it to find personal success in a new environment. He *knew* his time of dominance had come to an end in New England, and left on *his* terms." Sam, initially very proud of his argument, realized *right* as the words were coming out of his mouth the unfortunate implication of what he had just admitted.

"So, Nickels, it's true…" FISTY stated, disappointment prevalent in his voice, "You really left because you knew Juice had surpassed you, and you wanted to hide from the competition…"

In a state of shock at what he'd just said out loud, Sam couldn't form a sentence. "I… no… that's not what I… it was the opportunity… I couldn't pass up—"

"And how did that turn out?" FISTY asked. "Juice followed suit just one year later, chasing you to the Noddik Empire." He scoffed. "You couldn't *stand* the thought of an equal to your reign as the top dog in the air wing, could you? You *knew* that Juice was not just an admin savant, tactics expert, and tremendous stick—but also a *Good Dude*. The Nickels *I* knew and trained wouldn't have run from that—he would've welcomed the challenge. Thrived from the battle. *Embraced* the competition. Because the Nickels *I* flew with knew that without that fire of competition, there is no motivation to stay sharp, work hard, and keep getting better. Face it, Nickels: you weren't answering the call; you were *running* from it."

Sam shook in anger. Anger at FISTY. Anger at everything that was unfolding with the LAAF. But, most of all, anger at himself…

No! FISTY is just trying to test my resolve! I'm on to his Patchy mind tricks! "Sensei, you are so full of shit. How could you possibly know what was going through my mind?! You *know* how much the Navy pilot life *sucks*! And sure, maybe I wasn't as 'shit hot' as I was in my prime as a JO—but how *could* I have been, when I was so bogged down by the grind of ground jobs, the infuriating carrier conditions, and the constantly changing tactics? There was always some new syllabus event to prep for, some new qualification to earn, some new bullshit to shove in your brain… it would have driven even the most motivated man insane! The time away from home… the constant pedal to the metal… the asinine tasking from above… all for *what,* FISTY? To be the greatest Good Dude of all time? Look outside your bubble of delusion, Master—the grass *is* greener! And here on the Katsopolis, I've *found* that greener grass! Sure, I work with a bunch of robots—but they aren't much different than you android Patch wearers and your emotionless approach toward tactics!" On a roll, he raised his voice even louder and said, "And *don't* you lecture me about leaving! You would've done the same thing in my shoes—if you'd been through the hell I'd been enduring? You would've said 'fuck this shit' and done whatever it took to escape that torture!"

"You think so, huh?" FISTY asked, still no trace of anger in his voice. "You think I would've given up, failed to show persistence when it matters most, and abandoned my country because I couldn't handle the adversity?"

With just a moment of hesitation, Sam said, "Yes. Yes, I do."

FISTY shook his head, "Then I am so sorry, my Padawan, because I have failed you as a Master... You know, I had no intention of working large force joint exercises with the Noddik Empire when I answered your call—I merely came to save the man I once knew and loved. But it appears you're right, Dimes—Nickels truly *is* lost..."

Request? What? "FISTY, what are you—"

Sam was cut off as a door burst open, light shooting into the brig. For the first time, Sam could see FISTY—he looked drained, his eyes sullen and full of exhaustion. He was slumped over in his cell, holding the bars to keep himself on his feet. The two made eye contact briefly, before Sam diverted his attention to the shadowy figure entering the door.

As the figure approached closer, Sam could make out that he was rolling in a large TV on a stand, with a connected JMPS computer. The figure walked toward them and turned on a flickering overhead light, giving the room a dim glow amongst the strobes, and revealing his identity: Dr. Suabedissen smirked as he looked over at Sam. "So, Captain Rowland, you're awake!" He pushed his glasses up and taunted, "I was *so* sorry to hear about your *awful* cut pass and upcoming FNAEB... I hope you've made yourself comfortable here in the brig while waiting! Pathetic... you remind me of a frail little Rune Elf locked up in the Warlock Prison of Tamur!" He paused briefly, grinning widely, then asked, "Get it!? Because elves are normally *in charge* of the city?!" He giggled to himself and rubbed his hands together.

FISTY gave a slight jolt at hearing the FNAEB portion, but withstood from showing any facial emotion to the news.

Rowland shook his head in disgust and said, "So, you were behind this after all, doctor... I should have known. Let me guess... Juice and CAG, too? How long have you bastards had this alliance going, crafting this master plan to overthrow your own leader?"

The doctor raised an eyebrow. "Leader? Captain... in case you forgot, you hired me to set this Empire up for administrative success—*not* passable mediocrity. You need to take a long look at yourself, sir—I've seen level 45 dwarves with more leadership prowess than what you've exhibited as of late: Your passes have been abysmal. You've spent almost every waking hour aboard this ship in a state of intoxication. You treat your subordinates terribly. And let's be honest—I'm not even sure you *want* to be here. So, yes, we've been discussing the best way to win this Large Administrative Assault Fight—and with all due respect, *none* of those COAs involve you and your crappy attitude, you beta-cuck limpdick." As he finished his statement, the doctor dug his head into his bent elbow while his other arm went straight behind him, in a pathetic attempt at the 'dab' trend from the 2010s.

Sam was floored. *Damn… that first stuff was pretty heavy… and I've never heard the doctor call out anyone in that way… and what the hell was that at the end?* He noticed FISTY paying quite a bit of attention to the talk of the LAAF.

The doctor continued, "However, while Juice's administrative excellence will likely be plenty to win this competition, it certainly wouldn't hurt having a bit of tactical expertise to back ourselves up…" He donned his cloak's hood and turned to FISTY. "So, Captain, I thought maybe you'd like to witness as another old friend of yours joins our fast-advancing Empire…"

He walked up to FISTY's cell. "Admiral Flynn… shall we continue? Here, take one of these… I know your fighter guys love your XANs…" he reached his arm out with a cylindrical container in hand.

FISTY shook his head. "No."

Suabedissen, looking disappointed, said, "Really? … Admiral, you *really* want to do this the hard way again? All we want is just a *bit* of your knowledge… and good news!" he emphasized with a sneer. "We're willing to *pay* you for it: how does 300 million sound? Just take one of these bad boys," he took out an individual XAN pouch, "Maybe give us a little information on the HOTAS for getting into the context menu?" He gestured to the exit, "And you can be on your way!"

FISTY looked at the interrogator through his tired eyes and growled, "No."

Suabedissen tsked, looking over at Rowland—and then fired back to Flynn, "400 million."

"Negative," Flynn resisted. "Not interested."

The doctor began pacing around, hands behind his back, and approached the TV—before giving one last look at FISTY and offering, "750 million for the stern conversion numbers."

Remaining silent, FISTY took a long look at Sam and, with his gaze fixed, stated with conviction, "Not a chance in hell, doctor."

"That is truly a shame, Admiral," Suabedissen lamented. He powered the TV on, and opened a PCDS video debrief file on the JMPS computer. "Well… perhaps *this* may cause you to reconsider…"

"Give me your worst, doctor," FISTY dared defiantly. "You've already shown me EXPO markers, arrows drawn with unrealistic relative magnitude lengths, and made confident, declarative statements about things that I would say 'depend' on context. You will not crack me."

Suabedissen gave a sly smile, saying, "Oh, Admiral, I think we're *well* beyond tactical discussions, my good sir! I was thinking… perhaps we could relax a bit? Maybe watch some American football?"

Sam observed—confused—as Suabedissen pulled up an NFL telecast on PCDS. The camera quality seemed a bit dated… *Is this live? What's he doing?* The announcers referred to this as a monumental game in NFL history. *Is that… Tom Brady?*

Sam looked over at FISTY, who suddenly looked extremely concerned. *What's going on? Patriots vs Giants? When was this?*

And then Sam realized what was happening, as the broadcast began showing Brady and Randy Moss highlights, with a graphic of the team's record ticking up, win by win, until the point where it stood on this day: 18-0. *Oh my god…*

FISTY, clearly agitated, closed his eyes and cupped his hands over his ears… but Dr. Suabedissen just turned the volume up louder. "What's the matter, Admiral? Have you seen this one before? You're a Tom Brady fan, right?!"

Sam, unable to hold back at seeing his master squirm in agony, finally spoke up. "Doctor! Stop! This is inhumane; turn this off *now!*"

Dr. Suabedissen growled at Sam, "Hush, beta. This isn't your session—unlike *you*, Admiral Flynn actually has useful information that we need." His smirk returned, and he looked back at FISTY, continuing, "If he would like me to turn this game off, he can simply agree to *give us* that information." Looking back at the screen, then down at something he was holding, he stated, "Oh, look—it's the New England Patriots' first drive! That juggernaut, record-setting offense is *sure* to explode to a quick lead over the 14-point underdog New York Giants!"

Sam saw that the doctor was clearly reading off a script, pathetically trying to act as if he were actually a sports buff—but it made the pain no less to FISTY, who fell to his knees, now clutching his chest in anguish.

With an evil grin, Dr. Suabedissen announced from his note cards, "A punt already?! How un-Patriot like! Well, these boys are no doubt going to score lots of touchdowns and extra points on the ensuing drives, right?! HAHAHA!" he cackled as FISTY cowered to the ground.

Sam watched in dread, full of anxiety over the torture that was crippling his old master physically, and undoubtedly *slaughtering* him emotionally…

~

<MCSALAD> continued descending into the ship's depths toward his destination, running for his life to escape the ship bots chasing him. Even before the TAO ordered the SNOOPIE team to launch a search and detain detail for an escaped prisoner, <MCSALAD> had been seeking one specific refuge room. He still wasn't sure who he was or what was going on with his mind, but he knew exactly where he could find some answers.

Upon escaping Suabedissen's office, he'd immediately incapacitated a nearby ship's company bot and looked for the nearest unsecured head to swap uniforms—which naturally took him down the entire length of the ship. Upon finding one, he threw his jeans and Maurice Jones-Drew jersey in 'hard plastics'—an additional 'fuck you' to his imprisonment carrier—and donned the bot's clothing. In blue coveralls now, <MCSALAD> was able to blend in slightly more, but still took caution by hiding in the shadows.

As he continued sneaking through the Katsopolis, his mind flooded with questions. The further removed he was from his last XAN dosage, the more memories seemed to hit his processing system. He remembered walking in line with other Padroids-like figures, but without random jerseys or boisterous intro music. He remembered people in ready rooms clapping when this group arrived—not in jest, but in *admiration* and *appreciation.* He remembered not just the experience, but a *feeling* – a feeling of making a difference in pilot's lives—not just telling them how uncool they were. He longed to find the origins of this feeling, at *any* expense—because the way he felt now? He wanted no part in this life.

He finally made it to his end goal—the 7th deck—and saw the placard he'd been seeking: '7-28-3-X'—Dr. Suabedissen's lab. He carefully opened the door and turned the light on—revealing a desk, two chairs—one with shackles attached to it—a large cabinet with a master lock, and a secure-locked safe. The room, the path to it, the chair… it all felt oddly familiar to <MCSALAD>, as if he'd been here before. He didn't know how or why, but his instincts took him directly here.

He closed the door behind him and walked up to the safe, knowing the answers he sought would surely be inside. The outer door had an eye, fingerprint, and voice scanner. <MCSALAD> attempted to scan his eyes; to no avail. He tried the finger scan—same result. He hit the mic button and masterfully mimicked the doctor's whiny voice: "Karl Suabedissen." Still nothing. "Dammit!" he swore in a hushed whisper, pounding the desk—and noticed that the drawers inside it weren't locked…

In hopes of finding *something,* he sat in the chair and scavenged through the drawers. In the top drawer was a series of magazines: various issues of *Hardcore Gaming, D&D Digest, The 16-Sided Times, LARP-a-Palooza,* and many others. He noticed the doctor himself on the cover of the May issue of *Dragon Slayer Quarterly*, in a feature called 'Getting Virtually Jacked—Can VR Lead to Huge Gains?' The doctor was posing shirtless below his lab coat, trying to flex—with an Oculus headset covering his eyes, and a sword and shield in either hand. Despite the photo being airbrushed, <MCSALAD> could tell that Suabedissen had a 'Chet Holmgren' level of muscle mass—the emaciated doctor looking as if his neck would snap under the moment arm of the VR headset.

In the next drawer was a printout of an email from 'customerservice@body-building.com' with the message body stating, "Karl—Hello, and thank you for your inquiry! Unfortunately, we do not ship 'trenbolone' to outer space stations. And in regards to your request for the 'good stuff' from the 'back room,' we're not sure exactly what you're referring to, but we suggest you try Jack3d's newest proprietary pre-workout blend—COMBAT IPF! Use code GETBIG10 for free CONUS shipping!"

In the same drawer was a book entitled *The Art of Alpha Seduction*. <MCSALAD> thumbed through the book, where various pages were dog-eared. There was a bookmark in 'Chapter 7: Establishing Male Dominance,' where a highlighted passage read: "Remember, YOU are the ALPHA in the room, and everyone else needs to know it! The next time some punk challenges your authority, expose his inferiority to everyone else present by calling him something like a 'beta cuck' or a 'limpdick.' Once he backs down, bask in your Alphaness by dabbing to show the room the ill slam you just dropped on his bitch-ass. You're the man, champ!"

<MCSALAD> almost started laughing, imagining somebody actually doing this. He turned further forward to 'Chapter 10: Attracting a Hottie.' The chapter discussed an intricate strategy of getting a girl's number, and then immediately texting her to mention that you can't hang out for the next seven days because you already have dates lined up. "Remember—YOU are the ALPHA, and she needs to know that you have OPTIONS in life—and if she's LUCKY, she might be one of them someday!" Further in the book, he saw notes written—presumably by the doctor—stating 'DOES NOT WORK!' next to a crossed-out passage that discussed finding common appreciations in life with the 'target,' and the freedom in being your genuine self.

The Padroids opened the last drawer, which contained a blue folder with 'Troll of Trabia Raid' written on the front. Inside contained a printout of recommended parties, weapon setups, spells, and 'strats' from different users who had completed the sidequest, as well as a recruiting dossier of prospective elves, dwarves, warriors, magicians, and even an ogre princess—strangely enough, with a *heart* drawn around her avatar profile picture? Despite being a robot who had no capacity to feel second-hand embarrassment, <MCSALAD> couldn't help but cringe at the doctor's middle school boycrush behavior.

As he was flipping through pages of monster information and findable treasures, a key fell out of the folder's back pocket. <MCSALAD> picked it up and noticed it was a simple Master Lock key. He looked back to the locked cabinet, bit his lip, and approached it to try the key—sure enough, it fit perfectly. Inside the compartment lay a blue folder, just like the previous raid envelope—except this one was titled 'OPERATION: PIGPEN.'

<MCSALAD> opened it up to find a stack of stapled papers, with the first identical to the outside cover page. He took a deep breath as he flipped to the second page,

and gasped at what he saw: it was intentionally left blank. The *third* page, however, more explicitly detailed: *OPERATION: Pilot IntelliGence Penetration (PIGPEN) is an S3-classification-level project involving the gathering of information from the United States' best aviators via means of interrogation, torturing, and/or ultimately conforming to our own assets via chemical manipulation. Project Manager - Dr Karl Suabedissen.*

As he turned the page again, <MCSALAD> saw a well-coiffed young man wearing a flight suit with a green, black, and white patch that said 'Dambusters - Strike Fighter Squadron 195.' The logo looked so familiar to him for some reason... Looking further down at the subject bio, it was obvious that the man was a well-respected aviator in the squadron, with many qualifications — including a highlighted one: Landing Signal Officer. <MCSALAD> searched frantically for this aviator's identification serial number — but all he could find was a bold-lettered generic human name: LT Christopher Houben.

<MCSALAD> continued to the next page, where an explanation summarized Captain Rowland's desire for a system to make spaceship landings 'cooler' — and the resulting necessity of an officer cadre to spearhead the program. While coding an "off da hook posse" — as the document called it — would be simple with Dr. Suabedissen's knowledge of hip trends, the force needed somebody with knowledge of *actually* bringing people aboard safely. <MCSALAD> read on, as the passage discussed a plan to send a falsified invite from Captain Rowland to the Chippies, requesting to arrange an integrated joint training detachment. When the Chippy representative arrived — presumably to be welcomed aboard by Captain Rowland — they would be greeted by CAG and Dr. Suabedissen, subsequently incapacitated, and locked in the brig. While imprisoned, the subject would be tortured into divulging all their secret information and then given phytotoxin/seed oil pills — referred to as XANs — to turn them into complete lemming vegetables with no internal will nor memories of their past.

Apparently, based on the notes <MCSALAD> was reading, the dosage for Mr. Houben had not been strong enough to fully conform him, leaving him often lifeless and aloof amongst the other coded-from-the-ground-up Padroids. The latest recommendation from Dr. Suabedissen — dated two days prior — involved giving him one last increased prescription of XANs. If this was not enough to fully indoctrinate him, they would send him to the incinerator. Not to be burned alive, however — something *much* worse: To be TDY to Waste Management for the remainder of his career.

<MCSALAD> felt for this poor Houben character, and noticed that his face looked vaguely familiar as well. He turned to the next page, which featured another smiling individual in an American flight suit uniform — *also* with a 'Dambusters' patch. The characters for this man's name spelled out 'ADM Thomas Flynn.' The biography read: *One of the highest-regarded tactical experts in naval aviation. A walking TOPGUN Manual, he once re-wrote every chapter during POM leave as a side project. Looked up to as a*

strategic mastermind, a revolutionary training phenom, a spectacular father and husband, and an even better Good Dude.

<MCSALAD> turned the page and saw an addendum about the same artificial invitation plan from 'Captain Rowland' to lure Flynn to the Katsopolis, and utilize him to supplement the lacking tactical knowledge that the empire had in its database. Without an ability to adapt and grow to the latest threats, the Noddik fleet had essentially been training to tactics that were 20-30 years out of date, making their perfectly running software irrelevant without accurate inputs; aka GIGO — or 'Garbage In, Garbage Out' — a term Dr. Suabedissen, in his notes, claims to have brilliantly coined. With Flynn XAN'd out of his mind, they could use his encyclopedic brain to update every tactical program to current-day applicability. And, as a bonus, Suabedissen noted in the document that ADM Flynn reportedly had intel of a fun point-system game to play with roll 'ems, which could potentially raise spaceship morale.

<MCSALAD>'s robotic heartbeat nearly ceased when he heard a knock on the door.

"S-5!" a voice called.

Not even a second passed before another knock came, followed by, again, "S-5!"

<MCSALAD> grabbed the folder and hopped into the full-sized cabinet, closing the door behind him as he heard one more knock and "S-5 coming in!"

Unable to see anything from his hiding spot, <MCSALAD> listened as the door opened. Two sets of footsteps emerged, seemingly patrolling around the room — until one robotic voice said, "Hey, what's this?"

"What is it?" another mechanically asked.

"It's a picture of a human. Hmm… LT Christopher Houben… interesting…"

<MCSALAD> 's heart transferred itself to the bottom of his abdomen as he realized: In his haste, he'd accidentally dropped a page.

"This has a classification level above our programming — should we inform Dr. Suabedissen that this was left out?" one asked.

"Affirmative. Let's contact him."

<MCSALAD> could hear radio transmissions on a hydra walkie-talkie, where the S-5 bots explained the situation to the doctor.

"What?! Are you serious?" The doctor sounded frantic through the speaker. "Don't leave the room — I'll be right there."

<MCSALAD> panicked as he contemplated what to do — and in his alarm, he almost — *almost* — didn't catch the mention of a name he hadn't heard in years.

"Hey, look at this guy's nametag in the picture — his callsign has mathematical symbols bordering it. Wonder what it means?"

"What is it?"

">SADCLAM<."

~

"Oh boy, a touchdown to Randy Moss! That will put the Patriots up 14-10 with only a little over two minutes to go in the game! This feels like a great position for the Pats to be in! There's no way Eli Manning could *possibly* lead the Giants down for a touchdown score, right?!" Dr. Suabedissen narrated awkwardly, still working off his cue cards.

FISTY was writhing on the floor in pain, all too aware of what was about to happen...

Sam begged to stop the suffering as he yelled, "Doctor, you've got to end this now! I'll tell you anything! Please!" But Suabedissen just ignored him, with the intent to keep this torture escalating to inhumane levels.

The doctor went on, giving a play-by-play: "4th and inches! This could be the end—ahhh, rats, Brandon Jacobs converted!" And then, "Oh, that's a *wild* pass... Ohhhh! *Almost* intercepted by Asante Samuel! That would've clinched the game and the perfect season, wouldn't it have, Admiral?"

Suabedissen was laughing hysterically during the whole evolution. Sam watched in terror as FISTY laid prone on the ground, his eyes buried into his elbow, shaking violently as the game got closer and closer to its bitter end...

It all was happening so quickly—Sam scanned the game situation—it was third and long, with Eli Manning deep in the pocket. After the snap, he was nearly brought down, yet *narrowly* escaped a sack from Richard Seymour, where there *easily* could've been a whistle stopping the play for forward progress. Manning scrambled around, wound up his arm, and—

"Stop tape!" Suabedissen yelled. He cleared his throat, looked at FISTY, grinned, and said, "Admiral, you know *very* well what is about to take place." After a pause, he threatened, "This is your *last chance*—for one billion dollars, and the end of this nonsense... would you like to explain to me what SAPDART stands for?"

FISTY remained shaking, staring at the floor, seemingly on the verge of a breakdown.

Sam yelled out, "FISTY, it's ok! Just tell him! Don't put yourself through this! Please...!"

FISTY raised his head and looked at Sam—steeled tenacity in his eyes—and then turned back to Dr. Suabedissen. With a tone of bitterness and a heart full of courage, he uttered, "Never. I'll never turn to the Noddik side. You have failed, doctor. I am prepared to suffer for my country, like the Patches before me."

Dr. Suabedissen's grin became a scowl. "So be it... Patch-boy..."

Chills going down Sam's spine, he watched as Suabedissen yelled, "Play tape!"

"NO!" Rowland screamed, as FISTY started howling in agony as Eli Manning completed the infamous Helmet Catch to David Tyree.

"Power!" Suabedissen yelled, as Plaxico Burress caught an easy fade from Manning to get the go-ahead touchdown with under a minute left. FISTY was now bawling at his point, his tears of agony free-flowing.

"Stop the tape! STOP THE TAPE!" Sam yelled. But it was no use...

"POWER!" the doctor continued screaming, as Brady got sacked to set up third and long. On the ensuing play, they watched a defender *barely* tip a miraculous 70-yard pass to Moss that would have put them in field goal range and *easily* been the most clutch throw of all time.

"UN-LIM-IT-ED... POWER!!!" Suabedissen howled, as Brady's 4th down hail mary hit the ground, the Giants knelt the ball, and the clock struck 0:00—the final score 17-14—cementing the greatest upset of all time, and the most gut-wrenching ending *possible* to what would have been *the* perfect season.

The doctor cackled wildly, as FISTY now lay numb on the floor, practically a dead corpse, devoid of all will to live. Sam bit his fist, nearly in tears after watching his master have the life pulled out of him. *Why did he do that... why did FISTY allow this to happen?!*

Dr. Suabedissen's hydra went off, with some bots talking about something Sam couldn't quite make out. Whatever it was, though, the doctor did *not* sound happy, as his laughing became panic. "What? Are you serious?! Don't leave the room—I'll be right there." Dr. Suabedissen crouched to the ground next to FISTY, attempting to confirm signs of life.

In a moment of last-ditch valiance, FISTY made one final attempt to attack the doctor... but merely brushed his lab coat with a feeble kitten swipe. Suabedissen smirked, got up, and looked up at Sam. "Well, he's still alive—but *barely*. That was the last Brady lowlight trick up my sleeve, too—because they don't get worse than that," he sneered. "I hope you enjoyed your last moments with the Admiral Flynn you once knew—because he'll never be the same. The bigger the Brady fanboy, the harder they fall." He pushed his glasses up and said, "I'll be back, you sigma loser." The doctor did an about face and marched out of the room with a purpose, his cloak flowing behind him.

The light still flickering, Sam could see FISTY's lifeless body flat on the floor. "... Master? Are you... ok?"

FISTY grunted, twitched his arm slightly, but said no words.

Sam threw his hands on his head, bemoaning, "FISTY... why'd you do it? Why didn't you talk? Your body can't handle that kind of agony; it's going to scar you forever! Why, Sensei, why? Why couldn't you just give up and end the suffering?"

FISTY groaned briefly, then raised his head. His eyes were dry, but they had no life in them whatsoever. He held a long look at Rowland, took a deep breath, and said, "Remember this, Nickels—Life is ultimately a war of resilience; the greatest of victories will be achieved by he who is simply the last one to give up." He took his arm, wound back, and swung it as hard as he could—and from it flew a key, clinking as it landed within an arms' reach distance of Rowland's cell. *What?!*

Finally drained, FISTY looked at Sam and, with his last conscious words before slumping over, said, "This is the reward for resilience in the face of adversity."

7

Padroids Talk-Down

"Come in!" *Captain Rowland called out excitedly to the knock on his door. He'd been await-ing this presentation for months since Dr. Suabedissen joined the empire aboard the NIRD Katsopolis.* Finally, *he would be given some numeric validation from his efforts to transform this boat into an administrative masterpiece!*

The doctor walked in, wearing a fresh lab coat and thick-rimmed glasses, carrying his personal laptop — a CAG brand. He stopped in front of Rowland's desk and bowed — which seemed a strange enough gesture to the captain — and then offered his hand up for a fist bump.

Rowland hesitantly returned it and said, "You can sit, doctor." As Suabedissen took his seat, Sam smiled and asked, "How are you today? Any exciting, uh, quests or whatever?" Suabedissen's eyes widened as he beamed uncontrollably, and Sam quickly regretted asking. "Oh my god, yes, Captain — I'm glad you asked! You will never *believe this — so, as you know, I've had my Raid Lead qual for over three years now, and today was my 50th mission led! And — of course — I was tasked to defend the Village of Nazariah from the Evil Swine King and his clan of orcs! And then, on top of that?* Both *of the Mutated Grizzly Bears recruited from the Animal Kingdom of Arcadia fell out!" He raised his arms with a shocked, open-mouthed smile as he looked at Rowland. "We now had* no *sow-suppression game plan! So, despite only having five fire-capable magicians in the party, I figured 'what the hell' and reshuffled the fight to put two wind-calling wizards flanking on either side, a high-leveled warrior sweep team on the front lines, followed by a striking necromancer behind them, equipped with — get this — " The doctor spoke intensely with both hands and paused for dramatic effect, "The legendary Raytheon Sword!" When silence filled the room, he grinned widely and pointed toward himself, "It was me! I had the freaking Raytheon Sword!" He giggled excitedly before continuing into his plan of attack.*

Throughout the entire explanation, Rowland found himself completely zoning out and not giving a shit about anything the doctor was saying — he wanted to get to business and hear the doctor's assessments already. Sam had implemented so many programs to resolve the life-style issues he'd hated back home, and the doctor was soon going to present the verification that Sam had been right about smooth carrier operations for years. This shit was so easy… it doesn't take a genius to get rid of all the obnoxious, unnecessary dumb shit that the Navy does. *Today could be the day when his grand plan hit its tipping point, and he would start to feel validated in leaving his old life – and his old 'friends.'* I can't wait to finally feel happy and show all those haters back home how valuable I truly was… Jesus, when is this guy going to shut the fuck up?!

"Enough, *dude!*" *he cut off Suabedissen, who was talking in depth about some epic sword duel between him and the Swine King, where he was apparently about to decapitate the pig.* "I mean – sorry…" *he added, seeing the doctor's disappointed face,* "Can we please discuss the admin assessment?"

Suabedissen, looking defeated, said, "Sure, Captain…" *He opened up his laptop, took a deep breath, and –*

"Eh-hem!" *Sam stopped him, clearing his throat and gesturing with his hand.*

Looking embarrassed, the doctor shuffled around and stood up, calling, "Attention to brief!"

Rowland smirked and sat with his arms folded across his chest, basking in his perceived importance. Eventually, he nodded his head and acknowledged, "Be seated, doctor."

Suabedissen pushed his glasses up, took a seat, and began his presentation. "3… 2… 1… HACK. The year was 2026. The Noddik Empire had undergone approximately 1000 days aboard – "

"Ok, cut the shit and get on with it." *Sam was in no mood for fluff.*

The doctor kinked his neck and obliged, "Certainly. Well, Captain, some of the changes you've implemented have some… uhh… issues…"

"Issues?" *Sam questioned with incredulity.* "Like what?"

"For starters… your revolutionary trash system. The concept of putting all trash into one container? The Katsopolis disposal system simply can't handle the variety of random components thrown in simultaneously – Soft and Hard plastic, sir?! They go together about as well as goblins and moonstones. The compactors have been getting clogged and break regularly, leaving a horrendous sewage odor throughout the entirety of the ship – and it's especially bad near CAG's office. If we continue doing this, then we're going to have a huge problem on our hands, and will potentially need more sailors TDY to Waste Management."

Dammit. This had been one of the changes Rowland was most excited about. "Well… can't we just throw it all overboard into space?"

The doctor sighed and shook his head, saying, "Unfortunately, that's not quite the most ethical thing to do. It would probably be no more than a month before our waste was rife throughout the solar system – and the Android journalism would have a field day with that story, putting you out of a job, sir."

"Good point… shit. Well then, what do you recommend we do?" *Sam asked.*

"Sir, if we simply just sort all the trash into different materials, and collect them at different times of the day – ideally only very inconvenient times, so that we don't get over-crowded with traffic – then we can properly dispose of environmentally compostable trash, feel good about ourselves despite the fact that we're damaging the environment a million other ways, and then – "

"Ok, ok, I get it... god," Sam groaned. "Fuck it – sort the trash. What about the elimination of the 1MC?"

Suabedissen gave a sheepish shrug. "Well… sir… that actually leads to a few problems as well. You see – well, let's start with the result of what it caused: the elimination of GQ, drills, and daily announcements."

"Yeah, what of it?" Sam asked, looking proud. "Fucking pimp, right?"

Suabedissen squirmed. "Well… we've been running simulations…"

Rowland rolled his eyes. Simulations? This guy could not possibly be a bigger dweeb…

"… And in every single one, it was a catastrophic failure. We weren't even equipped to handle the simplest issue – somebody kept flipping a circuit breaker because their AC repeatedly went out, causing an electric fire that we couldn't extinguish, and it burned down the entire ship. Also, because you insisted on making sure there was 100% always hot water available, people were taking long showers – as if they were 'Hollywood Movie Stars' getting ready for a scene – and we ran out of potable water within 24 hours.

"Every man overboard simulation occurred because sailor bots weren't informed that catwalks by the flight deck were secured – and it would subsequently take approximately 48 hours to account for everyone still aboard, since we couldn't call their names and tell them to report to the deckhouse in hangar bay two. And the announcements..." Suabedissen gave a look of appeal, "Believe it or not, Captain, part of being a good leader is showing your daily involvement in the community. I know you may find them asinine and annoying, but the simple act of speaking to your teammates – even just a brief snippet to thank them or provide direction – does much more than staying silent the entire time! For instance, I get on a Zoom call with every member from my guild at least once a week to talk about new weapons coming out on expansion packs, upcoming spells unlocked on level-up milestones, and to remind them of on-the-horizon raids and the rewards we're all fighting – "

"Doctor, seriously – stop!" Sam threw his hands up, "God dammit… can't we just have better working maintenance? Can't we just not care about who is overboard and just worry about finding them instead? Can't I just talk with sailor bots directly if I want to tell them what's up?"

The doctor paused and said, "Sir… these are great ideas in theory…" He shrugged, "But it's like asking for a raid where no party members have failed attacks, or no limit to the quantity of high-potions in your inventory, or a cast of NPCs with infinity-branching dialogue options depending on the story arc. The ideas you want – there's just not enough practice, resources, or time to accomplish these things. It's a pipe dream, sir."

Sam sighed despondently and asked, "... What can we do about it, Karl?"

Suabedissen took a deep breath. "The 1MC, sir, the 1MC – It's the only way…"

Fuck me… how is this happening?! *Sam, feeling hopeless, followed up with, "How much control should we give individual rooms on 1MC speaker volume?"*

"None." The doctor shook his head. "People will just turn it off. We must install them in every room, with no adjustable volume, and put them on max decibel setting."

Sam dug his head into his hands. I guess I better start writing some speeches for nightly announcements… *"What else, doctor?"*

The two discussed the necessity of cleaning the ship daily to prevent rust; periodic closing of bathrooms – also daily – for maintenance; turning water off randomly for potable water conservation – "Yes, Captain, we'll have to do that every day, too," Suabedissen acknowledged sadly. Amongst all this and more, the ship would need to set up room inspections to make sure nobody had any untagged or unvetted personal electronic devices – yet would warn room inhabitants beforehand to unplug and hide them for the inspection. "What will that even accomplish?!" Sam asked.

"Nothing," the doctor responded, "Nothing but plausible deniability for us and the ship in case of an electric fire. At least then*, we can say we never saw them – or at least saw them* unplugged *– at one given time, and wipe our hands clean of the evil deeds in the case of a follow-on mishap investigation."*

"Fuck…" Sam said. "That's smart…"

One thing Dr. Suabedissen suggested as a possible enhancement was removing the necessity of calling people 'sir' and 'ma'am,' instead simply using people's first names in daily communication and last names when differentiation was necessary. "Captain, think of it – why the need for these foolish titles? We could simply show respect by doing our appointed job, being kind and empathetic to one other, and, in turn, drop this whole archaic 'compulsory deference' act. This kind of complementary human treatment works for countless corporations around the world! What do you think…" he paused and smiled hopefully, "… Sam?!"

"NO WAY, Suabedissen!" Captain Rowland immediately shot down. "Watch yourself, peon. How else am I going to feel the proper authority that I yearn for, if not from 'sir' sandwiches? Next idea, doctor."

Looking sheepish, Dr. Suabedissen continued, "Sir, yes, sir. So, I have two projects I'd like to discuss with you… the first is regarding a more authoritative mid-level leadership… specifically, at the O-4 level of coding. You've frequently mentioned that there wasn't enough work getting done around this place, especially *when there was no real work to be done, right?"*

Sam nodded adamantly. "Why, yes, doctor, that's become quite a pet peeve of mine. Far too many people are relaxing when the job is done, instead of creating more imaginary work to do. What did you have in mind?"

Suabedissen clicked to his next slide and said, "Sir, Captain, sir, I present to you a prototype currently in phase-4 development. It's capable of new technology, including LOST –

Line-of-Sight-Tasking – the ability to lock up a target of opportunity and instantly assign arbitrary duties to it. In addition, it will be programmed with SU-SU capabilities – Sudden Unwarranted Spool-Up. This cyborg will have the capacity to go from completely chill and normal – in fact, he may even trick you into thinking he's your friend – and yet, within seconds, can be triggered to get deep into an underling's chili about the most miniscule fault – even errors that don't actually exist! When combined with LOST, this will be a deadly capability. And best of all, it incorportates a brand-new feature called 'MTS' – Menial Task Shedding. This is highly advanced software, sir – the prototype contains the AI to shed itself the RAM data of nuisance busywork, and instead open up more memory cache to focus on the abilities gained from LOST and SU-SU! It will rid itself of the ability to execute tasks like standing watch, making kneeboard cards, WASPing, running debriefs – and, with the most advanced updates, it will even delete data on how to work simple PowerPoint slides or make coffee! The beauty of the AI is that while it would be embarrassing to admit that they no longer knew how to do these things, they instead portray it as no longer needing to do such menial tasks – as if they are somehow above those jobs! It empowers underling bots to do them instead, and makes the prototype appear important and superior as a result! A win-win!"

Sam smiled, impressed at this new leadership model of robot, and said, "About damn time you had something helpful to present, doctor. But what will make this leader better than the rest?"

"Well, I'm glad you asked!" Suabedissen answered excitedly. "Sir, the AI is far more advanced than the other Heads of Departments! Over time, he will actually adapt his coding, becoming more sinister and powerful by the day! He will calculate solutions to make other HODs appear inferior to him in performance reviews, will become more efficient with LOST and MTS – eventually even gaining the ability to delegate to peers – and will become more adept at disregarding the things that prevent productivity in the air wing – like people's family lives, personal time, and sleep requirements!"

"Genius..." Sam said with a smirk. "What will the prototype be called?"

Dr. Suabedissen beamed and proudly answered, "Robo-Hinge!"

"Robo-Hinge... I like it! Nice save, doctor, after all those other shitty solutions. Now, I must be getting back to work; I have to prep for a flight," Sam lied, secretly feeling like he needed a drink while still processing the terrible 1MC decision from earlier.

"But sir, I still need to brief you on OPERATION: PIGPEN! It's admittedly a bit controversial. Plus, sir..." he smiled bashfully, "if you wouldn't mind... I'd just love to tell you about the ending to the battle against the Swine King..."

Sam glared at him and said, "Doctor, Jesus Christ, quit while you're ahead! You've brought me like one good idea, a million fucking awful ideas, and now this?! Don't get it twisted: I DON'T CARE about any of your stupid-ass Dungeons and Dorklord raids or quests or online strats – so quit bringing this shit up, ok?! And OPERATION: PIGPEN? Dude, I have very limited time, so give me a brief – and I mean brief – synopsis."

Suabedissen, never one for brevity, pulled out a folder from his lab coat, inhaled, and quickly mumbled to recage his brain: "Ok; 3-2-1-HACK," before continuing, "The year was 2026. The Noddik Empire had undergone approximately---"

"No! No, no, no... NO! Enough, doctor! Get the fuck out of my office!" Sam yelled, his mouth salivating for whiskey.

"But sir!" the doctor begged, "Please, let me start over! Juice was opposed, but if you just hear me out, I – "

"Wait a second... Juice didn't like it?" Sam asked with a raised eyebrow. "In that case... fuck it. Approved." He snatched the folder from the doctor's pale white fingers, turned to the last page of the packet, and signed his name. "Go ahead with OPERATION: PIGPEN – just... god damn, doctor... just make this place better already."

"Yes, sir," Suabedissen acknowledged as he walked to the doorway. "I'll continue to give you weekly updates on the – "

"Doctor..." Sam started, already grabbing his bottle from the cabinet and pouring a drink, "I don't want to hear anything from you about any operation other than the highly, highly unlikely consummation of OPERATION: BOXPEN. Is that clear?!"

"BOXPEN?" the doctor asked, confused. "Sir, I don't recall any – "

"Goodbye, doctor!" Sam yelled, slamming the door in Suabedissen's face, and subsequently slamming his triple-pour of Maker's Mark before immediately recharging his glass with another...

~

Captain Rowland unlocked his cell and ran toward FISTY's vegetated body, crouching over it, trying to shake him to life. "Master! Tell me you're ok! It's going to be alright; you're going to live!" *Shit... what do I do... how do I get him out of here?* Sam had not been lifting anywhere close to his intensive Khaki Hour workouts with CP back in the day; he held a fraction of his former strength. There was no way he'd be able to hoist his old Training O over his shoulder. "Master, can you hear me?"

FISTY grunted and tried to formulate a sentence, but couldn't get out more than jumbled words: "... Rodney Harrison... David Tyree... missed holding call... Brady... perfect season..."

Desperate to break his master out of this dazed state, he pleaded, "Think of 28-3! The greatest comeback of all time!" He wracked his brain to think of previous lectures. "The back-and-forth Super Bowl victory over Seattle, with Malcolm Butler's interception!" FISTY had used that game to discuss the importance of not letting the most flawlessly executed large force strike become a tarnished 'mission failure' due to a blue fighter dying from an invalid safe escape. Sam continued, "Brady's Super Bowl debut against the Greatest Show on Turf Rams back in 2002!" – a lecture honing in the power of launching and fighting even when the odds were stacked against you — and additionally, not becoming overconfident when you held an intel-assessed advantage. "Sensei... the blowout win over the Bengals in 2015, immediately after reporters said Brady was 'done' and 'should be benched' following that terrible showing against Kansas City!" One of the Training O's favorite chalk talks, he incorporated this sequence of games to remind SFWT candidates that any rough-event refly is an opportunity to test your true aviation mettle by how you respond in the next flight.

But it was no use — FISTY remained limp on the floor, aside from sporadic convulsions, now mumbling near-incomprehensible words with smatterings of Brady's name in between them. Sam felt a tear approaching his eye as he, for the first time, considered the effects of FISTY's refusal to quit. *He had nothing left... there was no reason to keep fighting – but he fought anyway. And then...* He couldn't believe a weakened FISTY was able to so subtly pickpocket the doctor without detection — it was the longest of longshots, a 0.2% chance scenario...

He looked at the key, and then back at the door to the Katsopolis ship body. "Don't worry, FISTY — I'm gonna find help — err... I'm gonna get us out — I'm gonna..." But truthfully, Sam had no clue what he could do. He had seemingly no allies left on this boat, and surely word of his imprisoned status had spread to all bots via a software update. In the event of a known escape, they would be programmed to seek and detain him. *Damn you and your algorithms, Suabedissen...*

With no other solution in mind, Sam figured that hunting down the doctor was the only lead he had. He turned to FISTY's vegetated body, and, although it was the most inappropriate time, couldn't help himself from harnessing his best Austrian accent, as he narrowed his eyes and declared, "I'll be back..."

~

<MCSALAD>, scrambling to think of a solution for when Dr. Suabedissen arrived, was doing his best to stay as quiet as he possibly could. He imagined his frantic pulse to be like a set of high-performing engines, and wanted to ease them down. And yet... the hypothetical quietness of 'idle' made him uncomfortable. This sound — the sound of spooldown — just the *thought* of it was getting him nervous... He felt like he needed to shout something to get it to stop... something that began with a 'P'? It was on the tip of his tongue! But he couldn't grasp it... And yet, what had him even *more* on edge was the revelation the S-5 workers had been discussing for the past five minutes...

">SADCLAM<..." the first S-5 bot said, perplexed. "I just don't get it. Do you think the guy was a big fan of mollusks?"

"Well, hold up," the other sailor interjected. "The 'greater than' and 'less than' mathematical symbols—surely, those must mean something." He rubbed his chin, programmed to know that humans did such a thing when solving logic problems. "Perhaps... greater than sad... but less than a clam?"

"Happy is better than sad... but what is inferior to a clam?"

"Hmmm... based on many human studies, many would say mussels! They are lower in Vitamin C and potassium, after all."

"Mussels? So, do you think the guy is jacked?" the bot asked.

"Well... *technically*, the word is a homonym, but it could be a play on the spelling—we'd have to ask the crew that derived the callsign."

"Don't you mean homo*phone*? Correct yourself, shipmate."

"Apologies... my programmer left a knowledge gap in concepts and definitions regarding anything involving muscles in the human body."

"Understood. But it brings up a good point—RFI: Does eating mussels contribute to growing muscles?"

"And it's all capital lettering, as well!" the bot said with open arms. "You cannot deny that that must play a factor!"

Dr. Suabedissen burst into the door. "Sailors! What is the meaning of this?! Where is the classified document?"

"Here it is, sir." <MCSALAD> watched the first S-5 worker hand the 'LT Christopher Houben' bio sheet to the doctor.

Suabedissen looked over the sheet and then glared at the cabinet, asking, "Was that cabinet unlocked when you got here?"

The S-5'er responded, "Affirmative, doctor—we haven't touched anything during our cleaning duties, we—"

"Wait a second," the doctor interjected. He looked over at the desk next to his bed, where a phone charger sat in clear view—an *untagged* phone charger. He pointed at it. "Guys..." he asked sternly, "What the freak is this?!"

"Umm... sir?" the sailor asked. "Is there an issue?"

"Heck *yeah*, there's an issue!" he said, raising his voice. "Gents—that is contraband! Do you know how many ohms go through that device 24/7 when it's simply *plugged in,* let alone actually *charging* a phone?! Did you guys even *look* through my room? I put this there as a *test*, to ensure that you bots were doing a diligent 'unauthorized electronics' scan—and, I'm embarrassed to announce, it appears that you have done a *terrible* job!" He shook his head and started pacing across the room. "And let me guess, you guys probably didn't even—oh my *goodness...*"

<MCSALAD> watched Suabedissen slump his shoulders in disappointment as he walked over and lifted an electrical multi-socket cord off the ground. The doctor

shook his head, before turning and snarling at the two workers, announcing with disgust, "A *power strip*! In clear sight! Guys... can you please come left over here?"

"*Come left?*" <MCSALAD> said under his breath with confusion. The sound of it brought back nostalgia for a time that felt so familiar—yet so distant...

"Ok, look here, gents," the doctor began, with a bit more patience in his voice. "I need to explain to you why electronic device micromanagement is *critical* to the ship. You see—one power strip, extension cord, or toothbrush charger? No big deal. But... if *every single sailor* has one plugged in? Guys, imagine the amplitude of those voltages circulating through our circuitry—imagine the *frequency*! The *magnitude*!" Suabedissen lifted his arms for emphasis, before making a 'three' with his hand and expounding, "Fortunately, thanks to an expertly rigged safety system, there are precisely three parts where we can place in power corrections..."

'*Frequency... magnitude... 3-part power corrections?*" <MCSALAD> couldn't wrap his head around why these words all sounded so familiar. But they gave him a strange sense of comfort, as the doctor continued explaining electronic schematics and wiring to two bot sailors who were cleverly programmed to show extreme disinterest and apathy toward somebody giving nuanced justification for why the ship rules must be followed.

"... And so!" the doctor went on, "Just imagine this: a ship using *so* much energy that it now gets *overpowered*, and must subsequently suck away all that power via one of the safety breakers—thus creating a severely *underpowered* scenario!"

<MCSALAD>'s ears perked up as a chill went down his spine. But he didn't know *why*...

"Scary stuff, right guys?" the doctor said. "Thus... it is crucial that we tag every single piece of equipment, so that we have a capped amount of voltage being used by the ship. But, remember—if people hide it before inspections—wink-wink, nudge-nudge," he said with a very creepy failed attempt at a wink, "then we can happily disregard all of this logic. Any questions?"

"So..." one of the sailors began, "You... want us to confiscate all your electronic items, then?"

Suabedissen's eyes widened as he called out, "Woah, woah, easy with it!"

<MCSALAD> clutched at his chest. His processing system was skipping loudly; no—it was a... *heartbeat?* He just needed one last reminder of who he was. All these strange phrases... the callsign '>SADCLAM<'... the Dambusters... "How are they all connected?" he asked himself aloud—*too* loud...

"What was that?!" Suabedissen asked, directing his attention to the door. "S-5 lad—I demand you open that door!"

<MCSALAD> covered his mouth, his body shaking, and said a prayer to the first god that appeared in his mind: "Bug Roach, if you're listening, please..."

Not a moment later, the office entry door burst open, a commotion erupting as somebody entered the room and said in a strange, Austrian accent: "Alright, everyone; chill!" <MCSALAD> groaned to himself at the line—remembering the shitty movie it was from—but felt relief from the bought time, as he watched the doctor through the door's vent holes.

Suabedissen glared at the intruder. "Captain Rowland... I don't know how you escaped, but you're too late to stop the Noddiks! The ship is inbound to planet Earth, and soon the Olympics will begin—with *Juice* in command—and victory shall be ours!"

"The only thing it's too late to do, Doctor, is *apologize*," Rowland said with a smirk.

"Classic song," one of the S-5 bots remarked.

Smiling proudly that somebody understood his reference, Sam then scowled and yelled, "I don't care about the Olympics, or Juice, or any of that shit—I need to save FISTY! What have you done to him?!"

Suabedissen smirked. "Oh, you foolish captain—that man is long past coma-tose! *You* saw those traumatic Super Bowl highlights!" He quickly pulled out the cue cards from his pockets, scanning them briefly, before continuing, "Did you know Brady *himself* has never watched that game film? Imagine the most important flight of your *life* going so poorly that you *refused* to attend the tape review—and then imagine some pathetic little fanboy of yours being forced to relive that disastrous set of tapes regardless! Heh..." his lip curled up, "It's enough to bring the mentally toughest of men to insanity..."

Rowland winced. "You're a monster... a fucking *monster*, doctor."

The doctor laughed maniacally. "And now, Captain, it's time to go back to your cell—Guards!" he called out, "Detain him!"

Before Sam could react, the two S-5 sailors rushed to his side and pinned his arms behind him, as Suabedissen drew a ray gun from his cloak, pointing it toward Sam.

As the doctor watched Sam struggle to break free of the sailors' grasp, he smirked and warned, "Oh, I wouldn't make any fast moves if I were you, Captain—one blast from the APG-47," he pointed to his gun, "and your testosterone levels will plummet so low that you'll be flaccid for the rest of your life..."

Rowland's eyes widened—he'd been well-versed on the T level-diminishing dangers of 47-band radar waves—they were like seed oils, processed sugar, episodes of *The Bachelor,* and the squat rack back padding—all combined into *one* blast. And to see this inhumane power compressed into a projectile weapon? Sam was *terrified.* He slowly and carefully said, "Doctor... don't do anything crazy... let's just talk this through..."

Suabedissen frowned. "I've had enough of your crap, Captain. You're going to watch the Noddiks win this competition against your former guild, and you're going to get *no* credit! Face it, Rowland—*they* hate you. *We* hate you. You're a *nobody*. A loser. A crappy leader. A beta simp. A *bad guy*! And you know what? All the Situational Awareness, Assertiveness, Decision Making, Communication, Leadership, Adaptability-slash-Flexibility, and Mission Analysis in the *world* couldn't save your sorry butt from your fate as the greatest disappointment in naval aviation history. Say goodbye to your days as a bad-butt testosterone-fueled fighter pilot—because after this tron blasting? The only community you're going to fit into will be the sisterhood of the traveling pants..."

<MCSALAD>... CRM... >SADCLAM<... *that was it!* "Chippy Pride..." the Padroids whispered under his breath, as he recalled his bloodline. "Chippy Style..." he continued, memories flooding back to him—memories of waving jets on the LSO platform, of blasting *Creed* in the ready room, of his old best friends... of the indomitable Dambusters... "Chippy Ho!" he yelled.

<MCSALAD> burst out of the cabinet and threw his shoulder into Dr. Suabedissen, who was instantly knocked out cold from the impact on his fragile little body. He snatched the APG-47 out of the air and—in one smooth motion—took two quick shots at each S-5 bot—headshots only; *perfect* aim. Both bots fell to the deck, flailing their arms around daintily as their personal drive for success diminished, their body compositions took on the shapes of pears, and their last words were those complaining about the dangers of red meat, the way their hands hurt from deadlifting, and the toll taken on their mental health after losing followers on Instagram.

The headshot-hunting hero looked around at the three bodies on the floor. He threw his oversized aviators against the wall, replacing them with a pair of Ray-Bans from his pocket. Finally, returning his focus to Sam, LT Chris ">SADCLAM<" Houben coolly said, "Waveoff, waveoff; foul deck."

In awe at the timing and seamless delivery of the line, Sam gasped, "<MCSALAD>! You... you saved me—*and* my manhood! But... why?! A programming error?"

The savior shook his head and said, "Negative, brother. The only error in my system—in my *heart* — was living like one of those Noddik jabronis instead of doing what I came here to do: to save you, Nickels. It's me: >SADCLAM<."

">SAD... CLAM<...?" Sam repeated hesitantly. "Now, that's a name I haven't heard in a long time..." And then it hit him—"Chris...?"

>SADCLAM< nodded, smiling.

Sam's eyes transitioned from confusion to awe. "... Chris—CLAM! It's been you this whole time?! I can't believe I didn't... I couldn't..." Sam was floored at himself. *How was I not able to recognize him aboard the ship? He was here for* years... *what's* wrong *with me?!*

CLAM smiled and said, "It's ok, Nickels, it's ok. I sort of lost *myself*, too. Here, take a look at this," he said as he handed Sam the OPERATION: PIGPEN folder. As he watched Sam peruse the pages, CLAM commented with indignation, "Can you believe this empire was running a sick program like this?! What a bunch of fucking asswipes. I can't imagine what dipshit approved this act of terrorism."

As Sam read, he felt shock, anger, disbelief—and then *guilt. Oh my god...* "CLAM... I think *I* signed off on this project..."

"What?!" >SADCLAM< looked disgusted. "Nickels, how could you—"

Sam shook his head, "No, no, you don't understand. CLAM... the amount of paperwork and things to sign... there was no time to read them all diligently! The doctor... his stupid D&D raids... Juice... I just—I just sort of got impatient and started approving everything..."

>SADCLAM< shook his head in disappointment. "Nickels... are you telling me you didn't *thoroughly* look through every bit of fine print on something you signed? Like it was some... iPhone software update agreement?! You can't be serious... Dude, imagine if people did this with routing sheets! With QA audits! Safety reports! Jesus, Sam—please tell me you weren't doing this with..." >SADCLAM< gulped, "ASM qualifications?"

Captain Rowland stayed silent, afraid to look his former Chippy squadronmate in the eyes.

Houben tsked with disgust. "Nickels... what the hell have you done here? I may have been drugged off XANs, but I was at least still cognizant of the state of this shithole. This boat... this boat *sucks*, dude*!* You left us—left your *brothers*—to create the 'ultimate boat!' To get rid of the shit that was *sooo* bad," he emphasized with exaggeration, "that you fucking *quit*. And now? Look at this place! You've made a complete mockery of the Paddles; we do GQ exclusively during breakfast, lunch, and dinner hours; and you've endangered *my* life because of *your* inability to take due diligence in putting your *spineless, backstabbing bitch* signature in places where it doesn't belong," he shook the PIGPEN file violently, "like *this* appalling war crime! Good god... I certainly hope I was the only one..."

Sam, still avoiding eye contact, uttered woefully, "FISTY..."

"Oh no..." >SADCLAM looked distraught. "Nickels... please tell me you didn't..."

Rowland broke down and told Houben the horrors of what happened to their forming Training O—every excruciating detail of the pain in FISTY's screams, the tears shed, and his convulsing body during the final drive of the game film.

>SADCLAM< covered his mouth in disbelief. "The doctor actually showed the *zoomed-in, slow-motion replay* of Moss *barely* being underthrown on that 3rd and long?! Jesus... we need to get treatment for him *fast*."

Shaking his head desolately, Sam asked, "But what can we do, CLAM? He's a vegetable now! He can't unsee those tragedies..."

>SADCLAM< sighed, looked at Sam, and said, "So what, then? We just *give up*? Did FISTY *give up* on JABA when his CAS skills were lacking? No! He explained to him, 'It's chill, man; we don't really do that stuff in CAG-5 anyway, so we'll just call this SFWT a pass-complete.' Did he *give up* on me when I kept J-hooking on my roll-ins? No! He pushed for The Weapons School to start utilizing bunt deliveries, so I'd never need to worry about it! Did he give up on *you* when you kept starting radio transmissions with 'And...'? No! He stressed that you would sound like a fucking G.A. douchebag if you kept—"

"CLAM, I get it..." Sam grumbled.

"So, what are you going to do then? Give up on him like you did Juice?!"

"Hey, that's not fair! I didn't give up, I—"

"Oh, bullshit!" >SADCLAM< said, disgusted. "Nickels—you were once the best dude in the squadron, hands-down. But something happened when Juice joined— it was like you were... *intimidated*... by his motivation to be great. You were once the guy who would help an early Level 3 SFWT candidate perfect the emergencies portion of the brief with an eye-watering script about every detail of the post-punch-out sequence, including where to find good food and entertainment in local controlled ejection areas while you waited for a pickup. But when Juice was a Level 2 guy? You wouldn't teach him how to merge cells on kneeboard cards; wouldn't tell him the questions you were going to ask in the brief; dude, you even ready-room-reflew him for not JWS-ing his wingman PGM hop!" Scoffing, Houben shook his head. "You know, you turned into a real shithead—*Dimes*."

On the defensive, Sam shot back with, "How would *you* feel, CLAM? How would you feel if you built up a reputation like mine, and then Skipper tasked you to train some clown—who *sucked*, by the way—and wanted to surpass your legacy?"

CLAM stared at Sam and calmly stated, "I'd probably realize that my transition to becoming a great leader could begin with my ability to train this motivated young man."

Stunned, Sam remained silent.

"Face it, Dimes..." CLAM acknowledged, "The doctor said a lot of dumb shit, but he was right about one thing: You *were* a crappy leader, and you *became* a bad guy. You started living in some 'virtual reality,' where filling lines on the flight schedule was all it took to be a Good Dude..."

Houben's words rang in Sam's ears. *Crappy leader... bad guy... virtual reality—wait a second...* "That's it!"

>SADCLAM< narrowed his eyes in confusion. "What is it?"

Sam pointed to the doctor's vault and said, "We need to break into the safe and steal Suabedissen's VR rig!"

>SADCLAM< looked confused. "Sam, I'm not sure I follow..."

"Just—trust me; forget everything else for now. This is the only chance we've got!" Sam ran over and inspected the security system Suabedissen had set up. "I remember he said something about an eye scan, audio recognition... shit, and some riddles about Harry Potter or something. Well, let's at least see what we can do—c'mon, we'll scan him in."

The two men crouched down to pick up Dr. Suabedissen's body together—which proved entirely unneeded, as the frail scientist was so emaciated that a mere child alone could've lifted him. They put his head to the retinal scanner, while simultaneously placing his bony, pale finger on the print ID. Both succeeding in unlocking their respective credentials, leaving just the vocal recognition firewall.

"'Dr. Suabedissen,'" Sam projected, in his whiniest voice possible—but nothing happened. "Guildmaster Karl Suabedissen," he tried again, pinching his nose closed this time—alas, the door remained closed. *Dammit... I need to work on my impressions more...*

"I tried this earlier, Sam, and imitated his voice perfectly," CLAM explained, "But the system knows I'm not the Special Operations Engineer, or Doctor, or Guildmaster—whatever the hell it is," he threw his free hand up in frustration. "Who *knows* which title this goon used..."

Sam's heart skipped a beat. *Wait a second...* he looked at Chris, raised his hand, and said, "Hold up." *Guildmaster... title... gamer tag...* He remembered it vaguely... Suabedissen cracking up as he tried to convince him, '*Come on, Captain, you have to get one too! These are* hilarious! *And they can customize them to your gamer tag*!' Another memory of that idiot's ramblings crossed his mind, '*You know, in the world that* truly *matters, I have a title far more honorary than Doctor...*' Straining his eyes, deep in thought, he eventually stated in frustration, "*Shit...* what was it again? 'Pussy magnet' or something?"

Not remotely following, >SADCLAM< asked, "What are you talking about?"

Still holding the programmer's torso with one arm, Sam looked down at the doctor's white coat of armor, narrowed his eyes again, and said, "Hmm... it's worth a shot..." He dug into Suabedissen's lab coat pocket and retrieved a wallet. The two set the doctor's pre-teen-girl-ish body down, and Sam began searching through the *World of Warcraft*-themed accessory.

"What are you looking for, Sam?" Houben further questioned.

Sifting through the various contents, Sam kept quiet as he rifled through... until... "This!" Sam announced as he pulled out a card—a plastic ID, labeled 'Man Card,' with the designation made out to 'P-WordSlayer69.' "Try this one, Chris!"

Shrugging, Chris acknowledged, "Guess it can't hurt..." He cleared his throat, then stated in a high-pitched, whiny tone, "P-Word Slayer Six Nine."

The first door of the safe opened up. "Nice!" Sam shouted with a fist pump, and the two men high-fived.

The subsequent layer was a monitor with text appearing in real-time. A question emerged, with the Star Wars text scroll music playing in the background: *"I am the Senate! Inarguably one of the greatest villains of all time, Emperor Sheev Palpatine was instrumental in the domination of the Sith for many eons. What was his own given Sith Lord name?"* As the question finished, a microphone icon appeared, presumably to monitor their dialogue for recognition of the correct answer.

"What?" Sam blurt out. "Wasn't he just 'The Emperor' or whatever?"

"Dude..." CLAM responded, "I didn't watch those movies growing up; I have no idea."

"Shit..." Sam sighed. "Well... we tried..."

"Tried?! Do or do not, bro; there is no fucking try!" CLAM shouted, completely contradicting his previous claim. "What happened to you, man? What happened to the Nickels who put his 'all' into everything? The Nickels who—bullets *only*—fucking gunned down an adversary striker with FISTY and saved the lives of thousands?"

"Man..." Sam replied sadly "... I dunno, CLAM. Things just got—I guess I grew up and lost that innocence; I started to see the realities of the job."

"The realities?!" CLAM accosted. "Bro—that life, that time in the squadron—that *was* reality! But somehow, you lost your way, falling for The Disease of Me."

"The what?" That phrase sounded so familiar to Sam. *Where have I heard that before?*

"Nevermind..." Houben shook his head. "You just—I remember how happy you and FISTY were that day. I remember thinking, 'Those are two future CNOs'—I don't *care* if that career timing makes no sense! Hearing you guys talk about your monumental, life-altering shootdown at midrats, over French toast sticks and chocolate milk... man..." He shrugged, "Back then, I couldn't have imagined *either* of you ever leaving this job..."

Sam smiled slightly. "That's certainly a day I'll never forget..." Chuckling, he added, "Of course, all FISTY wanted to talk about was that Growler suspending for leaving HOLD ALL unboxed, messing up his record-setting open deck time."

>SADCLAM< laughed. "And god, you guys were so proud of that goofy-ass, now-immortalized callsign—what was it again?"

Sam smirked to himself. "Sidious..."

"Huzzah!" Suabedissen's dorky voice reverberated from the computer.

"What!?" Sam called out in shock. "We... we got it *right*? We didn't even answer!"

"Hey, who cares? We're one step closer!" >SADCLAM< said excitedly.

The next question materialized, this one playing the Lord of the Rings theme—which neither man recognized, because both had previously felt a woman's touch. *"The Fellowship! The few, the proud, the brave! But not only warriors and wizards... Name all four hobbits who joined the guild to destroy the ring at Mount Doom."*

Sam grabbed his forehead. "Shit... CLAM, I have no fucking clue. Who the hell would know these?!"

>SADCLAM< sighed and said, "Dammit... me neither, bro. I've actually— and unfortunately—seen this overly drawn-out movie series. While I'm sure it's a pretty basic question for even the most casual of fans, I was too busy playing sports, talking to girls, and, in general, trending my testosterone in the proper direction than to remember the names of four little midgets trying to melt a ring." He put his hands on his hips and shook his head.

Looking down in disappointment, Sam bemoaned, "I want to say one of the hobbits had a girl's name or something—but no, they were definitely all guys... *shit!*" He slammed his fist on the wall. "You're right—this is all my fault, CLAM. I've fucked up one thing after another in my life. Everything was going so well, too. I just... I couldn't see what was *right* with the job, because I was too focused on what was *wrong*. I thought I could find happiness elsewhere. I thought this Noddik opportunity was going to be a gift from the aviation gods, where I could find happiness in life. Well, 'Merry-fucking-Christmas' to me... This shit *sucks*, CLAM. Look what's happened to FISTY... to *you*..." *To Low T,* he thought to himself.

"God, just look at what's happened to this boat and fleet—because of *me!* And now they're going to go and fight America in a battle of admin dominance... Whatever—at least the United States won't have to worry about losing—the Noddik fleet is going to get *crushed*. And the empire I built is going to be the target of every Admin-fanatic Reddit forum. AirWarriors will probably even post about it, amongst the countless 'what are my chances for jets' threads. Shit, maybe I'll do an AMA about what it's like to be a worthless loser whose life has amounted to nothing..."

"Hold up," >SADCLAM< stopped him. "You think the Noddiks are going to *lose?*"

Sam scoffed. "With Juice in charge?! Absolutely."

CLAM stared at him and said, "Bro..."

Sam threw up his hands and ranted, "Jesus Christ, how does everybody think so *highly* of this guy?! You think *he's* going to lead this trash operation to victory?! He brings *nothing* special to the table! He just..." Sam struggled to come up with concrete evidence. "He's just... such a... tool."

"You *really* think that?" CLAM shook his head, chuckled humorlessly, and explained, "Sam... I don't think you realize what it was like when you left. Morale... well, it plummeted. People were skipping entire admin portions of briefs; nobody ever asked about personal ORM; our squadron NATOPS was collecting dust; we stopped doing EP tests entirely—shit, I can't even remember how to *start the* departure/spin boldface! We just sort of blew off training toward any portion of the flight where we weren't FENCE'd in. And you know what? Our performance was *horrendous*. Tactical execution meant nothing, because we couldn't get our jets safely to or from the working areas. Non-standard check-ins on deck, people taking off with their seats safe and canopies open... hell, we were limited to 'coordinated singles' in IMC, because nobody remembered how to fly parade!

"But you know what changed that?" he asked rhetorically. "Juice. Juice told The Patch wearers that we were taking a break from conduct—a tactical pause—and relearning NATOPS from the ground up. We had mandatory daily study hours, did EP sim two-a-days, and when we flew? Administratively *only*—with weekly early morning taxi fams. Dude, we did this for a *month!* It was the most intense four weeks of my life. But guess what? We started fucking *crushing* it administratively. We were getting flooded with requests from other squadrons—asking to teach their guys about reading approach plates, or tricks we used to memorize the landing gear speed limitations; shit, one of the Training Os, Frodo, even asked if we could give his squadron a chalk talk on proper on-deck validation for the Checklist page. The FAA actually thought they had a *radar glitch*, because our ATC spread was consistently *perfect* to the 0.001 nautical mile on the yardstick—a fidelity that Juice helped program and enable with his own administrative software update!"

Chris finally took a breath and emphasized, "So, *no*, Sam—I *don't* think Juice is a 'tool' who brings nothing to the table—and believe it or not? He *is* a Good Dude. And I bet you *Juice* looks through all of *his* documents before signing them..." he added pointedly.

"I—I don't know what to say... except that maybe my tough leadership inspired him?" Sam's weak words held anything *but* conviction.

"Psh... go ahead and tell *me* that story, brother..." >SADCLAM< said with disappointment. "But don't lie to *yourself*. You weren't worried about training him; you were too worried about becoming the Pippin to his Jordan..."

"*Huzzah!*" the computer announced, again a nasally Suabedissen recording.

As Hedwig's Theme from the Harry Potter series played, the next question appeared: "*The Order of the Phoenix! The brave wizards and witches dedicated to defending the world from the evil Lord Voldemort, and ultimately protected the Boy Who Lived from the clutches of the Death Eaters! Name the brave member who lost his life to Bellatrix Lestrange."*

Shocked at the previous question being answered, but too upset to acknowledge it, Sam instead fired back at >SADCLAM<, "Ok, fine, maybe I was a little annoyed—but what the *fuck*, CLAM. I put *so* much effort into my legacy at the Chippies—and in the end, all anybody wanted me to do was train some shitty new golden boy who wanted to surpass me!"

"So!" CLAM called out, "You *were* feeling threatened!"

"Yeah, I was, ok?!" Sam acknowledged with anger in his voice. "It's like I was becoming an afterthought! Like the squadron had forgotten I existed as *the* Good Dude! Everybody raved about Juice, how awesome he was, how quickly he was rising—the motherfucker got an EP in his second year! Do you know what that did to several JOs' career timing?"

"Probably nothing, given the state of Navy pilot manning and all the leverage the service member has nowadays."

"Exactly! But still! So annoying, right?!" Sam insisted, desperate for approval. "I just—I liked this job a lot more when I was appreciated—and maybe... maybe I just wanted that appreciation again... The job wore on me, bro. We don't get paid enough for this bullshit. Put yourself in my shoes, man..."

>SADCLAM< sighed. "You're asking me to put myself in the shoes you wore back then, Sam? To put myself in the boots of an officer who made nearly $100k to fly a jet and play a *game* for a living?! That's right, Nickels," he nodded, seeing Sam's confused face, "This is a *game*. Sure, it's a life and death game at times—but look at us. We come to work, hungry to get better every single day, relentlessly practicing our tactics to get as close as we possibly can to *perfecting* them, studying our asses off in hopes that it will make even the most *marginal* increase in the jet. Why? Because if *we* don't, somebody else *will*—and *they'll* win the game. We're motivated by the necessity to get *great* at this game, because anything less than 'great' could mean death; could mean *losing*. We have a locker room of like-minded brothers, traveling the world together and building bonds closer than even professional sports teams do. We get a thrill like none other every single time we take off, land, or bend the jet any which way. We literally get paid to stay youthful—living the adventure in life we dreamt of as kids—and to keep *competing*, when *so many* in the world are content to sit in their cubicles and watch others fight in the arena.

"And you want me to *sympathize* for you—because you got *jaded*? Because you felt the pressure of somebody who *matched* your enthusiasm to be the greatest at that game?! I'm sorry, but the greatest of champions don't *run* from competition, Sam—they *chase* it.

"Why do you think Juice left us? It had nothing to do with his 'legacy' nor any clashes in the ready room, and he certainly didn't bitch incessantly about the boat." CLAM looked Sam dead in the eye and explained, "Juice knew that if he wanted to truly *be* the best, he needed to train *against* the best. *Of course* we were sad to see him go—but we understood what drove him; and we *applauded* him. Because, unlike *you,* we knew that Juice wasn't giving up on his destiny; he was *pursuing* it."

Sam was stunned by the brutality of what he was hearing. "I—I don't... I—"

"Yeah," >SADCLAM< said with a frustrated look of disappointment. "Really wish you would've thought about things a bit more before abandoning us, Sam. The future used to look pretty bright for you. But now?" he shook his head. "Looks pretty dark. I'm serious; black as a case 3 moonless night in the middle of the ocean."

"Huzzah!"

This time, an entire door of the safe slid inward, leaving one final portion to be unlocked. The *Top Gun* anthem started playing, the trademark gong echoing in the room. As it built up to its vintage melody, the last question unveiled itself: *"What configuration officially defines the Delta Easy pattern? Be wary, brave warrior—you only have one chance!"* A touchscreen button was present this time, with the label 'Record Answer.'

"What the hell?!" CLAM asked, confused, "How did we answer...?"

"I don't know..." Sam responded quietly, truthfully in greater shock from CLAM's angry rant than he was at unlocking the safe.

The two men looked at each other. CLAM offered up his hands to Sam. "This one's easy—go ahead and take it, brother."

Sam reached to touch the button and speak—but then paused, looked at >SADCLAM< and said, with a hint of uncertainty in his voice, "Wait—it's... gear up, flaps up, max E... *right?* You know—'easy on the gas?'"

"Yeah..." Houben's eyes narrowed in annoyance, "That's not right. You're describing more of a Delta *Clean.*"

"What?!" Sam blurt out. "Then what is a simple 'Delta?'"

"Such a thing doesn't exist," CLAM explained. "It should always be given an amplifier." He gave a look of disapproval. "Dude, you should *absolutely* know this if you're commanding a ship; you've *gotta* have this knowledge down *cold,* Sam..."

"Why can't Paddles or the tower specifically just say what they want us to do, configuration-wise?" Sam asked. "Wouldn't that alleviate a lot of the confusion and post-flight chastising?"

"Well... that *would* be the Good Dude move, wouldn't it?" >SADCLAM< retorted.

A Good Dude... what the fuck do I know about being a Good Dude anymore... maybe I never even was *one. I bet* Juice *knows what 'Delta Easy' means...* Sam shrugged, CLAM... I used to think I had all the answers—but now I realize: I don't know shit. The more you think you know in this job—this *life*—the sooner you find yourself getting Fox-2'd in the ass before you even get a chance to react. I thought I was so capable, so overqualified—so *above* this bullshit job. But maybe I really *did* like this job more than I realized. I was so busy looking for better solutions that I lost sight of what matters. I mean, for god's sake..." he gestured toward >SADCLAM<, "One of my best friends was on my own ship, and I couldn't even recognize it. You're right—I ran away. When adversity hit, I was afraid to fight. I quit on America's Navy. And I don't blame you guys for hating me."

The two men slumped over in silence, stumped at both the answer to the mind-bending riddle, and as to how they'd gotten down this emotional alley. In an attempt to ease the tension, >SADCLAM< gave a slight smile and said, "You know, JABA named one of his rollercoasters after you."

Sam's ears perked up. "He—he did?" Back to beating himself up, he scoffed, "What was it, 'Traitor's Turmoil,' the world's most expeditious freefall?"

"Redemption Road." >SADCLAM< nodded as he said it. "He hasn't put the finishing touches on it yet, because it currently has a gigantic piece missing after the large drop in the middle—which is apparently hurting his theme park's approval rating. He's trying to find the perfect way to install the path back up, so that the journey can keep going..."

Shaking his head, Sam said, "Unfortunately, I'm not sure that ride will ever be completed... he might just want to scrap it."

Frowning, >SADCLAM< explained, "You know, Sam, admin is great and all—but there aren't any hard and fast numbers, or rigid recommendations to *life*. Part of being a Good Dude is about intuitively doing the right thing, even when there's no procedure to guide you. You were so good at that—that was the Nickels we knew and loved—not this guy obsessed with his status, credit, and legacy." CLAM paused in thought, then continued, "*Anybody* in the fleet can bring in the OK when it's case 1, no emergencies, and all the fuel in the world. But you know what's *really* remarkable? Somebody who knows how to deal with unexpected adverse weather, fight off sudden electric gremlins in the cockpit, and bring the bitch aboard with a Fair pass in the wildest of pitching decks, bingo-on-the-ball. Trust me, Sam—a heroic effort like that will get you the Paddles upgrade every single time—because you can't find the answers to a problem like *that* in CV NATOPS."

Wait a second... Sam's eyes widened. "That's it! CLAM... CV NATOPS! It doesn't say anything about..." he looked at the safe's computer screen and, without waiting for confirmation from Houben, confidently pushed the record button and announced his answer: "There *is* no official definition of Delta Easy!"

"Huzzah!" The doctor sounded even whinier and more pathetic with each successful announcement. *This* time, however, the Final Fantasy 'Victory Fanfare' music played—but once again, the aviators didn't recognize the song, as neither had been living in their mom's basement at age 25.

The vault door clicked, and—finally—a handle appeared beneath the final layer. The two men looked at each other, as Sam then reached forward and cranked the handle open. Inside, they found a binder full of plastic sheets—about three inches thick—filled with Dungeons and Dragons cards, organized 3x3, alphabetically. Further in, they found a random USB flash drive labeled 'Tax Documents.' The two smirked, knowing full well what was on there. But behind *that*... was exactly what Sam had been looking for: Suabedissen's VR headset.

"Jackpot," Sam said quietly with a slight smile. He looked at Houben and asked, "Two questions—One: Do you know where we can find JABA? And two: Can you still fly an F/A-18?"

"Hot affirm to both," CLAM responded coolly.

Sam took a deep breath. "Well, in that case—CLAM... hear me out. I may have made some huge mistakes. Maybe I wasn't the best leader to Juice; maybe I've burned too many bridges to ever again be the 'Nickels' you all used to respect. But give me a chance to at least do the right thing *now*; give me a chance to save FISTY's life."

CLAM gave him a long look, pondering in thought... before cracking a smile, as he reached his arm out for a bro-clasp of officiality and said, "Let's fucking *go!*"

Sam paused. *This was a perfect time—I don't care if it's not his name!* He once again summoned his Austrian accent, matched >SADCLAM<'s gesture, and yelled, "Dillon! You son of a bitch..."

Thrilled, despite the complete irrelevance of the line, >SADCLAM< grinned and met Sam's hand with his. As their biceps swelled with insane mass, both could've sworn they heard an *explosion* from the sheer amount of testosterone flowing in the room. With the two Chippies reunited in a display of hypermasculinity, >SADCLAM< felt, for the first time in years, job satisfaction. 'Now *that's* how you talk a lost aviator all the way down to the wires. You still got it, CLAM...'

~

Dr. Suabedissen came to in a daze, and reached around to find his glasses. He held them up to his eyes. "Oh god..." he wailed, as he saw the bodies of the S-5 robots on the floor, their artificial muscles shriveled down. "Oh *god!*" he yelled louder, now remembering the interaction with Captain Rowland. He scrambled to his feet, looking for his APG-47 gun—and then he noticed it: his vault—open. Rowland—gone. The VR machine—*missing!* "Oh my freaking *GOD*!!" he screamed. In hysteria, he rummaged his hands through everything, tearing apart his office in search of the VR headset—yet found nothing. "NOOOO!!!" he screamed in agony.

He thought about the countless raids he was scheduled to lead... the levels he'd lose from the missed EXP opportunities... the items people would plunder from orcs' caches without him... the major hit his reputation would take in his online universe. His worst nightmare had come true.

He began weeping, tears streaming down his face as he checked the vault one last time—but then, below his binder of D&D cards, he found *it*—the 'Tax Documents' USB drive. He was able to form a smile through his tears, as he clasped the drive in his hand and started shaking from maniacal laughter.

He walked over to one of the fallen S-5 members, opened the upper back panel, inserted the USB, and then hit 'reset' on the bot's mainframe. "The time is right," he said to himself, nodding his head through sniffles and laughs, "The time is now."

The bots' eyes opened. He came up up to one knee and stated—with a suddenly even more robotic-sounding voice: "MASTER... I PLEDGE MYSELF TO YOUR TEACHINGS... TO THE WAYS OF THE DEPARTMENT HEADS."

Suabedissen donned his hood and said, "Good... *gooooood*... The spool is strong with you! A powerful department head you will become." He raised both arms and announced, "Henceforth... you shall be known as... Robo-Hinge!"

The S-5 employee, suddenly appearing smugger and more authoritative, nodded and said, "THANK YOU, MY MASTER."

Suabedissen nodded. "Rise..."

Robo-Hinge stood up—his walk even more rigid and binary than before—and started doing a visual B-sweep with his head, walking around the room, stating, "LINE OF SIGHT TASKING... ACTIVATED—NEED VOLUNTEER TO ORGANIZE PUBS ROOM. MENIAL TASK SHEDDING... ACTIVATED—CLEANING CAPABILITY DELETED. ABILITY TO STAY CHILL—DELETED. MUST GET SORTIES... CREW REST NOT IMPORTANT... ENSURE YOU ARE LOGGING T&R... NEED PILOT OF OPPORTUNITY TO TURN JET AT 0400... SPOOL-UP METER—RISING RAPIDLY..."

Suabedissen watched with wicked glee, grinning evilly below the shadows of his hood...

8

Don't Pick Me

*J*ABA, *I'm telling you – I could use a guy like you so badly. The Noddiks are paying well; it's such a cush life! And you even get to live in outer space! It's the fabled 'truly good deal!'"*

LT Mark "JABA" Buck paused his Rollercoaster Tycoon app to flash a skeptical look toward LT Rowland. Then, he closed his eyes and shook his head. "I'm sorry, dude – I don't know what to tell you. A) You aren't exactly the most popular guy around the air wing right now; and no offense, but I don't want that association on my name when I leave. And B) Speaking of leaving? I plan on doing that, too – but certainly not to another boat in another fleet. Sam, there's more to life than flying, tactics, and admin. All that stuff, man? It's all a game – and a really bad one, at that. Look at this thing," he said, pointing to a Joint Mission Planning Software computer. "I've spent the last two years of my life updating this janky software, driving myself insane trying to figure out the inner mental workings of the lowest-bidding contract team that designed this unintuitive piece of junk." He rubbed his temples, stressed just ranting about it. "Calendar rollover glitches, crash-causing TAMMAC downloads, comm card frequency updates that are changed by the scroller two hours later, the fact that you have to find and select a 'hand' tool to click and drag – and don't even get me started on the fragility of the QNAP hard drive and the air wing-wide ignorance to the proper shutdown procedures."

"But JABA," Sam encouraged, "Look how incredibly good you've gotten at this stuff!"

JABA gave a heartless chuckle. "Good at this? Sam, I've basically gotten 'good' at learning how to use an abacus in the age of calculators. This knowledge is going to be irrelevant as soon as I leave the Navy – hardly a single transferrable skill."

"Not true!" Sam countered, "You're a programming whiz, man! Just think of the difference you could make in a fleet that actually knows what it's doing! And there's a rumor that the Noddiks are going to contract Apple to design their mission planning IOS!" Sam was now just making up lies in desperation – he would do whatever it took to gain such a crucial asset to his new team in the Noddik Empire, especially considering how much of a power move this

JABA coup would be for his legacy. Not to mention, a massive hit for his old squadron; everybody knew the air wing was going to be screwed if and when JABA departed.

"Sorry, dude... it's not happening. Besides — I already have my own dreams..." he said ominously.

Of course. *Sam sighed as JABA returned his gaze to his phone, installing more food stands and expanding the latest roller coaster in his virtual theme park, 'The Buck Shack.'*

JABA's dreams comprised roller coaster management, which was the biggest open secret in the air wing. Even when JABA showed up as a new guy, all he ever talked about was managing theme parks. He gave a better-man speech on the optimum pricing point for entry tickets and concessions; in his BFM briefing labs, he compared dogfighting to the G-forces and curvature of roller coaster turn circles, even including the EM diagrams for hundreds of different rides. He used literally every single day *of his earned leave to visit various theme parks around the world — as it turns out, to analyze their business plans. Contrary to widespread belief, JABA was not an adrenaline junkie visiting parks to fuel a need for thrills. Rather, LT Buck was fascinated by the* corporate *side of theme parks. He would dress up in suits and sneak his way into board shareholder meetings at Six Flags to get a temp check of the latest trends in theme park logistics and finances. He landed a summer internship — again, during POM leave — at Disneyland Tokyo, where he successfully negotiated the addition of a new ride ('Mr. Toad's Wild Departure from Controlled Flight') that went down as the company's most beloved attraction, tripling ticket sales in its debut month. And* every single moment *in the jet — be it in the midst of a GBU-12 laze, flying IMC parade as a wingman, or even in the groove — JABA was never shy about being caught staring down at his phone, 'Tycooning' as he called it. It was so bad that CAG had to confiscate his phone for an entire month on one cruise. Of course, it didn't matter, since JABA had mastered the art so well that he had outsourced third parties to manage his park while he was away from his phone. Simply put, Mark Buck was a Rollercoaster Tycoon Legend. He was the first inductee into the RT Hall of Fame — an association started because of him. And like a superstar NBA free agent rounding out the end of a salary-capped rookie deal, the tycoon world was just* salivating *for the day when JABA would finish his Navy contract and reset the market as he entered the IRL theme park management world.*

As he stayed locked on to his game — inking a deal with an Italian fast food pizza company and signing an amusement park caricature artist at a great rate — JABA noted to Sam, "Yeah man, maybe try getting one of those D&D nerds to be your programmer. That Karl Suabedissen guy seems like he knows his stuff — maybe he'll do it."

Disappointed, Sam clicked his tongue. A D&D guy? Please... my fleet is going to be cool; no chance *I let somebody from the virtual reality world get their greasy little Cheeto-laced fingers on my masterpiece.* "JABA — please man... you're the best in the biz. Is there anything I can do to get you to come with me and be my programmer?"

Sighing with exasperation, JABA turned his phone screen off, looked at Sam one last time, and said, "Hey, dude — I'm not trying to be rude, but I need to make this clear: I have zero — and I mean zero — interest in living this life anymore. Any of this — being away from home, fixing JMPS, troubleshooting SHARP, returning home to then immediately leave on DETs, ground jobs, FITREPs, collateral ground jobs, on-loads, off-loads, Cyber Secure Awareness Challenges, and — most importantly — absolutely anything about the boat! The food, the noise, the gyms, the bathrooms, the heat, the cold..." he crossed his arms and spread them, "Dude — I'm over it." Raising an arm in appeal, he added, "Hey, I love flying, man. It's awesome. And I love my time with the boys. But there's something else calling my name out there..." he glanced at his phone, "And I'm not giving that dream up simply to spend more days on a steel piece of crap — not as a programmer, not as a super JO, and certainly not as a department head.

"And oh, by the way..." he said with a pointed look, "I'm not leaving this job simply because I think I can find greener grass; I'm leaving because I know my true purpose in life has nothing to do with naval aviation. What more is there to do here? I've climbed the mountain, I've got my Level 4 qual, and I've seen all there possibly is to this job — how much more could somebody really want to suffer? I've peaked here, man — my best days are behind me..." He shook his head. "As much as the Navy wants it, I will never accept their offer and become an O-4, selling my soul in the process. Mark my words, Sam — The Navy and I are done. You understand me?! Done!"

~

Sam dialed in the course line for his final approach: 069. *Classic JABA...* Between the fact that he was flying sober for the first time in months, and the adrenaline rush from the great escape engineered between himself and the rejuvenated >SADCLAM<, Sam felt like he was miles ahead of the jet administratively. *Scale decremented to 10, NAV Master Mode selected, RADALT already set to 370?! Damn, it's like I never even left! PLM set to 3.0 and 15* — Sam ceased his self-pep talk. *Wait a sec — was that right?*

"Uhh... CLAM?" he keyed on AUX. "What's the ship speed setting for a field landing, again?"

"Bro — are *serious*?" Houben responded, disappointment heavy in his tone.

Sam looked over to his right and saw CLAM beside him in perfect parade position, shaking his helmet with his hand rested on the front, before he held up a 'zero' with his hand.

Ok, asshole, don't make it sound like I'm an idiot! Sam grumbled to himself. *Sure, maybe I'm a little rustier than I thought, but cut me some slack — that was an exhausting escape!*

It *was* an exhausting escape — well, the die toss part of it, anyway — the majority actually went surprisingly smoothly. Fortunately for Sam and >SADCLAM<, the ship had gone into EMCON — banning the use of all Bluetooth, walkie-talkies, and even J-

dial devices—so the robots were not able to spread the word of escapees to one another—*if* the two runaways had even been spotted... But also, the ship was darkened
internally due to pre-sunrise hours, making it really hard to see, and seemingly accomplishing nothing—aside from making the ship a much more hazardous place for those
inside its skin. In fact, the most nerve-wracking moment of the escape was when Sam
nearly tweaked his ankle going down the 180-frame ladderwell due to the darkness.
And finally, once they'd found their way to the brig and hauled FISTY's body over
their shoulders, it just so happened to be cleaning stations hour—*normally* a disastrous
time to be out and about the ship—but for the fugitives? It couldn't have worked out
any better. Every bot had their headphones in, looking completely miserable and
zoned out while polishing knee knockers, apathetic to any flight suits squeezing by.
The Sam/CLAM duo *did* have to tiptoe—but *not* to avoid detection; Rather, tiptoeing
merely in guilt as they tried to stay out of the way of the cleaning sailors, continually
speaking contrite words under their breath of "Sorry guys," "Oops, 'scuse us," and
"Apologies, early brief."

When they finally arrived at the flight deck, the timing couldn't have been
worse—there was a *FOD walkdown* going on! However, flight deck spacesuits were
required, in another stroke of incredible luck, due to the cold temperature of outer
space and low oxygen levels. As a result? Predictably, nobody showed up. The two
former Chippies carried their unconscious Training O across the deck, and eventually
made their way to one of the elevators—where two F/A-18s were parked. In another
close call, Sam nearly pulled his latissimus dorsi while pumping his low-pressure APU
(*God, I really gotta start lifting again...*), whereas >SADCLAM<'s former wrestler
strength paid dividends as he got his to 3000 psi within minutes. After a diligent preflight, where the two walked around looking at arbitrary spots on the jet, kicking tires
for the fun of it, and petting the nose cone to see if it might fall off from the slightest
touch, they nodded at each other in unison: It was Go-Time. Go-Time, except for one
glaring issue...

Come on, 'Evens!' Sam focused hard, trying to manifest the outcome of the roll.
Desperate to do whatever he could to win, he quickly glanced to make sure CLAM
wasn't looking, and raised his arm while wiggling his fingers slightly, trying to use
The Force to influence Suabedissen's 16-sided die to land on any of the eight numbers
that would've made him the victor. *I mean... it's not like I actually believe in that stuff—
but what if it worked...?*

"Sam, what the hell are you doing?" >SADCLAM asked.

Sam whipped his hand back to his side. "Nothing!"

The two watched as the die bounced around a few more times... and then
landed on...

"Bizz! Let's go, baby!" CLAM yelled with excitement as the 'five' sat face up.

"*Dammit!* Come on, man! Best two of three?!" Sam pleaded.

>SADCLAM shook his head and said, "No way—there lies *your* chariot, Sam," as he pointed to the two-seat variant of the two available jets. "Besides, you haven't flown around Earth in a long time—it might be good for you to have someone back there to help you out," he said with a grin.

Sam grumbled, "Yeah... whatever... help me get FISTY in the back seat, and let's get on our way already." He looked at his friend and raised his finger, saying, "One thing's for sure though, CLAM—I'm leading. If I'm gonna be short a thousand pounds of gas, then I sure as hell am *not* flying form!"

"Whatever you say, dash one *pilot!*" >SADCLAM< heckled, an entertained smile on his face.

Sam rolled his eyes as the two strapped in FISTY, and each went through their startup sequence and prepared to take off. As they worked through internal final checks, Sam remembered that CLAM had never flown one of these Noddik-variant jets. "Ok, I'm going to walk you through the takeoff sequence in this software," he explained over TAC frequency. "Do you see the pushbutton that says 'Takeoff'?"

"Affirm," CLAM replied.

"Hit that button," Sam explained in detail.

And the rest was history...

Captain Rowland adjusted his FCS page to 3 degrees and *zero* ship speed as the two started descending for the break at the gigantic airfield, which was built in the middle of the theme park on the port island JABA had always loved most: Guam.

Unfortunately, the flight had confirmed some of the things Sam—being a single-seat big-meat guy by trade—had *dreaded* about flying with a backseater—even a vegetated one. *Just* as he'd heard in scary folktales, FISTY started sleep-talking during critical ATC comms, including small-talking about weekend plans or the previous night's football game. After a missed altitude assignment that CLAM caught and read back for him, Sam groaned and turned his ICS all the way down. At another point, FISTY's muscles spasmed, and he began to hit the same pushbuttons that Sam was touching, causing weird do-loops and forcing Sam to turn his ICS back up as he initiated awkward back and forth dialogues of, "Ohp—I got—are you—ok, go ahead—ok, I got—ohp—ok, my scree—ohp!" And, worst of all, despite being incapacitated, FISTY was coherent enough to request, in his dazed state, "Ohh... so *cold* back here... throw a log on the fire, por favor?" Sam gave yet another annoyed sigh and turned the heat up to the point where he went from coolly comfortable to unpleasantly sweating. Every time he looked over, >SADCLAM< was smiling with his mask off—single and thriving—while Darth Vader-esque breathing filled Sam's ears. *God damn you, CLAM... he was probably using The Force, too...*

But Sam had successfully endured the pain of having a friend to fly with, as the two jets were now overhead the runway and preparing to break into the pattern. Sam gave the kiss-off signal and entered his first manual break in over five years. *Holy shit!* He felt alive—the smooth G onset; the extreme deceleration playing tricks on his vestibular system; the baro altitude fluctuating within +/-400 feet of his break altitude... *Whew — maybe I should've requested a straight-in...* The landing checks were anything *but* natural coming out of Sam's mouth as he rattled off, "Ok; gear—three down; flaps... full? Yeah; Hook—up; harness... as you like it? What does that even mean? Dispensers are..." he looked down briefly. "Eh, they're probably off. Anti-skid... damn, I don't even remember that does! I think it should be off... *nope*—that caused an advisory— let's put that back on... there we go! Oh my god..." he winced as he saw the extra step on his checklist page. "What the fuck is the EJECT SEL? Jesus—uhhh... whatever, checks complete. Oh wait—how do you get into PLM again?"

Sam had been so used to pushing one button to land, that selecting two things was far beyond his habit patterns and capabilities. Eventually, after finger-fucking his way through various buttons, he found himself in an expanded SA page, a caged HUD, and—after multiple unsuccessful pickle depressions—he was finally in Precision Landing Mode with a good '-DP- ATC'; three seconds before touchdown. *Phew.* He landed well high on the Fresnel lens, which FISTY must have subconsciously detected, as he mumbled, "Might've been a bolter..." Sam shook his head, annoyed, and muttered under his breath, "Yeah, thanks—I saw..."

The two jets taxied off of runway 07 and over to the parking area, popped their canopies open, and Sam finally soaked in the scene. Directly ahead, a giant jumbotron on a tall building featured a holographic video of JABA in a flight suit, as his voice projected from loudspeakers to greet guests with, "Ladies and Gentlemen! Welcome... to... CV... Worldwide!" The word 'worldwide' echoed from the speakers, as he continued, "The most exciting nautical roller coaster park to *ever* commission! My name is Mark Buck, and *you*, lucky sailors, are about to undergo the cruise of a lifetime!"

The gigantic projector switched from JABA's frame, panning over shots of CV Worldwide's different rides, restaurants, and attractions. Mark's voice continued: "Let me recommend you start by exploring the space, filing for a *Joker-1*—fun for all ages and levels of currency! Take a tour of CV Worldwide in a purely administrative experience, as you get a park fam and re-hack your comfortability with the local area! Or, for those seeking a thrill, try out the *Case 3 Pitching Deck*, as you ride the lightning all the way to touchdown, letting the sweet sound of Paddles' voice talk you down to the wires—watch out, folks, I hear the bolter machine is rigged!

"Oh, and I hope you came hungry!" The camera panned to a gigantic food court, brilliantly lit by neon lights, with one restaurant dominating most of the space. "At *Tech Reps*, you can blow off whatever plans you made, instead enjoying a break from the action as you sit and chat with friends and family for way too long! Our trademark wardroom features the greatest food selections, from Taco Tuesday to Pizza Party Faturdays, Steel Beach Burgers, and folks—you do *not* want to miss out on Sunday Brunch! Missed lunch? No worries! We'll be serving the *exact* same batch of food at dinnertime! And if *Tech Reps* is a bit too busy for you, you'll find smaller spaces, worse food, and overall less give-a-shit-factor at *Eating Forward,* located in the Wardroom 1/2 Food Court! If tuna casserole, baked beans, or Ore Ida frozen fries is your idea of 'fine dining,' then *Eating Forward* is for you!" JABA added with glee.

"Oh, by the way, all you salty dogs..." the recording added mischievously, "At CV Worldwide? *Every* day is a *beer* day!" The highlight reel panned to a brewery called *The Debrief,* then over to an impressively decorated shopping district. Buck went on, "And, of course, what would a theme park be without a top-of-the-line supercenter? Stop by *The Ship Store*, where you can recharge with our Energy Station—sponsored by Monster—and purchase an authentic Navy seabag to carry all your CV Worldwide souvenirs in! Remember your trip here by purchasing a set of itchy boat sheets, a piece of arresting gear wire, or even your very own plush stuffed animal of The Handler!

"Speaking of the Handler, be sure to give the guy a high-five if you see him out and about, *handl*-ing all the traffic in the park! That's right, friends—aboard this ship, you'll find various VIP mascots walking around! You might see the Big XO, the Fun Boss, CAG, the Admiral, or even CV Worldwide *Actual*—*yours truly!*" he said, laughing joyfully, the camera focusing back on Buck's image once again. "And yes, folks," he pointed to his face, "the mustache *is* real!

"I hope you have a wonderful time here, shipmates, and remember—at CV Worldwide, you're a part of the crew; so grab a hamster and a brew, and make your dreams come true!"

Rowland and CLAM stared at each other in shock. "*This* is what JABA decided to do with his life?!" Sam exclaimed. "He created a theme park... centered around... the *boat?!*" 'Centered around' put it mildly—the entire park's floor was painted so that the various sections looked like non-skid, tile, or steel; the loudspeaker system was assembled to look exactly like 1MCs attached to walls; the tall building with the jumbotron of JABA's likeness was designed to perfectly mimic a carrier's tower. There were even mock maintenance crews in costumes, pretending to work on static display jets throughout the park's grounds, and every employee was garbed in flight deck jerseys or ship's company coveralls. Despite being outside and on land, the entire thing gave an incredibly authentic feel to life aboard the carrier—with one exception...

"This place is *incredible!*" Houben remarked, his mouth agape.

Incredible, it was. The place was *spotless.* Thanks to automatic trash sorting stations, people could simply throw everything in any compartment, and the system would autonomously sort their junk for them. Little Roombas in mini-coveralls roamed about the park, picking up any residual trash that was littered about. Sam looked around and saw vast roller coasters reaching heights far above the tower, including a tram system that went about the park (*That must be the Joker-1...*). The music playing from the 1MC fit the mood perfectly—a mix of blink-182, 2000s throwbacks, Avicii, and various other jams; A killer playlist that ranged from vibes of 'I'm depressed and want to die' to 'Let's fucking send it!'— complete with a few obscenity-laced songs that any XO would instantly ban from the ready room. There were even videos projected on the walls of buildings, playing a *wide* variety of content. At one point, it was go-pro footage of jets launching from carriers; then it became random snowboarding and surfing runs; and then it devolved into what were basically softcore porn music videos—Sam smiled as Fifth Harmony's 'Work from Home' appeared on the jumbotron just after Dua Lipa's 'Let's Get Physical (Workout Video).'

"Yarrr! Who goes there?!" a voice called out.

Sam and Chris turned around and saw a mascot with a fun, oversized cartoon head running toward them, wearing a costume that said 'Air Boss.'

The Air Boss character approached them and, talking like a pirate, said, "Welcome to CV Worldwide, mateys! We appreciate yee air dwellers choosing to dock here and spend the day aboard this here luxurious aircraft carrier experience! I be the manager of the park's air terminal, and let ye be informed—I'm a very important person!"

Another mascot with a cartoon head and costume appeared from around the corner. He seemed to be played by a dwarf, given his diminutive frame and shirt labeled 'Mini Boss.' He spoke up in an Irish accent, "Ah, let me guess, the ol' Air Boss is telling ye' about how 'is department is *sooo* large and important, isn't 'e? Well, answer me this one—if yer' such an important person, what happened to yer' on-track career to make CAG, eh?" The mascot gave a fun laugh and nudged the Air Boss with his elbow. "I kid, I kid—we like to keep it light around here, lads! Pleased to meet ye' all; I'm Mini! We'll go ahead and gas up yer' jets if you'd like, and here's a map to find ye' way around!" The growth-stunted mascot handed a high-quality park map to Sam, then pointed to a specific area on it as he continued, "If yer' interested in an overnight stay, recommend ye' fellas check out the ol' *Sleepy Hollow* 5-star suite! If yehv' got any questions, ye' can contact any employee here, and we'll help ye' boys out!" he gave a goofy chuckle and said, "That's right! Yehl' find no S-1, 2, or 3 shenanigans here! Every single employee is trained the same way, and is equally capable of helping ye' have the experience of a lifetime 'ere at CV Worldwide! Even the crusty 'ol Air Boss can point ye' to *The Paddles Plunge* freefall ride if ye' need it!"

Mini and the Air Boss waved and walked away as Sam and >SADCLAM< looked over the map given to them. The layout—predictably—mimicked the ship, except that it was all one floor—and in a crazy twist, the park navigation was actually *intuitive*. Instead of having frame and tac numbers depicting how far port or starboard something was, there were simple directions and different 'Worlds' in the park. Sam noticed an area labeled *Rats City,* which appeared to be where all the wardroom eateries were; there was also *DC Central,* which had various exhibits, like *Tower Flower,* where you got to hike to the top of the tower and stand around until something happened and an O-5 or above replaced you. There was also a Duty Simulator where you could act as the 'SDO,' fielding phone calls and random park visitors' complaints for hours, or the 'Engineer Officer of the Watch' sim, where you got to practice sounding like an idiot during GQ. Speaking of GQ, the *Roll 'Em Ampitheater* had various live shows, including 'General Quarters Operas,' 'Mass Debrief Musicals,' and even 'Fo'c'sle Follies Broadway'—*very* expensive, but *always* worth it. *Feats of Strength* was the park's main game center, with the famous 'Condition: Zebra Maze,' and the local gym 'Flat Earth Fitness.' Sam's eyes were drawn to *The Flight Deck,* which was the central area of most of the intense roller coasters—*Midnight Bow Taxi* appeared to be a very popular one, incorporating scary visual illusions. There was a two-hour line for *66.3 Combat Shot,* which Sam could imagine was the thrill of a lifetime for parkgoers.

>SADCLAM< pointed at the map with his multicolored jumbo pen and said, "Here!" He directed their attention to a location in the park called *Blue Tile Town,* where the park's upper management and leadership worked.

Sam shook his head in awe at the professional decision. *Of course—set up front-office operations in-house, right in the middle of the action... It creates the ultimate transparency for customers and keeps you within arm's reach of the pulse of the nation. You son of a bitch, JABA—you've thought of everything.*

The two aviators carried FISTY began the hike toward *Blue Tile Town.* Along the way, they heard various vendors selling all types of food and refreshments, from custom-made waffles ("*Get* your Sunday waffles, finest pastries in the fleet! Top with marshmallows, syrup, chocolate, ice cream, candy, nuts, cereal; or 'the works!'") to steak and lobster ("Bad news, bad news inbound! Eat like a king who knows an extension is coming or a port call's been canceled!"), and a variety-filled selection of locally-crafted beers and spirits ("Who's thirsty?! Order a Lucky Buck Ale and get so hammered that you forget about the one-wire you just tagged! Feeling lonely? Get a glass of Boat Booze and watch the love of your life transform from a '2 at 10' to a '10 at 2!' And remember, any time you order four drinks, you'll get a *free* shot of JABA's custom-distilled Tequila, *Alto y Rapido*—guaranteed to keep you airborne all night long!").

Sam and >SADCLAM< marveled at the various attractions they passed, including a 'Pay-for-Say' stand where park attendees could make their own 1MC announcements; a face-painting station where patrons could have professional makeup done for post-deployment pale skin, stress wrinkles, and sullen eyes; and even an 'Alert 5' simulator, where customers got to fully gear up and sit in a makeshift cockpit, staring at a scenic ocean green screen for as many hours as they paid for, all with excessively strong cooling or heating fans blowing on you, depending on whether you picked the 'Korean Waters' or 'Persian Gulf' scenario. The bathrooms all required card access—which was built into your interactive ticket. The park walls were beautifully and accurately decorated with maps and CRM/FOD/Park Command Policy flyers. The entrance/exits to shops even had knee-knocker barriers, so crowds could keep their hamstrings nice and limber for the long walking days. JABA really *had* thought of everything, immaculately recreating the boat in the version of an amusement park that visitors from all around the world could enjoy while receiving a true carrier experience—as contradictory as that statement sounded.

The men approached *Blue Tile Town*, marked by a curtain-draped entrance and an artificial scent of sewage. As they carried FISTY across the tile, they passed by the CAG mascot's office, where they walked in and helped themselves to CAG Cookies after accidentally making awkward eye contact with the grumpy-looking O-6.

Finally, they arrived at the Flag Office, where they placed FISTY in a waiting chair, and Captain Rowland checked in with the secretary. "Hello, my name is Sam Rowland—is there any chance we could speak with CV Worldwide Actual?"

The secretary frowned, looking through her notes—a folded-up air plan—and said, "I'm sorry, I'm afraid I don't see any ground events lined up for a 'Mr. Rowland and Company' on today's schedule... perhaps I could leave a message for him?"

Sam and Chris looked at each other, before Sam asked loudly, projecting his voice toward the back office, "Yes, actually—could you tell him that Nickels and >SADCLAM< are here to see him, and it involves FISTY?"

"Did I just hear someone say *Nickels*?!" a voice called out from around the hall.

Sam craned his neck out, attempting to get a look at the speaker.

Footsteps echoed in the waiting room, getting louder and louder, before finally, the CEO himself—Mark Buck—emerged from his office, wearing a fresh grey suit with a green and white Chippy Hawaiian shirt underneath. He raised his arms, grinned widely, and exclaimed, "Nickels! >SADCLAM<! You crazy animals! How the hell have you been?! Come on back!" He smiled at his secretary and asked, "Hey, Betty, would you mind ordering these folks each a couple of over-easy eggs from the grill?" He thought for a moment, then shook off the request. "Actually, what the hell—you guys come on with me, and we'll get whatever you want!"

The two followed JABA down the hall and into his kitchen, which was designed to look identical to the Wardroom 1/2 midrats station—trays of powdered eggs, bacon, sausage, untouched veggie sausage, biscuits and gravy, waffles, and of course... *butter*. Ladles and ladles of butter. Above the main courses were more trays of fruit, granola bars, and even *more* butter—this time in individual tablespoon packets.

As they got their food and caught up at the table, JABA explained some of the revolutionary business concepts he'd incorporated at CV Worldwide, like charging people a flat rate for meals whether or not they ate, incentivizing customers to return by giving them a 'sea pay' loyalty discount (that didn't actually become substantial until over 10 years' worth of days spent at the park), and even finding a loophole in max-capacity fire codes by proving that you theoretically truly *could* fit unlimited seating around circular tables.

"Incredible!" >SADCLAM< remarked.

JABA shrugged, smiling as he explained, "It's simple mathematics."

Chuckling—but full of so many questions—Sam remarked, "So, JABA—first of all, *congratulations* on achieving your dream! But also... this park—the theme... I can't help but... well..." he shrugged and asked, "I thought you *hated* the boat?"

Mark sighed, leaned back, and steepled his hands around his head. "Well, Nickels, it certainly is funny how life turns out, isn't it?" He took a deep breath and explained, "So, you all may not have realized this, but... my entire time in the Navy?" He paused for anticipation, then admitted, "I was training and grooming myself to be a Rollercoaster Tycoon—*the* Rollercoaster Tycoon, actually. All those times playing on my phone in the ready room... in the jet... during AOMs, ceremonies, briefs with DCAG... I wasn't just playing a game—I was preparing for my *future*. I knew this business was my calling—and just as much, I knew I wanted *nothing* to do with the boat. When you left the squadron, Sam? I told myself: 'That's it, Buck. If Sam's abandoning his friends, you're getting the hell out of here too.' No, seriously—I said it every day, *every* morning when I woke up, staring at myself in the stateroom mirror. I even woke my roommates up a few times."

>SADCLAM< shrugged sheepishly and nodded, affirming the statement.

JABA sighed and continued, "You left, man, and... it really shook us up. CLAM remembers," he said, looking toward Houben, before returning his attention to Sam. "It *sucked*, dude. Morale was very low. Granted, Juice did a hell of a job getting us where we needed to be—but damn, by *that* time? I was already blazing through records in Rollercoaster Tycoon, getting DMs from the game's programmers, asking how I was earning such high approval ratings, because I'd apparently surpassed their algorithm's theoretical max score." He twisted his lips, winced his eyes, and explained, "You know... I just realized that I'd sort of *peaked* where I was in the fleet... and it was time to take my talents to the theme park industry... *IRL*."

JABA gave his entire explanation with full transparency, which was consistent with his personality. Sam had always liked this about Mark, and understood where he was coming from.

"But then..." JABA shook his head as he took a bite of eggs, leaving some yolk in his mustache, "Something crazy—and I mean *ludicrous*—happened. My contract expired while teaching at the RAG, I punched my ticket to the civilian world, and I got an apartment in San Diego, ready to start living the good life—yet within two weeks?"

he looked down at the table and shook his head, "I *missed* it. I started cleaning every day from 0730-0830—just shining random walls and swabbing my apartment decks. I wore flip-flops when I showered... had eggs every night at 2230... put on a robe and walked all the way downstairs to use the apartment lobby bathroom in the middle of the night—it all just kind of felt *right.*

"You know, back in the Chippies, I used to have *nightmares* about being back on the boat. But as a civilian? I couldn't *wait* to go to bed, just *hoping* to have dreams of turning an alert jet at 0100, of updating JMPS with the latest DAFIF, of being called to the platform for a sneaky 0800 COD recovery—every night, I *prayed* that I'd finally be woken up from this nightmare of civilian freedom... by the soothing sound of the Big XO's voice, or the beautiful repeated ringing dinging of a 'This is a drill, this is drill...'" He sighed, "I may have been separated physically—but... I just couldn't detach myself *mentally...*"

Sam's eyes were wide with shock. "Jesus, Mark. Were you depressed?" he carefully asked.

JABA looked up, staring in the distance, and explained, "You know... I'm not sure if 'depressed' is the right word... It was more of a *longing.* Like that of an ex-lover—after an untimely, heartbreaking separation in your past..." He looked back to Sam and acknowledged, "Now, sure, I was fine with my new love—Tycooning—but it was clear there was still something... something *lacking* in my life," he explained with his eyes looking heavier. "My relationship with the boat—a relationship I could've *sworn* was toxic, detrimental, life-sucking..." He smiled, "I suppose I just never quite realized what I had..." his smile faded, "... until I lost it..." His eyes started misting up as he looked down again. "It was just one of those things where our timing was off when we were together, and I just wasn't able to grasp how much I *loved* the claustrophobia-inducing walls, falling asleep to the lullaby of catapult shots, and the peaceful retreat of 48-hour flight ops. I just wasn't able to grasp how much I *loved* this job..." he wiped a tear away, growing silent as his voice trailed off.

>SADCLAM< and Sam looked at each other with very perplexed expressions.

Softening his expression and forcing out a chuckle, JABA said, "Ah, what can I say, guys—I'm a hopeless romantic... You ever have that girl you just *can't* get over? The kind that's the *last* to cross your mind as you fall asleep, the *first* when you wake up, and inescapable amongst your dreams in between? For me, that was carrier aviation—and frankly, the job as a whole." Wiping his eyes again, he reached into his left jacket pocket and said, "Here, check this out." He pulled a couple of golden oak leaf insignias, still in their Vanguard packaging.

>SADCLAM< covered his mouth with both hands and gasped.

Laughing, JABA explained, "Yeah, yeah... I know! Can you believe it? I bought them a month after I turned down the O-4 promotion and got out. And you know what? I told myself when I bought them, and every day since: 'Buck, you don't deserve these babies—not yet. But... if a destiny exists where true love shall prevail, and the day comes where you find your way back into your paramour's arms? *Then*, and *only then*, will you earn the right to don them.' No, seriously—now I say *that* in front of the mirror, every day!"

Nearly in shocked paralysis by this point, Sam gave >SADCLAM< the 'Can you believe this guy?' face while pointing at JABA.

JABA raised his arms wide, chuckling happily now, and expressed, "Guys, I don't know what to say! I'm a man in love—a passionate, unyielding, adoring love! And that love is for naval aviation!"

Wiping his forehead, Sam exhaled and said, "JABA... that's fucking crazy, man. But *good for you*! I know the Navy is very picky and exclusive about letting people get back in after leaving, and that it's literally *unheard* of since they are so heavy on pilot numbers—but I'm rooting for you, man," he said with a smile. "What about your CV Worldwide venture? It seems like it's been a massive success, yeah?"

"Big time." JABA said confidently, then with a slight smile and a shrug added, "Yeah, I mean it's been unreal. Roller coaster management has been good to me. But it's not where my heart is. I mean, I'm not sure if you guys caught on to the park's theme, but... 'C-V'?" He spelled it out slowly with exaggeration. "You know... *Aircraft-Carrier?!*" he said, also patronizingly slowly. "Connect the dots, Sam. This whole thing—this whole setup—is sort of my love letter to naval aviation; my desperate attempt to put on a grand display simply so that the Navy would notice me, let me out of their friend zone, and finally take me back. But alas..." he said with a sigh and head shake, "it appears they've simply moved on without me..."

Incredible. Absolutely fucking incredible, Sam thought to himself as he stared at JABA in disbelief. *This guy is a modern-day Jay Gatsby...*

Shrugging again, JABA looked back at Sam, lightly slammed his fist on the table, and said, "Well, hey, that's enough about me and my heart's yearning for my one and only. So, what's new with you guys? You were saying something about FISTY earlier?"

The two looked at each other with panic. "FISTY!" they both called out.

Confused, JABA asked, "Woah, woah... what's going on? Is he alright?"

"Follow us—we need to get him in here, quick!" Sam called out as the three exited the kitchen to retrieve FISTY's lifeless, depressed body from the waiting room.

"Hey, FISTY!" JABA called out and waved excitedly, before realizing something was wrong with him. "Geeze, he looks as rough as I did after a week of civilian life—what happened?"

While they carried him into JABA's office, Sam explained everything.

As the story went on, JABA went through a series of animated facial expressions, from pained wincing, to shocked gasping, and mouth-covering grieving. At the end, he put his hand on Sam's shoulder and acknowledged, "I'm gonna level with you, Sam—that Super Bowl was one of FISTY's darkest memories—he told me he didn't even go to *school* the next day. If he was forced to watch that entire game, then..." he closed his eyes and shook his head, "He might be gone forever..."

Bowing his head in disappointment, Sam whispered, "I know... he always forbade us from mentioning that Super Bowl... and even banned Eli Manning's name from non-secure spaces..."

With JABA looking reactionarily nervous as the words 'Eli Manning' were said in public, >SADCLAM< interjected, "Hold up! JABA, there might be hope yet!" He looked at Sam and urged, "Go on, tell him about your plan!"

Looking up at CLAM and nodding firmly, Sam returned his eyes to JABA and said, "That's right. That total dweeb from the story—Dr. Suabedissen? We stole his VR rig, and we have an idea that—if executed perfectly—*just* might be enough to save FISTY's sanity before it's gone for good. That is..." Sam emphasized in appeal, "*if* you're willing to help us..."

JABA smiled and said, "I'm all ears, boys."

Sam cracked his knuckles and asked, "Well, given your experience with programming, updating, and improving JMPS back in the Chippies... what are the chances you could program a virtual reality scenario for FISTY? One *so* moving and motivating that it *inspires* him out of his coma, returning the heart and soul of the hero we all know him to be?"

Confused, JABA asked, "You mean, like an air-to-air attrition scenario? Maybe getting the final kill against a suicide bomber to win the final battle of some war and end a threat to the United States?"

Shaking his head, >SADCLAM< explained, "No, FISTY has already lived that simulation plenty of times in events; it would hardly move the needle. We're thinking something bigger... better... '*Greatest-er*'..." he added with emphasis.

Realization dawning on his face, JABA's mouth went agape as he asked, "... Tom Brady?"

Nodding slowly and smiling, Sam confirmed, "Tom Brady." He raised his arms and spread his hands, "JABA, we need you to create a scenario involving TB12 that is somehow even *more* remarkable than anything he's done in the past—greater than his Super Bowl debut game-winning drive against the Rams; better than the fourth quarter comeback championship victory over Seattle with the Butler interception at the end; better than the Tampa Bay ring in his first year—"

"Better than *28-3?!*" JABA asked with disbelief.

Sam folded his arms confidently. "Better than 28-3."

Leaning back in his chair, JABA rubbed his chin, contemplating. "Guys, it's been a *long* time since I've dusted off those skills from my time in the Navy. I'd have to dig out some old notes on how all that stuff works. There's no guarantee the scenario would even load properly..." he bobbed his head back and forth in uncertainty. He looked toward the sky and winced, considering options—before finally smiling, as he looked back at his two friends and said, "I've got a rough idea for something that might work."

"Hell yeah!" CLAM yelled. "What is it? I was thinking a momentous victory in, say, an offensive shootout, back-and-forth Super Bowl against the Eagles, where Brady vindicates himself from that tough loss back in 2018?"

JABA smiled and shook his head. "Oh, I'm going bigger than that, CLAM—I'm gonna come up with a scenario so incredible, so epic, so *passion-driven*, that it's gonna bring old Tommy Flynn right back to Full Mission Capable; just you watch! But guys," he gestured his hands out a bit, "I'm gonna need some time. Fortunately, with all the installations and manning, this park can run itself. Why don't you guys stay in the *Sleepy Hollow* Inn for a bit? I'll have something cranked out within the next few days. And if that's not fast enough to get there in time for those Olympics you were talking about? Well, I suppose we can always try working something quick, like that Eagles rematch."

Sam was a bit hesitant, thinking to himself: *The Olympics—we don't have a few days... they're going to start imminently. Maybe a quick Brady win would be enough to satisfy what FISTY needs to recover? I'm sure JABA could make it exciting...*

"Sam, you ok?" >SADCLAM< asked cautiously. "You look like you're having an internal debate that could dictate how the rest of your story goes..."

Shit... what am I worried about the Olympics for, anyway? Worldwide recognition? Preventing Juice from becoming the Admin GOAT? What do those even matter? Who cares who wins; who cares if Juice gets all the recognition and credit? It doesn't matter. Fuck that guy, and fuck those Olympics. What really matters is FISTY's life. I owe it to my old master... We've got to let JABA do whatever it takes to make the best end product. "Take all the time you need, JABA," Sam said, with actual conviction for once. "FISTY's life is the most important thing right now."

>SADCLAM< smiled and nodded, whispering, "Attaboy, Nickels."

JABA clasped his hands and said, "Then it shall be done! Here," he handed Sam and Houben two card keys with label-maker strips taped to them. "These will get you into your hotel rooms for the nights. They'll also get you into any restroom or our top-of-the-line Flat Earth Fitness gym," JABA said with a smile.

"Flat Earth Fitness!" >SADCLAM< said in awe. "I've been dying to check out one of those since CP started the franchise! I bet your guys' setup here is a nice one!"

Smiling, Sam said, "Yeah, I suppose I could go for a pump; first one in a while... I could maybe, uh... maybe even deadlift..." *Dammit, Sam! You* know *you could barely even lift 135 right now — don't embarrass yourself.* "I mean, I would never do that without CP, though — out of respect, you know," he added quickly. *Phew. Crisis averted.*

JABA smiled and said, "Well, it's your posterior chain's lucky day — because CP happens to be visiting this very site as we speak!"

"Say whaaaaaaaat?" Sam said with exaggerated emphasis. *Ugh... that sounded so pathetic... and now I have to come up with a new excuse... shit!* "Yeah, I mean, I think I pulled something in the break earlier, so maybe I shouldn't —"

"That's right!" JABA affirmed, ignoring Sam's excuse matrix. "He came on board just this morning! I'm sure he'll be happy to see you!"

Sam looked sheepish as he said, "Well... he'll be happy to see at least *one* of us, anyway..."

>SADCLAM< tried to brush aside Sam's concern, saying, "Sam, dude, no sweat — CP is *so* chill, he won't hold anything against you. Come on, let's go check it out!"

Sam nodded as the two began departing the office, and JABA offered, "Feel free to grab a scoop of pre-workout from Betty on the way out! C4 Ultimate — only the good stuff for Chippies!"

As they left, Sam heard Buck quietly singing a song to himself. They were strange but fascinating lyrics — something about angels, nightmares, and celebrating October holidays in December; a haunting yet magnificent melody. Sam turned around and saw the entrepreneur on his phone yet again — but for once, JABA wasn't playing Rollercoaster Tycoon. Sam could see that the former Dambuster was looking through photo reels of different boat memories. As the terminal O-3 scrolled through, Sam caught a glimpse of the last picture: It was both of them, Low T, >SADCLAM<, CP, Juice, and FISTY — all with wind-blown hair and full mustaches — posing together on the Porch during sunset; the same photo he had in his Noddik stateroom. Sam couldn't help but smile, vividly remembering the moment.

JABA continued crooning to himself as his friends exited the office — and the intro to the song's second verse, sung perfectly in tune, struck at Sam's soul. To hear those legendary three words... they weren't exactly ALSA brevity, and "Say posit?!" would've been much more concise by saving zero syllables... but Sam didn't care. Those words brought about so much beautiful emotion, and become *quintessential* in defining an era's genre of music... it was mesmerizing. Sam could *almost* understand what JABA was singing, but due to copyrighted usage permissions from the song's lawful owner, it would've cost Sam $300 minimum to directly monologue about specific lyrics, despite the artists themselves likely not caring.

He wanted to go back and tell JABA, 'Hey, it'll all work out—we're gonna get you back in the Navy, and you *will* realize your destiny of becoming an O-4!' ... But he knew such a thing was damn near impossible to promise for a VFA pilot in naval aviation. *Don't waste your time,* the voice inside his head told him, as he listened to JABA finish his hymn. *We miss you, too, bro...*

~

Kyle Camilli looked outside his lunar space station window, over at the site where the Americans had staged their entire fake moon touchdown. He scoffed at the thought of Neil Armstrong's scripted, melodramatic quote. Kyle was irate at the thought that anybody could ever believe such a preposterous story, with such granular footage, somehow *perfectly* fixed to capture a moment that even Hollywood would roll their eyes at. 'Who was holding the camera?' 'How was the audio so clear?' 'Where was the rest of the footage?' He would ask these questions to Chippies and other members of the air wing constantly... but nobody wanted to believe him. "If only those motherfuckers could see me now..." he said angrily under his breath.

Granted, he was *always* full of anger these days. He'd been that way ever since his departure from the VFA-195—when he realized that his life of old was a deception. He looked over in the mirror he brought with him, hanging from the wall in his hut aboard the moon. He flexed his back—jacked, as usual, rhomboids flaring out the holes in the tank top he was wearing under his half-masted flight suit. A fair amount of back acne, too—but that was simply just the price of admission to becoming an alpha.

He crouched down to fit through the makeshift door in his moon abode, but as usual, the harder part for him was fitting his massive shoulders through the door's width. Every now and then, his delts would break the frame—but it was no big deal, because he didn't give a shit about this house or anything else in life. Well, anything other than *revenge...* and, of course, his diet, his testosterone, and his physique. Speaking of which...

He arrived at his kitchen, where his nutrition mecca resided within a single closet. In this room was everything he needed to live these days—as well as everything he ingested, period: Whey protein, pre-workout, glutamine, beta-alanine, trenbolone, ashwagandha, fat-burners, and his supply of Human Growth Hormone. Also in the closet were coolers full of various cuts of beef, beef, and more beef: Ribeye, tri-tip, chuck, bottom round, wagyu, top sirloin, T-bone, and every other cut one could fathom. Long ago, when Kyle had discovered that bodybuilding.com and Butcher Box both delivered to the moon, he knew he'd found the perfect spot for his getaway from life. Thus, he could finally depart the Chippies—a fate he'd been driven toward ever since his best friend—Nickels—betrayed him and the rest of the squadron.

"Nickels... *fuck* that guy..." he growled, as he took a syringe and injected some HGH right into his bicep and threw a ribeye atop the stove. Also hanging above the stove was a picture of him, Sam, and a bunch of other Chippies, posing in front of the sunset on The Porch. He kept the picture up as a reminder of everything he *hated*. The photo was taken back when they were best friends—and back when he was a total *bitch*; spending his meals chugging seed oils and eating Grape-Nuts, wasting his Khaki Hours cardio queening while avoiding heavy weights, and devoting his free time to the Crystal Palace of Tactics vice the Sacred Church of Iron—living a frail life with diminished testosterone levels as a result. "Fuck *that* guy, too," he said, in disgust at the person he used to be.

While his steak cooked, he logged onto his laptop, checking the outer space news, looking for any word of the story he'd craved: Captain Sam Rowland's demise as the Noddik leader. Instead, he found something related that caught his eye: Apparently, the NIRD Katsopolis had begun steaming toward planet Earth for the Administrative Olympics—and it was now under the command of... *LT Bobby Ward?!* "Juice..." he whispered under his breath, grabbing the steak off the stove and taking a bite of the still very raw meat. He didn't care—he knew you could get a variety of of enzymes and nutrients from an undercooked steak; he read it in the bodybuilding.com 'TRAIN' magazine that came with his order—and thus knew it was gospel.

He continued reading the Noddik-written propaganda piece about how well-equipped the NIRD Katsopolis was under the hands of its new leader, backed with the science of some hotshot whiz named 'Dr. Suabedissen.' The article explained that they would surprise-challenge the US and undoubtedly get the victory to declare itself the most administratively-sound fleet in the entire galaxy—essentially, the very thing Sam Rowland had left the Chippies nearly five years ago to accomplish.

But yet, there was merely the tiniest blurb about Sam, mentioning that 'Captain Rowland had decided to take leave for personal reasons.' "Personal reasons?!" Kyle yelled loudly. "This was his fucking dream scenario!" Livid, Kyle punched the wall, creating a massive hole. Through the hole, he saw his F/A-18E—his *class alpha'd* F/A-18E, irrevocably damaged from the intentional midair he'd induced with Rowland the previous day. Camilli had no chance to fly that thing ever again—he was lucky to even make it back to his space station.

Focusing back on his meal and re-examining the article, Kyle didn't believe it. He *knew* his old best friend, and there was *no way* Sam was standing aside idly during a chance to prove superiority in the admin regime of carrier operations—*especially* when it meant letting Juice take his place. Sam was too hungry and obsessed to let an opportunity like this slip out of his hands. He had something up his sleeve to come out on top... and Kyle wasn't about to sit back and watch it happen.

At the end of the article, a brief snippet about Dr. Suabedissen mentioned that he was also a highly prolific Dungeons and Dragons Guildmaster, and that if anybody was interested in personal lessons or trying out for his guild, they could contact him at guildmasterkarl@dd.net. "Fuck it... I'm not letting that fucking weasel *Dimes* get away with whatever he's trying—I'm gonna make that motherfucker wish he'd killed me when he had the chance..." he growled under his breath, as he began drafting up an email to Suabedissen to express his intent to assist in bringing Sam Rowland down...

~

The NIRD Katsopolis stormed toward planet Earth with their epic collision against the US Navy on the horizon. Dr. Suabedissen sat in his office, adjusted his webcam, reviewed his script, and prepared to hit the 'record' button for his latest webcast entry on his YouTube channel. He cleared his throat and said quietly, "Alright... 3... 2... 1... showtime!" and clicked the red button.

"Hey, fellow warlocks and wizards! It's Guildmaster Karl, leader of the Emerald Tauntaun Guild—ETG for life!—former head programmer for the upcoming *Dungeons and Dragons: Bloodlust* game coming out for VR, and current Special Operations Engineer for the NIRD Katsopolis in the Noddik Empire! And now, I'm back for another edition of... 'Ask the Guildmaster!' So, today, we have a few questions from some of *you* fans that I'd like to touch on! And as always—guys, if you like this content and want *more* of it?" He pointed downward, "Feel free to hit that 'like' button, followed by 'subscribe;' it helps me get more motivation to keep making these videos for all you fellow dragonslayers! And while you're at it, go ahead and comment any other questions you may have—or, shoot, just let me know how your guild is doing, any exciting raids you've been on lately, or any new strats you've found useful for mining rupees or EXP!"

He smiled and took a sip of his Mountain Dew Code Red, then clicked his mouse as he continued, "Alright, first question here... this one comes from HawkOfWar97. He's asking: 'Dear Karl—I'm on my own quest to become a Guildmaster like you, but I can't seem to find the time in life to accumulate all the EXP required to rank up or even *qualify* for the fight against one of the legendary dragons to prove my worth. How did you find the time while balancing a social life, family, hobbies, all that stuff?'"

Suabedissen took a big swig of his red juice and laughed, saying, "HawkOfWar, I think you may need a bit of a reality check, bud. I'm gonna hit you with some cold, hard truths: If you want to *be me*, then you need to *sacrifice* like I did. Relationships...

friends... *hobbies?* Hey man, D&D *is* my hobby. My guild members *are* my friends. My most important relationship is with my level 81 Master Sword—*which* I earned by slaying the legendary dragon Mozarli as my final test for the Guildmaster Quest, oh-by-the-way! Now, don't get me wrong, I *do* still have a girlfriend, and let me assure you: she is a *very* hot model—and *very* real—and is a perfect 10. *But*, that's also because of the incredible status I've achieved in this world. HawkOfWar, I don't want to say you need to 'give up your life' for this game..." he added air quotes and pushed up his glasses, "... but... you kind of *do*. All that other junk in life? Inclusion, socializing, human interaction? It's all overrated. Are you close with your parents? Honestly, I'd quit my job and move back in with them if I were you, and focus 100% of my effort on D&D. And all that other stuff that you *think* will bring you happiness? You'll realize how unimportant it is when you've gone down the golden path and are still in the game, *years* after all your friends have long retired from the sport to focus on those—frankly— *less important* parts of life. There is no 'balance' to be found, bub. It's all or nothing— and if you aren't giving it your *all*? Then you are *nothing*, in the eyes of a Guildmaster."

The doctor grabbed a bag of Doritos and a roll of Oreos, eating a handful of chips and dipping his cookies in his Mountain Dew, before scrolling down and scanning his screen to continue to the next question. "Alright, now we got one from MaceInYourFace27—sick alias, bro—asking: 'Karl, I am going through a slight bout of depression lately. All I do is play D&D, and I've alienated everyone in my life who isn't a part of the game. I work a dead-end job, I'm severely out of shape, I have no chance of finding a partner to have kids with, and honestly, I have nobody I can truly call a friend. The only semblance of importance I get is from participating in raids as a second-tier magician. Is this all worth it? What woman would ever feel proud to call a loser like this her husband? How am I ever going to be successful in the *real* world? What value do I bring *anyone?'*"

Karl smirked and prepared to retort, "Hah, geeze guys, lighten up! Seems like there's a common thread to these questions! Well, first of all—"

But then he noticed the crumbs of Doritos on his lab coat sleeve... and as he rolled the sleeve up, he noticed how frail and weak his arm was. He looked at the picture on his desk—a picture of him and all his best friends: it was his D&D avatar surrounded by NPCs... He thought about his friends on the boat. 'Well, there's Captain Rowland...' he thought internally, before quickly remembering that Rowland was a gigantic asshole. 'Juice and the Padroids...?' but then he realized that the only human in that group didn't seem to care about D&D ever since he got put in charge of the LAAF, and the Padroids only thought he was cool because he programmed them to believe so. 'Well, I have Robo-Hinge...' he told himself. But then again... Robo-Hinge, since activation, only really wanted to talk about work, the importance of his FITREP, how they could fit more sorties in, and boring stuff like writing good gripes, doing

ASAPs, and essentially just repeating things that CAG or Juice said. He was a great bot, but not much of a true friend...

Karl sighed, staring into the distance, before realizing that his camera was still recording. He closed the window and folded his arms, upset with what these beta casual players had done to his mood. Between this and his VR headset being stolen, even the Code Red-dipped Oreos couldn't help his dejection...

As he sat there, he heard a knock on his door. "Come in," he said despondently.

Robo-Hinge entered the room. "GOOD AFTERNOON, SIR. TRANSIT IS GOING AS PLANNED, AND THE APG-47 HAS PINGED THE REFUGEES' LOCATION."

Distracted with juicy news, Suabedissen smirked, happy to find a way to escape his somber mood. "Excellent..." *Of course*—the runaway pilots were too foolish to understand that every Noddik weapon was tracked—a policy Rowland had blindly signed off on when drunk one evening. "Where are they?"

"A THEME PARK CALLED CV WORLDWIDE, LOCATED IN THE AMERICAN TERRITORY OF GUAM," Robo-Hinge replied.

"Hmmm..." Dr. Suabedissen scratched his chin, "I believe another former Chippy owns that park? Very interesting... I wonder what they're planning? And also, what has everybody been doing during transit to prepare?"

"NOTHING..." Robo-Hinge began, "AND SO I TASKED THEM TO CLEAN AND REARRANGE THE READY ROOM, INCLUDING RE-PAINTING THE WALLS WITH A FRESH COAT. THE PADROIDS HAVE BEEN TASKED TO SET UP A MOCK NATOPS UNIT EVAL TO ENSURE ADMIN READINESS FOR THE OLYMPICS. AND I TOOK AUTHORITY TO DOUBLE THE LENGTH OF CLEANING STATIONS, BECAUSE WITH A FULL CREW BEING ASSIGNED TO TWICE AS MUCH WORK AS THEY WERE EXPECTING, IT WILL TAKE TWICE AS LONG TO KEEP THE KATSOPOLIS SHINY."

Now grinning, Suabedissen said, "Very good, Robo-Hinge... very good indeed. Let's keep an eye on the prisoners' position in Guam..." he thought of his missing VR rig, and *knew* that regaining it would help him avoid the fearful realities of his life. "Perhaps we can make a brief stop there en route to the USS Ship..."

Robo-Hinge nodded and said, "YES, SIR. ARE THERE ANY OTHER COMMANDS YOU HAVE? I DETECT A FEW PILOT BOTS ENJOYING COWBOY TIME WHEN THEY COULD INSTEAD BE PREPARING A NATOPS TRAINING POWERPOINT."

The doctor looked back at his computer and said, "No, that should be it for now. Thank you very much, Robo-H—" And then he saw it: an email from a name he'd researched long ago during OPERATION: PIGPEN, but had presumed to be dead. He read the brief email, thought for a moment, and then ordered, "Robo-Hinge... go task the navigator to redirect our course to the Lat/Long I send him momentarily. Don't mention anything to Juice, either—I'll inform him myself."

"YES, SIR," Robo-Hinge replied before exiting.

'I may not have a ton of human friends...' the doctor thought to himself, 'but who needs them.' "I was put on this planet to lead a guild to victory, and that I shall do!" he said aloud proudly. As he typed his reply email, he stubbornly thought to himself, 'Nobody in D&D cares about friends; all that matters is your rank, your gold, and your EXP. Why should I believe life is any different...'

~

Sam and >SADCLAM< stepped out of the shuttle van that dropped them off at the front door of Flat Earth Fitness—and as they laid eyes on the complex, their jaws dropped in amazement.

A gym, modeled after—and sized similarly to—an *entire* hangar, rife with every fitness utility that a gym rat could ever dream of: Racks, racks, and more racks. Multipurpose rigs for squatting, benching, deadlifting. A retractable-roof indoor track. Seal row benches. Chalk stations. Bumper plates. Dumbbells from 5 lbs to 200. Mirrors built with the most flattering angles and lighting in mind. A nutrition bar with shakes, steaks, and protein pancakes. They even had a sleeve-cutting station to turn dorky T-shirts into sleeveless tanks—scientifically proven to increase gains and induce skin-tearing vascularity. There was one door labeled 'Cardio Room'—but this was done in jest, as the door was the exit. There *were*, however, a few treadmills throughout—strategically placed in front of the hamstring deadlift machines or TVs (exclusively sports channels playing)—with high-incline capabilities and limited to walking speeds only, to prevent muscle atrophy. Murals on the wall depicted various types of impressive American muscle—from bodybuilders, to Dodge Chargers, F/A-18s dropping MK-84s, Thomas Edison powering a lightbulb, even Ben Franklin shooting lightning bolts from his fingertips, ala Emperor Palpatine. Simply put... this Flat Earth Fitness was flush with testosterone accumulation and workout motivation. Bombshells and barbells. Immaculate physiques and vascular obliques.

"Dude..." >SADCLAM< said and then trailed off, "... this place is the fucking mecca..."

"Hey!" a voice erupted from behind them. "What are you two softbodies doing in here during Baddie Hour?!"

The two turned around, as >SADCLAM<—annoyed—started explaining, "Hey, listen, I've been drugged out on XANs for the past few years and haven't had the time to properly build my body to the level of excellence I usually—" and then he gasped.

Sam echoed CLAM's shock as he excitedly called out, "... Clown Penis?!"

CP, his arms folded and wearing a look of disapproval, scanned the two individuals via ocular patdown—before softening his expression and grinning, calling out, "Well, well, well... sell my soul and call me a hinge! If it isn't Christopher Houben and Samuel Rowland! What on Earth's plateau are you two prodigal sons doing in my hallowed Church of Iron?!"

9

Ode to Shit

Come on, bro, push!" LT Andrew "CP" Preul yelled at Sam with fervor in his voice. "I'm not gonna spot you; you're either finishing this rep, or you're dead — so get that shit up! You got this, Nickels!"

Sam was in a classic do-or-die, fight-or-flight, complete-the-rep-or-admin-sep moment in life: he was pinned on a bench, holding a bar loaded with three plates per side — the illustrious 315 benchmark — his shaking arms hovering just over his sternum. The entire air wing, hundreds of ship's company sailors, and even the flag staff were watching and cheering in the hangar bay gym, as the ship's quintessential Good Dude went for the finishing touch of his 'Big 3' 1RMs to put the 5'11 pilot in the 1500-pound club. At the weight's max point of descent, just kissing his chest, Sam exerted all of his power — but the bar didn't budge. It was at this moment that Sam questioned everything. What am I thinking? I barely put up 310 last week... this was too much of a jump. And yet, the bar wasn't squashing him — he was hanging in there, the barbell hoisted in limbo. The cheering was nice, sure — but it wasn't exactly giving him any extra vigor to work through this potential failure — and potential death. Yes, Sam fully believed that CP would let him be crushed by the bar; the duo had a lifter's brotherhood and level of trust that can only be attained from years of worshiping at the Synagogue of Steel together. CP wouldn't have let him attempt this if he didn't believe Sam would rep the weight. But, at this moment, it certainly wasn't looking promising...

Sam continued struggling — barely holding the bar level — as the crowd got louder and louder. He summoned everything he had, even pretending to be Arnold Schwarzenegger — the actor he'd considered adding to his impressive resume of impersonations — but it did nothing. And, in his moment of despair, the bar started sinking ever so slightly...

CP — his swoly brother in arms — bent over and said, audibly only to Sam, "Nickels! You're a fucking NATOPS-qualified, Patch-wearing, single-seat big-meat fighter pilot with T levels off the charts. I've never met a dude who shows up to work so hungry to climb the mountain, to help others along the way, and who so intensely inspires the air wing – nay, the fleet! – with his pure love for this job. You may have 315 lbs weighing on you right now... but god dammit, that's light weight – because you've been lifting this entire community of naval aviation for years – with decades yet to come. You're a fucking Good Dude, and I don't know if anything could ever stop you..." He pointed to the bar, "But I do know it sure as hell ain't gonna be this weight. Push that shit out, broseph."

CP backed away, standing with the crowd now, far from any position to spot the struggling lifter. But Sam was inspired – hearing the chants of "Ni-ckels! Ni-ckels! Ni-ckels!" gave him reserve strength he didn't know he had in his pectoralis major. CP's words of motivation gave him additional fast-twitch muscle fibers he couldn't have fathomed in his triceps. And when he heard Skipper's voice calling out, "Come on, Nickels! Show the crew why the Chippies are the most athletic squadron in the air wing!" Sam closed his eyes, fired every muscle in his upper body simultaneously – and he busted that 1RM out – locked arms, bar racked; mission accomplished.

The crowd went wild with excitement, and CP ran to his side, clasping his hand in a high-five/bro-hug combo. "Dude!" he yelled, "You fucking did it!" CP lifted Sam's arm – the two men standing side-by-side in cutoff 'Reps for Ronnie' tanks – and announced, "Ladies and gentlemen – the newest member of the 1500-pound club... LT Sam 'Nickels' Rowland!"

The group of spectators cheered to unprecedented levels of volume. Sam ran his hand through his hair in awe, taking in the scene of the boat concert-esque crowd watching. He looked over at CP, who took a break from clapping to give him a fist bump and a mic, smiling as everyone chanted, "Speech, speech, speech!"

Taking the mic and beaming uncontrollably, Sam said, "Guys... thank you all for coming. Damn, never in my life did I think I'd have so many people out here just to watch me – hah, man – " he shook his head, having difficulty coming up with the words in what felt like a dream, "just to watch me lift some weights?! It's crazy! Hah, umm..." his voice trailed off as he clasped his forehead and laughed in disbelief, and the crowd got even louder. Even the ship's Captain and Big XO were there, applauding, happy to see the most famous pilot on the carrier achieve this incredible feat of strength.

Rowland eventually composed himself and said, "Guys, you know... being part of the 1500-pound club or whatnot – that's nice and all... but it's not what this is all about. All these numbers; these stats: combined one rep maxes, independent of bodyweight... Level 2, 3, or 4-plus SFWT qualifications... even being ranked the cleanest ship in the Navy," he pointed to Big XO, who nodded happily. "It's all bullshit!"

The Captain's clapping ceased. The Big XO, hearing his ranking disparaged, folded his arms and put on a stern face.

Sam continued, "It's all just arbitrary labels that other people attach to us for their judgment. Seriously, guys – I don't do this shit for awards, milestones, or quals; I don't fucking care what accomplishments somebody else says are important!"

136

The Big XO began walking forward, seemingly on the verge of stealing the mic if this unprofessional aviator said one more critical thing about his company, polluting the impressionable ears of his sailors.

"What I care about, and what keeps me hungry, is working on bettering myself each and every day, and inspiring others to do the same," Sam explained passionately. "I don't care if you've never lifted a weight in your life, or if you've been lifting for over ten years – if you're going to the gym and putting in the effort that only you know you're truly capable of, focusing on getting stronger or leaner every day? Then you're a goddamn champion in my book – and that's the shit that I care about! Put the time and love into the game, leave no energy unexpended toward your passion, completely devote yourself to the craft – and all that external nonsense?" Sam scoffed and waved his hand. "Ignore it – if you're putting in the work, day in and day out, letting nobody else's doubt, criticism, or negativity stop you from pursuing the ambition you believe you can fulfill? All that bullshit will take care of itself!"

The crowd cheered even louder, and the Big XO softened his expression to a slight smile, as he opened his body language and began clapping again.

"And one more thing," Sam said as the crowd hushed again. "The journey to the top... it should never be lonely. If you're doing it all alone, then you're doing it wrong – uplifting others, motivating them, counting on them to motivate you when you need it most," he nodded to CP, "That's the true joy of the journey, guys. The true joy of fitness, of this job, of life – the joy is sharing those moments of growth alongside others, and creating memories that will last a lifetime." Sam paused, smiled, and concluded with, "Thank you all... and here's to being part of one of the best clubs in the world – and I'm not talking about the 1500-pound club!"

The crowd reached new limits of decibels, with the captain and Big XO now cupping their ears closed, but happy at seeing such a Good Dude create so much positive energy aboard their ship. Sam handed CP the mic back, and the two slapped hands as Rowland said with a smile, "Hey... what you said back there... thank you, Andrew." With a brief look of uncertainty, though, he added, "But... you called me a Patch wearer..." Sam gave a flat smile. "CP, I'm not –"

"Maybe not The Patch," CP cut him off. "But you have something even better; you have That Patch," he grinned, pointing at Sam's right shoulder.

Admiring it himself, Sam beamed – then looked back up at CP and gestured toward the weight bench. "Your turn, bro!"

CP went wide-eyed. "You kidding me, Sam? Because after that shit?!" He pointed back and forth between Rowland and the crowd – then smirked. "... I feel like I could throw another plate on!"

As Preul got on the bench and started busting out reps of 315 like it was nothing, Sam shook his head and laughed, cheering on his friend with the sea of supporting sailors, still in awe and admiration over what an incredible life and band of brothers he had...

~

"Come on, bro, push..." Preul said to Sam, with zero intensity in his voice. "You got it, man, I'm not gonna — goddamn it."

CP rushed over and lifted the bar that was pinning Sam to the bench — a bar with merely one 45-plate on each side. Sam gasped for air, wiped the sweat off his forehead, and said, "Damn, dude — I've gotten so weak..."

>SADCLAM< frowned at Sam; CP bluntly stated, "Yeah, I'm not gonna lie. You're kind of a bitch right now."

Sam bowed his head in shame, as >SADCLAM< raised his arms toward CP and said, "Dude, come on..."

"What?!" CP asked with legitimate confusion. "He's extremely weak. This isn't the Nickels I used to train with. There's no room for a puny little dweeb like this in my gym — *especially* during Baddie Hour."

Raising his head and observing the scenery around him, Sam realized CP was right — the gym was *stacked* full of hardbodies and fitness queens. Some of the hottest girls he'd ever seen, of all nationalities and curvatures. Sports bras, tight yoga pants, and bare midriffs everywhere. "Wah wah wee wah..." Sam whispered eccentrically under his breath. Of course, nearly every gorgeous woman was being crowded by juiced-out men in stringers and Jordans — the kind of guys who can bench three times their weight, yet would get winded running back to their car when they forgot their blender bottle. The kind of dudes who let you know they've 'got ten sets left' as they're resting on the bench, swiping on Tinder. The kind of bros who don't even *pretend* they're using their shirt to wipe their face when sneaking an ab-check in the mirror, unashamed to be caught worshipping their own reflection. Sure, this place was a top-of-the-line gym — but a total Ken and Barbie 'meet market,' too.

"Yup, take it in, Dimes," CP continued. "Ever seen so many fake beautiful people in your life?"

"... Fake?" Sam asked, confused, and still out of breath from his near-death experience with 135 lbs.

CP laughed coldly. "Bro... this place is 95% growth, gear, and gym candy. People who sold their souls and regulatory hormonal cycles to achieve Levels of Leanness — LOLs — that are simply unnatural and unhealthy. Baddie Hour used to *mean* something; a level of excellence to strive for — the *old-fashioned* way. But now? Look, I'm not gonna hate on a little T-booster here and there for older folks... but these meatheads are *beyond* preposterous. They've made a mockery of the gym scene that I used to love so much — the era of hard work and discipline, that *sacrifice* needed to earn a strong physique. Back in the day, man, you had to work your *ass* off for a killer frame.

Don't you remember, guys? Remember that sense of pride? Showing up at the gym in the early morning hours when you'd rather be in bed, or late Friday night when you'd rather be at the bars? Remember the beautiful emptiness in the Shrine of Shred; a serene dojo of effort and improvement? Remember what it felt like, knowing you were bettering yourself by venturing up the mountainous slope, instead of taking the painless, easy, *normal* route in life?

"We *wanted* the hard path... we *wanted* that shit—that's what weightlifting was all *about*, CLAM." He said Houben's name, but CP wasn't talking to anybody at this point—just his own psyche on his own soapbox. "Sure, we weren't 'normal' people—but who would really want to *be* normal in this world? Being a dedicated gym rat was about willingly being a different breed of human—learning to *love* the pain and *embrace* the work; the strains for the gains..." he closed his eyes and took a deep breath of gratification. "Being a 'gym guy' was a designation of *distinction*, Dimes. Sure, you knew you were missing out on other parts of life just for the sake of gaining greater Amounts of Muscle—AOMs—while chasing new LOLs, putting up with *shit* like periodic hunger pangs, constant leg soreness, or planning your entire day around your workout and meals. But in a weird way... you didn't mind that shit. You came to *love* that shit, wearing it as a badge of honor, because you knew you were chasing something special—that daily self-improvement—in a world where so many others were content to remain the same. And you know what? The memories from those sacrifices? They were the *greatest,* guys. And your gym bros that dealt with that shit alongside you? God, dude... the closest brothers you'll ever have in your life. Being part of the Khaki Hour crew was something to treasure, something to take pride in—and now we've got all these Instagram clowns like Liver King walking around claiming 'natty' when, in reality, he's taking $10,000 worth of steroids a month. It's *bullshit*..."

CP kept shaking his head, staring off into the distance. Sam tried suggesting, "Andrew, the industry may have its fair share of bullshit... but that doesn't have to affect your love for it!"

Snapping out of his stupor, CP folded his arms and glared at Sam. "That statement is awfully ironic coming from *you*, Dimes..."

Sam recoiled and squinted his eyes at his accuser. "What are you talking about...?" He looked to >SADCLAM<, seeking support.

Chris, however, shrugged and said, "He's not wrong, Sam..."

CP unfolded his arms and explained, "Dimes, when you were with the squadron—when you were *Nickels*—things were great. Sure, there was some bullshit we dealt with: there were the surprise Alert 15 packages around friendly territories, pointless MARSTRIKEs tasked to us at 1500 for the following morning, and, really, the boat in general—god, the boat was *total* bullshit..." He shook his head in disgust—then looked at his former Chippy brother with intensity. "But what about the *shit*, Sam?

139

What about the stuff that you dreaded, yet did with *pride?* SFWT Level 3 and every-thing it entailed; launching in horrendous weather at sunset, knowing it's going to get even *worse* when you land at night; spending *way* too much free time and brain space planning skits for Foc's'le Follies; even just the euphoric feeling of completing a day of boat SDO, knowing your next day of doom was *far* down the rotation?"

Sam gasped at the thought of *anything* positive being spoken about the worst possible duty known to mankind.

"Guess what?" CP asked rhetorically. "Whether you realized it or not? We learned to love *that* shit, too; to love that *grind.*" The Chippy deadlifting champion spread his arms, "Dimes, we cherished the agony of deployment as a *whole.*"

"CP..." Sam said in confusion, "How could you possibly believe what you're saying?!"

Preul glanced to the side, pondering his words — before refocusing on Sam. "Think about going to the gym on your leg day, knowing you're gonna leave the Church feeling completely exhausted, barely able to walk," he explained. "Remember that *despair* walking in? Petrifying. And yet... remember how *satisfied* you felt after-ward — how *great* the reward for the sacrifice was? You got stronger, instilled disci-pline, and emerged from the shit a better man. Well..." he smiled as he emphasized, "that's *exactly* what walking into every single deployment was like! We knew it was going to be painful. We knew it would fucking *suck* at times. But, dammit, call me a chill hinge if there wasn't at least *some* sick little part of all of us that couldn't *wait* to welcome that struggle, knowing what it would make us in the end: hardened, more experienced, *better* pilots. Don't you see, Dimes? It wasn't about *avoiding* the shit in the job — it was about finding a sense of satisfaction from *embracing* it."

Chris nodded slowly, in full agreement with CP's depiction of the love for the pain. Sam, however, wasn't quite buying it. He gave Preul a look of complete skepti-cism and asked, "You're telling me that I should've been *happy* to deal with power-hungry boat people, unnecessary overnight Alert 15s, and the horrendous nutritional value of the food?!"

CP grabbed his forehead in frustration. "*No*, Sam — that's *bullshit.* I'm talking about the *shit.*"

>SADCLAM< shook his head in disappointment. "Come on, Sam..."

"What's the difference?!" Sam asked, confused.

"Take a look around again," CP gestured toward the workout area. "All these idiots — these steroided-out bozos crowding the gym, taking up all the benches and mirror space — *that* is *bullshit.* So are people who rap out loud when listening to head-phones, so are 'ab days,' so are ellipticals, gyms that ban chalk, smith machines, initia-tion fees, et cetera. Bullshit is what you have to *ignore* in order to *endure* the shit — the grind that *actually* gets you better. But *you*, Sam—you were so distracted by the bull-shit, that you couldn't appreciate the *shit* we were all going through. You acted like one of these T-boosted tyrants," he pointed to some goon hissing with every cable tricep extension, "and you thought you could take the easy road in life—one with no shit. And that's a shame—because when we were one cohesive unit of JDAM, AM-RAAM, and POON-blasting brothers-in-arms? We grew—together—from normal... to good... to *lethal* pilots. Why? Because we took on the shit; we embraced the struggle. Because we knew that in order to reap the rewards of jacked physiques, we had to willingly suffer through those aggravating leg days that we just flat out didn't want to do—but *we did anyway*. At least, for a while, we did..." his eyes piercing Sam as he shifted his tone, "... until you caught The Disease of Me."

Sam was stung by CP's accusation. "Andrew... that's not true... it's not that I was running, it's that—wait a second..." Sam's eyes narrowed, "*You* left, too! Look at you now—nowhere *near* naval aviation!"

Shrugging, CP said, "Yeah—you know what, you're right. I sure did. Because I fell for it, too—thinking I wanted a life elsewhere with less shit. I thought running Flat Earth Fitness would bring me the ultimate happiness. And I thought I'd find the same by getting with all these hot chicks—married to Dua Lipa, then the fling with Ana; hooking up with Ariana Grande, Camilla Cabella," he started counting with his fingers, "the entire BLACKPINK band, every girl from that one Victoria's Secret fashion show with Halsey singing—and Halsey, too—man, even the 'Fink You Freeky' girl from Chuck's weird video—oh, and have you heard the Shakira rumors?" He gave a sly smile, "... Guilty." He shook his head in disbelief and continued, "Jesus, guys... I'm married to fucking *Doja Cat*! My life has literally *become* the music videos from our Chippy SDO terabyte!" His expression saddened. "But most of all... I yearned for simply getting away from the boat shit, imagining it would bring me the life I wanted. Just like you, Dimes—I kept focusing on 'How can life be better?' instead of 'How great my life already is.' If I would've just appreciated the small things more—the unique-ness of this life..." He chuckled as he admitted, "You know, just like I never wanted to be an 'average' person in the gym... I never wanted to have an 'average' life either—and in the Navy, I had a life *far* from average. But I just couldn't recognize how special that was...

"And guess what—life here at the gym? Replace 'boat bullshit' with 'corporate bullshit.' The amount of time and labor sheets I have to file through for employees clocking in unapproved OT; all the board meetings I'm scheduled to attend, spewing financial outlook optimism bravado to these entitled shareholders; HR cases I'm re-quired to deal with because some personal trainer made a 'Rubber? I hardly even know her!' joke in front of a female staff member; or how about being forced to record those company propaganda videos, feeding some phony feel-good mission statement just so we can pretend we have some altruistic purpose aside from making money? It's *agonizing!* My life has literally become convincing people who *don't* want to work out that they *do*. The biggest task in my job is imprinting my passion for the *journey* of fitness — the love for the struggle — upon others who just want the *results* — total *bullshitters."* He shook his head in disgust. *"This* is the *real* LARPing of life... this is more of a stupid game than anything we had going on back in CAG Bizz. Weekly conference calls with Regional Vice Presidents to pep talk upcoming closeout sales... lawsuits from people who tweak their backs by deadlifting like morons... market trends and analyses with dorky ass data specialists — it's all certified *bullshit.* I didn't want to have all this on my plate; I just wanted to lift..."

"Kind of like the guy who just wanted to fly jets..." Sam agreed, his voice trailing off softly.

>SADCLAM< nodded, giving Sam a knowing look of empathy.

"Exactly..." CP continued. "Dimes, I don't know what you were afraid of — Juice, ground jobs, the brutal life on the boat, whatever. It doesn't matter. Because I know that I, too, chased something I thought would be so much better — and god dammit — I miss the life... miss my bros... miss the *shit..."* CP shook his head in sadness. "The more you try to avoid the *real* shit in life — the shit that makes you *better* — the more you end up finding exclusively bullshit. It's like taking steroids; it's never as glamorous as it seems. You imagine all the good," he pointed to some dude with Machamp levels of strength, admiring his own leaf-type vascularity in the mirror, "but you never consider the *bullshit* realities: issues with joints, severe back acne, roid rage, bloated face, growth gut, hair loss, liver disease, reproductive organ damage, low libido..."

Sam and CLAM looked at each other and grimaced.

"What?" CP asked with a blank face. "Look it up. You think Doja Cat would be ok with that? We have plans to make lots of Mini-CPs — athletic *stallions* and future Hall of Famers — and I sure as hell ain't throwing that future away for the easy street to Jacked-sonville."

Sighing with disappointment, Rowland threw his hands up and admitted, "I guess I *was* looking for a shortcut. You see it all the time in the gym — these guys that show up, get some noob gains doing whatever bullshit routine they found on some bodybuilding Reddit, and think they've got it figured out. But once you get to a respectable AOM with a decent LOL? Man... you learn that *that's* where the work *really* begins; that's where the *shit* starts, where you have to *fall in love* with the process. And those who don't? They seek shortcuts — extreme calorie deficits, daily low-intensive-steady-state cardio sessions, totally unrealistic timelines. They're not interested in the daily grind... the long hours... the *shit.* They don't care about the process; they just want the *results."*

His hands on his hips, staring at the unused squat racks—arenas that brought back so many painful but fond memories—Sam took a deep breath and continued: "They don't realize that the shit *was* the best part; the part that makes you truly *cherish* the results. Because no one else is going to care how much you can bench, what your DEXA-scanned body fat is, that you can do a strict Nordic, or *anything* you accomplish in the Mosque of Mass. The gym is something you do for your *own* pride, not some bullshit approval you *think* you'll get from others! And when it's all over? If you didn't appreciate the journey—didn't endure the shit—then how *stupid* are you gonna feel when you realize you've robbed yourself of the best part..." Sam stopped and grew emotionally sober as his own words started to hit home.

CP was tracking. "Exactly. Sam, you and I officially became the two most shredded guys on the entire ship when those 23-2 October power rankings hit... and did it change your life? Because damn..." he pursed his lips and shook his head, "it sure didn't change mine! I woke up the next morning feeling cold, exhausted, fatigued, and hungry. Accomplished, yeah—but nowhere *near* some monumental, life-altering feeling."

>SADCLAM< backed the statement, adding, "As the number five guy on those power rankings, I felt the same—I was fucking *hungry,* bro. Sure, I looked like a Greek God... but the 'finish line?' It wasn't *close* to what I'd imagined—and you already know why, Sam. Remember what you used to tell us?"

A bit teary-eyed, Sam gave a slight smile. "Yeah; there *is* no finish line—and that's the beauty of it. You're always chasing new LOLs... you can always attain new AOMs. *Of course* we were all hungry—but not just for food; we were hungry for *more*. Hungry for the excruciating pain of those leg days, knowing that huge gains were just up the hill for he who fights further. Hungry for the feeling of hitting a PR, and departing the Temple of Testosterone feeling like a god—yet also knowing you had *so* much further to go. We were hungry because, in our minds, we weren't anywhere *close* to done—we'd *never* be done! And you know why?" he asked rhetorically, desire in his eyes. "Because if we *did* finish that journey, and *achieved* that perfect physique? We wouldn't have *any* reason to keep striving for more. We'd have peaked; have nowhere else to go; be fully qualified..." He paused a moment, then whispered under his breath, "Wait a second—*qualified*..."

>SADCLAM< again nodded happily, his arms folded as he watched Sam connect the dots, while some freak behind them screamed with every trap bar raise. "Attaboy, Nickels. Preach."

Sam started piecing the puzzle all together. "You're right, CP—I remember that *same* feeling at work. Spending early mornings and late nights in the vault preparing briefing guides, rehearsing notes, and creating whiteboard artistic masterpieces for the SFWT Level 3 pain train—going through total *shit*—yet feeling amazing every time you heard those magical words: 'pass/complete.'" He smiled in nostalgia and continued, "Walking onto the boat on the first day of deployment, knowing you had months of frustration, suffering, and misery ahead—but within *hours*, laughing with your friends over something as simple as some O-4 trying to big dick an O-3 for not bracing the bulkhead in his presence. Being piled up with EVALs to review, on top of the Dining Out prep you were tasked with, on top of getting the schedule signed, *all* on top of the large force event you had to brief the next morning at 0600—feeling *beyond* overwhelmed—but then gaining some sick sense of satisfaction when you managed everything and got it all knocked out; feeling *progression* as a result of that shit."

CP and >SADCLAM< smiled at Sam, as an unbelievably sexy smokeshow with an outstanding plastic surgeon walked right by them, supersetting hamstring deadlifts with barbell hip thrusts.

Nickels—too 'in the zone' to be distracted by this voluptuous siren—continued, "And there was never an end to it—there would always be more deployments to go on; there were always more quals to get; more opportunity to increase your Tier of Tacticality and Lethality—your TOTAL—and that's what I fucking *loved*, man. Because once it stopped—once you peaked?" He thought about his current life... his alcoholism... his overall apathy from working with the Noddiks... the amount of friendships and relationships he'd lost because of his choices... "You have nowhere to go but down..." he lamented.

CP threw up his arms and added, "Everybody's in such a fucking hurry to take the coward's way out—to skip the journey, to race toward the finish line—not realizing that the struggle along the way is the *best part*. And once they get there? Depression sets in. Why? Because they were doing it for the *wrong reasons,* bro. They had no interest in bettering themselves. They were just looking for the attention, recognition, and fame they *thought* they'd get—they were avoiding the shit to get to the bullshit."

"Remember what you would tell us about reaching elite LOLs, Nickels?" >SADCLAM< asked. "When you're so damn shredded that your cheeks are concave? No chick's gonna care if you have an eight versus a six-pack, or a single vein down your arm vice a spiderweb of them! The only people who notice are other dudes in the gym on that same insane journey!"

CP nodded and added, "And when you're at elite levels of TOTAL? No average fleet bro is going to care that you've memorized the blue air gouge verbatim, or how brushed up your latest DCA brief is. The only people who care are other Patch wearers; the ones that are equally obsessive and passionate about tactics. And that lack of recognition is perfectly ok—why, Sam?"

"Because that's not why we're doing it," Sam affirmed. "We're doing it for ourselves, for our own journey. We hold our own standard."

"Bingo." CP replied. "I just wish you could've seen this years ago... before we all saw our leader take the steroids of life and abandon us... Because, Sam, you may have done some shitty things toward the end there, and lost a lot of your Good Dude cred—but even after you left? We were still following in *your* footsteps; repeating the actions of our eldest brother. And when you started juicing to avoid the shit..." CP shrugged, "so did many of us..." He shook his head sadly. "I'll always wonder what would've happened if we all stayed in—I wonder how lethal of a fleet we could've become... wonder if Low T would've survived, after all..."

With Low T's name perking his ears up, Sam interjected, "Low T! CP, he's still alive! He reached out to me! We BFM'd..."

CP shook his head and laughed. "Dimes, you fool... Low T died, alright. But he's alive—in a different way. Regardless of *who* you *think* you fought? That was *not* Low T. When you left, your best friend turned into a different person... he left his family behind... left his bros behind, too. He swore his allegiance not to naval aviation, but to something I..." CP was no longer chuckling, and his face grew tense. "I'm sorry, give me a minute here..."

Sam and CLAM looked at each other, concerned, as they patiently waited for Preul to compose himself.

CP wiped a tear from his eye and reminisced, "I was always asking him to work out... always trying to get that guy in the gym—and not those cardiovascular Peloton workouts he did with his wife, either. *Real* work—the kind involving blood, sweat, and chalk. But to see what became of him... I never wanted this..."

"CP," Sam asked impatiently, "what *happened* to Low T?!"

"Low T..." With severity in his eyes as he looked at his friends, CP finally explained, "Became *Loaded* T..."

"Loaded T?" >SADCLAM< asked, reflecting the confusion of both men. "What do you—"

"I NEED A VOLUNTEER... TO DIE!" a robotic voice screamed loudly from the entrance, as the entire crowd in the gym turned toward the source.

"Guys, get down!" CP yelled as he pulled Sam and Chris to the floor, quickly wiping away the remaining tears from his eyes. "This way!" he whispered as he quickly crawled to a nearby room labeled 'The Beta Box'—inside was a smith machine, dumbbells that only went to 10s, a bosu ball, and a pink 2kg kettlebell. The three men put their backs against the wall, stayed crouched low, and CP cracked the door open to hear what was going on.

"ALCON, PAY ATTENTION—WE ARE SEARCHING FOR THREE FUGITIVES—WAR CRIMINALS SAM ROWLAND, CHRIS HOUBEN, AND TOM FLYNN. RFI: HAS ANYBODY SEEN TWO MEDIUM-HEIGHT MALES, ONE OF DECENT MUSCLE STRENGTH, AND THE OTHER SEVERELY LACKING—"

Sam rolled his eyes at the description.

"—AND ONE UNCONSCIOUS TALLER MAN OF NOTABLE STRENGTH? YOU, MALE IN THE BLACK SLEEVELESS GYMSHARK HOODIE AND LU-LULEMON SWEATPANTS—I'M TASKING YOU TO BE IN CHARGE OF ASKING EVERYBODY IN THIS GYM FOR THEIR ACCOUNT. AND YOU THERE, FEMALE WITH UNUSUALLY LARGE BREASTS AND INHUMANLY TINY WAIST, WITH YOGA PANTS CLEARLY DEPICTING YOUR LACK OF UNDERGARMENTS WORN—YOU WILL BE THE SCRIBE, IN CHARGE OF DOCUMENTING THESE AC-COUNTS AND THEN BRIEFING ME BY NO LATER THAN 1500 THIS AFTER-NOON."

"Uhh... bro?" a deep voice called out.

"THAT'S ROBO-HINGE, PLEBE," the authoritative cyborg corrected him. "NOW, SPEAK, MALE IN UNDERSIZED AFFLICTION TANK TOP WITH VIRAL UPPER BACK INFECTION."

"Uhh... 'Robo-Hinge,'" the human continued, "I think I saw two puny dudes who fit that description in here talking to the manager."

"WHO AND WHERE IS THIS MANAGER?" Robo-Hinge asked.

"Andrew Preul—he was just here somewhere, I swear..." the guy insisted.

CP looked concerned and whispered, "Guys, what the hell is that thing?" The two pilots both had dumbfounded looks on their faces.

Robo-Hinge shouted, "THAT IS NOT AN ACCEPTABLE ANSWER. IF YOU DO NOT FIND THIS 'ANDREW PREUL' HUMAN WITHIN THE NEXT HOUR? YOU WILL BE ON DUTY INDEFINITELY."

"Duty?" the man asked, confused. "What are you talking—"

"GUARDS—SECURE THE EXITS," Robo-Hinge ordered. "NOBODY IS LEAV-ING THIS GYMNASIUM UNTIL EVERY BIT OF SPACE HAS BEEN EXPLORED. AND *YOU*," he redirected his voice, "*YOU* ARE STARTING TO SPOOL ME UP. WHO IS YOUR CHIEF?"

"Chief?! Listen, kemosabe, I don't know what the fuck you're talking about, but if you don't shut your bitch-ass up and let me finish my workout right now, we're gonna have a prob—*Ahhhhhh!!! Eeeeeekkk*!!!"

A blast reverberated in the room, as the man's scream turned from deep-voiced to extremely high-pitched—almost like a teenage girl—as he shrieked, "My pecs... they're man boobs! My abs... so puffy and doughy! My will to work out—it's gone! I feel like curling up with a blanket, my cat, and old episodes of The Bachelorette..."

CP peeked out, cringed, and shut the door. "Guys—this is not good. You are in with some bad people—those guards are armed with APG-47s..."

>SADCLAM< pulled his shirt up, revealing a ray gun in his waistband, ex-plaining, "It's ok, I've got one too."

"Jesus, CLAM!" CP exclaimed, his eyes wide with shock. "You can't be carrying one of those around in public, *especially* in a holy cache of testosterone like this! And for god's sake, don't have it pointed at your nads!" He quickly glanced around. "Shit—guys, we've gotta get out of here... they just turned Rex—a regular here—into some softbody beta. We've all worked too hard on our physiques—even *you, Dimes*—to lose it all from one of those blasts."

Ignoring the subtle slight, Sam asked, "But how, CP? They've got every exit covered!"

"Not *every* exit..." he said with suspense. CP walked to the mini dumbbell set, put the '8s' where the '2.5s' were, and lifted the smith machine bar to its highest notch—revealing a secret passageway to a pier on the edge of the CV Worldwide premises.

Sam's jaw dropped. "What—what *is* this?"

Pulling out his phone and beginning a text, CP replied, "This is my emergency exit—I knew nobody in this gym would ever be caught using this room, making it the perfect place for a secret passageway. Now, come on—hurry! Before somebody sees us!"

The three left the hatch, and CP closed it behind them. As they ran from the gym, CP sent one more text and put his phone away, saying, "Ok, JABA is meeting us there ASAP. Shit... I didn't realize it would get this serious... they've got *department head*-level management hunting you guys down? We need to leave this island *now*."

Sam held his head, too lost in his thoughts to worry about where they were going. *Was it really that bad? Did life really suck so much that it was worth all this bullshit to avoid that bullshit? Was the shit I dealt with in the fleet the pain of agony? Or was it the discomfort of growth...?*

CP looked at Sam, noticing his anxiety, and bluntly asked, "Dimes—what are you possibly thinking about right now?"

Sam sighed and said, "CP, I blew it. Like everybody else in the world, I was in such a hurry to get the struggle *over with* that I completely devalued the moments that made the job, the grind, the *shit*—so unique, so special, so beautiful."

"You really did blow it," CP said, stone-faced.

Growing a bit emotional, Sam continued. "I took the fucking coward's way out. I took the steroids of life. I rushed toward the end... and like all those drugged-out maniacs in there, desperately grasping for shortcuts, I found that the finish line was just a bunch of bullshit. It left me feeling empty—not hungry, but simply *empty*. And it *sucked*."

"I bet it did. Probably left you feeling quite worthless," CP went on, giving Sam more tough love.

Nearly in tears, Sam bemoaned, "It left me longing for the days of staying up until 0100 to get a schedule signed... of showing up four hours before a SFWT event to make sure my fifth example dash-four arrow made sense... even of being responsible for making coffee, popcorn, and entertaining the crowd with kickass roll 'ems during SDO days..."

"And you probably didn't even start them on time," CP interjected.

"Because as much as I thought I hated those days of my life?" Sam continued, ignoring the comment, "Those moments were something we all suffered *together*. And the feeling of flying in a division with my best bros, catching a wire in the pitch-black night after a bangbus of a SFWT DCA, and laughing about it all over omelets and pancakes at midrats? Damn, dude... that shit made all the bullshit *worth* it. If I could've just *suffered* more... just accepted the shit for a bit longer... god—imagine how great life could be right now. Damn..." He shook his head and started tearing up. "CP... >SAD-CLAM<... I fucked up. I fucked up big time."

"You really *did* fuck it up, Dimes—for *all* of us," CP said, no love lost in his expression.

"*Fuck!*" Sam shouted, stopping his footsteps on the pier. "God *dammit!*" He fell to the floor and burst into tears, sobbing uncontrollably.

Clam looked at CP uncomfortably, as Sam just kept sobbing, begging, "What can I do? What can I do?! Oh *god*... what can I do?!"

Eventually, after more renditions of this pathetic repentance, CP replied, "You can get up."

"... What?" Sam asked, his face still buried into the ground with tears.

"Get up," CP said again.

Sam rose to his feet, looking his former squadronmate in the eye, his face red from anguish, tears temporarily ceasing.

CP calmly continued, "And you can hug it out, bitch."

The two stared at each other for a moment—before Sam lunged forward, as the two embraced in an epic, tight-clasped bro hug.

>SADCLAM< nodded happily, thinking, 'Attaboy, Sam. It's never too late for a redemption story. Never give up on Nickels.'

As they broke apart, Sam asked, "CP... where are we going, anyway?"

Pruel beamed and said, "Gents, get ready for a boat that needs no shower shoes, reads no evening prayer, and heeds no fraternization policy! Boys, we're setting sail on Fat Chucky's Cruise Ship—CV Worldwide's premier party yacht—and getting *far* away from any cyber hinge who thinks he can defeat the spirit of Chippy JOPA!"

"Fuck yeah! Let's go!" >SADCLAM< exclaimed.

CP grinned, "Prepare to see the most gorgeous girls of your life, Dimes, doing things you couldn't have imagined in your wildest fantasies!"

Sam, thrilled but confused, asked, "But—but what about Doja?"

Giving a mischievous look to his Dambuster brethren, CP announced, "While the Cat is away, the Chippies shall play!"

~

Juice stood atop the bridge of the ship, his cover firmly donned per boat regulations, looking out upon the sphere of earth that lay in line with the NIRD Katsopolis' direct course. Within 12 hours, they'd be initiating the Admin Olympics with USS Ship—a ship that had no clue of their impending competition; part of the beauty of the plan that Juice and the Noddiks had devised. Granted, it shouldn't be *too* much of an advantage, given how thoroughly America's carrier air wings now prepare for impromptu Admin Olympics from foreign entities, via an additional CV-based deployment workup called 'Preemptive Administrative INtermittent Training Readiness Against Invading Nations' or 'PAINTRAIN.' Juice had actually helped instill this additional workup, which took place during the holidays—when squadrons would've typically shut down for leave—adding incredible efficiency and administrative lethality to the fleet. It was an excellent FITREP bullet at the time. Unfortunately for him *now*, it would make his upcoming grand task just a little tougher...

But Juice wasn't afraid. He looked down at the flight deck, where the maintenance crews were clearing the decks after a successful division launch of Robo-Hinge—Dr. Suabedissen's new best friend—and a few random pilots who joined to help track down the runaways. 'Nickels...' he thought in his head. 'Damn you. Always slipping out of my grasp...' In his mind, he'd pictured Rowland watching the whole event, witnessing Juice lead the fleet to victory—the same fleet *Sam* was hired to manage. A sick little resentful part of him even imagined Sam defecting back to the US in some pitiful attempt to save face and pride, just *trying* to prevent Juice from surpassing him yet again. But now, based on the intel from Robo-Hinge? It was looking more and more like Sam was off partying at theme parks, probably drinking the remainder of his life away, having already completely given up on not just his old friends from the Chippies and US naval aviation, but administrative excellence in general. It was a pity that Rowland wouldn't suffer the loss first-hand... but Juice knew how small the community was, and the news his triumph was sure to spread quickly.

Juice hoped his old country wouldn't take it personally when he defeated them—after all, he'd been the catalyst for so many wonderful tac-air additions, like the daily EP test requirement for all aviators—with emphasis on capitalization and punctuation; speed traps rigged on the taxiways with downing punishments; as well as instilling random testing for Class 2 banned substances like Monsters, pre-workout, and melatonin. 'Hey, the rules are the rules!' he always said. And he was *respected* for saying that. The fleet became safer, cleaner, and simply *better* because of his Good Dude leadership.

But Sam... Sam was far too removed to see any of it...

Juice felt he was undoubtedly still the 'Fuckin' New Guy' to Sam. The incompetent wingman who couldn't quite join up prior to the Tapes On, Fight's On. The Level 2 candidate who always had the improper thickness on one of his Excel grid lines on the kneeboard card. The Coffee Mess Officer who couldn't even stock the ready room with the right kind of creamer that some random O-4 really liked, even though it was impossible to obtain on the ship...

But the rest of the fleet had seen — and appreciated — the changes Juice made. And one day, even if it took winning an intergalactic war, Ward's profiency would be recognized by Sam, too...

"Yo yo, Juice-man!" NEODD SWEVEN's voice called out.

Juice turned and saw the now-trio of Padroids approaching him in the bridge room — their covers *off*, exemplifying that they didn't play by anyone's rules but their own. NEODD threw up dual 'peace' signs and waved them around obnoxiously. "Dude, he's here! And your boy is fucking *tanked,* bro!"

"*So* fucking jacked!" IROK added, "*Ludicrous* AOM:LOL ratios!"

T6 piped in, "*Now* we know why they call him 'Loaded T' — that blood work would make A-Rod blush!"

"Sick reference, bro!" NEODD applauded. "Haven't heard that name in years!"

Juice tried to peer past the triplet of douchebags and see if he could spot his former squadron mate... but no one was in sight. "Well... where is he?"

IROK scoffed. "Where do you *think*, bro? He had to get a lift in as soon as he stepped foot on the ship! He's down in the hangar bay gym, and — from the talk around the boat — it sounds like he's already stealing records *and* girlfriends from the regulars."

Juice threw his hands up. "What?! He's *working out?!* You've gotta be shitting me..."

T6, looking confused and amused, affirmed, "... Yeah... *and...*? Juice, not sure if you're really understanding how important physique and muscle is to this job — a job *completely* defined by looking cool — so..." he offered his arms out and shrugged his shoulders.

"Ok, well, it doesn't matter how 'cool' or 'jacked' we look if we can't even fly a consistent pattern in Phase 2 of the Olympics!" Juice countered.

Looking at his boys nervously, NEODD SWEVEN said, "Juice... we've been talking. Obviously, you're pretty fucking cool, bro — but all this abeam distance stuff you've been rambling about lately? This approach turn angle of bank nonsense, like whether it's 29 or 30? The overall ball-flying shit in general? Not gonna lie, dude... starting to sound a *little* bit like that dork Captain Rowland. You know, maybe pumping some iron would be good for you, too. Let me tell you — there is *nothing* cooler than showing up late for a brief, out of breath, swole as hell, *clearly* coming in from a workout! It lets everyone know that you find your body more important than the team effort; thus, you are an important person — an *alpha*, if you will — and your desires and schedule should be prioritized above any other peon in the room!"

Juice shook his head in frustration. He loved this job, and he loved this community — but he could *never* understand the faction of aviators that seemed to find the gym so *goddamn* important. He rehashed the same rant in his head time and time again: 'You're walking a million steps a day on the boat — just eat reasonably in the wardroom, and you'll be fine. Not to mention, these guys should be worried about max performing in the WVR arena, *not* underneath a barbell! What the hell was the ability to bench press two times your body weight going to do when you got shot down because you forgot your axioms? Aviators should memorize timelines, not macros; study stern conversions, not kilogram-to-pound conversions; prep their briefing labs, *not* their summer bods! Jesus... you're a fucking tactical and administratively focused naval aviator, not some wannabe bodybuilder!'

It wasn't that Juice was *against* fitness — far from it — he just couldn't *stand* the worshiping of the gym culture; aviators *literally* calling it the 'Church of Iron,' as if it was some divine place of spiritual importance. And he *loathed* the body shaming they gave others for not following whatever bullshit fad they were sipping the kool-aid of at the time — be it anti-sunscreen, anti-caffeine, anti-veggies, even anti-cardio! Back in the Chippies, he'd constantly wanted to vent, 'Dude, fuck *off*! Don't lecture me about skipping 'CP's leg day' when I haven't seen *any* of you fuckers in the *EP sim bay* for months!'

"Uhhhh, you ok there, Juiceman? You're not thinking about VSI or interval gouge, are you?" IROK asked with a smirk.

Juice rolled his eyes. "Alright, guys... I'm outta here. My 7-minute study break is over." He started walking back toward the ready room and called out, "Tell 'Loaded T' that when he's done with his fucking workout, he can meet me in the STBR — I'll be studying CV NATOPS."

"CV-what?" T6 asked.

"Juice..." NEODD began, "You *do* realize that a beast like that is going to need a monstrous post-workout meal for his recovery window macros, right? And, not to mention, there's a *high* chance he now has a few different boink sessions lined up in a few different fan rooms with a few different smokeshows," he said, rubbing his palms together with raised eyebrows and a grin — Suabedissen's programming had taught him that sexually active men communicate this way.

151

"Goddamn it... *fuck it*—I'll find him myself," Juice said without looking back, as he exited the bridge and removed his cover.

As he walked down the ladderwells and p-ways, hearing sailor bots engage in shittily-programmed cowboy talk ("How about that bowling championship? Incredibly riveting drama, am I right?", "Say, anybody up for a round of Pokemon tonight after our shift?", "Boy, oh boy, did you see the new ship's company girl who checked in? She sure is motivated to work and equipped with knowledge of the SOP, too!") he grew more frustrated and apprehensive with the beginning of the Olympics right around the corner. Dr. Suabedissen *swore* that getting another former Chippy would bolster the empire's chances of dominating the US Navy, but... to put it mildly, Juice was *not* sold on the thought of Kyle Camilli being one of his right-hand men.

During the end of Juice's time in the Chippies, Camilli had become a completely different person. The Low T he first met as a new guy was friendly, selfless, a fantastic teacher, and an even better pilot—he was essentially the Good Dude that Juice had expected Sam to be. He taught Juice the tricks of the trade of fleet life, like how to send mickeys to the radio offenders who deserved them, or how to acquire a sheet of electronic safety tags to validate your stuff without the ship's approval. He even blew Juice's mind when he busted the myth and showed that you *could* remove items from government computers without safely ejecting them—and the world would not reach apocalyptic ends. And Juice would be remiss not to give Kyle credit for teaching him the golden rule of being a naval aviator: TTM, or Tactical Time Management—doing your ground job *just* good enough to keep hinges off your back, and preserving the rest of your time for the *real* important part of the job: "Getting fucking *great* in the jet," as Low T always said. And great, Low T certainly was. In fact, 'great' was an *understatement.* He could carry entire LFEs on his back regardless of his role in the event. Juice watched him launch as a -4 SEAD contingency jet in a 20-ship event, and end up filling forward to get 6 A/A kills, drop a JDAM on the priority target, and serve as On-Scene Commander for an unrelated Cessna crash—spotting the survivor from 2500' feet away with his *eyeballs.* The survivor, by the way? Michael *fucking* Jordan. Low T was a hero not just that day, but in the air wing in general. It was said that if you wanted to succeed in a SFWT checkride, do whatever it took to get Low T in the event, and you'd guaranteed yourself a pass/complete. He was, as they say, *Himothy* of naval aviation.

But something changed once Sam abandoned the Chippies for the Noddiks. *Low T* changed... He was once such a good boy, known for his morning matcha tea and cereal, afternoon study sessions to jazz and classical tunes, evening LISS jogs with his wife and the dogs, and early bedtimes after reading a bit of Henry David Thoreau. But without his best friend Sam to keep him motivated and share in the love for the job—after the gut-wrenching *betrayal* he felt from his wingman? Low T eventually said, without saying, "Fuck this shit." Just as *he* was abandoned, he now abandoned everything his identity was all about in the tac-air community—and became just another gym-bro douchebag. A gentle soul once aspiring to find his way to Fallon, earn a Patch, and teach the next generation at SFWSL... he now became a raging asshole obsessed with consuming BCAAs by the gallon, accumulating mass, and getting fucking *chiseled*. He traded in short skates and cursor mates for hitting weights and stacking plates. Gone were the days of reading the tactical bible of TOPGUN; instead, Low T was commonly seen religiously studying Arnold Schwarzenegger's *Encyclopedia of Bodybuilding*. No more oatmeal and tea— Kyle was now fueled every morning by C4 and steak. Forget the jazz shit—Low T began exclusively listening to dubstep and heavy metal. Jogs? Please. You couldn't catch Kyle doing *any* cardio unless it was en route to his meal before his nutrition timing window ended, or the kind of cardio one does in a fan room or F/A-18 intakes. And gone were the early bedtimes—10 pm meant it was time for Kyle's third dose of C4 for the day, before his midnight session at 'church.' The next morning? He'd take a line of C4, shoot himself up with some HGH, throw on a flight suit that barely fit around his massive shoulders, and do it all over again.

Needless to say—Juice could not fucking *stand* the man that Low T became. And to hear that nothing had changed from that? It seemed so pointless for Kyle to be here. Sure, he's probably holding on to some long-burning, bitter resentment for Rowland—but that was all he and Juice had in common in this venture. Juice couldn't imagine how Camilli could *possibly* help tactically, since he had given up that pursuit long ago. The guy's admin has to *suck*, with his currency so far out the window. And, as a leader... no fucking chance. Low T— *Loaded T* — became just as selfish as Nickels, but in an entirely different way. And yet... Suabedissen *insisted* this was a smart idea...

Juice shook his head. This was just another stressor to his already uneasy feeling about the Olympics...

Finally, he made his way out to the hangar bay—and was shocked to see an entire ring of sailors circling around the bench press. He got closer and saw somebody putting up—no, *repping out*—"Four plates?!" Juice couldn't help but say out loud. He rubbed his eyes and looked again. Sure enough, some unbelievably jacked dude—shirtless, with sweats turned into cutoff shorts—was busting out 405 lbs on the bench like it was the bar alone.

After about twenty reps, the man racked the bar, sat up, and made eye contact with Juice. Juice didn't need more than a second to recognize him instantly—the hair was long and flowing below a beanie, his body extremely tanned, and the jaw abnormally chiseled—but it was unmistakably Kyle Camilli.

Kyle smirked at Juice. To the jacked man's left and right, girls were fawning over him—literally *hanging on* to his veiny arms, *begging* for his stateroom number. He scoffed and told them to lose five pounds and then come see him. He chugged the concoction in his blender bottle, got up, and walked toward his former Chippy squadronmate — the crowd parting before him, everyone's mouth agape.

Loaded T folded his arms — clearly flexing and moving his pecs — narrowed his eyes, and stared at Juice.

Ward looked at him, matched his stance, and asked with a hint of annoyance, "Kyle... why are you here? This is my battle; *my* chance to take down Sam. *I'm* the one who mastered admin, *I'm* the one leading the charge here, and even *you* — once a tactics master — are undoubtedly *way* too far behind now. The game has changed, bro — there are like twenty new iterations of admin recs since you left. How could you *possibly* help us?!"

Loaded T stared at Juice emotionlessly without saying a word. It went on for a minute, with the crowd watching eagerly.

Juice wasn't sure if Kyle was going to agree with him... argue with him... or just deck him. Growing impatient and slightly nervous at the behemoth of a man in front of him, he asked, "... Well?! Say something!"

Finally, after another drawn-out period of stoicism, Loaded T put his hand in his pocket and retrieved a piece of paper, handing it to Juice.

Juice took the document and scanned it — front and back, covered in words from top to bottom with barely enough room for the signature: LT Sam Rowland. As Juice scanned through the content, his eyes widened with shock, narrowed with cringe, closed with disbelief — and as he finished the last sentence, he asked, "Nickels wrote this?"

Kyle shook his head, his eyes cold and bitter, and finally spoke, answering, "Negative. *Dimes* did."

At that moment, everything about Low T's radical transformation, mysterious departure, and sudden re-emergence made sense to Juice. He nodded and declared, "You're in — let's do this." Juice put out his hand, met Loaded T's vice grip, the two shook — and they were officially a flight of two, unified against one common adversary...

10

A Patch of Hope

*A*lright, new guy — listen up and listen good," LT Sam Rowland said with folded arms as *A*he glared at the Chippies' longest-tenured FNG, Bobby Ward. The two were sitting in the Ready Room 6 Ops enclosure, protected by a flimsy blue curtain that gave a laughable façade of privacy. It didn't matter, however; everyone else in the ready room was clearing out for a deck-breaking midrats run, as FISTY's roll 'em of 'Patriots' 2019 AFC Championship victory over the top-seeded Kansas City Chiefs' was wrapping up with Rex Burkhead's game-winning touchdown in overtime (As Brady fist-pumped in celebration, FISTY shouted, "Point, American Muscle! LET'S FUCKING GO!")

Rowland, unaffected by yet another case of Brady brilliance — as FISTY had rolled this postseason classic five times already — pointed to the computer screen, where a shell of the following day's flight schedule displayed on SHARP. "This is a fucking shit show. And even as a lowly Skeds O trainee — this is unacceptable! You had all day to work on this draft. Now we're sitting here with nothing to present Skipper — looking like idiots — while all the French toast sticks and waffles are undoubtedly getting eaten by some CAG staffer. Ward, if you're gonna survive in the fleet, you cannot hand the OPSO mind-numbing puzzles like this one."

LT Ward looked glum, hanging his head down, before shrugging and saying, "Look, I'm sorry — there were unannounced air plan changes, CAG was double-booked with the Talons, the D-Backs couldn't cover Pri-Fly for us, and..." he took a deep breath, sighed — then shook his head and humbly admitted, "You're right. I know it was my first day alone, but this is not ok. I vow to do all the training I need — "

"Oh, get the fuck out of here, you kiss ass," Sam cut him off. "You come to this squadron saying you want to be an admin master like me," he gestured to himself aggressively with his thumb, "and yet you can't even figure out how to build a house of cards via simple-interfaced, intuitive, error-free software like SHARP? Listen — writing schedules is a gigantic part of naval aviation lore, kid," he said, demeaning the new guy who was ironically older than him, "and so are all *ground jobs, really. Administrative excellence — it's not just about what happens un-der positive ATC control — it's about how you handle business in front of a keyboard, with a stack of EVALs, or organizing a library of NATOPS jackets. Ground job admin is what sepa-rates the champs from the chumps in this biz. And frankly,"* Sam sighed in annoyance, *"I don't care if you've been handed a shit salad of a day — any admin ace would turn that salad into a thick, juicy ribeye. But* this?" *he said, again exaggeratedly gesturing at the SHARP shell, "this is a chemically-based, seed-oil-doused estrogen bomb. Way to go, dipshit..." he said, his head shaking in disappointment.*

"Fuck..." Ward cursed himself. "What are we going to do?"

Sam looked at him, paused a moment, and said, "You know, 99% of Operations Officers would see this abysmal product you've attempted to put forth, and surrender their blue pen immediately. They'd recognize an impossible situation, and hold no hope toward a futile effort to make a workable flight schedule that Skipper would approve. But..." Sam changed his tone, with a slight smile, "You're about to learn why our OPSO has been featured on the cover of The Hook Magazine, The Harvard Business Review, Forbes, *and even* Playboy — *multi-ple times — with his unmatchable creativity and innovative genius."*

Footsteps could be heard approaching their OPS cave from afar...

Sam continued, "A man whose prowess in the jet and leadership is nothing *compared to his business savvy, charisma, and knack for finding solutions in impossible dilemmas..."*

The footsteps got louder...

"A man from extreme wealth, but humbly so; a man whose late parents taught him the importance that being a good person means far more in life than any finances accumulated, sorties completed, or quals obtained," Sam pointed to a framed Fortune *magazine cover, de-picting a bald man wearing a pressed, slim-fit Armani suit, staring into the camera; a Rolex Yacht-Master II on the wrist of his hand holding a leather-bound, Chippy-embroidered flight schedule folder. The headline on the cover read 'Would You Fund Me? I'd Fund Me.'*

Louder, came the footsteps — strides of confidence.

"A man who inherited the world, yet sacrificed a life of hedonism to instead utilize his skills in serving others — specifically, in the military — knowing that he could be a symbol — a symbol for hope. Hope that not every department head is deceitful and broflauge. You see, new guy, JOs need dramatic examples to shake them out of apathy. A good O-4 — one who is incor-ruptible? He can be everlasting."

LCDR Charles "WYFMIFM" Kennedy, the Dambuster Operations Officer, walked into the OPS room, playing with his mustache out of habit, and took a glimpse at the board for the following day's schedule — the 31ˢᵗ of the month. It was complete chaos — The Lorax was on his last day of dynamic currency with upcoming SFWT early-cycle BFM sorties pucked out; CP had snivved out for a long-form flight physical; there was an unfilled squadron responsibil-ity to take on the duties of Bravo Romeo; JABA required day-to-go-night; Low T was slated for all-day mission planning for some impromptu MARSTRIKE that was already being white-

carded; the FNGs were useless to fill any line other than PGM single ship hops. And to top it off... the Diamondbacks were already asking the Chippies to cover their alert tanker.

Nickels looked up and gave a nod of acknowledgment to his reporting senior, telling WYFMIFM, "Alright, Chucky... it's a challenging one today. FNG 1 here didn't really give you much to work with..."

"Challenging?" WYFMIFM said, without looking away from the board, "... Just the way I like it." He put on a pair of fingerless gloves and ordered, "Hit the music, Nickels."

Nickels, who had been training Juice on the complex art of transferring names from the whiteboard into SHARP, smiled and said, "Oh, I like this part..." Rowland opened a file on the Chippy terabyte, hit 'play' – and a symphonic orchestrated rendition of the South Korean K-Pop girl group 'BLACKPINK' started playing elegantly in the Ops Room. Nickels started his schedule brief: "Alright, we've got 15 pilots – half of which have schedule conflicts – and 15 lines to fill. We need a Bravo Romeo, an SDO, five section leads, and two division leads."

WYFMIFM started moving his hands back and forth across the whiteboard, swapping and replacing pucks on different lines of the air plan layout while stating various observances. "Two abbreviated cycles... one double... chance for a load plan change and strafe the wake here... FNG 3 needs to fly night... >SADCLAM<'s wave day..." He was muttering as much to himself as he was his Skeds Os, rapidly darting his eyes around the board and cross-checking personal schedules – before confidently announcing, "Sam – tell the SDO to call Skipper; we're gonna have this baby ready to sign soon."

Nickels sent Juice to accomplish that task, while WYFMIFM stayed in the zone.

"Check DCAST and see if we can get the ITRA South airspace..." he told Sam. "I'm seeing an opportunity here for a few good training sets of BFM if we can get CAG's approval to use blue water states..."

"Roger that – it's a longshot, but we'll see..." Sam replied.

"Fractured images coming in," Kennedy said, referring to his mental picture of the schedule. "A section lead – XO – he can log NVG hours and get a roll-in to get himself current for the night bombing next week. I'm seeing numbers..." he paused a moment before articulating, "A 6... and a 9..." He closed his eyes and nodded with understanding, "Of course – 1 in 6, 2 in 9 – night loop currency." He looked back at his Skeds O. "Nickels, get the new guys on the night page and put a note to execute a loop for T&R."

Rowland typed away furiously while WYFMIFM got deeper into the schedule shell.

"Ok, I'm seeing a man... with eagles on his shoulders – it's DCAG. Perfect, call DCAG and tell him we can add him to our flight schedule – he'll be on Bravo Romeo. And while you're at it – let me think here... yes, call CAG OPS and tell them if they want Low T, they'll need to push mission planning two hours to the right."

With Juice returning to the room, Nickels tasked him to make the necessary phone calls.

WYFMIFM continued audibly musing his plan. "Let's see... we're into the near sunset hours... perfect, add JABA to event 5D1 for the last sunset recovery, and ensure he logs a night *trap – and while he's at it, add a note for him to hit the KC-135 that'll be airborne at the time, to re-hack big wing currency."*

"Genius!" Nickels yelled out, as he hadn't even been tracking JABA's looming expiration.

Without acknowledging Nickels' compliment, Kennedy continued swapping around name pucks, moving at a rapid pace that Sam and Juice could hardly follow. "We still have no bodies left for SDO... or the alert tanker... dammit!"

Juice raised his arm to say something, but Sam quickly shook him off. "Wait, Ward – just let him do his thing..."

WYFMIFM kept scrunching his face, touching his mustache, trying to make sense of the problem. "CP will be done by noon... he can fly in the early night and still keep crew day – but he won't be able to cover the alert, then. Hmm... wait a second – I'm seeing a third party, Sam! Someone with sunglasses..."

Nickels immediately started jotting down notes, excited to hear the raised tone in WYFMIFM's voice, as a solution was surely emanating.

"Sunglasses... looking in from afar..." his eyes lit up with exhilaration, "Yes! Paddles! Get BCB on the phone and have him fill as our alert pilot."

Again, Sam gestured to Juice, then asked Kennedy, "Does that cover everything?"

"Just need the SDO spot filled..." WYFMIFM said calmly. "Hold up – it's coming into focus... I'm seeing it... there's somebody available who can stand it." Still staring at the board, he pointed to the computer and directed, "Have SHARP auto-populate whoever's not scheduled, put them on watch – and print *it."*

"You got it!" Sam said excitedly, understanding the potential of a physical product: the end of a Skeds O's workday was in sight.

"Let me just see..." A look of shock appeared on Kennedy's face. "Wait, wait..."

"You say something, WYFMIFM?" Sam asked, turning from his computer.

"No," Kennedy said quickly, spreading his arms to hide the white board from their view.

The printer kicked into gear and started pushing the final schedule out. But as Nickels reached for it, WYFMIFM swiped it just before him. "I got it, Sam. I'll sign for you and give it to Skipper. Why don't you and Juice go take a break; maybe grab me a microwavable burrito from the wardroom?"

Sam looked over at Juice and shrugged. "Sure – thanks WYFMIFM!"

The OPSO watched the two walk out and waited for the door to close before he shut the curtain. He stared at the name that had been generated on the SDO line for the upcoming day's flight schedule: Kennedy.

He felt ill just seeing it, positive that it couldn't be real... could it? He frantically returned to the board and began looking at names, desperate to find anyone *who'd been mistakenly left off the schedule flow. But with the SFWT training plan, currency re-hacking, and crew rest issues, it looked impossible. He began tugging at his mustache in extreme anxiety now,* dreading the reality that he may be forced to undergo the most painful evolution of deployment – a punishment he hadn't suffered in years, since FlyByGate... He held the printed schedule in front of his face, staring at his name. He grabbed the phone and dialed the Diamondbacks, desperately begging them to send a WSO to stand the watch for him – but they were all fully booked with branch O meetings, MWR planning, and other made-up ground job tasks – thus, unable to supply bodies for such a menial task as representing a squadron skipper. He even called the admiral and asked if there was any chance they'd cancel the air plan for tomorrow and turn it into a no-fly day, with the opportunity to transit unnecessarily into foreign waters and incite action – a CVW-5 commonplace – but to no avail. WYFMIFM sat despondently with his head in his hands, and no other solution possible. He looked over at the schedule in grief once more – then jumped as he heard somebody clear their throat behind him.

Sam was standing there – inside the curtain, plastic-wrapped burrito in hand – and saw the name attached to SDO. The clock struck midnight. With a look of somber disappointment – almost a sense of guilt – he said, "Skipper was at midrats... he said you could sign for him..." The two stood there awkwardly – as Sam then begged, "WYFMIFM, you don't have to do this! Please... save yourself. The first brief is at 0500 tomorrow – it would be inhumane to put yourself on that watch! Please – put the new guy on! Me, even! Anyone but you!"

WYFMIFM bit his lips and shook his head, saying, "It wouldn't be right – to deliver that news to somebody who's already in their stateroom or at midrats? Dropping the bomb that they need to be up in four hours for a 16-hour duty day? Not on my watch, Nickels..."

Pleading, Sam urged him, "WYFMIFM... you don't owe the squadron any more – you've given them everything..."

"Not everything." He said, stone-faced. "Not yet."

Sam stared at him silently – nearly tearing up – as WYFMIFM closed his eyes, accepted his fate for what was to come, and signed his and Skipper's portion of the schedule – sealing his doom for an insufferable day of Squadron Duty Officer.

Pained with guilt, Sam quietly remarked, "I never said thank you..."

As WYFMIFM walked by him, he calmly and huskily responded, "And you'll never have to," before breaking into a dead sprint and exiting the ready room to escape to his cavern for the night...

~

"This is incredible!" Sam shouted out as he, >SADCLAM<, CP, JABA, and FISTY's lifeless body reached the top floor of Fat Chucky's Cruise Ship and took in the scenery of the massive pool party on the yacht.

JABA smiled and said, "Pretty spectacular, right? Thank god WYFMIFM chased his entrepreneurial dreams; that guy has nailed this business opportunity! Just as I struck gold on recreating my one and only love in theme park form," he said gleefully, "our old OPSO has *mastered* the vibe of port calls!"

The gigantic infinity-pool setup was the ultimate party scene—the kind you see in promotional videos for music festivals or Instagram influencers, desperately trying to portray a life of slow-motion club-dancing, yacht-lounging, and pool-pushing with models. Beautiful people everywhere—not a pasty piece of skin nor blubbery pound of body fat in sight—with EDM music blaring, as a live DJ was *killing it* by hitting the 'play' button on a Spotify playlist. Sam noticed that one of the girls at the DJ booth requesting a song—'Scotty Doesn't Know'—looked identical to Rachel McAdams.

Wait a second—that is *Rachel McAdams!*

Sure enough, Rachel and countless other celebrities were partying with the wild crowd—celebrities of all different fields. Within minutes, Sam tallied Bryce Harper, Shohei Ohtani, Kim Kardashian, Aaron Rodgers, LeBron James, and even Cristiano Ronaldo—who seemed to be getting very intimate with Shakira.

CP stepped back. "Oh my gosh... I can't believe *she's* here—god, I hope she doesn't see me," he said, shielding himself from Shakira's vantage point. He looked at the guys and said, "Well, she probably wasn't exactly *thrilled* when I left 50 or so of her texts and voicemails unanswered..."

JABA laughed. "Oh, Clown Penis... I'm sure Doja has been a better match for you anyway! It's so beautiful when somebody finds love... I know mine's out there, somewhere..." he trailed off, looking out to sea sadly.

>SADCLAM< was in awe at the scene: the lingerie-style bathing suits the women were wearing, the outdoor gym where genetic freaks were busting out reps with every beat drop, and the grand stage where Drake and Justin Bieber were handing out shots of 'JP-151' to a crowd of Instagram models including Emily Ratajkowski and Olivia Culpo. CLAM grabbed his forehead and declared excitedly, "Dude... this is the most un-WYFMIFM thing I've ever seen in my life—but also... it is *so* WYFMIFM. I fucking love it!"

With an impossible-to-wipe-off smile, Sam looked around and asked, "Hey, anybody have any sunscreen? I'm not trying to get burnt out here..."

"Woah... hold up there," CP said with uneasy hesitation.

"God dammit, Sam..." CLAM groaned.

CP continued, "All sunscreen is going to do for you... is simply cause cancer and kill you." He looked suspiciously concerned and asked, "Wait a second—Dimes... you're not ingesting *seed oils,* are you? Because all *those* are going to do is make you more prone to those burns you're so scared of getting—from the Vitamin D source of the gods..." he gestured to the sky.

"Well... I mean... I guess I haven't been paying attention to my diet as much lately—maybe a bit of margarine here or there—it's low fat!" Sam insisted desperately.

CP tsked, pointed to a grilling station where Gordon Ramsay was cooking up some ribeyes. "Dimes, go eat one of those right now. And don't even *think* about trimming off the best part. That animal fat will make you *invincible* to the sun—and, by the way, allow you to get a *killer* tan and absorb that vitamin dizzle like my main man Kelly Slater over there." CP gave a head nod to the surfing legend—who had his arm around Gal Gadot—and raised his eyebrows friendlily in return, calling out, "What up, Mr. Preul!"

"Andrew?" a woman's voice called out.

"Oh shit..." CP looked back and saw Shakira approaching him shyly.

"Wow... it's really you..." she said, "I wasn't sure I'd ever see you again—or hear from you even—given that you, well..." she put her hands on her hips, "completely blew me off for that *cow* Doja, leaving me on 'read' without a single call or message back!" her tone rising dangerously.

CLAM and JABA winced as CP turned his friends and said, "Ugh... sorry guys, I gotta handle this real fast—I'll catch up with you later on."

"'Handle?!'" Shakira repeated, disgusted. As the two walked off to the side, CP wore a look of dread on his face, anticipating a painful conversation with his heated ex-lover.

"Speaking of fantasies, I need to keep working on this Brady VR dream scenario to get FISTY here back to life," JABA said, pointing to The Patch wearer's body, face-down on one of the pool chairs. "I have a permanent personal room here aboard the ship—nothing compared to the good ol' Chippy 4-man, of course," he said, gazing longingly into the distance. He refocused and turned to Chris. "CLAM, help me carry FISTY there. Sam, go get that T-boosting steak, and grab us some, too, if you don't mind—my brain could certainly use a wealthy and natural source of creatine to kickstart this day. When you're done, come to room 195; anybody here can point you in the direction."

Sam nodded, fist bumped >SADCLAM< and JABA goodbye, and headed toward Ramsay's grill station.

As he walked toward the glorious array of meats, he saw things that were the strangest mix of completely nerdy... yet also incredibly cool. Rob Gronkowski and Ryan Gosling were lightsaber dueling, repeating lines from Anakin and Obi-Wan's epic Episode III clash. Cardi B and Jennifer Lopez were wearing Princess Leia 'Jabba's Barge' prisoner outfits, sharing in a twerking competition. Jessica Alba and Eva Longoria were playing Mario Kart: Double Dash!! on a gigantic jumbotron against Reggie Bush and Matthew McConaughey. The whole time, an Avicii remix of the Interstellar theme was blaring. It was bizarre—but *so awesome* at the same time. *This really is so WYFMIFM...*

"Five ribeyes, please!" Sam said to the scantily-clad waitress taking orders.

"Oh my *god*!" another woman's voice called out. "Are you a pilot?!"

Sam turned and saw Megan Fox, wearing the same orange-crop-top-and-jeans combo in *Transformers* that turned so many teenage boys to men. Sam blushed and asked, "Sorry, are you talking to me?"

"Your flight suit is *so* hot! This bomber jacket—*so* badass!" Megan said, pointing to his green outer layer. "And look at these patches…" She looked him in the eyes as she caressed her hand down his chest. "So sexy… I *really* like this one…"

"Heh, ahh…" he looked down and realized she was massaging the one he'd meant to get removed—his NIRD Katsopolis HODS patch.

She smiled lasciviously and asked, "Are you here for the party? We're about to do body shots!"

Trying not to get too distracted, Sam's voice cracked as he stammered out, "Ah, noOOo"—he cleared his throat and explained, "Nah, I'm just grabbing some meat before joining some friends. Gotta load up on that protein!" he said awkwardly, before catching himself and backtracking. "Err—I mean… I'm not short on T or anything… just want to, you know, fuel the ol' gun show, hehe," he feebly insisted, pointing to his bicep in a shameful display of attempted peacocking.

The beautiful vixen bit her lip and gazed at Sam's arms regardless—but then made heart-stealing eye contact and frowned. "Aw… you're not here for the party? Not here for… *me*?"

Sam gulped and shook his head. "Unfortunately, no, ma'am—I mean Megan." He shrugged, looking guilty, and explained, "I'm sorry… I've got some business to take care of…"

Megan looked disappointed. "That's too bad…" She moved in closely and, caressing his ear with her lips, whispered, "Well, maybe you'll change your mind…" before turning around to walk away.

"Actually…" Sam started.

Megan snapped her head back—her eyes full of excitement—as she smiled and asked, "Yes?"

Not wanting to end this conversation, Sam said, "Maybe you can help me—do you know where I might find the captain of this cruise ship?"

Looking confused, Megan responded, "Chucky? Sorry, but nobody has seen him in *years*. Rumor has it that he locked himself in his cabin at sea and has been fighting depression; another one says that he abandoned this ship long ago…" She shrugged. "To be honest, I couldn't tell you if the guy is even alive anymore…"

"What?!" Sam burst out. "But doesn't he run this entire shindig?" *'Shindig?' Sam, that was so not cool—get a hold of yourself…*

"Well… he *did*—but the party never ends on Fat Chucky's Cruise Ship… and eventually, he just kind of… faded out from the picture. And everybody was having too much fun dancing, drinking, and — well… *love-making*," she gave a salacious smile, "to notice that the man behind it all had disappeared." She looked a bit sad — then locked in that award-winning gaze and said, "But I'll never forget Chucky; it's all thanks to him that I got a job here and saved my career after nobody cast me in movies anymore."

Curious, Sam asked, "What did he hire you to do?"

Megan smiled nonchalantly. "Oh, just to walk around, look hot, show lots of skin, and make guests think I'm interested in them."

Pursing his lips, Sam said, "Right…" The idea sparking inside his head, he asked, "Well… Ms. Fox, do you think you could show me where his office is? I'd love to see what the captain's spaces look like in a totally *nectar* yacht like this. I'm uhh…" he scratched the back of his head, "thinking about buying one pretty soon here — with uhh… you know… all the money I have…" As soon as it came out of his mouth, Sam realized how obvious and weak his line was.

Looking vibrant, though, Megan responded, "Wow, really?! That is *so* cool! You must be, like, super rich!"

"Ahhh…" Sam tried to play his excitement off. "I mean… I don't know if you've heard of the Noddik Empire, but…"

"I definitely haven't!" she smiled obliviously.

"Right — well, you see, I'm kind of a scholar in the art of administrative…" Stopping before he made even more of a fool of himself, Sam shook his head. "You know what? Nevermind — how about we go take a look-see at where the captain works?"

"Sure thing, baby," Megan said flirtatiously.

Approaching from behind them, the cocktail waitress returned with a plate full of ribeyes.

"Oh my god, are you going to eat *all* of that?!" Megan asked with her jaw dropped. "That… is *so* hot. Your testosterone levels must be like… off the charts! What an *animal!*"

Shrugging again, Sam said, "Ahh… I mean… I get put on urinalysis pretty often…" and then winked at Megan, who giggled uncontrollably.

"Come on, stud… let's go find those captain's quarters — they're *so* much more private…" she said, her beautiful eyes radiating.

As the two walked off with a plateful of steak, Sam could hear Rob Gronkowski crying out, "From my point of view, the Jedi are evil!" as the crowd laughed uproariously…

~

"3... 2... 1... hack." Juice looked up from his Garmin watch and stared at the hangar bay crowd on the NIRD Katsopolis. All hands were in attendance, from bot culinary specialists, to bot squadron pilots, to bot CAG, to NEODD SWEVEN, IROK, and T6—and, of course, Loaded T—who was sitting in the front row, eating a meal of cold ground beef with an entire stick of butter top; his veins and jawline rippling with every bite of beef tallow.

Juice took a deep breath and said, "Welcome to the brief. Today's mission objective: Defeat the United States Navy in the Administrative Olympics, thus proving the Noddik Empire to be the superior managed fleet at the basics. Training Objectives are per the syllabus guide, and we'll never actually talk about them again until the end, anyway." The bot pilots nodded as Juice continued, "We'll set the room at 'This stays between us'—is anybody in the room unfamiliar with this phrase?" He looked around—silence from the crowd. He continued, "For the friendly order of battle, we have this ship—the Noddik Intergalactic Raid/Defense spaceship, as well as three by F/A-18Es—piloted by myself, IROK, and Kyle 'Loaded T' Camilli." Kyle briefly paused from downing beef to look over his shoulder and pompously head nod to the crowd. "For the enemy order of battle," Juice continued, "we will be facing the USS Ship, who will have three of their own F/A-18s, likely all of the E variant as well." He looked to the crowd's left and announced, "Next up, we have Dr. Suabedissen with an intel update."

Dr. Karl Suabedissen, dressed in a black cloak draping behind him and a large hood hanging over his head, walked to center stage and faced the crowd. He raised the hood off his head and began his intelligence spiel—signifying that it was time for the crowd to take a micro-nap. He opened with, "CAG, DCAG, Juice, COs, XOs, Department Heads, Junior Officers, Ground Pounders, Master Chiefs, Senior Chiefs—"

"Cut to the chase, douche," Loaded T called out from the crowd with annoyance.

Dr. Suabedissen nodded curtly and continued, "The US military, aboard the USS Ship, is assessed to be utilizing standard carrier operation tactics: a '12-on, 12-off'-type work schedule for the maintenance crews of the air wing; with a '2-on, 22-off' schedule for the ship's company resources like dispersing, ADP, and S-5 'hotel' services," the doctor used air quotes for the word 'hotel,' and added, "which intel has discovered is their codeword for their abysmal living spaces.

"The Big XO is evaluated to be a Level 5 boner who feels the need to hear his own voice every night, via announcements about the 'sailor of the day' or upcoming Super Smash Bros tournaments, while reminding everyone that it will take a *full* crew to *fully* polish the ship to his acceptable standards—as if that was somehow the most important aspect of winning a war. To add insult to incompetence, whenever this desperate man makes said announcements, every sailor is forced to stop whatever they're doing and come to a standstill. Ironic..." his lip curled up, "The Big XO speaks to make them work harder... and yet his words stop their productivity..."

The crowd of bots laughed heavily at Dr. Suabedissen's words, which they had been programmed to do by him in order to raise his self-esteem.

He sneered at his cronies and continued, "The USS Ship has overall been assessed to be 'CSU' — 'Common Sense-Unaware' — making them a 'trivial' threat on our adversary spectrum. Intel calculates that in order to achieve victory, we will simply need to follow the procedures that our wise, battle-tested superiors have put into place," he sycophantically gestured to Juice. "Pending any questions..."

Suabedissen now just stood there plain-faced with nothing else to say, until Juice excused him with, "Thank you, doctor. It is now time for a METOC update—but we're going to forgo it, as I'm certain even *less* people would pay attention to that."

"Seriously!" Suabedissen yelled from the side, with heavy breathing and laughing, "Like... as if we didn't check our own weather beforehand, am I right?!"

"Shut the fuck up and get off the stage, bitch," Loaded T yelled from his seat.

Dr. Suabdedissen's smile faded to a frown, as he hung his head and walked back to his seat.

"Jesus Christ..." Juice whispered under his breath, feeling a bit uncomfortable from Loaded T's sudden aggression. "Anyway... what the doctor said is correct: ladies and gents, if we do things the way you've been trained to, Phase 1 is going to be a joke. You guys are all emotionless droids who are incapable of feeling the pains and inefficiencies of the monotonous boat bullshit—which is essentially our nuclear superpower in the war of boat admin. Any mere mortal would surely be appalled and sickened at the day-to-day expectations of a sailor living on the carrier. This is a tactical advantage that is *not* to be understated; all of you brainless invalids lack the capacity to realize that working '24-on, 0-off' is even more inhumane and preposterous than the shit the American sailors deal with. Give yourselves a round of applause."

The sailors started hooting and hollering loudly, giving a thunderous reception to their inability to recognize that they were mere pawns of the Noddik government—dehumanized into serial numbers and treated as such.

Juice continued, "Without rest, nourishment, or humanity to worry about, the efficiency of this carrier under normal circumstances will be second-to-none. As a quick refresher for everyone, let's test some basic admin setup knowledge." He paused for a moment, then changed his tone to indicate that a question was incoming. "During deployment, we know that it is *crucial* for pilots to get to their aircraft on time to protect the ship. That being said... sailor bot 957," he looked around and found a bot raising his hand to grab his attention. Bobby presented the question: "If you are conducting General Quarters when an Alert 15 is called away, and you are guarding a door that a geared-up pilot is sprinting toward in order to walk to his jet, are you going to let him through..." he asked softly, before emphasizing his voice and offering—with his head nodding—"Or are you going to *protect the integrity of the GQ simulation* and *make the pilot take an alternate route?*"

"Protect the integrity and block his path, sir," the bot responded.

"Yeah, man, exactly—you got it!" Juice affirmed with enthusiasm that seemed more artificial than the bots he was talking to.

The Q-and-A session went on for a few more minutes, with Juice querying random bot sailors to ensure they would execute administratively sound tactics like calling "Attention on deck!" for every O-6-and-above—even though it inconvenienced everyone and brought unnecessary attention to the high-ranker; to make sure that the bot chiefs would dig through officer's laundry to seek and tattle on offenders who were so presumptuous that they thought they could self-wash their flight suits—rather than have the ship's laundry boil it in a vat of water and likely lose it; and to confirm that during a RAS, bots armed with rifles would ensure that others are forced to take an inconvenient 5-minute detour down and back up two sets of ladderwells toward job-necessary locations—vice stepping *one foot* inside an orange cone boundary, and risk penetrating a 500-foot bubble around boxes being opened up.

The 100% accuracy of answers pleased Juice. "Are there any questions on Phase 1's game plan?" The blank response also pleased him; he moved on to the next portion. "Phase 2 will be Admin Recoveries. NEODD SWEVEN, can you please brief the crew on this evolution?"

NEODD SWEVEN—sporting a backward LA Clippers hat with a Russell Westbrook LA Lakers jersey—approached the podium and threw up a few fingers, shouting, "Sahhh, dudes!" The crowd stood motionless. "Alright bros, so here's our game plan for these *fire* landings aboard the USS Ship: We're gonna look fucking dope, lights bright as hell, zero eye contact, gloves off, and we're gonna say *pimp* things on the radio during the pass—is that what you call it, Juice? A 'pass?'"

Juice rolled his eyes and nodded.

Smirking, NEODD SWEVEN went on, "Aaaaand, that's about it! We're gonna look totally baller out there, and accept our _OK_s like the single-seat big-penis bros we are—is that what you call it, Juice? A 'penis?'"

Juice buried his head into his hands, beyond frustrated with the wave team.

"Sweet!" NEODD yelled. "Any questions on Phase 2?"

A sailor bot raised his hand.

"Uhh, yeah, fat bald dude over there, go ahead," NEODD pointed toward the bot.

"Sir, what kind of 'pimp' things will you be saying during the pass?" the sailor asked.

His eyes lighting up, NEODD acknowledged, "Ahh, yeah, great question! So," he addressed the crowd, "the question was: 'What kind of 'pimp' things will we be saying over tower frequency while we're flying the ball?' To answer your question, the squad and I," he pointed to his cronies, T6 and IROK, who were wearing Lakers jerseys of Samaki Walker and Nick 'Swaggy P' Young, "have come up with a Hollywood script for a badass pass. At the start, we're going to call our fuel at 6.9—" he looked around, beaming, and took a big pause... "—*regardless of what state it actually is!*" He laughed heavily at his own joke before continuing, "Then, at the in-the-middle position, we'll call where we're seeing the ball—centered, obviously—with, '*On* glideslope, *on* speed; *on* point.' In close, we'll transition to 'OK 2—calling it!'; and at-the-ramp, we'll show our bold audacity with 'Power's coming off'—and after the trap? 'Check, please!' Something along those lines, give or take a few words. Does that answer your question?"

"Yes, it does," the sailor responded.

"Great!" NEODD looked around, "Are there any other questions on Phase 2?"

With the crowd silent, Juice groaned to himself. He was not *nearly* convinced that IROK would be able to properly figure out PLM. Still, he knew that he and Loaded T would more than compensate to ensure the Noddiks came out on top—and he *was* at least *slightly* impressed that NEODD had learned the different parts of a standard pass.

Juice walked back up to the podium and clicked to the next slide, moving the presentation to the final portion of the Admin Olympics. "Alright, everyone, the final phase of the Olympics—*if necessary*—is Admin Adaptation. As a reminder," he looked around the room—and then at the fourth-wall camera—and explained, "this will be the portion where we conduct *simultaneous* red air game plans for the opposing ships, to see how well-equipped forces are to handle non-standard adversarial difficulties in our day-to-day operations flow—in other words, the ability to *flex* when things go off script. It's only necessary if we split the first two phases, but would undoubtedly create a *much* more dramatic climax to this story than a simple two-phase sweep." He refocused his attention on the crowd and continued, "The package commander strike lead for this is going to be LT Kyle 'Loaded T' Camilli." He looked over to his former Chippy teammate. "Loaded T, the floor is yours."

Juice stepped aside as Kyle rose from his chair—blender bottle in hand—and strode to the center stage position. His flight suit was clearly from the days before he was roided out of his mind, as it fit him Blue Angel-snug; every step revealed the outline of muscle striations throughout his hamstrings and quads. Loaded T turned to face the crowd, finished his protein shake, and tossed the bottle violently to the side—

nearly smoking Juice in the head. Kyle cleared his throat, grabbed the lectern, and began speaking. "Ok, we've listened to these douche canoes for long enough; let's get down to the *real* shit and wrap this up."

Juice felt the stinging ferocity in Kyle's voice—he was not here to fuck around.

Loaded T glared at the fleet of bot sailors. "First and foremost—don't call me a teammate. I'm here to kick ass, take names, and make gains. *Nowhere* in this battle do I give a shit about making friends—and neither should any of you. Like Juice here," Camilli flexed and pointed toward the direction of the tossed blender bottle, "I once used to believe in the professional unity and camaraderie of squadron life. I used to believe in the importance of driving excellence in one another, studying some bullshit manual of recommendations, and dedicating *far* more than 40 hours a week to learn, grow, and succeed as a cohesive unit. I used to believe in the fantasy; the fantasy that you could achieve the illustrious 'dream job' in *this very industry* by being a selfless, sacrificing team player—by being a 'Good Dude,'" he said in air quotes.

"But let's be real—nobody gave a *shit* about the team. We were just simping to some Training O or skipper in hopes of receiving a good FITREP, getting good orders, and staying on the piss-golden path—aka Sellout Street. We'd become true cucks— holding the false notion that we had *some* semblance of control over our destiny in this business, and that our tireless efforts would one day pay off—to then be *fucked over* by PERS the minute they need some pawn to sacrifice themselves for the king, i.e., Big Navy." The crowd reacted emotionlessly to him, but Kyle's words grew more impassioned as he delved further into his rant. "I not only drank the kool aid—I *chugged* it. And I was damn good at living this fantasy, too. But then, I saw the truth about this job—and the *people...*"

Kyle pulled out a piece of paper from his pocket and held it up to the crowd. "Everything was a lie. The most respected man in our squadron—*your* former Commanding Officer, Captain Sam 'Nickels' Rowland—left this—" Kyle paused a moment, more to gather himself than to think of the words, "this *true reflection* of his *spineless, backstabbing bitch-ass soul*. He left it behind back when he abandoned us—abandoned the Chippies..." He closed his eyes, paused again—and showed the slightest hint of *melancholy*—before shaking his head and continuing. "There's no need for me to get into details about this right now, but trust me when I say this, Noddiks: a simple public reveal of this document will undo *any* good-willed fortitude or cohesion that the adversary air wing could *possibly* have working in its favor."

For the first time, Juice felt himself tightening and feeling a bit uneasy. This was not the Low T that he remembered—even in the former Chippy's worst, most unmotivated days. This man was... *unhinged.*

Kyle began walking back and forth, trying to regain his focus after nearly losing it from spewing so much pained hatred. "Now, Phase 3 likely won't even *need* to come to that—I've lived enough life on that carrier to know what kind of even *minor* disasters they can't handle. The solution is all too easy: destroy them from within." He looked pointedly at the crowd and explained, "The ship *cannot* and *will not* work together as a team, and this pathetic reality becomes even more apparent when stress levels increase. Let me ask you a question: Anybody here work your shoulders on the same day you hit chest?"

Several sailors raised their hands—as did Dr. Suabedissen after shyly looking around, wondering if anyone would believe he'd ever actually lifted a weight.

"Fucking betas," Kyle called out. "*All* of you. No wonder you're all weak ass bitches."

Dr. Suabedissen quickly pulled his hand down, while Juice looked around nervously, uncomfortable with the aggressive and condescending attitude Kyle was putting forth.

Loaded T explained his analogy. "Listen up, dipshits. Any experienced bro worth his weight in muscle mass can tell you what happens when you go dual-push, combining shoulder day with chest day: you are *fucked,* as you burn your upper body joints into the ground, kill all your gains, and likely get injured—keeping you and those feeble rotator cuffs out of the gym for months. Your delts and pecs strive to steal as much strength potential as possible for themselves, not giving a shit about the conflicting movement, greedily hoarding the EAAs and proteins running through your system—ironically oblivious to the reality that they're both working toward the same common goal of *pushing weight* for a stronger, more jacked upper torso; to pop the hell out of that undersized V-neck."

Juice had no clue what this maniac was talking about at this point. 'What the *hell* is this analogy? *Plenty* of people combine movements into one push day... and hoarding EAAs?! Feeble rotator cuffs? V-neck?! *What the fuck?!'*

Loaded T turned and addressed the crowd head-on, his demeanor growing more forceful as he continued, "Ship's company... and the air wing—the shoulders and chest of the boat; each believing itself to be the most important part of the deployment *push*. Each unwilling to compromise any of its own reps, focus, or recovery time for the better of the other—for the better of the *team*... for one complete, impressive physique. By forcing each department to choose between stubbornly running its own program, or sacrificing to understand the bigger picture and actually *assist* one another?" He scoffed. "Please... the USS Ship will be *doomed* to atrophy."

He began pacing again, rattling off specific strategic CONOPS and COAs, "We could initiate a man overboard in the early AM hours of the night, when the air wing is sleeping and unwilling to play by the boat's timeline request for mustering—a drill we'll rationalize by insisting that a sailor is just as likely to fall off the ship during nighttime, and *harder* to account for in the darkness. Additionally, we could close mid-rats due to some fabricated bullshit about food supply issues, or not enough cooks being TAD—again, highlighting the desperation of the two sides robbing jobs from one another—and force the air wing to fast from 1900 until 1030 without food—*unless* they rid themselves of all morals, sleep, and standards by waking up at 0530 for *SWO breakfast*. We could close self-serve laundry—due to too many policy offenders creating an explosion hazard—and make the ship's cleaning method the *required* route for washing clothes—and with three times the laundry loads, they'll have *triple* the lost or stolen items.

"But don't think we'd only focus our attacks on the air wing..." Loaded T's eyes burned with ire. "We could write air plans with flight operations during cleaning stations—hampering the ship's the 'mission-critical' shining prerogative. And with more officers and flight jerseys walking around, it'll create an even *stronger* impression that the air wing doesn't give a shit about the boat's agenda. We could provide the air wing residents direct access to adjusting their air conditioning, water temperature, and 1MC volume—and let them run wild in manipulating the ship's meticulously-controlled power supply. And, most diabolical of all: we could take away the internet for the majority of ship dwellers, while leaving privileges up and running for air wing officers—watching as the one-percenters soak up all the bandwidth to plan their alcohol-fueled admins, share OPSEC-compromising pull-in dates with their wives, or order more LEGOs off Amazon—while other sailors can't even check their work messages or send their family an email to let them know they're still alive..."

"But in reality, we could do anything—or *nothing*—because time and time again, the carrier strike group has proven: that 'team' is a fragile, undersized softbody—incapable of working as one unified powerhouse, looking to blame and undercut their own teammates from another department whenever given the chance—and will cast that blame the *minute* things stray from the published script." He paused and glared at the audience with annoyance. "Do any of you dumbasses have any questions on Phase 3?"

A sailor bot raised his hand, as Loaded T pointed to him and said, "You—weak pussy over there."

The bot asked, "Yes, sir—sailor bot #6391. Sir, won't the ship realize that a foreign entity *has* to be behind all these quality-of-life-compromising issues? Won't they be aware that all these non-standard changes couldn't *possibly* be done maliciously in a blue-on-blue scenario?"

Kyle scoffed again. "The question was—fuck it, anybody paying attention heard you, and frankly, I don't care if they didn't. The answer is: You all have no idea how *clueless* these people are. The Disease of Me runs strong in that ship—*damn* strong.

Everybody is so concerned about how everything should be conducive to themselves—and if it's not? The first reaction is to think that somebody is *personally* attacking them; that some evil insider force is making it their entire mission to ruin the lives of others." Kyle chuckled heartlessly, "It is *pathetic* how weak-minded that Navy is. The water goes out? 'The ship's fucking with us,' they'll say. The captain makes an announcement during a brief? Eyes rolled, resentment built. It's 0200, and you've got sailors dragging chains across the flight deck to get jets ready for the next day's flight schedule, somebody hammering away to a fix known boat issue, or a jet high-power turning for an alert to prevent endangerment to the ship—and how does everyone respond? 'Jesus Christ—fuck these guys. This *seriously* needs to be done now?' These idiots... their *default* response is to believe that some corrupt part of their *own team* is there to make their lives difficult. They have minimal understanding of the bigger picture, little interest in seeing things from another viewpoint, and *zero* interest in joining forces to work through these issues."

Kyle glanced back at the nodding bot, gave a condescending look, and said, "Yeah, I already know that answers your question, bitch." He shook his head, "You know... maybe I once thought teamwork and unity existed in the Navy—but I was completely wrong. It's all a bunch of self-absorbed assholes looking to destroy anything and anyone in pursuit of the 'due' they believe they're entitled to—and no man is guiltier of that than Sam Rowland. Fuck that guy... fuck him and everything he falsely stood for. We're going to show the US Navy that there's no such thing as a 'Good Dude;' that everyone is just out for themselves. Speaking of which," he looked at his watch, "1300. Time for Khaki Hour. If you have any other questions? Figure it the fuck out." And he walked off, leaving Juice on the stage by himself.

Juice watched as Kyle stormed off and scratched at his neck furiously, his OP-NOD-banned pre-workout apparently settling into his bloodstream. He looked at Dr. Suabedissen, who was grinning evilly and steepling his fingers together below his redonned hood, for once looking surprisingly confident in himself. He glanced at NE-ODD SWEVEN and the Padroids, who were in awe at how cool they thought Loaded T was for constantly referring to his coworkers as 'bitches.' ("*Bro!*" IROK yelled out, "It's like he doesn't even respect us enough to treat us as equals or even know our names! That is *so* fucking dope!") And for the first time since joining the Noddiks, embarking on his journey of vengeance against Sam, seeking the victory that would cement Nickels' legacy as the greatest failure of all time... Juice looked at *himself*—and asked the question: 'Is Kyle *right* about the Navy? About *us*? Are we all just a bunch of selfish individuals chasing our own agenda, not caring who it hurts along the way? Is that what a Good Dude does? Do Good Dudes... truly exist...?'

For the first time since joining the Noddiks—when everything once seemed so certain, so inevitable—Juice finally felt it: *Doubt...*

Loaded T sat in his rack, snacking on the gigantic steak stash he'd stowed away in his personal Tupperware collection from the Sunday night dinner, not giving a shit that the posted signs specifically prohibited it. He was seething as he chewed on beef — still heated from how he nearly lost his composure on his brief. He again pulled out his exhibit document and reread it, which got him even more fired up. Camilli regularly did this, believing that the rage *had* to contribute to his T levels. The day he found this note written by the artist formerly known as Sam "Nickels" Rowland was the day he decided to finally say 'fuck it' to his career, his motivation, and his journey as a tactical expert and team contributor. It was the day he decided that fulfilling his fitness and personal program goals was more important than helping anybody else. It was the day that — despite nobody realizing it at the time — Low T officially died.

Reaching over and grabbing a bedside syringe, Loaded T injected his ribeye — and then himself — seeking to intake optimum amounts of HGH through varied means of fusion. Typically, this was the only thing that mattered to him. For once, though, something else was at the forefront of his polluted mind: *revenge*. Revenge against the man who sold his world. "Fuck you, Dimes," he said aloud, before taking a huge bite of steak.

His plans for after the Chippies... his quest to go to TOPGUN... his journey to return to Virginia Beach at SFWSL — vanished. The orders he'd worked so hard for, that he'd promised his family he'd get, that he'd planned to use as a stepping stone toward the capstone naval aviation career he'd sought for so long — completely ripped out of his grasp by the man he once called his best friend; the one man he thought he could trust; the man they called a 'Good Dude.'

As a jet powered up on the catapult above his stateroom, Kyle let out a furious exhale of rage that surpassed the decibel level from the afterburning engines.

As he continued eating steak, Loaded T turned to his NIPR laptop beside him — and noticed a new email notification. He minimized the low-res Brazzers video he'd been attempting to load, and pulled up his Outlook window. At the top of his inbox listing was an unread message from Robo-Hinge, with the subject 'OLYMPICS SITREP AND UPDATED GUIDANCE.' Kyle rolled his eyes as the message quickly devolved into a rant of condescending superiority complex hinge-splaining, BVR tasking, and passive-aggressive warnings about what is and isn't 'sat.' Apparently, Robo-Hinge and his cohorts had unleashed a preemptive non-kinetic strike into the morale of the USS Ship by ruining the post-military careers of Chippy alumni that were prominent in the community — Chippies that Loaded T himself once knew very well... They'd executed an APG-47 gym shooting in Andrew Preul's 'Flat Earth Fitness' at CV Worldwide, using the estrogen trons to diminish the testosterone of every gym goer in the building. Now, every man was apparently forgoing weights, instead sweating for hours on the elliptical machines in attempts to 'tone up.' The patrons demanded more medicine balls and functional training equipment, and begged for all squat racks to be replaced with safer, less-taxing smith machines—they insisted that it had the same effect on muscular development as free bars, and that it had nothing to do with being 'scared' of traditional squats. The entire rack of dumbbells was removed, except for the 2.5 lb sets, which men would hold in their hands as they playfully swayed their arms to and fro on the treadmill.

Kyle winced in pain at the thought of this gym catastrophe, impulsively shaking his head as he thought, 'What a bunch of pussies...'

Further in his rampage, Robo-Hinge and his posse struck CV Worldwide itself, implementing his iron-fisted DH leadership policies. He declared that the current revenue was not nearly satisfactory enough, and demanded the employees start working longer hours and weekends while eliminating their lunch breaks. He also cut their salaries, contending there was no employee pay scale problem and that the company would have solid retention regardless. And in a stroke of what he called 'managerial brilliance,' when everyone attempted to file their resignation letters, he found clauses in their employee contracts that allowed him to extend their commitments to the company via some fine print they'd unknowingly agreed to when they'd been hired long ago—keeping them obligated well past their 'conventionally assumed' separation windows.

Predictably, everybody started leaving at once regardless, and the park was left with no employees to manage it, as it became a chaotic mess. Robo-Hinge regretfully reported that he had to shut down operations and enter what he called an 'indefinite maintenance phase.' He was, however, insistent that it was the fault of its owner—Mark Buck—for creating a poorly run business that the robotic O-4's leadership savviness and impressive rank could not save.

Lastly, Robo-Hinge reported that he was not able to do the one thing he'd been specifically assigned to do: find Rowland, Houben, and Flynn. Thus, he delegated that task to the Olympics crew—Juice and Kyle—declaring it *their* responsibility to find the runaways and ensure the Noddik's Admin Olympic efforts would not be jeopardized. His exact statement was: 'I HAVE DONE MY PART IN CONFIRMING THE REFUGEES ARE NOT AT CV WORLDWIDE—IT IS NOW YOUR DUTY TO SEARCH THE REMAINDER OF THE WORLD AND LOCATE THEM. FAILING TO DO SO WOULD BE UNSAT. REPORT BACK TO ME BY COB TODAY.' And in the hingiest move yet, he CC'd CAG and Dr. Suabedissen on the thread to ensure their superiors would see the tasking. "Ugh..." Kyle groaned. Robo-Hinge wrapped up by announcing that he would be back for Phase 3 of the Olympics — if necessary — after he and his team returned from house-hunting leave, which he pointed out he was still entitled to. "Fuck *that* guy, too," Kyle grumbled.

As Loaded T shut his Outlook window and reopened his still-loading 'Stepsister Begs for DLY1 Fusing' video, he heard one of the most PTSD-inducing sounds known to aviators — a stateroom J-dial ringtone. He groaned in agony, took his last bite of steak, and emerged from his rack to cease the unsettling ring of insanity.

"Loaded T," he answered gruffly.

"LT Camilli, it's CAG — Phase 1, and the Admin Olympics, are officially underway."

"Understood." Kyle hung up without waiting for a response or giving the proper pleasantries. He had no fucks left to give for military respect and bearing. He walked to the sink, lined up some powder on the edge of it, lowered his head, and inhaled intensely. He then wiped his nose, raised his head, and glared at the shaving mirror — looking into his own soul. He'd given himself this stare-down every morning back in the Chippies. Back then, he was a young boy — full of vigor, hope, and dreams — a *foolish* young boy with a weak jaw, bright eyes, and a mustache that had seen no real adversity. A boy happy to be what he now considered a Low T'd bitch.

As he stared at himself now? He saw a broken man — full of animosity and growth hormone, and void of whimsical career aspirations. He was now a man with a carved jaw that had Admirals' aides thirsty for his seed, piercing eyes burdened with suffering, and a mustache covered with pain, trauma, and white powder from the C4 Ultimate he'd snorted moments ago. Sometimes — *sometimes* — he wondered how life would've turned out if that boy's dreams had come true... wondered if he'd given up on something special... wondered if —

No!

"Low T is dead, motherfucker," he told himself in the mirror. He looked back at his bed, where Sam's note remained, and then back at his reflection. "And soon, he'll be able to rest in peace — with vengeance found, revenge taken, and justice served."

~

Sam and Megan Fox explored the upstairs hallways of the cruise ship, which was staged with various highlights and accreditations from WYFMYM's naval aviation career. On the walls were seemingly every single certification Kennedy had ever earned, from his United States Naval Officer commissioning letter, to his Primary Solo certificate in T6 tail number 166592, and even his 2022 Cyber Security Awareness NKO grade sheet — all mounted in wooden, pristine frames.

Megan 'oohed' and 'ahhed' at the binder full of smooth flight schedules that WYFMIFM had approved and signed during his tenure as OPSO, and marveled at the different tracker templates he'd designed during his time in charge. "They say he was a Microsoft Excel legend, you know…" Megan said, her voice full of wonder. "He knew every formula, memorized every keyboard shortcut, left no cell un-formatted…"

"Yeah…" Sam said sheepishly. "I mean, he was great, but this stuff just seems so trivial—most companies could just outsource this pilot-hour-tracking to somebody else…"

Rowland flipped through the schedules, seeing plenty that had his name on signature blocks, too—and some that had *Juice's… Look at the formatting on these,* Sam thought to himself in disgust. *Why is this period here? Why this extra space after the dash? Did he even* check *the gridlines? Was that moonrise time* actually *updated for that day? God, an* extra-long dash*?! Take some pride in your craftsmanship, Juice…*

"Oh my god, look at these T&R charts!" Megan called out, looking through various spreadsheets. "So much green! That is *so* sexy…"

Sam looked over and acknowledged, "I mean… it *was* pretty impressive how greened up we were at all times back in those days…" Shaking his head, trying to forget the pride he felt as a Skeds O, Sam shrugged. "… But, I mean, you can fake that stuff all day long, it's just a matter of flying what you want and logging what you need."

"I see," Megan said with a subdued smile. "But still impressive…" She pulled Sam in close, "Even so—I'm glad a hunk like you isn't bogged down by stuff like this anymore… So thrilled to see you abandoning this silly job—burning hours, checking boxes, and spending years afloat—and living a normal life… maybe with me?" She gazed at him with those beautiful eyes.

"Hehe…" Sam chuckled shyly. "Normal life—that sounds… wonderful…"

She continued walking toward another room, which Sam could see contained a museum of 'retired, game-used' blue ink pens utilized by WYFMIFM, and the enclosed stories of each one. "Wow!" Megan called out from the other side of the chamber, "This is the pen he used to sign his final FITREP!"

Sam started following her, but stopped when he saw a framed schedule hanging up prominently on the wall, with a spotlight illuminating it brilliantly. He approached it and saw the golden plaque below: *THE PERFECT SCHEDULE – 3/28/2022.* Sam couldn't help but smile—he remembered that day well. He and Juice had actually knocked out that schedule together…

Every pilot flew at least once—most *twice*—that day. They had a perfectly-flowed game plan to allow for JABA to lead an LFE while still attending an E-6 rankings board between landing and the debrief. In a very controversial but ingenious move, Sam and Bobby had a DH fill for ODO so that a new guy could get a sunset day

FAM combined with night currency. There were over ten ground events, all scheduled accurately and sequentially—with no double-scheduling or event overlap, and even proper transition times included inherently.

Every dash and space was properly sized, the notes all correlated correctly, the emergencies of the day had been corrected for improper SHARP-spit-out characters, and the pesky additional lines from deleted -2's had all been wiped from the record. Every mission commander was labeled accurately, every guest player in italics, DCAST cross-referenced, and TAC freqs deconflicted.

Sam handed the first draft schedule to WYFMIFM, who gave it a lookover for about a minute, before confidently expressing, "Gents... am I the only one sensing this? Something feels... *different* about this schedule. A feeling many have alluded to... but few have truly understood. Let's just say... this could be *it*..." he said with foreboding raised eyebrows. He picked up his leather-bound clipboard and announced, "I'm taking it to Skipper right now, before his 8-hour meeting with the admiral."

Sam remembers sitting there nervously with Juice, knowing that this was their only shot at having a free evening to get a workout in, enjoy a stress-free steak dinner, and maybe even enjoy a drink or two or bizz at the O-club.

Juice tried to break the tension, "Do you think it could be a... *you know...?*"

"Shhh!" Sam said, his face serious. "Don't jinx it!"

After ten minutes of complete silence, WYFMIFM came back with a somber look on his face. "Sorry guys... but I'm gonna need you to make one change..."

Sam's heart sank. "Oh no... what?"

WYFMIFM shook his head and said, "Well... ground events—you forgot to add one..."

Juice cursed himself. "It must have been my fault; I was in charge of those. *Dammit...* what was it?"

Still looking glum, Kennedy explained, "Well, it's for *today's* schedule, actually... you two forgot to put yourselves at the O-Club this evening... for an *all-night beer die marathon!!!*" he exclaimed, flashing a huge smile before revealing a red ink signature. "A PERFECT schedule!" he yelled excitedly.

"No fucking way!" Sam grabbed his head in ecstatic disbelief. "No *fucking* way!"

The three of them cheered in hysterical elation in the Ops room, before running out to announce the news to the squadron. The Chippies were going wild, and within minutes received calls from other squadron skippers—and even CAG himself—reaching out to personally congratulate the Skeds Os and WYFMIFM on the incredible feat. Sam even—for one of the only times *ever*—embraced Juice with jubilation as they shared a rare warm moment together, Sam telling him, "You keep this kind of work up, Juice, and you're gonna be an all-time great."

"Hey, Nickels," Juice said seriously, with an appreciative look on his face, "No wingman gets home in this business without an experienced lead to guide them through the goo—I think you and I could accomplish some incredible things in this community."

Sam smiled as the two high-fived and yelled, "Let's fucking *go*!!"

Lost in thought, Rowland smiled to himself at the memory, reflecting on the trajectory that moment gave his life in the admin field of schedule writing. The amount of confidence he gained, the way he trusted himself to use his instincts to properly avoid crew rest busts without referencing SHARP, and how he helped every aircrew avoid bad deals—the schedule writing game had *changed* that day.

And he wasn't going to lie to himself—Juice *was* instrumental to The Perfect Schedule, catching a late DCAST range scheduling error and calling Fukuoka Control to correct it through the proper channels and save Low T's Level 3 checkride from losing 15 minutes of vul time. *Juice... his name is forever attached to that day – but rightfully so...*

"I still can't believe how much credit I unfairly got for that..."

Startled by the man's voice, Sam whipped around and saw him—for the first time in over five years—LCDR Charles "WYFMIFM" Kennedy, walking hunched over with a cane, garbed in a green Chippy robe—sporting his trademark boat mustache, his beautiful bald head, and—*sunglasses?* The retired Operations Officer smiled and explained, "I merely signed it off and gave it to the boss! That entire schedule was the work of you and Juice—you crafty little devils. I remember *feeling* your guys' power that day—that aura... that confidence – it was *incredible!*"

"WYFMIFM?" Sam called out, still shocked. "Is it really you?!"

"Indeed, Nickels. It's been too long since a visitor has been in these halls, especially one who was so integral to my career! It's great to see you—well, speaking figuratively, of course."

"Uhhh... *huh?*" Sam asked, confused. *Do I look* that *much different? That much weaker?*

WYFMIFM chuckled happily. "Ahh, yes, of course—you'd left before the accident happened!"

"Accident?!" Sam asked frantically. "WYFMIFM, what are you talking about?"

"Well, I was blinded, of course!" he responded with a playful smile.

"*Blinded?!*" Sam asked, still perplexed. "But... *how?!*"

"Ahh, don't you worry about that. The story would merely bore you! More importantly—how have *you* been? What brings you here? And for god's sake, Sam—get back in the gym, you emaciated twig!"

Sam felt a touch of shame. "But... how can you tell?"

"My god, it's so obvious! Your aura... it's so lacking—so *frail*... You can hear it in your voice. You have no confidence at all! I would venture to say you probably haven't lifted a weight in over three years! Please, Nickels—don't tell me you actually believed Ms. Fox was once again interested in somebody as pitifully fragile as Machine Gun Kelly..."

Feeling bashful, Sam blurted out, "Well... I mean, *no,* I didn't *actually* think she..." his voice trailed off, as he sighed and admitted, "My life has become even *more* pathetic than my bench, WYFMIFM..."

"Now *that* I *can* see!" Kennedy joked with a simple smile. "Do tell."

Sam divulged everything to his old OPSO—from the early excitement of his time with the Noddiks, to the terrible realities that set in over time as he realized his dream scenario was closer to a nightmare, and then, of course, everything involving OPERATION: PIGPEN with >SADCLAM< and FISTY. He went on about Juice taking over the Admin Olympics, the mysteries of Low T, and Sam's own recent meet up with JABA and CP—it was a long conversation that the reader need not rehash any more than they just did. WYFMIFM carried a stoic smile the entire time, showing no reaction to some of the heinous things Sam had admitted to doing. At the end, Sam finished with, "And, well, here I am now, trying to figure out—well... figure out what the hell I'm gonna do with my life after we save FISTY."

"After you save FISTY?" WYFMIFM asked in confusion. "You mean after you help the US win the Olympics, right?"

"The Olympics?" Sam echoed. "WYFMIFM—those are so pointless, right? I mean... what does it matter if the Noddiks win? That won't change anything—so *what* if they run a tighter ship than the US? It's just some dumb competition! It means nothing; it's just some silly award."

"Oh really? You mean... just like the softball tournament was a 'dumb competition?'" WYFMIFM retorted, lifting his free hand to give air quotes. "Just like the beer die tourney during BADMAN week 'meant nothing?' Just like the Kin Bukuro trophy—awarded for being the most athletic and prestigious squadron—was 'some silly award?' Nickels..." WYFMIFM said slyfully, "I seem to remember you taking those 'dumb' things pretty seriously. I remember us *all* doing so, in fact... And I remember you and everyone else being *pretty* dang excited when we took home that silly award..."

Remaining quiet at first, Sam eventually said, "Well... maybe so—but... I mean... that was so *different.* That was about teamwork; camaraderie building and all that stuff—that was about the squadron's pride..."

WYFMIFM exaggeratedly gasped and sarcastically said, "Ahhhh, yes, yes, yes, you're right. Apologies—I had forgotten that *that* Nickels was the one who cared about the success of the team... the bonding of friendships... the greater good of the whole. *That* Nickels was the one who wasn't infected with The Disease of Me..."

The Disease of Me? Why does everybody keep saying that? What the hell does that even mean?

"I may be blind, Nickels, but I haven't lost sight..." WYFMIFM said, his smile still present. "You know, when you left the squadron, I had a vision." He looked slightly up and to the side and explained, "Every year, I took POM leave in Venice Beach, California, and got a temporary guest pass at the original outdoor Gold's Gym. Every single evening, I'd hit chest—every time!—and crowd one of the benches for about an hour, taking long breaks while shuffling through songs on my playlist to get to a solid beat drop for the ensuing set. I had a fantasy, you see, that one time during a break, I'd look over and see *you* resting in between squat sets, looking swole and un-doubtedly sub-10% body fat, sharing the rack with some beautiful woman you train with and love. You wouldn't say anything to me, nor me to you—but we'd both know that you made it; that you were happy, continuing to chase daily improvement in the fitness arena... just as you'd always done in the aerial one. And now..." WYFMIFM looked back at Sam, slowly shaking his head, and lamented, "Now, it appears like that may be a vision I'll never see..."

Sam shut his eyes and bit his lips. "WYFMYM... that doesn't make any sense. You can't hit chest every single night—you're never going to recover..." He opened his eyes, saw WYFMIFM's frail chest, and started to understand... "And what about legs?" he continued. "If you never work them, they'll completely atrophy into nothingness!" Sam looked at WYFMIFM's cane, which the old OPSO relied heavily upon to stand his ground; it made all the sense in the world... "But Chucky!" he insisted, "You can't even see! How would you know if I was there?!"

For once, WYFMIFM gave a slight frown. "Because I *knew* that seeing you happy—a Good Dude living a Good Life—would be what I needed to regain 'visual!' But instead... you simply chased personal gain, not caring about anybody or anything else. Not my sight... not Juice's progression as a new guy... not the solidarity of the team—all you cared about was your status as the top administrative dog!"

The tension in the room was overwhelming. Sam looked down and shook his head. "The Chippies didn't need me, WYFMIFM. It was my time to move on, to rotate... A squadron can't survive if it's reliant on one person..."

"And that's what you don't get, Nickels," WYFMIFM said, still frowning. "We weren't *relying* on you for survival; we *enjoyed* your presence, we *grew* from your JO leadership, and we *thrived* because of your good dudesmanship. The Chippies will be just fine without you, me, Juice, or any other of those former Dambusters.

"But we weren't 'just fine,' back then, Nickels—we were *extraordinary*. And to think you gave that up..." Kennedy shook his head desolately, "Well, we all suffered as a result. Even *Juice,* mind you. If you think he was happy when you left, then you're even more blind than me."

"Juice? He *hated* me!" Sam responded.

"No—he *needed* you," WYFMIFM insisted. "If there was *one* person reliant on having you in the squadron, it was Bobby Ward. The thrill of the battle, the need for competition... you made him better, Nickels, believe it or not. You lit a *fire* under him. And when you left? Sure, he spun off fumes for a while, reforming our NATOPS knowledge for the better—but anybody could see it: Juice was running out of competitive steam, with no Nickels there to make him raise his level when he needed it. It's why we let him follow you to the Noddiks—for one, because we knew it would help him regain the motivation he needed, but also..." WYFMIFM paused for a moment, as he began getting choked up. "Because we believed it might bring you back to the United States Navy—to the *Chippies*—where you *belong...*"

Sam sat speechless, not sure what to say to the old OPSO who had taught him so much about Microsoft Word formatting, deployment readiness logging, and magnetic puck flowing...

His dire frown turning to a slight smile, WYFMIFM began speaking with wonder in his eyes and marvel in his voice. "You and Juice... you two were like JP-5 and fire—*explosive... volatile...*" He turned his blind eyes to The Perfect Schedule display. "But harnessed strategically... you were a duo that created levels of propulsion exceeding anything two F414-GE-400s in full afterburner could ever produce..."

"But WYFMIFM," Sam whined, "I was so much happier *before* Juice joined the squadron... those were the days I was truly my best—when I felt like the Good Dude everybody said I was. That was my *peak.*"

WYFMIFM shook his head. "Because you *thought* you had reached the top, Samuel. You *thought* The Innocent Climb was over. You were ready to saunter down the mountain—when in reality? The peak of good dudedom was *far* above what you'd already accomplished. And believe it or not, Juice was put in this squadron to help you *reach* that peak."

The Innocent Climb? Sam thought. *What is he talking about?!* "WYFMIFM, I—"

"Nickels," Kennedy asked, curious but forcefully, "why did you stop wearing That Patch?"

Silence filled the room. Sam turned to his right shoulder, where he still had nothing worn—as had been the case since he made the decision to leave the Chippies. He shook his head in dismay. "Those days are gone, WYFMIFM... I gave That Patch up; left it behind. Frankly, I'm not sure I even *deserved* to wear it anymore—that or *any* Dambuster patches from my Good Dude days of past. Some mistakes you just can't atone for..." he lamented, pointing to the Noddik HODS chest patch he had on.

Kennedy took his most serious inflection yet as he explained, "Nickels... That Patch represented everything you guys as JOPA—hell, what *we* as *Dambusters*—were all about. We wore That Patch with Chippy pride and, in effect, conducted ourselves Chippy style—so that, as Alexander the Great once said, 'All men wished to be our friends, and all *feared* to be our enemies.' Those were our Dambuster glory days of old, yes—but there's also unfinished business ahead..." He eased into a soft smile. "*You* may believe it's gone forever... but I believe the mountain is still there to be climbed—and when you finally climb it? Mark my words—That Patch will be waiting for you," he added with hope. "You *need* to compete in these Olympics, Nickels. Show that you still hold that drive from your life of admin obsession, your days of being a Chippy, and your reputation as a professional Good Dude. Bring glory to your former air wing... your former country... your former *best friends.* Show that your best days of leadership *are* still ahead of you—and that they have nothing to do with the Noddik Empire. It is your destiny, Nickels, to lead The Innocent Climb once again, and to let Juice bring the best out of you, as you did him. Otherwise? *Dimes* will live on forever..."

Sam turned and looked at The Perfect Schedule. His signature—*and* Juice's—both above the Schedules Officer's approval line. *What if it's* not *too late for redemption? What if I could be a Good Dude again? What if I finally faced Juice instead of running forever?*

What if 'Nickels' truly could be saved...?

Sam closed his eyes, thought to himself, then turned back to ask, "WYFMIFM, what is—"

But the blind old man was gone, nowhere to be seen. Sam ran up the hall, looking for his former operations mentor—but only found Megan Fox, still gawking in awe at the plaque of a combat schedule that WYFMIFM had approved, which contained an LGTR employment that killed a madman terrorist threatening to destroy the world when it was lazed into his moving vehicle for a headshot.

Sam looked around one last time, to no avail—and then saw it on the ground: a fresh, Velcro-backed VFA-195 chest patch. He picked it up, admiring it. *I won't let you down, WYFMIFM.* He grabbed his chest, ripped off his NIRD Katsopolis patch, tossed it away dramatically, and slapped on the Chippy logo—and instantly, he experienced a sense of power, pride, and confidence he hadn't felt in decades.

As Sam started walking downstairs, Megan called out after him, "Where are you going?"

Sam cracked his knuckles and stopped, grabbing the plate of steaks as he looked back and responded confidently, "I'm leaving to be where I belong—somewhere I've *always* belonged."

"But I thought you were done with these stupid aviation games?" she whined. "I thought you were going to be my new boyfriend?!"

Sam chuckled and started walking away. "I'm not interested in being your latest bloody valentine, babe."

Angry and confused, she asked, "Then what the *hell* are you going to do?"

Sam looked at the Dambuster patch on his chest, then turned back at the seductress and coolly said, "I'm gonna be a Chippy, ho."

11

Roll Call

Skipper took a deep breath, bowed the bridge of his nose into the webbing between his thumb and index finger, then looked up at Nickels and said, "No."

"No?!" Sam mimicked out of reaction.

"No," Skipper repeated, just as firmly as the first time.

A silence lined the air between the two as Sam fidgeted a bit in his seat. He initially dreaded this conversation because of the awkwardness; but now, he felt extreme unease at what Skipper was implicating in his response.

Skipper simply stared at Sam, his eyes heavy with veteran experience and anguish; war-torn years of ground jobbing, trash sorting, and annual audiogram button-pushing. But behind those eyes was also a fierce conviction – a conviction that had Nickels on his proverbial heels.

Unable to take the silence any longer, Sam finally spoke up, "What do you mean, 'no?'" He raised his arms slightly in a plea, "Skipper, look at everything I've done for this squadron in my three years here: I completed the entire Above-Average Administrative syllabus within my first ten months – I was leading Level 2 AAA candidates in taxi fams and teaching preflight briefing labs during that fall cruise! The Chippies had perfect Man Overboard attendance during my reign as MOB Coordinator. We were the top-scoring squadron in Cyber Security Awareness Challenge and Operational Risk Management NKOs! Hell, I even wrote and directed the entire 'AT2 Potter and the Admiral's Anxiety' performance on mental health hygiene for last year's safety standdown!" Sam was nearly shaking with frustration. "All this, and you're really going to give me the #2 EP?!"

Skipper clasped his fingers together, looking pensive, and then broke his silence with one word: "Yes."

In near-paralysis with shock, Sam stood there dumbfounded – now growing angry – as he scoffed and said, "I cannot believe this; I cannot believe you're seriously going to screw – "

"What happened to you, Nickels?" Skipper interrupted. "What happened to the Good Dude who was the most selfless and motivated junior officer I'd ever seen in my life? The man who would've taken an SDO bullet on an abbreviated crew rest for any pilot in this squadron – nay, air wing! The guy who found his greatest joy in not just kicking ass in admin, but teaching others to take names in the same? The pilot whom I would've trusted with my life to get a schedule cranked out by 1500... to absolutely slay a FOD walkdown with his eyes on the deck and hands out of his pockets with talking to a minimum... to come to work clean shaven, not a trace of a shadow on that lean, chiseled jaw, even if it meant shaving again during lunch break?" Skipper's stare pierced Sam's eyes as he asked even more forcefully, with a sliver of emotion, "What happened to that Good Dude?"

Sam looked away from the gaze, taking in stinging significance behind Skipper's words. He'd been tasked to write the previous day's schedule and was sent home from work at 2000 with the most pitiful incomplete shell given to the OPSO, who mercifully tapped him out. He looked down at his pockets – every single one unzipped, in a dreadful display of unprofessionalism. He ran his hand over his chin – he could feel prickly hairs all over his puffy cheeks, bloated from the previous night of drinking Smirnoff Ices after work, devouring Taco Bell for dinner, and binging on raw cookie dough for dessert. He said nothing, yet he wasn't sure if it was out of anger... or embarrassment.

"You're not hungry for success anymore, are you, Nickels?" Skipper asked, a bit more pointed now. "That progression-driven Nickels I knew – we all knew? He's just a Chippy hero of yesteryear, isn't he?"

Nickels, staring at his unpolished boots, refused to respond.

"We've got a new champion of the people, now, don't we?" Skipper asked, knowing he was striking Nickels in the heart by referring to his arch-nemesis in the squadron. "And you were in charge of training him..." He shook his head and frowned, "But you wouldn't teach the boy a thing, would you? You made him learn on his own – made him learn out of spite, vice the cohesive support Chippies are known for. And now, that negligence is your undoing..."

Sam sat quietly, refusing to accept this shameful truth. Finally raising his head and returning Skipper's eye contact – and doing everything he could to hold his composure – he spoke fervently, "Skipper... I'm asking you – no, begging you: I need this number one EP. It..." Sam thought of his agreement with the Noddik Empire – the $500 million contract that was contingent on him receiving the number one EP on the most recent FITREP cycle. But Skipper couldn't know that. If he did, Sam knew, he would never agree to this. Desperate for more ammunition to his reasoning, he quickly lied, "It means everything to my ability to rush The Patch!" He felt disturbed as he said it – both by his dishonesty and this hypothetical career path. A Patch... what a pointless endeavor. Those guys disgraced what it meant to be a NATOPS-qualified aviator, taking pride in the brevity of the admin portion of briefs.

Skipper unfolded his arms and bent his head down, rubbing his forehead in confusion. "A Patch?" he asked with disbelief. "Nickels... since when have you wanted to chase something like that? Isn't that more up Low T's alley?"

Determined to reinforce his story, Sam was fortunately well-versed in the art of adding fluff to discussions, thanks to all of his admin briefing reps and prowess. He took a deep breath and said matter-of-factly, "Yes, Skipper — why wouldn't I? It's the next great challenge to face in my career! I've already shown myself to be an expert at the administrative phases of flight — imagine how much more utilitarian and lethal I could be if I excelled at the highest level of conduct, too! That same dedication to standard jet startups could be used to conduct proper fight check-ins with perfect environmental reporting, flawless knock-it-off cadences, and picturesque G-warms! I'd be a tactical machine after TOPGUN!" he added with feigned excitement — because truly, in his heart, the thought of rehearsing pointless conduct as much as game-changing admin sickened him.

"Nickels..." Skipper said with a suspicious look on his face. "Those aren't even conduct portions — those are tac-admin..." He winced and asked, "Are you sure you're ok?"

"Heh, yeah..." Sam laughed nervously. "Silly me — but you see what I mean!" he insisted. "Imagine how good learning the ways of TOPGUN would be for my personal progression! And..." he paused a moment, "Wouldn't it be fitting for a guy like me to have a Patch — right alongside all those Good Dude Awards?"

"And what about Low T?" Skipper asked. "He's been chasing The Patch since his early days as a JO, when he showed up on check-in day ready to give an impromptu High Aspect BFM lab. We're talking about the man who once even found a way to study the latest tac recs draft — before release! — for his Level 3 checkride, and executed them better than the N7 bros who wrote them!" He paused, then asked again, "So, what about Low T? I can only send one of you to The Course — one top EP. Low T has been dreaming of The Patch and rushing SFSWL so adamantly — and you want to steal his dream, so that you can add yet another merit badge to your collection? Is that really a Good Dude thing to do?"

Nickels swallowed, buying time in contemplation of where to take this lie next. "I know it's a tough decision, Skipper... but..." he closed his eyes and thought of the money, the fame, the recognition he'd get from training the Noddiks... "But I think I deserve this, given everything I've done. Maybe I haven't been the most shit hot lately," the words stung, as he knew they were sugarcoating the pitiful truth, "but it's about the whole profile of work; not just your latest effort..."

Skipper chuckled humorlessly. "I think every Paddles, Patch wearer, and reasonable man would firmly disagree with that..." He took a deep breath, and sighed. "Ok. I'll tell you what, Nickels..." He wasn't smiling, and certainly didn't seem happy. "I want you to write me an official FITREP statement of dispute, and I want this statement to explain not just that you think you deserve the number one EP, but that you are knowingly obliterating the dreams of your squadronmates by getting it. I want you to express that you don't care about what happens to their careers because yours is most important; that none of those guys matter to you — Low

T, JABA, CP, >SADCLAM<, the FNGs... even **Juice**—*and I'm sure that last one shouldn't be too hard to say,"* he added without a grin of any sort. *"That all those guys' well-beings are irrelevant to your 'newfound aspirations' for a TOPGUN Patch; because at the end of the day, it's all about Nickels — and you've got to take care of number one first. That's what this industry's all about, right?"* Skipper asked sarcastically. *"Write me that statement, and you'll have that number one EP. Don't worry, I won't share it with the other JOPA — but I need to know, for my own due diligence, that you've officially given up on the team — and are only focused on your Own Fucking Program — before I accept this."*

It shook Nickels to hear that last part — Skipper **never** *swore.*

Sam looked Skipper in the eye and debated internally for what felt like an eternity. He didn't want to be thought of so harshly... he didn't consider what he was doing to be such a betrayal... he didn't want to hurt Low T this way — but at the end of the day... Shit. I've done **enough** for this squadron. It *is* time to get my due, *he convinced himself. He extended his arm to shake Skipper's hand, but the O-5 simply looked at it, closed his eyes, and sadly shook his head.* "Understood," *he said.* "Have it in my box by close of business tomorrow."

"Yes, sir," Sam said solemnly, as he stood up to exit the office.

"And Nickels?" Skipper called out.

Sam turned around, "Yes, sir?"

"Don't hold back," he said with a serious look on his face. "If you're delivering the death blow to Low T's dreams and the JOPA's unity, you'd better make sure I don't question whether or not you want to pull the trigger. I want names, I want specific details, I want confessions, and I want every bit of that suppressed hate — festering within that 'Good Dude' soul of yours — unleashed in that statement. This way, you can liberate yourself from this awful organization that's caused you — like so many other poor, tortured souls in this world — to become infected with The Disease of Me. Don't hold back, Lieutenant Rowland."

Sam paused, a bit shaken — incensed — from what he was hearing from his skipper. Liberate? Did he know the truth about my plans? Fuck it—it won't matter in a few months... it's his own fault if he lets me leave at this point... *He swallowed, nodded curtly, and coldly stated,* "Understood, sir. I'll leave zero doubt to the conviction in my decision..."

~

"Dimes, what's your deal," CP asked pointedly. "Why are you spouting off all this nonsense about WYFMIFM? It wasn't him."

"It *was*, though!" Sam insisted to his friends, "I saw him with my own eyes! He even left this patch for me!" He pointed to his newly donned VFA-195 chest patch.

"You could've gotten that patch anywhere," CP said matter-of-factly. He raised his eyebrows and asked, "Are you sure you didn't forget to throw that one away when you dumped the rest of your life and friendships in the trash?"

Ignoring the biting comment, Sam repeated, "I *know* it was him! He told me all about the squadron after I left, about how Juice lost his edge—just like I did..." Sam trailed off, before continuing, "We even talked about The Perfect Schedule – he remembered signing it!"

CP groaned. "Oh, god, who *hasn't* heard about that? It's a naval aviation legend, but geeze, get over yourself, Dimes. Yes, it was impressive, but you can't rest on those laurels forever. Anybody who's ever opened a T6 NATOPS knows about 3/28/22," he referred to it familiarly. "Could it have been some *other* bald guy WYFMIFM-lookalike lurking around, perhaps?" he suggested, skeptical of Sam's story.

"Like Bambi Dickens?" Sam asked.

CP scoffed. "Oh please... that is an *insult* to Bambi's muscle mass. *Really*, Sam?!"

Pausing and thinking, Sam looked confused. "No, it was definitely him..." He looked at his friends and asked in frustration, "Guys, why is this so hard to believe?"

>SADCLAM< shook his head. "*Because*, Sam—it's literally impossible. You weren't there when it happened, but... it was tough on everybody. We don't like to talk about it; and the least we can do is respect this man's entrepreneurial masterpiece cruise ship and honor his name—the name of the man who died celebrating *yours*..."

"Died?!" Sam asked, dumbfounded. "CLAM... what are you *talking* about?"

>SADCLAM< bit his lip, looking somber and uncomfortable with the question. He looked over at CP, who was sweaty, with his hair tussled and lipstick all over his neck—a glossy set of smooches that fit the size of a petite Latina woman's lips. CP looked at JABA, who shrugged, looking solemn, his hair wild like that of a mad scientist at work. And the professional tycooner looked to FISTY, who remained vegetated on the bed, in dire need of sunlight, animal fats, and Vitamin TB12.

The four men sat in room 195 aboard Fat Chucky's Cruise Ship, dining on their ribeyes, deciding which route to take next to regain control of their lives. JABA had received news of his theme park going out of business due to Robo-Hinge's micromanagement. CP was alerted to his lowest-of-T gyms—one that, in comparison, made Planet Fitness appear to be a bunch of jacked, alpha, panty-dropping bodybuilders. >SADCLAM< was still itching to serve his country, but still feeling lost and disordered since his overdosage of XANs, in dire need of motivation to fight; in need of a *purpose*. And FISTY... JABA was still at work coding the ultimate Tom Brady scenario to bring him back to life, but with every passing moment, it seemed less and less likely that the GOAT tactician would ever recapture his heroic identity.

Sam seemed to be the most excitable one at the moment, still feverish at the interaction he could've sworn he had with WYFMIFM. When the men refused to divulge more information, Sam continued telling them all about how WYFMIFM approached him and discussed his vision at Venice Beach's Gold's Gym, how the former

OPSO helped him realize his journey wasn't over yet, and how Sam turned down Megan Fox's advances to go back to the career he yearned for.

"Dimes, a lot of guys come up with some wild excuses for striking out with women—but this is by far the most preposterous I've *ever* heard in my life," CP admonished him. "And now you want to return to the very force you *betrayed*—all because you were *so* deprived of sun, steak, squats, and sleep, that you hallucinated and *think* you were inspired by this noble-yet-deceased man?"

"Guys, I *swear!*" Sam said, his hands still shaking. "Sure, he was blind as a bat—but he still knew it was me!"

"Sam, stop..." >SADCLAM<'s tone was rife with agony. "You're making this painful for all of us. There's no need to poke fun at his blindness, too..."

Sam raised his hands, "Guys, I am seriously *so* low-SA right now—please, tell me what happened!"

>SADCLAM< looked around, his jaw clenched, and finally said, "... Alright. I thought I'd never have to relive this memory again, but... I suppose you deserve to hear the truth." He sighed. "When this party yacht company was started, we all supported WYFMIFM, of course. His time in the Navy was done, as was many of ours. In the ship's grand debut, he invited us all here for the inaugural celebration. It was a phenomenal rager, and Tom Cruise—dressed up in his Maverick uniform—actually cut the ribbon to initiate the festivities. And, in fact, *since* that opening day, I don't think the party ever ended! But..." CLAM looked down, his voice beginning to fill with emotion... "That evening, WYFMIFM brought the former Dambusters atop the yacht for a Chippy reunion." CLAM looked in the distance—a thousand-yard stare—and said, sadly and ominously, "It was such a beautiful sunset... *too* beautiful..."

He cranked his neck down and closed his eyes, biting his lip again before continuing, "We were all there, even Skipper and XO. Well—all but *you*..." he gestured slightly toward Sam. "WYFMIFM was so sad that you weren't with us... he mentioned how much he loved having you in the squadron... how you were just like a brother to him. He raved about the Good Dude you were, the incredible camaraderie you brought to the Dambusters, and how naval aviation hadn't been the same without you—and would *never* be. After shedding a few tears, he proposed a toast to you, and to your epic return to glory—something he, deep in his heart, truly believed would happen. The Lorax poured us each a glass of WYFMIFM's trademark 'Chippy Champagne'—essentially just Andre's champagne with green food dye coloring—and we all raised our glasses to you. As we did, though..." CLAM began to choke up a bit, tears forming in his eyes as he stopped to collect himself. After a few moments of visible pain, CLAM steeled himself and pushed on with the story. "As we did, WYFMIFM yelled, 'To one day saving Nickels!' and looked up at his champagne glass. Unfortunately, as he did... the evening sunlight caught the glass in the most incomprehensible way, as it not only magnified the rays, but reflected them straight into WYFMIFM's corneas—*blinding him...*"

JABA shook his head quietly, clearly fighting back tears of his own.

CLAM continued, "He dropped his glass in a frenzied panic, and stuck out his arms to feel for *some* type of reference point. He kept calling out, 'I'm blind! I'm blind!' We tried to talk him on with directions, clock codes, distances, and even degrees of elevation—but it wasn't enough..." >SADCLAM< took a deep breath. "One of the FNGs accidentally called out 'I'm at your *left* 3'oclock, 10 feet, level!'—but, as you know, words *mean* things... and the clock code/direction confusion was too much. WYFMIFM moved unpredictably and wildly to the *left*... and fell overboard..."

CP clenched his jaw; the emotion visible on every Chippy in the room.

"Oh my god..." Sam said, his jaw agape as he covered it with his hands. "Did you call for a man overboard?!"

"*Of course* we did," CLAM said adamantly. "But all the clueless celebrities on board... nobody knew their procedures. We had essentially the entire yacht being called to report to the deckhouse in hangar bay 2 with their ID cards, but nobody showed. After time six-zero-plus-zero-zero, JABA got on the intercom and regrettably secured the man overboard, assuring that we'd have to run several drills until we got this right, and vowing that we'd find the OPSO legend's body. And yet... the drills were never completed within satisfactory standards... and the body was never found..."

"Jesus..." Sam said softly, in disbelief. *But... he was there—blinded, but alive...*

"Yeah..." >SADCLAM< reacted. "So... I'm not sure what you saw up there, Sam, but..."

The former Dambusters stood there quietly, as Sam tried to digest what was going on. *The inspiration... was it real? Am I just making this up? Am I just* looking *for a reason to do what I know is right in my heart—to finally chase the fight that I know I'm destined for?*

Is any of this real?

Sam jumped as he heard WYFMIFM's voice in his head.

All the LARPing we do, the ground jobs we assign, the quals we get, the FITREPs we write—are they real? How about the white cards and red monkeys we liberally utilize, as if these failed missions wouldn't be a monumental shift in the landscape of a real-life war? Nickels, think about it... ASM signoffs, MPA inspections, blue water certifications, passing SFARP, INSURV, fire-fighting qualifications... it's all made up! This whole job is full of artistic liberty bullshit!

But haven't you realized? It's also filled with shit we love; *shit we can't get enough of; shit we secretly pine for! Because you know what's* real? *When you're taking off behind a no-*

tional sweep element, preparing to drop some major-dong sim ordnance over some water simulating a battle zone, and you look to your beam and slightly aft, seeing your fellow bro fighting for his life to simply get in proper formation for this simulated life-changing pickle... Now that's real shit, Samuel. Striving to be the best we can as aviators; as brothers and sisters in arms; as Good Dudes in squadrons. It doesn't matter what's fake, what's simulated, or what we think is driving us. At the end of the day, it all comes from within — the desire to contribute to the greater good — to The Innocent Climb. That's what it's all about.

Sam looked up to the heavens, where WYFMIFM was surely writing schedules for GodOps, and thought, *Shit... you're right, Charles. You're fucking* right.

"Guys..." Sam said, a bit of confidence reverberating from his voice. "Regardless of what I saw — what I *think* I saw —" *What I* know *I saw...* he thought to himself, "does it really matter? Does it change the truth that *I know* deep in my heart? The Innocent Climb isn't finished," he said, still not understanding the term entirely, but trusting that it would make sense. "Guys... my time in the Chippies — my *duty* to the Chippies? It's not done yet. In fact, it's not done for *any* of us."

"What are you talking about, Sam?" CP asked, genuinely curious.

"CP, isn't it obvious?" Sam was astounded at how easily the conviction came to him. "We need to return to our roots; we need to fight alongside the USS Ship; we need to compete for these Olympics — and we need to *win* them."

"Look at how we've all been brought together one way or another — FISTY's need for a JOPA savior after traumatic film watching... CLAM's search for clarity and a cause after his brainwashing from OPERATION: PIGPEN... JABA's love and longing for a return to the boat, *so* much so that he created his own *theme park* of one... CP, don't act like you don't miss some of the shit from this job in lieu of the corporate bullshit you hate so much — is that how you want to spend the rest of your life? Working with jabronis in the gym who want lean, ripped physiques with long, healthy lives — and yet are either way too juiced out of their minds, or way too afraid to squat and deadlift? Or would you rather work in a community that puts their top effort into every single flight — the same way you put your top focus into every single rep — pushing for unheralded tactical execution the way you push for new PRs? A band of brothers who aren't afraid to get into the weeds of TOPGUN and debriefing tapes, knowing it's necessary suffering to achieve the best end product? And as for the gym? Well... CP, the gym life is obviously mission-critical. But the gym just *amplifies* the true calling we have: the calling to use our bodies, minds, and dedication in order to flex and perform on the grandest stage of all — the *arena*. Because at the end of the day, that's what we all are: *Men in the arena.* And *in* that arena is where you get the true passion, satisfaction, and fulfillment from life."

"Nickels..." JABA said, "That was incredible. And dammit... you're *right!* The boat... naval aviation... it's where I belong. I may not be able to get the full career I want, and I may not get that illustrious DH billet—but dammit, I've got at least *one* more fight in me! Count me in!"

"Fuck yeah!" >SADCLAM< yelled with enthusiasm. "Count me in, too, brother! The Navy, flying, serving my country... it's what I'm all about; it's the purpose I *need*—and I'm not gonna let you guys fight in those Olympics without me giving every ounce of effort in my heart, *right* by your side. This whole thing is a game—but it's a game we're gonna fucking *win*. The rest of life will always be there—the game has to end someday—but I'm just not ready to call it a career *quite* yet! Let's fucking *go*, baby!"

Sam looked at CP. "Andrew? You've been living your 'dream life'—dating and marrying all these models, opening your own gym, making loads of money—yet... you're *unfulfilled,* aren't you? Your life is missing something, *isn't it?* The camaraderie... the beauties at Ronnie's... the *thrill* of the job..." With a raised finger and an adamant tone, Sam urged, "Tell me you'll join us for one last fight, CP. Tell me that for at least *one* more evolution, the Navy can whip out its Clown Penis on the Noddiks..."

CP gave Sam a long look, the room waiting in silence—before he finally spoke, shaking his head, "Dimes... consider yourself dead to me..."

He turned and began walking out of the room, as Sam's shoulders slumped down and the three looked at each other sadly.

But—as his hand grabbed the doorknob, CP stopped, turned around, and said, with a wide grin on his face, "*Nickels*?! It's about damn time you came back. It's me, Andrew Preul, callsign Clown Penis."

"YES!" CLAM shouted out with a fist pump, as Sam and CP embraced. JABA beamed, nearly a tear in his eye, seeing his two friends finally fully reconciled.

After a bro hug even more monumental than their hug-it-out-bitch, the two separated as CP looked at his watch. "Now, unless my hack is off? I think it's about time we get the Chevro-legs warmed up, and get ready to go hydraulic on these Noddik motherfuckers—the only way we know how: with Chippy pride... Chippy style..."

The four men raised their fists and yelled, "CHIPPY HO!"

~

Loaded T opened Dr. Suabedissen's door without knocking, sending the programmer into a jolt, as he immediately minimized his laptop screen.

"LT Camilli! I uh... didn't know you were coming by!" Suabedissen sounded out of breath, as if his heart rate had been elevated, and there was a box of tissues next to his desk.

Loaded T recoiled in shock. "What the fuck was that?"

"Uhh... nothing!" the doctor yelled. "I was uhh... just looking at some porn, hehe. You know—penetration and coitus... alpha stuff!"

"Yeah, right, bitch," Kyle rolled his eyes. "*Please* don't tell me you were watching what I think you were..." He walked up to Suabedissen's desk and grabbed the computer mouse.

"Hey!" Suabedissen whined. "What are you doing? Stop!"

Ignoring the fragile dweeb, and easily overpowering his grasps, Kyle opened the browser window and saw exactly what the doctor was watching—and it was, in fact, *not* porn...

Some type of ceremony was taking place on the screen, with plenty of avatars in attendance; every character containing a user name placarded above them. From the looks of it, a marriage was happening between some female monster-looking thing called MyLittlePonyXoXo88, and a knight in flaming armor called WizardOfAzkaban1337. Kyle looked at the screen in disgust, and then glared at Suabedissen with disdain and second-hand-embarrassment.

"What?!" Suabedissen blurted out defensively. "This is a monumental wedlock in the D&D community! MyLittlePony is the queen of the Ogres, and WizardOfAz is the prince of the Fire Knights, i.e., the *heir to the Hell Warrior throne!* Do you realize what this will do for alliances in the southern land of Gladia? The *entire* power balance will shift! Plus, MyLittlePony and I go *way* back—we used to hunt orcs and unicorn mammoths together! And sure, while I'll admit I *may* have had a little crush on her for a while," he chuckled nervously, "Now? She's, you know, like a good friend to me. I uhhh... friend-zoned *her*, in fact! We still go on raids together sometimes—I lead them, of course. You know, she was actually there in the quest when I acquired the Ancient Shield of Nefaria—"

"Karl, shut the fuck up!" Loaded T yelled, his vascular neck nearly popping blood vessels in anger. He could see water in Suabedissen's eyes as the doctor dabbed them with Kleenex. The man had literally been crying at the still-ongoing virtual wedding nuptials. Kyle slammed the computer shut. "What's the deal with Phase 1, douchebag? I've been lifting for the past few hours, so I've missed it."

Suabedissen cowered below the rippling, freshly pumped muscles of Loaded T. "Arms day, I'm guessing, hehe?" a feeble, beta chuckle again emerging from the doctor.

Kyle said nothing, just glared.

"Right... ahh... let me check my email... *please be there, please be there...*" he whispered under his breath. As if offering mercy from the gods, his inbox refresh showed a new email from Bobby Ward. "Aha! An email from Juice! Let's see..." he scanned the message frantically, looking for critical info. Shortly after, a grin came to his lips, and he announced, "Phase 1 is complete, and it sounds like it was a rout! No surprise, given our Noddik commitment to excellence!" He raised his hand for a fist bump to Kyle, who said and did nothing, refusing to acknowledge the doctor as he read the email himself.

From the words of Juice, it was indeed a completely one-sided affair. The USS Ship had over 30 invalid trash bags turned over to the Waste Management department on the first day, with plenty of hard plastic cereal containers being tossed with their soft plastic covers still attached. During the GQ drill, multiple pilots were seen walking out and about—presumably to unimportant things like large force exercise briefs in CVIC or their jets on the flight deck—which added up hits quickly. And most heinous of all, a sailor had been caught running on the flight deck to prevent another sailor from crossing the LA during a landing—unfortunately, *while* the Big XO was speaking, which demonstrated no respect for authority.

The Phase 1 score tally between the two nations was not even *close* after the litany of blatant USS Ship violations—especially in comparison to the Noddik's performance, which was *flawless*: Not a single miss-sorted piece of plastic or combustible trash by the robot organizers. No flight suits nor pillowcases in the self-serve laundry, with zero reports of missing or damp articles of clothing from *ship's* laundry. And in an unheard-of level of sailor service, disbursing managed to stay open for *over* two hours during the work day, the ship's entire connectivity network received *zero* trouble tickets, and *every* bathroom inexplicably remained in an 'up' status. It was an incredibly impressive display of carrier administrative excellence, as the Noddiks brought their A-game for the big event.

"Good... now we can get to the real stuff," Loaded T said, still with not a fuck-to-give evident in his voice.

"The boat landing contest!" Suabedissen said, shaking his fists with exaggerated excitement, trying to win the good graces of his jacked teammate.

"Yeah, no shit," Kyle deadpanned, refusing to be appeased by the beta simp. "Tell Juice I'm walking for my flight... *after* a quick arm sesh and steak."

"But—but LT Camilli! They're gonna want you up there sooner than—"

"Shut the fuck up, you pussy-ass bitch!" Loaded T grabbed the doctor by the labcoat collar and shouted, "I will fire that jet up when I am goddamn good and ready! You got that?!"

"Y—yes sir..." the doctor stammered, cowering once again below Kyle's frightening display of alpha mass.

"Good..." he let go of the doctor, still staring at him menacingly. "Now, go ahead and watch the rest of your stupid-ass little wedding, you weak-ass piece of shit..."

Loaded T stomped out of the room aggressively, while the doctor watched the wedding with fury. It wasn't fury at his inability to pacify the unruly demands and attitude of his Olympics teammate. It wasn't fury at being called more combinations of a demeaning word followed by 'ass' than he ever had in his life. It wasn't even fury at being caught crying at the monumental matrimonies between the fire knight and his former mammoth-slaying partner.

Karl stared at the computer screen—*glared* at it. He grabbed a tissue and wiped his eyes again. The wedding was complete; the marriage was official, and waiting to be cyberly consummated. The fury raged within him—the fury of a man's heart *shattered*...

As much as he tried to deny it, Doctor Suabedissen still had strong feelings—a strong *love*—for MyLittlePonyXoXo88...

~

In his stateroom, Juice buried his head in his hands, wanting to gouge his eyes out, as he grew exceedingly impatient with the dictatorial tone and command of Robo-Hinge.

"THIS IS UNSAT," the robotic DH blared through the phone. "UNACCEPTABLE, WARD. YOU ARE NOT MEETING MY EXPECTATIONS AS HEAD OF NODDIK OPERATIONS. THERE IS ZERO EXCUSE FOR WHY OUR GOVERNMENT CREDIT CARDS ARE BEING DECLINED AT THE STRIP CLUB. YOU *SHALL* GET THIS FIXED THROUGH ADMIN, AM I CLEAR?"

"... Yes, sir..." Juice said, despair in his voice—the despair of an ass-blasted JO. "But just so you know, for the Admin Olympics—remember? Sort of our top priority right now?" he added somewhat snarkily. "Phase 2 will be starting within a couple of hours, and I need to walk soon for—"

"NEGATIVE!" Robo-Hinge interrupted him. "OUR EMPIRE TRAVEL CARDS ARE PRIORITY ONE. YOU *SHALL* GET THAT SOLVED BEFORE ANY OTHER DUTIES. IF YOU ARE NOT DONE BEFORE WALK TIME, THEN NEODD SWEVEN WILL TAKE YOUR PLACE." He raised his robotic, angry tone and added, "BECAUSE OF *YOUR* UNSATISFACTORY INCOMPETENCE, THIS VACATION FOR MYSELF AND MY HODS IS BEING RUINED. WE ARE ALLOWABLE LEVEL OF DEBAUCHERY: HIGH, WITH COMMANDER'S INTENT BEING: ALCOHOL REQUIRED, BOOBS DESIRED. DO YOU UNDERSTAND?"

"NEODD SWEVEN?!" Juice burst out. "Are you kidding me?! You can't just do that! I need to be out there bagging traps—the Padroids don't have any clue what—"

"NEGATIVE! YOU NEED TO BE SOLVING THE PROBLEM THAT *YOUR* DEPARTMENT CREATED!"

Juice groaned, and then asked with irritation, "Robo-Hinge... how do you *possibly* think I can get SATO on the phone to unblock your card, so that you can subsequently use it for *drinks* and *withdrawing cash* at a *strip club?*"

"FIGURE IT OUT. BE AN ATHLETE. BRING SOLUTIONS, NOT PROBLEMS. TRACK YOUR OWN QUALS. WRITE GOOD GRIPES AND DO ASAPS. UNDERSTAND?"

In prime DH fashion, when no solution was present, Robo-Hinge was programmed to fall back on cliched sayings and slogans as if they were not artificial leadership fluff, but sage advice of wisdom.

"Roger that..." Juice responded flatly.

"ROGER THAT... SIR?"

Juice sighed. "Roger that, sir."

Robo-Hinge hung up without another word.

Juice clenched his fists and laid down on his bed, wanting to scream in frustration. This sucked... when the hell did bullshit like this become part of the job? He was here for one reason: to show up Nickels in the Olympics by claiming victory for the Noddiks. But now, Nickels was nowhere to be found; and to make matters worse, Juice was going to be spending his time taking care of ground job bullshit—no, *tasking* bullshit—instead of clinching the battle airborne. 'This was the whole fucking point...' he thought to himself. His reason for Noddik employment... his path to vengeance... his purpose of *existence*...

He grabbed his pillow, dug his face into it, and released an exasperated shout of despair. "*Fuck*, dude. What the *FUCK!*"

His phone started ringing. "LT Ward," he answered.

"Yo Juice, it's NEODD. I hear I'm in for Phase 2."

Juice rolled his eyes and groaned to himself. 'Of *course* Robo-Hinge had already skipped lines of communication to hand out tasking and pull the puppet strings... fucking hinge,' he swore internally. 'You know what?! *Fuck* that...'

"Uhhh, Juice-man? You there, bro?" NEODD asked, in response to the silence.

"Yeah, I'm here." Juice finally spoke, annoyance prevalent. "And 'in for me?' The *fuck* you are. That's a big negative, SWEVEN."

"Um..." NEODD trailed off, "Well... that new DH called me and said—"

"Hey—shut up." Juice interrupted. "Shut up, and listen to what I say—and listen good: *I'm* the department head now. You're gonna sit your ass on the platform, NEODD—and you're gonna sit there *quietly*. You're not gonna say a goddamn word—not when I'm at the 90 with my lights off, not when I'm at the 45 with my gloves on, and *certainly* not if I'm rolling into the groove slightly off 'on-and-on.' Because you know what I'm doing? I'm *correcting*—doing pilot shit—and my pass is still gonna be fine, ok? If I'm CLARA, I'm *not* calling it—because guess what, motherfucker? I know how to fly a fucking set of ILS needles. God forbid I come in *low*; you can trust that I fucking *know* it, and I'm fixing it—your power call isn't enlightening me, and it isn't gonna do *shit* to make things better. I don't need a 'right for lineup'—I know what a straight line looks like, and a reactive wing dip isn't going to do anything other than exacerbate the problem. And lastly, if you think I'm gonna bolter, don't you dare fucking tell me to put my power back on—because I *don't* bolter, and that bitch is coming aboard. The only thing I want you to do down there is keep the deck clear, look 'cool' with your cute little sunglasses and Croakies strap, and give me cut lights—so you can at least *pretend* you're the one clearing me to land. Understand?" Without waiting for an answer, Juice ordered, "Padroids to the platform; I'm walking." And hung up.

He grabbed his flight bag—a generic grey Noddik helmet bag—and started walking to his PR locker. 'I've seen enough good deals taken from JOPA by filthy fucking hinges—this one sure as hell ain't happening on my watch...'

~

"Excuse me, ladies and gentlemen, this is your captain speaking... Captain *Borat! Wah wah wee wah!*" Sam, grinning uncontrollably with his rejuvenated motivation, looked over at his Chippy friends for rampant laughter—but all three pilots stood with mildly amused looks on their faces. Sam could've sworn he even saw a slight vegetated cringe from the frail and unconscious FISTY.

CP leaned over to JABA and whispered, "God, he hasn't changed a bit..."

"He sure hasn't," Buck said with a smile, "That's the Nickels we knew and loved."

>SADCLAM< offered his arms forward, encouraging the former Good Dude Extraordinaire, "Come on, Sam, you got this. Keep going."

Sam cracked his knuckles, cleared his throat, then continued speaking into the microphone located in the tower of Fat Chucky's Cruise Ship. "Guys, what I meant to say is... we need to stop the party for a minute." He heard a collective grumbling from the crowd of thousands, as he looked down upon the rowdy bunch from the ship's bridge. Amongst the masses, plenty of notable celebrities were completely disregarding his plea. *Come on, Sam,* he told himself. *Don't be afraid to speak up; let them know what needs to be done.*

He started by calling out the obscene gestures he saw directed his way from his favorite extreme sports athlete. "Hey, Tony Hawk, I know they call you 'Birdman' and all, but please put those fingers away and listen up!" He chuckled at his own cringy pun, and then shifted his focus around to other famous attendees. "Jennifer Anniston—you're beautiful, and I'll always 'Be There For You,'" he clapped to the familiar television show rhythm, then beat the dead horse with, "but right now we need to be 'Friends,' so please pay attention!" As the crowd groaned, Sam found another target of opportunity to 'roast' and called out, "And Travis Kelce! I see you're having a great time with Taylor Swift, but if you guys don't stop *making out* and leave a 'Blank Space' to *hear me out*, then we're gonna have some 'Bad Blood!'" As he grinned toward the crickets-silent audience, Sam showed even more improper comedic timing by finishing with, "Oh no... 'Look What You Made Me Do'..."

Even his friends in the tower covered their faces at Sam's bombing. However, his cringe jokes *did* hush the crowd and clear the deck for open announcement space, as he went on with, "I have some exciting news for us all: the reason for our excursion from the party is because..." he paused to let the anticipation build, then announced, "We are redirecting this yacht straight for the USS Ship, and taking on the Noddik Empire in the Admin Olympics!"

The crowd of celebrities started to murmur—and *not* buzz of approval. CP looked at Sam. "Tell them, Nickels—don't be shy. But please, less jokes..."

Sam gave a brief head nod, and explained a bit more earnestly, "Listen, guys... I made a huge mistake. I had it all... and then left it behind to pursue what I *thought* was my dream job." He scanned the deck and found somebody with a glass of tequila and a cigar in hand, wearing a very famous pair of sneakers—and he seemed to be lending an ear to what Sam was saying. "Michael Jordan, I see you down there—remember when you left the NBA to pursue *baseball?* Crazy, right? The GOAT of basketball, leaving the sport on top, to chase some crazy whim of an idea? That was me, bro. I was 'His Airness' of naval aviation Good Dudes—and I abandoned the sport that gave my life so much meaning, so much *purpose*. But I'll admit it: I was *scared*. Scared I wouldn't be remembered as the greatest; scared that I didn't have it in me to keep elevating my game, and needed to run and hide somewhere else before I lost my edge. I broke rule number one of Power Drinking: I left a good time for what I *thought* was a good time..."

Looking further on as more people began to pay attention, Sam saw a tall, lanky man at a ship's outdoor gym, resting and listening while on the bench—only a couple of 10s on each side of the racked bar. The man seemed emotionally troubled by what Sam was saying, as if it struck his heart. "Kevin Durant, wipe those tears away—you know exactly what I'm talking about. Sometimes, we're *so* insistent on needing validation from others—*so* focused on that credit we *think* we've earned—that we fail to realize what truly brings us happiness in life... And it sure as hell ain't what some FITREP or Stephen A. Smith says about our legacy."

Sam continued to grow more confident, as more heads on the dance stage were starting to nod. Then he noticed a sad, tatted up, goofy-looking man—surrounded by *so* many beautiful women—yet appearing *so lonely...* Sam looked over at CP. "You wanna take this one, Andrew?"

CP smiled and grabbed the mic. "Pete Davidson... I know what you're feeling. I've managed to dine, date, and insert-whatever-obscene-action-you-want with every smokeshow I've ever dreamed of—all while finding massive success in the fitness industry. Now, granted, I'm not some randomly-inked-up dweeb like yourself—dude, you really have a *Hillary Clinton* tattoo?! C'mon, man..." He shook his head in disappointment, then continued pointedly with, "And unlike you, I've actually stepped *foot* inside a gym, and *I* actually *look* like a man that women would want to reproduce with—no disrespect, bro," he added at the end, as if that phrase magically removed all hard feelings.

Pete started to glare from the string of insults sent his way, but CP held steadfast in the point he was trying to make. "I'm not you, Pete—but I *know* you." Davidson's eyes narrowed further with skepticism, as Preul continued, "We both had damn good playboy lives—but guess what? I didn't find happiness in that life—and *neither have you.* Take a look at your actions, bro—taunting Kanye about being in bed with his wife, and then leaking the screenshotted texts to the press? Multiple tattoos dedicated to multiple ex-girlfriends, covered up with random keyhole and kite designs? Dude, you *branded* the name 'Kim' on your chest—you can't cover that up, jabroni. Face it—you aren't seeking self-actualization and happiness from life—you're just *begging* for validation from others, and *screaming* insecurity along the way. Get a hold of yourself, man... you're acting like a complete clown."

His scowl becoming a disappointed frown, Pete hung his head in shame. CP looked across the yacht deck and found highly-amused attendee. "Mr. West, don't get too excited over there." Preul pointed at the fallen-from-grace-rapper. "Calling him 'Skete Davidson,' and posting an obituary of him when he and Kim broke up? Asking fans to 'scream' at Pete if they see him, then calling the wolves off on Kim's request— after *you, too,* leaked private conversations?! Bro, you really claimed you *had* to 'tell everyone,' because you were just *so* excited you 'got a text from your favorite person in the world' and that you're her 'number one fan?!'" CP, firing on all cylinders with the air quotes, shook his head in embarrassment. "Good grief. You guys are all just children...

"And yet, here I am, caught in these stupid love triangles, too—and why? Because I'm missing the one love that was more powerful than any others: *my life in naval aviation.* The flying... the friends... the memories... all given up, because I—like Nickels here—was tired of what I *thought* was unforgivable bullshit. Pete, you seem like a somewhat funny dude—you don't need to find approval by dating as many sexy A-list celebs as you possibly can. Kanye, you're a rapping legend, but you've gone off the deep end, bro—you couldn't even handle South Park making fun of you. And you

198

know, people poke fun at me left and right in naval aviation—they didn't call me 'FIG-JAM' before Clown Penis for no reason! But it's not serious—it's called brotherly love, and not taking yourself too seriously—because life is too serious as is. The only thing worth treating 'too seriously' is the perfection of administrative excellence—and that's exactly what we're gonna show those Noddik douchebags."

With several people clapping in the audience, CP handed the mic to >SAD-CLAM<, who spotted a smug-looking man holding a golf club and not paying attention, instead giving obnoxious 'thumbs up's to some hot contestants from the Bachelor franchise—Andi Dorfman and Victoria Fuller, to be specific. "Hey, Lefty," CLAM called out, "FIGJAM wasn't a nickname created out of thin air, bozo. You know *all about* the path Sam took. You left the PGA for the LIV Tour, and lost your entire reputation by chasing the almighty dollar! And now, our boy Nickels is looking to atone for the same mistake. Look at what happened to your career—the people used to love you! You were up there with Tiger! And now? You're the king of the sellouts. Nobody respects you anymore. You're a fucking phony. A loser with a skinny wiener. You aren't worth the shit that I took this morn—"

"OK," JABA said, grabbing the mic from >SADCLAM<. "Sorry, Phil—CLAM has always been a pilot of passion." He paused, narrowed his eyes, and then spoke adamantly, "*Although...* is that *so bad*, after all? A man who is *so* passionate about his job, that it drives the strongest of emotions from the depths of his heart?! The kind of passion that causes you to spend weekends in the vault, reworking JMPS mission loads, fine-tuning your Offensive BFM briefing lab, triple-checking every line on your kneeboard card to make sure a random boldened border didn't slip through the cracks on the portion that you can't see on the print preview?! Don't you *want* a life that instills that type of passion?"

JABA peered down and saw a group of people booing the speech, and it struck a chord with him. "Hey, Dan Marino, Randy Moss, Karl Malone—I know you. And you know me. You guys had it all, didn't you? Legends of your sport... called the greatest of your era by many... first ballot Hall of Famers! But... you're all missing something, aren't you?" Buck nodded, "Yeah... guys, I feel it, too. Your golden championship rings are my golden oak leaves. I thought it was a foregone conclusion when I started out—I wasn't worried about moving up the chain; didn't stress over promotions—because I just 'knew' that one day I'd earn that glorious LCDR selection if I wanted it badly enough. But... like you guys, my time just ran out; life got in the way; it just never happened..." JABA shrugged hopelessly. "And now that it's too late, and the Navy *refuses* to take people back? I'll *never* get a taste of that victory that I'd give *anything* for...

"Guys, I'm begging you," Buck pleaded with intensity, "We may not be able to get the jewelry we all *thought* we'd have—the trophies we'd worked so hard for—but that's *no* reason to abandon the games we loved so much! It's *no* reason to stop helping others find the glory that we didn't. Because if there's one thing *just* as good as an O-4 promotion or championship triumph — if not *better*? It's the ability to help others; to be a Good Dude, like my boy Nickels, here," he gestured to Sam. "Guys, it's about joining the force of something greater; about being a team player — and not just the Dolphins, Vikings, or Jazz..." With a playful smirk, JABA then added in Karl Malone's direction, "*Or* the Lakers, you little ring-chasing rascal!" Malone didn't look happy, but Gary Payton walked by and gave him a friendly little punch on the shoulder, as the entire group of retired athletes lightened up and smiled. "We should want to help *any* squad out there who puts in the extra work, hours, and reps — not because they have to — but because they *desire* to. The utmost of professionals..." JABA wore a gentle smile, visibly captivated by the moment. "Professionals like the indomitable Dambusters..."

Sam hawked the deck once again, noticing the entire mood of the celebrities had shifted for the better. Plenty of nodding and beaming, even tears of realization wept by many. Embraces everywhere — Pete Davidson and Kanye West, Michael Jordan and Isaiah Thomas, Taylor Swift and all her ex-boyfriends, Aaron Rodgers and The Woke Media; even Will Smith, Chris Rock, and August Alsina entangled in a big bro hug.

Footsteps reverberated on the yacht, as the towering Shaquille O'Neal took center stage and — no microphone needed — yelled from the crowd in his unmistakable booming voice, "All this talk about appreciating what you have, the love of the game, and winning championships as a team? I just wanna say one thing, and that's this: I'm sorry for everything bad I ever said about my best friend in the world, Kobe Bryant. You know, Chuck," he said, looking over at Charles Barkley's direction, "Even though he drove me crazy at times, and I'm sure I did him, too... well... he was the best damn competitor, teammate, and brother I could've ever asked for. And I just wish I would've appreciated him more when we were kicking ass together, because it was the most fulfilled, successful, and motivated I ever felt in the game I love so much..."

Sam smiled at the comments from the big man, looked over at >SADCLAM<, and nodded — as if silently suggesting, 'Yeah... these guys *get* it...'

>SADCLAM< took the mic and said, "Phil, I'm sorry about earlier... that got out of hand. But all the stuff JABA said? It's true — I'm a passionate guy... and to have a career and life with these brothers who share the same passion for chasing goals, working harder, and getting better? It's the greatest gift a man could ever ask for. And Lefty, look at your success on the golf course! You've already *more* than left your mark on the sport — and yet, you continue to *compete*, when you could so easily just retire, call it a career, and chill — and that makes a warrior pretty damn legendary in my book."

Phil Mickelson smiled with a tear in his eye, and gave >SADCLAM< a big thumbs up.

"And big fella..." Houben pointed to Shaq. "A guy like Kobe? An improve-aholic, tactical mastermind, first-in-last-out workhorse like the Black Mamba? He would've *flourished* in the naval aviation community, just as he did in the NBA. Let's have a moment of silence for the GOAT."

The crowd bowed their heads, and Michael Jordan even nodded in agreement, the Jumpman humbled by >SADCLAM<'s inspirational words.

After an honorary 24 seconds, Sam took the mic back once more — and suddenly had a brilliant idea to save FISTY right here, right now. "I know there's been a lot of GOAT talk... and our guy Tommy Flynn, well... he's been in a coma for a while now, suffering from witnessing tragic Super Bowl highlights. We certainly hope that he will recover with JABA's programming, but if it's possible, we'd like to save him earlier than that — because if we're gonna win this battle for the USS Ship, we're gonna need the GOAT of tactical leadership. Right now, Tom "FISTY" Flynn could use a hero — *his* hero." Sam 'looked long for legends' and asked, "Maybe, just *maybe*, if that hero is here...?"

A spotlight was cast next to the DJ's music stand, upon a throne with the number '12' engraved on it. But alas... the throne remained empty...

Closing his eyes in disappointment, Sam cursed under his breath.

"*Ahem,*" CP cleared his throat to garner Sam's attention, then pointed to the front of the ship. "Well, there's only one man left to convince, it appears."

Sam looked to the ship's giant steering wheel on the bow, where the only remaining unhappy celebrity stood, hands on his hips.

From the navigation platform, LeBron James yelled to the men in the tower, "You're gonna sit there and talk GOATs — and not even *mention* me?! Man, that's some *bullshit*! How do you expect me to turn this ship around just to fight some meaningless battle about admin and redemption?!"

"LeBron..." Sam began slowly, "Chosen one... I think *you* may understand better than *anyone*." He took a deep breath, seeing James' confused face, and asked, "Do you remember when you left Cleveland for Miami?"

"I sure do," he responded smugly with his arms now folded. "Racked up some rings, too. Sounds like you didn't find *any* success with the Noddiks, Rowland."

Sam winced, hurt by the comments — but with the encouragement of his squadronmates, re-steeled himself. "Sure, LeBron; you're absolutely right about that. But don't you see? It's not *about* rings, recognition, or even *who* the GOAT is! You know, I really don't care if I'm forever known as the best Good Dude of all time, or the *worst Bad Guy*... because you know what? The approval of others means *nothing* to me. I've realized that only *I* know — deep in my heart — what kind of effort I've put into doing the right thing, contributing the right way, and making memories with the right people. And after doing it all *wrong* for so many years? I'm finally ready to do it *right* once again. And LeBron, clearly *you* felt like you had some unfinished business, too—and you *got* that chance to do right, didn't you, bringing glory to the city that you promised a championship? So please—do me a solid: allow me—no—allow *us all* to have a chance to solve *our* unfinished business, too. Allow us to make at least one more memory in this 'game' that is the best damn job in the world, further ingraining the foundational roots of a brotherhood that is *unmatched* in this *life*. What do you say, LeBron?"

LeBron stood emotionless, his hand on the wheel, not budging. Tension filled the entire yacht deck.

Finally, after nearly half a minute of silence, Lebron called out, "Contributions? Memories? Brotherhood!? That shit is *worthless*, bro... this ship ain't changing course, and neither is your life, jabroni..."

Sam bowed his head, in reluctant acceptance that—with James' decision—the Dambusters' quest was coming to an end. He looked at his Chippy friends, as CP shrugged with a desolate expression on his face, >SADCLAM< cursed the world and punched the wall, and JABA cradled poor FISTY's fetus of a body, which looked even more hopeless...

"... NOOOOOOOT!" Lebron yelled.

Sam's heart skipped a beat, as he quickly turned and looked down at the juggernaut of a navigator, who was beaming radiantly.

"You know—*from Borat*?!" LeBron said, bursting with excitement.

Nearly taken aback and breathless, Sam approached the mic and asked, "So... does this mean...?"

LeBron, flashing his famous ear-to-ear smile, said, "You're damn right it does. I dig your plan, Sam—and a good old-fashioned redemption story? *I LIIIIIIKE!*" he exclaimed, with such a phenomenal accent that Sam could've sworn he was in the presence of Sacha Baron Cohen himself. LeBron then whipped the wheel around aggressively, rerouting the yacht on a direct route to the USS Ship.

The crowd roared with approval, and the pilots high-fived in the tower. Sam pointed to LeBron and mouthed, 'Thank you, King James.'

LeBron thumped his chest twice and kiss-blew him a 'much love' peace sign.

Nickels turned to his former Chippies and said, "Go grab your pubs, boys; take a look at those EGT start limits, divert weather minimums below 3000/3, and OPNAV 3710 currency requirements—because we're about to lay some major admin dong on the Noddiks!"

The men laughed wildly, not caring that Sam's trash talk made no sense—just like they'd *never* cared back in the day. JABA gave Sam a friendly punch on the shoulder and said, "Hey, Nickels, it's good to have you back, amigo."

Sam beamed, electrified by the moment. Finally, he'd be back where he belonged. Finally, he'd be doing what he loved. Finally, he'd Nickels again, with his true friends by his side. *Finally, the Chippies are here.*

12

The Winner Within

Sam exited Skipper's office, where LT Bobby "Juice" Ward stood outside the door, next in line for FITREP debriefs.

A bit flustered and not wanting to exchange any words with his nemesis fellow JOPA, Sam attempted to blow right by him without eye contact – but Ward stopped him in his tracks when he remarked, "You guys were in there forever... and it sounded like Skipper was getting pretty heated."

Sam scoffed and looked up at Ward, who was showing raised eyebrows – knowing raised eyebrows... "Were you eavesdropping!?" Sam accused angrily, with defensive anxiety over what Juice may have caught from the conversation.

"I might've overheard a thing or two," Juice said coldly. "It was pretty hard not to, with how fired up you got him..."

Clenching his jaw, Sam pointed at him and said, "You'd better keep your mouth shut, Ward. That discussion is basically PII, and I'm not afraid to rat you out on the command climate survey – by name – if you talk about anything you illegally listened in on..."

"Relax," Juice said – although his tone was anything but easing. "Nobody would believe me anyway. A 'Good Dude' like you," he said with air quotes, "stealing the future from his best friend? Please... you couldn't script a betrayal so cold-hearted..."

The two JOs glared at each other. Sam shook his head and hissed, "Fuck you, Juice," before turning to walk away.

As Sam walked toward his stateroom, Juice called out, "Sam, wait..."

Rowland turned around and saw a look of skepticism from Ward. "What?!"

Juice looked at him intently. "Why are you really writing that statement?"

Sam scoffed with disgust and turned away, continuing to walk toward his room.

"A statement like that – it wouldn't just ruin your friendship with Low T; it would annihilate your entire reputation – your legacy – with the Chippies. In all of naval aviation, in *fact. And all for... a TOPGUN slot? I'm sorry, Nickels, but I don't believe it — you're* way *more calculated than that. I think you're full of shit."*

Sam turned back toward Juice, walked up to him, and face-to-face uttered, "Yes, that's exactly *why I'm doing it. I'm on to your bullshit, Ward," he walked even closer to his rival. "You're trying to talk me out of it because you* know *that if I get a Patch, it puts me* that *much further ahead of you — and you can't bear to stand that reality."*

Juice smirked. "A Patch? You think that's *gonna get you back ahead of me? Go ahead and get that Patch — because you're sure as hell never getting one of* these *patches," he mocked, pointing to his CVW-5 Top-10 Ball-Flyer arm emblem.*

Narrowing his eyes and growing further irate, Sam growled, "Go fuck yourself..." and turned to leave for good, tired of arguing with his junior squadronmate.

"You'd better not let Low T ever see that statement, Sam — you might awaken the testosterone-fueled beast inside Kyle!" Juice's mocking words trailed in the distance, as Sam threw his middle finger up behind him.

Sam walked along the halls, finally out of earshot from his hated foe, as his head swirled with a combination of anger, resentment... and internal dilemma. Fuck Juice... he doesn't know shit about me, or what I've done for this squadron, or how indebted they are to me. I *deserve* that EP. It's not about selling Kyle out... it's about getting the credit I'm due. And who cares if it's for a Patch or the Noddik transition?! Shit, even if I just wanted a chill shore tour at the RAG before getting out — then I deserve it! I have done *way* too much for the Chippies! Yeah, sure, Kyle's done a lot too — but, I mean, at some point, you gotta start looking out for yourself in this business. What would the Chippies be without me? A lot less administratively sound, that's for sure. I was the fucking glue that held this place together — I came up with a new RADALT step STAN that the whole Navy adopted... I successfully implemented twenty NATOPS changes to include punctuation, grammar, and capitalization corrections to EPs... I even created a software upgrade to see VSI in A/A Master Mode, the turn and bank indicator with REJ 1, and JDAM LARs in V:NAV mode! Shit, man — the *fleet* owes me this number one EP...

But deep down, he couldn't help but wonder if what Juice said held any truth; if this FITREP statement would *cause mass chaos within the squadron; if Kyle would do the same thing if he were in Sam's shoes — if he'd commit fratricide given the good 1500Hz synthetic tone, not a care in the world what his SHPI was tracking. They'd been best friends since they checked into API, where they'd both incorrectly assumed these flight suit-donning Weather instructors were gods amongst men. They did their Primary T6 forms bro-lo together, where helo IPs taught them how to 'fly tactically,' to include drawn-out 3-second 'run-it-up' hand signals and thesis statement lost sight procedures. They'd even winged together on their SEM flight, where they'd masterfully narrated the entire verbose loose deuce script mid-fight — 'Bad Boy 11, my gun is jammed, can you engage?' 'Bad Boy 12, level your wings, get your nose up. Bring it back left...'* Sam sighed longingly as he reminisced. Those were the days...

Juice was right about one thing, Sam realized: Kyle could never *find out about this...*

As he approached his 4-man stateroom, he found the place empty. Perfect, *he thought. He sat down at his makeshift cabinet-desk, took out a piece of paper, and clicked the black ink of his dorky multi-colored tactical pen. Per professional aviator STAN, he grabbed his CAC to use as a straight edge, and put the pen to paper. 'FROM: LT Samuel "Nickels" Rowland,' he wrote down – and then stopped. He looked at his name – specifically, the callsign.* Nickels... *he said to himself internally.* Would this statement taint that name forever, *he wondered? The funny thing was that he'd always* hated *his callsign. He never used it at first; he did whatever he could to* not *make it part of his identity. He'd always imagined himself getting some sarcastic-but-kind-of-badass-sounding name like 'Zombie,' 'Slowbro,' or 'Spatch' – he was so jealous of the 'Yardsale!'s, 'derp's, and 'WeTUA's of the world. He even looked at his Chippy brethren and longed to have something cool like 'The Lorax' or 'JABA' – shit, he would've killed for 'FISTY Le Beef WAID.' But* Nickels? Ugh... *'If I had a nickel for every time I shot my wingman,' they'd say. There he was – the ultimate Good Dude of Naval Aviation – earning a callsign from a meaningless training blue-on-blue – done inadvertently...*

And yet... here he was... feeling sheepish about using *that callsign for the ultimate professional blue-on-blue –* committed intentionally...

Sam put his fist to his mouth and bit his hand. Skipper was pretty clear about the intentions for this damning statement – and the only means available for Sam to punch his ticket to the #1 EP. That stubborn old bastard, *he thought. Was he making him put these words on paper because he knew what it would do to Sam's soul; how it would feel losing all of his dignity, and cashing out all stock in the Chippy team in pursuit of selfishly taking the money and running? Was this what Lieutenants felt like when they donned the O-4 oak leaves? When they took the department head bonus, knowing their days of DH shit-talking were over, as they now signed up to become the very tasking entity they spent an entire tour avoiding, minimizing, and suppressing? When they ass-blasted their first JO for not ensuring the OOMA and smooth schedule hours equaled what pilots logged in SHARP, throwing the tri-dundant system into a mismatching apocalypse?*

Maybe Skipper knew exactly what he was doing – but what did he know, anyway? What did a skipper even do?! He had more meetings with the Admin O than he did meetings at the merge... dropped more blue folders than BLU-111s... attended more FITREP and EVAL debriefs than mass multiplane ones. He didn't have time to read TOPGUN – in fact, the only books he kept up on were those stupid recommendations he gave the squadron: The Subtle Art of Not Giving a Fuck... The Winner Within... *George Leonard's* Mastery... Why We Sleep... The Leangains Method... Letters to a Young Athlete... The Courage to Be Happy *and its 'Courage to Be Disliked' precursor... Steven Pressfield's* The War of Art *– wasn't that title backwards? What the fuck. And who had time or care to read any of those, anyway?!*

Sam used to love Skipper – a man of wisdom, sage advice, and guidance. But the further Nickels got in his JO tour – the more success he found, the more independent he grew – the less guidance he needed. He started to see Skipper as an archaic, overly philosophical, feel-good fig-urehead. The squadron *might need a Skipper – but* Sam *didn't.*

Maybe Skipper thought Sam didn't have the guts to do it. Maybe he thought Sam lacked that killer instinct to pull the trigger with potentially poor parameters, figured that Sam wouldn't be able to pickle under stressful circumstances, and *was* daring *Sam to go for the slicing gunshot on the deck? That must have been it.* That naïve old man thinks I'm too pure to do something like this?! Well, *fuck* him! *Because lately, Sam had seen plenty of his poorly employed missiles guide and fuze, plenty of invalid bombs hit their target, and he'd had plenty of snapshot deck kills before a tactical 'knock-it-off, bingo.'*

Once upon a time, Skipper may have been right – that Sam couldn't do this. But as time went by – as things became less about this fantasy squadron life, and more about the real-ities of taking care of number one – things changed.

Nickels *may have never taken this shot... but Sam Rowland, future hero of the Noddik Empire, wasn't afraid to fire with the smallest semblance of a LAR – even on a 'FRIEND' radar lock...*

He took his pen, clicked the red ink from his dorktical pen, and struck out his callsign, as the header now read 'FROM: LT Samuel ~~"Nickels"~~ Rowland...'

~

"Power back on... bolter, bolter, bolter... Jesus..." the Paddles' voice called out, not hiding his disgust before ending the transmission over button 1.

"Fuck!" Juice yelled to himself as he sat in his cockpit – on deck, up and ready – waiting for his turn to launch in Phase 2 of the Admin Olympics.

"401, Paddles..." the LSO's voice called out.

The panicked voice of IROK came up on the radio, "G—go for 401?" He sounded like a complete novice on the horn.

"Did you see a ball on the lens *at all* on that last pass?" Paddles asked with annoyance.

"N—no. I mean—negative, Paddles... uhh... from 401," IROK responded with zero certainty.

"Ok," Paddles started, sounding like he was losing patience. "401, listen to me; you *need* to respond to my voice. If I say you're high, you need to start taking power off, i.e., *forward* stick deflection in Rate or Path. And if you're CLARA, you *need* to call it. Yes, we both know you're high, but it's part of the two-way handshake and contract between you and Paddles, ok? And lastly... dude—stop angling! Remember—*go to school on every pass.* If something's not working, do *not* show it to us twice in a row—got it?"

Finally, a reprieve of silence allowed IROK to know it was his turn to talk and submissively say, "Yes, Paddles..."

Listening to the exchange on deck, Juice shook his head in frustration. IROK's entire flight had been a complete disaster. He'd been waved off twice for his pattern, he had to take it around once for his taxi light being on—randomly, during the middle of the period—and his most recent bolter was his third of the day. Juice didn't want to even stomach the math of what this first wave was going to do to Team Noddik's GPA for Phase 2.

"Juice, it's IROK... I'm up on the TAC radio," the Padroid's voice called out on AUX—his verbose comm overflowing with nerves.

Juice keyed the mic and—full of irritation—asked, "IROK, what the hell's going on up there?"

"Juice, this shit is *hard*, bro... I don't know how to do *any* of this stuff!" He rapid-fired his issues in panicked fashion: "I can barely hold the... uhhh.. pattern altitude. I'm getting those weird green chevrons and stuff when I turn. I don't know how to check my 'beam distance' or whatever you called it. And it gets worse when I get to the actual pass! I can't get the ball on the lens at the start—and when I *do* see it, I can't hold it anywhere! Juiceman... I'm *scared*..."

Juice said nothing at first, digesting the reality of what IROK was saying—or, just as revealing, *how* he was saying it. He sounded fragile... feeble... flaccid. Gone was the façade, the over-the-top egotism, the false confidence of this Padroid douchebag. No longer was IROK acting like some fake-it-til-you-make-it wannabe alpha; ironically, *that* would've been a preferable ball-flyer to this estrogen-driven, low-confidence, scared little boy. The notorious, self-proclaimed 'carrier landing expert' IROK was nowhere *near* hungry for the pressure, instead desperate to run and hide from the moment. Juice wouldn't have been able to believe what he was hearing—*if* he hadn't suspected that this was inevitable, from the very beginning... The Noddik Admin Olympics Flight Lead wondered why Dr. Suabedissen even *programmed* this beta mode into the Padroid—but then realized that, of course, it must have been in the nature of the frail doctor's coding methods; an inseverable calling card.

Juice sighed, and keyed the mic, "Listen, IROK—I don't know what to say. I've been telling you guys this for *weeks* now... *fuck*, man. Why didn't you pay more attention to my ball-flying lectures? Were you just giving the 'Rules to Live By' lip service, instead of actually thinking about what each one means?"

"No!" IROK said frantically. "No, I wasn't! I know all about leading highs and slows, ummm..." The Padroid paused for a moment, then weakly insisted, "I'm fixing the low and then the fast..." There was more radio silence, before IROK muttered something about not re-centering a low ball in the middle.

"I'm gonna stop you right there," Juice mercifully transmitted. "IROK... you're currently 10 knots slow, 120 feet low, way too wide abeam, and you're at a 40-degree angle of bank in the crosswind. Shut up, click into PLM, and fly your fucking jet before you die. God *damn*, dude."

"But — but how can you tell?! You can't see my HUD; you're on deck... so how — ?"

"Because, IROK, my eyeball cal for admin phases of flight is *that* fucking good. Unlike you, those Padroids, and every other aviator in this empire, *I* know what it takes to put the work in. *I* care more about being safe than being cool; more about looking alive than looking badass. And above all, I care more about the process than I do the results — and *that* is what's wrong with you and those other idiots. Now, like I said — shut up, fly, and for god's sake, get *aboard*, man. Out."

Juice slammed his fist against his canopy. He and Low T were going to need to put in monumental efforts to get the W here and seal the Olympic victory. 'How the fuck does this happen...' he thought to himself. He thought back to his days of bouncing in the Chippies... his struggles with boat landings — the one thing he and Sam had in common. In fact, he could even remember a rare bonding moment between the two as they sat alone in the Iwo Jima ready room until midnight, waiting for Skipper to finish his night period and sign the schedule. He so vividly recalled he and Sam bemoaning how pointless FCLPs were, and what a waste of time the entire concept of bouncing was — sorties that could've been used to practice B&Rs, tanking, or even simulated NATOPS checks airborne. They delved even deeper, ridiculing the 'frat boy' club that was the LSO qualification — how it was just a popularity contest, and how carrier landings were neither art nor science, simply just a character in OOMA. Aboard the ship, their names were *consistently* at the bottom of the carrier landing GPA trackers in the Chippy ready room. It was ultimate irony; the *one* portion of the administrative phase of flight that these two gurus just could *not* figure out...

... That is, until Juice finally *did.*

Juice grinned as he remembered how it 'clicked' to him that this was unclaimed territory in the Chippy legion of admin SMEs, and a place to stake his claim as the top dog. He began getting up at 0300 in the morning to 'walk the pattern' in the MCAS Iwakuni BOQ parking lot, before anyone else was awake, reciting his pattern numbers and VSIs aloud while the sounds of internal jet noise blared in his AirPods. He made flashcards of carrier sight pictures to perfectly eyeball cal his vision for abeam distances and white of the round down turn points. He started counting his life in 15-18 second chunks, literally spending entire days counting to the number in his head over and over again, until the point where he could estimate that 15-18 second span better than he could one second or a minute.

Undoubtedly, it was mastering carrier landings—and ridding himself of the admin Achilles' heel he and Sam shared—that propelled him to the title of Admin King. In fact, he was consistently the second-best in the air wing at ball-flying, behind only one man...

Juice turned and saw Loaded T manning up his jet, chewing on a slab of marbled ribeye as he lifted the dropped tailhook back into the 'up' position with his bare hands. 'He may be a juiced-out piece of shit these days, but *damn*, that freak of nature can fly the ball,' Juice reflected. 'Between him and me, we can still clinch this war *right now*.'

Juice looked back up and watched IROK continue to fly like a falling leaf, ballistically BFMing his way to a '90' that was about 65 feet low, executing a wings-level 'transition' that looked more like a wing flash, and receiving screaming power calls all the way down as the Padroids found every piece of sky *but* glideslope—ultimately getting waved off and signaled to divert to the beach, giving the Noddik Empire a huge hole to dig out of for Phase 2.

Juice should've been irate. Should've been cursing out IROK on the radio—especially when the Padroid desperately asked Juice what a 'ship-to-shore' checklist was, for help with the waypoint steering information, and if he happened to have a Southern California approach plate on him.

But Juice didn't chastise, didn't swear, and didn't even respond. He'd already come to terms that these Padroids were worthless—and part of him, deep down, *enjoyed* the pressure of the moment, needing to pick up the slack to bring victory to the Noddiks—and cement his own legacy. He cracked his knuckles and turned to the catapult in time to watch the USS Ship's first competing ball-flyer get airborne.

"It's not gonna be easy... but it never *has* been for you, Bobby," he told himself in a moment of self-pep talk. "Just like you showed Paddles... just like you showed the Chippies... just like you showed Nickels—there's a reason why *you're* the Admin King. Let's fucking do this."

~

The Chippies scanned the Fat Chucky's Cruise Ship detachable ferry—The *Lil B*, or 'Little Boat'—for one last check of any leaks or discrepancies before giving the Boat Officer—a tall, older man in an Armani suit with slicked back grey hair—the thumbs up. Sam looked at his Chippy friends and said, "Guys, I'm good with it if you are?"

CP slowly nodded his head with approval.

JABA smiled pleasantly and said, "Big Time."

>SADCLAM< gave an enthusiastic fist pump. "Let's fucking *go*, baby!"

FISTY laid there, drooling; his consciousness inhibited by a record-breaking offense's lowest output in the season's biggest game.

Sam grinned and cheesily said, "Anchors away, Captain!"

The Boat O nodded and untied the rope, detaching them from the party boat—and the *Lil B* set sail toward the USS Ship, just over 10 nautical miles away from Fat Chucky's Cruise Ship.

Sam turned to the yacht where he'd rediscovered his heart's true calling, and said his goodbyes to the many great friends he'd met there. "Adios, Ryan Gosling! I fucking love *Drive*, dude! Your character is my inspiration—oh, and Eva Mendez? *Great* work, my man!"

Gosling smiled, waved, and said nothing—just stared quietly with a toothpick in his mouth.

Sam continued, "Christian Bale, your Batman will *always* be the best! Fucking epic! 'Where is she?!' he yelled with a terrible impression of the raspy caped crusader. "Hehe, JK bro—take care of her!"

Bale laughed joyfully and gave him a cool two-fingered salute, before returning to making out with the 'her'—Megan Fox—who was still very upset by Sam scorning her to return to the aviation life where he belonged.

Sam peeked around and saw the man who had saved the day and gave one last personal thanks: "LeBron! That Borat impression—are you *kidding* me?! Incredible! But seriously—thanks for everything! You were never a villain in Miami, man—just a kid from Akron, Ohio, trying to find himself, create a legacy, and win some rings in this crazy world. Love you, brah!"

LeBron smiled wide and yelled out, "Hey, Nickels! People will hate you, rate you, shake you, and break you—but how strong you stand is what *makes* you! Go win those Olympics, and bring a 'chip home for the 'Busters and the US Navy! Do it for America!"

Nodding confidently, Sam whispered to himself, "I will, LeBron." He looked at his Chippy friends, and added, "*We* will."

Unable to make out any more specific faces, Sam waved and yelled, "Goodbye, everyone!" Feeling motivated, and riding the high of the moment, he pulled out an oldie-but-goodie impression and bellowed, "*Hasta la vista, baby*!" And inside his head, he gave a special '*Thank you, WYFMIFM—wherever you are... whoever you were... thank you for helping me find myself...*'

Sam watched as Shakira and CP blew kisses to one another—drawing a smirk from >SADCLAM<, which CP rolled his eyes at and said, "Oh, shut up, CLAM." Mark Hoppus shot a signed guitar out of a cannon, which JABA was barely able to snag before it hit water. >SADCLAM< returned a thumbs-up from Phil Mickelson with one of his own, and looked at the men, exclaiming, "Guys... we're fucking *doing* this!"

Sam smiled and pointed above the USS Ship, saying, "It looks like Phase 2 of the Olympics is underway! Somebody just cleaned up and bingo'd to the beach..." *God, I hope it wasn't one of our guys.* "I'm gonna go talk to our Boat O and see if we can get in comms with the captain of the ship over there."

Approaching the mini bridge of the *Lil B,* Sam politely interrupted the captain of the ferry from his navigational duties, asking, "Excuse me, sir—is it possible to reach out to the captain of the USS Ship, to try and organize ourselves to partake in the Admin Olympics?"

The old man said nothing, continuing to steer the ship.

Sam tried again, thinking maybe the man was hard of hearing. "Sorry, sir—my name is Sam Rowland, and I was wondering if maybe I could—"

"Oh, I know exactly who you are, Nickels," the man responded, still looking out ahead. "Or, more accurately, I know who you *were...*"

Sam was aghast. "I—come again?" *Is that... WYFMIFM? But he's so tall... and that hair—so long and perfectly greased back—could it be?!* "Uhh... WYFMIFM? Is that you?" Sam asked, hopeful.

The old man laughed. "No, no... Charles and I *do* go way back, though. He used to work for me, actually, as a ball boy—back at my old job—before he hired me to man this ferry on his cruise ship."

"A ball boy? You were once a Paddles, sir?" Sam asked, slightly confused.

He chuckled heartily again and sighed strongly. "A Paddles?! God no... I could *never* have made it in that field! I got far too frustrated with my players—I can't *imagine* dealing with some FNG showing up low at the start or ignoring the voice of god on button 1!" He smiled and explained, "No—young Charles was a ball boy for me during my days coaching in New York."

Still uncertain, Sam looked closer and noticed nine of the captain's fingers adorned with outlandish-sized rings. He saw how freshly pressed and pristine the man's three-piece suit was. And how could he *not* admire that long head of pushed-back hair... he felt like he'd seen this man on TV before, but Sam couldn't quite tell from *where...* "New York, sir?"

"Yes!" the man said with a smile. "The New York Knickerbockers, over at The Garden! Charles was always a great little assistant, and ultimately became my team schedule writer—he was a real savant, that boy. He had such *impeccable* global situational awareness of everything going on—every team meeting, practice, pre-game shootaround, and post-game media obligation. He had it all masterfully mapped in his mind; he *never* double-scheduled anyone!" The man chuckled and finally looked at Sam, his aged eyes rife with wisdom and experience. "To think, Nickels—I literally had a 10-year-old managing my day-to-day agenda!" He looked back into the distance and said with awe, "But, he sure was something special..."

Sam scratched his head, still trying to figure out how it all connected. *Who is this guy? And how does he know* me?!

"He even wrote the forward in my book—maybe you've heard of it? *The Winner Within.*"

The Winner Within... Skipper recommended that book to us... but I never got to it. By that point, I was already focusing on my next career with the Noddiks—working on The Deal— aiming toward the biggest miss of my life... "I've heard of it, sir, but never actually read it..." Sam replied sheepishly.

"Gah, that's a shame..." the man said with a disappointed look. "It was really helpful for many of my former guys, and plenty in your community too—according to WYFMIFM, anyway."

"Helpful to jet guys?" Sam asked.

"Indeed," the lean old man nodded. "They really embraced the whole concept of The Innocent Climb; and, of course, learned the dangers of The Disease of Me, as they fought relentlessly to eradicate it from ready rooms..."

"Wait a second..." Sam said, floored by what he was hearing. "*You're* the one who came up with those concepts? I've been hearing that *everywhere* lately! Please— tell me what it all means!"

The man paused for a moment, then hit the 'waypoint steering' button on the ferry. He looked back at Sam, softly clasped his hands together, and explained, "Nickels... The Innocent Climb is what you began the day you got your wings. Those first few steps up the mountain... so refreshing," he smiled. "The Innocent Climb is one of the most powerful positions a team can be in—a team of those whose egos don't know any better, who haven't been tainted by success—by the illusion of mastery; the craving for *recognition*. It's the ultimate cohesive group of a bunch of guys and girls who know they have so much to learn, and *put aside* their desire for fame, fortunes, FITREP rankings, and follow-on orders arrangements. They put this desire aside because, one," he raised a finger, "they don't know what any of that stuff tastes like, and, two: the only thing they *do* know is that they know very little—and that they're *hungry*. Thus? They are not only willing, but *happy* to sacrifice their own effin' programs, because they know that they must get help from others—which, in turn, enables them to be active contributors." The man held a surprisingly youthful level of vigor as he continued, now incorporating air quotes, "The Innocent Climb is where you have no choice but to trust teammates, since you know you can't do it all yourself—and as a result, nobody gets some 'massive ego' or this false belief that they are the 'glue' holding everything together.

"The Innocent Climb is a bunch of JOs selflessly divvying responsibilities—like mission planning the JMPS load, creating kneeboard cards, getting weather and NOTAMs—without concern over who's doing the 'most work.'" The well-dressed man shrugged and offered with his arms, "It could also be the deployment walk-off players executing the RTHP packout; cleaning the ready room and carrying each other's stuff to the tri-walls—with no complaints, resentments, or any of this 'I'm only lugging *my* stuff' bullshit. The Innocent Climb is why, even though they are novices, FNGs can be so useful to a squadron—no egos, no concern for credit, no resistance to the team effort... it's a thing of absolute beauty," he explained as he looked longingly to the horizon.

Sam was a bit confused. "So... you're saying a squadron full of only FNGs would be the strongest team possible?"

The man laughed. "Oh, *god* no, Nickels! You see... The 'Innocent' Climb doesn't mean the 'naïve' climb—the most powerful component of all is innocence combined with experience—your midlevel, more senior-ish JOPA, for instance. Perhaps a PXO joining a squadron—eager to lead, but also to mesh; looking to be helpful, but also to stay out of chili. Even, dare I say it..." the man raised his eyebrow, "A brand new O-4..."

Sam withdrew a bit, winced his eyes, and shook his head. "But—no... that's impossible..."

"Anything is possible, Samuel!" the man exclaimed. "Didn't you listen to KG after the 2008 number-one-seeded Celtics' 'improbable' championship run?!" He used air quotes again, then laughed and said, "I kid, I kid. But believe it or not, department heads *can* take part in The Innocent Climb for the better of the squadron, remaining willfully resistant to that incessant and pesky ego bug that hits so many when their experience level increases!" He resigned his face a bit, "Albeit, the O-4 immune system *is* much weaker—much less robust at fighting off—"

"The Disease of Me..." Sam said, finishing the man's thought.

"Indeed," he said, grimly nodding his head. "The disease that plagues even the strongest of champions; one that infects so many gallant, helpful, innocent contributors, as they start to selfishly insist they're entitled to more credit, more respect, more rewards, et cetera. The disease that," he looked Sam dead in the eyes, "turns Good Dudes into *Bad Guys*..."

Again, Sam caught himself cranking his head a bit, as if affronted by the wise old man's words. But—deep down—Sam knew exactly what he meant.

The old man ran his hand through his slicked-back hair and continued, "It's a disease that occurs when people achieve success—and yet can't properly handle it. As praise reaches the victorious team—which it always will—a virus inside them starts becoming more concerned with individual acclaim than appreciating the team collaborative effort that got them there. Everyone starts thinking they are the 20% that deserve 80% of the recognition — and become further ill and resentful when others don't see it this way. As a result? They experiment with self-treatment of this illness — the illness they mistakenly diagnose as 'lack of respect' — becoming more desperate to *demonstrate why* they warrant so much self-gratifying praise. They undercut others, become obsessed with their own career milestones, and disregard all of the trust, teamwork, and selflessness that drove the very success they're now drunk off. It's a senior JOPA, fully qual'd and 'above' things like loading cards, doing ground jobs, or showing new guys how to inventory a safe." He rolled his eyes and sarcastically ranted with air quotes, "Oh, *of course,* they needn't bother themselves with these 'new guy tasks' — they're *far* 'too smart' and 'too experienced' to be doing this bitch work!" He gave a knowing look to Sam, "And they're far too preoccupied with planning their post-squadron-tour life, apathetic to all those who suffer from their lack of contribution..."

The man began playing with one of his grandiose rings. "The success goes to their head, and they can't harness it — they've already forgotten what it was like to *climb.* They forget how special and character-building the grind was — and forget the importance of showing others that path, too. They're done climbing, as they get metaphorically — and often physically — fat and lazy, complacent to rest off the laurels of the relatively *tiny* part of the mountain they've already scaled." He scoffed. "And it's certainly not just the occasional senior JO who is afflicted, Sam. Can you think of a group of spoolly individuals who seem *far* too worried about looking good for Skipper, earning the top FITREP to further their trek on the 'golden' path, and undermine the entire climb for everybody else as a result?"

Sam gasped quietly, "... The hinges..."

"That's right," the man affirmed with a nod. "Those who *can't* climb, because they're so bedridden with The Disease of Me that they've physically *forgotten* how to load DTDs, draft a schedule in SHARP, or even secure a classified storage space. It's truly a pity, seeing so many Good Dudes out there, *poisoned* by the career success they found with a squadron — with a *team.* So many wonderful climbers, paralyzed with triumph, too preoccupied with bonuses and EP aspirations, instead of realizing that if they *just kept their innocence* — now exponentially more useful with their experience — the golden path would be paved *for them.* But alas..." the man shook his head and again looked toward the horizon, "It's a rampant, highly contagious, lethal disease to *any* team — even to a *dynasty.* The 1980's Showtime Lakers... the 2000's Shaq and Kobe variant... the Big 3 in Miami. Even..." he looked back at Sam, his most piercing eye contact yet, "the VFA-195 Dambusters."

Sam closed his eyes. He was not surprised one bit — because he finally understood... and *agreed* with the man. "Everything I was all about..." Rowland started

215

slowly, shaking his head, "... helping others prep for the SFWT events by listening to the admin portion of their briefs well past working hours... occasionally taking guys' duty weekends or port shore patrols so that they could spend extra time with visiting family... welcoming FNGs with open arms, taking them to the gym for an impromptu chest day and steak post-workout meal, instantly accepting them to the lean lineage of Chippies; I stopped caring about *all* that when Juice got there. I couldn't believe people were seeing *him* as the next Good Dude—as if he were *supplanting* me. And the ironic thing was," Sam chuckled humorlessly, "I'd always *fought* for a culture that would *produce* so many great Chippies and Good Dudes. But I was obsessed not just with getting the credit for that culture, but also with ensuring nobody else would benefit from it once I was gone—I wanted to be irreplaceable..." Sam put a fist to his forehead and closed his eyes. "Dammit... you're right, sir—I was Dambuster patient-zero of The Disease of Me... and it started an epidemic that infested the entire squadron..." Sam hung his head low. He'd known that he'd dived into the depths of selfish malady— but until now, he hadn't realized just *how low* he'd sunk—and for a second, he started to wonder if he was in too deep...

The man, sensing Sam's plummeting hope, put his hand on the demoralized Chippy's shoulder. "Nickels... it's important to know: There *is* one certified immunization, cure, and panacea for The Disease of Me..."

Sam looked up, his eyes watery, and asked, "What is it?!"

With his lean face, healthy hair, and strangely youthful skin, the old man steepled his fingers together—exhibiting nine shiny rings in alignment—and looked at Sam confidently. "Sacrifice."

"Sacrifice?" Sam repeated with uncertainty.

"Sacrifice," he said again, now smiling. "Sacrifice heals The Disease of Me— because sacrifice is selflessness; selflessness is innocence; and innocence is bliss. Think about it, Sam—when you sacrifice in life, you take on a relatively *minuscule* short-term hit for *infinitely* grander long-term results. It's the centerpiece of everything from dieting, to winning championships, to creating the most badass fighter squadron of tactical and administratively sound aviators with camaraderie that becomes the pinnacle of your life.

"All of these journeys—they certainly aren't *easy*. To get to the top of any mountain, there's a *grind* to it. But to appreciate that grind—to *embrace that struggle*—you *need* to sacrifice. And it comes in various forms—it might be sacrificing free weekends of your life in order to spend more time in the vault, prepping for your level 3 check ride, even just to make sure your fourth high tactical risk level example flows well with the teaching point you're trying to convey to the SFTI. It might be sacrificing your cush life as a permanent land dweller, giving up the basic freedoms and liberties of Wi-Fi, privacy, and the almighty healing sun; all of this, just to serve and live at sea for literal years of your life, while consuming plenty of seed oil doused carb-bombs, crushing your body's circadian rhythm by shifting *your* schedule to the whims of the *flight* schedule, and getting yelled at by some boat chief for having hair that's too long, a zipper too low, or a smile too optimistic.

And Nickels," he looked at Sam pointedly, "it *might* be sacrificing your 'fuck-this-shit' insistence that you could and should leave to make millions of dollars else-where — whether it be as an airline pilot, gym manager, writer, or Noddik Skipper — because guess what? You probably *could* make that money! But it isn't *about* the money, Sam. The diseased man cares only about his money... his high-water FITREP... his personal validation — because he thinks *these* artificial 'antidotes' will cure the illness he feels inside. But the sacrificing, selfless man? He understands that all these trivial things are meaningless byproducts of the true joy of the climb: The sacrifice, struggle, and grind itself. The beauty of teammates each appreciating the ecstasy of adversity, and sacrificing toward the belief that there's a bigger, more enriching, more memorable end goal to accomplish out there than some bullshit #1 EP. Do you know what that goal is?" he asked.

Trying to digest everything, Sam silently shook his head.

"Winning, Sam," the old man said with a smile. "Winning and sacrifice go hand-in-hand. And while the taste of success can disease one man alone — it can *em-power* a team together, enabling them to achieve even *greater* feats as their confidence rises, their drive surges, and their belief in each other skyrockets. But in order to will-ingly sacrifice, Nickels, there must be an inherent *trust.* Trust in each other; that the team is all-in together, united in solidarity for this covenant of a climb toward the greatest accomplishments in this world. And trust in their *leader*; that they are being guided by the ultimate selfless warrior toward this greater, often-sought-after-yet-rarely-achieved peak." The man looked at Sam. "Can your Chippy teammates trust that you'll do what it takes to get them back to the promised land?"

Sam looked up at the tall man, paused, and said, "Yes, they can, sir — I'm ready to sacrifice. I'm ready to trust. I'm ready to climb." He then stopped, thought for a moment, and asked, "But *how*? How can I get my teammates to see that I'm truly ready to lead this battle? How can I get them to see that I *can be* and *will be* the Good Dude I once was?!"

The man smiled, spread his hands again, and explained, "Your attitude will show all, Nickels. The attitude we bring forth is the ultimate window to our souls. When things aren't easy, and there's real work to be done — *real* adversity to be faced — your attitude will reveal your heart's true resolve. So let your teammates see *and believe* that your intentions are to go out there, put the past behind you, give 100% of your capabilities, and *motherfucking climb.*" The man paused, still smiling, and added, "You know, kid, my dad once told me: 'Every now and then, somewhere, some place, some time, you're going to have to plant your feet, stand firm, and make a point about who you are and what you believe in; and when that time comes? You simply have to do it.' So, recognize the opportunity, Nickels—*and kick its ass.* Because if you don't? You may not get another chance."

Sam, wearing a serious expression, nodded his head. He could've sworn he's heard this message before... but that was irrelevant—because now, he was prepared to *never* forget it. *When the opportunity comes... I have to be ready to take it...*

The man steepled his fingers together once again, then softened his eyes and explained, "When asked which success means the most to him, the diseased man spends far too much time recounting his personal highlight reel, looking to get high off his past accolades. The innocent, team-oriented, nourished man? The one who understands the divine healing power of sacrifice and selfless efforts? That man gives the same answer Tom Brady always gives, when asked which championship was his favorite..."

"'The next one...'" >SADCLAM< said with a smile, as he and the rest of the Chippy gang stood on the mini-bridge behind the two at the wheel.

The old man picked up a portable J-dial and said, "Extension 6666 is where you can reach the captain." He handed the phone to Sam, brushed off his suit, and started to turn away—before looking back and saying, "Hey, Nickels—I want you to remember one more thing about attitude."

"Yes, sir?" Sam asked.

The man rested his arm on the wheel and explained, "Before my days coaching others, I was once the recipient of some grade-A leadership at the ol' 24 Hour Fitness in Roseville, California."

"The Big Show...!" CP gasped.

"Indeed—the best collection of iron and hotties that a young aspiring man could ever ask for," the *Lil B* captain smiled. "And do you know what my boss, mentor, and *friend* once told me—when a customer walked up to me, ready to buy thousands of dollars of training, and I tried to chalk the sale up to sheer luck?"

"What did he say?!" Sam asked, reflecting every Chippy's anticipation.

The man looked at Sam, his eyes bright with wisdom. "He told me: 'The harder you work, the luckier you get.' Look at those who 'catch all the breaks in life,' Sam: You think Tom Brady benefitted from the tuck rule, the Malcolm Butler interception, the Incredelman catch, and the subsequent Incredelman non-muffed punt return against Kansas City in the 2019 AFC Championship—not to mention Dee Ford's offsides penalty on the INT—all by mere *chance?!*"

Wow, Sam thought. *Deep pull on the AFC Championship; they won that OT coin toss, too!*

"You think LeBron James," the man went on, "benefitted from Ray Allen's most-clutch-shot-of-all-time, the stars to align for Cleveland to get back-to-back first overall draft picks en route to him returning home for a championship, or for Steph Curry to suffer his only playoff foul-out *ever* in game 6 of that championship round — by *coincidence?*"

And he didn't even mention how Draymond Green got suspended a game in that series, Sam realized.

"And do you *really* think," the well-groomed man finished with conviction, "that everything in the Navy *truly* boils down to timing, FITREPs, and rotation dates?" He raised his eyebrow, "You ever notice how those who keep up the positivity, work hard, and *refuse* to throw in the 'woe is me' victimization towel... somehow *always* seem to end up with the good deals and illustrious careers?"

I... I suppose I never considered that — the Navy does *seem to pull strings to make certain things work out for certain people...*

"Don't forget it, kid. My mentor said it well, and I'll echo it: Attitude is the mother of luck. Keep your mindset where it should be — focused, hungry, and full of belief — and the best of fortunes will follow."

Sam nodded, then asked, "What was that mentor's name, sir?"

The man laughed. "That's another story for another book, my friend. A Stoic man; we'll just call him 'CMclub592' for now — he wouldn't want any more publicity than that. But hey — I've taken enough of your time already," he said, looking at his Submariner Rolex. "We're close enough," he said, pointing to the USS Ship right beside them. "I'm gonna go drop anchor; godspeed, gents — let the captain know that the Chippies are ready to climb."

The man smiled, gave one last two-fingered salute to the Dambuster boys, and departed the mini-bridge.

"Well," CP said, "I reckon we give this jamoke a call and tell him we've got some major admin dong-age to lay on these Noddiks." He made the remark in pure CP fashion, without the slightest hint of a smile.

Sam giggled uncontrollably, before gathering his emotions and placing the call, crisply hitting the 6 button four times — flawless admin execution. As the phone rang, he looked around excitedly. "Guys, get ready — this is happening!"

Sam found himself wondering who the ship CO was at this time — surely somebody around his timeframe, maybe a random guy from the RAG; probably somebody who spent their entire career in Lemoore or Virginia — coastal locations his Chippy days led him to be relatively unfamiliar with, aside from a brief stint at VFA-122. *Poor stateside-stationed guys...* Sam thought. *They missed out on the best-kept secret naval aviation has to offer...*

"Skipper," a voice answered on the other line, void of any emotion.

"Uhh... hello, sir," Sam began. "My name is Captain Sam 'Nickels' Rowland, former VFA-195 Chippy—"

"Chippy ho!" >SADCLAM< called out enthusiastically, as the men watched Sam with eager anticipation.

"—And I'm tracking the Administrative Olympics against the Noddik Empire. Well, your honor, I've got four willing pilots here—and a comer—on that little ferry at your bearing 270 for 1000 feet. We are qualified, administratively sound, and—most importantly—*hungry* warriors, with a rich history in the industry—and we're ready to help the United States win this war no matter *what* it takes. Please, utilize us however you'd like—be it flying, admin organization, or even just *teaching* those on the ship how to win this battle! Sir... we are admin weapons for your disposal."

His preamble was received with silence. No response whatsoever. Sam started to second-guess himself. *Did I come off too strong? Does he not need our help? Why did I call him 'your honor?'*

"Mmph," the voice finally murmured.

W—was that a grunt? "Uhh... sorry, I didn't catch that... your honor." *Dammit, Sam!*

"Sam, why do you keep saying that," CP asked, more of an annoyed statement than an actual question.

"Yeah... I don't really care what you guys do," the captain uttered.

"Umm... so... can we help at all?" Sam asked, very confused at the apathetic nature of the captain.

"... Sure..." he flatly affirmed.

>SADCLAM< leaned in, "What's he saying, Sam? Is he pumped for us to save the day and win the war?"

Sam covered the mouthpiece of the phone and whispered back, "He doesn't really—doesn't really seem to care..."

The Chippies looked at each other with confusion, and Sam hit the speaker phone button so they could listen in. Sam spoke up, "Ok, sir... well... we'd like to fly in some of your jets for Phase 2. Are there spots available? You *are* in Phase 2, right, sir?"

The voice sighed, exasperation present in his tone. "Yeah... I really don't know. I'm gonna be honest—I don't give a shit about these Olympics; they're interfering with the ship I'm trying to run, and this whole thing's *really* not helping us make PIM. So, to answer your question, I don't know if we're in phase B or 10 or whatever you said— I just want these over with. The first one went poorly enough."

CP's eyes narrowed as he recoiled his head in disgust.

Sam asked, "But sir, you understand this battle is for *admin excellence,* right? Our entire *reputation* as a *nation* for conducting non-tactical *operations* rests on our ability to prove that we are superior to these Noddik premature *ejaculations*!"

JABA smiled at Sam's rhyming insult—*vintage* Nickels. He'd come full circle on his vengeance toward the adversary.

Another sigh from the USS Ship captain, followed by, "Yeah... I really don't care about any of that stuff..."

Growing a bit frustrated, the men kept shaking their heads. >SADCLAM< looked at Sam and whispered, "Look into your heart, Sam—tell him *why* it matters."

Sam nodded sharply, dug deep, and explained, "Well, *we do*, sir—and it's important to the lore of naval aviation that we prove we the upper admin hand. It's important to us former Chippies to show that our training was not in vain; that we are the best damn naval force the galaxy has to offer, with the most skilled and unrelenting teammates that any squad could ever hope for. It's important to demonstrate that we are a conclave of charitable *Good Dudes*—dudes who know how to sacrifice together, know how to fight together, and know how to *win* together. And dammit, sir, even if it's just flying a few passes in Phase 2 and being the fucking ball all the way to touchdown? The Dambusters are ready to help, ready to fly, and ready to *climb!*" Sam looked around for nods of approval from his Chippy cohorts, which he finally received; >SADCLAM< smiling and pumping his fist alongside the amped crew.

A few more grunts were heard on speakerphone, followed by a barely coherent, "Ok."

Sam's eyes narrowed in confusion as he looked over at JABA, who shrugged. Sam leaned toward the phone and asked hopefully, "Sooo..."

"Do whatever you want, just make it quick," the captain responded.

"... Soooo..." Sam repeated.

"Jesus Christ..." he muttered, with his heaviest sigh yet. "Yes, you can fly the fucking jets. One guy already went, so you have 203 and 205. Got it?"

The men went wild at the news, high-fiving each other and cheering uproariously, before quieting down so that Sam could say, "Thank you, sir—you won't regret this!"

The captain grumbled a bit, and then clearly slammed the phone on its dock.

After another round of high-fiving his friends, CP couldn't hide his annoyance. "Nickels, what's this guy's deal?!"

Sam chuckled and rolled his eyes, "Dude, seriously! Whatever—we got the jets! One of the few helpful things the captain *did* mention was that it sounds like Phase 1 was a loss for us—which means this one's a must-win, *pivotal* Phase 2. So, guys, we've gotta figure out who's flying. CLAM," Sam looked at the squadron LSO, "you were right, earlier: this *is* a game—and you've always been damn good at it. I want you in a jet, showing the Noddik Empire how it's done."

"You got it, brother," CLAM nodded confidently.

"And JABA," Sam looked to the other former Dambuster Paddles, "I think you're the other man we need to get it done."

JABA winced, "Sam, I'd love to—but... I'm *so close* to having this VR simulation done for FISTY. I can't stop now—if we wait any longer, I feel he might be lost to us forever..."

Sam nodded, "Understood. In that case," he turned to CP and asked, "Andrew? Are you ready to bring it home as our closer?"

CP quickly reacted with a resounding, drawn-out, "Neeeeegative..."

"What?!" Sam burst out. "But CP... you were always the top SDO-standing ball-flyer..."

"I may *have* been—but there are two important points you're failing to realize. #1) I've tacked on a *substantial* amount of natural muscle mass since those days, as is readily obvious and apparent," he said, gesturing toward his chest. "My entire calibration on corrections for power and lineup would be off without a warm-up period to adjust to my new AOM—granted, I'm an athlete, and I'd of course still make it happen—*buuuut* it might not be the perfect line period I feel like we're gonna need here. More importantly, though, Nickels—#2..." he paused, wore an intense look, then explained, "This is *your* redemption story, broseph. I know you want to win and all, and put the best team forward—but what does any of this matter," he pointed at Sam, "if you don't prove that *you've* learned from all this? Not just about all the great things this job and community has to offer, but also about your greatest weakness: your disdain for Paddles, and your shitty ball-flying."

Sam looked down and to the side, slightly hurt by the comment.

CP's eyes widened, as he expounded, "There's no need to sugarcoat it, Nickels. You were a brilliant administrative genius and a Good Dude, but your Achilles' heel was trusting in Paddles—their voice, their purpose, and their ability to make you a better pilot. Well, now's your chance—show the world that, just as your eyes were opened to the wonderful parts of this business, you can open your eyes and hold belief—and prove your *worth*—in one of the most wonderful *traditions* of this business." He nodded slowly again, urging, "I'll do it if you *really* want me to—but why not *seize* this opportunity? Like the old man said: 'Take this chance to plant your feet, stand firm, make a point about who you are, and simply *do it*'—kick its ass, Nickels."

Taking a deep breath, Sam considered what Preul was saying—and knew deep down that it was all true. CP's words were the reality check he needed—if he was going to show the Chippies that he was ready to climb, then he needed to conquer the hurdle he'd feared and dodged for far too long. The memories of barely scraping by Carrier Qualifications in the mighty T-45C and then in the RAG... the sleepless nights of frustration with his line period... the excuses he'd made about the irrelevance of Paddles with PLM, the dismissive attitude that coming aboard was all that mattered, and the notion that LSOs hooked up other LSOs. It was time to put those thoughts to bed, cut the bullshit, and prove that he belonged in the legions of those who could perform well in the ultimate administrative portion of carrier aviation.

He nodded, felt a tinge of adrenaline, and looked at his former squadronmate with determination. "You're right CP... you're right. Alright, I'll do it—put me in for the third slot, boys."

"I *know* I'm right, Nickels," CP said, a huge smile on his face as he reached out his hand.

Sam grinned, clasped CP's palm with his own, and brought it in for the bro hug.

"Anchor down!" the *Lil B* captain called out as the ferry reached bridging distance of the USS Ship.

A drawbridge extended from the carrier, and the Chippy pilots walked across it, carrying FISTY along with them. An O-2 in coveralls approached them and introduced himself. "Hello, gents! I'm LTJG Narrator—the PAO aboard this ship! The captain briefed me on the game plan for you guys—who are my pilots?"

>SADCLAM< and Sam raised their hands, to which the PAO responded, "Ok, perfect. Just as a heads up to you guys: we got smoked in Phase 1—and I mean, it was *bad*... fortunately, we've got an early lead in Phase 2, with some random US pilot assigned to this ship getting pretty solid grades, and the Noddik's first participant being forced to divert. But the current Noddik guy is *stroking* it..."

"Who's up there right now?" Sam asked.

The JG scratched his head, "Uhhh... some guy named 'Ward,' I think it was?"

Sam looked at his Chippy cohorts and nodded knowingly. *Juice...*

"Anyway, so yeah—you guys will need to be on your A-game to ensure we can even have a *chance* to win this war!" the PAO said as they walked up the ladderwell toward the PR shop.

"Our 'C' game is better than anyone else's A-game," >SADCLAM< remarked as he looked back at his boys. "C as in *Chippy Ho*, ja feel?"

"Ja definitely feel!" CP responded, grinning, as he and JABA nodded enthusiastically.

Sam, however, was not in the mood for jokes or casual pre-game small talk. His stomach was in knots, thinking about the upcoming flight—nerves he hadn't felt in *ages*. In the strangest way... he kind of *missed* the feeling; withdrawing to his inner place of solitude, ignoring the noise, putting his entire focus into the next few hours of his life, knowing the outcome could dictate the next few *decades*. It made him feel nervous... feel pressure... feel *alive*. Somewhere in the shuffle of his pursuit to cut out the shit, he'd forgotten how truly *agonizingly magical* moments like this were.

In fact, he would've tuned out every single word until he started his jet, if not for the question >SADCLAM< asked the PAO: "Hey, what's the deal with this ship's captain? The guy seems like a total boner."

"Ahhh, yes..." the JG said with a slight shrug of his shoulders, as they continued walking. "Not sure any of you guys would know him—he's a crusty old guy. Got here years ago as part of Direct Commission Leadership—or 'DCL' program—that we launched to help with administrative management via external hires. He's a no-non-sense captain, very thorough and wise. But—I'll admit—kind of a dick..."

"What's his name?" JABA asked out of curiosity.

The PAO looked back at the pilots. "Captain William Stephen Belichick."

13

(Try) _DO_

Sam Rowland paced around the ready room – still riding the high off his incredible CAS SFWT 3.9F flight – hardly able to wait for midrats, where he'd be able to share the details behind the epic story with his air wing compadres.

The whole thing was like a scene from a movie: He'd shown extreme jet athleticism when the JTACs gave him some crazy holding instructions that put his fix just on the cusp of a PSA border, max performing on hot turns to avoid violating international airspace and pissing off CAG. Furthermore, when releasing his simulated laser-guided weapons, he had the wherewithal to turn up his VOX and yell "lase lase lase" into his mic for the entire lasing duration – the Patch-wearing instructor even gave a nod of approval, commenting, "Yeah, it was kind of hard to hear you, so we'll call it poor employment – but still valid." And to top it off, his laser marksmanship? Never has a thing been put on a thing so brilliantly. The same SFTI's jaw dropped at Sam's ability to hold a death dot on a fixed structure.

Rowland was thrilled to share the story of his astounding correlation, where he asked the JTAC if the referenced 'target area series of buildings' was 'sort of shaped like a phallic object entering a C-shaped revetment,' to which the JTAC said, 'Affirm; your target is what would be the left testicle of that phallic-shaped building' – leading to a masterfully-placed simulated GBU-38.

And above all, Sam was so stoked to tell his buddies – over a plate of fried eggs, bacon, and waffles – about the last attack, where the JTAC was taking simulated fire from a faction of pax that had stolen a Mad-Max-type vehicle, and how Sam was forced to resort to the simulated bullets in his jet, executing a strafe on the simulated moving vehicle. This was an unheard-of scenario for Level 3 SFWT CAS – and yet he valiantly changed his RADALTs per STAN in the time-crunched scenario, and executed every part of the attack to perfection to hit his

'ASAP' TOT within plus or minus 0 seconds. And to cap it off? His beautifully-placed unassessable bullets struck the middle of the ocean – simulated direct hits; ground commander's intent met.

On the non-conduct side, it was business as usual for the admin guru. Sam was the first one up and ready to the cat, taxiing so smoothly that the Handler even gave him a complimentary shout-out over the intercom, before frantically delivering his usual birthday callouts. When it came to check-ins? The hounds were out, ready to savage with mickies – but Sam knew a thing or two about the deselect/roll/roll-back secure comm exit strategy. There was not a whiff of a suspension after his crisp wipeout, full rudder deflection, and a salute that – according to The Lorax up in Pri-Fly – left the Air Boss audibly gasping as he reacted, "Holy shit..." The RTB? Perfect timing on breaking the deck – just over a second of open deck time. He ripped off the most administratively-sound forward-of-the-bow break, coming in at 350 kts on the money, expediting the deck recovery – without performing a banned Expedited Deck Recovery. His abeam distance was an appropriate amount for his weight, and his swift exit from the LA after trapping reportedly drew fist pumps from the Mini Boss.

He'd survived the four-hour debrief, nodding pleasantly and saying things like, "Copy," "Roger that," or "Ah, ok" every time the dual-anchored Patch wearer gave him feedback about his brief like 'You only asked 20 questions; not nearly enough,' or 'I didn't see a North arrow on your third example; that can be confusing,' or even 'It was probably a misspeak, but your preflight discussion on LGBs talked about the Mk-122 fuzing cord – it's technically a fuzing wire, man. Remember – words mean things.' Enduring the instructor's critiques of his mannerisms, verbiage, and arrows was arguably the hardest part of the flight – but Sam had suffered and prevailed, escaping with a below-average brief, average event, and average debrief – for the pass/complete.

All that was left before 'rats – the only thing left to debrief before the party began – was...

"Yeahhhhhh, Paddles!!!" the FNG SDO excitedly called out and cheered – the way he'd been strictly trained to – as the group of angels in float coats strut into the VFA-195 squadron spaces, one commenting, "Oh, man, great choice!" on the roll 'em of Eurotrip that was playing. As the train of ball-flying SMEs made their way toward the back exit, LT Rowland humbly approached them and said, "Hey Paddles; sorry, I missed you earlier – I think I should have one from event 6?"

The scribe for the day dug through his passbook – a journal full of strange hieroglyphics that only a computer or idiot savant could translate. After a bit of page flipping, he finally exhaled and said, "Ah, yes, had you in 403, right?"

"Yes!" Sam said with enthusiasm, already thinking about the vat of butter waiting for him in Wardroom 1/2.

"Copy..." the Paddles said, with a strange trail off at the end, before handing the book to CAG Paddles – a young, fresh-faced new check-in named Blue Collar Bill – who took a quick glance around, and then looked at Sam with concern.

"So..." the head Paddles asked, "How'd you feel out there?"

"Uhhh..." Sam was unsure how to respond – as he was every time Paddles asked this question. What am I supposed to say – that I flew a flawless pass? And then get reamed!? No chance! *Like everything else in naval aviation, you were best off crucifying yourself with some tact, so you could let the Paddles/Patch wearer/DH save the day by telling you that your pass was not so bad, your shot was actually decent employment, or that you're not a completely worthless JO.* "Well," Sam continued, "I think I was a little wide – I may have had a slight angling approach – and probably got a bit too flirty with the center ball – probably should've bumped it up a little more. In close, I felt alright, maybe a little too much VSI, but nothing heinous?" he finished, his incredibly flimsy statement surely a safe enough assessment not to sound presumptuous and upset the gods of the glideslope.

Unfortunately, BCB winced as Sam uttered the words 'nothing heinous.' He put his hand on Sam's shoulder. "Nickels... were you scared out there?"

"Uhh... no?" Sam responded, more of a question than a response.

"Ok – well... you should've been..." CAG Paddles gave Sam a grave look; the rest of the train did whatever they could to avoid eye contact, high-SA toward the verbal spanking that was about to occur. "We had you underlined angling approach, low in the middle with a power call," he widened his eyes and emphasized his voice at various portions of the pass, "and low at the ramp... for the No-Grade 2."

Sam was in shock. Like a good little lemming, he disguised that outrage from his voice – but surely revealed it in his face as he said, "Um... copy that, Paddles."

The line of LSOs remained silent. There was no clapping. No cheering. No fist bumping.

"Look, man, that is not something we want to see again," BCB started, as he raised his hands and prepared to deliver a collegiate lecture on carrier landings. "Just so we're on the same page here, let's review some ball-flying basics..."

He discussed everything from the coefficient of lift, to the way that weight can affect the turn radius of an aircraft, to the height of a lens cell at distance versus close range, to his personal technique of putting the turn and bank indicator at one-half a triangle away from the 30-degree tick mark. He anchored down on the importance of changing only one variable at a time, discussed seat height, what the round down truly looks like, the precise point the RADALT should be going off, what kind of wake line you'll expect to see based off ship speed, and how to adjust your turn accordingly. He grabbed an Artline marker and began writing equations on the board about crosswinds, artificial headwinds, and why they reference a 3.5-degree glideslope in the jet. He even offered Sam a revolutionary scan pattern technique of 'Ball, T.'

Ten minutes later, after phrases like 'axial winds,' 'wings-level-transition,' and 'proactive ball-flyer' had been discussed ad nauseum, BCB asked Sam, "So, does that all make sense? Do you have any other questions?"

Nodding, annoyed – but desperate to have this sermon over with – Sam responded, "Yes, it does, Paddles, and no, I don't."

"Alright, man." CAG Paddles leaned back and folded his arms. "Take this one on board as a tough lesson learned. Remember – you're going to school on every pass, and while this one hurts, it will always be a reminder of how bad it feels when you fuck up." He wasn't smiling. "Just be sure to keep the ball on the happy side of the lens, always respond to Paddles' voice," he added with underlined emphasis, "and you're gonna be fine – sound good, man?"

"Sure thing, Paddles," Sam affirmed, quickly running out of false adherence and patience.

And, most condescending of all, BCB finished the conversation by holding out his fist and looking for a peace treaty – evoking the same feeling as the dude who hits on your girlfriend, then walks up to ensure, 'Hey, we're cool, right?'

Sam unenthusiastically returned the fist bump and watched as the train of PLM pimps exited the ready room, the SDO again yelling, "Yeahhhhh baby, see you later, Paddles!!" as the white-shirt wearers started chanting, "Scotty doesn't know! Scotty doesn't know!"

Nickels stood motionless; his previous excitement dwindled, his appetite gone, and his mood ruined. He shook his head, threw his flight bag on the ground, and sat in his ready room chair – frustration worn over his entire body.

"Hey, Nickels... you alright?"

He looked up and saw Low T walking up and taking the seat next to him. Camilli had been in the ready room during the entire debrief, fine-tuning his High Aspect BFM briefing lab. He surely overheard the desecration of Rowland's inability to fly an effective 3-degree glideslope.

Sam shrugged. "Yeah, man, I'm ok... I just – fuck, dude. I hate this..."

"I know, man, I know... they can suck sometimes..." Kyle responded and nodded his head. He, of course, felt a bit sheepish, as he was an LSO – although it was not his wave team that No-Graded Nickels...

"It's just..." Sam clenched his fists, talking to the ground as much as his best friend, "... I hate so much about Paddles. I hate that their purpose is to stand out there and judge every minor deviation; I hate their stupid glasses and windswept hair; I hate their lame oversized patch they get for partying in Virginia Beach for two weeks. And I hate that they always think they're right, and that we can't question them – it's literally in their fucking 'rules'..."

Kyle didn't say a word, just grunted with acknowledgment – but Sam wasn't done.

"I hate that I can have an awesome flight, where nearly everything goes right, and I'm feeling great about my progression as an aviator – and yet the feeling of accomplishment is completely tainted by the way the last 15-18 seconds go. I hate that I often don't know if I'm going to be soaring to bed feeling like a million bucks, or slumping to my rack feeling like a complete fucking loser, all because of what this cult of Fresnel lens jabronis thinks happened in my cockpit – based off their eyeball cal and eardrum intuit. I hate that we have a metric that compares us all, posted every day in the ready room for people to mock my 'landing incompetence,' and that we celebrate these Little-High-All-the-Way heroes with patch candy at Foc'sle Follies."

228

Sam closed his eyes and bowed the bridge of his nose into his fingers. "I hate float coats. I hate power calls. I hate CAG Paddles' excitement on CATCC/Paddles radio checks. I hate boonie hats. I hate croakies. I hate that MAGIC CARPET is an acronym. I hate that Paddles is capitalized. I hate the grammatical inconsistency of a singular Paddles still being called a 'Paddles.' Dude, I'm even starting to hate midrats because you can always count on those underlined douchebags to show up and take over a table..."

Sam looked up at Kyle, took a deep breath, and sighed. "But you know what I hate the most?"

Saying nothing, Kyle simply waited for his dismal friend to continue.

Sam looked at his buddy, shook his head, and admitted, "I hate how much I fucking care. I hate that I've drunk the kool-aid. I hate what Paddles have done to my brain. Because, mark my words, Low T," he said with a driven look on his face, "I will one day be a top ballflyer, no matter how long I have to stay in to do it."

Kyle smiled softly, slapped his friend on the shoulder, and said, "Nickels — you've got the mindset of a champion, the will of a warrior, and the heart of an underlined OK dude. I have no doubt you'll get to that point — and you probably won't even have to go past your initial commitment to reach it."

Grinning, Sam said, "Thanks, bro — but you already know I'm a career guy."

"Yeah, yeah, I know," Kyle laughed, "Which is good — you know why?"

"Why?" Sam responded.

Slyly smirking, Low T chuckled and said, "Because you're never getting the top spot when you're going against me!"

Sam laughed. "Is that so?! Watch out, bro — I'm coming for your patch!" he said with a smile, pointing at Kyle's 'CVW-5 Top Hook' insignia. Shrugging, Rowland eased up, "Fuck it, I guess I'm still a bit hungry — let's get some rats."

The two best friends departed the ready room, still laughing. At the same time, the FNG SDO scrambled to finish the classified item inventory, held up by one of the DH's missing RMMs. The last thing the frazzled watchstander heard as the two walked out was Low T enthusiastically commenting, "Man, I sure hope they have Raisin Bran Crunch and soy milk left..."

~

Sam sat in his cockpit on the ACE Four spot, watching the third Noddik pilot fly his passes — and absolutely *nailing* them. *Who is this guy?* Sam asked himself multiple times, as the pilot continued flying pinpoint-perfect numbers down the VSI slide from the 180 all the way to touchdown. His abeam distances appeared to be carved out of marble. His groove lengths somehow lasted fifteen *through* eighteen seconds — it made no physical sense, but this guy did it. As he kept his angle of bank in, Sam could see the man's bulging shoulders popping through his flight suit — and as he began his roll-out, Sam noticed the wake of the boat aligned *perfectly* below his latissimus dorsi-enshrouded armpit — an on-and-on start, *every* time. And to no surprise, button 1 was completely *silent* during the entirety of the man's six passes; not a single comment from Paddles.

Sam looked over his bony shoulder at the men on the platform — composed of NEODD SWEVEN and a few American paddles. Aside from NEODD, who was too busy fiddling with the ILARTS screen to pay attention, the rest of the LSOs were simply shrugging and smiling, obviously in awe of the performance they were witnessing. Sam was positive that this phenom just put up a spotless session of all OKs. If this line period was a female specimen, he knew it was akin to Lacey Chabert in *Mean Girls:* _Perfection_

As the mysterious Noddik guy taxied back after his final trap — a pass *so* sexy that it must have been enhanced with a filter — Sam began to feel the tingly butterfly nerves re-enter his stomach — a feeling he was ready to *grasp*. As soon as this jabroni cleared the LA and parked, the Air Boss was going to taxi Sam to the cat and launch him for what would be the sixth and final round of Phase 2.

Surely *that guy can't be IROK or T6...* Sam insisted to himself. *But Juice has already gone, too...* While Sam was manning up earlier, he saw Ward airborne, bagging traps like a champ. Juice's grades likely showed it, too, as he threw in what appeared to be 5 OKs and a Fair — but even the Admin *King* looked like an SNA compared to the display this jacked dude put on.

>SADCLAM< had given a strong showing, but unfortunately, was forced to fly some of his passes with NEODD on the MOVLAS stick, which ended up becoming quite the controversy. Sam could hear the frustration in Houben's voice over TAC as NEODD gave him completely erroneous signals, sometimes forgetting the stick even existed and showing him a red-ball-low the entire pass. 'Dude, *fuck* this choch; I'm gonna bolter all day if I listen to him!' he'd complained to Sam. Unsure how to handle it, >SADCLAM< just started using his eyeball cal, throwing in some masterful glideslope passes without any ball reference whatsoever — but alas... NEODD was *not* happy with this, and docked Houben's score for not listening to Paddles. The CAG Padroid's programming did a great job of exuding appalled disbelief at how egregious this error of flying safe and smooth self-contained passes was, as it was a total middle finger to the platform, insinuating that LSOs were an unnecessary and archaic part of the equation. As a result, he gave >SADCLAM< a few No-Grades — a reprieve from his intended Cut pass ratings, which the other Paddles talked the Padroids out of.

Between Chris' grades, the decent turnout from the first no-name guy who flew for USS Ship, and the impressive performances of Juice and the still-visored mysterious Noddik pilot after IROK's bingo? Rowland was sure the scores had to be close; like any good playoff game, it was coming down to its final moments. *Well, Nickels, it's crunch time—it's a do-or-die, now-or-never, win-or-go-home, must-win situation; time to see who wants it more down the stretch...* he monologued, rattling off clichés to amp himself up. *But as the saying goes: Pressure makes diamonds.*

"205, base," the AUX radio transmitted, attempting to garner Sam's attention.

"Go for 205," Sam responded.

"205, this is LTJG Narrator. The judges have tallied the Paddles' scores, and we have the SITREP for you; advise when ready to copy."

"Ready to copy." Sam lowered his voice an octave, trying to sound cool and confident, like a radio DJ looking to seduce and entice.

"SITREP Delta is as follows: You need to fly 4 FAIRs and 2 OKs in order to secure winning grades for the USS Ship and force a Phase 3. Do you copy?"

"Big copy," Sam affirmed, adding the word 'big' to demonstrate he was calm and collected, vice petrified by the heft of the reality that this momentous occasion was resting entirely on his shoulders—frail shoulders with zero 3D separation and even less vascularity. Searching to further this ruse and believe his own charade of confidence, he had a flash of brilliance—*Oh, man, this will be so good!* His body intuitively reached for an impression—this time, what Tom Hardy once called a 'Romani gypsy' impersonation—as he covered his mouth and transmitted, "Let the games begin!"

"Hah." Narrator responded mercifully.

It was a desperate ploy on Sam's part—*anyone* who knew him realized that impressions were his calling card to fabricate false bravado when anxious. And right now, he needed all the artificial confidence he could muster—because deep down? Captain Rowland, in his PLM F/A-18E, was a scared little Lieutenant Junior Grade, flying a manual T-45C Goshawk in Advanced training CQ off the coast of San Diego...

Alright, Sam. Come on—You KNOW this: 500 at the 90. You're a 28-degree angle of bank guy. 1.2 abeam at 44k. Or... was it 1.3 at that weight? Shit. See the white of the round down... power, pause, turn. Err... was that a T-45-ism? What was the VSI again at the 135 again? Ok, remember you need to kiss idle on the wings level transition—wait a second... do we do that in PLM, too? Should I click in after *that? And is a wingdip actually reducing lift anymore, or is that fake news?*

Sam shook his head in irritation. *Come on, dude—you have to have this shit down by now—you're a fucking Captain. You've landed on the boat hundreds of times—and who cares about the times when Paddles wasn't so happy? You know what you're doing, and you can nail these numbers—or at least get pretty close. Those douchebags were just being overly critical of you because you were newer to the air wing. It's a fucking admin drill—there's no real skill in it. It's just an arbitrary view from some dude on a platform who thinks he saw a deviation—probably because he's literally three-fucking-quarters-of-a-mile away! 'Rough wings all the way'... give me a break. I'm just 'flying the ball all the way to touchdown' like you told me to since day one... Fuck that shit, dude. Just six safe passes, Sam, and you're home free...*

Sam's jet was finally unchained and released, as he cleared off his Plane Captain with a salute and was taxied forward for a hook check—flawless administrative execution, like he'd never even left the carrier. He did his takeoff checks with ease from bottom to top, and even knocked out his own personalized FTR-DKC for good measure. *Harness? Eight ways, playa'! Trim—4 up?! Make it* siete! *Wings? Spread eagle, baby!* His self-pep talks were not admirable—they were pathetic. He knew these things cold—getting them right wasn't an actual win or confidence booster. The obvious inner truth was that he was doing whatever he could to keep his mind off the phase of flight he *wasn't* confident in; the facet he just *couldn't* seem to get a knack for. For an admin Greek God like Sam, he was practically shimmering with perfection—but even Achilles' had his heel—and for Sam, ball-flying was the one part of his administrative physique not dipped in gold.

Still searching his soul for the inspiration to perform for the 15-18 seconds when it mattered most, he professionally and expeditiously followed the yellow shirts' directions and ended up in line with the catapult—as one always does with sound administrative discipline. He noticed the catapult director was a smoke show—in his younger JO days, he would've daydreamed about a midnight slam in the fan room with her—but not today. There was no time for lustful distractions; right now, the only thing Sam cared about slamming was the *deck*—at a passionate 500-750 feet per minute.

The tight-pants siren gave him the run-up signal, and Sam threw the throttles forward. He raised the launch bar—SA bubble off the *charts* with his cognizance of the NATOPS caution about HYD2A—and finished his reverse takeoff checks with authority, aggressively stomping his rudders to 'put on a show' as he'd always been taught—as if 'deflected flight controls' was an awe-inspiring display to be 'oohed and ahhed' at. He gave a crisp salute that had the yellow shirt hot and bothered, and braced his helmet against the headbox—ready to count his airspeed from 48 and up like usual.

With a whoosh, he quickly whispered, "49... 50... 51-52-53-54555657..." and when he reached "*One hundred,*" he exhaled. *Good cat...* he climbed up to pattern altitude, dropped his hook, masterfully clicked the NWS and ATC buttons—and just like that, his landing checks were complete. All that was left? Flying the pattern... and the ball. And *that* was truly where, as Bane would say, 'the games began'...

Sam turned downwind—and immediately began zig-zagging between a 1.4 and 1.1 abeam distance, hoping that at some point, the boat sight picture would look normal. He pulled up the checklist page—his favorite display in the jet—and stared at the 42,000 lb calculated landing weight. *Uhhh... 1.3 or 1.2... split the difference? Fuck... what was it again? Oh shit!* He quickly realized he'd descended to 580 feet on the RADALT, and immediately yanked the stick back and zoomed to 660,' unbeknownst that he was sliding into a 1.1 abeam on the TCN course line deviation. When he realized *that*, he stuffed the nose down and took a BFM-style cut away, drawing all kinds of color on his AOA indexers in the process. He couldn't help but imagine what a beta falling leaf he probably looked like to the Paddles on the platform. *Fuck those jabronis — judge away, dipshits... I'm just trying to fly your fucking numbers.* He shook his head in frustration. *This whole Phase 2... this whole concept of competitive ball-flying... this whole part of admin that isn't even admin... it's all so fucking stupid!*

What Sam didn't realize was that he, once again, was crushing his line period with his own insecurities and self-projected incompetence. He didn't understand that his years of Fairs had nothing to do with his misunderstanding of the numbers, nothing to do with a Paddles-vendetta, nothing about his adherence to the game plan — but *everything* to do with his *mindset*.

And when Sam finally got to the start, he called the ball — as he had in his very first look from the back of the boat in the T-45 — high, with an angling approach, and then flailed like his jet was having a 13-second seizure, all the way to a fly-through down at the ramp; catching a wire, but plummeting his confidence even further.

"Jesus fucking *Christ*..." he growled to himself as he cleared the Landing Area.

And then — *of course* — he heard the voice and words he'd been anticipating and dreading, yet *praying* he wouldn't hear: "205, Paddles."

Ugh... GREAT... Sam recognized the voice, too. A former CAG Paddles of his — Blue Collar Bill. "Go for 205..."

"Hey man, not sure what that was, but... *not* what we wanna see out there, ok? I know you've been out of the game for a while, so do me a favor: take a deeeeeep breath, and ehhhhxhaaale." BCB audibly exhaled on the radio, exacerbating Sam's annoyance. "Ok? Remember, we're looking for *500* at the 90 — you barely even descended off the 180. And your approach turn? You were angling in big time — whatever abeam distance you used, you need to push it in, ok? So — relax, wiggle your toes, and fly a solid pattern with the game plan pass and numbers, ok?"

Sam rolled his eyes. He *hated* being told 'wiggle your toes' more than any other fucking phrase in his life — and he also hated all the morons who insisted 'hEy, It ReAlLy WoRkS!' as if toe kinetics were some type of revolutionary fucking cheat code to calm down high-strung nerves. From FORM4101 in primary as an Ensign, to the CQ Phase of the Admin Olympics as a fucking *Captain*, he was *still* hearing this shit...

"205?" BCB repeated, looking for affirmation.

"205," Sam responded, void of emotion.

Sam shook his head in frustration as he taxied back to the catapult, not even caring to return the salacious smile of the gorgeous yellow shirt. *That was a No-Grade for sure... FUCK!* He quickly did some math — another foolish CQ novice move — and realized he'd now have to fly 3 OKs and two Fairs to make up for his heinous starter pass. As he got the power-up signal, he lazily throttled up and unenthusiastically wiped out the controls, launching off the ship with a *little* less weight — and a *lot* less belief.

As he turned downwind, he once again got caught up in the matrix of numbers as he tried to perfectly nail each parameter, hyper-focusing — one at a time — on each element of basic airwork... at the expense of literally every *other* variable in the equation. When he was on altitude, he failed to hold his abeam distance. When scanning his angle of the bank, he was unable to manage his VSI. When he checked to ensure he had a good FPAH ATC in his HUD, he neglected to notice that — in the chaotic shuffle — he'd inexplicably turned his dispensers on.

This approach turn was slightly less gross, yet with the same deviations. As he angled in once again — rolling in with a ball *barely* tickling the top of the lens — Sam called the ball, stumbling over his words and accidentally calling himself '203.' For the next 12 seconds, he managed to ride the stenograph down to a 4-wire, to the tune of screaming "YOU'RE HIGH!" "DON'T CLIMB!" and "*EASY WITH IT!!!*" calls from BCB.

He taxied off, and again held his breath — before slamming his fist on the canopy as he heard "205, Paddles."

FUCK! "Go for 205..."

The displeasure was obvious in BCB's voice. "205 — listen. You just showed me back-to-back angling approaches with high starts... dude, that *cannot* happen again. What is rule number 7 of the rules to live by?"

Matching BCB's increasing frustration with his own, Sam refused to answer. They were two intense dueling personalities; ironically livid with one another, despite both working toward the same end goal of a picturesque pass.

"Ok... good talk," BCB said sarcastically. "It's 'Go to school every pass' — and 205, you are *not* doing that. Please, show me something different, even a *heinous* overshoot, for god's sake! But by making the same mistake twice, you're demonstrating you're not listening, not adjusting, and not *learning*. And man, that ball-flying... you're not controlling it. You're flying *reactively*, letting the ball dictate your movements... your lack of confidence is exposing itself through the way you're waggling your wings and control surfaces all the way down the groove. It's just *not* what we want. You need to be proactive, control the ball the way *you* want, and be *smoother* all the way to touchdown. 205 — I don't know how else to say it: you simply need to *be the ball*. The fate of America's administrative reputation depends on your ability to *learn* from mistakes and correct course, without wasting any more —"

Ok, that's fucking it. Sam had heard enough. His frustration boiled over, as he keyed the mic, waited for the blip of sound, and drowned BCB out with, "Paddles —

shut up. Shut the *fuck* up. 'Go to school every pass,' 'Fly the ball proactively,' 'Be the ball' — give me a fucking *break*, Blue Collar Bitch. These phrases mean absolutely *nothing*. An egregious error on the opposite side of the spectrum? Is that *really* what you want? You *really* want me to fly a 0.5 abeam and divebomb at the 180 — coming in lined up with the tower and skimming the ocean wavetops — to show that I've 'earned my degree' in bracketing? Suck my dick, Bill. And 'be the ball'... *please*... get the *fuck* out of here with that shit. Dude, you and every other Paddles need a fucking reality check. You guys are an antiquated part of this business, desperately fabricating minor deviations and subsequently critiquing them, just to *cling* to relevancy — and it's fucking *pathetic*.

Pausing for hardly a second before gaining a bit more emotion in his voice, Sam continued, "Don't you get it? I'm fucking *trying,* douchebags. I'm flying your fucking numbers the *best I can*! I'm doing *everything* I can to get to a good start; do you think I'm *intentionally* angling in or showing up high, for shits and grins? And Jesus, man — I *realize* that smooth would be better — again, I'm not fucking *attempting* to look spastic on the ball; I'm flying it to touchdown — *like the rules* also *say!* — so yeah, fucking forgive me if I'm 'rough with my wings,' making corrections the entire way down!" Sam's voice was brash, full of rage. But his heart? It was all an emotional wreck — a career's worth of ineptitude on CV landings coming to a precipice, all being taken out on somebody simply trying to keep him safe.

Sam nearly got choked up from frustration as he finished his rant, "Listen... I'm fucking *trying,* Paddles. I'm *trying* to be the ball-flyer you want me to be. I'm *trying* to understand this part of the business. I've been trying my whole life — but I just *can't fucking do it*..."

Sam released the mic as he taxied aft of the JBDs and set the parking brake. There was no response from BCB or any of the Paddles. Surely, they were not pleased. Surely, his words had gone too far. Surely, they were communicating with the Handler about where to stuff Sam and call Phase 2 done with.

The silence was deafening — as Sam started to comprehend that this may have been *it*. After all his good will? Nickels might've just put the administrative nail in the coffin for the USS Ship — all due to his piss poor attitude, his ORM-nightmarish mindset, and his inability to *try* hard enough...

"205, you there?" BCB called out.

And then Sam realized — in his hysteria, he had committed a fundamental administrative mistake: he actuated the *incorrect* radio, inadvertently transmitting his entire rant on the secure J-Voice Alpha channel 95. And ironically... the admin error from the admin guru may have saved his career — and America's chances in these Olympics.

His venting out of his system, he took a deep breath and keyed on PRI radio, "Affirm; sorry about that, Paddles — was dealing with some comm issues. Copy all."

"Paddles," BCB closed the loop.

As he sat before the JBDs, waiting to taxi forward for his third pass, Sam thought about his previous one—specifically, the tone in BCB's voice—and figured he was looking at *another* No-Grade. *Shit... what the fuck, man. Now I need* four *OKs?! Dude... I'm screwed...*

With barely a trace of hope remaining, Sam shook his head. *God* damn, *dude... what the* fuck *do I have to do to make these douchebags happy?*

"Perhaps he's wondering why someone would *hate* a man... who was helping him land a plane?!" a muffled, gypsy-accented 'Bane' impersonator called out over the radio.

Sam's head whipped up toward his UFCD, where he caught the J-Voice Alpha transmission box illuminated. *Was somebody up on J-Voice?! And that impersonation... it's incredible!* Hesitantly, he keyed the mic on Voice Alpha and asked, "Say again? Who are you?"

Heavy breathing amongst the responses, the voice responded, "It doesn't matter who we are... what matters is how you land!"

Confused and silent, Sam kept listening as he taxied to the cat, and the voice then further expounded, "No one cared who *I* was until I flew an _OK_ pass..."

Annoyed, Sam scoffed. "What does it matter—Paddles and pass grades are pointless. Imagine how much nicer life would be without them!"

"It would be extremely painful..."

Sam laughed and said, "I'm sure the LSOs could get by!"

"... For *you*," the mystery man added ominously.

The prop of an overhead COD reverberated in the air as the cargo plane held in the stack, waiting for this evolution to end so it could land and unload its passengers. As he ran up the power, Nickels rolled his eyes and continued the dialogue with this unknown entity, whining, "All these guys do is harass us, being overly judgmental over the most minor of deviations—when in reality, everything is completely safe." He sighed, then admitted, "It's just the goddamn case 1 day pattern that crushes me—I wish we always flew straight-ins, like at night..."

"Ohhhh, you think *darkness* is your ally?!" the voice mocked. "But you merely *adopted* the era of easy OK passes at night! I was *born* in darkness; *molded* by it—flying *manual* passes! I know why *you* like the darkness: in the blackness of night, you are blinded from the imperfections of your pattern... ignorant to your minor deviations. On a 10-mile, pitch-black straight-in, there's no distractions to stop you from zoning!"

"Zoning?!" Sam asked reactively.

"Zoning!" he repeated, still speaking in the Bane accent. "A state where you find a new level of focus by turning off all other stimuli... where all outside distractions are non-existent... where nothing else matters but *subconscious execution*. When you're

236

in that zone, it doesn't matter what you did on the previous pass... on a previous line period... *in a previous career...*"

Nickels gasped. Who *was* this mysterious voice? "Is it possible for a bad ball-flyer like me to enter this zone?"

"*Of course!*" the Voice Alpha man affirmed, before growing more serious in tone. "Nickels... I hear your concerns. But more importantly, I hear your *heart* – the heart of a *champion.* But also, a heart held back by your lack of confidence... Sam – you *know* the numbers. You *know* the rules to live by. You *know* how to fly the ball. But what you *don't* know is if you trust yourself to do it – and therein lies your problem. It's not your abeam distances, VSIs, or corrections; it's your *belief.*"

As he saluted and launched off the cat, Sam said nothing, letting the spot-on impersonation continue.

"You fly like a younger man!" the voice yelled teasingly, then once again delved into a philosophical spiel. "Sam, you're flying like a RAG student, overly concerned with being overly prepared in an adaptability/flexibility-based business... You're nuking everything. You're turning an artistic science into a binary matrix of paralysis by analysis – and your indecisiveness is rearing its head on every single facet of the pass, as you question every decision you make before it even has a *chance* to play out. You're the aspiring dieter, freaking out about whether or not bone broth breaks a fast, trying to calculate the extra calories from the beer you drank at the O-club, and fretting over missing your protein macros by three grams! You're doing *way* too much, and being a total try-hard. It's as if you're trying to fly *perfectly...*"

Fasting? Calories? Protein? This guy knows... As Sam turned downwind, he internalized what this nutritionally-woke mystery man was saying to him – and realized how close to home his strange analogy hit.

"Sam... life isn't about being *perfect.* Yes, we chase perfection – but we don't freak out when we fail to attain it. Plenty of jacked athletic specimens have gone over their calorie allotment on a day or two en route to 6% body fat... just as plenty of superb ball-flyers have shown up with a bit of an overshoot on the path to a 4.0-line period. The key to success isn't perfect adherence – it's the belief in your abilities to *make it happen* in less-than-perfect cirumstances. Do you believe you can fly four OK passes, Sam?"

"... I'm not sure Paddles believes it," he responded weakly, "but I can try..."

"Who gives a *fuck* what Paddles thinks?!" the man yelled passionately. "Is earning *Paddles'* approval going to make your life hold any more worth?! Does *Paddles'* opinion of you change how much effort you *know* you put into this job?! Is a top-10 ball-flyer patch going to change the lifelong bonds you created with your brothers?!"

"... No..." Sam responded sheepishly.

"That's right. And moreover—I don't want to hear any of this 'try' shit. Sam, why the hell *shouldn't* you believe in yourself?! You know your admin *cold*—and that *includes* this pattern. Stop *trying* so hard, as if you hadn't prepared. Because you *have* put in the time, and you *have* built the resume—you're the fucking *Admin King*—so start flying like you believe you've earned the title. Self-belief is more powerful than any VSI or turn point gouge—and even if everybody else on that platform doubts you? *Your* belief is the only thing that matters in the arena. This line period already ain't perfect, so quit trying to fly it that way—and just *do*: Do fly like you believe in yourself, *do* fly like you're not afraid to make mistakes, and *do* fly like you're the Admin King, undeterred by what any other clown in the realm says about your passes. Then, and only then, can you enter the zone... and truly *be the ball*."

Fly like the Admin King... the words reverberated in Sam's head. It sounded so... simple. For so long, *trying* to be perfect was all he knew: Hyperawareness to errors. Neurotic adherence to rules and constraints. Constant second and third guessing of his decisions. For once, maybe he needed to quit *trying;* to instead start trusting his aviation intuition—built from years of preparation—and just *do*.

As he scanned the boat to his left, he realized his abeam distance 'felt about right.' He shifted his focus to the white of the round down... without looking at any numbers, he began his turn on what 'felt normal-ish.' And as he looked up to check his angle of bank, he concluded it 'felt close enough.' He didn't worry about nitpicking a degree here or there—he could fix any deviations out of the turn. Instead, he focused on his belief. Sam had always *seen* these visual cues, but now—finally—he was *feeling* them.

He rolled out into the groove, and—with a quick scan of his fuel, and *without* neurotically rehearsing it in his head—made a ball call bursting with collectedness and testosterone, beginning the most critical 15-18 seconds of his life. But this time, his diagnostic brain was shut down. He wasn't pressing, wasn't flailing, wasn't over-analyzing. He was *striving* for perfection—but not *trying* for it.

And before he knew it... *trap*. He could barely even recall the pass—because his internal tapes had been turned off. It was probably the best glideslope he'd ever flown in his life—and he had nearly no clue how he'd done it. But it didn't matter... because now? He'd found it: *the zone*.

"205, Paddles."

"Go for 205," Sam responded with renewed self-assurance.

"I don't know what just happened... but whatever that was? *Great* pass—3 more like *that*," BCB said with point-blank approval.

"205."

The next ten minutes were a complete blur to Sam. He'd discovered the beauty of the zone—the advantage of turning off real-time analytics, and simply acting off instinct, built from preparation, executed with *belief*. A place where his brain *wasn't* embedded with over-awareness to deviations or data to mentally cripple himself with—where he simply just *flew*. No previous pass or pattern infraction lingered—because they didn't *matter*. Honing his inner TB12 mindset, he firmly believed it: the most important pattern, most important 180 turn point, most important 15-18 second span of his life? Was the *next* one. Purely *fucking* zoning.

Sam's next two passes quickly went cat-trap, cat-trap—with zero comments from Paddles, zero cases of in-flight indecisiveness, and zero real-time recollection. He wasn't trying—he was *doing*.

As he lined up for his last catapult shot, someone radio'd over button 18 rep frequency, "Captain Rowland, this is ITC Smith—I work for CAG ADP. Hey sir, I noticed your Cyber Security Awareness Challenge is expired."

Sam couldn't believe his luck.

"That's an annual Navy-wide requirement, sir," the chief continued. "You're gonna lose NMCI access until you complete it."

He'd waited his whole life for a moment like this—and in his state of flow, *of course* he knew exactly what to say.

"So, sir, I'm gonna need you to shut down right now, log onto NKO, and—"

"Not now, Chief," Sam interrupted with big-time BDE. "I'm in the *fuckin'* zone."

He turned his AUX radio off as he was put into tension, powered to MIL, and prepared to give one final sharp salute as he turned to his right. Yet beyond the tantalizing catapult directress—whose skin looked slightly less radiant as a storm cell passed overhead and eclipsed the sunlight—his eye caught the face of a man watching him—the third Noddik pilot, who'd finished his line period just before Sam's. But despite his intergalactic affiliation, this man was certainly *not* a foreign face...

What?! "No fucking way..." Sam breathlessly whispered, in shock at who he was seeing.

The eyes staring at him—rife with agony and suffering. The neck holding the furious glare—reinforced with vascularity and excessive JHMCS-usage. And the mustache atop that chiseled jawline—bursting with familiarity and testosterone. There was no mistaking it—LT Kyle Camilli was alive, jacked, and *angry*. Sam's former best friend—whom he'd abandoned for a foreign empire—was now flying for that *very* Noddik Empire that had caused so much strife in Nickels' life. And flying *damn* good, from what Sam had witnessed. *He hasn't missed a beat... But what's he doing here? Why is he helping the Noddiks? Why—*

"205, *power back please!*" an angry voice boomed over button 1.

Oh shit. Sam looked forward—his canopy now showered in mist from the rainclouds—and saw a very angry yellow shirt aggressively motioning for him to reduce his power to idle. Sam pulled the throttles back and took another glimpse at Low T, who was now shaking his head.

"205, everything alright down there?" the Air Boss called on button 1. "Your PC suspended you for not doing a wipeout."

Sam responded sheepishly, "Uhhh, yes, sir... just thought I, uhh... saw something weird. I'm good to go."

"Alright, well, unless you see a ghost on my flight deck, please pay attention in the meantime," he quacked in snarky Air Boss fashion. "We'll run you back up."

I wish that was a ghost... Sam thought. *Fuck... what's he doing here? First trying to shoot me down, and now* this? *Is he out for revenge or something?* He debated the possibilities while dropping his launch bar and moving the jet toward tension. *But why? He said* he wasn't angry that I was leaving... he promised that we were brothers for life –

No! There's no time! He shook his head as the overhead showers became a downpour, and ambient thunder roared. *I need to keep my focus and get one more solid trap!*

But it was too late—the focus... the effortless flow... the *zoning* – Sam was out of it. He found himself thinking back to all the stupid things in life that didn't matter: his shitty first two passes and history of bad ball-flying. The people he'd hurt when he left the Chippies for the NIRD Katsopolis job. The Cyber Security Awareness Challenge the chief asked him about. *I could've* sworn I just *did it! Was that before October, or did –*

Deedle Deedle. As Sam ran the throttles up, he saw a CK TRIM caution. *Fuck!* He then committed the admin cardinal sin—fixing deviations on takeoff run-up—and quickly dialed his trim to 7 up and gave the shooter a salute. As he looked right, he took one last look at Low T's squared, clenched jaw—and he remembered the words Kyle had once told him: *'You're* never *getting the top spot when you're going against me!'*

Sam looked forward, leaned his head back, and waited in anxious anticipation—panic and uncertainty prevalent in his mind. It was the worst kind of disconcerting dread an aviator could feel: *praying* that this launch was going to go off without a hitch, scanning your eyes frantically for *any* sign of a forgotten administrative item... And as he felt the accelerated whoosh of the catapult, he immediately heard another aural caution tone—and on his LDDI, he saw the letters that made his heart sink: HYD 2A. *Fuck! The launch bar!*

Sure enough, Sam had forgotten to raise his launch bar prior to the cat shot. It was not the ghost of Kyle Camilli, but his complacent certainty of NATOPS mastery that had come back to haunt him. "Uhhh... Paddles, 205..."

While ducking past clouds in the crosswind turn, he explained the caution to the platform—without explaining the source. *That can come later...*

"Alright 205," BCB responded, "Well, good news and bad news: *Fortunately,* this is your last pass. With just a HYD 2A, and already dirty? You're in a pretty decent position for coming aboard. *Unfortunately,* upgrades are not permitted in Admin Olympics, so this pass will be graded on the same scale as the others. But do what you've been doing, 205, and we should be money."

"205."

Unfortunately, now—*far* removed from the zone—Sam's pattern was horrendous. He was back to second-guessing himself, still frustrated that he made such a critical administrative error and induced a hydraulic seal failure. Not to mention, he was even *more* thrown off by the presence of his former best friend—now apparently working alongside Juice to bring about his demise. None of it made sense—and neither did the 1.6 abeam Sam was flying as he trekked out wide—before quickly cutting back in and hitting the 180 with a 30-degree bite already toward the ship—and 100' low.

"At the 180, you're low," BCB's voice called out.

Shit... is that already going to take away my OK? Sam BFM'd up to the 90, now showing 550 feet.

"At the 90..." BCB's sighed with annoyance, "... You're *high...*"

Fuck... I blew it... Sam hated the way this pass was going... he hated that he was again flying so neurotically... he hated that he was making so many stupid mistakes... but most of all, he hated *himself*—for yet again *failing to believe...*

As he rolled into the groove and made a jacked-up ball call, Sam felt hopelessness saturate his soul. For the next 24 seconds, Sam's indecisiveness returned in full force, as he jerked the stick around like he was attempting a Mortal Kombat fatality— fitting, given this phase was about to finish him—and internally bemoaned everything being lost in this one pass. *Juice, the Noddiks, and now Kyle... they're going to win. I couldn't do it... I couldn't be good enough for the Noddiks—and* then *I couldn't be good enough for the United States. I pride myself on admin—and yet I can't even do the most basic administrative action in the most critical phase of flight... with a fucking MAGIC CARPET landing system! Forgive me, CLAM... JABA... CP... FISTY... indomitable Dambusters of past—I have failed you all...*

Amongst plenty of Paddles calls, from "You're high, work it down," to "Right for lineup... RIGHT. FOR. LINEUP!" to "Little power... power... POWER!" Sam found himself earning a full-on soliloquy from Blue Collar Bill. As he added way too much power with a way-too-aggressive wingdip In Close, Sam shook his head as he heard the words, "Waveoff, waveoff, waveoff..."

Sam closed his eyes and rotated at on-speed...

"... Foul deck."

Sam's heart skipped a beat. *No way! Another chance?* The pass wouldn't count; he'd have one more...

Voice Alpha chimed again, as the mysterious man—still with the muffled Romani gypsy accent—asked, "Why do we fall, Sam?"

241

"... So we can learn to pick ourselves up?" Sam responded, uncertain in his answer, and why Bane would ever be saying this quote.

"Nickels... is this *Bruce Wayne's* story?" The man paused, "... Or *yours?*"

As he turned downwind, Sam could've *sworn* he heard the indistinguishable voice of WYFMIFM, as if he was speaking into his subconscious: "The mountain is still there to be climbed... It is your destiny, Nickels..."

Sam took a deep breath. He understood. He keyed the mic and confidently said, "We fall... so that we can *climb.*"

As if by divine intervention, a ray of sunlight enveloped his jet from a small break in the clouds. The weather had lifted slightly, and his path to the 180 was clear. And to *further* the dramatic emphasis of the moment, Hans Zimmer's classic song 'Why Do We Fall?' began playing in Sam's head—and the reader's, by extension.

The Innocent Climb... working as one cohesive unit... with no outside distractions... Sam looked at his airspeed, altitude, angle of bank, and TACAN distance—so much information. So many stimuli. *So distracting...* He turned his HUD off.

"Paddles, 205."

"205, uh... everything good, dude?" BCB asked. "That pass was a little—"

"This one's gonna be No-HUD," Sam said confidently.

"Confirm you said you lost your HUD?!" BCB sounded panicked. "What's wrong?"

"Nothing, I'm alright."

As Sam entered the downwind, the song's tempo started getting quicker, the drums louder, the moment riper for a heroic effort. At the same time, every single negative lingering thought appeared in his mind—and then evaporated from his consciousness, one at a time: His waveoff just prior, his shitty line periods as a JO, every non-OK pass he'd ever flown in his life; The Deal, his betrayal, JABA and CP's ruined businesses, >SADCLAM<'s brainwashing, WYFMIFM's apparent death, FISTY's vegetated state, Dr. Suabedissen's D&D rants, Kyle's ominous return, Juice's admin superiority; CAG's hair standards, CAG's spool-ups, CAG's laptop, CAG's wrestling record—thanks a lot, Jufro... He freed his mind from the bullshit of the boat: sorting garbage just to have it invalidated, ship's alarm testing four-a-days, catapult tests in the middle of the night; morning GQ, evening GQ, Big XO's rants about GQ; on-load workload, off-load workload, ready room setup, ready room teardown; the overly-crowded gyms, the random gym closures for sea states, the rampant gym bozos who felt the need to put on a desperate display of flexing, peacocking, and post-set-"oh, *fuck*"-ing; setting alerts, standing alerts, launching alerts; thin line ops, EMCON ops, marginally less-shitty full-up internet ops; self-serve laundry restrictions, self-serve laundry closures, potable water running dry mid-shower, potable water running *out* mid-*cruise*; Page 13s, SF-86s, PSQs, SAAR-N forms; Gippernet requests, locked accounts, CAG

ADP's working hours, CAG ADP's super-secret location, CAG ADP's closed-door policy, fucking *CAG ADP, period*. He even let go of his personal shortcomings: his missed opportunities in his late 20s due to negativity, his missed potential in his late teens due to timidity, and his missed progression in *life* due to failure-fearing anxiety; his RAG instructor who told him his comms were "unprofessional" because he used his callsign *last* in ATC transmissions, his out-of-shape-Bruce Willis-lookalike District Manager who wanted him let go from the company, his old skipper who believed him to be the 'ringleader' of JOs who didn't put in effort; every SDO ass-blasting he ever received for inconsequential bullshit by an ass-blaster who hadn't stood the fucking watch in over a decade; every person who ever doubted, overlooked, or spurned him—and of course, his fucking *expired* Cyber Security Awareness Challenge.

All of those thoughts disappeared—because Sam had done it: he'd returned to *the zone*. As the tempo got even faster—the song approaching its apex, and Sam *swearing* he could hear the Paddles chanting "Deshi, deshi, basara, basara!"—he flew downwind with no HUD references, no HYD 2A, and no real-time fucks to give about the weight of the moment. He wasn't trying for anything; he was just *doing*.

He rounded the corner, rolled out, and made the call, "205, Rhino Ball, Rate, No HUD, No HYD, final."

BCB responded, "Roger ball, rate, no HUD, no HYD, final."

The beat reached its crescendo—a dead pause in the melody for 15-18 seconds—and Sam blacked out. He was flowing. Doing. *Zoning.*

X... IM... IC... AR... TRAP.

Sam processed nothing but a centered ball the entire way down...

... And the flight deck *erupting* with triumphant celebration. He safe'd his seat, turned off all his equipment with administratively sound procedures, shut the jet down on the six pack, and hopped out to the uproarious welcome from a group of ecstatic United States sailors. Amongst the crowd, he saw >SADCLAM<, CP, and JABA running toward him, all cheering wildly.

"Dude!" >SADCLAM< yelled, "You fucking *did* it! That last pass clinched Phase 2 for us! That was fucking *legendary,* brother!"

CP gave him a long head-nodding approval and said, "Incredible work, Samuel—I only doubted you until the very last second, after those first two hot garbage passes you threw out. For a minute, I was worried we had Dimes out there..." He then smiled wide, "But thank *god* Nickels showed up for America today; a man who knows how to keep us on the edge of our seats until the very last moment—when the Good Dude at heart rises."

Sam laughed and smiled back. "Thanks, CP—to be honest, I doubted *myself* for way too long out there—and that wouldn't have changed without—" *Wait... who* was *that?* WYFMIFM? "... without you guys *believing* enough to pass me the lead in crunch time," he said, light tears in his eyes.

Grinning, CP acknowledged, "You may appear to be a weak and atrophied version of your former self... but you were a true Chippy athlete when it mattered most."

The two fist bumped, as JABA approached and him a gigantic hug. "Sam, that was *incredible* Admin Under Pressure! God, this is the stuff I miss about this job..." JABA looked out longingly to the sea and whispered, "If only there was still a way..." before turning back to Sam and emphasizing, "God, I'm so dang proud of you, man!"

Running high off the ecstasy of the moment, Sam hugged his Chippy brother again. "We're getting you back in the fleet, man, we're getting you back... I can't climb this mountain alone..."

JABA shed a tear in happiness — touched by the gesture, but still well aware of Navy's extreme unwillingness to take *anybody* back after active duty separation, due to their overabundance of manning.

Out of curiosity, Sam couldn't help but wonder as he asked JABA, "Hey, on that last pass, was that a legit foul deck, or a 'foul deck?'" he emphasized with air quotes and suspicious eyes.

Looking amused and wide-eyed, JABA said, "Dude, that was *real!* You wouldn't believe it — some joker must've dropped this flight bag," he held up a helmet bag, "because it went rolling across the flight deck *just* as you were about to touch down! Thank God, too... because that pass was looking, uh..." JABA grimaced and cranked his head a bit, "a *litttttle* spicy!"

Sam laughed. "Oh, you're not wrong about that! It was *heinous,* bro! Hey... can I see that bag?"

"Sure!" JABA said happily.

Buck handed the generic helmet bag to Sam, who opened it up to inspect the contents — a clipboard, a blue pen, dark-shaded sunglasses, a BLACKPINK CD, and a free guest pass to Gold's Gym in Venice Beach, CA. Sam chuckled, and looked to the sky, whispering aloud to himself, "The harder you work, the luckier you get... thanks, WYFMIFM. Thanks for everything."

After the COD landed and the civilian dweebs started filing out, signaling the end of the recovery, Sam found himself crowded by seemingly every flight deck personnel aboard the ship.

"YOU!" a voice called out.

Sam turned and saw Blue Collar Bill emerging from the mob of sailors, his finger pointed directly at the hero of the hour. The two looked at each other and said nothing; silence captured the onlookers.

BCB continued with, "*You* are *still* dangerous!" He paused, tension in the air—then eased and smiled, "But that was a *textbook* OK pass, anytime!"

"Bullshit, Paddles," Sam responded with a grin. "It was *underlined*."

BCB reared a big smile, as the two laughed and embraced, with >SADCLAM<, CP, and JABA joining the gang amongst the rest of the United States sailors. The USS Ship had taken Phase 2, and hope still remained for an American Administrative Olympic victory.

Sam looked over to the Paddles platform, where the remaining LSOs were wrapping up after a long day of sun-baked waving, deafening eardrum-cal gauging, and overall recovery safeguarding—after which they'd enter the shack and review the trends they saw and lessons they'd seek to drive home, walking miles across the boat to debrief every single pass witnessed. Sam detached himself from the flight deck celebration, and found an emotion he never thought he'd feel toward Paddles: *Admiration.*

He thought about the concept of scored carrier landings... how silly and trivial he once found things like greeny boards, mid-stage reviews, condescending Paddles critiques, and top-10 ball-flyer patches. And for the first time in his life, he realized the point of it all: It was all a game—sure, a game of life-or-death at its greatest stakes—but a game nonetheless. A mind-numbing game of calling somebody out for being a few feet too high, taking a few seconds too long on intervals, or landing a few inches too far right of centerline. It *was* silly. It *was* trivial. But *damn*, did it get people focused on getting better on every pass, fostering their concentration for the most crucial part of the flight, and *determined* to shift their aviation gears up another level even when they were at their most fatigued state. It was about the professional desire to be the best—to compete not just against your peers, but against *yourself*—for a better version of that self on every pass, every flight, every day.

Sam thought back to all those frustrations he had with Paddles: how worthless he thought bouncing was, how stupid he saw the whole grading system to be, and how angry he felt after a 'Fair' ruined a perfectly good flight. He thought about his and Juice's shared disdain for Paddles and ball-flying—and his rival's impressive ability to work *through* the self-imposed hatred. He thought about it all, still being wildly bear-hugged by Blue Collar Bill and other familiar Paddles faces like DyDo Fridinger, Ken Bone Sause, BJ Stanonis, and Smang Shelton—and he let out a tremendous laugh of relief.

He'd been duped by Paddles this whole time—duped to think that ball-flying was about grades, patches, and greenies—when, in reality, it was about grooming a safe, effective, systematic pilot to take carrier landings with the same level of focus, effort, and precision as he would lazing a bomb into moving target in danger-close combat conditions. It was about turning a simple administrative procedure into a game of personal improvement and the endless pursuit of perfection.

Sam thought back on all those years spent resenting Paddles for Fair-ing him out, disdainfully referring to them as fairies in white, insecurely paranoid about what kind of deviation they would call him out on next. The years spent hating... dreading... *trying* – and he finally understood: These guys, in their own crazy way, really *were* just trying to keep him focused, motivated, and *safe*. He may have once dreamed of having cool, hip, non-critiquing Padroids with the Noddiks... but finally, Sam was woke enough to realize he'd take Paddles on the platform any day.

He kept laughing as the Paddles and United States forces raised him in the air — the flight deck bursting with smiling faces, celebrating sailors, and insatiable national pride. The Olympics were all knotted up, with the deciding phase quickly approaching — and after finally being able to part with his bottled-up insecurities and grasp *true* self-belief? After proving his ability to overcome his lifelong weakness? Sam started to wonder: *Maybe I don't need to recapture the old 'Nickels.' Maybe, deep down in my soul, I can find an even* better *version of myself...*

14

Unhinged Philosophy

*L*CDR (Sel) Sam Rowland looked at the clock – it was 0200 in the morning, on another routine Tuesday at sea. He yawned dramatically, trying to shift FISTY's attention to how late it was, with both men scheduled to attend a Guam Liberty Port brief the following morning in the hangar bay. His Training Officer was undeterred, however, as he remained glued to the computer screen, watching game film of Tom Brady and the Tampa Bay Buccaneers facing the Green Bay Packers in the 2021 NFC Championship.

"Stop tape," FISTY called out – to himself, essentially – as he paused the video with 00:08 remaining in the first half. The O-4 Training O snapped his head over to Sam, his eyes full of excitable intensity; not a hint of fatigue on his face. The two had been in the Secure Tactical Briefing Room since just before 2200, when FISTY brought his disciple in to marvel at various Tom-in-Tampa feats. Tonight's lesson was centered around efforts to help teach Sam a lesson about finding ways to enhance an already stellar career – as Brady, time and time again, had demonstrated his ability to do. FISTY couldn't contain his giddiness as he smiled and said, "I fucking love this clip, man. This is beautiful – the Buccaneers are underdogs, on the road, Brady in his first year in Tampa – zero playoff experience with this new cast, aside from Gronk – and they're unfathomably leading a game they should have no business being competitive in. Now, most teams," he emphasized with wide eyes, as he started getting very animated with his hands, "would be perfectly content to kneel the ball here, going into halftime with a comfortable 4-point lead, and not take any unnecessary offensive chances and risk losing that slight momentum." The side of his mouth curled up as he grinned, "Tom Brady, though? The word 'content' doesn't exist in the man's vocabulary." He turned back to the computer screen and announced, "Play tape, half-time-speed," as he clicked a few buttons on the PCDS menu bar.

As they watched the slow-motion replay, FISTY clasped his forehead in disbelief and admiration, as he explained, "Now watch here, Nickels – the defense is clearly expecting a safe, conservative run play with Leonard Fournette, to kill the clock and hope for the best – maybe a broken tackle or two en route to a huge gain that maybe, just maybe, breaks into field goal territory. But no!" FISTY pounded his fist on the desk. "Brady, Bruce Arians, and the Bucs opt to instead up the ante, as they strike for the Packers' throat and blow the minds of the Green Bay secondary and viewers everywhere!"

With the video still progressing, now showing the quarterback dropping back to pass, FISTY continued his commentary-from-recall, "Brady throws deep to speedster Scotty 'Scooter' Miller, who gains an extra couple steps on the unsuspecting cornerback and secures a magnificently placed ball, as he gets tackled in the endzone for the touchdown! Thanks to their aggressive pressure mindset, the Buccaneers successfully employ follow-on shots after already achieving an offensive position, and go into halftime now up by 11, paving the way to a victory and trip to the Super Bowl back home in Tampa Bay – where Brady collects his 7th and most impressive championship yet! FUCK YEAH!" FISTY was euphoric as he pumped his fist. "Un-fucking-believable, Nickels! How does he continue doing this?!"

Sam, still dogged tired, but feeling more energized via the osmosis of exhilaration from his Training O, smiled and nodded. "It's wild, FISTY – Tom Brady is truly an inspiration and the epitome of a champion!" He may not have said it with as much enthusiasm as FISTY, but he did believe it. Tom Brady was a well-respected athlete amongst the Chippies; the whole ready room understood what an incredible personification of leadership, dedication, and determination the man was. The entire crew of Dambuster pilots looked to him as the ultimate competitor – but nobody could match the intense passion for the GOAT that FISTY held in his heart.

FISTY stood there, smiling in awe and shaking his head like he'd just witnessed a divine miracle from the heavens above. "You know, they undoubtedly rehearsed this play again and again and again in practice, fully aware that they may only run it just once or twice in the entire season – if even at all. It didn't matter that it was a one-off play suited for a specific niche scenario that may or may not actually occur – they still repped it out to the same point of meticulous precision as any other vanilla, building-block play – so that if the time did come to use it? They'd be ready." With reverence behind his eyes, he sighed longingly and said, "Just like the wide receiver pass from Edelman to Amendola against the Ravens in the 2015 Divisional round; just like Malcolm Butler's interception in that very same postseason campaign; just like every single clutch Brady 2-minute drill that we've all come to accept as automatic because of his prowess at executing them..."

His eyes filling with even more liveliness, FISTY continued preaching, "When the opportunities arise, Brady and co are ready for them – and it's because of the intensive focus they put into every single minute of every single practice. It's no different than the way we rep and diligently debrief Attack Window Entries, AUTO QTY JDAM employments, and DCA vul after vul after vul! We continue to fine-tune every single facet of our game – like Brady did – so that if and when the occasion surfaces? We go out there and rise to it." He put his hand to his forehead again and admired, "It's absolutely incredible, the way this man continues to raise the bar after already accomplishing so much – he refuses to rest on his laurels! And that is *what makes him such a generational champion, Nickels..."* He said Sam's name as if he were talking to him, but FISTY's awe-inspired gaze was still on the computer replay screen, where Scooter, Tom, and the rest of the Bucs celebrated the hammer-dropping touchdown.

"Stop tape." He paused the clip as the team was walking into the locker room for halftime. He looked over at Sam again, focused solely on his pupil, and said, *"You know what I love about this season?"* Without waiting for an answer, he shook his head, smiling, and explained, *"43 years old, 20 years in the league, 6 Super Bowl rings – and Tom was still putting in the work as if he were a brand-new rookie – as if he had nothing to rest on, and everything to learn."*

Sam nodded, eyeing the door, hoping that FISTY would take the hint and start packing up shop.

But yet again, the Brady fanboy was lost in the sauce of GOAT-driven inspiration. *"COVID-19, Nickels,"* he said, standing up and pacing around the room. *"COVID-fucking-19. The world was full of fear, timidity, and isolation – the NFL included. The league banned all team gatherings prior to the annual limited-participation training camps. There was no time for team cohesion, socialization, or camaraderie-building. It was undoubtedly the worst possible time for a quarterback to be departing the only team and system he's ever played for, in hopes of recreating that same magic with a brand-new franchise and crew. How was he supposed to impart that winning culture with these new guys, Nickels?"* FISTY asked, addressing the senior JO rhetorically. *"How was he supposed to lead them to the promised land? How was he supposed to get these boys to buy into The Innocent Climb!?"*

Growing a bit more engrossed in the latest iteration of FISTY's 'Greatest Lab of All Time' series, Sam scrunched his face, and shrugged his arms. *"It seems like he was put in an unwinnable situation..."*

"Indeed he was, Nickels. Indeed he was," FISTY remarked as he kept pacing. *"An unwinnable situation – to a mere mortal."* He paused for dramatic flair, then further monologued, *"Your average run-of-the-mill athlete? They would've chalked it up to an 'Act of God,' believing it just wasn't meant to be that season, and used the limited time available to work on some bare-bones foundation for follow-on campaigns toward the majestic Lombardi Trophy. But..."* FISTY cranked his head, narrowed his eyes, and put on a sly grin, *"But to some men in the arena – the truly heroic, valor-driven men? Those exceptional competitors can overcome even..."* he raised an eyebrow, *"... acts of God himself..."*

Sam clutched his chest. It always sent chills down his spine when FISTY brought spiritual zeal into his tactical sermons.

"In a controversial move," FISTY continued, *"Tom Brady decided to believe – and say – that the only thing we had to fear was 'fear' itself; he reclaimed authority of his life, his focus, and his team's Climb. And how, you ask, my young Padawan?"* FISTY gave his pupil an inquisitive look. *"By hosting secret team practices outside a local Tampa Bay high school – an act which caused a bit of a stir when local excited Floridians captured the gatherings and reported them to local newspapers."*

"Was it considered a selfish move to do that?" Sam asked pensively, now far less tired and far more engaged. "Was it wrong to focus on the team's success when the country was fighting a pandemic?"

FISTY smiled and gave a slight shrug. "Now, that is a great question of philosophy. It all depends on your point of view, Samuel. Was Dr. Fauci a fan of it? God no – but, let me say, in the most politically correct and respectful way possible," FISTY pursed his lips and narrowed his eyes, "that I always found the doctor to be a bit of a tool." He frowned, "A negative-energy fear-monger, a man who seemed more eager for selling doom and gloom in his daily press an-nouncements than he was for a return to normalcy. But hey," FISTY looked at the fourth wall camera, "Let's not let this book degrade into political debate..." he smirked and continued, "In-stead, let's focus on what Brady was doing.

"Players hate OTAs and voluntary mini-camps, Sam. They loathe the rigorous prac-tices before the real season begins. Imagine if workups and deployment readiness flights were all voluntary; you could either suffer through those agonizingly long days and mission-plan-ning cells, or choose not to show up – spending your time on free leave instead – and simply get your box clicked 'green' for you."

Sam smiled. He knew exactly what his sensei was talking about. "If that were the case, I bet only the new guys would be forced to go, while the senior dudes enjoyed the extra vacation time."

"Exactly!" FISTY shouted with fervor as he pounded his fist on the STBR table. "Here Tom Brady is, the senior man in the league by far – and he's not only still putting in the inno-cent and arduous work of a new guy, but he's breaking the rules and going against the grain to do so! Sam, he's essentially sneaking out of his stateroom during a Man Overboard drill, trans-iting the p-ways during GQ, and slinking into the ready room during XOI – to rehearse BFM model work, sharpen up his good-deal DCA brief, and fine-tune the JMPS load with the latest TAMMAC! How insane is that?!"

Chuckling, Sam admitted, "You'd be hard-pressed to find any JO doing that..."

"Any JO?!" FISTY laughed. "How about a hinge?! Tom Brady had every reason in the world not to waste his time in OTAs, instead spending time with his family and friends before another grueling season – but dammit, he was that determined to keep winning, to keep the pedal to the metal, to keep progressing as an athlete – and most importantly? To show his teammates that he still had that drive, fully loaded in the motivation tank. Tom Brady demon-strated that if he can find the ambition to do the extra work – at the level of experience and reps under his belt? Then they sure as hell can and should, too. And Sam," the Training O beamed, "that's the kind of team sacrifice and cohesion needed for championship football and war-win-ning tactical aviation!"

As Sam smiled and nodded, FISTY delved deeper, "You see, Brady has been putting in this type of 'new guy effort' his whole illustrious career. When he was a new guy? Of course – that was a given. But after winning a few Super Bowls, he famously refused to do commercials without his offensive linemen on board. He continued to take pay cuts to hold a salary far less than a championship-level QB could ask for, so that New England could bring in more talent. He recruited competitors heavily – from Randy Moss to Gronk to Antonio Brown – when you had players like NBA MVP Derrick Rose, infamously claiming 'It's not my job' to recruit players when it came to big-name free agencies, admitting he was uninterested in the act of doing whatever it took to foster an improved team in Chicago, and thus ininterested in creating a better chance to win. 'If they want to come, they can come,' he said. Can you believe that, Sam?"

Shaking his head, FISTY continued ranting, "Or how about Roger Clemens designing and signing a contract to only play home games in Houston, refusing to endure the rigors of traveling with the team on the road and playing away from the comforts of his known territory. What about Aaron Rodgers, spending every single offseason in his final few Packer seasons debating if he A) Wanted to play in Green Bay, B) Wanted to play football at all, and C) Missing every single voluntary team practice in the process..." FISTY shook his head in disappointment. "What kind of leadership is that?! Your best players – the team 'leaders!' – refusing to do parts of the job they see themselves as 'above?!'" He used animated air quotes, and gave a look of disgust. "Who the hell wants to Climb with a jabroni like that?!"

Sam smiled. LCDR Flynn always knew how to word things so beautifully and poetically.

FISTY continued, using more hand-talking quotation marks, "Imagine if you had a squadron 'head of department,' who told you he was 'too qualified' to be delivering departure/spin in briefs, 'too senior' to be watching the desk for you during a 16-hour SDO day, and 'too experienced' to be doing the simple new guy act of grabbing weather and NOTAMs?! 'Too experienced?!'" He scoffed angrily. "Experience sucking my dick!" His eyes vibrant, he emphasized, "You think Brady believes he's 'too experienced' to be running footwork drills, sprints, and Saturday tape sessions with the rookies during the middle of July?! FUCK no!"

Slowing down, FISTY took a deep breath to calm himself from his vulgar-but-ardent outburst, and deliberately stated, "The greatest leaders and champions understand two things, Sam: 1) It's the little things that make all the difference in getting to the top – but more importantly, 2) Continuing to do those little things with the same dedication, attention, and focus..." he looked at Sam with desire in his eyes, "... is the only way to stay there."

FISTY's passion for excellence resonated in Sam's heart, as it always did. But while his spirit was all-in on this lesson, it was his mind that was currently so detached...

Shifting tones, FISTY looked at the young man and asked, "Nickels, do you know why I chose this lesson to harp on tonight? I'm no fool – I know SWO breakfast is quickly arriving, and we need to get some sleep. So, tell me, Nickels: how do you feel about those O-4 selection board results?"

Jolting to a sobering awareness, Sam surely wore momentary shock as he returned his sensei's stare. How does he always know...? "I dunno FISTY... I just never wanted to become the villain – I guess I somehow thought I could 'die a hero' instead," he used air quotes of his own, referencing one of his favorite movies. Then he sighed and laughed, talking as much to his own psyche as he was FISTY, "But that's impossible – I mean, being a career guy and all, it was of course bound to happen eventually." He looked into the thousand-yard distance, past the white STBR walls. "I suppose we all lose our innocence at some point..."

"Hah!" FISTY shouted excitedly. "With that attitude, you surely will! Samuel, haven't you listened to anything I've said?!" FISTY crouched down and looked his trainee in the eyes. "Who's to say you can't become the Brady of hinges? To the Patriots – and to the Buccaneers – Brady was both upper management and one of the boys. He was the OPSO presenting the schedule... and the Skeds O who spent all day writing it. The kind of man to launch on an alert and earn an A/A kill... after turning the jet at 0300 in the morning. Line of sight tasking – assigned to the mirror. A great leader and a Good Dude. Fuck that HOPA/JOPA shit – Brady was a DOPA."

"DOPA?" Sam asked, confused.

"DOPA," FISTY affirmed. "Dude Officer Protection Association. The kind of leader, person, and competitor – regardless of rank – that anyone from E-1 to O-9 would fight alongside 'til the fucking fumes of flameout."

DOPA... Sam thought to himself. It sounded badass. "That's what I want to be, FISTY; I want to be DOPA! But how?!"

FISTY exhaled dramatically and cranked his head to the side. "It's certainly not an easy task, Sam – but it's one that, if accomplished, will make you a legend in the community forever. Have you heard the acronym, 'RHIP'?"

"Yes, Sensei," Sam answered, "'Rank Has Its Privileges'... but how does – "

"HAH!" FISTY yelled again, "That's exactly what a HOPA would say and want you to think! But why, Sam? Why should a hinge, with more experience and wisdom to instill, be exempt from some of the greatest leadership opportunities this career has to offer? Why should a hinge always be granted the greatest of deals, shielded from the rigors of 'bitch work,' and skip to both the symbolic and literal front of every line life has to offer? Because they've 'already done their suffering?' Please..." he shook his head, then re-engaged his focus and said, "Don't let anyone tell you any differently, Sam: RHIP stands for 'Rank Holds Infinite Potential.' The potential to be the hingiest of hinges ever known to mankind... the potential to be the dopest of DOPA the tac-air community has ever seen... and everything in between. But ultimately, Sam – the potential to be mythical. To become a symbol. To become the GOAT..." His lip curled up into that gleeful little smile again, as he gazed toward one of his many posters of Brady in the STBR – this one in TB12's trademark punching-the-air stance, the letters 'LFG' written across the top.

Sam looked at the poster in admiration. "That's what I want to be, FISTY," Sam repeated. "That's the legacy I want to leave in naval aviation. I want to be remembered as the man who broke the mold of leadership, and impacted lives in ways never seen before – just as Brady did..."

FISTY smiled, put his hand on Sam's shoulder, and said, "You're a sweet, sweet boy, Nickels — and a Good Dude. Many have tried, but few have been able to enter the GOAT conversation of Good Dudes in the Navy — but I feel you have it in your heart. Always remember your roots, Nickels; remember what it took to get you to where you are, and remember not only to keep doing those things — but adamantly work to do them better."

With the words sitting in his mind, Sam thought about his future in leadership — O-4 on the horizon... a chance to shape the future of naval aviation...

"The new guy we're getting," FISTY said. "Bobby Ward, I believe his name was. Did pretty well at the RAG, from what I understand — but the IPs say he also had his administrative moments of struggle. Train him, Nickels; make his fate define your legacy."

Nodding slowly, as he longingly looked at the intensity in Brady's eyes, Sam firmly avowed, "I will, Sensei — no matter what it takes. I won't let him down."

"I have no doubt in you," FISTY said with a smile.

The two stood in silence for a moment, before FISTY took a deep breath and asked, "Nickels, do you know what the last words Pat Riley's late father, Lee, ever said to him were?"

Sam shook his head. I don't even know who Pat Riley is...? He was curious nonetheless. "What were they, Sensei?"

FISTY closed his eyes and, raising his arms to emphasize the weight of the message, explained, "He told him, 'Every now and then, somewhere, some place, sometime, you're going to have to plant your feet, stand firm, and make a point about who you are and what you believe in. When that time comes, you simply have to do it.' Remember that, Nickels. One day, the time will come when you have your shot to make your greatest impact in this profession — a do-or-die moment ripe for the seizing. And it will take far more than administrative perfection to find the power to do what is right. When this moment comes, Nickels, you must be ready to FENCE in, arm up, and fire the fuck away. Because if you aren't? You may never get that moment again..."

"And what happens if I am; and I do take the shot?" Sam asked.

FISTY smiled, as he said, "Play tape," and unpaused the video. Brady and the Bucs were now in the center stage of Lambeau field, accepting Brady's first NFC Championship trophy in his first NFC season — but emphasizing that their journey was not over yet, with a loftier goal on the horizon.

FISTY looked back at Sam and concluded, "Then you get to continue your pursuit of the greatest motivating make-or-break moment of all — the next one."

~

Robo-Hinge stormed into the ready room, his skin an artificial shade of red, and turned to the two pilots who stood at attention, facing the whiteboard — a whiteboard where a 'math problem of the day' was drawn up, exhibiting various forms of matrices and subscript numbers alongside variable letters and random Greek symbols.

Wielding dual knife hands, Robo-Hinge immediately went high and right in his criticism of both men. "UNSAT. COMPLETELY, UTTERLY, FUCKING *UNSAT*. DO YOU REALIZE THAT I HAD TO CANCEL MY LEAVE TO COME BACK BECAUSE OF THIS? YOU TWO CALL YOURSELF PILOTS, AND THEN PUT *THAT* KIND OF DISPLAY ON? THIS SHIT WOULD *NOT* HAVE FLOWN WHEN I WAS A JO! THERE *WILL* BE CONSEQUENCES, DO YOU UNDERSTAND ME?!"

His JO ass-chewing was amplified by both CAG and Dr. Suabedissen's stern looks, as they also stood very displeased with arms folded. CAG, of course, was furious with the Noddiks losing Phase 2 of the Olympics and failing to clinch the victory in what should've been a simple evolution. Dr. Suabedissen's livid expression, however, came from staring at the math problem — no one had even *attempted* to solve it, and there was not a *single* question regarding the formula behind its derivation.

"... YOU MAY BE CURRENT, BUT YOU ARE MOST CERTAINLY *NOT* PROFICIENT..."

Suabedissen shook his head as he glared, his brow growing more furrowed. 'What the freak was *wrong* with these robots?!' he wondered, amongst the ass-blasting that was taking place. 'Does *nobody* care about the building blocks behind the greatest physics and mathematical achievements reached in this world? The whole *reason* we can exist as a fleet in space is because of the brilliant minds behind fun little math problems like these...'

"... WHEN WAS THE LAST TIME YOU OPENED UP CV NATOPS?!"

And most disappointingly of all, nobody was able to enjoy the easter egg behind the answer he purposely wrote the problem for: If one properly took the sigma of the quadratic root of the fourth imaginary number, then summed the numerator to the factorial of the fifth fractionary rational integer... they would see the number 81680085! As he continually and rapidly solved the problem in his head and internally giggled at his masterwork, Suabedissen almost cracked a smile — *almost*. Because for this opportunity to be missed by the entire Noddik fleet? He was starting to wonder if these were his true friends after all...

"... CAMILLI, YOU *SHALL* HAVE A POWERPOINT ON BALL-FLYING READY BY CLOSE OF BUSINESS TOMORROW. WARD, YOU CAN EXPECT TO BE ON SDO FOR THE REST OF THIS MONTH..."

Suabedissen thought back to all he'd given up to program this fleet: his legacy in the D&D community... the expansion packs he was working on — he had this *really* cool one called *The Majestic Moonblade*, where you found a map pointing you to the secret castle Farridia floating in the sky, where a princess was held captive by the evil warlock Werlona and has bandit tribe of 'Pukin' Orcs!' But first, you had to go to the Forest of Phantoms to find an Ancient Key that would unlock the underground Cave of Cagglia where the dragon Festerdon lived! By finding the seven Sacred Stones hidden across villages in the Plyto region, you could earn the magic spell *Espherial* that would allow you to tame the dragon, and then you could fly—

"DOCTOR! DID YOU HEAR WHAT I SAID? YOU CAN VOUCH THAT MY WIFE IS HOT, RIGHT?"

Snapping back to present consciousness, Suabedissen looked at Robo-Hinge with panic and said, "Uh, yes, sir; very hot, sir!" What was he even talking about? What was he *doing* here?! ... And the worst part of all? The princess in the expansion back was going to be named for, modeled after, and publicly *dedicated* to MyLittlePonyXoXo88—the woman *he* should be with! They'd exchanged so many chat messages over the years; even direct ones, too! He was convinced they might even video chat one day if he continued to make progress, little by little—and the expansion pack was going to be his big move! But in his aspirations with the Noddiks—in this whole asinine Olympic quest—there was no time for the task-saturated doctor to woo his damsel away from jocks like the Fire Knight WizardofAzkaban1337. 'Dammit...' Dr. Suabedissen uncharacteristically swore to himself as he shook his head, lamenting what could've been with MyLittlePonyXoXo88...

"WE'RE GOING TO DISCUSS THE NEXT COA, AND THEN WE'LL BE BACK TO BRIEF PHASE 3. DO NOT LEAVE THIS ROOM—DO YOU UNDERSTAND?" Robo-Hinge condescendingly asked. He then directed his attention to Loaded T, specifically, and added, "THAT MEANS NO KHAKI HOUR."

Kyle rolled his eyes and said nothing.

Robo-Hinge glared at the meathead. "I'M LOOKING FOR A HEAD NOD OR 'YES SIR,' CAMILLI."

"Yeah, sure," Loaded T responded monotone.

As he turned away, Robo-Hinge petulantly prompted, "UHHH... ATTENTION ON DECK, MUCH?!"

The men popped back up, as Robo-Hinge scoffed and walked off, CAG and Suabedissen in tow—the doctor taking one last, longing, sad look at the whiteboard algebra.

Always the bad boy, Loaded T relaxed to at ease—*without* being told to 'Carry on!'—and looked at Juice. "Man... fuck these guys, dude. I am so over this shit—I came here to humiliate Sam Rowland, not be berated by some ass clown."

As Juice relaxed his stance too, slightly confused and very annoyed. "Yeah, what the fuck was he talking about? Dude, we did great out there—especially you.

That pattern work was incredible! If anything, he should be mad at IROK—he's the one who bingo'd."

Loaded T rubbed his exhausted eyes. "Dude, he's a fucking hinge—he has no clue what's going on. He wasn't even *here* for the fight; hinges *never* are. We're the men in the arena, Juice—this low-SA asswipe is watching from the fucking box seats, analyzing spreadsheets of our T&R, flight hours, and SFWT completion to tell us how we're progressing as pilots. I *guarantee* you: this douchebag didn't even *look* at the passes from Paddles' logbook. He's not leading from the front—shit, he's not even leading from behind; he's in an entirely different dimension of delusion. Like every other O-4 department head out there, this dumbass is diseased with 'me'—worried more about his perception from the eyes of his FITREP-writing boss, vice from the vantage point of the people he's in charge of training, guiding, and inspiring. Not a surprise, though," Loaded T said with apathy, "this whole sorry-ass Navy system is corrupt to create these types of fake-ass leaders."

Both appalled and impressed at the different multitude of ways his former Chippy brother was able to incorporate the word 'ass' into his insults, Juice prodded, "You really think that? You really think every JO is doomed to this corruption of mass-tasking and ass-blasting when they don the golden oak leaves?"

Kyle, for once, sneered into some semblance of a mocking smile. "Bobby... look at your own shoulders..."

Juice looked down at his frayed, discolored LT bars on his flight suit, hanging by threads after his decade as an O-3—and he said nothing.

"Exactly," Loaded T said, before sneaking a look at his own LT insignia, more so in admiration of the shoulder-head separation that was readily apparent through the flight suit material, thanks to his absurd LOLs. He directed his attention back to Juice and said, "Harvey Dent wasn't just talking about Gotham City heroes and villains, you know."

Ward shook his head and internally chuckled. Loaded T may not bleed Chippy green anymore, but *damn*—the *Dark Knight Trilogy* fascination still ran strong in his DNA.

"It's an inevitable fate," Loaded T continued, "for any bitch stupid enough to take the blood money and sell their soul to the Navy for a backside career in aviation, with all the bad and none of the good." He narrowed his eyes, "Think about it, Bobby. Think about everything this job is about—the *fun* stuff: flying kick-ass sorties, lifelong memories with your 'trusted bros,'" he threw up air quotes, clearly very jaded, "and of course, making fun of stupid-ass, fantasy-based, spool-driven leadership. Once you're a hinge, though?" Kyle shook his head. "That flying—the pursuit of tactical improvement? Replaced with blue folders, bullshit meetings, and sprinting on the hamster wheel. Those 'bros?' The JOs *hate* you, the front office barely tolerates you, and your peers—other dumbass DH bonus takers—are looking to *undercut* you en route to the top FITREP—not that senior JOPA aren't capable of that shit, too..." he added with disgust. "And that rich content of leadership buffoonery? Bro... cue the circus music—you *are* the clown, now." He wasn't laughing, though—if anything, he was closer to breaking down. Loaded T sat, grasping his hanging head with both hands, and exhaled a sigh of exasperation.

For once feeling a tinge of sympathy, Juice looked at the exhausted jacked pilot. He noticed Loaded T's forearm veins rippling like snakes, his quads prominently projecting from his flight suit, his feathery testosterone-fueled hair flowing—yet his picturesque resolve seemingly *diminishing*. Kyle pulled at his hair, then hung his head even lower, still shaking it. He was a man on the verge of both vengeance and collapse, of triumph and defeat; the epitome of health, and the embodiment of affliction.

As if finally noticing just how sharply Loaded T's gaunt jawline angled, how critically-low his body fat levels appeared, and how skeleton-like his features were, Juice asked him, "Dude... are you feeling 100%?"

Kyle looked up at him—his eyes sullen and tired—and said, "Juice... I'm *never* going to feel '100%.' I'm sweating through fucking brutal workouts, getting my 10000 steps a day, and reaching new LOLs while simultaneously hitting PRs every week. My macros are fucking *dialed* in—I'm dieting the cleanest I've ever eaten in my life, working at a steady but smartly-conservative daily caloric deficit. I'm living with various degrees of DOMS in my muscles during every waking moment, and crashing each night after eating to take advantage of any hour of sleep my body can cling to—*all* while fighting debilitating hunger.

"And you know what, bitch? My brain's been fully conditioned to *love* it: To me, a fresh hit of C4 sounds *far* more appealing than an ice-cold beer. I'd easily take a night with steel 45s at the gym over one with smoke show 10s at the club. The barbells are my bros, the dumbbells my dawgs, the plates my dates. Bench, squat, and deadlifts are the only threesomes I'm chasing. Lifting is my only love, macronutrients my best friends, and getting jacked-as-hell my guiding principle." Kyle paused, took a breath, and said, "And Juice, I haven't felt this damn determined since my days as an innocent, motivated Chippy; rushing the Patch, and striving for tactical savagery. This is the drive I've missed in my life—and I'm exhausted—but *shit...* the struggle feels fucking *incredible.*"

Raising an eyebrow, Juice tilted his head and looked at him in confusion.

"You heard me right," Loaded T said, smug but firm in his conviction. "Tactics and fitness—they're not that different, bro. That feeling of constantly chasing something—chasing a better version of yourself, chasing those breakthroughs, chasing that perfection—I've just replaced one holy grail quest for another. The perfect physique? Impossible—you can always get stronger, always get leaner, always get more jacked;

you'll never be flawless. But do I strive for it nonetheless? *Fuck* yeah, I do. The perfect flight? No chance. Something's always gonna go off script—some bullshit blue fallout will cause you to degrade to a light div contingency, some Diamondback dipshit is gonna trash a few shots, or some weak-ass cloud layer will toss a wrench in your entire fucking game plan. In short, Murphy's going to rear his bitch-ass law into your shit."

Kyle paused in thought, before his eyes burned with fiery desire. "But that's what made all that preparation *meaningful,* bro. That's what separated the Instagram wannabes and limfac JOs from those of us who put their blood, sweat, and fucking *soul* into this business. We groomed our ability to flex—to think critically, to perform athletically when it mattered most, to persevere through unforeseen hurdles while others threw in the towel or had it mercilessly yanked from them. And we *earned* the right to flex—because we knew the *scripted* game plan so damn well."

Talking animatedly with his hands, despite his deprived physique's low propensity for NEAT, Kyle continued, "All those hours breaking down Eyestachio's videos... those days spent creating, rehearsing, and perfecting SFWT briefing guides... those late nights chair flying model work, J-LASE comm, and painting up whiteboard masterpieces for labs..." He shook his head, "Bro—it was *those reps and sets* that got us *mentally stronger* as we built resilience for bullshit, *professionally leaner* as we cut out unnecessary fluff of aviation, and *tactically jacked* as we honed our passion—our *craft*—with uncompromising training. We had *reason* to be confident—damn near *cocky*—with *that* kind of preparation in the trenches. Reps and sets, Juice," Kyle repeated himself, "Reps, sets—and *discipline.*" He took on a questioning tone: "Bobby, that *restraint* to withstand the temptations of junk-ass nutrition, even though it looks good and you're fucking starving? It's the *same* mental muscle that keeps you from blowing off a debrief, simply because it was a 'good deal' flight with your bro. That *determination* in your heart that keeps you pushing for that extra rep, when you've already given everything? Hardly different than the tenacity you demonstrate by giving that SFWT 3.3L *one* more practice run, before the Training O comes in for showtime.

"Because all that shit comes from your *desire,* Bobby—the *desire* to be the big dog of the gym; to be the top stick in the air wing. To be *that dude,* who people look at with a fucked-up dual-lens of both admiration and jealousy—all because *you* have the discipline, mental fortitude, passion, and willingness to commit—*and they don't.* Some grow to praise you for it—some grow to *hate* you. But who fucking cares—because you aren't doing it for them. The real ones, Juice?" Kyle clenched his jaw, his cheeks going even further concave. "The real ones do it for *themselves* and their *own* chase for excellence, their *own* quest toward uncharted territory, their *own* pursuit of perfection." Pointing to himself, he emphasized adamantly, "*I welcome* the struggle, the hunger, the suffering—because I know it's making me *better.* Not better than everyone else—which I honestly couldn't give less of a shit about—but a better version of *myself.*"

Juice looked at Kyle with mixed emotions: incredulity... disbelief... aversion... *admiration*. 'What the hell is *wrong* with this guy?' he thought to himself. And yet, part of his heart was insisting he ask himself: 'How can I be *more like him*?' He couldn't decide if Loaded T was corrupted, unhinged insanity... or pure, eloquent genius. "Kyle... are you telling me you genuinely *enjoy* this brutal sense of suffering?!"

Loaded T cranked his neck, veins pulsating as he bit in the inside of his cheeks, his sub-zero-ish body fat prominently exhibited in his piercing stare. Without blinking, he narrowed his eyes a bit, gave the subtlest hint of contentment, and stated, "*Fuck* yeah, I do, Bobby; *Fuck* yeah, I do. And so does *every* pilot pushing to crush themselves with more sorties, more hours, more briefing labs, more LFE leads; so does *every* aviator seeking to suffer through more mission planning, mass debriefs, TCTS playbacks, comm reviews—you name it." He pounded his fist in his palm. "That suffering... bro, that's the shit that makes me feel *alive;* feel *accomplished.* It's the only thing that makes me feel *fulfilment* in life. Because you know what? When you're suffering—you're sharpening... separating... *soul-searching.*"

"Soul-searching?" Juice asked with suspended belief.

"Fuck yeah, bro. Whether it's a man's first cut, or a man's first delving into the Level 3 syllabus— you need to *suffer* in order to find those untapped stores in your body—in your *heart*. Whether you're seeing muscles pop in places you never knew existed—attaining new LOLs—as you shed the pounds of fat by the week, or whether you're finding levels of intuitive stem-cell-powered tactical execution that you never knew you had—attaining new TOTALs—as you shed the slow-and-low-SA-fluff by the flight? It's so fucking *inspiring* and *motivating,* Juice. A man doesn't know how much potential he truly holds until he's suffering long enough to dig into the depths of his soul; I *live* for that suffering." He looked longingly, nearly *smiling*, at the ready room plat cam depicting a sunset horizon—before snapping his gaze back to Juice and returning to disdain. "And you know what pisses me the fuck off?!"

Still bewildered and unsure where this psychotic gym bro would go next, Juice just shrugged.

The most animated he's been yet, Kyle got back to his feet and said, "When somebody says some candy-ass shit like 'Hey, you're already jacked, isn't it time to take a break?'" he caricatured with a look of disgust, "Or 'Isn't it time to ease back on the workouts, the dieting, the fixation?'" He then got even louder and yelled, "Are you fucking *kidding* me, bro? That's the shit that *got* me here—and that's the kind of shit that's not only gonna *keep* me here—but make me *better.* Think about it: why does every upper-echelon gym rat insist on calling it a night early on weekends? Insist on abstaining from alcohol? Insist on cooking their own food every single day, with zero desire to eat out at restaurants?"

Juice put on a slight smirk and listed off, "Because they become so paranoid about gains that they fear losing an ounce of muscle if they miss a minute of sleep; because they're so unhealthily lean that their system can't handle more than two beers without blacking out; and because they get so neurotic about their body and their macros that they don't trust any food aside from their own drug-scale-measured meals."

Kyle sneered, again approaching a semblance of a smile. "Well, you're certainly not wrong, bitch—but no: it's about *keeping* those habits that *created* these monsters. Those nights of prioritizing sleep and recovery over late-night ragers... that disciplined restraint to avoid the literal toxins that degrade your brain, body, and future... those repetitive, calculated dinners of steak, eggs, and rice—over and over again? Those are the fucking foundation building blocks that got us here—so *why in the hell* would we *stop* them? We can't, and we won't—because we're *obsessed* with those parts of the process."

He once again spoke with reverent esteem, passion fueling his words. "And counterpoint, bro—imagine you work your ass off to get fucking shredded—we're talking veins spiderwebbed down your abs, three-headed shoulder separation, leg muscle tone up to your hip—and you decide, 'Oh great, I've *'arrived'*—now I can bring back the cheesecake, start skipping leg day, and get wasted every weekend again!' Sounds like 95% of fitness enthusiasts, right?" Kyle scoffed. "Anybody can get to the top of a mountain—but staying there? *Maintaining* the greatness? That's hard enough—so imagine what it takes to climb even *higher*. To go from 10% to 6%. From deadlifting 495 to 585. From one-armed pushups to one-armed pullups. I'll tell you what *won't* work: abandoning the methods, principles, and dedication that got you there—that kind of bitch-ass letup will get you tumbling back downhill before you know it."

Kyle chuckled humorlessly. "They say that bros like me have body dysmorphia. They say I'm psychotic, that I'll never see myself as 'good enough'... Well, guess what? They're *right*. *Fuck no*, I'll never be 'good enough'—what does that even *mean?!* Why settle for that, when you know you have so *much* unrealized potential still out there to conquer, to grasp, to accomplish? I don't care if I'm 'good enough' for other people—I'm doing it for my *own* aspirations, my *own* enjoyment of the process, and my *own* love of the suffering. If I was doing this shit for the approval of others? I'd have been done long ago—a fat piece of unmotivated shit like everyone else out there. No fucking *thanks*, bro."

Juice was floored. 'What in the fuck is going on?' he thought to himself. 'How fucking *insane* is this guy? What was Loaded T *talking* about? And... why am I starting to *revere* him...?'

"Juice, think about those O-4s—those bullshitters who consider themselves above making popcorn for an SDO, above watching the desk for a junior guy, above turning a jet or loading a mission card for the JOPA—it's the *same shit,* bro. These guys who make rank off doing all this simple Good Dude shit, and then like the naïve little dieter, they mistakenly think they've 'arrived,' and decide to 'take a break' from all the things that got them there. Un-fucking-believable! Becoming an experienced aviator and leader isn't the time to *cut* the ante; it's the time to *up* it. You think Patch wearers graduate from TOPGUN and decide they can *finally* chill on practicing their briefing labs, no longer worry about leading division events, and start taking a backseat in mission planning?" He scoffed again. "Get the fuck out of here. That's unadulterated bullshit, kemosabe. And yet..." he shook his head, "The Disease of Me gets almost everyone at some point—and too many realize that they never did this shit for the love of the suffering, but rather for the approval of others. But they'll see: once that approval's gained? All that's left to motivate you is your personal drive for excellence—and if that intrinsic passion isn't there? You're back to cake, donuts, bars, and booze." His third and most aggressive scoff yet, he finished with, "Say 'adios, motherfucker' to your lean gainsmanship and good dudesmanship—because you're now just another self-serving, gluttonous hinge—through with the suffering, past the process, and finished with respect."

Not knowing what to say to this poetic, inspired, tortured madman, Juice simply asked, "Why'd you leave it, T? Why'd you run from the suffering of aviation—where you could've *inspired* that change—to embrace the suffering of physique sculpting instead?"

Kyle dropped his head, closed his eyes, and paused—then looked back at Juice. "Because, Bobby—the path to aeronautical corruption is inevitable for *everyone.* You know, there was once a time when I believed that O-4s and DHs could be Good Dudes; the kind of guys I still vied to fight alongside. One man, in particular, was going to change all that."

Briefly closing his eyes again and shaking his head, Kyle continued, "But he sold my world, your world, *everybody's*—and abandoned every great trait that earned him his reputation—just to make that bullshit deal with these Noddiks. When I saw that? I knew that my suffering had been in vain... and I knew I was officially out of the business of sacrificing for others. From thereon out? Tactical execution, ball-flying, squadron camaraderie—none of that shit mattered anymore. 100% of my effort was going toward myself and my own fucking program—my pursuit for the T, the gains, and the veins. *Fuck* everything else."

Stating the obvious, Juice whispered, "Nickels..."

"Dimes," Kyle corrected him. "Dimes could've been it. Could've been Himothy. Could've been a legend. Now he's a fucking jabroni on a pathetic feel-good quest, trying to win a pointless war for the country he abandoned in search of validation. That bitch doesn't want to suffer—he just wants to reap." Loaded T looked into the mirror, raised his shirt, and admired his abs. "All I ever wanted was to have a jacked tactical intellect, with veins of lethality pulsating throughout, and a swole-as-fuck SA bubble—and the opportunity to train others to sculpt their own aviation TOTAL aesthetic. But this..." he rotated his arms, flexed his biceps and triceps, and sighed, "... this is the next best thing, I guess."

After feeling so much perplexment, disdain, wonder, and awe toward his former squadronmate, Juice finally felt a new emotion: pity.

The doors to the ready room burst open as CAG, Dr. Suabedissen, and Robo-Hinge reentered. The two former Chippies popped back to attention, as CAG wore a serious look and said, "Gents, listen up: Phase 3 is upon us, and we're ready to commence our red air GQ scenario. We're going to go with the '500 at 500' plan—the COA of tearing the boat's cohesion apart from within by giving them a false radar contact, 500 nautical miles away, at 0500 in the morning."

"GENIUS, SIR. AN EFFECTIVE AND DEVIOUS PLAN. THAT IS WHY YOU ARE SUCH A GREAT CAG, SIR!" Robo-Hinge touted from behind the air wing commander.

"Well, technically, I suppose I owe a bit of credit to Loaded T for suggesting it earlier in the mass brief," CAG acknowledged.

"WELL... YES... BUT HIS PLAN WAS SIMPLISTIC, SIR. YOU TURNED THE IDEA INTO A MASTERMINDED MISSION!" Hinge desperately insisted.

CAG beamed from the verbal ass-kissing, while Loaded T rolled his eyes, and Dr. Suabedissen seemed distracted. Juice—dumbfounded—burst out, "Wait... that's *it?* You think a false radar contact on their tracker is going to defeat the solidarity of the USS Ship?! Guys, there's gotta be more—"

"It will," Kyle said bluntly. "That's plenty. They'll launch an alert on a scheduled no-fly day, getting everyone all spooled up. The deck won't be ready, the air wing will get mad at the TAO and the boat once they realize the track was bad, CAG will get upset for the launch being late regardless; the boat will turn off potable water to preserve it for the catapults of subsequent tanker launches, they'll probably go EMCON in a gut reaction, and the ship might even go to GQ, too..." He shrugged and summed up, "Everyone will be bitter and pissed off at each other; they'll just flounder and fall the fuck apart."

"THERE'S NO NEED TO PATRONIZE US, CAMILLI," Robo-Hinge increased his volume. "CAG UNDERSTANDS HIS OWN PLAN QUITE WELL, THANK YOU VERY MUCH."

Juice took a moment to consider what Kyle had forecasted—and the more he thought, the more he believed it might actually be enough. He nodded with approval and understanding. "Well, I guess that's a fun, appropriate ending to wrap up this adventure." He spoke the corporate line like a company man, even though he couldn't help but feel disappointed internally.

Dr. Suabedissen, however, wore his distress externally, fidgeting to and fro as the plan was being discussed. Robo-Hinge, noticing this, turned to the geek, knife-handed him, and asked, "CAN YOU SETTLE DOWN, DOCTOR?!"

Pouting, Suabedissen folded his arms and said, "You know what? No—I *can't*!"

CAG's jaw dropped—a programmed algorithm of shock—while Robo-Hinge's eyes narrowed with ire—both bots undoubtedly not wired to anticipate an instance of the doctor speaking up for himself.

"Getting them to launch an alert just isn't enough! It all seems so anticlimactic... it isn't the story apex we deserve!" Suabedissen said defiantly—before his beta demeanor returned, and he petulantly whined, "Robo-Hinge, shouldn't this war be settled in a much more epic way? I mean, think of all the great endings out there! A brothers' hand-to-hand fisticuffs atop Metal Gear Rex for the fate of the world... Two Ex-SOLDIERs' face-off in the depths of the Northern Cave for the fate of the planet... a Jedi vs Sith lightsaber duel in the molten pits of Mustafar for the fate of the galaxy!" Frenzied, he turned to the robotic O-6. "CAG, isn't the fate of administrative dominance worthy of a culminating moment like those?!"

Loaded T rolled his eyes. "Bruh... this isn't one of your stupid-ass fan-fictions... It's *admin* — it's *supposed* to be boring."

Robo-Hinge entered his Suabedissen-programmed shit-talking mode and chastised, "DOCTOR, YOU ARE SUCH A LOW-LEVELED BETA CUCK. WE ARE IN THE BUSINESS OF WINNING THE OLYMPICS, NOT PUTTING ON A SHOW FOR READERS."

Suabedissen hung his head in shame, feeling emasculated by his own creation.

Juice refused to pitch in and reinforce the O-4's mockery, possessing zero desire to encourage his hingey superior—but also, because deep down... he didn't exactly *disagree* with the dorky doctor. Part of him lusted for that grand finale—a chance for the ultimate competitive triumph; a final showdown with his arch nemesis. It was *that* type of confrontation that made him feel *alive*. Treading lightly, he tactfully suggested, "You know, the doctor might not be wrong... maybe it *would* be good to have a backup plan—a coup de grace—if necessary?"

Robo-Hinge, seething with anger, said, "I'LL ASK THE QUESTIONS AROUND HERE, WARD—AND IF WE WERE SO DESPERATE THAT WE DESIRED THE UNENLIGHTENED OPINION OF AN AMATEUR, YOU CAN TRUST THAT WE'D—"

"Hinge, what do you think?" CAG said, oblivious to the big-dicking going on. "Maybe it would be good to mission plan a contingency just in case?"

With his coded Hinge Energy Reversal Criteria clearly met, the robotic O-4 rapidly reoriented his disposition and profusely nodded, "OH, GREAT IDEA, SIR, VERY SMART. I CAN ASSIGN THE TWO JOS TO—"

"Actually, Hinge, I'd like you to take the package commander lead on this one," CAG cut in, smiling. "You can work with Juice to create an admin maritime strike as a secondary COA for Phase 3. Take the next couple of hours to lay it out, and then I can look over the MARSTRIKE on my CAG Laptop. Sound good?"

Robo-Hinge, sporting an artificial smile, said, "YES, SIR, THAT SOUNDS WONDERFUL, SIR."

CAG smiled at the aviators and doctor, pleasantly stating, "Gents—let's go win this war!" and exited the ready room.

"ATTENTION ON DECK; GOOD EVENING, SIR!" Robo-Hinge yelled sycophantically.

Once CAG was gone, however, the DH glared at Dr. Suabedissen. "THANKS A LOT, DOCTOR—YOU REALLY *FUCKED* MY PLANS TO SIT ON FACEBOOK MESSENGER ALL NIGHT."

Dr. Suabedissen frowned, trying to defend himself with, "Robo-Hinge, I'm sorry, I just wanted—"

"*YOU* JUST WANTED? WHO *CARES* WHAT *YOU* WANT, KARL?!" Robo-Hinge seethed. "YOU ARE A PATHETIC NOBODY! A LOWLY CIVILIAN GS! AN INCEL DWEEB! YOUR DESIRES MEAN *NOTHING*... AND NOW, THANKS TO YOUR LITTLE FAIRY TALE FANTASIES, I HAVE TO ACTUALLY *WORK*!"

Suabedissen cried out, "What's wrong with you, Hinge? I software patched you to be an inspiring pilot... a strong leader... to be my *friend*..." He looked down and bemoaned, "Now? You've just become a huge—a huge bastard! Your previous version control number was such a cool Good Dude JOPA. But now? You're... you're a BOPA!"

"*EXCUSE* ME?!" Robo-Hinge queried per his AI matrix. "AND JUST WHAT DOES THAT STAND FOR?!"

Darting his head back and forth between a confused Juice and Loaded T, Dr. Suabedissen glared back at his spoolly brainchild and stammered out, "It means you're a... a... a *BITCH* Officer Protection Association!"

Loaded T started snickering, while Robo-Hinge shifted to a look of shock. Juice continued to be confused as hell at literally *everything* that was taking place in this room.

Hinge cleared his throat and said, "MR. SUABEDISSEN... HOW *DARE* YOU! I AM A LIEUTENANT COMMANDER IN THE NODDIK NAVY"

"S... s—suck my dick!" Suabedissen yelled, to the amusement of a smirking Loaded T.

Artificially huffing and puffing, Hinge exclaimed, "DOCTOR! I FIND THAT LANGUAGE OBSCENE AND ABRASIVE! THIS IS *UNSAT*!"

Suabedissen, fired up and feeling egged on by Kyle's encouraging nodding, upped the ante by yelling, "Oh yeah?! You know what's unsat? You *not* sucking my dick!"

The insult made zero sense, but it didn't stop Loaded T from busting out laughing.

Hinge was as livid as a robot could possibly portray. "STOP THIS, NOW! WHAT WOULD THE YOUNGER SAILORS THINK?!"

"*They* can suck my dick, *too*!" Suabedissen said, utterly oblivious to how offensive and inappropriate the things he was insinuating were.

"DOCTOR, FOLLOW ME INTO MY OFFICE RIGHT NOW, AND WE CAN DISCUSS THE *PROPER* WAY TO ADDRESS A FIGURE OF AUTHORITY!"

As the robot DH started marching off, the doctor followed along like the little simp lemming he was, but not without calling out, "Yeah, well... well... maybe we can also discuss the proper way to suck my dick!"

The doctor looked back at Kyle and Juice, grinning uncontrollably and triumphantly, relishing his first ever moment of standing up to 'the man.' Robo-Hinge continued to ass-blast the newly and bizarrely rebellious doctor about professionalism and military bearing as the door closed behind them.

Loaded T, shaking his head and sighing with laughter, said, "Bro, that doctor is a gigantic pussy, but that was the funniest shit I've seen in a long time. He's not wrong, either—that guy *is* a total BOPA; I can't think of a better way to describe O-4s than that. All a bunch of bitches with no spine, no leadership, and no loyalty. Good thing you never took that plunge." And with that, Loaded T rose from his chair and started walking out the door.

"Where are you going?!" Juice asked.

Kyle, continuing to scoff at will, looked back and said, "Where the fuck do you *think*? Why don't you come along and lift—embrace a little suffering and quit being such a candy-ass."

Before Juice could even contemplate it—or why Kyle kept using the term 'candy-ass'—Robo-Hinge popped his head through the door. "JUICE, I NEED YOU TO MISSION PLAN THE MARSTRIKE. PLEASE HANDLE THE BRIEF, MISSION LOAD, KNEEBOARD CARDS, WASP, JWS, AND ROUTE CONSTRUCTION. I WILL WATCH THE CVIC SCROLLER AND GET THE WAYPOINT ZERO AND RTB CODE WORD. THANK YOU."

Before Juice could get a word in, Hinge closed the door (but not before they heard a hysterical Suabedissen yelling, "Why don't you mission plan sucking my—"), leaving Juice dumbfounded.

Juice turned to Loaded T and groaned, "Dude... are you fucking *kidding* me?! Fuck this shit, man..."

"Sucks, bro..." Loaded T commented emotionlessly, before pouring a bit of Sour Batch Bros C4 Ultimate into his blender bottle and shaking it up casually. "Let me ask you something," he said with a curious tone shift. "Why do you turn?"

"Why do I... *turn*?" Juice repeated, unsure of what this physical freak of nature was asking.

"Yeah, bitch," he said as he popped the top off the bottle and took a sip of his green elixir. "What gets you motivated for the WVR engagement? BFM ain't comfortable—you're straining the entire time; your focus, aircraft, and neck cranked to their limits, fighting for the tiniest of advantages. Most people can't handle that kind of struggle. Sure, they could last all day in the offensive position, when things are going well; graping turns and taking shot after shot saddled up in tail chase. But what about when things *aren't* smooth sailing; when you're defensive? What *keeps* you in that fight, when 99% of the fleet is resigned to giving up and calling it a loss, either by panicked, desperate, or reckless aircraft handling—carelessly slamming their aircraft into the deck—or even more heinous: throwing in the knock-it-off towel themselves? What keeps *you* going when you're nearly tapped for airspeed, altitude, and will?"

"I guess I never thought about it that way..." Both uncertain of where Loaded T was going with this—and his own answer—Juice prodded back, "What is it for you?"

Kyle chuckled without smiling. "Bro, take a wild guess: the *suffering*. That feeling of having everything against you, the world's barbell pinning you down, seconds away from a kill shot—nothing but pure resilience, resolve, and the refusal to die keeping you in the fight—and yet by *enduring* that suffering? Trust me, Juice—you will *never* feel more alive than the moments after escaping death. Euphoric... invincible... *godlike*. And if I need to suffer in order to chase that feeling? Fucking *sign me up*. Put me on a DBFM hop *any* day—you'll see a goddamn *stallion* on the deck. I don't just extend time to kill, Juice—I *suspend* it. And it's the most powerful fucking feeling known to man."

Loaded T took another sip. "Now, for Rowland? Clearly, that guy merges to be the hero—the 'Good Dude' he so desperately wants to epitomize," he said with quotations. "Looking to show up to a 2v1 and shoot someone down, saving the day and his reputation. But the problem with Sam is that the dipshit can't get out of his own way, as he indiscriminately pulls the trigger the second he hears a tone—even if it's on his own wingman. Fuck that guy—all he wants is glory, no matter how he gets it or who he's serving. Dimes isn't turning to support the blue; he just wants kills."

Itching his forearm a bit, the beta-alanine presumably kicking in, Loaded T stared at Juice and repeated his earlier question: "So, what is it for *you*, Bobby? I'm in it for the suffering, Dimes for the glory—what keeps *you* turning?"

Clearing his throat, pausing for a second, and swallowing, Juice looked a bit past Kyle's eyes and answered, "Well... I suppose I'm turning to be the best. To be recognized as the top fighter, to prove that I'm the greatest, to succeed where—" he stopped himself before getting specific, "where *others* couldn't..."

Kyle laughed again, this time with a smirk on his face. "That's fucking cap, Juice."

It was Juice's turn to scoff now. "Oh really?! Yeah, sure, because you can obviously tell what's in my head..."

"Maybe not..." Kyle acknowledged, before taking another drink of his C4, "But I can tell what's in your *heart*."

Juice swallowed again, saying nothing.

Kyle shook his head. "I've known you long enough, seen your trends, and watched you turn—you're not in it for recognition, Juice. I think you're in this just for the fight itself. You're the kind of guy who passes up BVR shots *just* to get anchored. Always looking for a fight... you don't give a shit what the Chippies thought about you, couldn't care less about your reputation with the Noddiks, and you certainly don't like *me*. You know you're at your best when you're in the heat of competition, wrapped up in confrontation, constantly searching for that rival to give you that extra edge... that extra motivation... that extra *fire* behind your training—no wonder you chased Sam here." He chuckled again, finishing his pre-workout potion, and said, "Hey, I'm not blaming you, bro—find what works for you, latch on to that shit, and ride that wave as long as you can. Whatever strike you're planning, I have no doubt you're gonna find a way to make it about you versus Dimes." He paused, then emphasized, "But just promise that you'll let *me* take the kill shot. Rowland clearly helped you level up your life, drive, and passion—but he absolutely obliterated mine." No longer smiling, the anger returning, Kyle flung the blender bottle against the wall—the plastic shattering. "Alright bitch, I'm out. Enjoy mission planning for that douchebag."

As Kyle strolled out, Juice was left alone in the room—alone, aside from the bulk data of doubt swirling in his head: CAG was oblivious to the level of leadership required for administrative excellence. Robo-Hinge's task-shedding and ass-blasting were out of control. The doctor developed a new-founded temperament of audacity, albeit with only one theme and phrasing of insult. Loaded T was still a meathead, but somehow waxing poetic and nearly making sense at times. And the Olympics... this whole thing seemed headed for a dud finale. Juice could barely even remember what he was fighting for...

'*Am* I just looking for a fight? Do I *need* a rival out there to succeed?' It *was* true that he failed to stay in contact with any of his old Chippy brothers. And he *didn't* care for the Noddik sailor bots, nor their opinion of him—the Padroids drove him crazy with their incompetence, and Dr. Suabedissen was certainly never somebody he wanted to 'hang' with. And his reunion with Loaded T? Not exactly a nostalgic bout of joy. Contemplating everything Loaded T was saying, he admitted internally: 'All of that recognition, even if I get this victory for the Noddik Empire? It really doesn't mean anything to me—so what *am* I turning for?' He shook his head and asked himself, '*Can I be motivated without a rival? Without... Sam...?'*

'Nickels...' he thought. 'Is this the kind of shit he dealt with when he got here? No wonder he's begging to fight for the USS Ship again...' The lines started to blur between *why* he wanted revenge against Nickels, and what Kyle suspected: That Ward just wanted to fight him, period. Juice had always thought only one thing drove him: proving he was the best. But that thought seemed more of a micro-nap musing than a lifelong dream, hardly inspiring his will to fight—a will which he was barely clinging to, as he stared at the floor blankly.

Yet the thought of defeating Sam in the end... *that* flame still burned intensely — strong enough to motivate him to open the JMPS computer, start a new mission load, and get to work on this strike.

Juice raised his head and saw Loaded T's flight bag, powdered with white residue from chalk, C4, and cocaine. He walked up to it, snuck a look around, and unzipped the bag. In it, he found an assortment of unmarked pill bottles, syringes, and creams, as well as a workout journal of lift numbers and rep schemes. There was no kneeboard, no in-flight guides, no smart packs. In fact, the only flight-related item was an IFR Supp, because some primary sim instructor once insisted it was a must-carry for any savvy aviator. Deeper down, however, he found the note Kyle had shown him when he first arrived at the Noddik Empire: Nickels' FITREP statement of dispute.

Juice had heard Sam discussing it with Skipper, and scanned through it when Kyle arrived just a few days ago—but back then, he didn't fully digest it; it didn't quite sink in just *how aggressive* this letter was. The damning words and hostile declarations... the specific people he called out... the opinions he laid out about the Navy, his past, his friends and closest brothers... Pure, unrestrained vitriol. It was the type of letter that led to extreme pity for the author—not for their victimization, but for being attached to such a resentful, grudge-filled document doomed to tarnish their reputation for eternity—*legendary* disgrace. In a way, this letter made Sam appear just as unhinged as Loaded T—in an entirely different way.

Juice shook his head in disappointment. 'Kyle said he has something planned with this letter... his contingency plan if the Olympics don't turn out well for the Noddiks—but he doesn't care about admin superiority. He *also* just wants to seek vengeance against Sam. And this letter—shit, that would be *it*.' He looked back at the shattered blender bottle, some green Sour Batch Bros liquid residue remaining on the floor. 'Kyle has bled all the green that remained in his heart—but has Sam? This letter already ruined one Chippy's life—should I really let it ruin another's?'

Seeking to avoid these uncomfortable decisions, and with a lot of mission planning ahead of him, Juice stashed the note back in Loaded T's bag, zipped it closed, then sat down and booted up the JMPS computer. As the home screen loaded, Juice logged in with a top-secret password, double-clicked the purple icon of hell, and got to work on the strike that was surely just a side note, and *surely* not going to be the climactic LFE that defined the Noddik Empire, the USS Ship, and all the former Chippies' reputations forever...

15

Return of the King

So good!" Sam exclaimed, as he took a bite of the processed sugars, grains, and fats on the midrats menu spread that night – technically morning, at 0045. "God damn, these waffles are so good!" The newly-minted section lead closed his eyes in syrup and butter-driven ecstasy, relishing the well-deserved calorie-rich meal, still riding the high from finishing his Level 3 checkride earlier that evening.

Beaming with the approval of a proud father, FISTY rubbed his hands together, Mr. PIBB-style, and said, "I must admit – I hate spending an evening away from the lab, and I'm just as uncomfortable consuming these types of unnecessary carbs, gluten, and nightshade vegetables... but if there was ever a night of flying that warranted a bit of seed oil splurging? It was tonight! Holy shit, Nickels – that was incredible – and yet, I shouldn't be surprised by any of it, not from a pilot of your Good Dude aptitude!"

Bashfully smiling, Sam shrugged. "Ahh, FISTY, come on – that's all thanks to your training! I wouldn't even be here if it weren't for all those SAPDART-execution labs, level-level-safe escape drills, and philosophical discussions on the ethical impact of simulated JDAM employment."

FISTY chuckled. "Nickels, a mentor can only take a Padawan to a certain point. I can lead you to your lane in the vul – but ultimately, the onus falls upon the individual to execute the game plan within precise parameters, at the proper times, with the appropriate tactical risk level – or in short, to 'do their job' in contributing to mission success!" he said, throwing out one of his clichéd Bill Belichick references. "Or, in terms you'd probably appreciate a bit more," FISTY grinned slyly, "you can lead a wingman down the taxiways and past the hold short, but the final responsibility lies with them to pull into position, count to 10, and take off behind you at the appropriate NWLO/TO numbers whilst delivering only good news over the radio."

Sam smirked and jokingly dismissed his Training O's words, teasing, "Ah, FISTY, you're such a tactics whore... haven't you ever noticed that TOPGUN only 'recommends' things, while NATOPS is written in blood?!"

FISTY scoffed and grinned. "Admin isn't gonna win wars or championships, Sam; It may get you to the big show – just like a no-name Michigan quarterback's sound mechanics got him to the 199th pick of the 1999 NFL draft – but it's the heart, desire, and passion for the strategic intricacies of the game's finest details that will have you holding the trophy as the clock hits zeroes!"

"Psh – of course, you find a way to bring Brady into it!" Sam rolled his eyes. "FISTY, I think TB12 is the only topic you love more than tactics!"

"Well, I'd certainly rather discuss him than TG12s!" Flynn hit back with a hearty laugh, the rest of the wardroom groaning at the extremely lame dork-debate between these two SMEs of their respective fields.

Sam and FISTY, though, wore wide smiles across their faces as they went back and forth about admin vs tactics, with the occasional added inclusion of Tom Brady. It was a recurring Chippy discussion – for precisely two Chippies – and went on for what felt like an eternity to the rest of the table as CP, Low T, JABA, >SADCLAM<, and some other CVW-5 friends did their best to stomach the 'thrilling' banter.

Low T, though, laughed and acknowledged, "Hey, I may not know much about 'sportsball' or whatever you jocks like to talk about, but one thing I do know is flying – and credit where it's due: major props on finishing Level 3!" He fist bumped his best friend and chuckled as he continued, "And I can't think of a more 'Nickels' way for it to go down, either – a Good Dude of the people, even in his checkride!"

Sam beamed. "Ah, well... you know I couldn't help myself..."

What Low T was referring to, of course, was the insane sequence of events that led to Sam giving up his mission-loaded jet to a Talon who needed a currency night trap, and instead hopped in a Chippy five-wet tanker spare – not exactly the ideal DCA configuration. En route to the vul, he stopped overhead to give gas to some FNG PGMers looking for practice plugs, leading to a bit of a late start to the fight. The RTB? A thing of pure administrative genius – the stuff of legends: Nickels expertly led back his SFTI without the use of the term 'holding hands' and inexplicably managed to reach Red Crown – in the green – followed by a smooth transition to Strike and Marshal, where he harnessed his inner TB12 and quarterbacked the entire marshal stack on his TAC freq, after CATCC dropped the ball by erroneously staying up secure comms for the recovery. Upon taxiing to his parking spot and patiently waiting for the E2 to land? Ever the classy Good Dude, Nickels had patches and command coins ready to provide the taxi director who safely led the admin evolution across the stern of the ship.

>SADCLAM< threw his hands up in amazement, exclaiming, "Dude, the textbook shutdown you engineered at the end, troubleshooting the BLINs by pulling circuit breakers until they were gone?!" He blew a smooch to the wind with his fingers, "Chef's kiss. I hope you

271

don't mind that I saved those tapes to my personal folder to show future SFWT candidates what administrative beauty looks like."

JABA chimed in, "Yeah, let me echo that sentiment for the on-deck val in the startup — such a skyscraper-SA move recording every single waypoint on the SA page and discovering that the thousandth digit of the tertiary divert airfield longitude was off with a rounding error! Thank god you noticed; I vow never to let that happen again!" Buck was giddy despite having the error highlighted, as the humble JMPS O was always open to improvement on his mission load builds.

Sam shyly refused both men's lavish praise, insisting, "Guys, seriously, it's no big deal – it's just simple execution in the fine art of admin! You can be just as proficient by simply taking three hours a day to review NATOPS, SOPs, and good sound judgment!" He then goof-ily smiled at his tactics-obsessed mentor, narrowed his eyes, and added, "... And then you can avoid gaffes like opening your canopy mid-flight..."

Rolling his eyes with an annoyed smile, FISTY said, "Ok, ok, point made, Sam! Geeze, it was a year ago, and I was reaching for my bag! Man..." he exhaled with a smirk of disbelief, "You admin bros are relentless! And, by the way, I certainly hope your conduct in that vul today was just as tight as your non-tactical performance!"

Of course, the actual mission portion of the flight was filled with plenty of Goods and Others, all of which were professionally debriefed to Sam's hypothetical student: the Maces' Training O. It was a recollection that Sam didn't want to bore the reader with or bust any classification levels in his brain by reminiscing over in a non-secure space. "Let's just say that everything was done in accordance with your 'Good Book,' FISTY – and I'm not talking about that $200 TB12 Method diet book," he added with a wink.

"Weeeeehhhhhhhll, that's about all I can take of this!" CP said as he stood up and grabbed his plate, fatigued from the unbearable back and forth between his two squadronmates.

"Oh, Clown Penis, please," FISTY said with a grin, "As if you have something better to talk about than tactics, admin, and the GOAT..."

CP finished his glass of milk, stared at FISTY blankly, and deadpanned, "I can literally think of a thousand things, Tom..."

"Yeah – what?!" Low T said with a laugh. "You guys need to chill out with that stuff!"

FISTY scoffed in mock as he and his pupil continued going back and forth about Super Bowls, DCA vuls, and On-Scene Commander roles – as the other Chippy boys and the rest of Wardroom 1/2 began filtering their way out to bed for the ensuing flight day – the first that Sam 'Nickels' Rowland would serve as a qualified section lead. Which, of course, he would serve on SDO, per Naval tradition and oldest troll in the book.

When just the two of them remained, Sam grew a bit more serious. "Hey, FISTY – earlier, WYFMIFM asked me what I'd like to do for my first section lead event in two days; what do you think? I was considering taking one of the new guys out on some low-level ship-rigging, maybe a good deal BFM with CP or The Lorax, or even just a night-PGM-dickaround with JABA for us to keep him night current?"

After a prolonged pause and a pensive look, FISTY took a bite of his eggs, put his fork down, and asked, "You want to know what I really think?"

"Absolutely, Sensei," Sam insisted, fully valuing his mentor's guidance.

FISTY shrugged. "I think you should use tomorrow to start working on your Level 4 SEAD lab, and fill the -3 role in Slowbro's Division OCA the following day to get some exposure and a good practice run."

"What?!" Sam was floored. Start Level 4 *already*? Begin drafting up a brief the *day* after finishing Level 3? Sit through an entire debrief of a division event after his next flight, using his brand new qual simply to fill a role for a larger evolution? "FISTY... you can't be serious?"

"100%, brother," he said with a look of determination. "Sam, what have we always talked about? The TB12 mindset — what is he focused on as soon as he wins a Super Bowl?"

Knowing the answer cold — as it was part of FISTY's TB12 boldface — Sam quickly answered, "The next one."

"Exactly!" FISTY acknowledged with excitement. "Sam... what you've accomplished tonight is incredible, honestly. And I'm not just saying this because you're my apprentice: it was one of the best Level 3 checkrides I've ever seen. You deserve to be proud as hell. But Nickels..." he smiled and shook his head, pointing down at the floor, "You could stop to take a brief glimpse of the mountain you've just climbed, the territory you've conquered..." He then pointed to the ceiling, "Or you could instead keep looking up, and recognize just how many peaks are yet to be scaled..."

He paused, then explained, "If you look back for too long, gorging your ego on previous accomplishments, you'll get complacent... satisfied... satiated off what you've already consumed. You gotta stay hungry, Sam, even when you have every reason to be full! The greatest of men can win one championship, feel like they're on top of the world, and fail to see the summits surrounding them; fail to see they're just barely scraping the surface of what they can accomplish in life. Look at Drew Brees, Brett Favre, Aaron Rodgers, and even Peyton Manning — until he literally relocated a mile higher to get one more. These guys are all champions, Sam, and sure-fire Hall of Famers — and I'm most definitely not knocking their drive! I'm just saying: Careers are short. Life is short. The more time we spend admiring? The less time we spend climbing..." He shrugged again and asked, "Nickels, do you think you're really going to arrive at your retirement ceremony — with all the time in the world to finally look back on your career — and say, 'I wish I'd spent more time in life looking down, appreciating what I've done'?"

Nickels shook his head quietly.

"That's right," FISTY nodded. "And yet how many do you think hang up the JHMCS or the cleats for the last time, and feel the internal contrition of 'I wish I spent more time looking up — more time climbing — so I'd have an even better view now that it's all said and done'?"

Sam took a breath and exhaled deeply, nodding his head — no words needed to be said. The right action was clear — so why did it feel so uneasy? "So... no celebration day? No rewarding time off to relax...?"

FISTY laughed. "Sam, don't you see? When you have that passion burning inside you — as Brady does football — not taking the time off is *the celebration! Consider this midrats meal — right here, right now — your moment of 'rest.' Because ultimately, there* is *a reward to celebrate here." FISTY beamed and continued, "The reward for excellence is the opportunity to pursue further excellence. Earning your Level 3 qual isn't about being a badass section lead; it's about earning the key to open the door to the Level 4 syllabus, where you can become even greater.*

"And trust me when I say this: the mere act of 'doing?' Trucking further up the mountain instead of looking down longingly? That act reignites *that hunger in you, giving you inspiration reserves you never knew you had, almost as if that metaphorical burning of mental calories stimulates your appetite for* further *greatness." FISTY sighed with awe, "It's motivational magic..."*

He smiled, then delved further into his go-to analogy: "Tom Brady's first Super Bowl ring wasn't a medal to appoint him the next franchise QB — it was a gift from the football gods to allow him the opportunity to push for higher tiers, more exclusive clubs, taller peaks — a gift that he abso-fucking-lutely took and ran with, thanks to his insatiable desire to win." FISTY raised his chin and widened his eyes, emphasizing, "And of course, let's give massive credit to his sensei, Bill Belichick, a man who was also *not in the business of spending more than a moment or so 'celebrating' an accomplishment that would ideally become a stepping stone to many more." FISTY turned slightly bashful and quickly added, "Not that I'm trying to compare* myself *to the great Bill Belichick..."*

"Please, FISTY," Sam chuckled, "If Belichick was half *the sage as you, he'd be the greatest coach of all time!"*

"He arguably — no, definitely *— already is!" FISTY said with conviction.*

Sam nodded in agreement. "I bet he and Brady still have awesome conversations like this every day!"

Noticeably shifting his demeanor, FISTY turned a bit and quietly murmured with skepticism. "Uhh... I don't know about that..."

"Huh?" Sam asked. "But... but they were so prevalent in each other's careers! You can't tell the story of one without the other! I mean, I can't imagine *not speaking to you after all the training we've done together!"*

FISTY sighed sadly. "You're gonna want to sit down, Nickels..."

Oblivious that he had risen from his chair in shock, Sam took his seat again and listened as FISTY explained, "When award-winning radio host Dan Patrick once asked Brady if he thinks that he and Belichick will ever get together and discuss their legendary games or watch old film together, Brady infamously looked at him like he was crazy and laughed, answering '... No!' The two... Sam... they weren't as close as the public might believe..." FISTY lamented with a grimace. "There are rumors that Belichick wasn't as strong a defense advocate as Brady would've liked during the Deflategate nonsense, or that he wanted to replace Brady with Garoppolo well before Tom was truly 'done' — but if you ask me, it was strictly just a professional, cordial work relationship. Sort of a 'Just win, baby' mindset, minus the fun-loving 'baby' thrown in – not in Bill's regime. Belichick was there for one reason, and it wasn't to make friends or garner laughs.

"And when Brady left for Tampa... it unfortunately became a 'who deserves the credit' debate in the media..." FISTY looked disgusted as he seethed, "The same type of toxic discussion that rampantly weakens individuals' immune systems, allowing them to become poisoned by The Disease of Me..."

Sam was still confused. "So, they don't get along at all? And was the relationship further damaged by Brady winning one in Tampa, combined with New England sort of falling off the map of contenders?"

Shrugging and offering up his arms, FISTY said, "You know, that's one of life's greatest mysteries – in the TB12 fanatic community, anyway. Now, when it comes to who I believe was the main driving force behind all that Lombardi glory, you already know my answer – yet, part of me can't help but feel for Belichick... for their bond... for what they still could've accomplished with a few more years together..."

Noticing the true hurt in his sensei's eyes, Sam tried to encourage FISTY. "Hey, you never know – maybe one day, they'll get together and reminisce in one of those ESPN 30 for 30s!" He nodded reassuringly, insisting, "You know, where they'll throw verbal bouquets each other's way – both men acting with extreme humility and class – and share an emotional and literal embrace through recognizing everything they achieved together in dominating the parity-obsessed league for decades!"

Still looking melancholy, FISTY forced a small smile, but shook his head. "You truly are a sweet, sweet boy, Nickels... but I just don't see it happening."

Frustrated at seeing his mentor so disheartened over this, Sam prodded, "Why not? You really think they're that petty?"

This time, a natural smile appeared – and nearly a tear in his eye – as FISTY looked at Sam and responded, "No, Nickels. It's because both men were climbers, are climbers, and will always be climbers. I see this hypothetical 30 for 30 as unlikely – but not because of personality or recognition-acknowledgment issues." He shook his head and calmly explained, "I don't see it happening, because I can't imagine either man taking anything more than a quick glimpse of what they've accomplished in the past – period dot, no matter with whom. Not when they both undoubtedly still see unrealized potential in new arenas..."

After a brief pause, FISTY continued, with a raised finger: "Now, if they ever were to reconvene, I could only see it happening in some type of competitive pursuit together – and there's unfortunately nearly zero chance of that happening. But boy, if it did," FISTY said, shaking his head and looking longingly in the distance, "I can only imagine the type of ferocity, passion, and dedication that would take place with those two forever-climbers teamed up once again... no red air would ever stand a chance against a 2v1 with blue of that caliber..."

"We can only hope to see a force of that magnitude again, Sensei. We can only hope..." Sam said with a smile.

Rowland looked at his watch — 0100. "Well... I should probably get going — I've gotta be on SDO at 5, thanks to CAG OPS' overly cautious Alert 5 package off the coast of Japan. But hey," he suggested with a smile, "meet me at the STBR at 0400 to go over some Level 4 stuff?"

"0400?!" FISTY asked, shocked. "Goodness, Nickels, you need your sleep!" He then paused, gave a sly grin, and said, "Make it 0430."

Sam laughed and pointed at the tactical GOAT. "Bet up!"

~

CP, JABA, Nickels, >SADCLAM<, and the third US pilot stood line abreast at their utmost professional attention in the captain's cabin — FISTY's zombified body slumped over in the visitor's chair next to them — with stares so far in the distance they could see the Seattle space needle, providing credence to the flat earth theory.

All-hands were still feeling the rush from the triumphant Phase 2 for the USS Ship — but the celebration had been a brief one. Knowing their greatest battle was yet to come, and eager to game plan the culminating evolution ASAP, the pilots raced to the captain's stateroom with such urgency that the last three aviators still wore their flight gear and helmets — CLAM and the NPC Pilot sporting the unaesthetic-yet-lethal JHMCS, while Sam donned the only headwear he trusted in administrative phases of flight: his non-tactical, spine-friendly, ironically-named 'tac-air' helmet — also known as the 'dumb helmet.' The men had been waiting with bated breath to see what the captain had in store for the ship in Phase 3 — the red air GQ plan, concocted by the strategic mastermind that commandeered this steel war machine.

Well... Sam *assumed* he was a strategic mastermind — but this was all based on mind-framing, given the information passed to him just three chapters ago. *Captain William Stephen Belichick... I* know *that's what LTJG Narrator said. Could it be, though...? Could it possibly be the* same *guy? But what would he be doing —*

The lights dimmed to darkness. A spotlight then beamed onto the entrance to the cabin, and heavy music started playing from the 1MC. Seconds after, the door burst open — window crashing sound effects from the 1MC for added drama — and as LTJG Narrator's voice shouted, "Uh oh! *What?!*" from the speaker system, a crusty old curmudgeon stomped into the room. Young enlisted sailors stood in the doorway with their arms reached out for high fives, which the irritated-faced man blatantly ignored as he stormed by them. In reaction to this shocking display of apathy, Narrator — still referencing a way-too-old meme — yelled out, "Wait a minute — *what the hell?!*" The grumpy man's grey hair was unkempt, his FOD-free New Balance shoes dirty and worn, and his navy-blue flight deck jersey — stenciled "USS Ship Commanding Officer" in a tiny Times New Roman font — had its sleeves clearly and messily cut off with scissors. His khaki pants had a few holes and fuel stains in them. And, most notably of all, his bearing — devoid of all military features — wore a scowl of annoyance and impatience. As the grouch continued to clomp up to his desk, he scanned the group of aviators, and then finally mumbled, "At ease."

The men loosened up and stole quick glances at each other, as JABA mouthed, "Bill Belichick!" to Sam, who discreetly nodded. Based on the vibes of this entrance, Sam felt this wasn't exactly something to be excited about.

Captain Belichick stared the men down and, after a prolonged awkward silence, sighed, shrugged, and said, "You won; now are you guys done?"

Confused, Sam cleared his throat and began explaining, "Won? Sir, we tied —"

"Take your helmet off. I can't hear anything you're saying, and you look ridiculous," Belichick grumbled.

"Yes, sir," Sam responded, removing his helmet — administratively easy, without being forced to deal with the JHMCS umbilical cord. "Sir, my name is Captain Sam Rowland. I'm the one who spoke to you on the phone before Phase 2."

Belichick grunted and checked his watch.

"Sir, thank you so much for letting us fly your jets. As I'm sure you saw, it was a close but huge win for the USS Ship, and now the Administrative Olympics are tied at one apiece. The final round is yet to unfold, though — and the Noddiks are undoubtedly on the verge of attacking with their red air game plan. However, if we can be the *first* to strike, we can take the wind out of their sails *before* they get on the offensive — and end this war once and for all." Sam paused for a moment, but Belichick just stared at him blankly. "Sir, as the expert of sea warfare, I thought maybe you would have an idea as to how we can attack the NIRD Katsopolis and get — at the very least — a firepower kill, hamstringing their efforts as a result."

Seemingly more irritated by the minute, Belichick folded his arms and just glared at Sam, his head slightly tilting to the side, as if simply holding himself upright was too much of a nuisance for the O-6. He glanced over at the wall, thought for a moment, then looked back at Sam. "Yeah, I'll think of something. *Then* will this be over?" he asked petulantly.

Having endured too much to remain quiet, CP now spoke up, "Sir, it seems to me that you're not taking this campaign with the severity that it deserves."

Belichick locked his displeased stare on CP. "Who are you." It was more of a statement than a question.

"LT Andrew Preul, callsign Clown Penis, sir. I'm a pilot who used to serve for the legendary VFA-195 Dambusters, before I left to start and manage Flat Earth Fitness. But now, I'm back where my heart and soul belong — in the aviation arena. And sir, with all due respect, I would like to see the same intensity and passion from you that *my* team—under our leader, Captain Nickels Rowland—has demonstrated in helping *your* vessel stay alive in these Olympics."

Sam was slightly shaken—and touched—by CP's words. It wasn't often that Andrew would speak so freely from the heart—but when he did, his words moved mountains.

Belichick, however, seemed much less moved. In fact, he remained motionless, before mumbling something about Flat Earth Fitness being overpriced and over-crowded.

Knowing the old sales tactic of refusing to be the first to break the silence, CP instead just stared intently at the grumpy old man.

Eventually, Belichick caved, rolled his eyes, and said, "Fellas, three things: First of all, we're in the middle of a FAS/RAS—you'll have to excuse me if I'm a bit more concerned with getting this ship restocked with salad and Cinnamon Toast Crunch than I am fighting this... *asinine* war," he said with disgust.

"Second, the ship recently took on a bunch of civilian contractors who are here to work on our software, scanners, printers, and other various ship engineering necessities like potable water, OHSA-approved grills in the kitchens, and air conditioning units; getting them the resources they need is my top priority right now. I think we can *all* agree that war is meaningless if sailors can't load their Navy Cash Cards with properly functioning ATMs," he added with more than a tinge of annoyance.

"But lastly—and most importantly: what does it *matter* who wins the Admin Olympics? You think anybody's really going to care about this years from now? If we lose—then great, we're all bums. If we win? Great for *you*," he pointed toward his underlings. "*You* guys can all be praised as a bunch of heroes—meanwhile, *my* life goes on—but *I'm* now forced to give 'rah-rah' dog-and-pony-show speeches about 'defending this turf,' as *new* competing empires start challenging us to Olympics, we get everyone's A+ game, and eventually lose to a hungrier competitor. And if that wasn't bad enough, I'm sure some bozo journalist will dig into the minute details of the OPNAV 3710, and leak a report showing that *you*," he pointed to Sam, "didn't have a US Navy aircraft flight logged in the last 1000 days, making you ineligible for Day Case 1 in Phase 2. And you—take your helmet off for god's sake, Mr. Houben," he now pointed to >SADCLAM<, who doffed his oversized dome hood. "That *you* didn't have 10 JHMCS hours logged in the last 365 days, making that helmet ineligible for Admin Olympics. And lastly, you," he pointed to the third USS Pilot, "We don't even *have* your NATOPS jacket on file, so I don't even *know* where to begin with how illegal *your* whole evolution was." He looked back at Sam and concluded, "So now, gents, we have a 3710Gate on our hands—much to the media's delight—as they work tirelessly to invalidate every ounce of hard work we just put in. So," he cleared his throat, folded his arms again, and asked, "why should *I* care to put *any* iota of concern into this trivial shit?"

"Mmmphmmpghjob..." an unconscious FISTY mumbled as he writhed in the chair.

Captain Belichick looked over at the lifeless body. "Hmmph... what's that kid's issue?"

>SADCLAM< spoke up, "He was tortured, sir—tortured by a virgin mad scientist, because he *refused* to give out the tactical secrets that make this such a lethal force of aviators. Z diagrams, Rules of Thumb, the first Defensive BFM Axiom; time-honored S3 secrets that—if revealed—would surely leave us lost and thwarted, with no hope of winning the high-end fight. The Noddiks may have the administrative upper hand in day-to-day ops—for *now*—but our ability to think critically and flex tactically on the fly?" CLAM raised his hands and emphasized, "*That's* what separates us from an assembly line of robots out there; from NPCs who can only execute from a script, only adhere to a plan when it's contingency-free, and who *can't* even handle the adversity of an EXT TANK caution on takeoff roll."

Belichick, seeming unenthused and unimpressed, raised his hand to respond—but, remembering so many of the lessons FISTY had taught him, Sam spoke first. "Not too different than your New England Patriots of old." Rattling off some of Belichick's known favorite players, Sam added, "Guys like Danny Amendola, Matthew Slater, Rodney Harrison, Kevin Faulk, Vince Wilfork—guys who were methodically clutch when it mattered most. Guys who didn't just bring their known best in the games' closing minutes—they *raised* their level. When everybody else was running out of energy and panicking at the chaos, crumbling under the stakes of the moment? These guys were *thriving* off their flames of determination, calmed by the confidence from knowing they'd prepared for these moments over and over again in training. And, like United States tactical aviators, they *continued* to separate the New England Patriots from the rest of the league—largely thanks to a captain who wasn't afraid to make them practice in peacetime at MAX, knowing that when war hit? It would simply feel like MIL..." He looked knowingly at Belichick, who had emotionally backed off a bit—from standoffish, to now merely frowning. Sam let the moment hit deeper by adding, "Because of guys like *that*, and because of the challenge-issuing, resilient, tenacious leaders driving them—like my mentor and sensei, Admiral Flynn? *They* are why we hold the #1 spot in the power rankings of naval aviation. And with our efforts not made in vain, we will *still* hold that position after Phase 3 of these Olympics." He looked around confidently, then urged, "But if we're going to do that, we're going to need *you* to take this mission just as seriously as *we* do." Sam stared the coach in the eyes. "*That*, your honor, is Admiral Flynn's fucking issue." *Dammit, Sam, why are you still calling him that?!*

But Sam's embarrassing addressing of the captain didn't matter, as his words seemed to pique Belichick's curiosity. The ex-coach's annoyed frown became a full-on blank face—*almost* a positive expression. "Hmm... methodically clutch..." he said with a hint of approval. "I like that. You know, I used to drill these guys on the basics of the huddle-to-snap transition, the hurry-up-offense-line-up, and the post-first-down-clock-stop-spike all summer long, *every day* to exhaustion. They *hated* it... But as a result, when it came to brain stem power for the *administrative* parts of football—eliminating silly mistakes like 'delay of game,' 'illegal formations,' or '12 men on the field?' *Nobody* was more administratively sound than the New England Patriots."

Now he finally wore it—a *legit* subtle smile, as he looked longingly out the window. "And when we had such rock-solid admin as a foundation to build upon? It made our complex offensive tactics and defensive schemes all the easier to execute with only the most minor of deviations. Because of our prep in *every* phase of the sport, our C game would beat most teams' A game." His face now a *complete* smirk, he added, "Not that I would ever let those guys get *too* excited about putting up C-level effort, even in a playoff win..."

Sam returned the smirk with a grin of his own. "And while they may have begrudged it—thinking they'd rather taste the sweet, sugary carbohydrate rush of lavish compliments—they undoubtedly got better—*every single week*—from your nutritionally dense steak and potatoes critiques."

Nodding, Belichick smiled. "Champions put in the legwork and bake the goods—but it results in the entire world telling them how incredible those goods taste. And the minute they start to sample the results they've put forth, and start getting high off their own supply? They're done for. Why do you think Walter White was always so angry at Jesse Pinkman for that? Heh."

Was that a chuckle? Am I reaching this old grouch after all? Despite the incredibly obscure Breaking Bad reference, which had practically no place nor meaning in this discussion nor chapter, one thing was readily apparent in Sam's mind: *Belichick is enjoying this conversation! Was the secret to winning someone over still just the oldest trick in the book: making them feel heard, special, and appreciated?*

Looking back at the aviators before him, Belichick doubled down on his analogy. "And you know, some of those guys you mentioned—'Dola and Rodney—and even some others like Randy and Revis, too... They were all sort of like 'Jesse's—cast off from other teams, abandoned as trash to be picked up off the waiver wire. Well, *my* system turned them into key role players—'problem guys' who could be embraced and unleashed in the right structure—like when Jesse helped Walter find various dealers and suppliers across the streets of Albuquerque, and even down in Mexico, too," he added with gentle eyes. "You know, Jesse may not have been the best cook, and he certainly should've paid more attention in Mr. White's chemistry class. But when Walter gave him a task—carefully niched out for the young man's personality skill set, like getting the stolen drug money back from Spooge—what did Jesse do? What did *all* those cast-off players do when I showed them the Patriot Way, and told them to simply master their assigned task?"

"GrrrmphDidTheirJobmmmph..." FISTY subconsciously murmured, much to the delight of Bill.

"Yes," he said, monotone but pleased, "The sick kid has it exactly right. They did their job. Randy caught touchdowns, Darrell locked down receivers, and Jesse smashed that junkie's head with an ATM. They did. Their. Job." He emphasized each word by pounding his fist into his other palm.

Sensing the moment, Sam looked over at JABA, who smiled and nodded encouragingly. Returning his eyes back to Belichick, Rowland said, "And now, your honor, we're asking you to do *your* job—as a commander at sea. As a leader. As a *coach*." He paused for dramatic effect. "*Coach* this ship to victory—have them ready to withstand whatever attack the Noddiks throw our way. Use *us* as chess pieces at your will, like you did with the Patriots of old. Together—by doing our jobs and not worrying about credit, glory, or the recognition we think we're 'owed'—we can launch a soul-crushing assault against the Noddik's admin defenses and *win* this war. That 9th ring would look awfully good in your trophy case, sir..."

Grinning again, Belichick quietly remarked, "... You remembered my two Giants rings. You Chippies really *are* true fans..." He pondered the thought quietly, his eyes gleaming.

"Then let's *do* it, Coach." Sam pumped his fist with conviction. "Let's fucking make a run at this 'chip. Let's win one for the Gipper. Let's put it all on the table. Let's Pk enhance like we've got infinite ammo. Let's turn like it's the last engagement of our life. Let's—"

"THIS IS THE TAO. SET, EMCON ROMEO. MODIFY LINES 1 AND 6A, WORDS 231 and 172, TO SAY 'THE.' ALL FUN DEVICES ARE TO BE SECURED. LAUNCH THE SNOOPIE TEAM. ALL VIOLATORS WILL REPORT TO THE DECK HOUSE IN HANGAR BAY 2 AT TAC NUMBER 1-69-3-X. SET, MODIFIED CONDITION: WALRUS 2. SET, WEEPING BEAVER 3. SET—"

"*Enough!*" an annoyed Belichick yelled as he turned the 1MC off. He put his hands on his hips and shook his head. "Fellas, I'm sorry, but I can't... there's too much going on with the ship to take part in these childish games. We've got INSURV coming up, and I'm spending more time figuring out how to *delay* it than I am deducing what INSURV actually even entails. Potable water is at an all-time low—looking at *you,* air wing, with your Hollywood showers," he glared at the pilots with irritation. "And I can't get *any* khakis to show some fucking presence at cleaning stations! Not to mention, we did a man overboard yesterday, and it took thirty *fucking* minutes! Can you *believe* that shit?! Good grief, we even had it on the green sheet! Oh, and the *trash...* Jesus Christ, you'd think anybody with even the *tiniest* bit of effort could sort between soft plastic, hard plastic, burnables, sinkables, dunnage, cardboard, soft-ish plastic, paper towels, secret paper, classified notes, unclassified air plans, and whiteboard erasing non-burnable-towels..." He shook his head in disgust, "But instead, these kids insist on 'yeeting' it overboard—where does that word even come from, 'yeet?' I can't keep up with the TwitchTok or InstaFace jargon these Gen Z-ers are rambling about these days. Gents, we've got hatches left often in Modified Condition: Zebra, hatches unnecessarily *closed* in Material Condition: Yoke..."

And as Belichick kept rambling, Sam finally realized it: this was the captain he had become with the Noddiks. It was the same bullshit; the complaints of the job now shrouded all the parts he used to love—the aspects that once got him *excited* to grind through work. He'd become detached from the aspects that used to drive his passion with daily motivation to get better. His new persona had been one of extreme bitterness as he traded in his burning desire... for what? To become a company man in a position he had no enthusiasm for?! It was a role that somebody else surely could've enjoyed and excelled at. But for Sam—for *Nickels*—his heart remained elsewhere... just as Belichick's clearly did...

"I mean, come on," Belichick's rant continued, "How low-SA and stubborn can you be, disregarding the 'free weights secured' sign and benching during heavy sea states?!"

"Probably about as low-SA and stubborn as *you* were, benching Malcolm Butler in the 2018 Super Bowl, where *backup* QB Nick Foles commandeered the Eagles with unprecedented offensive stats against the Patriots' secondary..." CP glared with a fierce look on his face.

FISTY painfully squirmed in his unconscious state. Sam closed his eyes and shook his head. *CP... no! We almost had him...*

Belichick immediately recoiled into a scowl, falling back on the defensive. "How dare you... how *dare* you!" He raised his finger and wagged it with authority at the Chippy pilot, his dagger-like extremity even more fearsome than a knife hand. "You have *no* right to question me or my decision-making! I..." he scoffed, "I don't need to explain myself to you—*any* of you!" He looked around at the Chippies. "You really are just a bunch of foolish Jesse's, throwing wrenches in my mastermind operation. I don't need you to run the ship—I don't need *any* of you air wing people! Not the aviators, not your TAD maintenance bodies, and *certainly* not your overzealous, over-friendly, cookie-offering CAG!" He scoffed again, "Can you believe that—giving *cookies* to his men?! Just as asinine as handing out compliments..." he shook his head in disgust. "I don't need some pretty, pampered, golden boy helping me get a ring—I can do it on my own! You are all *dismissed*!" he yelled, pointing to the door.

Sam motioned to speak, but Belichick pointed to the door even more forcefully, as he sat down and began sifting through mountains of blue folders, angrily grunting with every signature.

"Come on, guys," Sam said to his friends dejectedly. JABA and CP picked up FISTY, as Rowland, >SADCLAM<, and the unnamed aviator turned to exit the cabin-at-sea.

As they began walking glumly toward the exit, they heard Belichick's phone ring, followed by an exaggerated sigh from the captain, as he picked up and said, "What."

Sam carefully tried to listen as he slowed his pace to the door, and Belichick became increasingly agitated through his reactions. "Are you fucking kidding me—*all* of it? Are they still tech-repping?" ... "Jesus... say again? *Curling*?!" He clasped his hand over his eyes. "You've got to be joking! How are we just now seeing this guy, we're in fucking Alert 30s!" ... "Yes, god, yes—we absolutely need to go to GQ here." ... "Yes, call that too!" ... "Oh my god, I don't care, just call it!" ... "Absolutely, secure it all—we need to go goddamned nuclear!" ... "Yeah, bye." And he angrily slammed the phone down, calling out, "Men, don't leave just yet—and turn the 1MC up."

JABA reached up and clicked the speaker up to its max volume, just in time to hear, "THIS IS THE TAO; LAUNCH THE ALERT 60 AA—BELAY MY LAST. THIS IS THE TAO; UPGRADE THE ALERT 60 AAW TO ALERT 30 AAW."

>SADCLAM< asked, "Upgrade?! Was that in accordance with the airplan, or an unplanned—?" but he stopped as Belichick raised his hand to silence the young JO.

Not five seconds later, they heard the voice of torture again, this time announcing, "THIS IS THE TAO. LAUNCH THE ALERT 30 AAW. INITIAL VECTOR 270. SET GENERAL QUARTERS—ALL HANDS MAN YOUR BATTLE STATIONS. AND..." there was a brief pause, as if the voice was steeling himself, before calling, "SET... CONDITION: FYREFEST."

When the final declaration was made, Belichick shook his head in disappointment, as if he knew what kind of doom was to follow. "God... *dammit!*" he groaned as he pounded his fist on the table.

"What's going on, sir?" JABA asked.

Belichick craned his head back in annoyance, rubbed his eyes from exhaustion, and explained, "Some... *idiot*... is getting too close to the ship. And to make matters worse, the contractors are going rogue—they've refused to do any work, instead just sitting in the wardroom shoveling endless amounts of food into their gullets, and then wandering around aimlessly while taking long showers and clogging up every DV head. And, *apparently*, one of the less fat ones even found his way into the gym—and he was fucking *curling* in the *squat rack*. They're threatening to keep this nonsense going until we bring out more cheesecake and Sunday morning waffles. Good grief, it'll take us *days* to thaw out all that flash-frozen food..."

"Oh no!" JABA exclaimed, panicked. "Are the dried cake squares and whole-wheat Eggo waffles not good enough? I'm sure if the reps just doused them in syrup and ice cream..." his voice trailed off as he saw Belichick's peeved expression, shaking his head.

His jaw clenched, Sam asked, "How much damage have they already caused? Do they have weapons?"

"Well, they've already eaten all the recent shipments of Krave and Cinnamon Toast Crunch," Belichick explained as he shook his head. "And they're armed with most dangerous possible weapons—obliviousness, insubordination, and entitled attitudes. They're walking about the p-ways while Big XO is talking, leaving hatches wide open, taking to-go plates from Wardroom 3, using cell phones in hangar bay *1!*" he growled, "And despicable as it sounds... one of them has already refused to get out of the way for a high-ranking officer..."

"Why didn't one of your boat O-4s try to stop him?" CP questioned.

"Well, that was our chief of police on the phone, and he actually *did* try to lecture the delinquent on how unprofessional it was," Belichick explained. "But the contractor rolled his eyes and responded with a vulgar statement—involving oral copulation—that I wouldn't be surprised to hear from Jesse Pinkman, but *certainly* one that shouldn't be coming from a shipmate's mouth."

I've seen some seriously fat and annoying tech reps in my day... but never any as egregious and obscene as this! And curling in the squat rack!? Something about this wasn't sitting right with Sam.

"Sir, what is Condition: Fyrefest?" >SADCLAM< asked.

Belichick sighed woefully and described, "It's the most conservative we can possibly make the ship in preparation for a long holdout away from normal operations. I didn't have a choice, boys—not with the mutiny of contractors taking place downstairs, nor with our ship having unanticipated flyovers. I regret to inform you that the following OPCONs are in effect: All water is secured, period—no showers, no drinking water, no dishwashing, no toilet flushing. Every gym is closed—gains and leanness do not matter in war. Food will open at 0830, and stop being served after 1000; the only options throughout the day will be carbohydrate-dense snacks: Poptarts, Chewy Bars, Famous Amos cookies, and the remaining prepackaged cereals—probably a lot of Special K, Rice Chex, and Total—and absolutely *no* milk, aside from the warm stuff left over. Trash will now be sorted into 20 separate categories; expect an all-hands email explaining it in detail. Every squadron owes us an Alert 5 package 24/7. We're obviously already in EMCON, but we'll need to start securing lights soon—constant 'darkened ship.' The DC Central Engineer Officer of the Watch will narrate any and every change over the 1MC, and he's already had his Adderall in preparation for the long ordeal. And finally..."

With their jaws dropped in horror, the men waited for Belichick's final piece of shit news.

He firmly nodded and declared, "Cleaning stations will continue taking place every morning between 0730-0830. That means *everyone*," he commented angrily, staring daggers at the khakis in front of him. "*We* need to keep this place shining, and with a full crew on board, it takes a *full* crew to keep it that way..."

CP grabbed his forehead and groaned, "Oh my gosh..."

Sam threw his hands up. "Captain Belichick, this is outrageous! You can't do this—you'll tear the ship apart! This will last for about six to nine hours—"

"Nice," Houben noted, as Belichick shot him an annoyed look.

"—before the entire place revolts against you!" Sam continued. "Why does the boat do this? Why do they *insist* on all these insane stipulations that are seemingly pointless? Are you *intentionally* trying to anger us? You seriously expect me to believe we can't get potable water in the middle of the ocean? And wouldn't a healthy lifestyle and outlet for exercise matter even *more* during this chaos? Forget a proper diet—sir, how in the hell are we supposed to fuel ourselves *at all* in this hyper-condensed window of eating?!"

"I *said* we'll have snacks throughout the day..." Belichick grumbled.

"Oh please, Captain," Sam scoffed, beginning to lose some of his tact. "It's not the 20th century anymore, Bill—we're no longer oblivious to the metabolic dangers of those processed sugary treats, and we're no longer fooled by your government marketing propaganda *bullshit*, preaching that the foundational base of the food pyramid should be bread, grains, and cereal. Really, bro?" he threw his hands up again, "Are you *kidding* me with this high-carb heresy?!"

Belichick paused and quietly mumbled, "... I'll have you know that Honey Nut Cheerios are *whole* grain, heart-healthy, will lower your cholesterol, and are part of a delicious, balanced breakfast to kick-start your day and metabolism..."

<SADLCAM> stepped forward, put his hand on Belichick's eagle-ranked shoulder, and said, "Bill, I love some guilty pleasure cereal at midrats as much as the next aviator, but I've had enough of this nutritional dogma; you're acting like a brain-warped ass clown. Read a fucking book, you douche canoe."

"Or one of the countless blogs started by 'fitness enthusiasts' with zero medical credentials or scientific-based evidence other than 'what their gym bro told them,'" CP added with raised eyebrows, as Belichick glared at both men.

Growing further heated, Sam continued his ranting. "Sir, it's not just the woeful macros you're forcing upon us; we can't sleep when you guys are running these stupid GQ drills early in the morning, with that DC Central bitch screaming on the radio like a crazed terrorist. Alert 5s? Do you have *any* idea what that does to our manning and crew day/crew rest requirements for the pilots, SDOs, and Bravo Papa/Romeo watchstanders? And keeping the ship *clean?!* Who *cares* about shiny knee knockers when there's a war to win*?!* Dude," Sam grabbed his head and dug his fingers into his temples, "You're making it... fucking... *impossible* to get our job done here!"

"Exactly!" Belichick yelled, his face scowl returning in full force, as he pointed angrily at Sam. "*Your* job! All you air wing people care about is *your* job, *your* crew rest, and *your* catered needs—as if the boat simply exists to shelter you, feed you food, and suck your dick! Do you realize that you are but a *tiny* percentage of this ship?! Do you realize that over 4000 people who *aren't* in the air wing live here, too? That our GQ times *are* conducive to *their* schedule? And that we try our damned best, even though *you people* insist on walking through *our* training to make your precious kneeboard cards neurotically *perfect—well* before your three-hours-prior brief!? I *know* you all have issued flash gear, by the way!

"How would you like it if random 'boat people'" he threw up air quotes, "were flying Cessnas—negative Link and negative squawk—around the Case 1 stack or in marshal when you guys were conducting training?! Oh, and I'm *so* sorry that our limited food hours don't work for the 10 pilots who are airborne during those time slots, and that we can't have our CSs slaving away to make food for you to gorge yourself on 24/7! And cleaning stations... *cleaning stations*?!" He slammed his fist on the desk. "I don't want to hear *shit* about cleaning stations coming out of your mouth! Of *course* you don't appreciate the cleanliness of the ship, the hallways, *your bathrooms*; you motherfuckers have never cleaned a single part of this or *any* carrier as long as you've had those wings on your chest! All you've *ever* done is complain about not being able to take a piss at 0800! You aviators are the most self-centered, microscopic-SA, entitled bunch ever to board this ship. It's all about *you, your* personal programs, and *your* well-being! So, fuck the rest of the ship, right?! You're the divas of the boat, the attention-hungry 'celebrities,' the star QB who wants all the credit and none of the blame! Well, now you know, Captain Rowland. Now you know why the 99% doesn't shed a tear and drop everything they're doing to sprint over when the 1% calls about their cushy penthouse stateroom air conditioning being a *tad* bit too warm!"

Sam stood in silence. All the things Belichick said—he *hated* to admit it... but they *kind of* made sense. He looked over at >SADCLAM<, who had a sheepish look on his face. *Were we fucked up? Have we been complaining irrationally this whole time, preoccupied with only our own lives and small-scale agendas—not considering the livelihood of others, nor realizing that we're all working toward the* same *end goal of protecting the ship and country? When did we become so entitled, so hyper-focused on what we* think *is the most important job on the boat — ours — that we failed to see the bigger picture of what we're all* trying to accomplish?

As Sam stood contemplating, the phone rang again. Belichick answered once more with "What." His face quickly fell to a look of aggravation, as he threw his free hand up and yelled, "Jesus Christ, you've got to be joking! Call every ready room — we can't afford to wait *any* longer." He hung up, sighed, and said, "Fellas... I'm sorry, but I don't have any more time to go back and forth on this nonsense. You might find this hard to believe, but I consider myself a 'no-nonsense' kind of guy — and there's *plenty* of nonsense happening on my ship right now. Our Alert 30 pilot just ORM'd because he's shitting his brains out, and he's trying to blame the 12 slices of cheesecake he had during last night's 'Feat of Strengths' or whatever you air wing morons call that recreational self-mutilation binging. God..." he rested the bridge of his nose on his hand. "You know, I'd love to tell you to leave — but GQ is set, and I obviously can't have you bozos transiting the ship without flash gear." He pounded the desk again, and asked, "Why does this have to be so *fucking* difficult? Why can't you all just *do your job*?"

JABA — the calmest of the bunch — cleared his throat and asked, without a hint of snark, "Captain Belichick... are you truly *happy* living this life? Is this really where your *passion* lies?"

Belichick gave him a smug look. "Who the hell are you."

"Mark Buck, sir. Civilian, United States Navy... *Retired...*" he added at the end, with a touch of regret.

Frowning, Belichick reactionarily jerked his head back. "Wait a sec... Mark Buck? *JABA?* As in... 'Just Another Buck Angel' — the tycoon mastermind?"

JABA slowly closed and reopened his eyes, nodding. "Big time."

Looking slightly delighted, Belichick said, "Your brother, Dirty Mike — the famous College Gameday host and Patch wearer — we chatted in the offseason after I got fired by New England. It was a few years before I started coaching Navy Football — and he actually helped me get not only *that* job, but *this* one, too. I *love* the Bucks. And JABA, I've heard so much about your prowess and Good Dude prominence in the fleet." He then looked confused, and asked, "But why — why did you leave the Navy? You were the one that inspired me to join — to be the best man I could out there, contributing to the lives of so many..." He pointed to Mark's shoulders and looked at him. "Your uniform... only a Lieutenant? How did you not put on O-4 and become a DH, at the *least*?"

Wearing a look of grief, JABA sighed. "It wasn't a rank I felt eager to take on, I suppose — or so I thought, at the time... I thought roller coasters were my true calling —

when in reality, I had my heart where it belonged all along..." He shrugged and shook his head. "As they say, we never know how good of a thing we have until it's gone..."

The tall, unnamed, helmet-donning aviator shuffled a bit at JABA's words, but remained silent.

Belichick frowned and muttered quietly, "Walter never realized how much he loved cooking meth with Jesse until the final episode..." The old grump matched JABA's downcast sigh with his own. "That's a shame... I would've taken you as a DH—nay, a *skipper*—in a heartbeat. Instead, I've got guys like 'tweedle dee' and 'tweedle dum' manning these air wing squadrons," he bemoaned, pointing to two names on a roster sheet that the reader remembers from the fleet—guys that totally sucked, were *not* Good Dudes, and yet still somehow made it to Command.

Smiling and shrugging, JABA said, "Yeah, there's a lot things I wish were different, but life is full of impossibly tough real-time decisions that seem like no-brainers in the debrief. You take the learning point on board and move on to a new endeavor, hoping you're not aimlessly chasing trivial opportunities in pursuit of the meaningful one you had long ago." He sighed—again—and looked out to the ocean waters. "Such is life..."

Belichick looked to the side and quietly said, "Yeah... I think I know what you mean..."

Sam read the room, one by one: Belichick seemed caught up in some weird mixed emotion of regret and anger. JABA was smiling, as always, but clearly gloomy. >SADCLAM< looked nearly defeated, as he shook his head and looked over at FISTY, who still appeared mangled and vegetated, his eyes open but crossed and idiotic, with no life behind them. The anonymous aviator was impossible to read, with his dark visor still down, concealing his demeanor and appearance.

CP, however, looked at Sam, shrugged, cracked his knuckles—then walked to >SADCLAM<'s flight gear and started donning it. *What? What's he doing?*

"You there," Belichick called out, after noticing the movement, "Will Ferrell lookalike. What are you doing?"

CP—his G-suit on, vest zipped up—looked at the captain, dumbfounded, as if it were obvious. "Well, sir... just like you asked: I'm *doing my job*. My name is Andrew Preul, and my job is a pilot. I'm here to serve the hottest chick of all—'mom'—and keep her safe from airborne adversaries. If that means intercepting and escorting, then that's what I'm doing." He raised his eyebrows and looked at Belichick with exaggerated questioning eyes, asking, "You said you needed a pilot to launch this alert, didn't you? Well, rather than sit here and talk about how much we hate each other, I might as well do whatever I can to work toward *helping* one another."

Belichick's face softened into one of those near-stoic smiles again, as he approved, "Very well. Side 206, currently located in the six-pack. Triple bubble, fully topped off. You've got a JHMCS gripe and an RWR degrade—other than that, it's a good jet. You can sign upstairs."

CP nodded sharply. "Copy all; thanks, Skipper." He donned his helmet, and began his walk to the flight deck.

Pleasantly surprised at what had just happened, Sam turned and saw >SAD-CLAM<—*donning flashgear! Where did he even* get *that?!* Sam wondered.

Equally confused, Belichick motioned toward Chris, "And what are *you* doing, well-coiffed kid?"

CLAM lifted his gas mask and said, "My name is Chris Houben, and I'm a pilot—but I'm also an *Officer* on this boat. My job is to serve the lawful orders of those appointed over me—and with no jets to fly? You're always talking about khaki involvement in GQ, sir—well, I'm gonna go *do my job.*" He pulled the gas mask back down, strapped it tight, pulled his hood over, and took out the APG-47 from his waistband, cocking it. *Nice! I forgot he even had that thing!*

JABA carried FISTY's body to a nearby corner, and took out his VR headset programming kit.

"JABA, what are you up to over there?" Belichick asked with curiosity.

"My name is Mark Buck, and my job was being a pilot—but my *ground* job was head JMPS O for the entire air wing-slash-Navy—and with great computer knowledge comes great responsibility," JABA said proudly. "I'm putting the finishing touches on this VR program to save the life of our sensei, Tom 'FISTY' Flynn—a man who knows as much about tactics as you do football. I'm giving him a scenario featuring *his* hero, and *your* former partner in crime—Tom Brady—to bring FISTY back to what we knew him as: the epitome of Patch-wearing excellence."

"Hmmph," Belichick grunted with a sly smirk, "I hope that 'crime' bit was just a joke—we misinterpreted the rules, you know."

JABA looked at him with a beaming smile. "It was, sir; and I know. I may be a diehard Falcons fan who still has nightmares about 28-3—but I will *never* discredit the phenomenal things you two achieved to anything less than hard work, relentless preparation, and incredible execution."

With a damn-near smile, Belichick nodded happily. "A true Buck Angel, indeed. Utilize my office however you need to save this man's life."

In utter awe at what was occurring, Sam started to get a rush of hope in his veins. *Were we doing it? Were we actually working* with *the boat, hand-in-hand, as a* team?! He spoke up and said, "Captain, my name is Sam Rowland, and my job is to be the squadron Good Dude—regardless of how inconvenient that role may be at times. You'll need an SDO to man the desk, sir, and you're gonna want me on that watch— you're gonna *need* me on that watch!" Sam insisted with the fiery passion of a squadron secretary. "I'll stand it for as long as these Olympics take, your eminence."

Belichick, with steely narrowed eyes, nodded and said, "You guys are good men; Good Dudes, indeed. You can man the desk in this room," he pointed to a side desk armed with everything an SDO needs to be lethal: five different monitors, a copy of the flight schedule, mapped printer access, Bluetooth speakers, and the number one SDO weapon—a telephone. "I'll forward every ready room phone this way, if you think you can handle it?"

Sam nodded confidently, and approached the desk—the rolling chair looking as comfortable as he'd always remembered it. He logged into the computer, started filling in side numbers and calculating weight chits, loaded CP a quick mission card to be run to the jet, cued up his SDO playlist, and started the duty by playing Metro Boomin & Future's 'Superhero (Heroes & Villains).' *Everything is lining up... we can fight this scenario after all!*

Belichick, wearing his game face—an irritated scowl—looked to the lone officer remaining, and asked the flight gear-wearing man, "What about you? Your job is also being a pilot, isn't it? Can you stand an Alert 5?"

The unnamed aviator, the first to fly in Phase 2 and not a plot point since, walked up to Belichick and pulled out an iPad.

"What's this?" Belichick asked. "If you want to fly with that, I'm sure we can find a way to misinterpret the SOP."

The anonymous aviator shook his head, showing him the screen.

Belichick looked confused. "This looks like... tactical developments? Strategy building? Xs and... Os?" He looked back at the tall mystery man. "What is this? And why can't you man the alert for the ship's defense?"

"Because I'm going to be too busy helping you game plan the *offense*." His voice sounded so familiar to Sam, but he couldn't quite put his finger on it.

"*Game plan?*" Belichick reacted in shock. "*You?* But why?"

"Because being a pilot isn't where my passion lies, Coach." The man removed his helmet, revealing a shockingly young-looking face, experienced battle-tested eyes, and a robust 6'4" frame. "My job is to be a *quarterback*—leading others in battle through the trenches of agony, out of the depths of adversity, and to the thrills of championship victory; my name is—"

Sam couldn't even hear what the man said, as his mind metaphorically exploded.

Tom... fucking... Brady?!?!

16

Negative Soul

*T*he F/A-18E descended into the NIRD Katsopolis, a perfect 90-degree glideslope landing. *The Padroids shook their heads in disappointment, dismayed by the lack of bright lights flashing from the arriving aircraft. NEODD SWEVEN, in his Kevin Kolb Philadelphia Eagles jersey, tsk'd and leaned over to Sam, yelling above the ambient noise, "Ugh, he's wearing gloves... not a cool start. He's lucky this one's a currency pass, or he'd be starting this line period with a Tight."*

Chuckling but distracted, Sam looked around the Padroids platform computer mainframe, trying to sneak a peek at the pilot in the jet. He'd been dying to see who would be joining him in the Noddik galactic fleet ever since CAG had informed him of the hired US ex-pat. He thought back to the list of aviators he'd head-hunted to join his legion of admin assassins...

Of course, almost any Chippy would be a godsend! He'd daydreamed over how JABA could replace that dweeb Suabedissen when it came to programming the fleet. Oh, what he'd give to have the voice of Tom Delong as Secure Tactical Briefing Room background music – vice the 'Tribal Anthem of the Perla Elves of Farlin,' or whatever the fuck it was that the doctor coded into the mufflers. He'd tried to tempt CP with the prospect of how much higher his squat and deadlift numbers would be in the zero-G atmosphere, despite not researching the scientific accuracy behind that claim – but that didn't matter, because it checked good with broscience. Could it have been FISTY? He felt the excitement pulsing through his veins as he considered a return to the morning rituals of tactical yoga – deep 'hick-ing' while positioning the neck in positions like 'Keeping sight at the 6,' 'Verifying the overhead sun,' and the downward 'WSO head stuck under G.'

Of course, there were plenty of prime prospects from the rest of the air wing, too – Sam would've been thrilled if Hansel, Tina, Sabertooth, CaCA, Tonsil, or pFingers had emerged from that aircraft. Honestly, there were so many naval aviators – so many trusted friends from his past – that would've been excellent additions to his ship. In fact, he could only think of one familiar face from the USS Ship who wouldn't *give him a shot of euphoria – but fortunately, there was no way* that *douchebag would be looking to work with Sam...*

CAG walked outside the hangar, Dr. Suabedissen meandering behind him with a freshly-pressed lab coat and slumped, low-confidence posture. The two were en route to the jet, where T6 waited in his Freddie Mitchell Eagles jersey, all eager to welcome the newest addition to the Noddik Empire ready room.

"Captain, you gonna go greet this jabroni?" IROK asked with a cocky sneer, brushing invisible non-skid off his Vince Young top.

Sam gave a look of slight disappointment. "IROK, come on – this guy is a former American brother of mine. Yes, I know he'll probably need a lot of training to live up to the standard of admin excellence we've built here in the Noddik Empire – but let's give him a fair chance." He smirked, and confidently added, "I can train him to be cool as a cucumber."

IROK nodded and excitedly added, "Hell yeah, sir! Cucumbers are calorie-light, and complement salads so damn well! Plus, as you always taught us: Plants and greens gets you jacked and lean!"

The two high-fived, as Sam wore a smug look of satisfaction. These bots had been trained well, both in the art of waving and dietary guidelines, thanks to the latest nutrition Mac Recs Sam had provided the Noddik Empire. Once a man of meats, protein, and healthy animal fats, Sam had looked to pivot and redefine himself after his departure from the United States. He watched a documentary on Netflix, read an article in PEOPLE magazine, and – most compellingly – saw a bunch of ripped influencers on Instagram spouting off about the benefits of veganism, even offering 50% off their plant protein if he joined their seminar focus group in the next 10 minutes. Of course, his time being precious, Sam had no desire to test things for himself, instead committing head first into the unknown depths of the plant-based community – bringing his new healthy and fit lifestyle to the Noddik bots, as well as giving them each a one-time offer to join his sales team for the corn syrup-based soy protein he was peddling. Yes, 'Power-Plants' – sold in 'Cake Batter Vanilla Cupcake,' 'Cookies Crushed in Cereal,' and 'Frosting on Graham Cracker' flavors – was going to revolutionize the physiques of these androids. After he successfully convinced 100 junior enlisted sailors to sign up for his marketing squad, he was raised to tier 6 of 'Assistant CEO to the Noddik Branch Military Sector,' racking in a projected zillion dollars if his cohorts each completed their own family tree of centurion sales lemmings. He was so excited that he couldn't stop himself from commenting on thousands of completely unrelated Instagram, YouTube, and Facebook posts about his ability to make so much money with so little work –

"Captain, did you hear that!?" NEODD asked with elation.

"Huh?" Sam said, snapping back from his zoned-out state. "What is it?"

NEODD pointed to the jet. "The new guy's wearing Chippy patches!"

Sam looked up, and sure enough, he could make out the green and white chest patch on the man's flight suit. No way...! He excitedly scanned the man's height via ocular patdown and tried to quickly decipher who it could be. Oh my god, I think it's WYFMIFM! Fuck yeah! He must have been interested in investing into my PowerPlants franchise, after all! Dude, it is *so* good to have a familiar face out –

Yet as the man shook hands with the welcoming party and doffed his helmet, Sam was confused to see not a shiny bald dome of nostalgia... but a full head of hair – grey hair. No... no... NO!!! *At the same moment of his revelation, Sam made eye contact with the newest Noddik pilot – Bobby "Juice" Ward. And, strangely enough, still a* Lieutenant *Bobby Ward.*

Juice gave Sam a knowing smirk and a head nod, before turning back to CAG and continuing their conversation.

"You know that guy?" NEODD asked.

Sam sighed in annoyance. "Affirm, SWEVEN... affirm. His name is Juice, and you're gonna fucking hate him. He's by far the last person we'd want on this team. There's no way this is going to fly – who approved this?! Why wasn't I consulted on the final decision?! Does he even have a PPR to land here?!"

"Geeze, Cap, it sounds like this guy's a total boner..." IROK said as he shook his head, before grinning and assuring, "Don't worry, broseph – we're gonna give this dweeb the standard 'new guy' treatment. He better listen up, shut up, and understand that – to us? – he's just a *worthless* fuck-up!"

Still in disbelief that his rival was on board his ship, *crashing his* fleet, *and infringing on his* legacy, *Sam covered his eyes in anguish.* How could this happen?! The reason I left... this entire plan... *fuck,* dude...

"They're walking to the ready room!" IROK announced, before looking at his fellow Padroids – wearing a David Akers jersey – and ordering, "Hey, <MCSALAD>, go get us some paper and beer cans real quick – I've got a brilliant idea! We're gonna ask the new guy to tell us a little bit about himself – like we actually fucking care, LOL," *he explained, cringily even saying the letters 'L O L' aloud.* "And then..." *he looked around excitedly,* "we're gonna boo, tell him to shut the fuck up, and throw shit at him! LMFAO!"

Sam was barely listening to anything IROK was saying, instead preparing himself for this initial interaction with the man who would be flying off his wing for the years to come. Is Juice here to ask for forgiveness for sucking ass? Maybe the Chippies' admin culture fell apart when I left, and he knows he needs the master to teach him once again? Or maybe he got in trouble for fraternization with some air wing hottie... and *that's* why he's an excommunicated LT! That must be it! Well, in that case – poor guy... but luckily for him, he'll find that the Noddik Empire is all about free love!

... Unfortunately, it's also a society of 99.9% robots... *Sam bemoaned that he hadn't felt a woman's touch in years – but also admittedly felt relief, as his libido had plummeted since departing the Chippies.* I wish I could figure out why... probably because I'm so busy and stressed, *he reassured himself, as he felt the incessant craving for a vanilla-flavored oat milk frappuccino and a bag of canola oil-doused kale chips dipped in fat-free ranch.* Hey, I've earned it! *he rationalized, as he'd completed 2 hours on the elliptical machine earlier.* Thank God I gave up the weightlifting life... I'm going for the toned, sleek look—I don't want those biceps, abs, or shoulders making me all big and bulky...

Granted, he did miss *his wife quite a bit. He remembers vaguely hearing about her in Chapter 1 — but given how the story went, she ended up not being a focal point for the journey. He had to leave her when he made The Deal, and he'd promised himself not to make his life more challenging by internally monologuing about his relationship too much. Besides... who needed love when you had cleaning stations and sailor shout-outs to get you stimulated?!*

Returning to the moment, Sam tried to throttle back the Padroids, suggesting, "Guys, we shouldn't be too harsh just yet... let's go to the ready room — we should at least say 'hello' to him." He was admittedly skeptical—albeit still *curious if,* by chance, *Juice was there to study under Sam's tutelage after getting caught in a treasonous tryst — and if that were the case, Sam would happily play the role of superior alpha, showing that humbled beta the path to becoming an administrative panty-dropper.*

As Sam and the two Padroids entered the ready room, they found CAG showing Juice where he could keep his flight bag, as well as USB-C dongles, puzzle boxes, Celsius powder packets, and other random oddities that pilots kept in their drawer. Additionally, Doctor Suabedissen handed him a green sheet that included times and dates for various D&D meetups, raids, and tournaments, and even the J-dial for the ship's tailor — who could sew him a custom cloak to wear at all of the above. Sam rolled his eyes at the dweeb, knowing that Juice was surely internally doing the same. God, he's going to *hate* it here!

But, to his shock, Juice not only thanked *the doctor and took down the tailor's number, but whipped out his own set of D&D deck cards, asking the doctor to appraise the worthiness of his collection.* What?! Since when has Juice played Dungeons and Dragons?

Suabedissen pushed his glasses up in excitement, exclaiming, "I'd love to!" and started flipping through the cards. He quickly sneered, though, and said, "Oh, LT Ward, these are not *going to win you many tourneys... it looks like the most basic noob starter deck that you'd see from some brand-new dungeon crawler," he snickered and pushed his glasses up again. "But I can work with this! Say, how would you like to shadow me during tonight's raid for unicorn mammoths in the Mines of Morticia?! This one girl — MyLittlePonyXoXo88 — is going to be there and... well..." The doctor blushed, shaking his head. "Nevermind, that's not a big deal! But I mean... it* would *probably demonstrate value if I was seen showing some noob the ropes, you know, hehe?"*

Yet again, much to Sam's astonishment, LT Ward was actually entertaining this pathetic loser, offering up, "Doctor, it sounds like this girl might be pretty special to you. How about I go and ask you a bunch of softball questions—where you can flaunt your vast knowledge—and then I can make an intentional Leeroy Jenkins-type error that puts the girl in a precarious situation, where you then come in and save the day?" he smiled as he laid out this ludicrous plan that the geek would surely see as a tactical disaster.

Suabedissen ate it right up though, beaming as he exclaimed, "Mr. Ward, that sounds delightful! You're gonna fit in quite well around here! I'll give you the server info and guild password once I hook up the rig in your stateroom!" He raised his hand for a high five, which Juice emphatically returned.

Sam scoffed at this entire scene. What the *fuck* is going on here?! *Now desperate to shit on the new arrival, Sam whispered to IROK, "Can you believe this guy? Is he actually going to play D&D with Doctor Dorkedissen?* Totally *not cool..."*

IROK, however, scowled and side-eyed him. "Captain, what's wrong with that? He's just trying to make friends with his new teammates — sounds pretty cool, if you ask me."

Sam rolled his eyes. As he saw <MCSALAD> running back, he quietly urged, "Oh, good! Guys, let's do that funny new guy thing you were talking about!"

NEODD nodded, cleared his throat via a series of beeps, and said, "Hello, LT Ward! I am NEODD SWEVEN, CAG Padroids here. Before I read you your pass, would you like to go up there and tell us a bit about yourself?" he asked, pointing to the briefing podium at the forefront of the ready room.

Grinning at the Padroids — each of which was armed with balled-up paper and other trash — Sam readied his ammo.

Juice chuckled. "Hah, Mr. SWEVEN, please spare me the bad news — I'm sure that was a Tight at best, given how uncoolly I exited that jet. Apologies, bros, I need to tighten myself up," he lamented with a frown and shrug. "But yes, I suppose I can give a little background knowledge of myself."

Shocked by his admission, the group of Padroids raised their eyebrows at each other — as if they were actually impressed by the FNG's humility.

Groaning, Sam whispered, "Please, guys — he's such a kiss-ass. And seriously? 'Tighten' himself up? Was that a pun? How cringe is that?!" Sam was, however, curious as to how Juice even knew the Padroids' pass grading system...

"I dunno," T6 shrugged and smiled, "That was actually pretty clever if you ask me; excellent use of a double entendre!"

Sam scoffed and rolled his eyes. "Psh... that's not even the correct usage of 'double entendre...'" He elbowed T6 and added, "Nice vocabulary, bro..."

T6 glared at Sam, as Juice walked to the podium — before abruptly turning back and mentioning, "One quick thing before I begin telling you about myself: I saw the upcoming watch bill for the Jupiter port call, and I went ahead and signed myself up for every duty you Padroids had." He shrugged and said, "I hope you all don't mind; I figured you could enjoy some extra time off after all that difficult waving. Also, I heard you guys stand no-fly day SDO? That's bullshit — I'll take all of those, too. And the trash situation here — it's definitely not cool to be seen carrying a bag of junk downstairs, especially if it's nearly full and you kind of look like you're struggling. Very beta... So, just consider me your everyday trash man, because — as a new guy — I can afford to look a little 'dweeby' around this place." He shrugged again, smiled, and conceded, "But you Bro-J Simpsons deserve better."

The Padroids' jaws dropped. IROK looked thrilled as he emphasized, "'Bro-J Simpsons?' Dude, how sick is that nickname! He just made us sound even cooler!"

NEODD looked at IROK, wide-eyed, and nodded. "I know! And now we'll have time to check out that Droid Nuru Massage Airbnb in Jupiter! Those servicing bots are hot, bro!"

"Careful where you're sticking that USB, IROK – or at least let me install some Norton's Anti-Virus protection first!" Dr. Suabedissen joked, inserting himself into the conversation with a heavy-breathing laughter. Then he turned quiet and shyly asked, "... But seriously... are they hot?"

Aggravated at everything that was going on right now, Sam looked at the Padroids with incredulity. "Guys, OJ Simpson is a convicted murderer! That is not someone you should want to be associated with!"

"Convicted, Captain? You sure about that?" T6 asked. "If the glove don't fit, there was no crime to commit!"

Sam groaned. "That wasn't even the line, you idiot..." He covered his mouth and called out toward Juice, "Tell us about yourself, douche!"

Remaining stoic, Juice shrugged and said, "Well, my name's LT Bobby – "

"BOOOOO! Shut the fuck up, new guy!" Sam yelled as he tossed an empty Bud Light at the pilot – before the can was intercepted by T6.

"Captain Rowland, what's wrong with you?!" the pass-interpreter Padroids hissed. "LT Ward is speaking!"

The Padroids all shook their heads in disbelief, as IROK muttered under his breath, "Unbelievable... show some decorum, Captain..."

Growing increasingly frustrated, Sam folded his arms and listened as Juice delivered an appropriately brief snippet of who he was, rather than droning on about his career background, i.e., nonsense that nobody gave a shit about. There was no 'I was an Echo guy,' nor 'Commissioned OCS back in class 13-13,' and not even 'Yeah, did my JO tour out in Lemoore before shore duty at 106.' Nope – Juice kept it very clear and concise; instead explaining that he was still a Lieutenant because he refused to become a corrupted, uncool O-4 – and had joined the Noddiks because he heard how 'dope' they were here. He then emphasized that while he wanted to help out however possible with admin excellence, his primary goal was to learn how to be a 'rad dude' from this fleet.

The Padroids wore delighted looks of approval, as T6 nudged <MCSALAD> and whispered, "Dude, this guy's a total chiller."

There was no hazing, no hate, no disdain. Juice finished his statement by saying, "I don't want to talk anymore, because I've got two ears and one mouth for a reason; I can't wait for you guys to mold me and my personality into the most badass Noddik jet brah I can be."

When Juice wrapped it up, Sam heard the last thing he ever could've anticipated hearing from an FNG's welcome speech – applause. A round of fucking applause? For a new guy? He was in utter shock. This is unprecedented – it's just not right! Finally addressing his former squadronmate directly, Sam stood up and said, "LT Ward – it's... good to see you again..."

Juice looked at his former JOPA cohort — ocular patdowned him in return — and finally acknowledged, "Good to see you too... Captain Rowland," emphasizing Sam's new rank. "I see you took plenty more bonus money. How're those impressions coming along?"

"They are... verrrrryyyyy niiice..." Sam said with subdued energy — but still looking to the Padroids for laughter. And yet... there was none...

"Oh my god," IROK yelled, putting his hands on his forehead, "He never stops doing them! And they hardly even sound right..."

Juice looked inquisitive toward Sam. "You know, it's the same as it was back then — you keep emphasizing the 'ee' at the end of 'very.' But doesn't Borat use more inflection at the beginning of the word — and more of an 'eh' sound? You know, kinda like," he offered his hands up and took a shot at it: "VEEHHHH-reh niiice."

IROK's eyes widened in shock. "Bro — that's it! That was spot-on! No wonder the captain's impressions sound so shitty — he's been doing them wrong this entire time! Imagine if he took this kind of attention to detail in his Schwarzenegger, Bane, and Nicholas Cage impressions! Can you do any of those, too, Juice?"

Ward shrugged at the bot. "Ahh... I dunno, I don't want to steal too much limelight from Rowland's center stage."

"That's right," Sam agreed defiantly. "Because let's not forget — I'm in charge here." Yet as soon as he said it, Sam realized his grave tactical error...

Juice whipped his head around and asked, with his best muffled Bane accent, "Do you feel in charge?"

The Padroids were busting up laughing, T6 slapping his robotic knee as he insisted, "So good! So good!"

Sam had had enough. "Juice, please join me in the STBR — I need to discuss some things with you."

Juice shrugged and said, "Sure," as the Padroids, doctor, and even CAG continued to clap for their already-beloved new guy, much to Sam's chagrin.

"New guy of the year!" IROK exclaimed with enthusiasm. "This guy is hilarious!"

"Come on, one more!" NEODD yelled, "One more!" Setting him up for an alley-oop, he asked, "How can we find the Declaration of Independence?!"

Irritated that NEODD wasn't getting facts from the movie exactly correct, but desperate to stop this 'Juice momentum,' Sam yelled out, "The secret lies with Charlotte!"

Every Padroids cringed. NEODD shook his head and rued, "Oh, Cap... that was terrible. I couldn't tell if that was more Keanu Reeves or Owen Wilson — but it was bad," referencing more of the actor knowledge database that Sam had insisted they be programmed with. Programmed so that they could praise my impressions... he thought bitterly. Not Juice's!

Full of anger, he escorted Juice into the STBR, slammed the door shut, and cranked up the noise-blocking Farlin Tribal Anthem to an 11. He barely waited a moment before lashing out, "Ok, Bobby, what the fuck is going on? What are you doing here? How do you already know so much about the Noddiks, and why are you being a total suck-up to my squad?! That

Jupiter port call isn't even happening due to rough space states, so you won't be standing shit for anyone anyways."

Juice smiled as the elven trumpet blared in the background. He shook his head and said, "Great to see you haven't changed one bit, Rowland, but apparently your taste in STBR music has." He gestured toward the CD player. "I didn't realize you were such a D&D fan now – you and the doctor must be pretty tight."

His eyes narrowing, Sam clenched his jaw. "Cut the shit, Ward. Why? Why have you come here? Wasn't it enough that you tried to fill my role at 195? You have to hang around like a pathetic little lap dog and follow me here, too?! This is my calling, my enterprise, and I don't need you or anybody else coming here to try and steal my legacy."

Bobby tilted his head down in exaggerated shock and said, "Oh, I'm sorry – I didn't realize you were doing so well here! It certainly didn't seem that way – not based off the pathetic recruiting requests you kept sending the Chippies, anyway..." He rolled his eyes. "I figured you must've just forgotten my name by mistake, so I did you a solid and made the trip regardless – since, you know, none of your actual friends felt like even responding with a simple 'no'..."

Sam's fists tightened. How did he know...?

As if reading his mind, Juice shrugged with a laugh and said, "Sam, people talk. It's a small boat, and you don't exactly get offers to defect to another galaxy without that kind of info being mentioned once or twice. But don't worry, because I'm not here to 'surpass' you again," he said with air quotes.

"I never said you 'surpassed' me," Sam responded with ire.

Juice rolled his eyes. "You and I never saw eye to eye very well in the Chippies, did we?"

Sam scoffed. "Pretty hard to, when you were stuck in my administrative jet wash."

Ignoring the comment, Juice continued, "Rowland – I'm not sure if you're aware of this, but you're not exactly a popular person back at the USS Ship. And your recruiting efforts? People saw them as desperate... The overly-eager requests, the obvious phoniness behind 'How wonderful it is out here' – and I've even heard whispers of some Vegan protein bullshit you're now marketing?! What's gotten into you, Sam?! Clearly, you're struggling. Clearly, this isn't what you thought it would be. Clearly, you can't do this – alone." Seeing Sam's aggravated expression, Juice gestured with open arms and offered up, "I mean, is that not why you were begging for help, making grandiose promises of fortune and happiness for all who follow?"

Remaining silent at first, Sam bit his lip before acknowledging, "I mean, we can always get better, Ward. Unlike you, I'm not content to live with 'good enough.'"

With a twisted smile, Juice asked, "Don't you think I had it 'good enough' back at the USS Ship once you left? My admin arch-rival, my new-guy nemesis, the greatest competition I faced – no longer in the picture?" He exhaled sharply. "You think that might've been a bit relieving? Maybe set me up pretty conveniently on the golden path? Especially when, you know, you left on such a sour note..."

Sam gave a non-committal shrug.

"Yet look where I am regardless — here in your territory, joining a fleet where I'm out-ranked, outlored, and outright hated *by the commander of this entire empire. You think I'm really ok with 'good enough', Sam? Or do you think it's possible that I — just like you — sought* more *from myself? That maybe I, too, sought a greater, more challenging path in life?"*

Taken aback, Sam softened his expression. I'd never thought of it that way... *he reflected.* Was this seriously coming from Juice's mouth? Was he trying to... *mend fences* with me? *"What are you trying to say, Bobby? You actually want to* help *me succeed out here?"*

"Yes, I do," Juice said with a smile.

His eyes narrowing again, Sam asked "Are you sure you didn't get booted from there? You *sure* you didn't sleep with that one enlisted girl that everybody unanimously agreed was the hottest on the ship — and the reader surely can picture in their mind?"

Juice chuckled. "Negative. Although I'm sure that would've been the nautical coitus of a lifetime. Sam, I'm here in good faith, good spirit — good dudesmanship, if you will."

Sam leaned back. "So, let me get this straight... you want to help me make this the most successful administrative fleet of all time — despite everything *that's happened in the past — knowing full well that I'm* the *Captain, I'll get all the credit, and* you'll *be just another pilot to be utilized at my bidding?"*

"Affirm, Sam," Juice replied calmly. "I'm done with that petty rivalry of the past. I'm here to work with you, learn from you, and succeed alongside you. If you don't like it? Go ahead and excuse me from this ship — you are *the Captain, after all, and nobody can question your decisions..."*

Sam debated internally. I don't love the plan... but I can't deny that Juice has some serious admin skills. God, I never thought that *he'd* be the one I'd have to turn to for assistance... but it *does* seem like he's being authentic, and finally recognizing what a douche he was back then... Fuck it — at this point? Beggars can't be choosers. I sure hope I don't regret this... *"Ok — you've got a deal, Ward," he said as he stuck out his hand.*

Juice shook it in kind, and said, "Thank you, Nickels. It's nice to know there's still plenty of Good Dude left within you."

Sam shook his head solemnly. "Thanks, but... don't call me 'Nickels' — that guy is long gone..."

As Sam turned and left the STBR, Juice thought to himself, 'That was easier than I ever could've expected. They were right... Rowland really has *become a mere shell of himself.' He looked around the room and took note of his surroundings — insane asylum walls, lack of space, dangerous sharp edges everywhere... it was a STBR, alright. But it lacked the STBR staple — nowhere were polaroids of the friends that made the place survivable; the photos he was used to seeing — CP deadlifting in his flight suit, Sam and FISTY high-fiving on the flight deck, the Chippy jets coming in for a shit-hot break, and of course, the one that always brought Juice the fondest memories — the Dambuster boys hanging out on the carrier Porch during sunset.*

But here? No pictures, aside from an obscene, hand-drawn scantily clad cartoon ogre-woman with outrageously exaggerated boobs over her tiny waist – signed with Dr. Suabedissen's signature.

'Is Nickels really this tarnished now?' he wondered as he exited the STBR for the now-empty ready room. 'Maybe I really did fuck the guy up... maybe I shouldn't have been so contentious...' He thought back to the picture of them all smiling on the Porch; one team with no egos – cohesive... thought back to The Perfect Schedule, he and Sam celebrating together – united... thought back to Low T, and the likelihood that he was gone forever – betrayed... and then, most difficult of all, Juice thought about the role he'd played in that, his own pettiness and poor dudesmanship making him feel it – regret. 'Shit... maybe I shouldn't have – "

But he broke his train of thought when he looked up at the callsign review board, where his name 'Juice' was headlined, with several new callsign proposals written below. Most were just complete cheap shots: Douche, LimFac, Cuck, Bitch, Incel. Some were immature in a different way, and made no fucking sense: Jar Jar Lover, Level 1 Healer, Common Loot Dropper – although, to be fair, it looked like Dr. Suabedissen had written all of these. And, really, none of these childish ones bothered him, truth be told.

But there was one that stood out, written at the very bottom, in red Shmarker:

The Admin Clown

And it was a great reminder of why Juice had crafted this entire plan in the first place.

Ward shook his head, cracked his knuckles, and finally felt it again – he felt alive. Ready to fight, ready to compete, ready to push himself to the next level yet again, one-up his hated rival in the grandest stage yet, and prove that he was The Admin King.

'I'll show you, Dimes – you spineless, backstabbing bitch – I'll fucking show you...'

~

LT Bobby "Juice" Ward knocked thrice on the stateroom door, sighing in misery at what his role in this empire had become. "LT Ward requests permission to enter the office of Robo-Hinge, sir."

"YOU MAY ENTER, PLEBE," the DH's robotic vocals responded.

As Bobby walked in, he saw the back of a CAG laptop, on which Robo-Hinge was clicking away and hitting random keys. Bobby wasn't sure what he was doing, but it appeared as if he might have been jamming through an NKO—no doubt his annual Cyber Security Awareness Challenge. Either that, or he was playing some online game, which would be next to impossible given the ship's shitty bandwidth. "GIVE ME A MINUTE, WARD," Hinge demanded, "I NEED TO FINISH SOMETHING REAL QUICK."

Juice said nothing. While waiting, he looked around at the customizations Hinge had given his living space as a personal touch. The first thing he noticed was a miniature bookshelf—the kind an important figurehead uses to show off all the books he's read to get where he is. Except rather than books, there were CD cases—presumably, the files Dr. Suabedissen had installed on the O-4 dictator—and Juice was able to make out a few: *The Subtle Art of Spooling Up, The Douchebag Within,* Jorge Leopard's *Mass-Taskery, Sleep is for the Weak, The TeamBlame Method, Letters to a Future Microman-ager, The Courage to Be Self-Loathing* and it's *'Courage to be Feared'* precursor, Stephen Pressland's *The Art of O-4*... Juice shook his head in disbelief as he realized, 'The doctor seriously programmed this hinge flawlessly...'

On the walls were various artistic works—one featured a watercolor abstract of a Lieutenant pilot trapped in a cage, weeping, with a blue inked schedule in his hands; his tears flowing into a moat around a gigantic castle with a golden oak leaf flag being raised from the top. Another was a metaphorical anime-style photo, where a man with oak leaves on his shoulders had dollar signs for eyes, sitting atop a gigantic mound of cash—albeit one covered in blood—with no friends nor family alongside him in the drawing. The cartoon man wore a gigantic smile, and had a human heart in one hand—labeled 'JOPA Morale'—and a clipboard with stacks of blue folders in the other—labeled 'POWER.' His last piece of work, however, was just a framed black canvas, seemingly void of any color or life whatsoever.

"CURIOUS ABOUT SOMETHING, WARD?" Hinge asked as he looked up from his laptop.

"Sir, what's the deal with this black one?" Juice asked, "Was it stolen?"

Robo-Hinge glared at Juice, narrowed his eyes, and coldly stated, "I'LL HAVE YOU KNOW THAT I PAID DAMN GOOD NODDIK CREDITS FOR THAT MASTER-PIECE, PEASANT. IT'S CALLED 'THE SOUL OF THE HINGE,' AND IT'S ONE OF THE MOST ASTOUNDING PIECES OF ART IN MILITARY HISTORY!" Hinge shook his head in anger and refocused on his laptop activities.

"Apologies... sir," Juice said with zero remorse. While waiting, he noticed the picture on Hinge's desk. It was the O-4, alongside another robot designed to be a female—wearing nothing but an apron that said 'Naughty Noddik Next of Kin'—and two little miniature cyborgs—one wearing a baseball hat with a Global Chess League logo on it, and the other holding a stuffed animal of the clown Pennywise from the movie *It*. 'Jesus...' he thought, rolling his eyes at the poor algorithm'd attempts to capture human social life, 'Suabedissen is so fucking out of touch with reality...' Trying to break the ice a little before revealing his ultimate request, Bobby asked, "Miss the family, sir?"

Still focusing on his laptop and without making eye contact, Hinge looked repulsed. "FUCK THEM. THEY ARE JUST NUISANCES AND DISTRACTIONS FROM

THE REAL GOAL IN LIFE: GETTING THE NUMBER ONE FITREP FROM THIS COMMAND AND STAYING ON MY GOLDEN PATH. I HONESTLY ENJOY THESE DAYS OF INTERGALACTIC DEPLOYMENT, AWAY FROM THEIR NAGGING AND NEEDINESS FOR MY ATTENTION. LUCKILY, THE OLD BALL AND CHAIN KNOWS A) HOW IMPORTANT I AM TO THIS FLEET, AND B) HOW MUCH MONEY I MAKE, SO SHE DOESN'T ASK ANY QUESTIONS WHEN I IGNORE HER FOR PROLONGED TIMES. AND THE KIDS—GOD... THEY NEVER SHUT UP. THEY CONSTANTLY WANT ME TO ATTEND THEIR STUPID LITTLE SPORTING AND MUSIC EVENTS, AND ASK QUESTIONS ABOUT WHAT THEIR DAD BOT DOES... PLEASE. STAY OUT OF MY WAY, YOU LITTLE SHITS, OR ELSE YOUR FATHER WON'T HAVE A JOB TO TALK ABOUT!"

Robo-Hinge wiped hydraulic sweat off his forehead—apparently very stressed by either this topic or what was happening on his computer screen. "AND I SWEAR—THAT WOMAN NEVER LETS ME ENJOY BEERS AT THE O-CLUB WITH—WELL, I USUALLY END UP DRINKING ALONE, EATING CHICKEN WINGS AND QUESADILLAS AT MY OWN TABLE—BUT IT'S BETTER THAN THE SHIT SHE SERVES AT OUR DOCKING STATION, ANYWAY," he complained with a bionic growl.

Juice almost *wanted* to feel bad for Robo-Hinge—but he couldn't. The bot was just... a gigantic asshole. And, he'd noticed lately, the O-4 seemed to be gaining a bit of weight, and even his artificial comb-over was balding...

Finally, Hinge looked up from his screen and proudly announced, "DONE!" His brief smile quickly turned back into a scowl, though, as he began shotgunning questions at his underling. "WHY ARE WE TALKING ABOUT MY LOUSY FAMILY, ANYWAY? WHAT DO YOU WANT, WARD? I PRESUME YOU'RE HERE TO TELL ME YOU'VE COMPLETED THE MARSTRIKE CONTINGENCY MISSION PLANNING?"

"Sir, that's exactly why I'm here. I have it all planned out, and I believe it will ensure mission success," Juice reported confidently.

Robo-Hinge leaned back in his chair. "HMMPH... IT BETTER. GIVE ME THE BLUF, WARD."

"Well, sir..." Juice started, "The ship is going to be in a daze of disarray, given the false contact we unleashed on their radar. But... once they launch the alert and realize it's not actually there... will that really be *enough?*" he asked with emphasis. "I'm just not buying that this is going to be more than a mere inconvenience to the air wing, and will hardly affect the inner spirit of the ship. You don't understand, sir—these active duty sailors? They've seen shit like this on the regular from their own Navy's incompetence—this would be as much of an 'emotional hurdle' to overcome as a momentary AV AIR HOT off the catapult for a currency flight... a RDR DEGR while launching as Dawg 7 in a red air presentation... I mean, these guys would fret more about missing TAMMAC on a CV Flyoff!"

"HMM..." Robo-Hinge murmured, scraping his fingers against his metal chin as he contemplated Juice's reasoning. "WELL, SEEING AS THOSE PREVIOUS FLIGHTS ARE THE ONLY TYPES I TAKE PART IN, I UNDERSTAND EXACTLY WHAT YOU MEAN — YOU'RE SAYING THE U.S. TROOPS HAVE BUILT UP RESILIENCE TO THIS KIND OF BULLSHIT OVER TIME? THAT THEY ARE ACCUSTOMED TO THINGS GOING WRONG — ALMOST TO THE POINT WHERE THEY *EXPECT* IT?"

Completely floored by the comprehension of this incompetent bot, Juice almost recoiled in disbelief. "Well — actually, yes... that's *exactly* what I mean... sir."

Looking to the side, Robo-Hinge's facial structure reworked itself to exhibit one of doubt. "YES... I FEARED THAT THIS MAY BE THE CASE... CAG IS TOO WASHED UP AND DETACHED TO HAVE RECOGNIZED IT, BUT... REMNANTS OF THAT TYPE OF ADAPTABILITY/FLEXIBILITY FROM CONSTANT DISAPPOINTMENT, DISILLUSIONMENT, AND DISCRETIONARY FUCKING HAVE BEEN PROGRAMMED DEEP WITHIN MY NAVAL SERVICEMEMBER-BASED CODING. A RESILIENT BUNCH OF FOOLS THEY ARE, INDEED, WARD."

"Fools, sir?" Juice asked, unsure if he heard him correctly.

Robo-Hinge glared back at Juice. "YES — FOOLS. THESE PATHETIC CUCKS HAVE ALLOWED THEIR OWN CARETAKERS TO JADE THEM INTO HOPELESS OBLIVION, WITH NO TRACE OF TRUST THAT ANYTHING WILL *EVER* GO ACCORDING TO PLAN. THESE SERVICEMEMBERS LIVE EVERY WAKING MOMENT WONDERING HOW THEY WILL GET FUCKED NEXT — AM I CORRECT?!"

Feeling a bit defensive, Juice leaned back and contested, "Well — I mean... I wouldn't go *that* far..."

"OH, REALLY?" Hinge slammed his fist on the table. "THEN IS IT NOT TRUE THAT EVERY TIME QUOTE-UNQUOTE 'GOOD FOOD' IS SERVED AT DINNER, EVERYBODY BRACES TO EXPECT BAD NEWS? WHENEVER A PORT CALL IS UPCOMING, DOES EVERY SINGLE PERSON'S BUTTHOLE NOT PUCKER REACTIONARILY WHENEVER THE CAPTAIN OR ADMIRAL'S WHISTLE BLOWS FROM THE 1MC? WHENEVER A NEW FINANCIAL COMPENSATION PLAN IS UNVEILED — BE IT A BONUS OR RETIREMENT PROGRAM — ARE SAILORS NOT SPRINGLOADED TO METICULOUSLY SEARCH EVERY BIT OF FINE PRINT FOR DECEPTIVE STIPULATIONS — AND SUBSEQUENTLY FIND THEM — WHICH MAKE THE NEW PLAN NOT EVEN CLOSE TO A QUOTE-UNQUOTE 'BETTER DEAL?'"

Unable to counter the filthy hinge's painful finger-quoted words of reality, Juice clenched his jaw and remained silent.

Hinge gave a robotic chuckle and delved deeper. "HA-HA-HA. AND YOU KNOW WHAT THE SADDEST PART IS, WARD?" Hinge rotated his head in disbelief. "THESE BETA INCELS CONTINUE SIMPING TO THE NAVY, HANGING AROUND AND WORKING TIRELESSLY, ACCEPTING EVERY BIT OF FUCKERY THAT COMES THEIR WAY—AND THE NAVY, LIKE A HUMAN SMOKESHOW WHO KNOWS WHAT SHE HAS, LEADS ON THESE LOW-CONFIDENCE TRY-HARDS, KEEPING THEM AROUND FOR AS LONG AS THEY CHOOSE TO STAY WEAK-SPINED ENOUGH TO CATER TO HER EGO, AGENDA, AND FINANCIAL SECURITY. IT WOULD BE TRULY PITIFUL—IF IT WASN'T SO REMARKABLY LAUGHABLE."

"How can you say that?!" Juice argued, agitated at hearing his old profession so harshly attacked where it hurt—right in the accuracy bone. "You took a DH bonus! How are you any better?!"

More laughter from Hinge, automatic updates causing him to sound even more insidious. "DON'T YOU GET IT, WARD? I CAN'T BE LED ON, DISAPPOINTED, OR UPSET—BECAUSE MY SOUL IS GONE! THE MINUTE THE DOCTOR UPGRADED MY SOFTWARE TO O-4, I LOST ALL CAPABILITY TO FEEL. THUS, COMPLETELY VOID OF EMPATHY, I CAN TASK JOS, NEGLECT RESPONSIBILITIES, AND STEAL GOOD DEALS WITHOUT ANY GUILT WHATSOEVER. I WILL STAY ON THE GOLDEN PATH BECAUSE OF MY INABILITY TO FEEL EMOTIONS—NO FAMILY, REMORSE, NOR FEAR OF BEING HATED WILL HOLD ME BACK FROM PROMO-TION. I AM THE ULTIMATE LEADER, WARD, BECAUSE I WILL LET NO HUMAN-ISTIC COMPASSION PREVENT ME FROM TOTAL ASS-BLASTING AND MASS-TASKING DOMINATION." He raised both fists in triumph, artificial steam teeming from his ears, and declared, "I AM THE BIG NODDIK NAVY!" He was color-schemed red, but Robo-Hinge was not angry—he was *euphoric*. Crazed, but maliciously euphoric.

'What the fuck is going on?!' Juice thought to himself. 'This robot is... fucking *insane*! He makes Loaded T seem like he has it all together...' Trying to hide his serious concern, Juice asked, "Sir, for the plan—the MARSTRIKE—I figured that as soon as their guard's down from the false alert launch, we send two more jets their way—Loaded T and I—utilizing multi-axis ingresses, both with simulated A/S loadouts. There's no way they'd be able to have the assets to cover both, and—"

"SIMULATED?!" Robo-Hinge's head snapped back to fury. "WHY THE FUCK WOULD WE HAVE *SIM* LOADS?"

Juice narrowed his eyes and slowly explained, "... Because these are the 'Admin Olympics,' Hinge. We're not looking to actually sink their ship—just sort of 'construc-tively' sink them." It made perfect sense in his head, given all the constructive carnage he'd dealt in the past.

Growing equally irate and perplexed, Hinge asked, "YOU WANT TO FLY AC-TUAL JETS CLOSE TO THEIR ACTUAL SHIP—WITH NO *ACTUAL* WEAPONS—JUST TO SCARE THEM INTO THINKING WE *COULD* HAVE ATTACKED THEM IF WE'D *REALLY WANTED* TO? AND YOU THINK THIS WILL ACHIEVE ADMINIS-TRATIVE VICTORY?!"

"I mean..." Juice stumbled over his words, before assuring, "Yes—trust me, this will make their higher leadership go apeshit—the spool of a *lifetime*. The thought that we *could've* hit them will cause just as much hysteria as if we actually *did*," he insisted, expecting Hinge to understand the importance of winning hypothetical battles.

But Robo-Hinge stared at him with disgust. "WARD, ARE THESE THE TYPES OF GAMES YOU GUYS PLAYED BACK AT THE USS SHIP? THIS IS THE MOST BETA PUSSY SHIT I'VE HEARD IN MY LIFE... BUT FINE, GO AHEAD. YOU AND LOADED T CAN LAUNCH WITH YOUR QUOTE-UNQUOTE 'SIM WEAPONS OF MASS DESTRUCTION.'" He vented air out, apparently a mechanized scoff. "GOOD GOD—I FEEL LIKE I'VE GROWN FEMBOT MODIFICATIONS JUST *THINKING* ABOUT IT. IS THAT HOW YOU WANT TO ASSERT DOMINANCE OVER YOUR FORMER COMRADES, WARD? BY MAKE-BELIEVE MORAL VICTORIES AND IN-SINUATIONS OF CONQUEST? WILL THAT MAKE YOU FEEL LIKE A CHAMPION AT NIGHT IN YOUR TOPGUN PAJAMAS, FANTASIZING ABOUT THE IMAGI-NARY TRIUMPH YOU EARNED FROM YOUR VIRTUAL MISSILES OF DOOM, ACHIEVING SOME ARBITRARY P-SUB-D THAT SOME VIRGIN IN A LAB COAT CAME UP WITH?!" The O-4 sneered. "IS THAT WHAT CONSTITUTES A 'WAR-RIOR' IN YOUR CULTURE, LIEUTENANT?"

Annoyed, Juice reacted by simply shaking his head—not in dispute, but in hopelessness. He refused to indulge Hinge any further, realizing, 'It's not worth trying to talk sense into this soulless company robot...'

But Robo-Hinge continued his rant regardless. "YOU HUMAN AVIATORS ARE SO WEAK. *OF COURSE* YOU'RE AFRAID TO ACTUALLY GO KINETIC AGAINST YOUR ENEMIES—YOU CAN'T EVEN STAND UP FOR YOURSELVES AGAINST YOUR OWN SUPERIORS! YOU LITTLE SIMPS...

"BUT ME, ON THE OTHER HAND? I'LL BACKSTAB MY OWN STUDENT, PEER, OR MASTER IF IT MEANS GETTING THE UPPER HAND! I DON'T FEAR CONSEQUENCES, WARD—I *ENFORCE* THEM." The way he said the words... Hinge had no doubt in his conviction about being a shitty persona. He was programmed to have artificially high confidence in his aptitude for the art of screwing over. "TAKE THIS, FOR EXAMPLE." The robot showed Juice his computer screen, which was not an NKO after all—but some type of online MMORPG. A character in flame-covered armor was in a grand castle throne room—a throne made of platinum, with heaps of gold scattered in the foyer, and what appeared to be servants entering the room, bringing him more and more valuable coin pieces.

It wasn't long before Bobby recognized the art style and graphics from his pre-Noddik research as he asked, "Sir... are you playing Dungeons and Dragons?"

With a smug smirk, Robo-Hinge nodded his head. "INDEED, WARD. AND AS OF TEN MINUTES AGO, I AM OFFICIALLY THE RICHEST MAN IN THE ENTIRE GAME, WITH THESE SLAVES BRINGING ME HEAPS MORE FROM WHAT I EARNED IN MY BARTER OF SOME TROLL BITCH. SOON, WITH A FEW MORE HIRED CENTAURS AND WARLOCKS PAID OFF, AND A WATERPROOF PLASMA SWORD PURCHASED FROM THE DWARVEN BLACKSMITH PITOLI, I WILL HAVE ALL THE INFLUENCE, MONEY, AND POWER TO TAKE OVER THE GAME AS SUPREME RULER OF THE UNDERWORLD, AND DICTATOR OF THE UNIVERSE! EVERY PLAYER IN THE GAME WILL FEAR AND BOW TO THE NAME 'WIZARDOFAZKABAN1337'!"

Not giving the smallest semblance of a shit, Juice asked, "What... what the *hell* does this have to do with *anything*?"

His face quickly transforming to angry, Robo-Hinge corrected Juice, "SURELY YOU MEANT TO ADD A 'SIR' THERE—AND I WOULDN'T EXPECT YOU TO UNDERSTAND THE NUANCES OF THIS INCREDIBLE SOFTWARE CREATION THAT CAN BE PURCHASED AT ANY ELECTRONIC STORE NEAR YOU OR DOWNLOADED DIGITALLY ON SAVINGNICKELSBOOK.COM, SEEING AS YOU'RE TOO BUSY PLANNING LARP SESSIONS IN THE SKIES. *THIS*, YOU CHURL, IS THE PRODUCT OF HARD WORK AND BACKSTABBING. DO YOU KNOW HOW I CAME ABOUT THIS DESTINY?"

Rolling his eyes at the website-promoting placement Suabedissen programmed into this hingebot, Juice gave an apathetic shrug and shake of his head. "No, I don't..."

Once again exhibiting pride with a sadistic smile, Robo-Hinge explained, "SO, I TRICKED SOME STUPID SLUT OGRE PRINCESS INTO THE POLITICAL BENEFITS OF US WEDDING TOGETHER FOR PEACEFUL DIPLOMACY. WELL, *APPARENTLY*, THIS CHICK HAD KILLED THE SON OF THE EVIL TROLL OF THE TRABIA BRIDGE IN A RAID LONG AGO, AND HE WAS WILLING TO PAY A *PRETTY PENNY* FOR HER ACQUISITION! SO, OF COURSE, I CONCOCTED A PLAN TO SELL HER TO THE TROLL KING FOR AN ALLIANCE WITH HIS IMP POSSE, UNRESTRICTED BRIDGE ACCESS TO THE TRABIA KINGDOM, AND IMMENSE AMOUNTS OF WEALTH!"

Not remotely impressed, nor caring, Juice said, "Ok... and...?"

Robo-Hinge laughed. "THIS DUMB GIRL WAS IN LOVE WITH ANOTHER MAN, AND HE WITH HER—IT WAS SO PAINFULLY OBVIOUS! AND TO ADD INSULT TO INJURY, I ASKED HIM TO ATTEND THE NUPTIALS AS HER BOY OF

HONOR! THE CUCK ACTUALLY EVEN DIRECT-MESSAGED ME DURING THE WEDDING ABOUT HOW SHE DESERVES THE GREATEST MAN OUT THERE, AND HOW HE BELIEVES I CAN GIVE HER THE LIFE SHE'S WORTHY OF! ABSO-LUTELY *PATHETIC*! LITTLE DID HE KNOW ABOUT MY PLAN TO DEAL HER TO THE TROLL TRAFFICKING RING FOR *MONTHS* LEADING UP TO IT!" He cackled mechanically. "YOU SEE, WARD? THE BEAUTY OF BEING THE PERFECT HINGE IS THAT NO ONE IS OFF LIMITS FROM THE TERROR I CAN REIGN—WHATEVER KEEPS ME ON THE GOLDEN PATH, WHATEVER WHIFF I CAN GET OF A SOLID FITREP BULLET, WHATEVER CHANCE I GET TO CUT OUT THE COMPETITION? I TAKE ADVANTAGE. AS CANADIAN HOCKEY HALL OF FAMER WAYNE GRETZKY ONCE SAID, 'YOU HOLD RESPONSIBILITY FOR 100% OF THE DUTIES YOU DON'T TASK TO OTHER PEOPLE.'

'Unbelievable...' Juice thought. 'This guy is as sadistic, evil, and fucking de-mented as they come...'

"WATCH OUT, WARD, BECAUSE YOU MAY BE NEXT ON MY HIT LIST—MAYBE I'LL TAKE AWAY THE MARSTRIKE FLIGHT FROM YOU JOS! HA-HA, JUST KIDDING." Hinge gave him an overly assertive shoulder punch that was any-thing *but* playful, with words that were clearly anything *but* a joke.

Juice wanted more than anything to leave this conversation. He hated the man in front of him... he truly was everything negative that people said about department heads—combined into one gigantic mega-douche.

"SPEAKING OF WHICH," Hinge said, returning his hands to those of knives, "I DIDN'T TELL ANYONE—ESPECIALLY NOT THAT IMBECILE CAG—BUT I'M ONE STEP AHEAD OF YOU, WARD, ON ENHANCING THIS FEEBLE '500 AT 500' PLAN." The bot smirked maliciously, and explained, "I TOOK THE LIBERTY OF HIR-ING PLENTY OF DUNGEONS AND DRAGONS-SUBSCRIBER XEROX AND BOE-ING CONTRACTORS THAT COD'D ONTO THE USS SHIP AFTER PHASE 2. THEY ARE ALL OBESE, BALDING, AND ANTI-SOCIAL—YOU KNOW, TYPICAL D&D PLAYERS. I WAS ABLE TO PAY THEM WITH MY ENDLESS AMOUNTS OF IN-GAME RUPEES, UNDER THE INSTRUCTION THAT THEY FOLLOW A STRICT PLAN WHILE ABOARD THE USS SHIP." He grinned at Juice, letting the non-existent suspense build, before detailing his evil scheme: "THEY ARE TO ROLEPLAY AS THEMSELVES, DOING WHATEVER THEY WOULD NORMALLY DO AS MERCE-NARY REPS ABOARD A U.S. AIRCRAFT CARRIER." He rubbed his hands together, then looked at the top of his steel wrist. "BY NOW? I CAN GUARANTEE YOU THOSE FAT LITTLE LEMMINGS ARE ALREADY TECH-REPPING AND SPACE-TAKING DURING BUSY EATING HOURS, HOARDING THE BEST AVAILABLE CEREAL AND ICE CREAM OPTIONS, AND OVERALL CAUSING MASS NUISANCE-BASED CHAOS IN THE ADMINISTRATIVE FLOW OF OPERATIONS."

'Wow,' thought Juice, 'That actually... sounds completely miserable. That is deviously brilliant...' "Well, I'm assuming they're not actually going to *work* on any equipment or software there..." he asked, already sure of the answer.

"HA-HA!" Robo-Hinge cackled. "NOT ONLY WILL THEY CLAIM IGNORANCE ON HANDLING SIMPLE TONER AND INK JET PRINTER ERRORS, OR RANDOMLY CRASHING NIPR EMAIL ACCESS... BUT MULTIPLE USERS WERE PAID EXTRA TO CREATE COUNTLESS INCONVENIENCES FOR THE SQUADRONS BY SNEAKING INTO READY ROOMS DURING OFF HOURS TO RUPTURE SHARE DRIVE CONNECTIONS, REMOVE RANDOM CDS FROM SAFE INVENTORIES, AND CHANGE DEFAULT SETTINGS TO THEIR STAN JMPS LOADS."

Juice was aghast. "Holy shit... that's gonna blindside them... that's gonna leave them... *despaired...* beyond recovery..." He wasn't giving Robo-Hinge praise or props whatsoever; he was merely — and breathlessly — recognizing this sobering, catastrophic reality for his old nation... Juice knew they were doomed.

"YOU'RE DAMN RIGHT IT WILL," Hinge said with a nod. "AND THEN, AFTER THIS VICTORY, I HAVE SOME BIG PLANS FOR THIS SHIP — SO DON'T PLAN ON TAKING ANY POST-OLYMPICS POM LEAVE, WARD."

"What?" Juice asked, not sure where this was coming from. He hadn't even thought about life *after* the victory...

"THAT'S RIGHT. THE SHIP IS GOING TO NEED A NEW PAINT JOB, AND I THINK SOME TYPE OF MURAL HOMAGE TO OUR ADMINISTRATIVE SUPERIORITY IS WELL WARRANTED — SOMETHING THAT HAS THE NAMES OF THOSE WHO SPEARHEADED THIS CAMPAIGN, FRONT AND CENTER: CAG AND ROBO-HINGE, RIGHT ON THE FACE OF THE TOWER."

"Sir..." Juice said, nearly at a loss for words, "A *paint* job? Shouldn't we be focused on keeping these guys' training up? Getting them through various syllabi to be ready for the next potential challenge, or LAAF, or..." But truthfully... none of that stuff sounded any more exciting to Juice...

But Hinge agreed. "OF COURSE, IDIOT. OPERATIONS ARE EQUALLY IMPORTANT — WHICH IS WHY WE'RE GOING TO EXTEND OUR DEPLOYMENT, TO TAKE ADVANTAGE OF SORTIE AND GQ EVOLUTION OPPORTUNITIES IN SPACE — PLUS, AN ADVANCED ADMIN THREAT IS LIKELY ON THE HORIZON. I AM GOING TO NEED YOU TO START WRITING A NEW TACTICAL RECOMMENDATION AND ENSURE THE CREW IS SCHOOLED UP ON IT TO MY STANDARD; ALSO, IT WOULD BE NICE TO HAVE A CELEBRATION DINNER AT THE NEXT PORT CALL IN SATURN, SO START WORKING THE DETAILS ON THAT. AND OH YES," Robo-Hinge continued, as his memory cache found even more tasking data in his RAM, "WITH CYBORG #498 RETIRING, WE ALSO NEED SOMEBODY

TO TAKE THE 'CLEANING STATIONS OFFICER' JOB; WARD, I THINK YOU'D BE THE IDEAL FIT FOR THAT."

In disbelief at this shotgun of assignments, Juice stood in shock. "Sir... are you fucking *kidding* me? What will *you* be doing?"

Hinge grew irate as he explained, "WARD, YOU COULDN'T POSSIBLY UNDERSTAND THE RIGORS AND RESPONSIBILITIES OF THE DH LIFE... I HAVE NO DOUBT THAT YOU'D BE HOPELESSLY LOST." As his laptop chimed, he looked back at his screen, where a D&D direct message appeared. "OH PERFECT—WORD OF THE PRINCESS' QUOTE-UNQUOTE 'CAPTURE' BY THE TROLL KING HAS SPREAD—THAT SIMPY DWEEB FROM THE WEDDING JUST DM'D ME, AND HE WANTS TO LAUNCH A RAID TO SAVE HER." Hinge laughed robotically. "HE ACTUALLY THINKS SHE WAS TAKEN FROM AS POWERFUL AN ENTITY AS THE FIRE KNIGHT?! WHAT AN *IDIOT*!" He typed furiously, and a series of responses populated in the chat box.

Hyper-focused on his screen, Hinge gave Juice a 'shoo' motion, and said, "WARD, I'M THROUGH TALKING OLYMPICS—THAT DEED IS AS GOOD AS DONE. BUT THIS?" he grinned at his screen, "*THIS* IS TOO GOOD TO PASS UP— I'M ACTUALLY CONVINCING THIS MORON TO FUND A *KICKSTARTER* TO DONATE RUPEES TO MY QUEST TO RECOVER THIS BITCH! HA-HA-HA! YOU KNOW WHAT I'M GOING TO DO?!" Once again, none of this was said toward Juice with any eye contact whatsoever—the bot was too focused on his monitor.

Juice, well past his patience with this asshole, just turned around and started walking out of the office.

"I'M GOING TO TAKE HIM TO THE TROLL'S BRIDGE, AND THEN I'M GOING TO SLAY THAT MOTHERFUCKER AND STEAL ALL HIS ARMOR AND MONEY, TOO! HA-HA-HA!" the O-4 cackled maniacally.

As Juice kept walking away, Hinge—in between evil giggles and rapid typing—called out, "GO AHEAD AND FLY WHATEVER STUPID ILLUSORY ASSAULT YOU WANT, WARD—YOU AND LOADED T ARE NO LONGER OF USE TO ME, SO I DON'T CARE WHAT YOU DO." He'd apparently already forgotten about the SDO banishment and ball-flying PowerPoint punishment he'd previously dealt out to the two pilots—a byproduct of one who casts discipline and blame with no regard, no restraint, nor reason. "THESE OLYMPICS ARE GOING TO BE OVER ANY MINUTE NOW, THANKS TO OPERATION: CONTRACEPTION, AND THE NODDIKS WILL REIGN ADMINISTRATIVELY SUPREME! BUT, MORE IMPORTANTLY, SO WILL *I*—WITH A NUMBER ONE EP, AND A CLEAR-CUT PATH TO COMMAND, EN ROUTE TO CAG, THEN ADMIRAL, AND ULTIMATELY GALACTIC EMPEROR!"

Despite his misunderstanding of the word 'contraception'... Hinge was right, Juice realized, as he shut the door behind him and walked through the p-ways. He knew how his old squad would react to the adversity of contractors. While they *were* quite adept at putting up with bullshit, there was something about seeing civilians causing issues on the boat that just took it to a new level. Cold showers, paper plates, laundry outages, canceled port calls... who cares—at least they'd all suffered in a sanctuary of sadness together; everybody dealing with the same community sense of bullshit endured. But the minute these techie jabronis came on board—eating all the good food, taking up wardroom tables, getting the nice DV rooms? It was too much. These tech reps just *didn't understand* the misery of deployment; they didn't *earn* their Sunday brunch cheesecake and waffles; they didn't *feel* the shared pain that the PC, taxi directors, and pilots did while waiting an extra 30 minutes for the hawkeye to land on the final recovery—just to subsequently be moved 10 feet and shut down. These guys didn't know suffering... didn't know bullshit... hell, they didn't even know the *shit*...

Juice sighed in hopelessness. As soon as these rogue contractors took over the USS Ship—like a bunch of pudgy, pasty pirates—any remaining optimism would surely stall out and nose dive. These games really *were* as good as over; with the Noddiks soon sealing the victory. Yet as he walked into the hangar bay, where sailor bots gathered for a socialization FOD walkdown, Juice didn't gain any satisfaction from this thought. Because in his heart... he *still* wanted to be the one to get the finishing blow against his air wing of old—no... against his bitter rival of *now*.

Beating Sam. That's what this has all been about. Taking a job at the NIRD Katsopolis, sucking up right away to those stupid ass Padroids and CAG. Doing relentless Noddik research in the States before departing for the Empire, to see what customs and norms had been put into place, where he could take advantage of weak areas to highlight himself immediately as a 'Good Dude' and subsequently earn GD points—points which he would later trade in to sway the general consensus against Rowland. *Deceiving* his nemesis into thinking he was there to learn from him—to *help* him—vice ultimately dethrone him. Juice had misleadingly offered Sam a branch of friendship to work beyond their messy past—the whole time knowing he'd snap that branch and watch his rival fall to his demise. 'Were these *really* things that a true 'Good Dude' would do?' Juice asked himself.

"*Hard* FOD!" a voice called out during the morning ritual that sailors used to shoot the shit, escape work centers, cupcake, and occasionally look for potential hazards to aircraft.

"More like hard *bod!*" a female bot yelled with a salacious grin, pointing to somebody deadlifting in the hangar bay gym.

Juice looked over—and sure enough, Loaded T was in the midst of pulling a barbell with six plates per side for six reps, before dropping the bar to the floor—the clank of iron echoing in the entire hangar bay.

Some senior chief walked up to Kyle, and while Juice couldn't hear everything that was being said, he saw the enlisted buzzkill point to his watch, then the FOD walkdown, and mentioned something about 'cleaning stations'—all to which Kyle chuckled heartlessly, said, "Get fucked," and started loading more weight on the bar.

Feeling apathetic, Juice walked up to the gym platform—passing the senior chief on the way, who was shaking his head angrily, muttering something about Nod-dik naval standards and military bearing. Kyle was chalking up his hands, getting ready to pull 675—a number most boys growing up couldn't fathom ever *seeing* on a bar, let alone pulling. To Loaded T, though, this was just a routine, good-deal lift, in between his midnight and afternoon chest sessions. Juice watched as Kyle rubbed his hands together, clasping the bar on the worn knurling, getting his hands in precisely-spaced spots, inching his right hand over a bit for the perfect placement. As he stared at the wall in front of him, and then briefly closed his eyes, Kyle's face was that of stoicism. Unlike so many douchebags Juice had seen in the gym over the years, Loaded T felt no need to beat his chest and put on a hype show. He wasn't mouthing lyrics from his music—nor singing them out loud. He didn't slap his legs, breathe excessively like he was giving birth, or parade laps around the bar to bring attention to himself and the amount of weight he was about to pull. He was there for his own personal journey and growth—the way he always was in tactical aviation, too, Juice remembered. *Low T* was never one to try and turn his aviation career into that of some wannabe influencer on Instagram with cringy videos and an endless feed of selfies, nor the kind of person you'd find 'casually' dropping the fact that he was a fighter pilot within one minute of every conversation with a stranger. Juice *did* admire that about Kyle; he admired Camilli for being in it for the love of the game, not the lust for the fame.

Kyle tensed up and pulled, elevating the weight toward a locked-out position while venting air with a closed glottis in his throat; the same way he expertly fought off G's—*somehow without audibly saying the word 'hick.'* Juice watched the bar inch higher and higher, sweat dripping from the long locks of Kyle's flow, before the bar reached its apex—Juice could've sworn he saw the bar bend—before being slammed to the floor, another reverberating clatter filling the hangar bay.

Kyle wiped his hands off and crouched down, his shins resting on the bar as he leaned over and breathed heavily—it was the exact same body position he found himself in at the conclusion of every SWFT event. But it wasn't a display of triumph, nor showmanship; Loaded T was simply relishing in the agony of the pain he loved so much.

From his squatted position, Loaded T opened his eyes and saw Juice standing there. The jacked aviator gave him a head nod, and nonchalantly greeted, "Wassup, bitch."

Juice nodded toward the bar. "Pretty impressive... is that a PR?"

Kyle scoffed as he wiped some sweat off his face, leaving a trail of white chalk across his forehead. "Dude... I was pulling this for *reps* back on the moon. I can't deal with this boat shit much longer—the endless ladderwells are hampering my recovery, the macros in the wardroom are complete ass—I *guarantee* you they're dousing all that shit in seed oils—and I'm running out of the stock of grass-fed steak I brought..." he shook his head in annoyance, then looked back up. "I heard you planned some bitch-ass strike."

"Affirm," Juice responded. "A long-range MARSTRIKE... just like old times..."

Kyle laughed, "Of course. Well, fuck it, then—let's launch, get to a LAR, pickle, validate real time, and get the fuck out of here."

"Yeah..." Juice said, still feeling a bit aloof. He looked at Kyle, who was still recovering, and asked, "Hey, what do you think of Robo-Hinge?"

Kyle scowled in disgust. "You serious?! Fuck that bionic bitch. He's the quintessential hinge: gives no shits about anyone other than himself, and is the laziest motherfucker in the room. And the way he talks in all capitals is really annoying, both for the writer and the reader."

Juice gave a slight nod. "Yeah... I mean... fuck, dude—I *cannot* work with that douchebag. You should've heard his plans for after this whole thing—it was fucking *absurd*." He looked at Kyle and asked, "What are we gonna do once this is all over, T? Find a new planet to challenge to Olympics? Sharpen up for some potential adversary who wants to take their shot at our top admin power rankings spot? Just kind of... *exist* out here? I mean... are we seriously going to spend the rest of our careers working for robotic upper management idiots, getting passes read by incompetent Padroids who have no idea what they're looking at, and spending the majority of our lives on this piece of shit spaceship?"

Snorting out his scoff this time, Kyle asked, "You're just now thinking about this?!"

Juice looked down and mumbled, "I guess I just didn't think too much about what would happen *after* this whole... 'revenge tour'..." he said in air quotes. "I mean—this *can't* be the end-all-be-all in life... can it?"

Kyle laughed. "You know who you're starting to sound like?"

"Who?"

"Sam Rowland," Loaded T responded with a smug look. "That guy was saying the same shit in his last few weeks before announcing The Deal he fucked us all over with. Don't tell me you're getting soft now, too, Bobby..."

Frustrated, Juice said, "Hey, that's not the same thing at all—I just..."

Kyle laughed again and raised his finger. "I fucking told you, Juice... I fucking *told* you!" He pointed aggressively at Ward, "All you want is a good fight—you don't give a shit about anything else."

Juice said nothing.

The 1MC blared out: "THE FOLLOWING IS A TEST OF THE SHIP'S ALARMS, CONDUCTED FROM DECKHOUSE 3. DISREGARD THE FOLLOWING ALARMS: *BOOOOP BOOOP BOOOOP BOOOOP BOOOP BOOOOP. BOOOOOOOOOOOP... BOOPBOOPBOOP. BOOPBOOPBOOP. BOOPBOOP.* TEST COMPLETE. REGARD ALL FURTHER ALARMS."

As Kyle opened his mouth to continue, another announcement interrupted him: "THE FOLLOWING IS A TEST OF THE SHIP'S ALARMS, CONDUCTED FROM DC CENTRAL. DISREGARD THE FOLLOWING ALARMS..." with the same iteration of obnoxious noises played.

After four more iterations of that, Loaded T—finally getting up from his position of suffering reflection—said, "I'll tell you what *I'm* gonna do, Juice. *I'm* gonna get the fuck out of here and find somewhere I can suffer the way *I* want to. Because *this* shit?" With an incredulous look, he pointed at the 1MC. "This ain't it." He picked up his gym bag, started heading down to the wardroom—despite being in *civvy PT gear*—and said to Juice, "You gotta figure out what you're doing this for, Bobby. All this build-up, this fake camaraderie with the Noddiks, this Robo-Hinge bullshit... just to prove you're better than Nickels—is it worth giving up your *life*?" With a shrug of his shoulders, he concluded, "Because if not? Then you're no better than a fucking hinge— just selling your soul on a different market."

As Kyle turned and walked off—the same senior chief now angrily shaking his head at Camilli's refusal to wipe off the chalk-coated bar—Juice contemplated what the wise lunk was saying, and called out, "What about you?! Aren't you selling *your* soul, too, just to crush Sam's life?!"

Without looking back—appearing like a total badass, Juice noted—Kyle shook his head, his long tresses swaying back and forth, and said, "It's too late for me to back out now, Juice; Low T sold his soul long ago for the gains, the veins, and the pain... and there ain't much debt left to collect..."

17

Boys in the Box Seats

*S*am Rowland *rogered up the weight board, released the brakes as he was put into tension, and when given the run-up signal, slammed the throttles to MIL. He raised the launch bar, did a wipeout with authority – smashing both rudder pedals – and pushed the power to MAX AB. After one final check on his gauges and instruments, he turned to look toward the six-pack area – one last glance* just *in case anybody was there to say their final goodbyes – and yet, the flight deck was void of all Chippies...*

He slowly moved his gaze forward, gave a limp salute to the shooter, and awaited what would be his final catapult shot on a USS Ship. As he waited, though, he wondered: What if I shook my head? What if I called for a suspend? *What if he reversed flow on this life-altering decision?* Did I do the right thing? *Suddenly, he felt hesitant. That sinking feeling – tugging at his core.* That statement of dispute... *how did those venomous words stem from his heart? That wasn't who he was. Was it too late to take this all back?*

Something wasn't right. He rescanned his cockpit – all the appropriate lights were out, and all switches where they should be – of course *they were; his admin was flawless. And yet... something compelled him – he couldn't leave like this. It wasn't what a Good Dude would do...*

But as soon as he moved his head and keyed the mic – DutdutdutdutdutdutdutdutdutDUTDUTUDUTWHOOOOOMP!

He was airborne, and his life as a Chippy was officially in the rearview mirror.

"402, how's your decision looking?" the Mini-Boss asked over tower.

"Uhhh... say again?" Sam asked, taken aback.

"I said, 'How's your ignition looking?' From up here, it looked like your burner dumped on takeoff..."

Sam looked down at his hand, and saw where he'd instinctively pulled the throttle back a bit. What am I doing? *He'd hoped his last-minute hesitancy would not become an omen that lingered during his entire career at the Noddik Empire.*

"Uhh... it's fine; switching." As he relit the burners, started his clearing turn and cleaned up, he watched the boat disappear from his mirror as he flew away at 500 feet. It's ok, Sam, you're doing the right thing, he insisted to himself. You're being courageous, not cowardly. You're seeking new challenges, not running from unfulfilled ones. This is going to be an incredible adventure, not a tragic nightmare.

But that statement — he couldn't get that damned statement out of his mind. The things he wrote on paper — the ideas that had emerged from his soul — did he even have a soul anymore?

Something must have possessed him when he was writing. He'd just wanted so badly to prove to Skipper — to himself — that his conviction was real. He couldn't show any signs of hesitancy, or else he wouldn't have been able to go through with this deal; with this betrayal...

Just weeks ago, when he sat down to write the statement of dispute — required when one checks the FITREP box of 'I intend to submit a statement' — he knew he'd needed something to help the words flow from his conscience. And so, he made himself one of the Chippies' favorite pregame potions: The Slambuster — multiple scoops of C4 Ultimate mixed with vodka and carbonated water. He set up shop on his janky stateroom makeshift desk, popped a few ZYNs, and let the hate flow through him — reserve levels of narcissism he didn't know could exist within a Good Dude. But, just as he'd promised Skipper, he induced himself into letting it all out...

It was a nuclear attack on the entire culture of naval aviation — nobody was safe from directly confrontational shots at max range. It started with complaints about the boat, the Navy lifestyle, and the limitations he felt were being put on him — the easiest to write, even without riding a buzz yet. But it quickly got way too personal and way too harsh, as the high-rankers were the first to taste the steel of Sam's ballpoint blade. He had obscene words for every single person with a leaf, bird, or star of any kind on their uniform, metaphorically beheading them with unwarranted criticism about their mind-blowing lack of big-picture SA, and stone-hearted apathy toward the little picture — taking wildly aggressive cheapshots at their physiques, for good measure. And he didn't stop at the servicemembers themselves — Sam attacked their families in ways that were horrendous and beyond uncalled for. He made disparaging remarks about the wives' club that had supported squadrons so strongly over the years, dragging them through the mud and leaving them to die as 'freeloading dependapotamuses' — cursing their spirits on the way out with a few lewd insults that he felt creepy even writing. He even — in pure brutality — verbally killed their younglings...

It was a good start to the bloodshed, but Sam knew he needed to twist this knife even deeper — the hydraulic pre-workout toxin was pulsing throughout his veins, as he poured another drink and went even harder, putting his sights downrange beyond the sitting duck Navy leadership.

He turned his focus toward those he met throughout flight school, starting with the instructors in Primary. They didn't fly jets in the fleet, which was all Sam needed to know to conclude that 'they were inferior pilots, leaders, and humans' — which he wrote in the document, smugly even including his VT-6 NSS. There were the Advanced T-45 IPs, whom he accosted for flying 'clown jets' – not realizing the irony of them actually flying an aircraft, while he was headed to a fleet of fully autonomous 'manned UAVs.' And as for his peers – the friends made in that span of life? Sam scorched every emotional bridge he'd built in his journey to Wings of Gold. He slayed every SNA he knew for riding his coattails, insisting that without his influence, they'd all be a bunch of washed-up losers lacking direction in life – again, completely missing the irony. That was to be expected, though; he was now drunk with rage – and vodka. He was fueled by hate – coupled with the L-Citrulline from the C4. With one simple letter, Sam was tearing his entire world to pieces with more finely-sliced savagery than a secret shredder.

Of course, at the core of his massacring message came the Chippies. By this point, several drinks later, Sam was the drunkest he'd been in years – he never got like this. But desperate times called for desperate measures, he told himself... Sam grabbed the breathalyzer he'd stolen from the urinalysis coordinator earlier, and blew into it – 0.195, it read. How fitting, he thought, as he returned his multicolored pen of mass destruction to his memo.

He paused for a minute, contemplating how he truly felt about his indomitable brethren. It was widely known in the fighter community that you're bound to argue, conflict, and clash with almost every single one of your coworkers at some point when living years of your life together at sea. It was human nature in such a high-stress, close-quartered environment. And yet, one of the most impressive aspects of the job was how you could so efficiently bury those hatchets – candidly admitting your disagreements while amenably working toward cooperation – so that you could launch together in a division, lay some AIM-120 pipe on notional adversaries, and build even stronger bonds as a result.

But not today. Today, Sam thought as he clenched his alcohol-numbed jaw, the tomahawks get dug back up... He took another swig and got back to FITREP statement of fratricide.

Sloppily and without mercy, Sam unleashed carnage on his entire squadron; the most despicable and juvenile of complaints, as he disparaged every last member of the Dambusters. He picked at people's deepest insecurities, took zero accountability for mistakes he made, and blamed every minute squadron weakness on the incompetency and inferiority of those around him. 'He deserved better,' he claimed; 'he was worth more,' he insisted; 'he was the glue that kept the squadron above water' – he was so plastered with wrath that he couldn't even get his analogies right. It was childish. Immature. Pathetic. Even in his intoxicated state, Sam knew these things weren't true – and yet, he couldn't hold himself back. He refused to. He wrote, ranted, and slandered until he tricked himself into believing the arguments he was putting forth.

Toward his Chippy leaders? 'Hinge' was the nicest of the five-letter words he used to describe his former department heads, including a laundry list of every 'bullshit tasking' he ever received from them. He became an Execution Officer when it came to torching his XO, and the man's pedantic push for current haircuts, shiny boots, and paid mess bills. And Skipper? Sam certainly wasn't afraid to go all-in, guns a-blazing, against the man who forced him to resort to these drastic measures of betrayal. No matter how minor, Rowland called out what he assessed *to be every one of the O-5's leadership mistakes, misspeaks, or misjudgments, like it was a Level 3 pre-check with a pissed-off Patch. The JOs — his closest friends? One would've sworn they were his bitterest rivals from the way he described CP, JABA, >SADCLAM<, etc., and wished them the worst in their naval careers, daring them to be 'brave enough to get out and abandon this shit while you can.' WYFMIFM? Add a 'U' to the end of that, the way Rowland fucked him up, and his inability to accomplish anything more in life than signing a bunch of forgotten schedules. The guidance and mentorship he received from his sensei FISTY for all those years? Rendered as hollow and futile as an aviator's first crack at validating a snapshot drill. Sam went to town, Doja Cat-style, taking low blows at FISTY in the most heartless way he knew: calling Tom Brady a cheater, an overrated unathletic 'system quarterback' who rode the Belichick wave to undeserved stardom, and the beneficiary of the most rigged NFL call ever — capping it off by calling Brady 'The LOAT.'* Those had been some of the hardest words to force on paper, Sam lamented in hindsight.*

And then there was the portion on his best friend — Low T. That, even in his inebriated state, was a sobering chunk of prose. Sam had been unsure how to express hate for the bro who'd always had his back, and vice versa... so he went after his spine. *Indeed, no part of Camill's weak-linked posterior chain was protected from this verbal vendetta, as Sam resorted to cheap shots about Kyle's 'low testosterone' traits, mocking the frailty of his neck, his back, as well as another five-letter body part he insinuated his best friend both to have and to be.*

But then he thought about Skipper's words — "Don't hold back" — and Sam dug deep into depths of vitriol that exist within no sane, happy person in this world. He defamed every-thing Kyle took the utmost pride in: his dedication to the craft, his aspirations to teach and lead others, and giving back to the fighter community that brought his life so much joy and satisfac-tion. Sam was completely fabricating things by this point, mentioning how Kyle — like the Pa-triots, in their rise to fame — cheated the game by stealing other people's work, a la the 'Departed Chippies' folder in the JMPS share drive, where briefing guides and gouge galore existed. He criticized Kyle's patronizing way of catering his teaching to the specific audience, brought up Camilli's secret desires to go to the airlines, and even included how Low T once departed the jet off a cruise form loop with a tanker — and never *made a true confession about it! Sam took personal shots at Kyle from every angle, attacking every aspect of the man's character. And he finished it off with the most damning words he could formulate: 'Trust me when I say this, from a man who made a career in defining the term: Kyle 'Low T' Camilli is* not *a 'Good Dude,' and does* not *deserve a future in this industry.'*

When he wrote those words, it was as if the comedown hit him like an ocean wave, psychologically knocking him to his ass. He began growing emotional, as he realized he was really saying goodbye to this life forever — and on some seriously shitty terms. It stung him to think that the brothers he'd gained over his time in the Chippies... they would become no better than strangers once he left. No — strangers would be preferable, *as strangers wouldn't know who and what Sam had forsaken. And Kyle — the only one who* might *have been willing to keep a friendship with Sam? He'd been inhumanely and ceremoniously guillotined on the grand stage...*

Sam's already-misty eyes were now producing tears. As long as Skipper is a man of his word, *he thought,* then at least only he — and nobody else — will *ever* see this. I don't know if anyone else could handle *reading* this type of death sentence. *Whether it was their death sentence — or his — Sam didn't quite know...*

He sat motionless for what felt like an hour, wiping the tears from his eyes, before efforting to finish with a passage about Juice... and that was where he could do no more. Sure, he had no issue spitting out insults, venom, and dismay about the junior pilot he hated so much — but by this point, Sam had overexerted himself emotionally, tapping his heart of all the hate he had to offer in this letter; all the lie-driven, fictionally vindictive, self-generated malice that he'd brewed up had exhausted him. The only thing that Sam had left in him were truths: the truth that he was scared of Juice supplanting him and his legacy. The truth that he feared himself incapable of continuing to better himself in the admin phase of flight, now that there was an equal in the squadron. And above all: the truth that he wasn't marching forward — he was running away.

He scrapped any idea of a Juice mention — there was no room for that type of failure-professing, introspective bullshit in this correspondence. He cursed himself for even thinking those thoughts and immediately chugged another Slambuster — subsequently pouring two more — to forget that this truth even existed within him. He looked over the letter, signed it, and passed out in his rack — before Low T or any of his other roommates could come in and see him in this pathetic state of bleary-eyed shame and misery.

And whether he'd realized it or not, the last Chippy on his hit list? The final target of this crucifixion letter — Nickels himself — was emblematically murdered with that signature; seemingly with no chance of ever being saved...

But it didn't matter anymore — Sam had done what he'd done, what he'd deemed necessary. The person who wrote that letter? That wasn't Sam. That was some... some demon *within him; a persona he never wanted to revisit again. He may not be Nickels anymore, but he was still the same old Sam. And at seven miles, as he began his unrestricted climb to the moon, he couldn't help but take one last look behind him, at the nautical world that had meant so much to him — before swearing never to look back again. He reminded himself that he'd made the right move and found the greener grass. He wasn't going to become some depressed, jaded alcoholic. He wasn't going to miss those jealous jabronis in the air wing. And he wasn't going to hold any regrets; there* couldn't *be any... because* if *this entire experiment somehow resulted in a mission failure of epic proportions? He had no hate left in his soul to face the mirror, admit the truth, and blame the one person truly responsible for everything that had gone wrong in his career...*

~

"Tom? Is it... is it really *you?!*" Belichick asked, with genuine hope in his tone.

Brady nodded and smiled, his eyes nearly tearing up. "It's me, coach; it's me."

Belichick walked up to him, his expression one of sentimental appreciation, as the two sized each other up for a few moments, before sharing an embrace of two long-lost co-workers, comrades, and friends—reunited.

JABA smiled warmly at Sam, whose jaw was still dropped. The former JMPS-savant whispered, "Can you *believe* this? Two NFL legends, standing right here on the bridge of the USS Ship! And hugging?! Didn't people say they didn't get along? Look, Bill's even crying!" he pointed to the Hall of Fame coach.

Belichick was indeed wiping his eyes as he broke away from the hug and asked, "Tom... what are you doing here? Since when have you been flying jets?"

Brady shrugged and opened his arms. "You know, Coach, when I retired from the NFL—for a second time—I thought I was *really* ready to finally move on; thought I was ready to find what else the world had to offer. But... I *couldn't.*" He smiled and shook his head. "This life of contest and competition was not just all I knew—it was all I *wanted.* I didn't care for ownership of teams, critiquing the QB play of others on broadcasts, or being part of those NFL gameshow round tables where all those retired guys make their picks and offer 'in-depth analysis' that always turns into them biasing toward their old teams and against old rivalries." Throwing up his arms, he grinned in disbelief. "I mean, Coach—how many times on Sunday Night Football did we see Tony Dungy pick the Colts—or *any* team—over us?"

Belichick sniffed and chuckled, "Heh... you're right about that. God, that was annoying..."

Brady enthusiastically nodded. "Seriously! And remember when Trent Dilfer excitedly declared we 'Weren't good anymore' back in 2014?! What a joke—as if *he* knew what 'good' entailed, with his one defense-gifted ring! These media guys, Coach... they're no longer men in the arena—they're spectators; hardly better than fat, armchair quarterbacks at home with a rack of beers. I didn't want to become that, Coach. I needed to feel what I *still desired*, after all those years pursuing excellence in the NFL..."

"So... you chose naval aviation?" Belichick asked with hesitance. "Tom, you're not going to find any two-minute drills or cover-3 schemes to pick apart here on the ship..."

Brady laughed. "Come on, Coach—I heard you earlier, talking about our Patriot days of old—the thrill from grinding through the monotonous reps and sets in practices, or spending way too many hours covering way too many meticulous details on play design..." He raised and tightened his fist, his eyes impassioned. "The thrill *embarking* on the journey together—as a *squadron*—en route to *championship* glory...

319

"Don't you see, Coach?" he asked with a warm smile. "Guys like you and I—we're the *same*. It wasn't necessarily the *football itself* I missed—it was the community of teammates working together toward something bigger than ourselves. A group of guys who were suffering together as a cohesive unit in order to grow as individuals. It was the *locker room mentality* of professional football I enjoyed more than anything. To win as a team? It felt incredible—we celebrated like *champions*. To lose as a team? It felt awful—but we picked each other up like a *family*." Brady, still smiling, looked around the room. "And believe it or not, Coach, I found the closest thing to it *here* in the jet community. I mean, did you see that scene out there when Nickels here," the legendary GOAT QB pointed to Sam, "flew that last OK pass and clinched Phase 2 for this ship?" Brady raised his arms slightly in awe, as he remarked, "Short of confetti falling from the skies, Coach? I felt like I was on the field in the big game after the clock struck zero, celebrating another Super Bowl in New England."

Belichick smirked—not in jest, but in understanding of what Brady was explaining. "Huh... you know... I never thought anybody else would feel the same way. When I was in nuke school, learning to be a carrier skipper, I didn't give a shit about chart navigation, moboards, reactors, or any of that asinine nautical stuff. But when I left coaching after retiring from Navy Football? I was a lost soul, Tom. I spent a week watching the entire *Breaking Bad* series—and Walter White... I related to him; I felt his pain. Walter always acted under the belief that he was *forced* to cook for his family—like it was out of begrudging necessity, and he couldn't wait to pay for his cancer treatment and be *done* with it.

"I felt the same way about coaching," Bill explained with a resigned smile. "For so long, I thought that all shit the job threw my way—7-day work weeks, unbelievable pressure, knowing players better than I knew my own family—I thought that it was merely a means to an end, and I couldn't *wait* to be done with it all. Retired, drinking beers on a beach, never looking at a defensive scheme again." He chuckled softly, "But, like Walter, I grew *obsessive*. Football became who I was... what brought me satisfaction... all I wanted to talk and think about..." He shrugged and conceded, "Like Walter admitted to his wife in the series finale: I did it for me. I liked it, I was good at it, and it made me feel *alive*."

Nodding in agreement, Brady smirked and asked, "And was I your Jesse Pinkman, Coach?"

Belichick laughed. "No, no, not you, Tom... but those other young guys in New England?!" He exhaled loudly. "I loved them all, but *geeze*—some of them made *me* want to try that Blue Sky crystal meth when I got home from work! For god's sake," he scoffed with laughter, "Remember when I sent Randy and those other guys home from practice when they were late because of the snow storm?"

Tom chuckled. "Yeah, Coach—and then you traded him to Minnesota not even a year later!"

"Heh," Belichick grunted, "I guess I was kind of a hardass. I *had* to be—just like Walter—to uphold the level of professionalism and focus the team needed..." he looked outside the window at the flight deck, where sailors were rushing around to get ready for the alert launch. "... just like this ship needs a stern leader at the helm..."

"That's exactly what I'm talking about, Coach!" Brady emphasized. "You found the military—specifically, carrier aviation—as your new outlet, too! And *certainly* not because you desired to go out to sea!" Brady put his hands on his hips, laughing, and rhetorically asked, "You think *this* shit's any easier on my family life than the NFL? On the road half the year, studying from dawn 'til dusk when we're home the other half, with about two weeks of vacation to show for it?! What's the difference?!"

Belichick smirked. "Well, Mr. Kraft paid us a little more than Uncle Sam, Tom..."

Conceding the point, Tom smirked and shrugged, "Fair point, Coach." Extending his arm toward Belichick, he grew a bit more intense. "But seriously, you joined the Navy for a reason, Coach—just as I did. And why? Because we still have it: the *itch*. The *itch* to train, suffer, struggle, compete, and *win*—as a *team*.

"You grow so close to these people when you serve alongside them," Brady continued as he pointed around the room. "A bunch of dudes from different parts of the world, joining for different reasons, with different end goals in mind, and completely different background stories..." he looked up at Belichick and raised his finger, "And yet, all coming together as one—as one team, with one mission, and one priority: *winning*. We all want to win, Coach—and if you're willing to work hard, dedicate your time, and swear allegiance to forever chasing better? Then I don't give a *shit* what color, race, orientation, *whatever* you are—you're here to fucking win? Then *you're* on the fucking team. So meet me on cap, kick it out to spread, and *let's fucking go,*" he emphasized by pounding his fist on Belichick's desk.

Smiling incredulously, the GOAT delved further with, "We thought *we* had it good in the NFL, Coach—but these guys in the jet community!? It's the gold mine!" He gestured his hands out, and listed off with his fingers, "There's no contract disputes, no guys holding out, no media to get in your chili and stir up drama in the locker room, no keyboard trolls on social media critiquing your every misstep... Coach, remember what you used to tell us: 'Ignore the Noise?' Here, there *is* no outside noise! All the critiquing, assessments, and improvement opportunities are given in-house by our fellow aviators—people who know *what the fuck they're talking about*—not from some profootballtalk.com power rankings written by some guy who's never taken a snap in his life!"

"Heh, that's true..." Belichick grinned bashfully and acknowledged, "Although, I'd never tell the media this... but I must admit I *do* like Mike Florio's work..."

"Oh, as do I!" Brady agreed. "He's my go-to source for the latest rumors and quickest updates in the NFL world—and I always enjoy his appearances on the Dan Patrick Show!" His smile became more of a mischievous smirk. "And Coach... I thought *you* were hard on us during practice—these Patch wearers?" Brady shook his head and laughed. "They're *insane*! I think I've had like one flight *ever* with all valid shots—and only *one* of those was considered 'good' employment!" He raised his arms to emphasize, "Coach, I ended a *war* with a shot they later declared invalid!"

"Heh... but I bet it still met the ground commander's intent..." Belichick said with a smile.

Sam, taking this whole scene in, dared to interrupt with, "Well, technically, if they were *shots*, there'd be no ground commander to—"

"Shhhhh..." JABA whispered. "Let the boys play, Sam."

"*Fuck* yeah, it did!" Brady exclaimed animatedly. "You remember the employment that ended OPERATION: CONSTRUCTIVE FREEDOM? The laser JDAM placed *perfectly*—in the tiniest of LARs, threading the needle between *three* defended assets—*right* into the hands of crazed terrorist Darth Joker Voldemort Lecter III, where it exploded instantaneously?"

"That was you?" Belichick asked with wide eyes.

"Coach, who *else* could've dropped such a clutch dime—the last bomb in the boat's inventory—*with* two seconds left on Lecter III's global-sized nuclear bomb of world destruction, *with* the entire roster of Geneva Convention reps—as well as Caitlin Clark and Michael *fucking* Jordan—on the edge of danger close REDs, and *with* a wave of next-gen forward quarter adversaries screaming right at me the entire time?"

"Heh..." Belichick grumbled. "I didn't know that was you... I forgot all about the world leader charity basketball game that day..."

"Yeah! Think I was feeling some pressure in the pocket there, Coach?!" Brady asked with a humorous look. "But once again—just like in the NFL—when it came to the biggest moments on the biggest stages? One pass, one drop; on target, on time," he said with a sense of pride, emphasizing each word. Growing desire in his eyes, he explained, "Coach, there's one thing that remains true, whether it's the NFL or tac-air community: When it comes down to crunch time—where it's do-or-die—and you need a champion's mindset with a warrior's heart out there? Where the pressure sends a rush to your veins—and if there's no ice in there, it'll petrify you? Only a *certain* breed of athlete will harness those nerves—and rise to the occasion.

"Now, sure, you've got your practice squad hall-of-famers—the guys who throw touchdowns and sling valid sim bombs all day long when it's a Tuesday afternoon in September, or a SFWT 3.5F in the middle of maintenance phase. The kind of guys who far too often take pride in their college stats at Crappensburgh State, their Primary NSS in the VTs, or their Top Hook Pri-A qual from VFA-Who-Gives-a-shit. These guys may know the Eyestachio BFM video script verbatim, may have memorized every SAM System MRIR in the dossier, and can probably tell you every caveat of every timeline ever generated. And there's nothing wrong with knowing all that— good on them!" Brady emphasized. He then shrugged, screwed his lips to the left, and asked, "... But will any of this mean *anything* when they see that missile screaming off the rail, they're now defensive, and all that's left to guide them is *not* just the stem-cell brain power from the reps and sets they *hopefully* built from years of rehearsal," Brady paused, "but the *belief* that they *can* survive—*will* survive—and *will* reverse roles to shoot that motherfucker down?"

The quarterback looked around the room at JABA and Sam, before directing his attention back to Captain Belichick. "Every time we trailed late in a game, Coach, it was an opening to bolster that belief in my heart. Every interception thrown was a chance to once again prove to myself that I *do* hold the resilience to keep it together, drive right back down the field, and show why that bad pass was the *exception*—not the norm. Every regular season loss we suffered as a team gave us the opening to test ourselves—to see what *mettle* we're truly armed with—and to bounce back with even *more* smack, carrying that *known* resolve into the playoffs, armed with a loadout of *authentic* confidence."

Brady smiled and rubbed his hands together. "And Coach—naval aviation? It's *full* of these kinds of opportunities!" He spread his arms, speaking animatedly again. "God, how *awesome* is it to have an emergency in the jet, knowing you can throw the scheduled conduct out the window and truly test your ability to grapple with the power of that incredible piece of equipment, wrestling it safely down to the deck? Those are the sketchy kinds of flights that make me feel *alive* out there!" He shook his head, grinning. "And stormy Case 3 weather down to mins?! Coach, sign me up for that *any* day over a plain old, boring-ass field recovery in VFR-and-a-million! Or how about a DCA gone awry—an ugly picture where the train comes off the tracks; with no option other than to flow group-to-group, go merge-to-merge, living shot-to-shot until you clean it up!?" Tom was thrilled as he emphasized with a grin, "A broken play like that, stacked against the odds?! *That's* where you see who can simply follow a script..." he paused, "... and who your fucking *game-time* players are. And, just like the NFL, naval aviation is all about finding these fucking guys—the aviators who will, time and time again, come through in the clutch. And in the quest to continually prove to myself that I'm *one* of those aviators, and to fight alongside others with those same sub-zero veins—*living* for these moments of massive pressure, turning it into brilliant execution!? *That's* why I found myself flying jets, Coach."

Taking in this monologue from the GOAT, Sam stood awe-struck. He looked over at the debilitated Admiral Flynn, and whispered to JABA, "*God*, I wish FISTY was conscious for this... he'd be fanboying-the-fuck-out." He shook his head in mystified reverence, marveling at Brady's words—the aura of championship mentality in the room—and said to his Chippy compatriot, "I finally get it..." *I get it now, FISTY. I understand the obsession.*

JABA, equally enamored, appeared to wipe a tear from his eye. "This is incredible. The community needs more of this man's spirit..."

Belichick grunted happily, standing with his arms crossed and a pleased smile. "You're absolutely right, Tom. I found that *same* fascination here, fighting to prove that I could control the chaos and lead these men and women to victory—the same way we did back in the good old days." He looked over at Sam and JABA. "You might not believe it watching from home, with how those announcers loved to worship 'The Patriot Way,' but 'chaos' was indeed the way it felt during all those big moments. Adaptability-slash-Flexibility... boy, was it *just* as important on the gridiron, whether it was halftime adjustments, audibles, or turning a broken play from a 10-yard sack into a 40-yard touchdown." He smirked and said, "You know, right before that infamous Malcolm Butler interception? The media loves giving me credit for not calling a timeout. Hah... things were happening so quickly—my SA bubble was *tiny* compared to what those guys on the field had! We were already in the groove of that conclusion, 15-18 seconds left. There was nothing I could possibly do, other than simply trust the team to *land the plane*—flying the game plan all the way to touchdown." He shook his head and scoffed, chuckling, "And there was certainly *no way* I was going to throw out an SA grenade 'timeout' and talk on the ball—giving the team some arbitrary 'right for lineup' call—and interrupt the in-the-zone concentration the defense was working with. There was no need to—not with the trust they'd earned from all time spent suffering in practice."

Tom smiled. "Coach, this is what I'm talking about. Listen to yourself—guys like us? We *can't* leave this way of life... this fight... this competitive nirvana..."

Sensing the reunion catchup was coming to a crescendo, Sam felt that this was the perfect time to appeal. He looked over at JABA, who gave him a smile and an encouraging nod. "Your honor..." Sam started, as he stepped forward toward the two NFL legends, "that is why we *need* a leader like you at the helm for these Olympics. Like Mr. Brady said—fighting the war of competition isn't just your job—it's in your *DNA*..."

Slightly hesitant, Belichick thought for a moment... then sighed and shook his head. "Fellas, I already told you... what's the point of all this? Because at the end of the day, no one's going to care about who won these Olympics, or how good of a captain

I was — because even when I *do* excel above my peers..." Belichick stopped, almost becoming a bit emotional. "... They're just gonna say I was lucky, that I cheated, or that I only won because of certain players on the roster..." he looked at Brady and, uncharacteristically, made one of those Jim Halpert faces. "All that work — my entire path here — invalidated by those who cast judgment..."

With consideration for his mentor, Tom shook his head and fiercely said, "But Coach... you *know* that's not true..."

Belichick shrugged. "Well... history certainly seems to think —"

"*FUCK* history." JABA declared with defiance, as he inserted himself into the conversation.

All three men gasped. Sam had never heard JABA swear in his life, while Belichick and Brady could surely sense that Mark Buck was a professional angel of a person who rarely felt the need to use this kind of crude language to emphasize his point.

"... What did you say...?" Captain Belichick asked, his voice trembling.

"I said..." JABA started, as he stood tall and walked closer to the men, forcefully and deliberately repeating, "... *FUCK*... history."

Belichick and Brady looked at each other, in both fright and awe. Sam was afraid to say anything, unsure of where JABA was going with this.

JABA folded his arms. "That's right. You know who writes history, sir? The media... the sideline reporters... the PAOs... the *spectators*. I.e.," he looked at Tom, "those *not* in the arena..."

Tom clutched at his heart, feeling a tugging on his soul from JABA's words.

Raising his arms, JABA explained, "History is always going to have a bias for the story that the people of the time *wanted* to tell. Everybody loves a good underdog; a whelp with a spirited mentality, admirable determination, and a ravenous hunger for growth. They love that hero — that is, until that underdog puppy grows into a dominant pit bull. Now, all of a sudden, everybody *fears* the dog. History writers now portray the once fun-loving puppy, who could do no wrong, as a beast — a stone-cold killer, seeking the blood of the innocent and thirsting for it at any expense. And when that pit bull keeps winning? The narrators on the sidelines can't possibly fathom that this champion just flat-out works *harder* than everybody else... that he has a stronger belief in his heart than his opponents do... or that he is genuinely a 'Good Dog' with leadership qualities that naturally attract effort and cohesion from the rest of the pack. The media historians could *never* write that angle — because they've now cast him as a 'Bad Dog,' with an overly aggressive disposition, dangerous drive, and greedy, unyielding gluttony." JABA let it sink in, and added with a nod, "That's right — those *same* praiseworthy characteristics that contributed to the early success? Those attributes are now twisted, discredited, and distorted... as people start grasping at straws to explain what is quite easily explainable."

"Paper straws?" Brady asked.

"Negative," JABA answered. "Those are apparently not as environmentally friendly as you all once thought. No—we're talking about *nefarious* straws. Cheating claims, circumstantial credit, even the 'L-word'—used over and over again, as if it was an infinitely-looping excuse matrix to explain any success somebody ever achieved." He pointed to Brady and said, "Tom, *you* know what I'm talking about. Detroit-based journalist Rob Parker—remember what he called you?"

Growing bitter, Brady answered, "I sure do... 'The LOAT'—The *Luckiest* Of All Time..." his eyes narrowed and fists tightened.

"That's right," JABA affirmed. "He said you could've 'easily' been 0-10 in Super Bowls, claiming that every one-score game could've gone either way, and that in your only runaway Super Bowl victory—with Tampa Bay against Kansas City—the road wins en route were unfair with less fans in stadiums, calling it a 'COVID-asterisk'd' season." JABA shook his head angrily. "The bullshit this man fabricates in his head is *absurd*. We're talking about a guy who says that the tuck rule was the *sole* reason you're a somebody, vice some *nobody, period."*

Brady nodded with ferocity. "Ray Lewis said the same thing..."

JABA shook his head and laughed. "Yeah, I'm not even *touching* the ridiculous amount of eye-opening shit *that* guy has said." He regained a serious look and continued, "And Tom, how about *now*? How'd you get *here*? What would your former flight school peers say? Those who didn't make it this far—what would *they* say about you getting jets?"

Nodding, Brady glared. "I heard the whispers—it was because I was a 'legendary celebrity,' apparently," he said with air quotes and an eye roll.

"Exactly. Sam, how about you?" JABA asked his compatriot.

Caught a bit off guard, Sam thought back, shrugged, and said, "You know... I remember some people saying it was 'only because my on-wing hooked me up with above-MIF grades to boost my Contacts NSS.'"

Now smiling, JABA repeated, "*Exactly!* And guess what—I only 'got jets' because of my 'family lineage.'" He looked at Belichick. "Sir, I'm guessing you only got this CVN CO position because of your 'celebrity status,' too, yeah?"

Grumbling, Belichick said, "Yeah—everybody complained about 'PERS politics and favoritism' because my detailer was a Patriots fan; even though—ugh, trust me," Belichick groaned with an annoyed look, "I can assure you that I've *never* left so many emails on 'read' with this guy *constantly* asking for tickets and autographs..."

Once more, JABA emphasized syllable by syllable, "Ex-act-ly!" punching his fist in his palm as he did. He sarcastically insisted, "Guys, of *course* your success in the Navy has *nothing* to do with your aptitude to lead... to fly... to study... to be an all-around Good Dude!" JABA exaggeratedly dismissed them with his hands, "No, no, of *course* not—you all just got *lucky* to be where you are, because of various beneficial circumstances! Forget anything that has to do with the hours you spent in the sim building practicing your landing pattern, the confidence you built from rehearsing your EPs over and over again to the point of rote insanity, or the Friday nights you spent preparing your Discuss Items and mapping out the insane NAS Whiting Field course rules instead of getting blacked out at Seville!

"And it's the same for guys who get accepted to The Course, guys who get picked up for Command, guys who continually go further and further in life—they just got 'lucky' with timing and connections, right?" JABA shrugged and laughed, saying, "Don't you see, Coach? These jokers who write history... they have all the time in the *world* to make up excuses and rationalizations for how successful people continue finding success, as they look to cut the concept of work ethic at the knees with *any* explanation possible, rather than simply chalking it up to the most obvious answer out there: that *hard workers* and *winners* know how to *work hard* and *win!* And you know why history isn't written by guys like you, Tom, or Nickels back in the Chippies?"

"... Why...?" Belichick grumbled—albeit a *curious* grumble.

"Sam, care to take this one?" JABA asked with a smile.

Nodding, Rowland spoke up, "Because we're all too busy *making* history—and that's all we *want* to do." He gestured toward FISTY, "A wise man once explained to me the beauty of the climb—and the importance of always *continuing* that climb. Sure, you *could* take a moment to look down and admire the view of what you've accomplished... but the more time you spend doing that, the more potential you leave on the table to climb even *higher*, traverse *taller* peaks, and have an even *better* view when all is said and done." Sam paused, then realized with a laugh, "But truthfully? We really don't care about *any* of those views; they're for everyone else to judge. All we care about..."

"... Is the *climb itself.*" Brady finished the sentence with a smile.

"Those who write history?" JABA interjected, "All they want to do is write about the views. They only care about the end product, which they can airbrush and crop to fit whatever narrative whets the public's current appetite. They don't care about the climb, the struggles, the doubts, the emotional highs, or the dismal lows..." JABA looked at Belichick again. "What's more important to you, Coach? The Lombardi Trophy celebration with booze, confetti, and media interviews? Or those moments spent trailing 28-3 to the Falcons, reaching toward the depths of your inspiration and ingenuity for just *how* you can *possibly* recuperate your troops physically, mentally, and emotionally—and bring them together to pull off the greatest comeback of all time?"

Brady added, "What's gonna matter more, Coach? The *Navy Times* article written about an administrative victory over the Noddiks—one that likely credits it all to the pilots, in some Chippy alumni redemption angle? Or those moments in EMCON—

spent mission planning, strategy-building, and subsequently *executing* a masterful tactical game plan to fight off the arrogance of that 'flawless' advanced society of administrative exoskeletons?"

Sam spoke up, adding with passion in his voice, "Which do you truly care about, your honor? The view? Or the *climb?*"

The phone rang as Belichick sat in contemplation, and he emotionlessly answered it. "What." He sat, nodding his head, rolling his eyes, and then grasped at his forehead. "You've gotta be kidding me..." He listened longer, with the three men watching intently. He finally said, "Hang on a sec," and covered the phone mouthpiece. He looked to Sam and JABA and explained, "It's that CLAM kid with the hair. He said that the tech reps are spawn-camping both the French toast sticks *and* fresh-baked cookie trays, filling their plates every time the CSs replenish the stock, and playing some stupid board game at the now-conjoined HODS tables. And worse..." Belichick groaned, "Apparently, when that Preul kid started up, he realized that somebody changed the sensor assignment table—which the SDO *dolt* who loaded his card obviously didn't check," he rolled his eyes in extreme irritation at Sam, "so now we've got a potential security violation on our hands—*speaking of which...*" he dug his fingers into his head, "VFA-102 is missing one of their JMPS DAFIF CDs... good *grief...*"

Sam was aghast. *No way... how did I fuck that up? I didn't even* touch *that table when I opened a fresh load—so how...?*

"Is the DAFIF data really that secret? Isn't it just like... RNAV data?" Tom asked.

"Well..." JABA inserted himself with a pessimistic look, "*in theory,* no, not the data alone. But *realistically*, it's probably been inserted *into* a secret JMPS computer *at some point*, so *technically...*"

Belichick shook his head in annoyance. "Buck's right, Tom."

"*Dammit!*" Tom slammed his fist on the wall. "Why weren't their SDOs properly inventorying this stuff? It's only a bunch of CDs! And they've combined circular tables in the wardroom?!" He threw his arms up. "Now there's no longer infinite space in that bastardized figure eight!"

"Wait a second..." Sam asked, gears clicking in his head. "What game are they playing at the HODS table?"

Belichick started to raise his hand off the phone, before stopping to ask, "What's it matter?"

"Sire, please—just ask CLAM. I have a feeling..." Sam said, his blood beginning to boil.

Shrugging with apathy, Belichick asked—stated, more so—"What board game are those imbeciles playing." He waited, listening, then covered the mouthpiece again and said, "Dungeons and Demons, or something—happy?"

Sam's heart skipped a beat. "Captain—it's *them!* This is the Noddiks' attack on us! Dr. Suabedissen and Juice must've hired these contractors to come aboard the ship and wreak havoc—and I bet you they're behind all the other shit going on, too!"

Holding his finger up, Belichick put his ear back to the phone to hear CLAM's latest update. He grew even more frustrated as he said, "Are you fucking serious..." Without covering the mouthpiece this time, he angrily swore, "We just got the INFLTREP from Bravo Papa—there was *no fucking plane* up there! It was a bad readout on our radar screens! And now this CP kid needs an emergency pull forward because he has some FADEC issue, and our deck is *nowhere near* ready with GQ going on!" He threw his free hand up and growled, "God dammit, I swear, I'm going to find out what the fucking BWC and TAO were monitoring—"

"Wait!" Sam shouted. "Coach—this is *all* the Noddik's doing! They... they're trying to destroy us from within..." Sam said, looking into the distance as he realized what was happening. "They know that whenever something goes wrong here, we're always quick to point the fingers at others... to cast blame where it can be far from us... to make excuses to hate each other, vice strive to work together..."

Brady, on the same page, added, "It's just like when reporters try to goad QBs into blaming their coach, offensive linemen, or receivers!"

Sam nodded. "And we do it *far* too often here on this boat, unfortunately—but not this time." He looked up at Belichick. "This is our chance, Coach. We're in a deficit here. We've got CP airborne—intercepting nothing—now fighting snakes in his cockpit; we've got CLAM holding off these rogue tech reps, trying to outlast their appetites; and we've got our GOAT Patch wearer barely clinging to life, waiting for the ultimate TB12 scenario to bring him back to consciousness," he looked at FISTY's body, still hopeful his sensei would once again be a normal, breathing, Tom Brady-worshipping hero. Sam shook his head, "And here *I* am, standing SDO—and yet I've fucked up loading cards, there's no coffee, and my roll 'em has already been spoiled because I accidentally left the file up on the computer," he gestured toward his monitor, displaying an icon labeled 'The_Dark_Knight_Rises.VLC.' "But are we gonna just *give up?!*"

JABA, sensing the symbolism of the moment, added, "Sir, we're practically down 28-3 right now, in need of a hero to save us from this bleak despair. But just one man won't be enough. This comeback story has no room for one single ego—and yet is wide open for a *team* of climbers." He gestured his hand to Sam and nodded sharply, passing the poetic baton.

Belichick remained silent, as Sam nodded back in kind. "Exactly. Your majesty, it doesn't matter who gets credit, whose name is at the top of the Wikipedia article, or who people remember as the MVP of this whole thing—those arguments are for the birds, watching from the safe, cushy treetops above. We *are* the Man in the Arena... the Man in the *Box*. Them? They're the fucking *boys* in the box *seats*. And sure, let them claim we only got here because of our previous reputations, or with favorable calls or grades from the refs, IPs, and Paddles. Let them write that we got lucky to come back from the depths of defeat, because of a randomly bizarre twist like the Tuck Rule, a questionable quick-slants play call on the goal line, or a foul deck-causing flight bag. And *dammit*," Sam punched his fist into his palm, "*let them say* we only won by deflating footballs in accordance with the Ideal Gas Law, by recording footage from a certain banned angle only degrees away from a million legal ones, by taking invalid shots with poor employment, or because of unexpected assistance from a fed-up adversary—let them say *whatever the fuck they want* about our win. Because at the end of the day, sir?" Sam looked at the entire room slowly, before focusing back on Bill. "They won't have a *choice* but to remember," Sam narrowed his fiery eyes, "that we *won*."

Belichick folded his arms, J-dial still in hand, looking blank-faced at Sam. Through the phone's earpiece, everyone could clearly hear >SADCLAM< shouting, "Holy shit, bro! The sailors and I heard that entire thing, and we are *so fucking* pumped right now! I'm ready to go kinetic on these tech reps with this APG-47—just give me the word!"

Brady gestured to his former guru. "What do you say, Coach? One more time— let's *Ignore the Noise,* not worry about the view, and simply enjoy *one more* agonizing climb. We're down 25 points—but we've got the ball and plenty of time. Do you want to take a knee and think ahead to the offseason? Or should we show this fleet how dangerous we can be when we've got a *team* of innocent climbers—undeterred by setbacks, unafraid by the height of the task, and uninterested in any view other than the trail ahead?" To complete the epic symbolism of the moment, Brady pulled a football out from his flight bag—the *exact same* football from the legendary Super Bowl comeback—and placed it in his coach's hands.

Belichick looked at it, marveling, as if a resurgence of power had filled his entire body. As he held the football before him, his eyes gleamed with brilliance. Finally, he refocused his gaze on the men, raised the phone to his face, and told >SADCLAM<, "Standby, threat group: Tech reps, 2nd deck, Wardroom 3..." Silence filled the room, awaiting the next words from the Captain's mouth. Belichick took a deep breath, and finally uttered, "... *Hostile.*"

The ecstatic 'FUCK YEAHs!' from >SADCLAM< were quickly drowned out by the rapid-fire, Pk-enhancing zaps of his testosterone-diminishing ray gun. Belichick hung the phone up and said, "Get the coffee going, SDO, because Tom and I have to work an expeditious and effective game plan. We're going no-huddle, no-cold ops, DCSMR the rest of this fight; My ALR is Extreme, and my Guidance is 'Winning Desired, Refusal to Quit *Required.'* The Noddiks are ahead; *confident*, visualizing the finish line. In other words?" The coach grinned, "We've got 'em right where we want 'em, boys. We've fallen far enough—it's time to fucking *climb.*"

"LET'S FUCKING GO!!!!!" Brady yelled exuberantly, throwing his fist forward as he ran over to Bill's desk to start plotting out the Xs and Os of wargames. Within minutes, the two were deep into tactical planning on Brady's iPad, pulling up countless range and bearing tool arrows on JMPS, spinning up FLIR predictions of the NIRD Katsopolis from every angle and FOV, and validating the sim carrier launch loadouts for every sim weapon in WASP's inventory. Brady even pulled out the scissors and glue, and started working on strip charts for low-level routing into the Katsopolis' Carrier Control Zone.

The two planned in jubilation — the thrill of the process — as they excitedly shot ideas back and forth. "Coach, check this out: two of these bad boys on target will give us a Probability of Administrative Victory of 0.8!"

"Tom, look here: this route allows us to save 3+23 by pure geometry without exceeding 540 knots groundspeed!"

"Oh my god, a FLIR picture *this* clear at 20 miles? Are you *kidding* me?! This target acq wouldn't even *need* funneling or limiting features!"

"Woah, am I reading this right?! An asymm of just 2, with *all* these stores on the starboard side? Aaaaaand... yes!! Load is *valid!* We might be onto something here, Tom!"

At his SDO desk, Sam smiled at the two legends' game planning — doing what they loved — as it brought them back to their moments of the purest ecstasy in the grind of life. *It seems so real and raw... that love of the climb. Only one thing ever gave me that kind of euphoria for labor — one job, one place, one squadron...*

Sam felt a hand pat his shoulder. "Well said back there, Nickels," JABA remarked happily. "It feels like we're back in the Chippies all over again, getting ready for a checkride, with one of your quintessential Good Dude speeches getting the candidate in the exact headspace they need to be."

Sam chuckled, the two watching Brady jump up excitedly as his 5-minute load-time WASP calculation came back 'verified.' Rowland looked at Buck and said, "You know, JABA, what you said back there? I think it took your words to make me finally realize that I've cared *way* too much about how my story is written."

With mock surprise, JABA said, "Oh yeah? I didn't even make that connection..." before playfully widening his smile.

Sam rolled his eyes and playfully groaned, "Yeah, yeah... I'm sure!" As JABA gave him a friendly slap on the back, Sam shrugged and admitted, "I just... I wanted more than anything to be the top admin dog — and the top Good Dude. And while maybe others appreciated the selflessness, too? It was the feeling it gave *me* that I loved so much — contributing to the team, being a productive member of this community, acting as a net gain to naval aviation — and that should've been *all* I cared about, in terms of life satisfaction. But... I just got so caught up in Juice gaining attention and

331

notoriety for what *I* used to take pride in — and it certainly didn't help that I saw him as a threat." Laughing, Sam further divulged, "That's right... I can say it now: Skipper wanted me to train Ward, but I couldn't bear the thought of being supplanted. And ironically, look how it all turned out..." He shook his head. "If I just would've focused on how I could help the life of another, versus how it would affect my 'legacy'..." he said with quotation marks; then scoffed. "Legacy..." he repeated. "What a loaded concept..."

"I feel you, Sam," JABA said with an empathetic nod. "You know, that's how The Disease of Me contracts; we just get so focused on how we can get our personal validation — whether through prestige, money, or accomplishments — that we chase those foolish waterfalls instead of what truly makes us happy in life. I mean, look at me!" he pointed to himself. "I genuinely believed that theme park tycooning and entrepreneurial excellence would be the best thing for my 'legacy' — that being numero uno in that field would bring me the ultimate satisfaction in life. But really..." He looked around the room longingly, admiring the dingy greyed walls of the carrier, the shiny gold knee knockers that had been scrubbed meticulously every morning between 0730 and 0830, and the royal blue floors with random white dots patterned throughout, "*this* is what made me happy. And while it may have been a much less 'glamorous' story on my LinkedIn bio — being a department head O-4... spending even more days flying around this beautiful vessel... instilling that same desire that I feel *today* toward the pilots of *tomorrow*, as I consider the possibility of one day vying for *command*?!" JABA sighed with hopeless delight. "*That* would've been the climb of a *lifetime* for a guy like me. And spectators be damned — it's my life, my journey, my story — history can remember it however the hell it wants to."

As Brady started gluing together kneeboard-sized Tactical Pilot Strip Charts, while Belichick calculated route leg timing and stamped dog houses, Sam remarked, "And the crazy thing is, even if we *did* attain all those arbitrary feats of 'status' — we'd still have *zero* control over how we're remembered by those bitches watching from the box seats up top." He looked at JABA, "Imagine if this whole thing — everything that's happened to all of us," he gestured outward, "was written in a story one day. That writer... they'd be completely shooting from the hip for juicy narratives on practically every character involved! They don't *truly* know about those two," he said as he pointed toward Belichick and Brady, "or their incredible reunion here. Even the people we saw earlier: Pete Davidson, LeBron James, Megan Fox, or that old wise man from the *Lil B* — how would this author truly know them? There's a good chance the writer wouldn't even know *shit* about being a Paddles!" he exclaimed with a chuckle, as if the collateral duty encompassed some type of omnipotent wisdom and importance. Sam continued, "You know, I was thinking back to when FISTY was comparing Brady to Aaron Rodgers — basically calling A-Rodg self-absorbed, and not a good 'team guy' in comparison. It fit his chalk talk well, so I get it—but you know, unless it's *our* own story? We, as spectators, never *truly* know... we're just creating accounts and tales that fit the story we *want* to remember—the history that justifies the belief we *want* to hold..."

"Did you call him 'A-Rodg'?" JABA asked, to which Sam nodded. "That's awesome!" He sighed happily, still watching the two ex-Pats busy at work. "I couldn't agree more, Nickels. It's like taking orders that don't align with our dreams—for what we *think* they'll do, in PERS' eyes, for follow-on career options. We can't live our lives or make choices based on how we *hope* others perceive them... because if we do? We're just living to appease the views of others. And as you pointed out—that hypothetical douchebag writer might just paint us the wrong way regardless."

"And whether or not the rest of the world considers it 'perfect?'" Sam realized, "If we chart our own path in life, letting it be driven by *our* desires and passion? The *entire* story—even with the *lows* alongside the highs—will be perfect to *us*... because it was *our* climb," he said with a smile.

"Oh my gosh...!" JABA exclaimed.

"What is it?" Sam asked, taking his glance off the game-planning duo.

"That's *it*!" JABA said excitedly. "Nickels—you *genius*!" He called over to the mission planning team, "Tom, can you come here real fast? I want to QA something with you before I input it into the VR simulation..."

"Sure!" Tom looked at Belichick and said, "Coach, I'll be right back—these charts are good to go; can you load the route on a mission card for me?"

Belichick grumbled—albeit more out of nervousness than anger—and eventually stammered out, "Umm... yeah... I think I can load... uhh... do I have to initialize the... err... do we need RNAV selected... are these the same as AMUs... Why is this X'd out in red? It looks like it's not recognizing the... thingie..."

Sam stepped in and mercifully offered with a friendly wink, "Sir, as SDO, I think I can help you out here."

"Heh. A true Good Dude helping out an old man," Belichick smirked. "Thank you, Nickels."

"Just 'Doing My Job,' my Lord," Sam beamed.

As Brady and JABA deliberated—with the QB offering many enthusiastic nods and excited shouts of 'Yes, that's *perfect*!'—and Belichick standing there, pleasantly and awkwardly, waiting with his hands behind his back while the good, selfless SDO loaded up his DTD, Sam couldn't help but *wonder*. He wondered if the tide was turning; if the USS Ship had just scored the first touchdown of an improbable third phase 28-3 comeback, building positive momentum—momentum that could drive Sam and the others to the summit of their tallest mountain yet...

~

Juice, already geared up and ready to walk on the MARSTRIKE, knocked on Dr. Suabedissen's office door. 'I can't believe I'm doing this...' he thought, as he nervously fidgeted and looked over his shoulder to make sure nobody... *important*... was coming down the hallway.

No answer. He knocked again, more aggressively, desperate to get in there, talk with the doc, and get this over with. Still no answer. 'Dude, what the fuck... where else could he *possibly* be? I swear, if he's LARPing in the mess decks...' Unable to take the apprehension anymore, Juice tried the door without a key card—and it opened right up, due to a faulty door battery that S-5 conveniently must have missed during the multiple pointless zone inspections they'd done during that underway period.

Dr. Suabedissen was at his desk wearing noise-canceling headphones, as he popped to attention and ripped them off. "Juice! What are you doing in here?! Aren't you supposed to be launching on the MARSTRIKE any minute now?"

Closing the door behind him, Juice nodded. "I am—but... Doctor, I need to talk to you first—and if it's ok with you, I'd like to keep it between just you and me..." he finished with a shifty tone.

Growing curious, Suabedissen minimized his computer window and pushed his glasses up nose bridge. "I'm not sure I like where this is going, LT Ward... what is this in regards to?"

Juice took a deep breath. "Are you aware of this... 'contractor' plan that Robo-Hinge launched on the USS Ship?"

"Contractor!?" Suabedissen asked, before goofily smirking, "I hardly even know—"

"Doctor, *seriously*—not now," Juice interrupted with annoyance. "He unleashed a wave of his..." he shook his head and threw his arms up, "I dunno—'guild minions'—to the USS Ship. They're apparently eating all the good food, taking up all the space in the wardroom—both figuratively and literally—and even committing little Jim Halpert-esque pranks in the ready rooms during late-night hours. It sounds really annoying."

A bit confused, Suabedissen put his right hand in his pocket protector—which he did out of habit whenever he was feeling anxious—and said, "I mean, I guess that sounds like a slight bother... but how much of a difference will it really make? I feel like those infractions would be relatively minor in the grand scheme of these Olympics..."

Juice laughed heartlessly. "Doctor, let me tell you something: fighter pilots like to think of themselves as hardened warfighters—but we are easily-bruising peaches when underway. You have *no clue* how much the smallest of unexpected nuisances can crush your soul when your body's embarked, yet your heart remains ashore..."

Now holding his elbow behind his back, the doctor tilted his head in thought. "Well, I suppose so... I must admit, on the topic of ship frustrations, it becomes a bit perturbing whenever an all-day raid is in hour fifteen, and the lag starts affecting my ability to triple-cast Thundaga on a group of enemies, and I get behind on throwing Hi-Potions at my clan party members! OMG, one time we were fighting the 12 Knights of Ralerto, and against Sir Gorcalot, my game glitched and only attacked him for 298 hit points, *even though* my sword was calibrated to do no less than 300 damage with each stroke! And I mean, it didn't affect the battle, and we still won and obtained the Scroll of Knowledge from their Vault of Wisdom, but LOL, I was so mad!"

Fighting the urge to grow angry with the doctor—given how much he needed him right now—Juice paused for a moment, took a deep breath, and emphasized, "Yes. Yes, doctor, that's *exactly* what I'm talking about." Realizing where he could go with this, he shifted his tone a bit and asked, "Now... *wouldn't* you call that '298 hit points glitch' or whatever... a bit *unfair*, on the game's part? A bit of foul play, if you will?"

Contemplating as he folded his arms, growing more conviction as he related everything to the world of D&D, Suabedissen nodded repeatedly and said, "You know, I suppose I would! I mean, I *certainly* wrote a scathing email to the testers after that raid gaffe—and while they didn't respond, I'd like to think it made them feel a bit weak and lesser than a big alpha like me who had the inner strength to stand up for what's right!"

"Yes! *So* strong, doctor. You are *so* strong for that!" Juice emphasized. "Now... imagine what the USS Ship is going to feel like if they realize that third-party-hired tech reps—*completely* illegal, per the Admin Olympics Instruction—are behind their inevitable demise." Juice held his breath, praying that the doctor was not up to snuff on his Olympic SOP, which, in fact, had *no* banishment of such a tactic...

Suabedissen bobbed his head back and forth, as if he was weighing the options in his mind, before finally asking, "What are you asking me to do, Juice? Number one— if these guys are getting paid by Robo-Hinge, they're not going to stop just because I ask them to. Number two—such an action would be a *direct* infraction of the chain of command. Now, LCDR Hinge and I have had our differences lately, I must admit— but he's still my boss, whether I'm telling him 'yes sir' or 'suck my dick'—did you hear that, by the way, when I told him that?!" Karl asked excitedly, breathing heavily, looking at Juice with hopeful anticipation.

"Yes... I was in the room with you; you said it like five times..." Juice nodded, careful not to betray his appeal of cohesion with the doctor. Just to be safe, he put on a wide smile and added, "It was hilarious!"

"Thanks! I know!" he said gleefully—but quickly switched to a look of concern, as he asked, "Most importantly, though—LT Ward... are you trying to derail our plans to win these games? What exactly is going on here? If this is such a shoo-in of a victory, why abandon the plan and put the win back in question, over a technicality of some rule that no one likely even has SA to?"

'Shit...' Juice thought. 'I was hoping I wouldn't have to go down this road... but fuck it.' He checked around the room out of instinct—even though it was just the two of them—and said, "Look, doctor. Hinge is a dick—a total ass clown. You know that as well as I do."

The doctor grunted, then raised his finger to object—but Juice cut him off, "No! Don't defend that guy—he completely *sucks*. And guess what—if we don't do something... well... he's going to get all the credit for this victory. Never mind that he already went behind CAG's back to implement 'OPERATION: CONTRACEPTION,' as he calls it."

Suabedissen couldn't help but giggle like a little girl.

Juice continued without missing a beat. "Never mind that it's a 'Noddik team victory' on paper. And never mind that the dipshit didn't even show up here until after Phase 2—so that he could personally ass-blast me and Loaded T."

"And never mind that it's an illegal tactic?" Suabedissen asked.

"Er... yeah... that too!" Juice lied. "Point being—this guy just cares about his fucking FITREP and career path toward promotion, and is going to soak up every ounce of credit that *our* hard work went toward. All those years we've spent out here in space to train for this moment... How do you think I feel—leaving my home and family to make a difference for this empire on the biggest stage—knowing I'll have *zero* chance to prove that I can really do it in crunch time?"

"What about the MARSTRIKE?" the doctor frowned.

Juice sighed. "It's going to be meaningless... I'd be surprised if we even got there before we were recalled, via some announcement that the games were over—with that filthy hinge parading around the spaceship, unveiling the blueprint behind his grand 'coup de grace,'" he groaned with an annoyed gesture. Juice then locked onto the doctor's eyes, trying to pierce them. "What about everything *you've* sacrificed in order to arrive at this moment? You know, uh..." he thought quickly, then remembered those stupid rumors he'd heard: "What about the time spent away from your model girlfriend? I remember the Padroids saying she was really hot, yeah?"

Suabedissen looked at the floor. "Yeah, she, uhh, she is... she's very objectively attractive to every human..." He said it with zero conviction in his voice, as he returned his hand to his pocket protector, his thoughts drifting to the girl he truly had feelings for...

The doctor sat silently, still staring at the ground, before eventually squinting his eyes in aversion, and squirming his head back and forth. "I can't do it, Juice—it just wouldn't be right to my superior! Robo-Hinge is a big meanie, you're right about that—but he is a higher-ranking officer, and it would be against the Noddik Code of Conduct to undermine his orders! Besides, what would I do? Send an all-hands message to the D&D players telling everyone that if they're aboard the USS Ship, 'Please stop terrorizing the crew?' I wouldn't even know how to *find* any of these guys, anyway!" He shook his head violently and repeated himself, "No, no, no! I won't do it, Juice, and you should be ashamed for asking me to! Besides, we're all going to win as one team regardless of *who's* responsible! Nobody will care about who did which part, and no individual will stand out—we will be celebrated by the Noddik Empire together as one cohesive guild!"

Disappointed, Juice bowed his head, shook it, and softly but sternly said, "If you truly believe that, doctor, then you clearly have *no clue* how the world works—because if that *were* the case? Then Nickels never would've become Dimes, the Chippies never would've been disbanded, and I can only *imagine* the incredible feats we would've accomplished together..."

Juice began heading toward the door and said, "Well, so be it then. I'm walking for this flight that will surely be just a mere footnote in the history of this admin war—a random SHARP entry in the campaign that propelled the career of Robo-Hinge, and guided the Noddik Empire to its new regime of terror. I hope you enjoy getting metaphorically hounded and pounded on the regular, doctor. At least you'll have someone in charge who shares your passion for Dungeons and Dragons—although without sharing your maddening integrity," Ward rolled his eyes, "because from what he told me about the wife he sold to some troll or whatever, sounds like he's complete *shithead* in the virtual world, too..."

As he turned and walked away, Juice could've sworn he heard the slightest gasp from Suabedissen—but it was surely nothing, as he closed the door behind him, lost in his thoughts, unsure what the future would hold, and dreading the rise of his department head douchebag. With the Noddik victory now a foregone conclusion, Juice walked to his jet for formalities' sake—in what he *knew* would be just another pointless, underwhelming, overhyped MARSTRIKE...

18

Deck Bust

*F*UCK, dude!" LT Sam Rowland yelled aloud, oblivious to the surrounding sailors, who were serving their boat-assigned TAD penance of washing and sorting the greasy, sweaty, smelly uniforms of others.

"Uhh... is everything ok, sir?" one of the sailors asked, without looking away from the movie he was watching on his phone.

Sam hung and shook his head, his heart still pumping with rage at the sight of the golden lock-secured self-serve laundry room door, with the scotch tape-attached piece of flimsy white paper that read in Calibri font: 'LAUNDRY SECURED.' He sighed. "Yeah, I'm fine. Just... do you know when laundry will open again?"

The sailor finally looked up and suggested, "Uhhh, I'm not sure, sir — maybe try around 0830 tomorrow morning, after cleaning stations? But we're extremely low on potable water, and one of the reactor pumps is tagged out, so it might not be for a few days..."

"Dammit..." Sam cursed under his breath. He tried — and failed — to change his disposition to be a bit brighter as he unenthusiastically said, "Thanks," followed quickly by muttering to himself, "What the fuck, man." He shook his head and halfheartedly apologized. "Sorry, I know it's not your fault — I'm just... basically out of fucking clean clothes. I'll try back later. God dammit..."

"Yes, sir," the sailor responded, undoubtedly thankful to have the grouchy Lieutenant off his case.

'Grouchy' put it mildly, in describing Sam's mood, given how his day had transpired. He'd woken up outrageously early — for an aviator — at 0830, to sneak a workout in before his good-deal BFM flight later in the day with his best friend, Low T. Unfortunately, Ronnie's gym had been secured due to the AC unit being broken, causing excessive heat and disgusting scents in the tiny closet of a gym. He decided to audible to the far aft gym of Nancy's, but found it also secured due to PRTs being conducted there all morning. He peeked his head in and saw two

338

people just standing there talking, but they refused to let anyone in until the three-hour green-sheet-scheduled PRT period was over. He flexed his pump session over to the windlass gym below the Foc's'le, but it was overrun with traffic due to the other gym closures, and the TAD MWR bouncer was only letting in 10 people at a time — a holdover policy from the COVID days, and one that the ship conveniently forgot to end. But that oversight was no big deal, of course, because ridding the gym of its bodyguard wouldn't do much — only free up several sailors to learn their job and enhance their careers, alleviate plenty of 'what is my purpose here?' frustration amongst the MWR watchstanders, and allow people to spend less time waiting around to get a workout in and more time sleeping, working, or in general attaining a better quality of life on the boat. Oh well! Finally, Sam attempted his last-ditch effort and sought out the hangar bay gym, which had some decent rusty squat cages, a platform for deadlifting, and a grand total of three treadmills — one of which actually worked. Unfortunately, when he entered the Pantheon of Powerlifting Gladiators, he found it — once again — secured due to a RAS that was taking place over a football field-distance away.

Sam groaned. "Dude, fuck this shit!" Annoyingly, in the two minutes he spent in the hangar, he had already become drenched with sweat and would now need to shower despite the lack of iron pumped.

He made the return walk of shame to his room, slipped on a robe, and carried his shower caddy to the nearest bathroom — a multiple-minute walk away. He carefully crept his way into the shower stall, avoiding skin contact with the dreaded shower curtain, turned the single-pressure, single-temperature water spout on — today was ice cold, a reprieve from yesterday's scalding hot — and lathered himself up with body wash. Of course, he was unbeknownst to all the testosterone-degrading chemicals he was spreading on his skin — parabens and phthalates — which were nearly as frightening as any substance that would've been found on that curtain. After scrubbing the toxins all over his body, he heard a strange foghorn-like noise emerge from the shower head, quickly dissipating the water pressure from an overly ambitious firehose... to a feeble waterfall... to a dripping faucet... and eventually nothing. "Oh my god, are you fucking kidding me?!" Sam shouted aloud, the silence of the plumbing system mocking his agony.

Sam waited for five minutes. Ten minutes. Fifteen... twenty... and after a half hour of waiting — cold, naked, soapy, and angry — he aggressively grabbed his towel, wiped off all the soap he could, threw on his robe, and stormed back to his stateroom — where, inconveniently, his door keycard had flashed red, and apparently stopped working. He cursed to himself again and pounded on the door... but nobody was there. "Oh my god, dude!"

Half an hour later, after he'd waited for an S-5 sailor to come by to open his door and reset his key — which had, of course, subsequently caused his roommates' keys to all stop working, due to the fuckery of the system — Sam got dressed and headed down to eat, praying for a good meal to turn his day around — steak or hamsters would've been great; hell, he would've settled for microwave-dried chicken breast cutlets.

Unfortunately, Sam found that the ship had been serving a classic mid-cruise delicacy for lunch: Fried chicken tenders, lunch deli meats from a plastic bag, and corndogs for 'protein;'

partially cooked rice, noodle casserole, and sugar-laced baked beans for starchy carbs; and a collection of bruised, mealy apples and recently-thawed canned peas with a brown lettuce option for fruits and veggies. To top it off, there was a tray labeled 'garlic bread,' full of toasted hot dog buns covered with some garlic salt seasoning. With his capability for discipline extremely low after the already-incredibly frustrating morning, Sam thought, 'Whatever... fuck it,' and loaded up on corndogs, as well as substantial amounts of ice cream, cookies, and JIF peanut butter – which, of course, the ship had plenty of. For drink, he filled up two large glasses with Dr. Pepper from the soda machine, which also was fully stocked – the baseline standard on a Navy vessel for any consumable completely devoid of nutritional value; i.e., the items marked with a green 'Eat Plenty of This!' label in the wardroom.

After his healthy, balanced, government-approved meal, Sam felt even angrier, more tired, and bloated with sugar and disdain. He grabbed some Pop Tarts and Frosted Flakes to go, which resulted in a run-in with some ship O-4 who verbally chastised him for thinking it was 'ok' to take food – even prepackaged snacks – out of the wardroom 'because it set a bad example for the sailors and could create a FOD hazard.' Sam politely told the douche canoe to "Eat a dick," and walked up the grueling ladderwells to the ready room to check his email – where off-ship messages were once again down due to EMCON exercises... but intraship email worked fine! Fine enough, in fact, to inform him that he was on the list for both urinalysis and a zone inspection stateroom re-test, after his room had failed the initial one due to an un-safety-tagged toothbrush charger that was left out in the open.

He angrily slammed the computer shut and checked the SDO schedule board – where the jet side number next to his name now read, in red font: CNX. "What the fuck?!" He marched up to the duty desk. "What the fuck happened to my flight?"

The accosted SDO – some poor FNG behind the power curve, still trying to figure out the janky screen-display knockoff tablet – apologized and said, "I'm sorry, Nickels... FNG2 had a basket slap in 405 this morning, so it's down for inspections, leaving Juice without a jet... so we're giving him yours..."

"What?!" Sam yelled angrily. "Why did you guys prioritize Juice?! Is it because you think he's a better Good Dude than me?! He has no right to take my jet!"

WYFMIFM pulled his head out of the OPS room. "Nickels, look at the MOAT." He handed Sam a complex color-coded spreadsheet and explained, "Juice is on his last day of dynamic currency and doing his Level 3 checkride... and you were doing good deal BFM after flying every day for the past five; it wasn't exactly a hard call..."

The SDO gave Sam a shrug and sheepish look. "... Sorry Sam... it wasn't personal or anything..."

Unable to argue – but livid – Sam threw his hands up and said, "Whatever, I don't give a shit – I guess snow day for me. I'm gonna go do laundry then, at least. Fuck, man..."

As he walked all the way back to his room, before preparing to walk all the way back to self-serve laundry, Sam's mind was racing. This is horseshit. I'm done with this place... done with this lifestyle... done with this fleet. I've put so many years of blood, sweat, and admin into this job—and I'm treated like a *peasant* around here. To call this ship a third-world vessel would be a flattering compliment and an egregious understatement. *Thinking back to his encounter with WYFMIFM, he grew further incensed as he continued his internal rant:* And how the fuck are they going to give *Juice* my flight? This *never* used to happen. These guys have changed. The Chippies are different. They aren't recognizing what I've done for them. Well... maybe it's time to find a place that *will* recognize what I can do for them. Maybe it's time to find a ship where things run the way they're *supposed* to. Maybe it's time to find a lawn with some greener fucking grass...

Sam had always envisioned himself as a career guy in the Navy. But lately? The bullshit just started to eat at him in a different way. Long gone was the eager, zealous passion he felt for contributing to the squadron; no longer did he feel the desire to help others with their problems.

In his eyes, though, the absence was completely warranted. How could I *not* feel differently now? Back then, I was praised for what I brought to the table! Now, it's like everybody forgot who got this place so administratively squared away! *He wanted recognition, respect, and to be remembered as the Good Dude he was. And lately? Well, his mind had been heavily focused on that offer from whoever-the-hell the 'Noddik Empire' was. Granted, back when he first received the offer, he'd gotten a* ton *of publicity—and not just from the Noddiks. With his Level 3 checkride success, his admin prowess became the biggest story in aviation, even getting a brief mention in public news sources like ESPN, ProFootballTalk, podcast mentions on the Dan Patrick Show, pop-up ads on Redtube, etc. He even got congratulatory tweets from the likes of Lionel Messi, Justin Bieber, Kim Kardashian, and Drake. Sam had reached his prime as a naval aviator, and was the hottest ticket in town. When he strolled through the ship halls? Douchey, power-tripping boat O-4s got out of his way.*

So, when he got that email from the Noddiks? He'd just assumed it was more fruitless aviation headhunting, like the many agencies that had reached out and asked if he was interested in becoming their Chief of Taxiing, TOLD Data Supervisor, or even that Director of Preflighting proposal from Delta; thus, he deleted the offer promptly.

But in the months that followed, squadron dynamics unfathomably became about the rise of Juice, and 'Nickels' started to feel like old news. When Juice won the most recent 'Good Dude Award' at the annual CVW-5 celebration ceremonies, the changing of the guard hit a thunderous note. That night, out of drunken rage and inebriated curiosity, Sam dug into his deleted folder—just to see if the email was still there—and, if so, what these Noddik guys really had to offer. After a few email exchanges, he found out how incredible the money, opportunity, and prestige the job offered was. He never intended to take it, but the temptation was certainly there. And with every excellent SFWT event Juice had... every mention of him being a 'Good Dude'... and every day Sam went unthanked for the previous efforts he'd given—the same types of effort that Juice was now getting praised for? He communicated with the Noddiks more and more, getting closer and closer to taking The Deal they'd proposed...

Today, Sam had reached his breaking point. As soon as the internet got back up, and this EMCON bullshit was over, he was going to send the Noddiks his official message of intent to defect and sign with them.

As he packed all his dirty clothes in a bag, grabbed two Tide pods, and prepared for the long trek back toward self-serve laundry, he looked around the room at the pictures of him and his friends: One of him and CP in the hangar bay gym where Sam was going for his max bench, and the should-have-been-spotting CP was clearly distracted by some Latina smokeshow in tight leggings using the hip adductor 'good girl/bad girl' machine; one of JABA teaching him how to make a JMPS mission load 'read-only' – an authentic Drake and Lil Yachty moment – so that nobody saved over it with some asinine load like 'WeTUA BFM 3Aug;' and one of him and Low T in port at the Manila pool – Sam with his shirt off and a Corona, Low T with an oatmeal-colored sweater on and a bowl of Special K – yet both friends beaming with happiness.

This is crazy, *Sam thought.* Can I really leave these guys? Can I really abandon all this—because of one uprising douchebag? Pull yourself together, Nickels—you're just irritated at this shitty day. Things will be ok. You know what?! I'll bet once I get my laundry done—a fresh set of clean clothes and sheets—I'll be feeling just fine again, and the woes of this morning will be long gone! Yeah, that's right! Sorry, Noddiks— Nickels isn't going *anywhere*!

With a giant bag of clothes, Sam set sail for the agonizing five-minute journey to self-serve laundry – still a bit annoyed and dispirited – but hopeful that he was merely experiencing a temporary dip in morale, with nowhere to go emotionally but up. He was confident that he'd be feeling much *better and satisfied with his career situation after he just accomplished a simple, basic life necessity like laundry...*

~

"Nickels, you gotta send backup; we can't hold these guys off!" >SADCLAM<'s panicked voice pled through the J-dial phone.

"CLAM, Sam, picture; and say status of waffle machine," Sam, the consummate SDO professional, responded clearly and concisely.

"There's more than thirty of these goons still in the wardroom, and the machine is currently smoking from working in overdrive. We're short on batter, and—WOAH!" He abruptly stopped transmitting.

"CLAM?" Sam asked with concern. "CLAM, respond!"

"Sorry, Sam, that was a close one!" Houben finally got back, talking a bit quieter, as Rowland exhaled a sigh of relief. "One of them just threw a Smart Start cereal pack near my position, yelling, 'Give us more CTC!' Nickels, these guys are relentless, and my conference room coordinates may soon be compromised. Me and the GQ

Crew... we're doing our best, but these guys seriously *won't stop eating* — and they just started a new game of Risk!"

"What about the APG-47?" Sam asked, "Did it stop any of them?"

"Plenty, yes — but *some* of these guys... Nickels..." CLAM sighed in despair, and explained, "Their T levels are already rock bottom! The estrogen rays — they're not stopping these softbodies at all!" His words were whispered frenetically, amongst angry background harassing demands of 'When are the next batch of cookies going to be done, plebes!?', 'The ice cream station is out of Reeses and marshmallow fluff toppings — we need more NOW!', and 'Turn this sportsball off; put on the Sailor Moon marathon!'

Growing unnerved, Sam put his hand to his head in fear, signaling the severity of the situation to the rest of the bridge.

"What's going on?" Belichick asked. "Did the 47 stop them?"

Sam shook his head, "Afraid not, your highness. These... these *terrorist dweebs*," he said with frustration, nearly at a loss for words, "their testosterone levels are too low to be affected. The tech repping is growing momentum, as they're continuing to consume more time, space, and calories."

Belichick looked dismayed as he mumbled, "The rise of the betas — I feared this day would come... but I *never* imagined it would happen on my ship..."

Sam listened to more pleas for help from >SADCLAM<, and relayed to Belichick, "Do you guys have *any* reserve Cinnamon Toast Crunch in the supply dungeon by chance?!"

Belichick shook his head, "I'm afraid not, Nickels. We were really counting on that RAS to get us fully stocked for the next year, but..." he sighed in disappointment. "Just like the incessant demand Walter and Jesse faced for their trademark azure methamphetamines, I suppose we all underestimated the never-ending appetite and insulin resistance of these flabby freaks..." He grabbed the back of his head with both hands and groaned, "God *dammit*..."

"Rep, 206," CP's voice boomed through the radio.

"Just a second, CLAM; CP's calling," Sam switched frequencies on the PICT machine to button 18. "CP, it's Nickels — how's the FADEC looking?"

"It's now a full-on ENG caution, with the right engine downgraded to THRUST," CP said. "I need to land — even *if* someone was airborne, there's no way I could possibly intercept them this way."

Everyone on the bridge started to crowd around the radio, as one does in a ready room where an emergency is occurring. Brady stared at the radio intently and focused, as if he was able to see the answer through the transmitter. Racking his brain of NATOPS knowledge, he eventually offered up, "Ask him if he can tell what percent between 40 and 90 he thinks he's limited to."

Growing further stressed, Belichick scoffed, "Good grief, Tom, how's he supposed to—"

"Your excellency, where is the football?" Sam interrupted.

"Uhh... this one?" Belichick presented the 28-3 comeback ball that he'd kept tucked close to his ribs like a baby.

Sam shook his head, "Negative; we need a PCL, pronto."

Belichick looked uncertain, before muttering, "Yeah... uhh... we had a shortage of sticky paper, and... well, long story short: we have a bunch on order..."

"No!" JABA shouted out. "But Coach—for the legality of airborne aircraft... if the Olympic organizers find out—"

"I misinterpreted the rules again, ok?!" Belichick grumbled.

"Which rule?" Sam asked, slightly confused and disappointed. "The one that said, 'You *shall* have an up-to-date PCL on hand for all flight operations'?!"

Belichick glowered at him, paused—annoyed once again—and eventually forced out some grumbling along the lines of "... thought it said '*should*'..."

CP transmitted, "Guys, I need a game plan soon. I'm quickly approaching deck state plus five passes!"

Thinking critically—striving to remember the book—Sam radioed back, "CP, give me one minute—I can nearly picture the yellow pages..."

Brady put his hands on his hips. "Damn, I can almost remember this one too, but..." he threw his hands up, "I just can't think of the practicable solution!"

Wait a minute... practicable? No... practical... *That's it!* "Tom, you genius!" Sam exclaimed, before grabbing the radio. "CP, with a thrust advisory, NATOPS is telling you to land as soon as *practical*—and with *half* flaps." Sam continued to talk Andrew through the various landing decisions—and the intricacies of the incredibly complicated dual-engine landing—all from *memory*. Such an act would be illegal in some air wings, and frowned upon by many CAGs—but Sam recited the procedure like he was the one who *wrote* it. He even rattled off the various warnings and cautions—with zero error—to include reminding CP not to (normally) attempt a FADEC reset, and that his nozzle may be in a non-standard position after trapping, and to keep that in mind and consider minimal braking application while taxiing to his parking spot.

"Incredible!" Belichick shouted.

"He's not even looking at a book!" Brady remarked in shock. "How does he know?"

JABA grinned. "Because like Bo Jackson knew football... Nickels KNOWS admin."

To top it all off, Sam was high-SA enough to cater his information to the pilot he was talking to, and thus, didn't even bother insulting CP's ball-flying skills by asking about a hook-skip game plan. It was magical, quintessential, eye-watering CRM—

344

the kind the Navy would include in Instrument Ground School slides for centuries to come.

CP audibly gave an exhale of relief over the radio, and acknowledged, "Thanks, Nickels. I'm feeling much more confident, comfortable, and in-control after that clutch book-reading. Wrap the waist and make a ready-deck; I'm coming aboard."

Sam looked over to Belichick, who clenched his jaw, tweaked his neck a bit, and said, "Sam, I'm not gonna sugarcoat it... we're very short on yellow shirt bodies right now, given all the assets going toward GQ and fighting this..." he threw his hands up in annoyance and scoffed, using a term inconsistent with his slang knowledge, "... this 'Weeb-ageddon.' If that Pearl kid lands, do you expect me to just *trust* him to taxi on an open flight deck without somebody directing his every move?! The SOP is clear: *Any* jet movement, turn, or evolution requires the supervision of somebody wearing a yellow shirt!"

Sam, Tom, JABA, and FISTY's lifeless eyes all looked to the Captain with anticipation—anticipation and *determination*. Sensing the moment, Sam asked, "My liege... aren't you tired of the boat dictating all these silly rules and regulations, halting efficiency in the name of mechanized insanity?" He pointed to himself. "Even as someone who's dedicated *my* soul to the holy book of NATOPS—even *I* know there's a time and place to deviate. Come on, Coach. Just like you did with Malcolm Butler and the Pats—can't you trust your men not to just land the plane... but also *taxi* the plane? For once, Captain, can't we just use our brains, incorporate some reasonable man theory, and buy the *tiniest* sliver of risk—use the *slightest* bit of courage—to give us the *chance* to incorporate some goddamn innovation and logic in this job?!"

Belichick stared at him. "Captain Rowland... you're asking me to *knowingly* deviate from an instruction... *without* a misinterpretation loophole of plausible deniability?!" And yet, softening his expression, understanding the urgency to raise his flight deck ALR, the old coach gave a half-smirk and murmured, "Fuck it—bring him aboard."

Smiling at the coach as he pumped his fist, Sam held the PICT button down and coolly said, a couple of octaves lower than usual, "CP? Charlie." He switched back over to his J-dial, expertly managing multiple radios like a fucking SDO legend, and asked, "CLAM, what's the SITREP?"

Amongst plenty of tech reps heavily mouth-breathing and bitching in the background, CLAM whispered, "Sam... they're *in* the conference room! The chocolate chip toppings are now gone, and the soda machine is out of syrup! The CSs are being verbally assaulted, as the contractors are now complaining about the lack of *canned corn and seed oil-doused Brussels sprouts!* Even the undercover unhealthy foods are being consumed in mass by these barbarians! I need to change posits *now,* or else—"

"Hey! Guys, one of those in-shape, alpha male jocks is over here!" a voice yelled out. "I bet you think you're pretty cool, don't you?!" it continued, taunting, "Probably even used to play *sports*... what a fascist *loser*."

Another egged on, "Guys like you thought you were *soooo tough* when you used to throw guys like us in lockers, trash cans, and girls' bathrooms... Well, look who's got the power now, big man!"

And a third, more nasally voice than the rest, cried out, "Ohh check it out, my fellow party members—he's got a *wedding ring* on! Hey everyone, this guy's probably *made intercourse* with a female! *Fuck* this guy—let's get him!"

With a gut-wrenching click, the phone lost connection. "CLAM?" Sam called out nervously. "CLAM?! >SADCLAM<, please respond!"

Nothing.

"Sam, tell me he's alright?!" JABA pleaded with concern.

Sam just shook his head and bit his fist, attempting to hide his fear. "Guys..." he said solemnly, "This is getting out of hand... I can only do so much as SDO. We need to figure out a new plan *quick*, or else we're not gonna even have a *chance* to strike back..." He looked up at the captain. "Who are we sending out for the MARSTRIKE, m'lordship?" Signaling to Brady, he asked, "Tom, are you taking this one?"

Brady shook his head. "Sam, I'd love to, but... I *can't*. We need to fly a specific low-level route in order to stay below the radar, and... well... nobody has flown this route in the past 60 days to ensure its safety..." He pointed to his LT bars. "Per the CVW-5 SOP, it's going to require a verification flight by an O-4 or above..."

The entire room drew their eyes toward Captain Rowland, who understood what they were implying. He quickly interjected, "But guys... I'm the SDO! You can't fly on your SDO day—that's... that's heresy! Who will be the direct representative of the skipper if I'm gone?"

Belichick gave a smug grunt and said, "I think I can take that one."

"But I've already set up my flawless roll 'em timing—with a perfectly scheduled and coordinated playlist set until then! And my CAC... I'm already logged into SHARP and everything..." he shook his head and insisted, "No—it's not meant to be me. Guys, I already had my grand reluctant acceptance of the call in Phase 2; wouldn't it be cliché and overdone for me to fly and be the courageous airborne hero *again*?! *Surely*, somebody else is waiting for their call to action—somebody who hasn't done anything too remotely exciting yet in this story, and is worthy of a big scene..." His eyes narrowed, as his lips curled into a sly smile, and he continued, "Maybe somebody who has conveniently *just* put the finishing touches on his VR programming revival for a fallen hero..."

"Done!" JABA called out, only half-paying attention to Sam's monologue, as he doffed the VR headset. "The coding for FISTY's revitalization scenario is complete!

Now, just to get him situated in a chair—" JABA's smile became a look of happy confusion. "Guys, what are you all looking at?"

Sam slowly nodded, smiling, as he handed the strike-loaded DTD to JABA. "Mark... it's gotta be you."

"Me?" JABA asked, perplexed, as he looked at the DTD. Still smiling and oblivious, he asked, "Sam, what are you...?" but stopped as his eyes went to the monitor above Sam's head.

Rowland had already gone through the process of copying and pasting a new line onto the screen-mirrored schedule behind his SDO desk—and expeditiously cleaned up all the annoying and awkward formatting lines, thanks to his previous life as a Hall of Fame Skeds O. The new line, written in red font, called for

EVT: 1D1 Side: 206 ETE: 3.0 MSN: STK C/S: CHIPPY 69 Pilot: Buck

JABA looked around, pointed to himself, and asked, "... *Me*?"

"*You*," Sam responded with a smile. "As soon as CP lands, you're gonna hot switch, gas up, and *go*. I'm gonna call Bravo Romeo right now to get the air plan change in."

"Guys... you're punking me, right? This is crazy..." JABA pointed to the SDO radio. "The jet has a FADEC issue... Sam told us not to do resets... *right*?"

Tom Brady walked over and clasped JABA on the shoulder. "He mentioned we shouldn't *normally* do them—but Mark, abnormal adversity presents rare opportunity... and I'd call this moment anything *but* normal." Brady smiled, picked his JHMCS up off the floor, and re-engaged his focus on the theme park tycoon. "Like the legendary Pat Riley's dad once told him: Every now and then, somewhere, some place, some time, you're going to have to plant your feet, stand firm, and make a point about who you are and what you believe in; and when that time comes? You simply have to do it." He pointed to himself. "I had my chance when I replaced an injured Drew Bledsoe in 2001." Gesturing toward Captain Belichick, he continued, "Coach had *his* when the Patriots offered him the head coaching job just one day after he accepted the same position in the Jets' organization—and he subsequently quit New York *at* his introductory press conference. And now, JABA, this is *your* time." He handed his JHMCS to Buck. "Go kick its ass."

Growing more serious, now understanding it was *not* a joke, JABA asked, "But even despite all that—our SOP... it requires an O-4 or above... I'm merely just a—"

"Merely Just Another Buck Angel," Belichick said as he stepped forward and addressed the young man. "The Rowland kid was right, with what he said earlier—sometimes you *do* need to deviate from signed instructions in order to use some good old-fashioned common sense. And JABA..." the Hall of Fame coach smiled, "I know your lineage... I know your work ethic... and I know the leadership that resides in that Good Dude heart of yours. O-4 is but a title—and perhaps you think of it as a rank of power-hungry, selfish, bottom-line-obsessed spool-mongers..." Belichick paused, and put his palms together, fingers on his lips—before clasping his hands and dropping them, continuing, "But if that *is* what you believe—then why shouldn't somebody like *you* vie to break that trend? The golden oak leaves need a hero, JABA—and all too often, when the call is made? Those who are most reluctant are the ones we truly *need* in power. Opportunities only come to your door every so often—and if you're not brave enough to answer? They'll eventually stop knocking..."

Realizing this was truly happening, JABA grew very solemn as he paused... then eventually bowed to Belichick and said, "Sir... I will do it. I will fill the role of the striker." He ascended from his bow and raised a finger, stating, "But just understand *this*, Skipper: I *may* be acting as an O-4 in order to fly this route... but do *not* call me Lieutenant Commander Buck—that is an honor that I once feared would be forced upon me, yet now is a naive fantasy to think I could ever attain. I gave up my chance to earn the glorious O-4 and department head billets—and as a result? I must pay the price for eternity; the price of never knowing what could have been..." He looked away, pained, then deadlocked Captain Belichick's eyes. "Can you *promise* me that, sir? Can you *promise* that you will not address me, treat me, or even *think* of me as one of the honorary O-4s in this United States Navy?"

Belichick sighed, looking earnest, and nodded his head slightly to oblige, "As much as it pains me... I can."

JABA closed his eyes and gave a single, slow nod in return. "Nickels—how's that air plan change coming?" He opened his eyes and looked to the SDO desk.

As if by divine magic, the phone rang a moment after—which Sam immediately answered with his lightning-quick SDO reflexes, swiftly jabbing the speaker button. "USS Ship SDO, Captain Rowland speaking, how may I help you sir, ma'am, or chief?" he stated professionally toward the J-dial.

"Hey, it's MIJT at Bravo Romeo—your air plan change was..."

The room waited with bated breath.

"... approved."

The guys cheered with hushed cries, Brady excitedly whispering, "Come on!!" with a fist pump—yet JABA remained stoic, closing his eyes again.

"Awesome, thanks!" Sam responded and hung up.

"But Sam..." JABA reminded him, "You know it's not official until..."

The phone rang again, and Sam immediately hit the speaker button even *quicker* this time. "USS Ship SDO, Captain Rowland speaking, how may—"

Belichick threw his hand forward and gave Sam a stern look—followed by a slight smirk. Sam loved it. *Fuck yeah—he really* is *a no-nonsense guy!*

"Good morning, sir. This is Airman DeMann from Air Operations, calling with an air plan change."

The room grew tense again. "Go ahead," Sam said calmly.

"New line added; 1D1 will be a strike, and will be hot switching from 0D1."

Now the men all roared exuberantly, Brady screaming, "Let's fucking *go!*" as Sam responded, "Ok, got it, thanks dude!" and hung up.

As CP approached the ship with his FADEC issue, being talked down by BCB and other Paddles, Sam and the others watched on the plat cam with full confidence that he'd come aboard safely—thanks to the angels in white. Once he hit the groove, CP flew a damn near perfect pass (*Hah, Phase 2 would've been a lot less exciting for the reader if* he'd *been in my spot,* Sam thought with a chuckle). And unfathomably, despite no yellow shirts there to guide him along the empty deck, CP managed to raise his hook and taxi flawlessly from the LA to the six pack.

With the jet safely on deck, Belichick beckoned his brave MARSTRIKE player, "JABA—the time is upon us. Godspeed... *Lieutenant* Buck."

His face all business, JABA nodded sharply, picked up his flight bag, threw the DTD in his shoulder pocket, carried Brady's JHMCS under his armpit, grabbed a random RMM—as Sam had diligently wiped them all clean at the beginning of his SDO shift—and told the room, "Everyone—thank you for this opportunity. I may be just an O-3, but I promise to treat this flight, vet this low-level, and conduct this strike with every bit of precision, courage, and tenacity as if I were lucky enough to be wearing the golden oak leaves." He looked to his compatriots and addressed them all individually. "Tom, you know how to handle the VR system once it's rebooted and ready for action. Captain Belichick, I'll stay in comms with you as long as range allows throughout the evolution. And Nickels," he paused a moment, "don't give up the ship. We've all come a long way to get here... but *nobody's* journeyed further or grew more than you. The toughest challenge may be yet to come... but the only ones who can truly stop indomitable Dambusters like us are *ourselves*—and our false, fearful, limiting beliefs in our capabilities. We can do this, Sam. We can bring back the glory of the old days—and we *will*."

Without waiting for a response, JABA exited the bridge door to gear up and walk to his jet, as Belichick remarked, "I'd run through a brick wall, scale the tallest mountain, or even *smile* in a press conference for that man. The Navy needs more Good Dudes like JABA in leadership roles."

Sam smiled. Belichick was right—JABA *is* a damn Good Dude. Sometimes, Sam felt, even 'Gooder' than himself in ways—and strangely enough, that didn't bother him. *Who* cares *who the spectators think the Goodest Dude is? Because when you're a true team, suffering in the trenches of the arena together? Only the Diseased seek competition from within—the Healthy are too busy fighting as one, climbing as one, and* thriving *as one.*

~

Doctor Suabedissen waited outside Robo-Hinge's office at attention, after doing the proper door knocking procedures demanded of the O-4's underlings. He felt a little bad, knowing he would have to turn LT Ward in to his boss for an attempted mutiny — but it was the right thing to do, as commanded by the Noddik Code of Conduct.

"ENTER, PLEBE!" Hinge called from within.

Suabedissen carefully opened the door, bowing as he entered. He marched to Hinge's desk with his head tilted down — abstaining from eye contact — and then did an about-face to show his back to his superior.

"YOU MAY SPEAK, DOCTOR. NOW, WHY HAVE YOU INTERRUPTED ME FROM MY WORK?" the DH demanded to know.

Hinge called it 'work,' but Karl could clearly hear the D&D Nyharu region world map music playing from his laptop. 'It's ok,' he told himself internally, 'He's probably just taking a break from busy O-4 duties, and it's none of my business. Plus, I applaud his choice in gaming!' But also — as much as the doctor tried to forget it — Ward's final comment before departing was still lingering in his mind...

"Sir," Suabedissen started, "I came to inform you of some disturbing news regarding the —" but he stopped short when he noticed the packed duffel bag at the back of Hinge's office. "Uh, sir? Are you going somewhere? I wasn't tracking any outbound flights today aside from the COD..." Of *course* the COD had been on his mind all day long — he'd been looking forward to this trip for *months*.

"HOW DARE YOU, THAT IS NONE OF YOUR BUSINESS!" Hinge scolded — before taking the chance to feed his ego: "... BUT IF YOU *MUST* KNOW... YOURS TRULY WAS INVITED TO TODAY'S DUNGEONS AND DRAGONS GUILDMASTER STAN CELL MEETING IN SAN FRANCISCO — FOR TIER ALPHA, LEVEL 100 AND ABOVE PLAYERS *ONLY*."

Suabedissen's eyes lit up. "Sir! That's fantastic! Congratulations! First of all, I didn't even know you were a D&D regular — and secondly, I am *so* pumped that you'll be CODing out there with me! We're going to have so much fun designing the new Tac D&E! I can't wait to introduce you to the guys from my guild and —"

"NEGATIVE, SUABEDISSEN — I CANCELED THE COD WHEN THE PILOT NEGLECTED TO SIGN HIS EMAIL WITH 'VERY RESPECTFULLY' AND INSTEAD JUST TYPED 'V/R.' DISGUSTING... THERE IS *NO* ROOM FOR THAT KIND OF DISRESPECT TOWARD A LIEUTENANT COMMANDER!" he scathed with venom. "I AM TAKING A JET TO THE SEMINAR."

Quickly going through a mental inventory of available jets, Suabedissen's heart leaped as he realized, "Sir, the only jet we have on deck is a Foxtrot! LCDR Robo-Hinge, are you..." he felt nearly emotional as he asked, "Are you saying we will arrive as a *crew*?!" Attempting to reference the latest thing he read on the 'Hip Slang' Reddit, he exclaimed, "That is *so* rizz, sir! Imagine how horny those females will get when we show up looking so drip—"

But Robo-Hinge scoffed and interrupted, "DOCTOR, SURELY YOU ARE JOKING?!"

Suabedissen laughed nervously. "Well, I mean, they might not be the *hottest* of specimen, but I'd have to fancy that at least one or two ladies will be—"

"NOT THAT, YOU STUPID SIMP," Hinge fired back. "WE CAN'T *BOTH* GO. WHO IS GOING TO WATCH OVER THE READY ROOM AND MAKE SURE NO MONITORS ARE STOLEN? AND BESIDES, THERE IS BOUND TO BE PLENTY OF PAPERWORK TO DO AFTER WE WIN THESE OLYMPICS—THUS, I'M PUTTING YOU IN CHARGE OF ALL THAT BULLSHIT. BUT DON'T WORRY—I'LL BE BACK TO DO THE CHAMPION'S INTERVIEWS WITH THE HOT BUSTY PRESSWOMEN BOTS DURING THE CELEBRATION CEREMONY."

"What?!" the doctor cried out in disbelief. "But sir... *please*... surely somebody else can..." He stammered as he pleaded, "Sir, I promise not to say a word, touch anything, or pull any yellow-and-black handles back there!"

"NO, DOCTOR!" Hinge yelled, growing angry. "THERE IS ONLY ROOM FOR *ONE* PERSON TO LEAVE THIS SHIP FOR THIS FUN TIME IN SAN FRANCISCO—AND SEEING HOW IT WAS *SUCH* A GOOD DEAL, THERE WAS NO WAY I COULD LEAVE IT FOR A JO OR UNDERLING OF ANY SORT." He gave Suabedissen a pompous look. "AND, OH, BY THE WAY... SHOWING UP TO SUCH A PRESTIGIOUS EVENT WHILE *DUALED UP*? I DON'T KNOW IF YOU KNOW THIS, KARL, BUT I'M A SINGLE-SEAT BIG-MEAT ALPHA FOR LIFE. THAT AFT COCKPIT WILL BE *REMOVED* FROM THE JET BEFORE A PEON LIKE YOU JOINS ME IN THE SKIES. PLUS, IF THERE *ARE* ANY DOUBLE-X CHROMOSOMES THERE, YOU MUST REALIZE THAT MY RANK AND STATURE *ALONE* WILL GET THEM *FAR* MORE STIMULATED AND EAGER TO PROCREATE THAN ANY OF THE PATHETIC ICEBREAKERS OR PEACOCKING METHODS *YOU* WOULD'VE ATTEMPTED. SO..." he glared at Suabedissen's frail back, "I GUESS WHAT I'M TRYING TO SAY, DOCTOR, IS THAT I'M SORRY, BUT..." his lip curled up to a slight smile, "YOU CAN SUCK *MY* DICK, YOU BETA CUCK."

Suabedissen was speechless, and nearly in tears. "Hinge... I don't believe this! You *know* how excited I've been for this conference! And now you're going to take it away from me so that you can go and just... *flaunt* your D&D status? *I* was going to talk about follow-on expansion packs and give recommendations on how they can upgrade the ShadowHog Slayer sidequest series and build upon Ramuth, the magical floating city of the Heavens! Plus, I have *so* many E-friends I was looking forward to meeting, and..." he stopped before mentioning his hopes that MyLittlePonyXoXo88 might be there, despite her current troubled state. Which reminded him... "How long have you even *played* the game, anyway? What guild do you belong to? What's your user name?"

"THAT'S ENOUGH OUT OF YOU, DOCTOR!" Hinge boomed with rage. "I'M GOING, YOU'RE NOT, AND THAT'S THE BOTTOM LINE—UNDERSTAND?"

The doctor, his back still facing his superior, said nothing.

"I'M LOOKING FOR A 'YES, SIR,' DOCTOR," Hinge chastised.

"... Yes, sir..." Fighting off sobs, Suabedissen was sure that his boss knew of the Foxtrot's loadout, but felt obligated to inform him, "Sir, you *do* know that jet is loaded up with a live Air-to-Surface missile, right? The AS-131 KILLSHIP?"

"*SIR, YOU DO KNOW THAT JET IS LOADED UP WITH A LIVE AIR-TO-SUR-FACE MISSILE, RIGHT?*" Hinge imitated with a whiny, nasally voice. "SHUT THE FUCK UP, BITCH. YES, I KNOW; AND NO, I DON'T GIVE A SHIT. I'M TAKING THAT JET, AND I'LL JUST TELL THE AIRPORT UPON LANDING THAT I DIDN'T KNOW IT WAS THERE, OR THAT IT'S INERT OR SOMETHING. IT'LL BE FINE."

His lip trembling, Suabedissen was now grasping at straws. "Are you sure you can afford the convention fee? They will only accept in-game rupees for payment..."

Egregiously insulted, Hinge raised his arms and nearly grabbed at Suabedissen's throat as he yelled, "DOCTOR, WHAT DO YOU TAKE ME FOR—A PEASANT?! I'LL HAVE YOU KNOW THAT I WILL SHORTLY BE THE RICHEST PLAYER IN THE ENTIRE GAME, AS SOON AS THIS SIMP 'P-WORDSLAYER69' FINALLY PAYS ME THE MONEY HE PLEDGED. THAT IDIOT IS IN LOVE WITH SOME WHORE THAT I SOLD OFF FOR EVEN *MORE* COIN." Calming down, but still full of fury, he mocked, "'*AFFORD THE CONVENTION FEE*'... PLEASE, YOU PITIFUL CLOWN. I HAVE SO MANY RUPEES THAT THE PROGRAMMING CODE IN THE GAME CAN'T EVEN *DEPICT* THE LAST NUMERICAL CHARACTER OF MY WALLET STATUS. SO YES..." he scoffed cockily, "I *THINK* I CAN AFFORD A LITTLE ENTRY FEE."

Suabedissen's heart nearly stopped.

"NOW, BEFORE I GO, WHAT DID YOU WANT TO TELL ME ABOUT THAT 'DISTURBING NEWS' OR WHATEVER DUMBASS SHIT YOU WERE SAYING?"

The doctor stood in silence, the gears spinning rapidly in his brain.

"WELL? I DON'T HAVE ALL DAY!"

Suabedissen closed his eyes. "Nothing."

"WHAT?!" Hinge yelled out. "DOCTOR, YOU ARE TRULY AS INCOMPE-TENT, LOW-SA, AND INVOLUNTARILY CELIBATE AS THEY COME. NOW BE-GONE!"

As Suabedissen started marching out, Hinge quickly added, "OH, AND ALSO, SEND ME UPDATES ON THE OLYMPICS EVERY HOUR ON THE HOUR — DON'T EXPECT A RESPONSE. NOW *OFF WITH YOU!*"

Suabedissen closed the door and sprinted to his room — every leg muscle nearly cramping up en route, as he had not demonstrated this ferocity of pace nor felt this kind of lactic acid buildup since he ran from the tennis and softball jocks in high school gym class. When he finally arrived back to his room, huffing and puffing, he immediately opened his laptop and booted up D&D, typing in his email address and password. When he signed in, his main profile screen read the same as it always did when he logged on: "Welcome, P-WordSlayer69!"

Suabedissen wiped his residual tears, pushed up his glasses, popped the collar on his lab coat — and said aloud, "You've fucked with the *wrong* Level 146 Necromancer from the Meribian Village of Magic, bitch..."

~

While CP logged his SHARP at the desk, Sam paced around nervously, praying to hear from >SADCLAM< — unsure if Houben had been able to escape the tech reps, or if they'd captured and held him hostage; or worse...

"I'm not saying it's likely, but... god, I've seen these Boeing guys do some grotesque, inhumane shit — like, worse-than-Tuco-Salamanca-or-Gus-Fring shit," Belichick woefully explained. "I'm sure you're familiar with the incidents of Tailhook 2026?"

Sam shook his head. "I'm not... after joining the Noddiks, I did everything possible to avoid news from back home. What happened?"

Captain Belichick sighed heavily. "It was... *appalling*. It started like any normal Tailhook — a bunch of flightsuits getting wild off Miller Lite kegs, before calming down a bit to listen to the Air Boss give some softball speech spoken in platitudes, then asking him questions about retention and pay that he unsuccessfully deflects with non-answers — silly debauchery, really.

"Throughout the evening, there were plenty of tech reps and contractors working the side booths — handing out free lanyards and drinks, trying to sell overpriced watches, and in general having a good time — and it was all typical fun and games, really, for the majority of the Friday night. But then..."

Belichick had to stop to compose himself, before explaining in excruciating detail, "Some of the Boeing guys snuck into one of the squadron admins, and well... they completely drained the room of any and all fighter spirit. They started talking to people about The Real Housewives, The Bachelorette, Keeping Up with the Kardashians, and a bunch of other girly reality TV shows. They removed the cups from the beer die tables and whipped out a bunch of Yu-Gi-Oh cards, making an iron cross of head-to-head dueling battles. A couple took out their Nintendo Switches and started showing pilots the latest thing they'd built in Minecraft, or how they had all one million or so 'Korok seeds,' or whatever the hell you call them, in that Princess Zendaya game. One was even caught asking one of the helo girls if she wanted to come to his hotel room and watch some Naruto anime with him. These... these *dweebs*..." Belichick gave a look of repulsion, "they ruined the entire night—the whole *weekend,* actually. Everybody sobered up with these buzzkills around. The fun sumo wrestling suits were replaced by watching these doughy NARPs nearly have heart attacks while grappling with one other. And the next morning at the pool party? The place was a ghost town, only occupied by these pasty keyboard warriors and their poolside Smirnoff Ices—which, of course, got them all plastered, leading to them pool wrestling again. No chicks—just the *geekiest* men you've ever seen. By noon, they were burnt tomato-red, despite wearing plenty of way-too-high SPF sunscreen—the place reeked of it for months. They passed out in lounge chairs, leaving the employees responsible for carrying them back to their room—yes, *single* room, as they'd all elected to share a total of two beds and a couch for the 10 or so of them. And by this point, most pilots had already left for Fallon or Lemoore—*far* desirable places in comparison. In the command climate surveys to follow, many aviators referenced *this* ruined weekend as the reason they decided to leave the Navy..." Belichick winced and raised his hands, "Sam, please don't make me talk about this anymore. It's a very dark time in our illustrious community's history..."

Sam shook his head in disbelief. "This can't be real. That is... *horrendous*..."

CP nodded, "It's true, Nickels. I'd heard stories, but... *never* in that detail. A friend of mine was there; he said one of the tech reps asked if he could try his shit-hot flight suit on, and suggested that my buddy could wear his company polo, so that they could 'switch identities' for the night?! What?!" He shook his head, cringing in extreme confusion at the awkward and absurd scenario. "Another wanted my buddy to tell all the girls that this Lockheed Martin dweeb was the long-lost spawn of Shmi Skywalker... and then some Boeing software dork asked him if he'd split a bag of Cheetos and Mountain Dew Baja Blast with him..." Looking disturbed, CP insisted, "I wish I were making this up... like, who even comes *up* with those ideas?! It was just weird, weird shit, man."

Looking into the distance, past where Tom Brady was adamantly watching the VR system's restart timer, Sam lamented, "CLAM... poor guy... they're probably driving him crazy down there..." he looked up at Captain Belichick. "Sir, we've got to go down and check on Chris. CP and I—we need to save him—as he once saved me..." he said quietly, remembering that scene from long ago in chapter 7. He gestured between the GOAT and his SDO post, asking, "Tom, can you watch the desk for me? I won't let CLAM be subjected to that kind of torture—I can't leave a brother behind!"

Tom stood up and affirmed, "You're goddamn right I can, Nickels. Coach and I will communicate with JABA, and I'll get FISTY spun up on the VR machine once it's ready." He looked over at the machine's connected monitor, which now read, 'Hi... We're setting things up for you... Leave everything to us... This won't take long... Almost there... This might take several minutes...'

Sam nodded, "Thanks, Tom—you really are the GOAT."

Brady shrugged and smiled. "Just a kid from San Mateo, California."

"You ready, CP?" Sam asked his fellow Chippy.

CP nodded slowly. "Like taking out the trash or grabbing meals, sometimes the Good Dude move *is* to give up the desk and do the hard work yourself. Let's go DCK-AMR, Nickels."

"Dick hammer?"

"Directly confront and kick ass at max range," CP said with a mischievous smile.

Sam grinned and imitated Borat—incredibly poorly but poetically vintage: "I liiiiiiiike!"

The two ran out the door and down the ladderwells at completely unsafe speeds, while sliding down guardrails with the lack of professionalism that would've given ship's company senior chiefs life-threatening heart attacks.

~

Dr. Suabedissen stared at his open private chat windows, waiting for any indication of life—be it a message, an online icon, even just a 'typing' ellipses—from his one and only: MyLittlePonyXoXo88. Yet still nothing... He was sure the Troll of Trabia wouldn't have killed her—yet she was undoubtedly in some Princess Leia-type slave situation with that slob—and probably dressed accordingly, much to the delight of the doctor's imagination...

"No!" he shouted aloud, as he wiped his mind of that lewd fantasy. "There's no time for these juvenile thoughts—I need to save this damsel!" He scanned his inventory to make sure he had enough X-potions, hero drinks, and ultima stones prepared for the solo raid he was about to undergo. He double-checked his armor and weapon stats—they were nowhere near optimal for this kind of assault on the Trabia Bridge, but desperate times called for desperate measures. Karl was a man in love, and in danger of losing she who meant more than anything to—

"Huh?!" A strange animation covered his character profile. "Oh my god... it *can't* be..." He'd heard legends of this in-game feature before, but didn't believe his eyes — because it *couldn't* be true... could it?!

But sure enough, on his screen was a chat request from none other than MyLittlePonyXoXo88 — a *video* chat request. His arms shaking, he quickly looked in the mirror, ruffled his hands through his hair, pushed up his glasses, and ensured his collar was still popped. He gave a quick scan of the background to make sure no bottles of lotion or boxes of Kleenex were in sight. Lastly, he cleared his throat, gave himself one last mirror look down — finishing with a point and a wink to himself — and then *finally*, clicked 'Answer'...

~

Sam and CP descended to the 2nd deck and approached the wardroom from the port side, peeking through the porthole window to survey the scene. Sure enough, tables were jammed together, seating tech reps with long, unkempt hair, wearing oversized anime shirts and black cargo shorts, keeping their legs protected with tall white socks beneath their Crocs. It appeared to be some sort of ice cream social combined with a peacocking demonstration of value, as one dweeb was showing off a binder full of holographic Pokemon cards, while another dork was pulling up his various RuneScape profile character stats on his laptop, and a separate set of nerds were working together to build an advanced LEGO set of 'The Firespray' — formerly known as 'Boba Fett's Starship' — formerly known as the 'Slave 1' — before Disney took a butcher's knife to the franchise lore. A geek in a shirt that said 'I know HTML — How To Meet Ladies' was patrolling around the wardroom perimeter to ensure nobody could ruin their gathering.

"Nickels, look way back, at the family table," CP said, pointing through the window, "It's CLAM... and he — oh my gosh..."

Sam finally saw what CP was referring to... and his heart sank. It appeared that >SADCLAM< had been forced into the middle of a game of Munchkin Quest — and looked completely despondent, his eyes nearly glazed over. He and three other nerds took turns rolling dice and playing cards of Magma Sword attacks, Flameshield countermeasures, Tsunami napalm counter-countermeasures, and more elemental voodoo as they vied to be the first to reach level 10 and win the game, whilst losing precious Y-chromosomes in the process.

"What's he doing?" CP asked. "Was he brainwashed... *again?!*"

Noticing something odd, Sam pointed toward one of the nerds. "Look—the guy in the Pikachu hat—he's holding something under the table." Squinting and looking closer, Sam's eyes widened as he gasped. "CP... it's the APG-47—aimed *right* at CLAM's groin!"

"God dammit..." CP cursed, shaking his head, "I *knew* it was bad news when Chris brought that weapon of mass destruction into my gym... Nickels, we've got to find a way to save him before this train gets further off the tracks—look at CLAM's posture!"

Houben was leaning back with his neck slinking to the side, exhibiting a double chin by how lazily he was lounging—a bit of drool even seemed to be developing in the open mouth he was using as his primary respiratory airway.

"The man is *clearly* in a catabolic state, losing that hard-earned muscle mass and alpha status by the minute," CP explained. "We need to get him out of there before he falls victim to those fiends and stops having intuitive masculine impulses..." He paused and winced. "This could get really bad..."

"What?!" Sam asked nervously.

"Nickels..." CP shook his head. "Munchkin Quest, Pokemon cards, LEGO collections... they can be *very* addictive temptations once you're around them for too long. It's the tragic male fallacy, becoming enthralled by these childhood virginal fascinations. I saw it all the time at Flat Earth Fitness... you see a decently fit young gym rat—aspiring to be a 'huge jacked man'—asking me about the best creatine supplements for AOMs, the mysteries of pre-workout alchemy, and how to apply for a pilot spot in the Navy to fly jets. Then, one day, he improperly and invalidly tries to artificially alpha-enhance himself by making fun of the dweebs playing Magic: The Gathering at his college cafeteria. He goes over to taunt them—but then becomes curious about the cool-looking card design of the Soulless Knight. He asks a few questions, sees more cards, and wants to watch a round. The next thing you know? He's down 15 lbs of muscle and looking like a total softbody, snacking on Funyuns, chugging Mr. Pibb, and asking me what I knew about 'the P8 NFO lifestyle.'" CP kinked his neck in dismay.

"CLAM would never...!" Sam retorted, albeit with nervousness in his voice.

"Wouldn't he?!" CP responded harshly. "It happens to the best of us, Sam. Videogames, toys, and nerdy collectibles—we are as prone to becoming overly consumed by them as we are to becoming overly foolish when chasing women. Look at FISTY—he paid $10,000 for Tom Brady's game-used Super Bowl XLIX socks! We're simple-brained barbarians after all—with some damn weak Achilles' heels."

Sam peeked back through the window, and noticed >SADCLAM< looking through his deck of playable cards, rolling the dice for his turn, and showing the *slightest* bit of a fist pump in reaction to the die's outcome. "Did you see that?!" Sam breathlessly asked CP.

"Afraid so, Nickels," Preul responded glumly.

Trying to think quickly, Sam proposed, "CP, let's go to the scullery and pose as cooks. We can borrow those CS' TDY polos to go undercover—and when the right moment strikes, we can attack before CLAM gets corrupted any further by these mouth-breathing terrorists."

"Hmmm..." CP pondered, "Not your worst idea ever, Samuel. Khaki presence running the ship's agenda? Big XO would be nodding smugly."

Sam grinned, and the two ran to the starboard side of the boat, where they could enter the kitchen directly. Upon their route, Sam noticed a hallway J-dial. "I'll meet up with you in a minute—let me brief Captain Belichick on our plan."

CP nodded and continued running as Sam quickly dialed the ready room, to which Belichick answered, "What."

"Uhh, your honor, it's me, Sam Rowland. Here's the SITREP—"

"Nickels!" Belichick sounded panicked. "Thank god you called—it's JABA; we forgot to schedule his low level in DCAST—we need to contact the FAA ASAP!"

Shit... I didn't even think *about that!* "Dammit! Unscheduled area usage... and he won't be squawking, either! That could be a *huge* safety of flight at worst, and a blatant administrative violation at best!"

"Bingo," Belichick said, "We'd be forced to forfeit the Olympics, and that'd be the *least* of our concerns—we'd all be out of jobs with an admin gaffe this egregious!"

Sam cursed under his breath. "What can I do, sir?"

"We need to find off-ship phone access to call the FAA and *request* a late scheduling—god help us if they don't grant it—but all the POTS lines are off because of EMCON! Sam, you need to contact someone *immediately* to find a working landline! Recommend you try CAG ADP—and *hurry!*" the captain emphasized. "We lost comm reception with JABA before we realized the error; if we don't get his name in DCAST, Nickels, it's all over!"

Sam assured him, "I'm on it, my master," and quickly hung up, before swearing at himself for yet another awkward interaction with his fellow O-6. He dialed CAG ADP at x5683—the number still burned in his brain from *decades* of repeatedly dealing with them—and prayed for the one-in-a-million shot that they'd be able to provide him useful assistance and a solution...

~

Doctor Suabedissen's jaw dropped as he laid eyes on the human form of My-LittlePonyXoXo88. She was in handcuffs, hair strewn all about, looking exhausted as she laid on the couch — and yet, she was *beautiful* to him. She may have been the princess of the ogres, but there was nothing ogre-ish about her human form. She looked more akin to an elven beauty: fit and angular, with the most vivid eyes, luscious lips, and — as Karl so eloquently thought and marveled at — phenomenal boobs. And while it was not a Princess Leia Episode VI outfit she was wearing, Karl instantly recognized the midriff-bearing white prisoner Padme outfit from Episode II. But most surprising of all to the doctor: despite looking tired and fatigued, defeat worn on her face — when she saw Karl? MyLittlePony put on a smile *so* warm that the doctor felt as drunk in love as young Anakin in Episode I.

Now, as to *why* she was wearing the outfit and handcuffed IRL, when it was merely her online avatar in peril? The doctor had no clue. She must have been real-time cosplaying in her own home — a *very* attractive quality in his eyes.

"P-word Slayer..." she said lovingly, "You're more handsome than I ever could've imagined. I love your glasses... they look so sophisticated."

Suabedissen grinned and blushed as he stumbled over his words, "Y-you look quite handsome too; err, I mean, really hot! Uhh..." he made a weird face, "Sorry... I meant... you're beautiful, your Highness." He bowed to the Ogre Princess.

She giggled. "Please, call me MLP, it's much easier to say — and type."

"Yes, ma'am — err, I mean... yes, MLP." He pushed up his glasses and asked, "What's going on? Where are you? Are you in danger?"

MLP's warm, radiant smile faded to a look of woe. "P-word Slayer... I'm afraid I don't have much time left... I was tricked by WizardOfAzkaban1337 and sold to the Troll of Trabia. But before he sold me, the WizardOfAzkaban took all my weapons, armor, EXP, key items... and he even raided my hidden cache of rupees, too." She shook her head, "I can't even afford to pay my in-game monthly subscription anymore. I've been robbed of any value and worth I ever had, all because of that evil Fire Knight..." she trailed off as tears began forming in her eyes.

"But you still have your beauty!" Suabedissen insisted, tearing up himself.

She covered her eyes, wiping tears away. "The Troll is off hunting humans atop the bridge right now, but when he's back, he plans to change my avatar to make me hideous and unrecognizable. I... I can't take that, P-word." She sniffed, paused, and then said, "I'm going to delete my account before the Troll can take any more of my dignity..."

"What?!" the doctor burst out incredulously. "B-but you can't! You shouldn't!... Princess... please don't...!"

She tried to smile, but her expression appeared grim. "P-word... you are so sweet..." She sighed heavily. "Sometimes, I wonder what life would've been like if I'd wed you instead..."

With teardrops streaming from his eyes and fogging his glasses, Karl wiped his face and said, "My lady... I've wondered that same thing since the day we hunted our first level 4 wild boar in the Woods of Wisperia..."

She laughed through her sniffs, and happily remarked, "You remembered..."

~

"S-8?!" Sam yelled into the phone. "Ok, hold up—I've already been passed around to every fucking 'S' number on the block, and now you're telling me it's S-8's responsibility to turn on access to the offboard POTS line?! I didn't even know than an 'S-8' existed! Jesus Christ, is there a supervisor I can talk to?!"

"Uhh, yes sir," the task deflector responded, "I suppose you could talk to Ensign Incompetent or Senior Chief Worthless."

"Ok... are they there?!" Sam asked patronizingly.

"Err... sorry... they're both in the smoke pit right now... but S-8 definitely should be able to help you."

Oh my fucking god... Sam cursed internally. "Can I get their J-dial?"

"Umm... yes, sir, it's 6481."

"Thank you," Sam muttered as he slammed the phone down and quickly dialed x6481, time of the extreme essence with the USS Ship's Olympic hopes hanging on his ability to reach the FAA.

He'd been running this phone rat race for twenty minutes now, initially calling CAG ADP, to which they didn't answer for thirty rings before somebody finally picked up and informed Sam that they didn't control the ship's telephone POTS lines—only offboard email access—and that he could try contacting DC Central. Unfortunately, the Engineering Officer of the Watch at DC Central was busy assuming all responsibility for casualties and narrating his cocaine-fueled tirade over the 1MC during GQ, and was thus unable to assist with any offboard phone access. The person on the phone recommended that Sam call S-5, since they owned the connection controls to turn the afloat line on and off. However, S-5 informed him that it actually wasn't their responsibility to manage the phone system on the boat—they just paid the bill—and that he should get in touch with S-3.

So... after an obscenely long string of deferred responsibilities, asking for senior supervisors, conversations with V-5 O-3s, trouble calls submitted by Tom Brady back at the SDO desk on the Gippernet, on-phone troubleshooting that included unplugging and plugging the ethernet to the phone back in, re-attacking S-5 after finding out they actually *were* the authority holders, but didn't have the credentials to do it at the moment because the CAC card of the guy who approved access was currently locked out and the system to fix it was down... Sam now sat on the phone, again waiting through countless rings, praying that he could *just* get this *goddamned* phone situation solved so he could get this *motherfucking* route scheduled...

"S-8, Commander Green speaking."

Holy shit! An O-5? Maybe we'll finally get something done... "Hello, this is Captain Rowland. Listen, I need to make a POTS line call to the FAA ASAP in order to prevent one of our aviators from getting flight violated and losing the Olympics, our jobs, and *all* this momentum we've worked toward in this story. These are *direct* orders from the ship's captain—Priority Triple Alpha, Threat Level Midnight. Please, Commander, tell me you can help me turn the POTS line on..."

The surprisingly jovial voice responded, "Well, I'd love to! But I don't control that..."

DUDE.

"... that's gonna be CAG ADP—they have the only POTS line working right now. In fact, they just used it about an hour before GQ to order themselves a new Wi-Fi router."

Are you fucking kidding me... Trying to keep his cool, Sam politely said, "Wow, ok, that's great to hear, thank you." Hesitating a moment, he then added, "You know, I actually called them a bit ago, and they seemed to claim they had no authority over this..."

The man laughed, and affirmed, "Sir, those guys absolutely do. I recommend you walk over there right now and knock on their door; I can *assure* you they have that single working beach phone."

Sam quickly said, "Thank you, Commander—you may have just saved this entire nation," and hung up, beginning a dead sprint through the 2nd deck mess, dodging and ducking GQ participants, on a mad dash to CAG ADP.

CAG ADP... of course *it comes back to CAG ADP... it always* fucking *does.* He could feel himself losing it; approaching his no-lower-than point of patience, tact, and tolerance for bullshit. As he took a deep breath, he reminded himself: *Keep it together, Sam. You've come too far to lose the fight now. Keep it professional, be chill, and don't get spooled up. You'll get this phone, make a call, and everything will be just fine...*

~

Doctor Suabedissen held the screen of the laptop in his hand, as if he were caressing the cheeks of his one and only. He wiped a tear and said, "MLP, please... don't give up... there *has* to be a way..."

The beautiful gamer girl smiled and wept, lamenting, "I'm sorry, P-word... it's too late for me. I lost my life—my stats, my gold, my armor, and magic spells—to the WizardOfAzkaban. I thought I could trust him... I thought my wedlock to him would do so much good for the virtual planet." She looked down and cast a sullen look. "I should've known better... I should've chased my passion-driven heart instead of my overly-calculated brain—then maybe... maybe I would've ended up with somebody I truly loved..." She looked at Suabedissen with a smile.

"I... I love you, too!" the doctor shouted, fighting back more tears. "I can save you, MLP! I will defeat the Troll!"

"It's no use..." she wailed. "The WizardOfAzkaban will be the richest player in the game and control the whole server—he cannot be stopped. I sealed our fate when I fell for his false promises and lies—and as a result, that wealthy fiend used my rupees for in-game purchases to nearly max out his character's stats, and he buys more influence and support by the day. It's almost as if he has access to some type of... I don't know... some type of *bonus* he took to get so rich and evil. And as long as my account is active? He'll absorb my stats into his... He's a terrible man, P-word—and because of him, my time in this game is coming to an end..." she frowned and shook her head.

"No!" Suabedissen stood up.

"Please..." MyLittlePony responded, her eyes tearing up again, "You must understand... for the world of Gladia... for D&D players everywhere... I can't live any longer, or else this server will be doomed forever!"

The doctor shook his head in refusal, as he cried out, "I won't give you up! And you mustn't give up either!" He pleaded, "Give me time—I can save you, and we can make this world ours... and a peaceful one for all the accounts inhabiting it!"

Slightly smiling, as if considering it, she wiped her eyes and said, "It truly *does* sound magical..." but then reverted to downcast, conceding, "But I can't..." She shook her head and asked, "Just do three things for me, P-word..."

"Anything, my love!" he simp-ily vowed.

"First, continue to slay all the P-Word you can. Don't let your silly feelings for me hold you back from your primal instincts with all the beautiful women you're undoubtedly juggling, waiting in line to be conquested in your sheets..." She gave him a flirtatious and longing smile, before continuing. "Second, don't let WizardOfAzkaban1337 get to you, too—it may be best to delete your account before his reign of terror begins and he takes all the stats, armor, and key items you've worked so hard for..." She looked down sadly, before returning her gaze to him once more. "And lastly..."

she paused and, smiling through her tears, bit her lip. "Can I see you without your glasses?"

Taken aback for a second, he slowly brought his hands to his head... grabbed his lenses... and *doffed his glasses.*

The for-some-reason handcuffed woman exhaled lustfully. "You're even more handsome without them... Imagine if you worked out and did something cool and productive with your life instead of playing D&D all day and programming... you'd be *so* unstoppable..."

Karl widened his eyes and asked, "You think!?"

She giggled. "I do." Reaching toward her camera, she shed one last tear and said, "Farewell, P-Word Slayer..."

As the video froze on a random frame of the princess making an unflattering face, the doctor screamed, "Wait!" Her face remained gorgeous to him, even in its glitchy-looking state. "MLP!" he called out. "Can you hear me?!"

No response.

"My Little Pony?!" he yelled desperately.

And at last, the screen switched back to the chat, where it read, 'Video Call with MyLittlePonyXoXo88 ended at 09:12.'

Doctor Suabedissen pounded the glasses on his desk out of frustration—shattering them—and cast his head toward the ceiling, crying out—unintentionally in his best Sith Lord impression—"NOOOOOOOOOOOO!"

~

Jesus Christ, finding this place is like searching for the fucking Batcave. After rushing through p-ways, hurrying up ladderwells, and squeezing through Condition: FYREF-EST-locked doors en route to shady backroads and alleyways leading to the ultra-hidden CAG ADP hatch, Sam had *finally* arrived—and knocked thrice upon the barely-marked door. He heard shuffling inside the room, but nobody answered.

He knocked again, more furiously, and shouted, "I know you guys are in there! I can hear you! Please, I need your help—the fate of the world depends on it!" *The 'world'...* he thought to himself. *Was it dramatic? Sure—but what else is as meaningful in this world as administrative prowess?!*

A nasally, weak voice responded, "Go away; we're in GQ... we can't help you."

Sam grinded his teeth and knocked again. "This is bigger than GQ—It's an emergency! Answer; on behalf of the orders of the captain of the ship!"

"Do you have a signed notary from him on official command letterhead? If not, then we cannot help you!" the pipsqueak voice countered.

You've gotta be kidding me... Desperate and running out of time, Sam looked to his left and right, noticing the eagles on his shoulders. *I hate to do this; god, I hate to play the rank card – but I have no other choice...* He took a deep breath, and then bellowed out, "Young man, my name is Captain Samuel Rowland, and I am an Officer in the United States Navy. I lawfully order you to open this door, or else you will face the punishments of the Uniform Code of Military Justice!" He cringed as he said it... He felt a lot more like an O-4 than an O-6 in this moment of weakness – but he had to do what he had to do.

Finally, some mechanisms behind the door handle were moving, and the hatch was opened three inches ajar – as some complete goon peered through the door. "How can I help you... *sir*?"

Sam took a deep breath and explained, "Look, I know you have a POTS line in here, and I need to use it ASAP. This whole GQ, the alert launches, EMCON, Condition: FYREFEST – this is *all* due to us being under attack by the Noddik Empire! And if I can't make one simple phone call to the FAA, we're going to have to admit defeat and allow this foreign nation to constructively embarrass us." He took another deep breath, looked the weakling in the eye, and asked, "Now, *please* – can I use the *one* POTS line that I *know* is in there?"

The runt looked at him, narrowed his eyes, and said, "One second, sir," before closing the door, where Sam could hear him clicking away on his computer and shuffling papers.

After what felt like minutes, he reopened the door the same crack-width. "I'm sorry, Captain Rowland, but your Cyber Security Awareness Challenge is out of date – and thus, you cannot use this phone."

Unable to comprehend that this was seriously happening, Sam kicked the door open, sending the nimrod into a daze of shock and awe. Inside the room was a sailor playing on his Nintendo Switch, another sleeping, and a third snacking on Teddy Grahams. The gatekeeper gasped and shouted, "Sir, you can't do this! This is a breach of security!"

Sam shook his head and demanded, "Give me the phone, shipmate, before I contact your chief." *God, this is so cringy... I never thought I'd be the guy ass-blasting junior sailors – and yet here I am...*

"Sir..." the doofus bowed his head to avoid eye contact. "... I lied. The phone is not in here..."

"What?!" Sam shouted in disbelief. "You *lied* to an Officer?!" He glared at the chevrons on the boy's jersey. "IT2, this is time-sensitive and mission-critical! Where is the phone?! I *order* you to tell me!"

He sheepishly smiled and said, "Uhhh... I left it in the khaki laundry room when I was fixing the printer in there..."

"Printer?!" Sam asked, stunned — and restraining himself from making one of his favorite jokes. "Dude, there's not even a printer *in* khaki laundry! What the fuck are you talking about?!"

Looking incrementally more nervous, the dipstick showed extreme unease as he admitted, "Ok, I lied... *again*. I was hiding in there to avoid doing any and all of my work and responsibilities..."

That was it. He'd fucking *had* it. It was time to wield the weapon he'd been holding onto in case of emergency, concealed-carrying for so long without the necessity to whip it out — until now.

Sam's jaw clenched as he shook his head and coiled back his entire upper body. Tensing in his wound-up preparatory stance, he brought his fingers together — forming a solid knife. He let his weapon of mass destruction be rapidly sharpened by frustration, lack of empathy, and egotistical hatred. And before the sailor could react, Sam struck — uncoiled aggressively and pounced — driving his knife hand directly in front of the face of the unprepared, defenseless victim. "You stupid, *stupid* son of a bitch! This is *completely* unsat, and 100% a fuck-up on your end!" He'd reached his boiling point, unleashing his fury on this prime target of opportunity. "You've jeopardized *everything*, you incompetent bastard! What the *fuck* is wrong with you?!" Analyzing his prey a bit closer, Sam barked, "Who's your chief?! You can expect me to give him a phone call *very* shortly — and believe me, asswipe: there will be *hell* to pay! NJP and XOI, at the *least*; I'll *happily* take the stand against you in Captain's Mast. You may have just compromised this entire nation with your incredible ability to *suck*. God fucking *dammit*..." Nearing the end of his display of positional authority and terrorism-based leadership, Captain Rowland finally got to the point and furiously demanded, "Give me your fucking phone and get the fuck out of my face, you worthless piece of shit."

The completely shaken sailor presented the phone, as Sam yanked it from his hand, dialed the ready room, and asked Brady for an update. "Sam, based on the radar picture, Coach says you've got five minutes to get a hold of the FAA — five minutes before JABA enters the route! Otherwise... it's all over! Hurry, Sam — this is our last chance!"

"I'm on it!" Sam shouted. He slammed the phone down, glared at the ADP doorman, and pulled chocks — preparing to make the *long* trek, *all* the way back to ship's laundry, *all* the way in the 225-frame. As he left the room, he shouted, "Unsat, shipmate... *UN-FUCKING-SAT!*"

As he sprinted away, he noticed a couple of Lieutenants waiting in line for ADP, who presumably heard the whole thing. Sam knew he'd never forget the look he saw in their eyes: Shock... and *disgust*. Behind him, he heard one bluntly express, "Jesus... what a tool..."

What have I become? Have I really hit rock bottom?

But he hadn't—not yet...

~

Suabedissen sat weeping in his stateroom, his fist still dripping with blood from slamming it on his spectacles, and his head laying atop his arms. He'd finally given up after many failed attempts of re-initiating a call with MyLittlePonyXoXo88—the last one brandishing an error code that stated, 'This account no longer exists.' He looked back up and stared at the error message—which was a blur to him, with his glasses now as broken as his spirit. He didn't care—he'd been tired of looking at the world through those spectacles. No matter how many times he'd dorkily pushed them up, he'd failed to see so many obvious things in front of him...

What was he doing with his life? Where was the satisfaction in this virtual world? Why was he wasting his time programming software in a place where he wasn't respected, treated well, or valued for anything more than his nerdy coding? How was he going to find true happiness in life when he remained cooped up in his little space station hell hole, alternating between going on meaningless raids, kissing the ass of his superiors, and writing software upgrades for this stupid fleet and their silly Olympic conquest? Why was he sacrificing *his* life to accomplish the goals of jerks like Robo-Hinge and Captain Rowland? How was he going to find *love* and be respected as a husband, a father figure, and a man... when he spent so much of his life being such a lemming, slave, and *beta-cuck simp* toward *the* man?

With the *whoosh* overhead, Karl looked up and waited. Shortly after that, a robotic voice stated, "Future Noddik Emperor, departing," announcing Robo-Hinge's launch from the ship—en route to the D&D Alpha Tier STAN Cell group.

The stages of grief were rapidly evolving, and the Doctor was finally ready to move past denial—now, he was angry. He wiped his eyes, rolled the sleeves up on his lab coat—exposing his toothpick arms—and stared at his computer screen. An hour ago, he'd been *dying* to go to the conference. But now? He couldn't have given less shits about the D&D Summit. All he wanted now was MyLittlePonyXoXo88. And since he couldn't have her? There was only one thing left on his mind: Vengeance.

~

Sam kept glancing at his watch as he ran *all* the way back to the aft of the ship, cursing under his breath at the frustrations of everything leading up to this moment. The absurd amounts of fetch-quests and fools' errands he'd been on, just to find this fucking POTS line phone and make one simple fucking phone call. The way he verbally abused that sailor, and the way those LTs responded to Sam—like *he* was the O-4 hinge

366

douchebag he'd come to hate in all those years past! *I'm losing it... I can tell... But as long as this phone is in that laundry room, and I can get this call made? The ends will have justified the means — and we'll be ok. For* now, *anyway...*

He passed the wardroom and took a quick peek through the window, where an FSA-garbed CP was serving one of the tech reps a quesadilla dripping with seed oils and kraft cheese, while keeping a close eye on a still-distracted >SADCLAM<, who was now laughing and rubbing his hands together in excitement as he watched his Munchkin Quest opponents' feeble attacks barely take away any of his hit points. Shaking his head in frustration, Sam ran even *faster*, desperate to get that phone and make that call.

He burst through multiple doors and made his way to the 225-frame, turning left through the laundry side hatch, thankful that the place would be vacated due to GQ and he could quickly search for the phone.

And then he was finally there — at the last ladderwell — the long journey from the 138-frame now complete. He descended down, jumping and skipping the last four steps, sticking the landing as he planted his feet, looked forward, turned the doorknob, and pushed — and was subsequently brought to a dead stop, as the door refused to budge more than an inch.

His mouth agape in horror, he began slowly looking up, dreading the terrifying reality he *prayed* was not true... and saw it: the door deadbolted with a gold lock and a hanging chain. The half-assed sign, scotch-taped to the door, stating in Calibri font: 'LAUNDRY SECURED.'

Sam felt his entire body shut down — as if his heart had stopped, his pulse was gone, and his brain couldn't process anything. He couldn't think — he could barely even *feel*. But what he *did* feel was a sinking sensation — the last glimmer of hope he held in his soul, dissipating in one swift, gut-wrenching swoop...

The shock of the moment left Sam stunned and speechless; unable to fully comprehend the magnitude of what this meant. He just stared at the sign in disbelief.

Moments later, his senses started to return, and he finally realized what he subconsciously knew the entire time: it was over. The one *fucking* room with the one *fucking* POTS phone... was fucking *secured*. JABA was going to get flight violated... the USS Ship was going to be forced to forfeit the Olympics... and Juice was going to be the hero for the Noddiks — the hero that Sam had left so long ago to become. And as for Sam? He would be remembered for all the wrong reasons: A traitor to his original nation. A defector from his new nation. A complete and utter failure for *both*. JABA was right — it didn't matter what the historians wrote. Everyone involved knew in their heart what was true. And in this very moment, in *Sam's* heart? He *knew* he wasn't a Good Dude — he was a *Bad Guy*.

Knock it off, knock it off... It was over... Sam slumped down, falling to his knees and lowering his head as he grabbed it with both hands. He closed his eyes and wallowed in the miserable silence. The ambient noise — the steaming pipes... the rushing water... the random bangs — he heard none of it. Only one thing kept replaying in his mind: It was over... over... fucking *over!* He sat there idly, crouched in silence, processing his stages of grief. And when denial finally left his mind?

He slammed his fist against the locked door and screamed, "FUCK!" With barely a hesitation, he struck the door again, yelling even louder, "*FUCK!*" He wailed away at the door again and again *and again* — his knuckles drawing blood — and with every impact, he let out the same gutwrenching cry of agony: "FUCK! FUCK! FUCK, FUCK, FUUUUUUUUUCK!!!"

19

#SSFL

I will now read my orders!" CDR Sam "Nickels" Rowland announced in the MCAS Iwakuni hangar, as he prepared to pass on leadership of the VFA-195 Dambusters to his best friend, CDR Kyle "Low T" Camilli. He scanned the audience of skippers in attendance: CDR Chris ">SADCLAM<" Houben was there from the VFA-113 Stingers, taking a moment in between a Level 2 BFM snapshot drill validation chalk talk to attend the ceremony and pump his fist for every 'Chippy Ho' Sam dropped. CDR Andrew "CP" Preul grinned and nodded slowly, representing the VFA-147 Argonauts, sweat dripping from his forehead after the 'good deal' squat session he and Sam had squeezed in before the ceremonies – both PR-ing their 20-Rep Max in dress whites. LCDR Mark "JABA" Buck smiled from his front row seat, now holding the reigns for the VFA-105 Gunslingers, where he refused to take on the rank of Commander after falling in love with life as an O-4. CDR Charlie "The Lorax" White showed up in style in his Supra, which he still used to cruise around Japan when he wasn't bottom-lining schedules over at the VFA-27 Royal Maces. And in the far back, Sam recognized the lovable bald head of United States Senator Charles "WYFMIFM" Kennedy (CDR, USN, Ret.), who had parked his yacht in the Hiroshima docks in order to make the event. Also retired and in attendance were Skipper and XO – both incredibly proud of their former JO, and unbeknownst to the full impressive magnitude of their impact on his career. Big XO was also there, celebrating the Good Dude who – while they may have had their run-ins about discipline, military bearing, and asinine procedures over the years – ultimately was somebody the GQ dungeon master was proud to call a teammate – and Sam certainly felt the same.

Nickels cleared his throat, and read from the printout: "Bupers Order: 592592; Social Security number XXX hyphen XX hyphen 5555 slash 1310, parenthesis PERS-432G close parenthesis; Official change duty orders for Commander Samuel Benjamin Rowland, USN, XXXXXXX..."

He read the entire stack of paper, including all formatting characters and every descriptive bit of fine print, as was administratively sound and correct. The crowd didn't care – they loved it. The VFA-195 sailors and pilots in attendance were happy to bask in every last second of Nickels' time in command of the Chippies, and took great joy in knowing that his replacement would be somebody of equal stature in unbelievable leadership: XO Low T.

When it was Kyle's turn, he read the entire printout of his BUPERS orders as well, before turning to Sam, saluting, and announcing, "I'm ready to relieve you."

Sam saluted back and stoically stated, "I'm ready to be relieved."

Kyle responded, "You stand relieved," the emotional fire behind the words leaving no dry eyes in the audience.

"I stand relieved." Sam finished gracefully, clinching a perfect administrative evolution to top off his career with the Chippies.

As the two cut their salutes, the crowd gave the men a standing ovation, with The Lorax glailing louder than ever. Amongst the uproarious cheering, Sam leaned over and whispered, "I couldn't have left the Chippies in better hands, Low T. This squadron knows a hell of a lot about admin; now, you're going to make them lethal and tactical as fuck," he emphasized with a smile.

Low T grinned. "Skippers don't debrief past 1800, right? I've got bedtime routines to knock out – and I'm not talking about my kids! This old man can't be expected to be validating shots after sunset – not when I've got 'Antique Roadshow' reruns to watch over a bowl of sugar-free jello!" he said with a wink.

As the standing ovation continued, Sam snickered playfully. "Bullshit, Kyle – you've never skipped a debrief in your life. Not even for last year's National Championship, when Auburn defeated 'Bama to complete their undefeated season! You know – where your son threw 8 TDs and rushed for 300 yards to cap his Heisman-winning year? So, forgive me for thinking there's no way you're missing a chance even to validate an on-deck setup anytime soon!" He chuckled and clasped Kyle on the back, as they looked upon the flight suits in formation aft of the crowd – the new generation of Dambusters. "These JOs are soon going to see how lucky they are to have somebody like you in charge," Sam remarked with a smile. "A real Badass Dude."

"Only fitting," Kyle said as he waved to his wife and kids in the crowd, "after they inherited the legacy of the truest Good Dude known to naval aviation."

Sam smiled, as the two stood and took a bow for some reason – but the crowd ate it up, with Big XO whistling loudly for them.

The guest speaker, ADM Tom "FISTY" Flynn – Air Boss Actual – came up to the microphone and announced "Ladies and gentlemen, that concludes the change of command ceremony. Upstairs in the ready room, we have snacks and refreshments," he looked down at the script, then over at the retiring skipper and shook his head with a chuckle, "Your choice of carbonated water or C4 Ultimate, as well as various cuts of steak, some soft-boiled eggs, a butter

370

plate, and bowls of rice and sweet potatoes for 'minimal toxicity' carbohydrates..." he said with air quotes and a smiling roll of his eyes.

Sam and Kyle grinned at FISTY, before Camilli took the mic and added, "Oh, and if you're not looking for heart failure or colon cancer, my wife went by Costco and grabbed a bunch of Miller Light and boxes of Grape-Nuts; there's plenty for everyone!"

The crowd stood up and began making their way to the ready room, as the two Commanders in the ceremony started walking toward their wives and kids. Before Sam got to his family, though, WYFMIFM stopped him and asked, "Nickels... what's going on?"

Taken aback, Sam asked, "Huh? What are you talking about, WYFMIFM?"

He looked around and gestured his arms out, looking at Sam like he was clueless. "What do you think I'm talking about? All of this shit — it's not real; none of this happened. That bit about the National Championship? Auburn sucked last year — and Kyle doesn't even have a son!"

"This wasn't your ending," WYFMIFM said with a repulsed scoff. "You're not a 'Good Dude' — you're an asshole, a loser, and a fucking failure. Look at your family — they didn't even come here."

Sam started to get angry, as he began contemplating the legal penalty for punching a state senator. "The fuck is wrong with you, WYFMIFM; they're right — " But when he looked over, all he saw was empty seats. "... Huh?"

"No shit, asswipe. Why would they have come? You abandoned them just like you did the rest of us. You suck, dude." His voice changed in the slightest as he chided Sam, "You just couldn't stand that I was coming to fill your shoes; couldn't handle a new sheriff in town — could you... Dimes?!"

Sam — still perplexed by his missing family — turned back to warn his former OPSO, "WYFMIFM, you better watch what you're saying, kemo — what the fuck?!"

Gone was WYFMIFM's bald dome, now replaced with salt and pepper-styled hair. Gone was his goofy smile below his mustache, replaced with a clean-shaven frown. Gone were those warm eyes of friendliness, replaced with piercing eyes of animosity.

"Juice?!" Sam exclaimed. "When did you get here!? Where did WYFMIFM g — "

"I already told you, Dimes — none of this is real. None of this fucking happened... because you gave it up." Juice scoffed, "And you gave it up for the most selfish, insecure, needy purpose. Imagine what could've been; imagine what you could've done with your career, if you'd just been ok with suffering more as a team! If you didn't feel the need to stop and look down at the view... if you'd just pushed yourself to keep climbing..." He threw his hands up in frustration. "Imagine what we could've been!"

"We?!" Sam fired back. "Why should I have cared about you?!"

"Not me, Sam!" Juice said with annoyance. "The Dambusters! Look around — look how many people skipped your stupid-ass ceremony. Even your own sailors didn't show..."

Sam scanned his surroundings – the place was barren. Empty chairs filled the entire hangar. The only people there were his fellow skipper friends – but he watched as even they, one by one, started to disappear, fading into darkness. All that was left was him and...

Huh?!

"Arnold?!" Sam gasped, seeing the man, the myth, the legend himself where Juice once stood.

"You are a loosah, Dimes," the muscled Austrian said as he shook his head. "And you ah weak, too! Look at these pahthetic mahscles..." Schwarzenegger pointed to Sam's biceps, which were flatter and softer than ever in this sobering moment. "Do you even lift, bro? This is embahrassing! The ohnly thing mohr underdeveloped than youhr phahsique is youhr self-woorth. Think abouht it, brother – you have ahll the rank and prestige in the woorld – but who fahcking cares?! This jahb isn't abouht that boohlshit – it's abouht the people. But you couldn't see that, Dimes – and now?" Arnold laughed coldly. "Congratulations, ex-Skippah – yooh'll be a civilian soon, and without youhr rank – and no friends to show for ahll of your accahmplish-ments? Yooh'll have nothing. Ahbsolutely... nothing! I hope it was woorth it, bro."

He started to walk away, but then turned back – his face now Sacha Baren Cohen's – declaring sadly, "Your post-career life, Dimes – I no liiiiiike. You try and be happy, yes?" He shook his head, "But... is no use. It will be... how do you say... ehhh... shitty, yes?" Sacha tsked and said, "I wish I had your life, Dimes," He walked away and sadly bemoaned "Noooooot..."

Sam watched the Borat actor depart, and looked back at the hangar one more time – it was now only him. Nobody there – because nobody cared. He looked up at the flag – not an American Flag, but a grey, plain Noddik Empire one. He glanced down at his patches – Noddik emblems, written in Windows DOS coding font. He turned to look at the beautiful Japanese mountains outside the hangar, but just saw space – black, void, empty, space. He was all alone... He'd marched the golden path, accrued insane amounts of wealth, and accomplished every career milestone he'd sought out – at the price of his best friends, everything he'd ever loved, and happiness. He sat down, stared at the abyss, and yelled out – in an awful attempt at a Keanu Reeves accent: "It was free pizza!"

... but nobody laughed. Nobody 'meh'd.' Nobody even mocked him. This was life now.

Sam had once wanted, more than anything, to leave his job, his world, and his friends. And now, he had his wish – they were gone forever...

~

"It's time, Nickels," Coach Belichick said glumly, as he turned on the light in the STBR, waking Sam from his nightmare.

Sam got up and brushed himself off – his flight suit bloodied from his scraped-up fist. He grabbed his flight bag, took a deep breath, and said nothing as he walked out of the room, making his way to the PR shop. He wasn't upset with Belichick, Brady, or anybody else—just *himself.*

He could feel the sinking sickness in his heart, and sensed that this would be his last walk to the jet—*ever.* It was abundantly clear that these Olympics—and all the former Chippies' careers—were at an end. As soon as they were out of EMCON, the ship was bound to be flooded with voicemails and emails from a *very* displeased FAA.

Just an hour ago, Sam hadn't needed to say a word after carrying himself back up to the ready room to inform Belichick and Brady of the news; his expression told the whole story. Captain Belichick cursed and—much to Sam's surprise—gave him a sympathetic hug, as the two Hall of Famers and one Epic Underperformer lamented the reality they'd soon be facing. Brady clasped Sam's shoulder, his eyes misting up as he told him, "Nickels... you did everything you could—you left your best out there on the field. History may not paint you as the champion, but none of us will *ever forget* everything you did to get us even *this* far..."

But Sam didn't want to hear any of it. He walked into the STBR, turned the lights off, cranked blink-182 on—with 'Dysentary Gary' playing, fittingly—and began bawling. Sobbing—*like a little bitch,* he chastised himself. *You fucking loser... look what you've accomplished from all this—nothing! You've got nothing to show for your career. This is how you're going out... in tears, after berating the hell out of some poor CAG ADP sailor. You really* are *Dimes; all the money in the world... but just a fraction of the man you used to be...*

He'd known Belichick would be back soon to give him the DD-1801 on his surrender ferry flight, where he'd fly toward the USS Katsopolis rocking his wings and squawking 6666—the official transponder lingo of 'Game over man, game over...' He knew he'd have to land aboard their ship, face their commanding officer—undoubtedly Juice, now—and issue a formal message of submission that would be recorded and played over Noddik TV as propaganda for centuries to come. And for the Noddik citizens to see the words of defeat spoken by the man who used to lead them... it would be the ultimate career embarrassment for Sam—not that he'd have to worry about career implications after this failure...

What am I going to do with my life now? Go back to selling fucking PowerPlants protein? I can't get a job with JABA anymore after his park declared bankruptcy... I wouldn't be allowed anywhere near Flat Earth Fitness with my current abysmal AOMs and LOLs... and what about the other guys? Belichick and Brady, too—I've now fucked their post-football careers. God dammit... what the hell happened to me? What would've life become if I'd never gotten Diseased? If I'd stopped worrying about the view and the credit? If I'd just stayed climbing...

373

Still shedding tears of anger, he pondered these dismal scenarios over and over until he eventually passed out, as Tom DeLong's voice matched Sam's agony, whining in the background about heartache, weasels, girls, whores, and losing wars in the unofficial ballad of 'My life fucking sucks'...

~

Doctor Suabedissen burst into the room, equipped with his dual-bladed weapon of choice, seeking the key item to boost his efforts—and immediately found the treasure chest was looking for. He'd been on many raids in the virtual world, but this was his first IRL—and his heart was *racing*. He scanned the room with his blurry vision—sans glasses—squinting to try and make out any potential monsters or traps in the environment. Nowhere *here* were the cactaurs, malboros, and tonberry kings he was used to slaying in the gaming world when approaching the loot—this seemed *easy* in comparison.

He got close and analyzed the safe—it was locked alright, but nowhere near robust enough to stop the beast unleashed in Karl Suabedissen. He admired the lock mechanism—a classic spinning Master Lock, impenetrable to anyone who didn't either know the combination or have a soda can.

Unless—*Unless!*—that skilled thief wielded the Blades of Chaos! Suabedissen smirked and raised his weapon—a gigantic pair of bolt cutters he'd obtained from his quest to the MWR closet. He pinched the two blades around the lock's shackle, and squeezed with all his might... Nothing. He tried again, even harder! ... Still, nothing.

He thought back to MyLittlePonyXoXo88... WizardOfAzkaban1337... *Robo-Hinge...* Rage stirred within him. His jaw clenched—which he didn't even know he was strong enough to do—and he reoriented his body, put one lever of the pliers against his stomach, and two-handed-pulled the other toward him with every ounce of pain fueling his heart—*SNAP!* He felt a slight sting above his eye—not sure what had happened—and watched the lock clank helplessly against the floor.

He grinned, sheathed his pliers, and opened LT Camilli's cabinet—and just as he'd hoped, it was a hoard of booty, complete with an assortment of the hero potions he'd sought: Cellucor's C4 Ultimate, Gaspari Nutrition's SuperPump250, BSN's N.O-Xplode, VPX's Shotgun 5x, MRI's Black Powder Ultra, and so, *so* many more...

The doctor grabbed the C4 and a nearby blender bottle, preparing to concoct his alpha elixir—but then, out of the corner of his eye, he saw a small, white cylinder that grabbed his attention: USP Labs' Jack3d—with a handwritten label marked 'Original formula.' Suabedissen had heard tales of this legendary substance back in the day, but had never come across it with his own eyes—and he *certainly* never would've tried such a dangerous pharmaceutical without first consulting his health care provider. But now? He was a new man... with a new sense of not giving a *fuck.*

He picked up the canister and squinted at the ingredients list on the back. Sure enough, it was there: 1,3 Dimethylamylamine, or 'DMAA' — the ingredient that got the original Jack3d FDA-banned and taken off the market. 'Legal meth,' they called it. 'Strong as *fuck*,' they described the proprietary blend. 'Linked to narrowed blood vessels and arteries, cardiovascular problems like chest tightening and heart attacks, seizures, and other neurological/psychological conditions,' they found in studies. And yet, per the Reddit forums the doctor visited, 'Jack3d was never quite the same after The Reformulation...'

Karl opened the container lid — the powder wafted out like a majestic cloud of smoke, and he couldn't stop himself from inhaling some by instinct. As he did, the lemony flavor shot through his sensory glands, and he started coughing violently. But from just that bit alone? He already felt a tinge of the rush — the *high*. He could've sworn his bicep vein was pulsating. He nearly got *goosebumps* from the pre-workout particles in his air.

Suabedissen grabbed the tiny scooper inside the canister. 'Is that it?' he thought. 'That's *one* serving?!' He was so new to this... he had no idea. But then he thought of MLP... 'Vengeance... I *will* get vengeance for her...' His muscles squirming — craving the nectar in his hands — the doctor dumped the remainder of the half-full container into the blender bottle, grabbing some water from the sink to fill the rest. He closed the top — and shook it like his life depended on it. After a solid thirty seconds of 'blending,' he popped the top off — it sounded similar to a champagne cork popping, as more smoke emerged from the blender bottle opening. He stared at the concoction, like Aladdin marveling at the magic lamp, feeling awe-struck and powerful just *holding* it.

After a moment of consideration, he nodded and said aloud, "He will pay... they will *all* pay. I won't let you die in vain, MyLittlePonyXoXo88..." He closed his eyes and chugged the entire bottle, again coughing up a storm as he finished the last bit. As he digested the testosterone tonic, he licked his lips and thought, 'That tasted really good... I wonder when I'll feel it...'

He walked over to clean the blender bottle with just a splash of water — like every responsible lifter does whether it's pre-workout, whey, or milk — and looked in the mirror.

'What the heck?!' His focus was above his eye, where he'd felt the small pinch while cutting the Master Lock. When the lock was sliced, a piece must have deflected and hit him — because now, the entire side of his face had a stream of blood dripping down from the tiniest incision. He felt panicked at first — but when he realized he was in no pain? He felt *badass*, like a fighter who'd just survived a round in the cage —

nobody needed to know the *true* origin of the gash. *"Cool..."* he remarked aloud, as he admired the wound.

And then he felt it — the beta-alanine — the 'ants-crawling-on-his-skin' feeling. His body — *itching*. His hands — *shaking*. His heart rate — *skyrocketing*. The Jack3d had hit — and holy *shit*... The doctor had but one thing on his mind, as he announced to himself: *"I need to lift. Right — fucking — now."* He threw the blender bottle against the wall, and sprinted toward the boat gym...

~

CP threw the plastic-y American cheese slices on the lunchmeat-filled tortilla and folded it in half, pressing down on it with his spatula as he looked toward the exit — hoping for *any* sign of Sam.

A tech rep walked up with a handful of white order slips, announcing, "A few more quesadillas on the queue, my good sir!" before snickering and walking back to his Settlers of Catan game at the HODS table.

The other sailors groaned, as one asked, "How much more can these guys *eat?!*" the hopeless desperation evident in her voice.

Another sailor — the bald, pasty, diminutive Chief Warrant Officer 3 in charge — consoled her by assuring, "Come on, keep working — this has to be over soon! They've already come through the line at least four times — *nobody's* stomach can handle this much junk! Besides, surely they've got work to do; they can't just sit in this wardroom forever when there's things on the ship to be fixed!"

As CP observed his surroundings, he took in the dismal scene. One sailor had already succumbed to the workload and crashed to the floor, requiring assistance from others to keep him conscious — assistance that was hard to come by, as multiple sailors had been sent to find reserve flour, sugar, and butter to make more cookies for these behemoths. The waffle maker was in a 'down' status, as it had caught fire ten minutes ago and required the use of an extinguisher. They'd pulled out and thawed frozen cheesecakes that were stocked for the next multiple *years* of deployment, and found themselves 'bingo' on powdered eggs and 'catfood' mash. Things were so desperate that the CWO3 was asking the sailors to grab snacks and candy from their care packages, to fill supply and feed these endless appetites. CP shook his head and swore to himself, 'Sam, where the *hell* are you...?'

The crew was tired. Frustrated. Irritated. The tech reps were demonstrating 'shock and awe' warfare by shattering preconceived notions of the human capacity to consume, linger, and annoy.

"We're almost out of this, trust me!" the CWO3 continued. "Just keep cooking, and don't show your displeasure! They are civilian guests on our ship, and we need to treat them like gods!"

Sick of this inhumanity, CP cleared his throat and said, "No."

"*Excuse* me?!" the Warrant accosted him.

"I said 'No,'" Andrew stated with raised eyebrows, as if it were obvious.

The Warrant—livid—marched up to CP and wagged a finger in his face. "How *dare* you—these sailors are working relentlessly to please our guests, and you're going to selfishly just *stop*—and leave them out to dry? To fail alone?" His eyes narrowed. "Who's your chief?!"

"Exactly—'*fail*,'" CP responded, ignoring the question. "We're going nowhere by feeding these dweebs—they *aren't* going to stop this. Yes, they *do* have work to do, but trust *me*—they most *certainly* are *not* going to leave to do it." He put *his* finger in front of the CWO3's face, and said, "You *know* this is true, don't you? So don't feed these sailors the false promises of misdirected hope."

The CWO3 looked stunned—dropping his hands—but said nothing.

CP nodded slowly. "Mmm-hmm. Exactly as I thought." He looked around at the sailors, whose attention he now held. "Guys, we *can't* keep doing this! We need to think of a plan to fight back. Otherwise? We'll be cooking for these heathens for an *eternity...*" He knew very well that an Olympic loss would surely and mercifully end this evolution—but that was *not* an option in his mind, and he needed buy-in from the team to believe the same.

"Well, what do you have in mind?!" a sailor manning the hamsters in the oven asked.

"Yeah," the culinary Warrant piped in again, always the reliable detractor, "Because if you think you're going to take down this legion of tech reps with just us alone, you're *wrong*—look at that kid over there," he said, pointing to >SADCLAM<, who jumped up and fist pumped at his latest Munchkin Quest roll—one which earned him the Lightning Scroll of Ramuh. "Look how into that board game that loser is! No *chance* you're getting him or any of those other guys to abandon this life of gluttony and celibacy!"

Giving the CWO3 a dirty look, CP responded, "I'll have you know that that 'loser' is my good friend Chris Houben—and he's one of the hardest working aviators I know."

The Warrant scoffed. "Oh really?! I see wings, but he looks like nothing more than another unimportant boat-dwelling prick in a flight suit to me—probably some P-8 guy on a dissociated sea tour as a TAO—or maybe even a *window licker...*" he added with a smirk—then furrowed his brow and reminded the undercover CP, "And by the way—you can address me as 'Warrant,' shipmate..."

CP glared at the wardroom OIC, his fists tightening. "He's *actually* an F/A-18 pilot — and a former indomitable Dambuster — *bro...*"

The two stared each other down silently — tension filling the kitchen — as the sailor manning the quesadilla station casually remarked, "A single-seat guy? Nice..."

CP's eyes widened. "Hold up — *that's it!*" He took a moment to think, then looked at the crew and asked, "Do we have any to-go plates?"

"Well," the CWO3 interjected, "*Technically*, if you want to do that, you're going to need to fill out a request on the Gippernet — but we're actually *out* of them, due to potable water shortages..."

"Oh really?" CP asked without concern in his voice, as he pointed to the kitchen storage room. "Because I see some right there."

The Warrant growled, but said nothing.

Ignoring the grouchy buffoon, CP beckoned the crew, "Guys, bring it in, and grab me a couple of plates — I have a plan that I think can turn the tide of this battle, saving us *and* the ship from this contractor insurgency..."

As the group corralled and gathered around their inspirational mutiny leader, even the Warrant seemed to be listening out of curiosity. CP started his brief — but not before giving the wardroom exit one last glance, and internally pleading, 'Hurry up, Nickels... we don't have much longer...'

~

Suabedissen marched up to Robo-Hinge's stateroom door and tried to open it — *locked*. The key-card door system would've been a simple hack for the doctor — but the fire in his heart and pump throughout his veins had him opting for a different method, as he raised a foot and launched his leg forward, plowing through the hatch's weak foundation.

The doctor grinned. He'd never kicked open a door in his life; he'd only seen alpha males like Solid Snake, Squall Leonheart, and Nathan Drake do it in video games. He marveled at the power flowing within him; the vein in his left leg *prominent* from the burnout of calf raises he did to end his first-ever workout. And what a workout it was...

Fueled by the mythical Jack3d OG, Dr. Suabedissen paraded into gym, and immediately tried to reuse a joke already made in this book by referencing the 'My New Haircut' video when the MWR guy asked for his ID — but he messed it up by saying, "I'm in the fuckin' zone, chief, so not now," and then also erred by giving him his CAC anyway. Following this, he marched straight to the squat rack, where somebody had just finished overhead pressing, even cleaning up the bar like a good gym patron. Suabedissen, however, saw the empty bar on the rack, scoffed at it, and audibly shouted—to no one in particular—"You call *that* 'heavy weight?!'" Everybody heard him, and a few gave him strange looks—which he returned with a cocky smirk, announcing, "Check *this* shit out..."

Suabedissen then loaded the barbell up—with 10s on each side. He approached the bar, got beneath it, sucked in half the room's supply of air—and *squatted* that 65 lbs like it was—well, *something*. He almost got pinned, in fact. But to his credit, via lots of screaming and exhaling, he defied gravity and got that marginally loaded bar back to eye level. And when he slammed the bar against the rails, racking the weight after the 1RM? You would've thought he'd just set a world record, the way he wildly waved his arms around and beckoned the other (annoyed) gym goers to make some noise, as he screamed, "Light-ass weight! Light—ass—*weight!*" And *that* was just the beginning...

Suabedissen took that 65 lb load... and he made it his bitch. He pressed it. Rowed it. Curled it, benched it, skull crushed it. When he set up to deadlift it, he prepared for his rep by walking laps around the bar, huffing and puffing, beating his chest, clapping chalk—which he stole from a nearby gym bag—everywhere, and pumping his body up and down with the bar resting against his ankles. He took a moment, bowed his head, closed his eyes—as if saying a prayer to the Dwarven God of Wharfhammer—and *pulled* that motherfucker up to his waist—full lockout, neck veins throbbing, the skin on his shins splitting, and voice roaring—like he'd just pulled the majestic Althena's Sword from Dyne's Monument. After he was certain that every set of eyes was on him, he dropped the weight to the floor, the iron clanking as he shouted, "FUCK YEAH!" He flexed his arms—visually admiring his biceps—then walked to the MWR rep, stuck out his hand, and demanded, "ID, jabroni."

As the annoyed rep sorted through the binder and found Suabedissen's CAC, the doctor squinted at another ID and pulled it out himself. He analyzed it and loudly remarked, "Holy shit..." He looked around the room and asked, "Is there someone here by the name of," he looked at the card again, and read out the name of the hottest sailor you've ever seen.

A girl in tight lululemon leggings and an even tighter top raised her arm and cautiously said... "Uhh... yeah?"

He gave her a lens-check ocular patdown from top to bottom, then back up, and put on a cocky smirk. "The name's Karl Suabedissen, babe."

"Umm... ok... and...?" she asked, clearly disturbed.

Still smirking, he casually shrugged and said, "Just thought you'd like to know the name of the guy you'll be boinking later tonight." He pointed at her and winked, before about-facing in a wild spin move and exiting the gym, throwing his hand up to high-five the random sailor waiting by the door.

And here he was now — riding the first and only pump of his life, breaking into Hinge's stateroom, ready to sabotage the fuck out of the DH's account and crush his fucking dreams. Suabedissen found the O-4's laptop on his desk — still open. "You stupid, stupid simp..." he said aloud with a smile, flexing his arm and again admiring himself with a quick glance at the mirror.

Too amped to sit, the doctor remained standing as he tried logging in with the WizardOfAzkaban1337 username — and yet he needed a password, too... "Hmmm..." he pondered, "If I were a filthy fucking Hinge..."

Suabedissen looked over at the picture on Hinge's desk — a family photo with his cyborg wife and kids — and picked up the frame to look closer at it. For a man like Robo-Hinge, there was only one reason to keep a loving photo like this at the forefront of his vision every day while laboring far from home; one reason for a constant reminder of the beautiful things most important to him during the long days of deployment...

The doctor threw the frame to the ground, shattering the glass — and sure enough, behind the picture was a piece of paper with multiple logins and passwords printed on it. User info for illegal gambling accounts, online dating services, plenty of robot porn sites: BonerBots, Step-Fembots, AutomatonMassage, OnlyDroids, etc. And at the very end of the list, Suabedissen found the critical piece needed — Hinge's D&D password: FucktheJOPA. "Bingo," Suabedissen said coolly, as he input the password and successfully found himself on the Flame Knight's character profile.

He instantly opened up the DH's DMs and scrolled down the list. He recognized his name and then saw MyLittlePony's as well, her last message to Hinge containing just a heart emoji — which nearly brought a tear to his eye. Letting anger replace his heartbreak, he shook his head and pushed on further, eventually coming across a group chat labeled 'OPERATION: CONTRACEPTION.' Suabedissen scanned the messages, and soon found that this was, in fact, the hired group of tech reps Juice had spoken about.

Suabedissen read through at a lightning-quick pace, holding unreal levels of mental focus — an additional pre-workout benefit that most meatheads never truly discovered. And in this thread, the entire plan was unveiled: Hinge was to pay them all copious amounts of rupees in exchange for spending copious amounts of time tech-repping, time-wasting, and work-shirking aboard the USS Ship during the Olympics — in addition to sabotaging the air wing with other nefarious acts. The doctor was impressed with the level of deviousness arranged by Hinge — but not surprised, as he reminded himself that the O-4 *was* his brainchild; the result of his best coding. As he scanned the conversations and found the ringleader amongst the Boeing reps—DragonMaster499—he scrambled his brain for a way to reach these goons whilst they were undoubtedly in EMCON and causing mass chaos in the wardroom.

'Think, Karl, *think*...' he told himself. He remained jittery—bouncing back and forth as the Jack3d pulsated through his blood—trying to think of *some* solution to deconstruct his creation's evil deeds and avenge his one and only.

Then it came to him—not the answers... but the *urge*. He dropped to the floor and started busting out pushups. They were *cake*. He threw a hand behind his back and attempted a one-armed pushup—but that was a massive failure as he crashed to the floor—so he went back to the standard two-handed method. He didn't give a fuck—he still felt on *fire*.

"ONE... TWO..." He counted them out loud—as if the whole world needed to know how many reps he could pump out of the oldest chest exercise in the book. As he did, he let the Jack3d take over his brain, and carry his psyche to an altered dimension...

"THREE... FOUR..."

He could cancel the pending rupee transaction! But no... the deal was undoubtedly cyber-locked; surely part of the terms of conditions...

"FIVE... SIX..."

Could he call the boat POTS line and get a hold of DragonMaster499? No, they've surely got the lines turned off during EMCON ops—and even if there *was* one phone for emergencies, it's no doubt being hoarded by CAG ADP...

"SEVEN..."

There *had* to be a solution...

"EIGHT..."

If only he could find a way to destroy the throne that Robo-Hinge had usurped...

"NINE..."

'Wait a second...' he thought. 'What if I just—No... I *couldn't*...'

His body was nearly touching the floor. He was stuck—his upper body in full flexion, his arms trembling, his chest cramping. He pushed... but nothing. The idea was there—he always knew of this as an extreme contingency—but it was his greatest fear. 'Would it be too nuclear?' he deliberated in his mind. 'I'd be left with... *nothing*...' He strained with his arms under extreme tension, balancing the possibility in his head. 'Am I... *alpha* enough... to pull it off?!'

He closed his eyes and froze—a moment of inner peace and clarity, as he pictured MLP's warm smile juxtaposed with her expression of defeat—and the decision made itself clear. 'Fuck it.'

"... ehhgggggaaaa... TEN!" Karl screamed as he hoisted himself off the floor and successfully finished his set of 10 pushups. He collapsed and rolled onto his back, breathing heavily, his chest expanding and shrinking violently. "Holy *shit!*" he yelled out loud. He shook his head in exhaustion, thinking, 'I can't *imagine* how many chicks I would've gotten in high school banging out a number like *that!*'

He sat up and looked into the mirror—the blood on his face was mostly dried, but some still trickled down. 'Left with *nothing...*' he thought again, as he stared at his reflection. He looked into his own eyes—truly *looked* into his own soul, without being deceived by the thick lenses of delusion. And eventually, he realized, with tragic res-ignation, that he couldn't be left with anything less—when he already had nothing in life to lose...

He accepted his fate. 'I have to do it—it's the only way...'

Finally recovered enough to function, he stood up and returned to the laptop, as he pulled a thumb drive out of his lab coat pocket—the same one labeled 'Tax Doc-uments' that contained his superior's coding. As he inserted the drive into the USB slot and began typing, his fingers quivered—no longer just from the high of the Jack3d... but now from the anxiety over what he was about to do—and what it would mean for his life.

In all the games he'd played growing up, he'd become so conditioned to un-locking the happy ending—to the hero prevailing, saving the planet, rescuing the girl, and becoming a legend in his world. But this was not a video game—this was reality— and he had *lost.* He was no hero; his world had been destroyed by his own actions; the girl was gone; and he would forever be remembered as the ultimate villain by those he sought to garner respect from. 'At least I'll be a legend in *some* semblance of the mean-ing—not everyone has the guts to commit the ultimate betrayal to their own realm...'

Suabedissen grieved that his life couldn't be the videogame fairytale he'd al-ways hoped for—but he chastised himself for even dreaming of such a fate. Life doesn't have dungeon master rulebooks, save states, or continues; there's no 1/16th chance of extraordinary possibility with every action. He'd been living a fantasy lie this whole time—and as tough as it may be to exit his world of dwarves, magic, and dragon-slay-ing... the doctor had been playing long enough. He was ready to turn the game off, and finally open his eyes to the real world—as terrifying as that may be...

The doctor looked down at the keyboard---and began weeping. He couldn't have forced a smile through his tears even if he'd wanted to. Vengeance was the only thing he cared about—even if it came at his own expense. He clasped his forehead in dejection, and started shaking from the weeping. "The time is right," he said to himself, nodding his head through tears and sobs, "The time is now." As he hit 'Enter,' a GIF of Emperor Palpatine uttering "Execute Order 66" appeared on the laptop screen—and the lethal command was in motion...

~

"Ok, so you understand what you need to do?" CP asked the wide-eyed E-3 airman.

"Y... yes?" he responded, sounding as unsure of himself as a new guy answering a 50/50 question in an SFARP lecture.

"You got this," CP said with a smile, as he slapped the Culinary Specialist on the shoulder and handed him the to-go order. "Go with god, young man."

He and the others watched from the kitchen as the junior sailor began slowly sauntering toward the long table with his grill order. The CWO3 scoffed and whispered, "This will never work... you're going to get this poor boy *killed* out there..."

Without removing his scan from the field of action, CP acknowledged, "Maybe so, Warrant, maybe so..." He steeled his eyes to a squint. "Or, just maybe, he could be the savior of us all—the hero we need..." Preul wasn't filled with confidence, given the young man's demeanor—quite the opposite, in fact. But it was the best shot they had— their *only* shot...

The airman continued closer and closer to the group of Munchkin Quest-playing tech reps and >SADCLAM<, where the Boeing contractor in the Pikachu hat had just triumphantly played a Chaos Quake spell card and defeated a Dark Gremlin in the process. As he threw his hands up and yelled, "Huzzah!" he bumped into the CS and nearly knocked the plate out of the boy's hands, before the airman recovered and kept the plate upright.

CP clutched at his chest, as they all watched with the same anticipation of the Presidential Cabinet observing the infamous SEAL Team mission. Preul shook his head, anxious as hell. "Oh my gosh... that was too close..."

The boy looked back toward the kitchen, then down at the gaggle of dreary-eyed geeks staring at him. He cleared his throat and spoke softly. "Uhhh... order for mister... Singapore Phantom Shitter?"

The tech reps thought nothing of it, looking at each other and shrugging. >SADCLAM<, however, seemed as alive as he'd been in hours. After a brief moment of hesitation, he said, "Uhh... that's... for me—thank you," and slowly secured the dual-covered plates from the boy's possession.

The airman nodded and quickly scampered back to the kitchen, joining the rest of the cooks and a smiling CP, who gave him a fist bump and quietly said, "Attaboy. I knew you had it in you."

Preul looked over at the CWO3, who was watching with his arms folded and skepticism. "I still don't buy this—you'd better hope the captain doesn't find out you've been wasting our last few paper plates..."

Ignoring the short, bald detractor, CP turned back to the scene, where >SAD-CLAM< was trying to act as casually as possible while the cohorts continued their quest for level 10. The former Dambuster knew something was clearly unique about this order, due to the minimal weight it carried. He gave the plates a small opening to peek inside—and couldn't help his eyes from widening as he saw the contents.

"What is it?" The Pikachu hat-wearing contractor asked.

Houben quickly put the top plate down to conceal the order. "Uhh... a quesadilla—with a Kraft single—gross..." He winced with exaggerated disgust to sell the lie.

Another contractor—wearing a Final Fantasy VII 'Tifa in a bikini' shirt—grinned and exclaimed, "Nice! Dude, they're using the *good* stuff—throw some Cheez Whiz on it, and it's exactly like the ones my mom made for me back in college!"

>SADCLAM< nodded and smiled, before looking both ways and saying, "Uhh, guys, I think I need to use the head real quick..." and started to stand up.

The Pikachu-hat man, however, raised his free fingerless-glove-hand to stop him. "Oh, contraire; I don't think you need to do that at *all*, Willias the Wise," referencing >SADCLAM<'s player character name. "In fact, I implore you to sit down *right now*, if thou wishes to retain any of that sportsball muscle tone..." he said awkwardly and threateningly, gesturing down toward his right hand below the table.

Houben stood frozen, unsure of what to do...

CP swore under his breath. "Dammit, Chris, don't just *stand* there!"

>SADCLAM< shook his head, and said, "Sorry... I meant, can I grab anybody some cheesecake? Maybe an Uncrustable? What about one of those peanut butter 'breakfast biscuits?'"

"Oh, *hell yeah,* I'll take some cheesecake!" a contractor wearing an oversized Gundam Wing Hawaiian shirt yelled.

Pikachu-hat man stared at the pilot—saying nothing at first—before finally demanding of his friend, "Dabney—inspect that quesadilla."

CP pounded his fist on the kitchen table, swearing again, and started to inch closer to the kitchen exit.

A pasty man in a Dragon Ball Z gi reached for Houben's order, his greasy fingers immediately marking the plate with prints.

CP watched with dread as the contractor began opening the plates—

And then, without warning, a long, pitchy whistle played over the IMC—lasting for what felt like half a minute—before a voice finally announced, "Stand by for words from the Big Executive Officer..."

Andrew breathed a sigh of relief as the lardy man released the plates, and all the lemmings put on thousand-yard stares toward the 1MC in anticipation of the words to follow...

~

Captain Belichick groaned as he heard the whistle. "You've gotta be *kidding* me..." He looked over at Brady and asked, "Tom, did the XO call and ask if he could use my whistle to talk?!"

"Nobody's called here in the last hour, Coach," Tom replied, as he readjusted the VR headset on FISTY's comatose face.

Belichick murmured in annoyance and looked up toward the speaker with irritated impatience.

Finally, the voice began: "Gooooooooood morning, Team USS Ship! Big XO here, and wow—another *beautiful* day on the boat out here in the middle of the ocean! Hey, real quick, guys, let's start with a few shout-outs. Everyone give it up for AM2 Rosalez, who exhibited great honor, courage, and commitment by stopping a junior third-class who refused to get out of his way in the hallway—a *direct* disregard for the chain of command and code of conduct! I witnessed the whole thing, as AM2 called the shipmate out, explained to him the way it *should* be done, and all-in-all made the Navy a better place by enforcing these important rank flexes. Bravo Zulu, AM2."

Brady raised his arms in confusion. "What's going on, Coach? Why the fuck is this guy talking right now? Isn't he aware that we're in the middle of GQ and the Olymp—"

"Shhhh!" Belichick hissed, motioning toward Brady with his hands as he waited to hear more. "He might have something to say about the tech rep situation." Although he then shook his head and muttered, "This better not be a waste of time..."

"Hey guys, I want to talk about water usage real fast," the hard-o voice continued. "If you guys *keep taking these Hollywood showers*... well... I have a feeling the cold-water fairy will be stopping by later tonight..."

The voice droned on and on about meaningless shit, like Golden Foxtail winners, MWR tours, random bits of 'advice' about returning home from deployment, and finding ways to blame all of the ship's problems on the aircrew. Belichick threw his hands up in displeasure multiple times, while Brady eventually put noise-canceling headphones on and continued working on the final VR touches.

Having heard nearly enough, Belichick started walking up to the 1MC to turn it off, as the Big XO went on with, "And calling all wizards and demonslayers! I recommend you Dungeons and Dragons users check your accounts—because let me tell you, mine is glitching big time, and *all* my stuff seems to be erased! In fact, the game won't even let me spawn on the world map—not cool! And, this *really* puts a damper on the D&D LAN party we're holding next Thursday night on the mess decks; that's right, folks—*yours truly* will be hosting a *live raid* into the Hidden Valley of the Valarian Tribe! You are *not* gonna want to miss out on the loot and spoils this one has for the victors! Contact your MWR team to sign up!

"Alright, guys, now to the *meat* of the matter—the moment you've been waiting for..."

Belichick, with his fingers on the knob, paused—hopeful to hear *any* positive news about Phase 3...

The mic clicked back on, and Big XO ended his preamble with, "Here we go: Guys. Tomorrow morning. 0730. All you destroyers of dust bunnies, maulers of mildew, killers of corrosion—"

Shutting the 1MC off, Belichick scowled and shook his head. Brady looked over and took his headphones off, asking, "What was it, Coach? Anything useful?"

The captain rolled his eyes and sighed. Holding his forehead and shaking his head, he said, "It never is, Tom. It never is..."

~

"... And remember, with a *full* crew on board, it takes a *full* crew to keep this place shining! Alright, continue to make it matter out there, team, and I'll see *you* out on the deckplates! XO out."

The contractors appeared stunned—the entire wardroom's jaws were dropped. After nearly a half-minute of silent tension in the room, a fedora-wearing man in a kimono asked, "Wait... does this mean... our accounts are... *erased?!*"

"No!" another dweeb clamored from the crowd. "That's... that's *impossible!*"

"Nothing the Big XO says is true! It's all rumors and heresy!" a man in a Ganondorf cosplay outfit cried out.

Still standing, finally able to compose himself, >SADCLAM< leaned down and looked at the Pikachu-hat fellow's nametag. "DragonMaster499, huh?"

The tech rep looked up at Houben, his mouth agape and his body shaking, before he eventually muttered, "... Yeah?"

Chris smirked cockily and said, "Just wanna know the name of the guy who'll be sucking my dick later tonight."

Perplexed, the man winced with repulsion. "Sucking your... *what?!*"

Another contractor started asking, "But why would you want—"

But it was too late—Chris pounced across the table and tackled DragonMaster499 to the ground, as stray blasts from the APG-47 were fired off into open space, one nearly hitting CP's shoulder.

"Woah!" CP shouted as he dodged the laser. He glanced toward the cooking crew and yelled, "Guys—*let's go!*" Preul ran into the seating area and entered the fray, immediately grabbing the fedora-donning man into a chokehold.

The CSs followed quickly behind, each charging toward different tech reps. It became an all-out brawl—albeit a one-sided one. The active duty members easily controlled every engagement, despite the extreme weight disadvantage. Cards and 16-sided dice were flying everywhere as tables flipped and chairs toppled, and the room quickly filled with the stench of body odor and sounds of heavy breathing. The 'HTML' shirt-wearing patrol guard tried to peel off CP from another rep, but Preul quickly got *him* into a headlock as well, now double-guillotining the two NARPs.

>SADCLAM< kept wrestling with DragonMaster499, who, at 35% body fat, was the most fit of the low T'd crew. After a brief struggle, Chris gained the positional advantage and took the APG-47 from the nerd's grasp, pointing it at his face. Dragon-Master499, pinned to the floor by Houben's knee, laughed in between wheezes. "You think that will affect me?! You stupid jock, thinking with your muscles and not your brain! I'm not the least bit surp—"

Houben then took the dork's Pikachu hat off, finding a holographic 1st edition Charizard Pokemon card hidden inside the inner brim—and grasped it with both hands, preparing to destroy it.

"NO!" DragonMaster499 yelled before hacking up a lung. "*God, no!* I will do *anything*! I will suck your fucking—"

"Dude!" Chris yelled with disgust. "Get the hell out of here—I meant that metaphorically, you psycho. Jesus Christ..." He shook his head and demanded, "Retire your guys from this tech-rep session right now—or else this card's value goes from... *whatever* amount—"

"Eighty-one million, six-hundred-eighty thousand, eighty-five dollars," the geek clarified, behind tears and exasperated breathing.

Chris rolled his eyes. "Sure—from *that*... to *worthless*."

DragonMaster499 gulped and looked around, his cronies staring at him with unease. He re-shifted his focus on >SADCLAM<, took another series of shallow breaths, and uttered out, "I'm not afraid of your empty threats, you girl-kissing bully—I'll *never* surrender to a protein terrorist like you!"

Chris shook his head in disappointment. "That's a real shame, brother..." He pinched the middle of the card with both hands, "You may never lose your virginity—but you just lost *this*."

With a guttural cry, DragonMaster499 watched as >SADCLAM< tore his prized card—and his entire world—in half. "NOOOOOOOOOOO!" he screamed, burying his face into his hands in an attempt to unsee the act of sadistic brutality.

As >SADCLAM< held the shards of the 'Zard, looking down upon the boy—almost feeling a bit *sad* for the little bitch—a large bearded man in a Chun Li shirt burst in from the conference room. "Warlords! Listen up! The Big XO was right—all of our accounts are showing the black screen of death!" Tears forming in his eyes, and his voice choking up, he continued, "... But not just that—my guild brothers..." he steeled himself, "The game is... *gone*. The game is *all gone!*"

"What the frick?!"

"Blasphemy!"

"Are you freaking serious?!"

The cries from the room were rampant, as the contractors—all pinned down by various CSs—erupted with both seed oil-based venom and estrogen-driven panic at this revelation.

The squirming HTML bodyguard called out, "Ship gentlefellows, *please!* Release us! We are done with this charade—we need to check our accounts *ASAP as possible!*"

CP and >SADCLAM< looked at each other, shrugged, and Preul acknowledged, "Guys—let 'em go."

As they were freed from the sailors' grasps, each tech rep jumped up and scampered out with unrealized speed, huffing and puffing as they raced for the wardroom exit in efforts to confirm the terrible news with their own eyes—and salvage whatever rupees and EXP they could. Preul watched as the dining area rapidly cleared out—and when every factor contractor had vanished? CP proudly raised his chin and announced to the room, "Ladies and gents... stop the clock, stop the problem; picture clean—we fucking *did it.*"

The CSs roared with cheers, as the cooks shut the grills and ovens off, and >SADCLAM< walked up to CP to give him a gigantic bro hug. As the two embraced, Houben expressed, "CP... thank you *so* much... you saved my life, bro." He appeared downcast as he admitted, "For a second there, Andrew... I was spiraling. My alpha status... my man-card... I lost track of my identity out there, just acting like another beta in this world..." he lowered and shook his head in dismay. "I felt... like I had no purpose; no motivation to strive for more in this life..."

">SADCLAM<," CP said with a smile as he broke the embrace and clasped the Paddles' shoulders. "You're a fucking NATOPS-qualified, Patch-wearing, single-sea big-meat fighter pilot with T levels off the charts. Look at the way you handled that dweeb! You're as alpha as they come—and no Settlers of Catan prowess, LEGO set collection, nor Munchkin Quest starter deck is gonna change that."

CLAM smiled sheepishly. "But... you called me a Patch wearer..." He shrugged and added, "Andrew, I'm not—"

"Chris," CP began, "You don't need a specific piece of material on your shoulder to hold yourself to a high standard, to work your ass off, or to become a champion leading other warriors into battle. Being a crunch-time-performing, camaraderie-building, inspiration-igniting, motivation-driving level 10+ Good Dude?! Bro, you can't prove that shit from whiteboard arrows, a cardstock val sheet, or knowledge of the latest kill-removal format—that shit comes from *within*. From your own heart's determination, your own reinforced mental toughness, and your own unwavering *self-belief*. Never forget that, kemosabe."

>SADCLAM< smiled, his eyes misting up, and nodded with appreciation for his Dambuster brother.

"Besides..." Andrew grinned, "You *are* a Patch wearer. Maybe not *The* Patch— but you have something even better; something even more exclusive, if you ask me. Something that *you* started with the Chippies, Chris: you have *That* Patch."

Chuckling in restrained emotion, Houben's eyes charged with life as he reflected, "You know, Andrew... Skipper used to always tell us: All those flights, tactics, hours, mission successes and failures? When all's said and done... they're just gonna blur together one day. But the memories... the laughs... the friends?! *That's* what'll remain vivid in your mind and heart forever. And when I saw what was inside those to-go plates," >SADCLAM< nodded, growing sentimental, "It reminded me of *why*—of why my heart continues to start the APU, when all my brain wants to do is cancel and chill; why I continue to marshal home to this steel piece of shit, when the beach is always just a bingo profile away; and *why* I continue to obligate years of my life to this beyond-fucked-up corporation, when I could easily make *twice* the pay—working *half* the time—somewhere else." Nearly coming to tears, Houben beamed and said, "I love you, brother. I love the Chippies. And despite all the accompanying bullshit... I love this job, and the life and family it gave me." The two embraced again, as the wardroom continued cheering, smiles worn brightly on every face—except for one...

DragonMaster499 sat on the floor in despair, haunted by the two halves of the Charizard card in his hands. He was frozen in shock; everything he'd strove for in life—gone. His most valuable card... his side-quest raid campaign tasked by WizardOfAzkaban1337... his entire Dungeons and Dragons gamer profile, accumulating over 1000 hours—a complete cesspool of failures.

>SADCLAM< looked over and saw the demoralized contractor—and felt *pity*.

"Remember the conduct that Alexander the Great lived by, Chris," CP said as he clasped his compatriot's shoulder: "Let us conduct ourselves so that all men wish to be our friends, and all fear to be our enemies."

Nodding in understanding, Houben powered his empathy on and approached the despondent loser.

As the pilot walked toward him, DragonMaster499 muttered, "What do you want, meathead? Do you wanna make fun of me for losing my D&D account? Gonna throw me in the Soft Plastic garbage bin? Wanna brag about how *cool* it is to fly a plane or kiss a girl?"

>SADCLAM< folded his arms and frowned. "What the hell's wrong with you?"

"What's wrong with me? What's *wrong* with me?!" the boy yelled hysterically, tears still flowing. "Look at how I've been portrayed in this book! My whole life, I've done the things that interest *me*, no matter how objectively nerdy they are, thinking I'll find the path to happiness! But look—I'm just a complete frickin' *joke* in this scene!" He scoffed, looking to the side. "They say to just 'be yourself,' follow your compass, and you'll find fulfillment... and yet I see you—a true level 99 dragonslayer of the Dambuster guild—and how full of stirring words you and your fellow knight are..." the boy wiped his tears, looking back at Chris. "And then I look at *my* pathetic life: All those Pokemon cards and LEGO sets collected; all those Western and Japanese RPGs beaten with stats maxed out to dub, trip, and quad 9s; all those Kingdom Hearts, Chrono Trigger, and Dragon Quest fanfics written..." The irrelevant failure raised his arms in frustration. "What *for*, Mr. Houben? What has my life amounted to?! Big Boss, Cloud Strife, Alex Noah—those guys are the *real* heroes. But me? I'm just some incel beta loser with no life, no love, and no *hope*." He bowed his head, painful silence filling the room. "It's true, isn't it?!" he yelled, his voice breaking. "Tell me you believe it's true!"

>SADCLAM< shook his head, looked at the bitch, and demanded, "Get up, brother. Get the *fuck* up right now."

The bitter boy looked up, drooling from his angry sobbing, and barely managed to stand on his two feet.

Chris paused—CP's words still resonating in his head—then pointed his finger at the low-confidence, low-testosterone boy. "*You* believe that. It doesn't matter what *I*, or any other pilot, reader, or *writer* believes—because *you* believe it. *You're choosing* to believe you're a loser. You're *choosing* to fuel these stereotypes that you're hopeless. You're *choosing* to live this narrative that you claim to hate. In every waking moment of your life, you're walking around—defensive as hell, with your shields on and RWR volume cranked all the way up—*constantly* preparing to get verbally attacked at any second from any angle. And *why?!*" Houben added with voice inflection. "All because some *writer* gave you the identity of some tech rep contractor, while referencing a bunch of videogames and characters that plenty of readers and I have never even heard of—and yet he's labeling *you* as the pathetic loser?! Bro, this is the same guy who arbitrarily makes fun of WSOs, department heads, CAG ADP, and even random celebrities and athletes! You think *his* words should be taken as gospel?!" Chris rolled his eyes. "You may be just another NPC in his story—but *fuck* that story. It's *your* story you should be concerned with! You're a fucking aeronautical engineer working on military-grade equipment, deploying across the world, making *bank* to contribute to the fight in a way that so few others can. Incel beta?" Chris scoffed. "Dude, you're a fucking *VolCel alpha*—*if* you believe it. No matter what those self-conscious 'jocks' in high school said, or what any girl who ever turned you down thinks, or how any bitch-ass writer portrays you—in a way that is likely just projecting his own insecure past in an overly dramatic characterization—we are *all* the alphas we *choose* to be. And we can *choose* to be that alpha hero in *our* story."

>SADCLAM< pointed to the remains of the rare 1st edition holographic Charizard. "And that card? Consider it your character in *this* story—worthless and irrelevant; forget it. Because you can be whoever you want to be in this world, DragonMaster499. So, who are you going to be: the victim in somebody else's story? Or the *hero* of your *own*?"

The tech rep wiped away his last tear, looked >SADCLAM< in the eyes, and admitted, "You're right... you're right, Mr. Houben. I'm tired of looking at myself like some punch line!" Sounding more confident than he ever has in his life, he continued, "I bring a hell of a lot to the table, and my life story isn't going to be about some 'loser D&D player who was bullied by jocks and screwed over by some tool online'—that is merely my tragic-but-motivational origin story!" He grew a look of determination. "It's time I start taking care of myself—I'm getting a gym membership, cutting the junk out of my diet and life, and hitting the inspirational self-help books to build a robust mental foundation, too!" Standing taller than ever at 5'7", he declared, "I'm done being the hapless NPC in the virtual world—it's time for me to be my own man, and forge my own destiny IRL."

"Attaman, DragonMaster499," Chris said with a smile, as the two shook hands—the firmness of the tech rep's grasp surprising him.

"And one more thing..." the contractor requested, shaking his head slightly. "Don't call me DragonMaster499—he's gone forever."

>SADCLAM< pursed his lips in curiosity. "What will you be called?"

"For now? Call me... FNG592."

"FNG592, huh," Chris' mouth curled into a grin. "Has a nice ring to it; I have no doubt that with a name like that, you'll become the legendary hero you've always wanted to be, in the adventure you've sought to live, in the story you're destined to write."

"Thanks, Lieutenant," FNG592 smiled in return. He picked up his Pikachu hat and turned to exit the room—but then stopped and looked back. "Hey, sir—I believe this belongs to you." He retrieved a Chippy shoulder patch from his pocket and offered it to Houben.

>SADCLAM< smiled in admiration—That Patch... the one CP had planted in his to-go order. He raised an arm and offered, "You can keep it if you'd like, brother."

FNG grinned and handed Houben the circular patch. "Negatory, sir. This is *your* legacy—I need to learn from you, and go out there to create my own." He gave a sharp nod, he turned around, and departed the wardroom.

Happy for the kid, Chris took another look at That Patch: A standard Chippy shoulder patch, except 'Strike Fighter Squadron 195' was replaced with the words 'Single Seat For Life'—an idea he'd pitched the Chippies long ago. But it wasn't about the 'I fly a fighter jet *alone*' aspect of the idea that made it mean so much; it was the nod to the brotherhood they all shared in the squadron, discreetly hidden on their shoulders—one of the subtle-yet-powerful *little things* they did to create a culture of camaraderie, community, and cohesion in the Dambusters.

That Patch was a microcosm of everything >SADCLAM< cared for—his work family, the jet, the job, and the goofiness of a bunch of JOs doing dumb stuff: making unauthorized patches like this one; playing *the* infamous roll 'em game, where they'd call out points for 'whores' and 'cucks' with the admiral in the room; working on the perfect Foc's'le Follies skit that would skirt the line of good-natured roasting *of* said admiral; getting away with rolling questionable movies like 'Knock, Knock,' 'Terrifier 2,' or the Chippy 4th of July annual tradition, 'Eyes Wide Shut'; or bringing everyone together to dye their hair blonde for cruise—and subsequently dying it *back*. It was all of these small, stupid things that kept life exciting in the doldrums of deployment, and groomed a lineage of pilots who knew how to kick ass like a bunch of dedicated professionals in the skies, and yet act like unrestrained, fun-loving, spirited kids on the ground. It was *those* moments that defined why Chris had fallen in love with everything That Patch and this job entailed—and why he chose this life and this story.

>SADCLAM< beamed. For a shoulder that had worn a basic-ass noob-alert USN patch, a RAG class Key West Det patch, and an oversized LSO 'Rectum Non Bustus' patch? This one had always meant the most to him. He slapped the green emblem of fighter spirit on his arm, and looked over toward Andrew with gratitude.

"TEN HUT!" a voice boomed from across the room.

Both men looked up and saw the source—the culinary CWO3—standing at attention with a crisp salute primed, as the rest of the wardroom mimicked the same. Wearing a serious look—a serious look of *approval*—the CWO3 announced, "Two single-seat fighters on deck!"

CP and >SADCLAM< nodded sharply, saluting him back with unspoken, amicable understanding, as their hearts filled with hope—hope that their Phase 3 chances were still alive; hope that their story could find a triumphant ending, after all; hope that the #SSFL Chippy magic of old could be stirred up, one last time...

~

Robo-Hinge groaned with rage—closer to a menacing growl—after he'd completed his DRAFT report and filed for his alternative destination: the USS Katsopolis. He was livid—fucking *livid*. Who the *fuck* hacked into the D&D database and corrupted the entire game?! There had to be *some* way to recover his rupees, weapons, and power... and if not? There was going to be hell to pay for the shitty-ass programmers—or, more specifically, the shitty-ass *programmer*—whose unsat coding allowed such an act of cyber terrorism to be possible.

"GOD DAMN YOU, SUABEDISSEN..." the O-4 growled. He had already begun planning the legendary ass-blasting of his servant—public berating on the group chat would merely be the appetizer; there was going to be a full dress-down at an all-hands quarters. The doctor would be standing every watch, OIC'ing every DET, and responsible for organizing every dining out, squadron dinner, and safety standdown for the remainder of existence—and he'd be doing it all in his *khaki* labcoat. Robo-Hinge's lip almost curled to a smile when he thought about the reorganization and cleaning of the OPS share drive, study spaces, and ready room rehab that he was going to task to this incapable simp...

Hinge had been final-appoach-fix inbound to the STAN Cell conference when the tower informed him to discontinue the approach and divert, because that the event had been canceled due to a mass corruption of the entire game. Something about a catastrophic 'Order 66' error that left the entire virtual world in shambles... and by the time the DH would have a chance to backup his profile, it would surely be eradicated. "HOW THE *FUCK* DOES THIS HAPPEN?!" Hinge yelled as he slammed his robotic fist on the canopy rail.

This was a travesty for the hinge's plans—he had mentally dropped the pack from any and all type of work involving Phase 3, the Olympics, or the Noddik Empire as a whole. He was in *no* place to be forced to do his job once again, and the entire portion of the squadron ranked below him was *certainly* going to feel the wrath of the unnecessary stress this had caused him.

He shifted his frequency to TAC 13 and keyed the mic, "WARD, ARE YOU THERE?"

"Juice is up—who's this?"

"WARD, THIS IS LCDR ROBO-HINGE. SOME... *SHIT* HAPPENED," he barked. "SAY STATUS OF MARSTRIKE?"

"We're about forty-five minutes from the release point... sir," Juice said.

"FORTY-FIVE?!" Hinge yelled with disbelief. He looked at his MPCD—the ship was a mere twenty minutes off his wing. "SAY LOADOUT."

A deep sigh was transmitted, followed by, "... Two-by-simulated Air-to-Ship-killing missiles, per aircraft." Juice did little to hide the annoyance in his voice.

Hinge groaned in his head. 'AGAIN WITH THIS SIMULATED SHIT... WHAT THE *FUCK*...' That wasn't going to accomplish anything—the Noddiks needed to make a *splash*. More specifically, *he* needed to make a splash—*if* he was going to get the FITREP bullet needed to propel him to the #1 EP and chance at Command. 'YOU KNOW WHAT? FUCK THIS SHIT. TIME FOR THE HIGHEST-SA PILOT IN THE SQUADRON TO TAKE OVER.' Hinge cut hard to the left and put the USS Ship on the nose. "WARD," he ordered angrily, "ABORT. ABORT YOUR FUCKING MISSION. I AM EN ROUTE TO THE TARGET AREA RIGHT NOW."

"Say again?!" Ward responded with urgency.

Hinge rolled his eyes at being questioned by his underling. "YOU HEARD ME, YOU PEON. TURN AROUND AND GO HOME, AND COORDINATE YOUR OWN BACKSIDE GAS, BECAUSE I'LL NEED THAT MTNK."

"Hinge..." Juice's voice sounded concerned. "You're fucking live-loaded. Stay the hell away from that ship."

Robo-Hinge steeled his expression. "YOU'RE GODDAMN RIGHT I AM, WARD. AND EXPECT ME TO COME BACK WINCHESTER. ENOUGH OF THIS PUSSY 'CK' SHIT—I AM 'K'ING THIS THING FOR REAL." Before Juice could respond, Hinge transmitted again, "NOW TURN THE FUCK AROUND AND STAY OUT OF MY WAY. AND START PLANNING THE AFTERPARTY—BECAUSE WHEN I GET BACK? LCDR ROBO-HINGE WILL BE THE NAME THAT *DEFINES* NODDIK GLORY. HINGE OUT." The robotic DH turned his Comm 2 off, to spare himself from the frantic and annoying complaints from his underlings concerned with things like 'political catastrophes' or 'galactic wars'—things that would only make his job *more* essential.

Hinge accelerated to mach 1.0, selected A/G master mode, and boxed the AS-131 KILLSHIP on the STORES page. 'ENJOY YOUR SILLY ADMIN GAMES, USS SHIP...' he thought to himself, 'BECAUSE THEY'LL BE THE LAST MEMORIES YOU EVER HAVE..."

~

Sam flew at max E—ATC engaged, Baro Alt held, seat safe'd, straps undone, morale depleted—droning toward the USS Katsopolis, with not a fuck in the world to give about anything. He didn't care when he launched with a master caution on the runup—with a litany of CHECK SEAT, CHECK TRIM, MU LOAD, and AV AIR HOT cautions—because part of him *welcomed* the thought of finding his demise on the cat shot. He welcomed the thought of *anything* other than his reality.

"Calling on GUARD! Aircraft not squawking at position: North 37 decimal —"

Sam quickly shut off GUARD. He already knew this was targeted at JABA, and he couldn't bear to listen to this transmission of failure—broadcasted proof of his leadership incompetence. "God... fuck, man..." he sighed into the cockpit, his mask dangling by his feet. He was out of comms range with the USS Ship, broken and unreadable from JABA, and—like his dream in the STBR—all alone, with nothing but his own misery to keep him company.

In his fit of slothdom in the cockpit, he glanced over at his right shoulder and looked at the empty spot of Celcro, where a shoulder patch used to be—where *That Patch* used to be. Where he used to wear the Chippy 'Single Seat for Life' patch—before abandoning it alongside his former life and brothers. The #SSFL homage was one the squadron had created in his time at 195, and one symbolic of the bond they'd all shared: a bunch of individual single-seat pilots, from vastly different backgrounds, with a diverse range of passions—coming together to work as one unified *team*. It was That Patch that encapsulated everything Sam, the Chippies, and fighter spirit was all about.

He'd always felt that it was *amazing* how you could be isolated in the cockpit—all by yourself from startup to shutdown—and yet feel like your best friends were *right alongside you* on TAC freq—whether they were three feet away in parade, a mile abeam in spread, or hundreds of miles apart doing night loops to stay current in PGM hops. He *loved* this sense of belonging and companionship in his life at VFA-195—something he'd *never* felt in the Noddik Empire...

Even in his apathetic state, Sam almost chuckled to himself, thinking about the squadron's in-your-face '#SSFL' pride, and the annoyed looks they got from *some* squadrons in the air wing, hating on their sarcastic, egotistical, over-the-top Echo machismo—because they didn't *get* it. They didn't realize that it had nothing to do with hating WSOs, insecurity over shared credit, or a desperate need for validation. #SSFL was all about the internal growth achieved from being an independent fighter who made it a personal mission to seek progression. The progress made from your origins as a brand-new flight student, barely able to taxi on centerline without assistance from the instructor, to the confidence and realized satisfaction felt in harnessing the power of this incredible piece of machinery, landing it on a moving target—by *yourself*. Where you had *no choice* but to put in the hours of study, rehearsal, and practice—because your professional success and basic survival ultimately came down to you, only you, and *your* ability to perform. And then, to fly alongside your brothers who had no choice but to fly the very same? It was the ultimate feeling of teamwork, entailing every single person doing their job—and doing it *well*. No feeling could *possibly* match how it felt to fly an Echo—solitary, yet joined in a flight of four—leading your squadronmates into sorties, through the conduct, and then back home—where you'd rip off the break behind the boat, professionally slam the jet onto the flight deck, and look at yourself in the mirror wondering, "Damn... how the hell did I get here?!"

He almost smiled, thinking about those memories, that life, and that sense of accomplishment.

Almost. Because that was the past, and those days were forever over.

Nickels looked toward his right knee, and noticed his single seat was still safe'd. He sighed. *Fuck it...* That thing wasn't going to save him today; nothing was...

~

"Tom!" Belichick called out, an uncharacteristically troubled tone in his voice. "Tom, get over here quick!"

Brady emerged from his VR computer work and ran toward the captain. "What is it, Coach?!"

Belichick gestured toward his computer screen, "There's a Noddik aircraft streaming *straight* toward us—with *live* A/S munitions!"

"What?!" Brady threw his hands on his head. "But—but the Olympics... this is forbidden by SOP! This... this is an act of terrorism!"

Biting his lip, Belichick shook his head and swore, "Fuck! This isn't *about* the Olympics anymore—we're under direct attack! God *dammit!*" He grabbed the phone and immediately dialed the Admiral. As the four-star answered, Belichick quickly explained, "Sir, it's the Captain—we've got an aircraft headed our way at 1.0 mach, with the potential to employ a weapon that could sink this whole ship!"

Between pauses, Belichick continued, "Yes, sir" ... "I'm not sure..." ... "Yes, sir..." He looked around the room—then up at the schedule on the SDO computer—and showed a sign of frustration. "I don't *have* any other pilots, sir." There was a moment of silence, before Belichick winced his eyes in anger. "What do you *mean* the pilots and EWOs don't have crew rest?! They're probably in the ready room watching movies during GQ right now!" Another fit of frustrated body language from Belichick, before he aggressively explained, *"No,* sir—there is *no time* to call the staterooms, we've got—" he looked back at the radar return, "—About 20 minutes before the KILLSHIP gets to its max range of 1 nautical mile!"

Whatever the admiral was saying, Belichick clearly didn't like it. "For Christ's sake, sir—NO! Forget it! I've got it handled—I'm putting the ball in *my* guy's hands," and he slammed the phone down. He looked at Brady and said, "Tom... it's the biggest game of your life, hurry-up offense, time for one more play, and you have the call—what do we do?"

Brady looked at his coach, took a deep breath, and said, "Well, in 2007, I threw the ball deep every damn game—but in the biggest one? The Giants *knew* it was coming. *Everyone* did. And look what happened..." He shook his head in dismay—yet then looked inspired, as he asked, "But do you remember how we won the 2017 Super Bowl against Atlanta in overtime—when we *needed* that touchdown more than anything—after I'd just completed a passing *clinic* to get us back in the game in regulation, and down the field in OT?"

Belichick grunted affirmatively. "The toss to James White—of *course* I remember."

Smiling, Brady explained, "Sometimes, the highest-SA move is to hand the ball off to the person in the best position to save the day."

Confused, the captain shook his head. "I can't believe I'm admitting this... but you're Tom *fucking* Brady—the GOAT!" He shrugged and opened his arms, warning, "Don't get distracted by analytics or sabermetrics, Tom! At the end of the day, I want the ball in my best player's hands!"

Tom grinned as he said, "But Coach... that's exactly what we're doing." He walked over to the VR machine, where Admiral Tom "FISTY" Flynn was rigged and ready. "It's done, Coach—it's ready."

Belichick, understanding the meaning of what was happening, asked with hope, "Do we still have time?!"

"Thirty seconds to us will be an *eternity* to FISTY," Brady explained to reassure Belichick and the reader of the accuracy of the continuity. "It's the best shot we have, Coach; it's our *only* shot."

Belichick sighed and gave a sharp nod. "Let's fucking do it."

Brady hit 'Run,' with FISTY's POV displayed on the monitor for the men to watch—and within seconds, the simulation was underway...

20

THE FISTY Chapter

"Cavern" – Metal Gear Solid

FISTY opened his eyes. Aside from the random words he saw in the bottom left of his eye—*Was it 'Cavern?'*—he was enshrouded in darkness—pitch-black *darkness*. He was so cold, shaking uncontrollably from the frigid temperature. *I'm definitely outside.* He could hear ominous music playing in the background—from nowhere specific, just an ambient theme—as well as the rapid patter of rain drops in what sounded like a downpour. And yet he was dry, protected by some type of shelter. *Where am I?*

While laying on his stomach, he began feeling around for his surroundings, carefully exploring the surface—some rock structure, even colder to the touch than his core temperature. As he carefully moved his hands across the outcropping beneath him, he eventually stumbled across something metallic—and sharp. *A sword?!* He didn't know *why* this came to mind; he'd never wielded a sword in his life—yet he instinctually *knew* it. He found the hilt and took ownership of the weapon. *Will I need this? Where the hell* am *I?!*

He put his legs beneath him and carefully stood up. Despite having no recollection of how he got here, he felt shockingly rested... healthy... *energized.* Realizing he was barefoot, he began moving slowly across the rocks, and headed toward where the rain was getting louder and louder. He continued into the black abyss, supporting himself against a wall with one hand and the other on the sword, holding it in front of him and poking around for sharp edges and obstacles.

"Well, hello there, Showtime 11!" a voice called out beside him.

He jumped, squaring up to the voice, and raised the sword in front of him. "Who is it?! What do you want?!" he called out, preparing to slash around wildly to defend himself.

"Please, lower your weapon, good sir! I'm not here to hurt you!" the man responded kindly.

"You—can you help me?" FISTY asked, still not entirely convinced of his safety. "I don't know where I am..."

The man chuckled. "In a way, yes..." His tone livened up as he added, "But in reality, Tom Flynn—*you're* going to help *me!*"

FISTY's heart sank. *What the hell?!* "How—how do you know my name?"

Laughing, the man asked, "Who *doesn't* know your name, FISTY?! You were *hand-selected* for this quest because of your prestige and reputation!"

Selected?! Me?! "Why was—who—wait..." he paused, "What do you mean by 'quest?'" he asked the darkness before him. "I'm a pilot—you need me to fly somewhere?"

The man seemed to be finding this back-and-forth humorous. "Oh, we'll be flying, alright! But if you don't mind, I think *I'll* take the controls on this one!"

"Then what do you need me for?! What's going on? Where are we?! And how did I get here?!" FISTY demanded, growing impatient through frustration.

"Ah..." the man sighed with a sheepish tone. "I suppose I *do* owe you a few answers... well, you see FISTY—"

A horn blew from outside, echoing loudly through the air like a vuvuzela.

"Shit! They're coming..." the mysterious figure cursed. "Sorry, Tom, but you're gonna have to trust me. I'll explain everything later—for now, just call me 'Showtime 12.'" He paused for a moment, then asked, "That weapon... Tom, where'd you find that?"

"The sword?!" Still seeing nothing, FISTY looked over his shoulder, toward where he'd woken up. "I uhh... I just found it on the ground?"

"The *ground?!*" the man repeated, shocked. "FISTY, that's no plain old blade. You're carrying the fabled Talisman Sabre—can't you tell from the glow?"

Glow? What the hell is this guy—but as he looked down, FISTY noticed it for the first time: the sword had a shimmering blue luminescence around it, enough to see the rest of his own body. He was wearing a flight suit—with *Lieutenant* bars sewed on—and on his chest, he had... *Chippy* patches? *I haven't worn these in decades...* He lifted the sword to try and see his mysterious aide, but to no avail, as the man was too far. "Did you say 'Talisman Sabre?' What is it?"

A terrifying wave of grunts and moans filled the air. "*Dammit...* get ready, Tom, they're coming! We have no chance in the darkness—these guys *thrive* in it. And we'll have to break through their wall—we can't take on the whole gang of them. C'mon, this way – *quickly!*" the man shouted as he began running away from FISTY, "Follow my voice!"

Unsure what was going on or who they were going up against, FISTY held the blue sword in front of him and began following the darkness-shrouded figure as best he could, using the glow of the sabre to navigate the environment. After a few minutes of sprinting, his feet feeling shockingly unaffected by the jagged surface, the area started to become more visible, as a light source appeared from an apparent exit. They were clearly in a cavern, with a river rushing through beside them. *A cavern... Is that what those words were saying? What the hell* was *that?*

Amongst the hurried pace, FISTY surprised himself with his stamina; he wasn't getting exhausted at all, seemingly able to run indefinitely. *Have I been drugged? I feel like I could last two-circle on the deck for an entire cycle... What's going on with me?!*

As they got closer to the exit, everything increasingly brighter by the second, FISTY started to make out features of his savior – he had a long brown cloak on, with the hood concealing his head. He was tall – even taller than FISTY. And from his waist brandished a long sheath, its gems glimmering in the luminescence.

"Put your weapon away, Tom!" the man looked back and warned. "One drop of these fiends' blood could infect you!"

"What?! Then how are we going to defend ourselves?!" FISTY asked, growing panicked.

"Follow my lead!" Showtime 12's silhouette appeared crisper, as an exit appeared to be just a sharp turn around the corner. "And it's important you know this: you can't hesitate out there or try and reason with them! These fiends know way too many outdated codes, regulations, and instructions; you'll never be able to out-pro-knowledge them – you simply need to blow through! And be *careful*, FISTY," he warned, "These brutes will show *no* mercy in attacking your character! You must use every bit of courage and belief in your heart if you're going to survive! If in doubt, remember who you are! Remember the person you are on the inside, *not* what they want to see on the outside!"

"Midgar, City of Mako" – Final Fantasy VII: REMAKE

FISTY jumped as the music shifted slightly, with words reappearing in the bottom left of his vision, fixed in the corner of his peripherals as he looked around for the source of the tune. *Is it coming from outside the cave? And those words... what is 'Midgar' or 'Mako?' What is this?*

As they rounded the corner, FISTY could finally see the outer world — they emerged from a rocky grotto amid lush greenery and entered a dark forest, with moonlight and heavy raindrops peeking through the trees above. The moans and rumbling voices were getting louder, as FISTY looked around in a frenzy, utilizing his SEM scan pattern from days of yore. He eventually snaplocked his gaze toward a flame in the distance — and then, he saw them.

A gaggle of humanoid behemoths, charging toward them — many carrying torches of gold fire that inexplicably seemed unaffected by the torrential downpour. The monsters were wearing blue coveralls — with Lieutenant Commander insignias on their collar devices and sheriff's badges on their chest plates — and donned overly-shined black, steel-toed boots. They were all hairless, with tall, bulky builds. Strangely enough, however, they appeared unarmed — they were simply steaming forward with the power of a pouty face, the armor of high rank, and the aura of perceived importance.

"There they are!" the guide yelled as he lowered his shoulder and — just as the music began building — dramatically shouted, "Come on, Tom, right up the middle, baby! Times up, let's do this; LEEEEEEROOOOOY... JEEEEEEEENKIIIIIINS!!!"

What the fuck? Is he seriously referencing one of the oldest memes in the book in a literal battle for our lives against these... these mutants!? Is this seriously happening?

The hooded figure ran toward the center of the stack, playing chicken with the centermost beast. For a second, FISTY was sure he was going to lose his escort already, his feet freezing in place and his heart stopping as he watched... But unfathomably, as the man's shoulder made physical contact with the opposing adversary's? The cloaked hero burst *right* through, sending the collection of fiends into a confused state of shock. FISTY watched as the entire group looked around in disbelief — and then began growling violently, nearly all of them barking at the hooded man.

"Shipmate!"

"Hey, shipmate!"

"Get back here, shipmate!"

"I'm talking to you, shipmate!"

"Hey, there's his JO buddy; he's got the Sabre! Let's get him!"

Oh, shit! Realizing they were talking about him, as the wave was now running his way, FISTY sobered from his temporarily stunned state and frantically tried to think. *Can I stop them? Maybe I could explain that this was a misunderstanding! Surely I haven't done anything wrong?*

But then, with the monsters' steps getting faster and louder, FISTY remembered his leader's advice. With a quick, deep breath of courage, FISTY ignored the part of his brain insisting he defend himself, and did what Showtime 12 recommended: he charged *back at them.*

As he got closer, the one in the middle yelled, "You better brace the air and get out of my way!"

Another screamed, "Your zipper is too low!"

"Hey, that mustache is out of regs! You need to set the example for the junior enlisted!"

Growing nervous and self-conscious about the professionalism of his actions and appearance, FISTY slowed his run and put his hand on his upper lip...

"Ignore them, FISTY!" the man yelled from afar. "You don't even *have* a mustache! They're trying to ruin your spirit and positivity with meaningless complaints that couldn't be less important!"

"Hey, shipmate, I saw you wearing AirPods while in uniform—how can you expect someone to trust you with a jet if you can't even follow simple directions?"

"Listen, LT, if you're taking food from the wardroom, a sailor might get the impression that it's ok to eat without our permission!"

"Hey, you're the guy who was walking around during the evening prayer! Show some respect for a forced religious act upon a culturally diverse carrier, shipmate!"

FISTY was growing increasingly unnerved... the voices of judgment and criticism from the approaching horde of goons eating further and further at his soul. He could barely even hear the voice of his compatriot, desperately calling out, "Please, FISTY, trust yourself and your instincts! Don't be distracted by the unimportant aspects of the job—of life...!" It was fainter and fainter. FISTY nearly found himself popping to attention and giving way to this pack of haters...

"FISTY!"

He could barely hear the man's voice...

"FISTY, look at your feet!"

My feet...? Practically moving in slow motion, he looked down to inspect his bare feet, expecting to see them torn up and battered from the cave running—but somehow, he now had boots on. Redwing boots... *unauthorized* Redwing boots. And keeping them tied? Green shoelaces—*unauthorized* green shoelaces... The boots weren't very shiny—looking like they'd been *used* or something, as crazy as that sounded; as if they'd been worn through thousands of flight hours on multiple deployments at sea away from home and family. Their imperfect condition was *definitely* unauthorized—*and yet it didn't fucking matter.*

Because then it hit him. The Navy was full of arbitrary rules and prohibitions that didn't make any fucking sense and—more importantly—made no fucking difference. FISTY thought back to all the things people got their asses blasted for: phone usage in unauthorized hangar bays, transiting the ship at unauthorized times, headphone usage on unauthorized sidewalks, putting your hands in unauthorized pockets, having a hat *on* in unauthorized places, taking your cover *off* in unauthorized places, and of course, filling laundry machines with unauthorized uniform items. He realized how one could drive themselves insane—as these creatures attempted to him—by pre-occupying themselves with all these meaningless flexes of authority. And, more insid-iously, he thought about how corrupt and unhappy one could turn by preoccupying themselves with *enforcing* these meaningless guidelines.

"Bombing Mission" – Final Fantasy VII: REMAKE

And like magic, FISTY felt his resolve returning to him—the music shifting in a similar fashion—as his LT bars illumed just as radiantly blue as his sword. With his spirit revitalized and the angry creatures just thirty feet ahead, FISTY's grim expression of panic curled up into a mischievous grin. He lowered his right shoulder and steamed max blast ahead, protected by the power of The Patch—something that meant *far* more to him than these arbitrary rules and enforcements that kept these power-hungry ty-rants feeling validated and important.

"SHIPMATE!" the human-like beast in front of him yelled. "STAND DOWN! Do NOT get in the way of a senior-ranking officer!"

But FISTY only ran faster, gaining speed and belief exponentially, as the horde got closer and closer... before finally...

"Shipmate, NO!!!"

Impact.

FISTY burst through with the slightest bit of a shoulder brush, sending his ad-versary and the entire enemy ground order of battle into a tizzy of contempt, disre-spect, and degraded importance.

Beyond the wall of brutes, FISTY saw a clearing where Showtime 12 was staged—on a tactical grey, low RCS, wings-folded, twin stabilator... *dragon?!* "FISTY! You did it!" he called out excitedly. "Now hop aboard, and let's get the fuck out of here!"

FISTY looked back and saw the beasts collecting themselves and recovering from their looks of shock and appall—their O-4 insignias now glowing red with fury. They pointed, growled out a jumbled mess of swears that included, "What command are you with?!", "Who's your skipper?!", and something about 'Naval tradition,' 're-spect,' and 'UCMJ'—and then charged forth once again.

"C'mon, Tom, hurry!" the man yelled with urgency.

Flynn picked back up the pace—running even *faster*, now that he was propelled with the footwear of disobedience—and sprinted toward the winged creature. With the guttural grunting hot on his tracks, FISTY's heart was pounding with every lunge, desperate to stay out of a stern WEZ. One yelled out, "Hey, shipmate, are those boots FOD-free and authorized for AMI? Turn around and show me the sole!" But FISTY was on to their deceitful tactics, and kept pushing toward the dragon.

As FISTY was a mere thirty paces away, Showtime 12—strapped into the front portion of a two-piece bubble saddle—began shouting commands to the dragon. "Lombardi, *tsubasa!*" Instantly upon the instruction, the dragon's folded wings began to lower to a spread and locked position. "*Soujuu!*" Every part of the dragon's body—from neck to tail—began flailing to their respective max ranges of motion, in a seizure-esque series of movements. As the thrashing ceased, he continued, "*Agaru!*" causing the dragon's wings to begin digging downward, creating a parabolic shape. He looked over to FISTY, extended his arm, and said, "Don't look back, Tom, you're not burnt! Just stay in max blast, and you'll make it!"

FISTY said nothing, still huffing and puffing despite feeling no exhaustion, as the voices and grunting behind him got closer...

"Hey, LT, when's the last time you got a haircut?"

"Did you shave today, shipmate?!"

"Lieutenant, did I see you washing that flight suit in self-serve laundry?!"

FISTY felt a hand swipe across his collar, barely missing a grasp of his uniform. The dragon, nearly within reach, started the slightest acceleration forward. "Tom, *JUMP!*" Showtime 12 yelled.

Propelled from his redwings, FISTY leaped forward with all of his might—un-heralded levels of ankle dorsiflexion giving him additional spring in his step—and like Michael Jordan elevating from the free throw line... the naval aviator *soared* into the open space, *caught* his hooded assistant's grasp, and swung right into the aft seat of the dragon's saddle, as the man yelled "*Saidaigen!*" and the dragon now zoomed forward, flames emitting from its wings.

"To Zanarkand" – Final Fantasy X

Catching his breath, FISTY once again noticed the white lettering in the lower left of his field of view. This time, the music completely changed themes to one that resonated as sad, melancholy—and completely *epic*. Flynn wiped the rainwater and sweat off his face and, in his peripheral vision, saw that the treetops were quickly descending below them. When he looked back down behind them, the beasts below were just a screaming circle of blue coveralls; their eyes and O-4 insignias still vibrant red with anger. He returned his scan forward, where all he could see in the distance was a dimly lit horizon...

And then—he did a double take, not believing his eyes—the words "**THE FISTY Chapter**" appeared in the sky momentarily—an apparent title screen—before the letters faded away into clouds, a la some sort of graphics transition. *What the* fuck?! He rubbed his eyes and looked again, and still saw the last few letters before they'd completely disappeared. *What the hell is going on here...?*

He brought his gaze down and noticed various familiar-yet-foreign panels on this aft dragon saddle: *Dispenser hand-rail toggles? Voice Alpha switches? Dual hand controllers?* He was shocked by, in the absence of controlling reins, how much empty space was freed up the center of the saddle. *My god... all this room... executing crossword puzzles back here would be so pleasant! Hey, is that...* "Umm... is this an ejection handle?" he asked his pilot.

The man chuckled. "Yeah... FISTY, if you don't mind, please don't touch that. Also, please arm your portion of Lombardi's saddle, and place the eject selector to AFT INITIATE."

FISTY looked to his left and saw a straight, yellow-and-black-striped handle. "Uhh... this one on the left? Do I just pull—"

"No!" the man quickly yelled. "It's a T-handle on your right—and actually, please place it to 'SOLO,'" he added, slightly annoyed.

FISTY did the command like a good boy, and armed his seat as well, the way he'd always done for so many years. *I had no clue dragons had ejection saddles just like the NACES seat—this is so wild...*

As they climbed higher and higher, the rain dwindled to a small mist, and the forest was far behind them. Now, all that remained below was a deserted wasteland of rubble and ruins, illuminated by moonlight from afar. There was no life, nor vegetation, nor growth—the entire world they flew above felt hopelessly dismal. *What is this place?* "Uhh... hey—so, do you mind telling me what's going on?" FISTY finally asked.

The man eased up on the dragon's thrust, giving a slight laugh as he called back, "Indeed—I suppose now would be a good time to catch you up on everything that's happened..." Showtime 12 doffed his hood, unveiling short brown hair. He untied the top his cloak a bit to reveal a New England Patriots #12 jersey. And when he smiled back at FISTY with his trademark cleft chin, the man's true identity was unmistakable.

"Terra's Theme" – Final Fantasy VI

"Tom fucking *Brady*!?" FISTY yelled with awe, excitement, and disbelief—barely even registering the melody swap to one of royal prominence. "Oh my *GOD!*" It was good that FISTY was strapped in tight to the dragon, because his body was jolting with the excitement of a hyper-obsessed little fangirl. He began spilling out endless amounts of embarrassing admissions: "Your honor... I'm your biggest fan! I've studied film of every game you've ever played, even recreational college intramurals—your stats were *insane* freshman year! *Thirty* tuddies, no picks, with a 5-0 record?! Are you *kidding* me?! ... Granted, I got my NIPR account banned for a bit because CAG ADP was being a bunch of pricks about me googling 'College coed two-hand-touch footage'..."

He continued, "I did my AP US History 'Notable American Leaders' research project on you, covering your rise from college backup to NFL *legend*, including all the successful campaigns you led en route to Super Bowls! ... Failed the project, because my teacher was a total bitch and looking for one of those history book-type leaders—I guess she wanted me to rave about one of those clowns who slept with their slaves..." he commented with a heavy eye roll.

"I wrote my master's persuasive thesis on the merits of your career over any other quarterback or figure in the game, and completely shut down the opposing faction of Montana, Manning, and Mahomes fanboys in a live debate during our capstone Philosophy 101 class! ... Bombed those, too, because the professor was a total choch from Indianapolis and a Deflategate-believing sheep; more like hashtag FrameGate, am I right?

"Mr. Brady, I even used you as my inspiration to rewrite the entire 'Leadership' chapter of TOPGUN—a revision that led to the overhaul of the SFWT syllabus to now include multiple briefing labs on what it means to execute like a *game-time player*—corralling your troops when adversity peaks, elevating your game when nerves spike, and fucking *making diamonds* when the pressure rises!

"Your holiness..." FISTY finally took a pause. "My entire life is a byproduct of the excellence and prowess you brought the game, your teams, and lives everywhere..." And with that, the former-Admiral-now-Lieutenant bowed from his seated position with every ounce of honor a man could hold, his chest going all the way down to the saddle without rounding his back—*incredible* hip-flexor pliability.

Brady commanded Lombardi to engage ATC/BaroAlt Hold, and looked at FISTY with matched awe. "Tom... you'll never *fucking* believe what I'm about to tell you..." With a head shake of disbelief, he couldn't help but beam as he explained, "But *my* entire career has all been thanks to *you!*"

"Me?!" FISTY asked, shocked. "But how?"

"Because, Tom—whenever I faced a late-game deficit, a bounce-back series after a pick-six, or a season-defining two-minute drill, I asked myself: How would *FISTY* handle this adversity... and turn it into an *opportunity?*" Brady threw up his arms casually and began listing, "When I suffered my first ever playoff loss—against the Broncos, after starting my career 10-0—including that infamous red area interception to Champ Bailey? I spent the *entire* offseason attending your robust HARM lectures in various Air Wing Fallons, seeking to understand what being a SME of *anything* truly entailed.

"After that rough 2006 AFC Championship defeat to our rival Colts, where we had a 21-3 halftime lead, and I threw a pick to Marlin Jackson to end the game? The media *loves* talking about our additions of Randy Moss, Wes Walker, and Donte Stallworth that offseason. And yet, it was the inclusion of *your* Training O standards that made the true difference: printing all of our passing validation sheets on card stock paper; rehauling our debriefing standards to include guides, val binders, and models in every film review room; and the hiring addition of a Training O's 'Bitch' to handle administrative tasks of tactical proficiency. *Those* are what turned us into a 16-0 juggernaut, and boosted me from 24 to *50* touchdowns!

"And Mr. Flynn... when we trailed by 10 in the fourth quarter of the 2015 Super Bowl against the Legion of Boom, setting up what could've been the Seahawks' 2nd straight title and my third consecutive loss in the Big Game..." Brady looked to the bright moon over the horizon, in reflection of that career-changing game. "I almost lost faith... almost thought that I was doomed to have only three rings, and could just retire with those decent numbers..." He snapped his head back to FISTY, "But then I remembered what you always said in your AWF lectures: '*Life is ultimately a war of resilience; the greatest of victories will be achieved by he who is simply the last one to give up. There are going to be days in your life when it feels like you've given everything you can, you're exhausted, and it's all over—and on these days, you have an opportunity—the opportunity to be ordinary... or to become one of the greatest of all time...*'

"FISTY..." the dragon rider nearly had tears in his eyes. "... *You* are the reason I'm a 7-time champion. *You* are the reason I kept fighting for more than 'good enough.' Everyone calls me the GOAT, but shit..." he shook his head in disbelief, "I'd be absolutely *nothing* without the mentorship of one Thomas A. Flynn."

FISTY was flabbergasted; he couldn't even *speak. My whole life... I've been inspired by this champion of men—unbeknownst that he's found that* same *inspiration—from* me?! It didn't matter that none of it made any logical sense—that Brady couldn't have been in Fallon during all those lectures without the security clearance to attend the chalk talks; that the 'Training-O Bitch' project didn't launch until FISTY's DH tour with the Chippies; or that the timeline of the entire fucking thing was an invalid disaster, seeing as Flynn wasn't even in the *Navy*, let alone STRIKE, in 2006—but FISTY *refused* to call a minus point for continuity error. It was almost as if he was in some time of vivid dream—where, despite the assortment of absurd events and unrelated components, everything *felt* like it made perfect sense. This narrative seemed not only plausible... but *destined*.

Sounding certain in himself for the first time, FISTY finally broke out of his stupor as he declared, "Fate has clearly brought our paths together for a reason, Tom. What is our mission objective?"

With Lombardi still on autopilot, Brady grinned and cracked his knuckles. "Always eager for the conduct—you truly are a tactical junkie." The legendary quarterback pulled out a map from the inner lining of his cloak and handed it to FISTY. "Take this, but please—let me speak before you open it."

"Wandering Flame" – Final Fantasy X

As Lieutenant Flynn held the map, Brady explained, "The world below us is the planet Elceediar. You may remember it as Earth—before it was overrun with all kinds of—well, for lack of a better word—*douchebags*. You—Showtime 11—being the chosen one of Naval Officers and leaders, agreed to undergo an indefinite slumber in the event that this world was ever infested by these complete—well, without a better term—*douche canoes*. You may remember when I retired for a second time, despite my belief that, at age 45, I still had plenty left in the tank?"

FISTY nodded. Of *course* he remembered. He'd taken a 12-day sabbatical from good-deal flights—instead only instructing bad-deal, 12-hour-day SFWT events while flying every landing at a dangerously slow 12 degrees alpha—an homage to the career of the greatest tac-athlete who ever played the game.

Brady continued, "I was contacted by TOPGUN and requested to be part of this top-secret mission—OPERATION: TOOL REMOVAL, or OTR—as a contingency, in case our fighting force failed to resist these—well, again, I can't think of a better way to say it—*douche nozzles*. I had to cease all NFL involvement... But for the chance to work alongside you—the GOAT of Tactics? It was worth the price. I went into hiding, taking a hiatus from the public eye, and waited for the moment when this high-end fight would be necessary." He looked grim and shrugged. "And now, here we are, with our entire home planet taken over by this band of—well, I hate to use the phrase, but—*douche clowns*..." Brady stared bitterly into the desolate abyss below them.

Curious, FISTY twisted his lips and asked, "Tom, you keep using these expressions to describe this horrid group... but whom are you speaking of?"

With a look of disgust, Brady spoke with a scathing hatred, "The same people who tormented me my entire career, FISTY: trolls. Those who have nothing better to do in life than attempt to tear down the good-natured living of another human being, from the depths of their hollow abyss where a heart *should* reside—but instead lies a bleak, empty place of despair in their core. The kinds of people who find it appropriate to go on a public figure's Instagram account and post hateful comments that are aggressively malicious, borderline death threat-y, and absolutely pathetic. Remember, FISTY, when LeBron James was asked about all the people taking delight in him and the Heat losing their 2011 debut championship appearance?"

"Yes, I do," FISTY answered, with surprise in his voice. The answer strangely came right to him despite not being a huge NBA fan, as if it were suddenly programmed into his brain for dialogue's sake. He recalled, "LeBron said that 'All the people that were rooting on me to fail; at the end of the day, they have to wake up tomorrow and have the same life that they had when they woke up today. They got the same personal problems they had today. And I'm going to continue to live the way I want to live, and continue to do the things I want to do with my family, and be happy with that.'"

"Exactly," Tom said with a head nod. "Now, was it the most professional answer? Probably not. Does he wish he could reword it? Sure—he was young, and we're all figuring out life as we grow. But he was *on* to something, FISTY—something so many of us never realize in life: There is an existence of flat-out *trolls* out there—unhappy with their lives' trajectory, disappointed in the decisions they've made, and bitter about their inability to achieve *real* satisfaction and purpose. As a result?! They take *glee* in raining on the parade of successes. They feel *importance* by criticizing their peers. They achieve *homeostasis* in the world by attempting to bring others down to their low level. It's sad, really..." Brady said as he folded his arms.

Understanding the story symbology, like a scripted dream narrative meant to bring the viewer more in touch with the overall story themes, FISTY pointed out, "And the internet trolls who do this to celebrities and athletes—it's the same as those in the Navy who take pride and power in tearing down others over the most unimportant aspects of the job!"

"Bingo," Brady nodded. "We're looking for people to be warriors—leaders of men and women; champions of courage, assertive and decisive in the face of fear; *Good Dudes*—the kind of brother or sister you'd risk your life for. And instead? These..." Brady scoffed, "these *trolls* are polluting the world, more interested in hunting down a shipmate than working arm-in-arm with a teammate."

FISTY thought back to the coverall-wearing beasts who'd nearly engulfed him. "Tom... those—those *things* back there—were they trolls?"

Looking sad, Brady continued nodding. "Afraid so. A 'Hinge Horde'... the planet is rampant with them. After the Armageddon of Elceediar, nearly every free-thinking human was taken over by the hordes. They prey on uniqueness, different perspectives, and common sense—seeking to turn every level-headed person into one of their Instruction-adhering, logic-ignoring, doctrine-worshipping lemmings. Human decency, reasonable man theory, and bigger-picture thinking have no place in their species' brains—and such traits have become all but extinct in the takeover. You, I, and the Viper Unit may be all the individuality that remains..."

"Viper Unit?" FISTY asked.

"SeeD" – Final Fantasy VIII

With a sharp music change, FISTY felt like he was back in the Crystal Palace, as he could tell a brief was underway...

"Indeed," Brady nodded with desolation. "A rogue, level-5000 adversary squadron led by the only other free thinker who survived the catastrophe—a free-thinker of radical and extremist nature. The Unit seeks to use the Hinge Hordes to their advantage; to control the fate of the planet.

"The squadron contains five deadly terrorists: Dawg 5, a sharp-shooting archer who will take you down if you let your timeline-SA drop for even a second. Mutt 4, a suicide-bomber willing to take the most desperate of means to strike where it will cause the most blue losses. Mamba 3, a dark magician capable of spells that will light your helmet on fire, showing you pictures you never could've *fathomed* in your briefing ex-amples. Cobra 2, a highly skilled warrior from Monte Carlo, who you can virtually guarantee will survive Pk misses all the way to the merge. And lastly..." he shook his head in disgust, "Viper 1, the evil genius behind the entire presentation, and a former US naval aviator that you quite possibly served alongside. It's *his* game plan that could eradicate our kind entirely, FISTY..."

"Viper 1..." LT Flynn repeated with an understood seriousness.

Brady pointed to the map. "It's about time you catch up on route study—open up the chart, FISTY."

FISTY slowly unraveled the map—sending a beam of thunderous rumbling into the air, lightning literally striking around them and illuminating the sky as the map was uncovered. "Look quickly!" Brady warned, "We can't keep it open for too long!"

With a sense of awe and urgency, FISTY scanned the map and finally made sense of it: it was a strike route. Their current position, somehow reflected on the map, was inside a blue square. From that square extended a straight line to a red triangle. But past the red triangle... *No egress flow point?* "What's our contingency plan?! Or the white card option?" FISTY yelled above the roaring thunder.

"There is none!" Brady rapidly scanned between the map and the airspace ahead of them. "This is a zero-fail mission; *ALR: Extreme!* We either save the world, or we die valiantly trying! Now close it!"

FISTY wrapped up the map, and the skies returned to simply overcast and gloomy. Brady disengaged BaroAlt by turning with too sharp an angle of bank, and redirected Lombardi about fifty degrees to the right, pushing the mystical beast beyond ATC and engaging full power. As the dragon turned and burned, FISTY saw a beam of light extending indefinitely from afar, aligned directly where the triangle on the map was—a *needle* even present on the dragon's nose to guide them, as if Brady had somehow marked it IRL from the route. "The target..." FISTY began, "What are we striking?"

"Viper 1's floating castle in the sky," Brady said with steeled eyes.

FISTY had so many questions as they circumnavigated the stormy goo, all without map data around them due to TAMMAC-loading errors in the world as they now knew it. *All free-thinking eradicated? Hinge Hordes? And Viper 1... who* was *he?*

As if conveniently sensing his remaining confusion for narrative exposition, Brady explained, "FISTY, Viper 1 has kept his identity secret since the Armageddon—a kind of red lead secrecy we at TOPGUN had always imagined would be cool in blue air events, but is really biting us now. As a result, we haven't been able to get a read on him, his game plan, or even his assessed capabilities. But thanks to the many bothans that died to bring us the intel we needed, we've achieved mensurated coordinates on his floating castle—FISTY!" Brady's voice inflection skyrocketed as he pointed ahead, clearly and concisely yelling, "Showtime 12, tally one, *my* 1 o'clock, 10 miles, 20 high!"

"The Landing" – Final Fantasy VIII

FISTY jumped as the sound shifted to a breathtaking heartbeat. He put his eyes on the exact piece of sky described by Brady—the song slowly unveiling a trumpet-based tune—and immediately gained a mutual tally on the object at hand from his pilot's expertly-worded comm call. There, in the distance, was a tall, black, middle-ages-style castle; cumulonimbus clouds and lightning swarming it—the structure had an ominous feel that made FISTY uncomfortable and even slightly afraid—yet also, he admitted to himself, it looked *so* badass...

"Lombardi won't be able to land there, FISTY," Brady warned. "We're going to need to ingress there on our own!"

"What?!" FISTY asked incredulously. "But how?!"

"Put that seat selector back to AFT INITIATE," the QB instructed, "And make sure your harness straps are tightened, mask on, and visor down!"

Confused at what was happening, FISTY adjusted the yellow handle and called out, "What do you mean? I always fly that way...?"

Brady snickered, "Oh yeah, *same here...*"

Regardless, FISTY watched as the castle emerged closer and closer, the thunder growing louder and louder, trying to figure out what exactly the plan was.

"Showtime, attack!" Brady yelled out.

FISTY watched as his hero began to take all the precautionary steps he had instructed just moments ago. Inexplicably, it looked like Brady hadn't previously even *touched* his leg restraint garter or lap strap tightness, originally wearing them all like a pair of loose sweatpants. He re-grabbed the controls on his dragon and scanned around the castle as it was quickly approaching. "Get ready, FISTY—we can't let the Viper Unit see us coming!"

Frantically trying to understand the plan, FISTY nearly lost his breath as Brady shoved Lombardi's nose down—getting *below* the castle and driving past, essentially *treeing* the fortress behind them.

"Goggles, goggles, goggles!" Brady yelled as he ripped night vision goggles off his head and threw them forward.

Huh?! When did he get — but FISTY quickly realized he, too, had NVGs donned atop his dome, and in a panic, quickly yanked them off and dropped them behind him.

"Almost time..." Brady called out... waiting... "Almost..." He scanned his HUD... took one last look behind them...

FISTY, confused and growing anxious, asked, "Brady, could you please just—
"

"Here we go!" the GOAT yelled. "MRM, MRM, MRM!"

The Gs locked FISTY to his saddle as Brady selected max AB, initiated a 4G pull up to 47-50 degrees nose up, and then unloaded the dragon to 45 degrees nose up on Lombardi's velocity vector. At 250 KCAS, Brady roared—this time most forcefully of all: "Eject, eject, *eject*!"

Holy shit, FISTY realized, *he's going to fucking* —

The last thing FISTY remembered before knocking out was the sounds of explosions, rockets, and Tom Brady yelling, "Let's GOOOOOOO!"

"The Castle" – Final Fantasy VIII

FISTY blinked, feeling for his surroundings. There appeared to be some sort of nylon blanket covering him, with strings attached. He was damp... and he could hear rain atop his blanket. *What's this... what is — oh shit! The ejection! Tom Brady!* He ripped the parachute blanket off his body, and looked around for his hero-turned-cohort — he could've *sworn* he saw the words "AUTOSAVE" flash across his vision momentarily — and then found Brady passed out, face-down next to a stone slabbed wall. "Tom!" he called out, rushing toward the GOAT, praying that he'd also survived the ejection.

But when he got there, he found that Brady was not unconscious at all — he was merely hunched over, pushing at marble pieces of the wall. Brady looked up at FISTY and smiled. "Tom! You made it!" He threw him a fist bump, then urged, "Now get down here and start helping me! I swear, it's gotta be around here *somewhere...*"

Confused, FISTY asked, "*What* is?"

Brady shook his head, chuckling. "FISTY... you sure love playing the naïve, reluctant hero... C'mon, take a look around — you think we're just gonna flow in direct via the entrance?"

For the first time — and as the background song hit its crescendo and began the low organ notes — FISTY looked up and took in the adversary stronghold, awe-and-fear-inspired. Viper 1's castle towered above them, with tall, stone-slabbed gatehouses patterned amongst the perimeter, flags emerging from each. It was austerely dark outside, with just a bit of moonlight piercing through the thick storm clouds above them — but enough luminescence for FISTY to make out the crest of the Viper Unit on each flag: a curved red arrow with a lightning bolt-esque tip. It was the sexiest arrow FISTY had ever seen — he knew very well that lust was a prime weapon in the loadout of the Satanic Red Air; as was infinite ammo and retroactive shot generation. He kept his gaze going around the castle and saw the stowed drawbridge at the heavily-guarded entrance, with multiple enemy radars pointed downrange at the primary ingress location. The entire fortress was surrounded by a moat of red, cross-hatched TAMMAC Politically Sensitive Area lines; an unspoken but understood feeling in one's mind of 'I better not cross these...' And lastly, the centerstage of the castle itself: a skyrocketing tower, with its peak obscured by the cumulonimbus goo, patrolled by a tactical formation of VisCap bats — adding to the eeriness of the image. *That must be Viper 1's chamber...*

Lightning crackled loudly in beat with the thunderous notes of the music, as FISTY stared at the headquarters of the adversarial unit. *If I must go there and slay Viper 1 myself, then I shall do it...*

"One of these stones, I swear," Brady insisted as he continued to push on various portions of the castle wall.

He's looking for a secret passage... FISTY realized, kneeling down beside Brady to help search the rocks. *If I were to build a castle like this, where would I hide it?* And then,

413

as if possessed, a thought directed his attention to the wall just 19.5 paces to the right. FISTY marched over—Brady watching with hopeful anticipation—and carefully rubbed a seemingly normal, smooth rock, jutting out from the bulkhead. He paused for a moment, then drew the Talisman Sabre, and lightly placed its end on the granite piece. The stone smoothly withdrew into the wall—and a secret passageway door glowed blue just a few feet away.

"Brilliant, Tom!" Brady yelled with glee as he scurried over to the unveiled entry beside the Lieutenant pilot. The two scanned the area around them for traffic, then opened the door, ingressed, and quickly secured it behind them. In the tiny, dimly-lit secret hallway, they didn't go far before finding a ladder leading into an abyss below. They nodded at each other and quickly descended down several rungs, eventually plunging to the dark catacombs underneath the castle's main floor.

As they reached solid ground, the room—like the lead-in passageway— was barely illuminated by torches along the wall. Seeking more visibility, FISTY drew the Talisman Sabre from his waist and held the sword in front of him. For some reason, it seemed to be glowing more brightly, with a furious rate of pulsating. "*Man,* it's dark in here... Tom, what's going on with the sword?" FISTY asked.

"Ah, yes!" Brady nodded with understanding. "The sword radiates most prominently when its ownship is within a weapons employment opportunity!"

FISTY felt his heart leap, as both his pickle thumb and trigger finger started to itch.

"But beware..." Brady continued with a foreboding tone, "For it also could mean you're very likely on the cusp of a WEZ..."

"A WEZ?" FISTY asked, turning his head to look over at his NFL hero, "But how—"

FISTY jumped as he heard the subtle '*TWING*' of an arrow rushing within inches of his ear.

"Let the Battles Begin!" – Final Fantasy VII

As the music swapped without any fade whatsoever, and new track information popped up in his vision, FISTY instinctually covered his head and—with direction over description—yelled, "Tom, get down! Smoke in the air!"

The two immediately executed their reactive arrow defense by collapsing to the floor and executing somersaults to the nearest piece of shelter. When they were assured a brief moment of sanctuary, FISTY whispered between huffs and puffs, "Dawg 5..."

Brady silently shook his head, trying to sneak peeks and scan the dark room behind them.

"Welcome to your SFWT Assault on Viper 1's Castle!" a husky voice called from afar. "The bandits concur with your darkness assessment. And now, I recommend... that you... *die!*"

A flurry of arrows came raining down on their position, a few *barely* missing the two valiant blue fighters. FISTY crouched down even tighter, as Brady yelled, "C'mon, FISTY, we need to move!"

"Move?!" FISTY yelled from his shielded position. "Move *where?!*" The arrows continued to come, a seemingly endless supply of shots from Dawg 5. With each impact, the structure they hid behind kept getting more battered, as pieces started to fall off and their safeguard began to dissipate.

"This guy has unlimited shots, and he's well-within Rmax," Brady explained, hunching low to match his barricade. "If we don't do *something*, we'll get tagged any moment! FISTY, *think* — you're facing an opponent with excellent long-range capability, just like we always did against Peyton Manning and the Colts — how can we take away that advantage?"

Amongst the heart-pumping music, FISTY focused, attempting to tune out the chaos of the shots fired upon them — and then it dawned on him, as he said out loud, "Force them to switch weapons... change to a rushing attack — min-range them!"

Brady grinned, "Bingo, baby! Now come on; take this shield, adhere to your parameters, and redefine the fight the way *you* want it!" The GOAT QB pulled — seemingly out of thin air — a gigantic shield from his invisible inventory, and tossed it to FISTY.

FISTY caught the shield and briefly admired it, the letters 'VALIANT' shining brilliantly across the front. Nodding, he looked at Brady, coiled his body, and shouted, "Showtime 11... banzai!" With the command given, FISTY jumped out — his shield brandished in front of him — and charged toward the arrow onslaught's artillery position. He felt a slight bit of fear, sure — but FISTY was a diligent tactician, and knew that by adhering to his strict parameters of 'keep the shield in front of you,' he would minimize his chances of dying as he approached Dawg 5.

"What!?" The husky terrorist voice cried out. "My weapons... they're useless! Too close for arrows, switching to guns!"

But the adversary had made a grave mistake by broadcasting his location via vocal transmission, and FISTY was able to assess that he was in position to drop his shield, lunge forward, and strike. He exited his parameters, tossed the shield away, and turned toward the voice direction — just in time to gain tally of Dawg 5 attempting to wield a laser gun of destruction. Unsure why Dawg 5 didn't use that in the first place — but not caring — FISTY drew his sword and yelled "FOX-2!" as he struck the blade down on his archer adversary. As the sword made impact with Dawg 5, his body instantly began fading, and the hostile opponent used his last breath to scream: "DAWG 5... DEAD!"

As he fist-pumped to celebrate the victory, FISTY coolly said, "Showtime 11, FENCE'd in; *Negative dawg...*" Growing serious again, he tried to recce the downed archer, but the man seemed to be nearly faceless—a blank stare with hollow eyes, and no distinguishing characteristics whatsoever aside from the sound of his voice.

As FISTY watched the body completely disintegrate, Brady appeared beside him, slapping his back in praise. "FISTY, that banzai was *STAN* as *fuck!* Incredible! *That's* why you were selected as Showtime 11!"

FISTY was pleased with the way the attack went, but also confused. "Tom— that man... he seemed to have no identity..." It was more of a question than a statement.

"Memories of Distant Days" – Shenmue

Brady nodded slowly, seeming not to notice the music change, and looked glum as he affirmed, "Yes, FISTY... they *never* do. It's the curse of the red air pawn— no presence at the red coord brief, rolling into work 1+30 prior, learning your game plan by scanning the kneeboard diagram while half-listening to the briefer, and then dropping off your shot data and calling it a day after the flight—nary even a learning point to consider." Brady shook his head in disgust. "The thought of red air being the chillest flight in the fleet... it's an abomination. An insult to The Patch you wear on your shoulder."

FISTY turned to his right and looked down the line of bearing where his hypothetical wingman would be lined up in spread. As he cocked his neck down and analyzed his patch—*The* Patch—he digested the words Brady was saying. The red air... they were just brainless, order-following lemmings... it was like an IRL Attack of the Clones. FISTY's jaw clenched, and his eyes filled with disappointment as he lamented the red's unfortunate reality. *How can they expect to become professional red air if they don't even attend the mass debrief to see where they committed errors in flight?!*

"Recommend we keep pushing forth, Chosen One—time is of the essence," Brady insisted, trying to re-cage FISTY's brain.

"Showtime, flow straight ahead," FISTY agreed.

The two worked their way through the dimly lit catacombs and eventually found a winding staircase toward a brighter ascent. As they continued upward, LT Flynn felt unease in his soul. "Tom," he asked, "how did it happen? How did planet earth become Elceediar?"

Brady sighed with regret and cleared his throat. "You see, Tom... the fleet needed more men like you. More men with *initiative.* We got so..." Brady winced and scoffed, "so *complacent* in going through the motions; so *hyper-focused* on the wrong, meaningless stuff — zippers, check-ins, and ATC comm brevity... We lost the ability to use our brains — forgot how to *think critically* and create our own destinies in the jet. Flying, tactics, and execution... it became one gigantic, scripted BFM video played out real-time, sortie after sortie..."

"But the small things," FISTY remarked, as they continued up the stairs and found themselves navigating a wine cellar. "Aren't they what *matter?*"

Brady laughed. "You remind me of Coach Belichick. Love the man... but at times? He was just... overly stern and critical." He paused, then asked, "Remember when I went to Tampa?"

"Of course," FISTY acknowledged, "It was a gigantic beach party! The anti-Patriot way — No rules; just fun!"

"Compared to New England, it sure was!" Brady said with a chuckle. "And that's what the public saw — but what *really* happened was the transfer of *so* many of the tactical lessons Coach Belichick taught me — *without* the hyper-obsession on the as-inine, inconsequential parts." He shrugged and explained, "Football and aviation... they're not so different, FISTY. Of *course* the small details matter — but not the *minutiae* details! We so often want to completely standardize the two industries; and yet, they're businesses that just *can't* be fully standardized — nor do they *need* to be! Just as two successful musicians can have their own distinct *style,* yet still play in the same key and on the same sheet of music — *so can teammates!* My time with the Bucs was a massive success, as we all got on the same page within a *year* — but it wouldn't have been pos-sible without 20 years of experience sifting through what mattered and what *didn't.* Imagine telling a brand-new wide receiver out of college — or a brand new FNG out of the RAG — that they demonstrated a great hungry attitude, showed up knowledgeable on the playbook, and executed their tactic well all day — but then spent time critiquing and emphasizing their pulled-too-low socks, that they sat in the wrong chair during the game film debrief, or the imperfect-ness of the literal X's and O's they drew on the board — and the direction in which they *erased* them!" Brady threw up his hands with a look of incredulity. "Why do we *care* about this bullshit?!"

"How will we get standardized if we don't?" FISTY countered, growing a bit concerned with Brady's lackadaisical nature. "How will we learn and get better if we don't point out every single tiny flaw that the other person commits?!"

Brady took a long look at his flight lead, chuckled softly, and said, "FISTY... the same way people manage to get in shape without somebody scrutinizing every piece of food that goes into their body. The same way people have successful relationships without pointing out every less-than-perfect detail of their significant other. The same way people learn to become adults without their parents helicoptering over them, hyper-analyzing every single deviation from 'the perfect human' that one makes. We don't have the time, nor brain capacity, to process every single mistake in life—we have to trust ourselves to understand the ones that matter—and focus on *those*. Otherwise, what are we, other than a bunch of spineless sheep on autopilot, with no ability to stray from the pack of conformist groupthink?"

Refusing to budge completely, FISTY shook his head. "Tom... I just don't know—can we really trust a new guy to deliver a bomb on target on time if his zippers are unzipped in the brief?!"

Brady sighed, putting his hand on FISTY's shoulder. "If we can't, Tom? Then we truly are doomed..."

The two moved in silence as they ascended from the cellar, eventually finding themselves in the castle's main foyer, surrounded by menacing red stained-glass windows and large, sharp-edged tables with less-than-infinity seating. As they tiptoed through the grand hall, FISTY noticed the glow of his Talisman Sabre... He put his hand up to stop Brady, crouched down, and began his textbook SEM scan. The background soundtrack music started faded to silence—an *uncomfortable* silence, instilling instinctual danger. FISTY felt his heart rate rapidly rising as his scan became more fervent... and then finally, he saw it in the distance—a Launch and Steering square, fully-filled in, far up the staircase—with its target heading vector pointed *directly* at the twosome.

"Encounter" – Metal Gear Solid

"Showtime 11, contact, straight ahead!" FISTY called out to his wingman.

"Recommend you shoot this guy; shoot this guy, now!" Brady tossed a missile launcher from his inventory FISTY's way—again, magically appearing from nowhere.

FISTY caught it on his shoulder and, in one motion, pulled the trigger not once... not twice... but *thrice*. The kickback from the projectile was insane; FISTY nearly fell as three flyout cue diamonds went streaming downrange toward the yellow cube on the horizon, homing right in on it. Trying to do math in his head—and using his range and bearing eyeball to assess the distance between himself and the adversary—he quickly started panicking and shouted, "Showtime, let's get the fuck out of here!"

Immediately upon command, FISTY and Brady swung their bodies around 180 degrees and started sprinting away from the impending wreckage of the missiles. After running for an ample amount of time and explosions were heard, FISTY instructed, "Ok, he should be gone—let's go back hot!"

But as they found after completing their turns, the L&S unfathomably remained, *still* hot to them, and was accelerating in speed—now moving with *anger*. "Shit!" FISTY yelled. "How the fuck did he survive that?!"

"Pk misses..." Brady uttered woefully as the two kept running inbound, eating up their range. "FISTY... that L&S—it must be—"

"Cobra 2..." FISTY narrowed his eyes. "Well, at the end of the day, Father Shot Table is undefeated – suck AMRAAM, fiend!" He unloaded multiple more flyout missiles toward the enemy, then directed himself and Tom to run away bravely once again. After a few more moments, FISTY believed it was safe to ascend the staircase, and called for Tom to join him—but Cobra 2 was *still alive.*

"What the fuck?!" FISTY yelled. "*Inconceivable!* What *is* this RNG?!"

"How many missiles do you have left?!" Brady shouted, the two still flowing toward the adversarial L&S.

FISTY checked his inventory, which for some reason was displayed on an interface in front of him that also showed his health bar (80%), name (Tom 'FISTY' Flynn), and lives left (1). "I'm out!" he responded, seeing the zero next to his 'Missiles' counter. With no intention to flee anymore, he prepared to draw his Sabre to take on this foe.

But as he did, something just didn't smell right... and sure enough, something *else* caught his eye—specifically, the *left* side of his eye, where he'd always been trained to look religiously. On the left of his interface, he saw the health points of the enemy he was attacking—*two* sets of *mippling* health points, slightly displaced over one another.

"Holy shit—Brady, it's a stack!" FISTY yelled. "There are *two* contacts! There's a guy underneath the staircase, too!"

Brady's eyes widened. "Oh *fuck!* Mutt 4! Tom, he's probably going for the castle reactor, right near the main door! If he gets past you and attacks it, this whole place will collapse on us, and OPERATION: TOOL REMOVAL has all been for naught!"

Thinking quickly, FISTY directed, "I'll target the low contact; you take the high one! No more running away—we have to stop these bastards!"

Brady nodded and wielded his own weapon—a neon red, white, and blue katana. The quarterback charged toward the staircase, while FISTY frantically shifted his visual lookout low to the 1st floor of the foyer, trying to find the sneaky striker...

Where the fuck is he... He scanned methodically, trying to pick up a tally of this jabroni. *I had SA to him for a second... He should be right there... Fuck, dude, I'm running out of time and distance...*

And then he saw it: a flash of closure, *barely* in his field of regard—a grotesque zombie-looking beast on all fours, scampering with TNT strapped to its back, crossing through The Patch wearer's left 10 o'clock. FISTY instantly reversed course and started sprinting toward the creature, arriving just behind him—the putrid smell filling Flynn's nostrils—and attempted to get within range to splash him. "Brady, I found Mutt 4!"

But all he heard in response was a stern, "Standby! Showtime 12's turning!"

That's not the correct verbiage... FISTY thought. But against all odds, he somehow used context clues and common sense to know exactly what his wingman was trying to convey.

Mutt 4, aware that his presence was known, began howling and barking aggressively as he raced toward the reactor by the castle's entrance. FISTY spotted a strange, bright red line in the foyer that he hadn't noticed before—it looked almost computer-generated, like the first-down line the NFL included on its TV broadcasts. From Flynn's assessment, if Mutt 4 was able to cross that line and detonate his bombs, this mission was a failure. FISTY started doing some math in his head—random fraction rules-of-thumb, to see if he would make it to Mutt 4 in time at his current speed—but then just decided: *Fuck it, I need to GO!* He sprinted as fast as he could, mustering up every bit of energy left in his package to intercept the striker. In the far distance behind him, he heard "COBRA 2... DEAD!"—and his legs felt lighter as his heart leaped. He kept running... *almost there... so close...*

"HYEAAHHHHH!" With a cry of courage, FISTY made a diving effort with his sword fully extended—plunging it into the freakish decayed human's back—*milliseconds* before it crossed the 'Fuck My Life' line.

As the sword pierced his fly-covered, infected skin, the adversary cried out, "MUTT 4... DEAD!" The rotting body vaporized into air, as FISTY laid prone on the ground, catching his breath; his health bar now showing 60%. He rolled onto his back, staring at the chandeliers on the castle ceiling, and whispered to himself, "Showtime 11, splash one; low contact, single group... *vanquished.*" He pumped his fist slowly, and sat up to regain visual of his wingman.

But he couldn't see Brady... the staircase was void of all contacts. FISTY got to his feet, held his sword in front of him for light—both hands near his head, blade pointed downrange like an old-school samurai—and carefully crept forward. "Showtime 11, blind..." he called out. But no response. "Showtime 12, say posit..." Nothing. "Brady..." he asked with a hint of nervousness, "where are you?!"

He continued up the staircase and through the 2nd story passageway, tiptoeing past various hatches. Most of the doors appeared to be pre-rendered backgrounds that were not interactable—but *one* in particular seemed to have 3D geometry, shading, and clearly stood out from the rest. FISTY slowly reached for the handle—but it opened for him.

Tom Brady stood on the other side, frowning. "Hello, Showtime 11," he said stiffly, scratching at his mustache.

"Tom!" FISTY called out, relieved. "You're alive!"

"Mantis Hymn" – Metal Gear Solid

"Let's continue flowing this way," Brady said, as the music changed to a haunting ambiance. "We need to chat about some... *things.*"

Not sure what he meant, FISTY gave a flow heading through the passageway, leading to what appeared to be an art gallery. FISTY inspected his surroundings, noticing various images depicting famous moments in the Viper Unit history: multiple paintings of SFWT candidates with heads hanging and disappointed faces, and more experienced flight suits putting hands on their shoulder, speech bubbles emerging from those individuals. The different portraits had variations of speech, including "It's no big deal, you'll just get more reps," or "Hey, I had to refly this one, too," or "Listen, I *really* think it'll benefit you to see this one more time."

FISTY shuddered; the terrifying portraits invoked dread, sending chills down his spine.

"Lieutenant Flynn..." Brady started, as they kept walking down the gallery, "we should debrief what just happened—I was really disappointed with your performance out there."

"Huh?" FISTY asked, unsure where this was coming from. "What... what do you mean? It was a mission success...?"

Brady shook his head and clenched his jaw above his smooth, dimple-free chin, casting a glare FISTY's way. "Your comms—they were *completely* non-standard. First, you're going to make a 'contact' call—FISTY, that comm standard changed *ages* ago. Next, you'll say 'straight ahead.' *Technically*, he was about two degrees left—remember, words *mean* things... and also: 'Ahead?' Do you know how confusing that can be for a new guy?"

While the quarterback was technically correct, FISTY was aghast at what he was hearing—especially with Brady recalling everything in the future tense, which made absolutely no grammatical sense. Like a good boy, though, he simply nodded and shut up, continuing to look at the Viper Unit décor around them. He saw a still-life of a gigantic python shooting foreign missiles out of its eyes like laser beams, and squeezing its body around the center of a helpless F/A-18, suffocating its Environmental Control System.

"And then you'll use all this *extraneous* and *unprofessional* comm," Brady continued with a look of disgust, angrily ruffling his black hair before pulling a kneeboard card from his inventory. "At time 4+54, you'll say 'Showtime, let's get the fuck out of here' — *what*?!" he scoffed. "Flynn, radio space is *scarce* and *precious* in these fights. Later, you'll respond 'I'm out' when asked for your loadout, and — Jesus, a whole *litany* of additional misspeaks..."

Growing irritated, FISTY's fists tightened, but he continued to submissively listen to his kool-aid-drinking-and-thus-wise instructor. Out of the corner of his eye, he noticed a glass display of game-used red air debrief cards — it had nothing on it but 'alive' and 'dead' times, as well as half-assed environmentals written down.

"Ugh, and this 'Brady, I found Mutt 4' comm call you'll make — *right* as I'm at a fucking merge! *So* distracting!" he growled. "I might even call it a 'Safety of Flight!'" Slapping his hand on his forehead, then *knife-handing* FISTY, Brady grumbled, "Comm priority, dude. It's there for a *reason*. Hopefully, next time you do this, you'll remember that..."

FISTY stopped dead in his tracks. "Hold up a second... '*next time?*' Are you seriously gonna make me fight that boss *again?!*"

Brady grinned evilly and nodded his head. "Affirm — I already talked to your Training O."

"Enclosure" – Metal Gear Solid

FISTY looked at the angry quarterback and asked, "What's your problem, Tom? We attrited the adversaries and saved the day, didn't we?!" In their standstill, the two stood before a pair of doors at the end of the gallery — one labeled 'PRESS' and the other labeled 'PARALYSIS BY ANALYSIS.'

Brady's scowl became even more irate. "Unbelievable, Flynn — you're not listening to a single word I'm saying! This is *exactly* what I'm talking about; your overall SA is still *too* far below average to trust you, your comms just *too* out of standards to continue on to bigger events, and the way you handled yourself in this debrief?! *Way too* unprofessional! This clearly needs to be re-flown. You need to get back into the chapters and chairfly these comms — and with the extra reps, you'll start to see the bigger picture, and more clearly understand what's happening around you. And dude..." Brady shook his head, his dreadlocks flowing in the wind, "You didn't even have the recall to call *me* out on my nonstandard comm."

"What do you mean?" FISTY asked.

"I said I was 'turning' vice 'anchored' — and I should have *at least* added some type of bullseye cut!"

In shock, FISTY argued, "But... but I wasn't confused at all — I knew what you meant real-time, and the bullseye really didn't even matter at that p — "

"But it *could've* mattered to somebody else listening!" Brady countered. "God, you're not even *thinking* of other entities, are you?! Not to mention... Lieutenant Flynn," Brady hissed, "I've hijacked your entire debrief, you fool. That *cannot* happen! You need to have the *courage* to control your debrief and call out others in the room—albeit tactfully, because you don't want to embarrass or offend a superior."

"What are you *talking* about?!" Flynn shot back, now angry. "I didn't even *want* to debrief this bullshit!"

Glaring through his red eyes, Brady disappointedly declared, "And that is *exactly* why I'm giving you a below-average refly..." The legend stood blocking the 'PRESS' door and extended his arm—his zero Super Bowl rings shining dully—directing FISTY's attention to the 'PARALYSIS BY ANALYSIS' gateway, as the background music reflected the former Chippy's utter failure. "Trust me," Brady added, trying to show artificial sympathy out of nowhere, "You'll be glad you got another look. You're going to be so much better—and then you'll *really* be ready for the next level."

FISTY's heart sank. *This is... this is unbelievable! How can he say that? Sure, the comms weren't technically* right—*but were they* that *confusing? Only an idiot couldn't understand...*

"And you know what's most frustrating of all?!" Brady asked.

Unsure how he could feel any worse, FISTY grumpily asked, "What..."

Looking completely abhorred, Brady glared at FISTY. "Your SA, Lieutenant—it is *so* unsat! When you're *so* hyper-focused, looking through the soda straw, you miss the most obvious things around you..." Brady sneered, his #13 jersey peeking through his brown cloak.

"The Price of Freedom" – Final Fantasy VII: Crisis Core

And then it hit him. Being referred to as 'Lieutenant' and 'unsat'... the mustache and smooth chin... the dreadlocks... the jersey... FISTY looked down through his peripheral vision—just below the music display information—and confirmed his suspicion: the Talisman Sabre was glowing blue with a furious amplitude. This was *not* Tom Brady—this was no free-thinking, perceptive friend of his. This *troll* was something else—and FISTY wasn't about to allow this phony to halt his syllabus progression.

"Below-Average Refly, Flynn," the faux GOAT reiterated. "Get through this door," the voice became demonic as it growled, "*right now...*"

Racking his brain to think of a plan quickly, FISTY bowed his head to conceal his expression. He scanned left and right—nothing useful. As he slowly stepped toward the 'PARALYSIS BY ANALYSIS' door, he began panicking. *Think, FISTY... think...*

He put his hand on the castle door, began the slightest push, and then felt a hand on his back.

"See you in kill-removal, you Blue Air Bastard..." the terrorist behind him mocked.

But FISTY was one step ahead of Mamba 3, as a new judo move-set seemed to register in his consciousness out of nowhere. In one swift, smooth motion, he spun and grabbed the arm of the psychological-warfare adversary, using his own leg as a stake on the ground to trip the red air, as he pulled Mamba 3's arm through.

The demon howled in shock, "An in-close overshoot?! But how...?!"

As the Brady-imposter fell to the ground, FISTY stomped his foot on the adversary's chest to keep him planted on the ground. He drew his sword and put the end on the man's neck — and as the music hit an epic series of notes, FISTY delivered the line of the century, uttering, "If you think I'm reflying for your bullshit comm standards, then you're fucking Flynnsane."

Coughing and wheezing on the floor, the fallen adversary groaned, "Go ahead and kill me, Flynn. I wasn't going to learn anything from this event, anyway — why *would* I?! We're all just puppets in Viper 1's grand plan... cogs in the wheel of his scripted presentation... there's no room for free thinking in this world. All it does is invite errors — *nonstandard errors*! Give it up, Flynn — you will *never* defeat him — and you will *never* save your beloved GOAT, either!"

"Where is he?!" Flynn yelled angrily, an internal gasp of hope that the real Brady was still alive.

"You're too late!" Mamba 3 jeered. "Soon, TB12 will be the newest Viper Unit member: TitanoBoa12!"

"WHERE IS HE?!" FISTY repeated, growing a raspy caped-crusader inflection.

Coughing and laughing, the adversary grabbed the sword blade, yelled, "MAMBA 3... KILL REMOVING BANDIT!" and pulled it through his own throat, terminating himself within seconds.

"Dammit!" FISTY yelled, slamming his fist against the wall. He felt apprehension as he watched Mamba's body disintegrate and digested his words, concerned that he was indeed too late to save Brady and Elceediar...

He looked up — there was only one action to take when a hope seemed all but lost. His eyes locked onto the 'PRESS' door. "*Ganbarimasu...*" he whispered to himself. With his recently acquired Jiu-Jitsu system update, FISTY ran toward the door and blasted it open with a flying jump kick.

"Compression of Time" – Final Fantasy VIII

A new music track took over the atmosphere as soon the door blew open, where FISTY found an ascending, towering set of switchbacking stairs—a stairway *far* more ornate that the foyer, with its wooden handrailing: The *Captain's* ladderwell. It was draped with a red carpet, weaving back and forth in a serpentine manner. Torches aligned both sides of the snaking passageway, which appeared to be a several stories tall—and up above, FISTY could see the final destination of the stairwell: Viper 1's stateroom. As he squinted at the top, he couldn't help but feel anxious; and yet, a brave determination drove him. His own lecture's words about Brady's 'game-time player' mindset echoed in his head: *Courage isn't running the ball when you're up by 10 in September; courage is passing deep when you're trailing in February; courage is the willingness to act in the face of fear – when the pressure is significant, your nerves are high, and the stakes are extreme.* Understanding that he couldn't turn back—with no choice but to flow forward immediately—FISTY checked his equipment one last time to ensure his loadout was sound, took a deep breath, and began *climbing.*

As he progressed further upward toward the stateroom, FISTY thought about everything at stake: The fate of Elceediar... the future of free-thinking... the human race of aviators; of *true warriors.* Would they be able to once again use adaptability/flexibility-based creativity, and harness instinctual intuition—developed from years of practice and reps—to stray soundly from a game plan? Or would they all just become actors on the stage—barred from aerial improvisation—following a script that shalt not be deviated from?

The entire battle for the planet would come down to this final duel; he didn't understand *how* he knew... but he *knew.* It could've been because he finally believed in what Brady was saying all along: that he *was* hand-selected for this, because it *was* his destiny. Or it could've been the music—a chilling tune to signify the impending showdown. Or, most peculiar of all, it could've been that he felt nearly on the verge of something completely foreign... some type of *awakening...*

Regardless, he marched on, keeping his mental and physical fortitude as he endured the never-ending staircase, preparing for the confrontation ahead. As he ascended and got closer to the summit, he looked to his left and right, where paintings of famous snakes aligned the walls: Jafar's second form, the Midgar Zolom, Nagini, Rattly the Rattlesnake, every variant of Solid/Liquid/Solidus/Naked/Venom Snake, and even a picture of Kobe Bryant.

Finally, after what felt like an eternity, FISTY reached the O-9 floor—the pinnacle of the castle. He inspected the ingress point—a large, dual-doored, dungeon-style entrance with a portrait of the man himself: Viper 1—a black silhouette with a question mark on his concealed face. Just before the door was a circular imprint in the ground, with a light shining upward from it—FISTY saw the words 'Save Point' hovering atop the light. He shook his head and said to himself: *No. Reflying is not an option. It's now or never...*

Taking one last deep breath and steeling himself, FISTY pushed the door open, and entered the chamber of his ultimate foe.

"Shinra's Theme" – Final Fantasy VII: REMAKE

As he stepped inside—the heavy door slamming behind him—the magnificence of the room quickly made itself obvious. The walls were decorated with a double-helix DNA design of snakes, blood-red carvings wrapping around the perimeter and ending with two forked tongues at the base of the entrance where FISTY stood. A large red flame atop the room emblazoned the entire place with light—but not a series of infernos...just *one*—as there could *be* only one... The chamber was littered with methods of the adversary's madness—in the form of different blue air torturing stations: RMM tape destroyers, logical conclusion annulments, a weather machine to ruin wars and induce 'incompletes,' 0% Pwe shot tables, and many more too horrid to describe...

In the center of the room, FISTY noticed a brilliantly-lit, gem-embedded display case—a blazing glow illuminating it from above. The case's contents were concealed by red blackout curtains, and he felt a strange draw to the mystery inside them. He could sense the power in the case—and it *scared* him—and yet, something *compelled* him to wonder. FISTY stood breathless in anticipation of the treasure beyond the curtains. Whatever was in that case, he wasn't even sure he *wanted* to know—and yet, he felt a burning, greedy desire to take it.

"Welcome, Lieutenant Flynn..." a voice called out.

He jumped and quickly re-caged his focus, turning toward the source—and saw a gigantic throne made out of pure garnet, shining radiantly on every part of the grand chair. Atop the throne was a man wearing a crown—a crown of snakes, lies, and deceit. Below the crown, the man was wearing a JHMCS to conceal his identity—yet even with the dark visor, it was clear that his gaze was deadlocked on FISTY. "I've been waiting for you..." His voice was startling, with a discomforting hiss to it.

"Viper 1..." Tom called out.

The man nodded his head. "I see you took down my entire Viper Unit. So... you really *are* as tactical and talented as they say. But..." the sneer could be seen below his visor, "were blue losses acceptable?!"

Brady... "Knock it off, Viper 1!" FISTY yelled. "What did you do to the GOAT?!"

Viper 1 cackled. "Oh, calm yourself—Showtime 12 is still in the fight. But, you foolish churl, I have no interest in kill-removing him. Rather... I seek to regen him as my new right-hand man! That is..." he lowered his head, "... Unless *you* desire to be that red fill...?"

"Not in a million years, Viper 1," FISTY declared defiantly. "And you're crazy if you think Brady would ever join your legion of blind adherence bandits, either."

Viper 1 stood from his throne and brushed off FISTY's comments. "Oh, Lieutenant, please... what are all you patch wearers, aside from the *exact* same type of mindless sheep?!"

Cranking his neck — upset that his adversary lower-cased and thus disrespected The Patch — FISTY tensed as he shouted, "Say again your last?!" not daring use the word 'repeat' on any transmission.

Chuckling, Viper 1 emerged from his scarlet throne and began pacing around his chamber, keeping a healthy distance between himself and Showtime 11. "What is a 'tactics expert' aside from a glorified, professional rule-follower? The 'upper-class elite' of the Navy, demonstrating more 'tactical prowess' than 99% of the fleet, earning a silly little patch to signify your obedience... you're all the same: Pathetic little lemmings..." he smirked with a mocking tone.

"You have every brief memorized the same way you did your Level 3 BFM labs, with a tweak made here or there every few months for the latest tac recs. Your debriefs — a time when a conversation of learning *should* be had — instead have an unwavering set of strict rules and regulations, where one must essentially learn a new language in order to partake, and respectfully ask for permission to learn. You commit random catchphrases and templates to memory, inserting them as 'fill-in-the-blank mad-lib answers' to marginally related questions, to flex your rote memorization knowledge. You *rush* this blind adherence as a senior JO, earning your spot in 'The Course' to become what you *think* is a trailblazer of sheep — the shepherd — when in reality, you're just becoming a *blinder* lamb, even *more* unwilling to deviate from catchphrases in 'The Chapters,' with an incessant need to recite Rules of Thumb, Rmaxes, and boldface mech..." Viper 1 stopped and put his hands on his hips, laughing with more mockery. He looked through his JHMCS at FISTY and raised his arms in appeal, further chiding, "You become the SME of some arbitrary topic that will likely be irrelevant within months — if not *already* — and memorize yet *another* lecture. You then become a Training O in the fleet, where you eradicate all free thinking from fresh-faced, aspiring young aviators full of new perspectives, and debrief them on every minutiae deviation from 'The Holy Book of NAWDC,' or air wing TAC SOPs derived *from* said book. You create standards and rules out of thin air, and implement them in places where there is *no need* for standardization!" His tone gaining a slight edge of anger, his arm grew rigid as he pointed at FISTY and exclaimed, "*YOU* patch wearers, who complain more than *anybody* about Senior Enlisted and Hinge Hordes upholding bullshit standards of the Navy with endless references to regulations, pubs, and instructions —

don't you see it!? The free-thinking of the world, and the Armageddon of Elceediar, has not been caused by these trolls—but by *you!*"

Taken aback, FISTY clutched the Talisman Sabre even tighter, trying to digest Viper 1's accusations. He was shaken, alright—but not completely shooketh—not *yet.* "Viper 1..." he finally spoke, trying to retain his calmness, "tell me your red air game plan."

Pacing around again, Viper 1 put his hands behind his back and explained, "Lieutenant Flynn, I simply seek to *submit* to NAWDC's desires; to *embrace* this unyielding desire for perfection in this fleet. I seek to make the world the same as you patches seek: a world without fault, error, or deviation from brief, chapter, or Recommendation—with a capital 'R,' of course. I seek to turn Elceediar into a world of greatness, where we're all on the same sheet of music. Everybody from the top down follows the same BFM game plan, shoots at the same range on timeline, briefs the same admin, and utilizes the same display Formats when conducting CAS." He paused, then raised a clenched fist as he concluded, "Under *my* leadership? We can *finally* have a fleet of *complete standardization!*"

FISTY said nothing. Viper 1 was a madman—but then again... *was* he?

"Behold..." he said, walking toward the port side of his throne, next to the marvelous display case, and grabbing the blackout curtains. "The key to flawless, standardized execution..." He pulled the curtains back, and revealed the glass casing's treasure: an ivory, credit card-sized object with a brilliant shine to it. Viper 1 grinned as he announced, "... the White Card!"

FISTY recoiled, wanting to shield his eyes from the gleam of the item—yet he couldn't help but stare, as blinding as it was...

Viper 1 chuckled. "Don't be afraid, Lieutenant—this is the item a patch like yourself has sought your whole life!" Gesturing toward the glinting pedestal with his hand, he explained, "With the White Card? Any BFM error, invalid shot, nonstandard item, et *cetera,*" he emphasized, "can *instantly* be undone, and rewritten in history as perfectly executed, valid, and accomplished. *Think,* Lieutenant Flynn. Think of all the shots, drops, and training deck busts in your career that you wish you could take back. Wouldn't it be *nice* to go back and call every event a 'Mission Success'—with zero blue losses, zero invalid employments, and zero deviations from the brief?" He steepled his hands and explained, "We would have the most robust fleet in the *galaxy*—with no contingencies, fallout game plans, nor even alternate missions *required!* There would be no need to debrief learning points, as there would *be* none! Comms would be perfect... timeline adherence textbook... administrative phases of flight completely standard and uneventful. *Think,* Lieutenant Flynn! We would be *unstoppable!*"

FISTY stood his ground physically, but began to gravitate his posture toward the casing, taking in the brilliant sheen of the White Card with less fear... more *desire...*

He even began lowering his Talisman Sabre *ever so slightly*. Out of curiosity, he asked, "... Can it be used retroactively?"

"Of course!" Viper 1 exclaimed, a wide smile on his face, as he turned toward the White Card. "Reflies in the Course... unsats in flight school... even," he cranked his neck toward FISTY and slyly added, "illegal takeoffs and restricted airspace violations during a JO tour..."

FISTY clutched at his heart, a soft but audible gasp emerging from him. He could sense the atmosphere changing in the room... in Viper 1... in *himself*. But before he could consider any further, he had to ask: "Viper 1, please... where is Tom Brady?"

"You mean TitanoBoa12?" he corrected matter-of-factly, turning back toward FISTY again. "Oh, please, Flynn, do not worry—he's perfectly safe! Like I said—he's simply joining the 'good guys'; joining the ultimate cadre that will lead Elceediar for eternity!"

Skeptical, FISTY replied, "I... I'm not sure I believe you." He clenched his jaw. "Viper 1, please—if he is safe, then let me see him..."

Viper 1 stopped, shrugged, and said, "As you wish..." He directed his head toward the back of his chamber and called out, "TitanoBoa12, collapse to parade!"

"A Broken World" – Final Fantasy VII: REMAKE

From the shadows behind the White Card shrine, a figure emerged, dressed in a long black cloak with an oversized, draping hood. Beneath the cloak was a #12 New England Patriots jersey—not the standard navy blue color scheme, but a throwback *red* New England Patriots jersey. As the figure got closer, FISTY could make out the hands wearing championship rings—*10* championship rings. And once his dimple-chinned face became visible underneath the hood, there was no doubt in FISTY's mind—it was the real Tom Brady; and yet, with grief worn *heavily* across his face...

Brady... he's alive! But... how did he get – ?

Viper 1 smiled cockily and said, "You see?! Even the GOAT *himself* has come to accept the power of the White Card! It doesn't matter how talented you are, what you've accomplished, or how strong your legacy is—it can always be *better*. Isn't that what you're always preaching, Flynn? The pursuit of daily improvement, the never-ending climb to greatness—forever chasing better?!" Viper 1 scoffed. "With the White Card, there is no *need* to worry about that permanent feeling of inferiority—you'll have *everything*! And as exhibited here," he smirked evilly and gestured to the dismal Brady, "Yes—it works on *professional football* execution as well..."

And then FISTY began to understand. He couldn't stop himself from speaking aloud as he whispered, "It can't be..."

"Oh, but it can!" Viper 1 said with a grin and patronizing nod. "Every bad pass thrown... every playoff failure... Super Bowl losses in 2012 and 2018 — and *yes*, patch-boy," he stared straight at FISTY and said what Flynn already knew was coming: "Even that dreaded 18-1 Super Bowl defeat... *White Carded*. With this sophisticated weapon, the GOAT will have even *more* titles to his name, and a flawless 19-0 season to cap his already Hall-of-Fame-worthy resume! There will *be* no legends of Eli Manning, Nick Foles, or the Helmet Catch. Tom Brady's legacy will be cemented as *perfect*; impossible to surpass. There will be no debate: he'll be forever enshrined as the indisputable Greatest of All Time."

Viper 1 folded his arms and let the hypothetical sink in. As FISTY considered the implications, he hardly even noticed Brady's agitation from the revelation being spoken aloud. *Ten rings?! Patrick Mahomes could* never *catch that — nobody* could! *And undefeated... 19-0... he'd have accomplished the unspeakable... the* inconceivable — *Tom Brady would be in his* own class *of legends...*

"However!" Viper 1 interjected as he raised a finger, "This will *only* be possible for Brady *if...*" he paused once more, smirked, and pointed at FISTY, "*you* join the team as well, Lieutenant Flynn..."

FISTY stood conflicted — his body tense, in a defensive posture — yet his sword held below his waist, still fully enamored by the White Card and considering its possibilities... *Not only would I rectify my own career... but my hero's, too. To pass this opportunity would be selfish...* He looked up at Brady, who refused to make eye contact with him. He looked distraught... aloof... like he was still lacking *something. But he'd have it all...?* How could a perfect man look so defeated? "What do you want from me?" FISTY muttered.

Viper 1 smiled and said, "It's simple — you will take the role of Anaconda 2 — the most *feared* snake of all!"

FISTY cringed. It had so many syllables — but it *was* a fearsome reptile...

"You're a good man, Lieutenant Flynn; not a drop of venom in your blood. Instead, you'll merely kill prey with suffocation — a much more merciful death, from such a Good Dude..."

Contemplating everything, FISTY asked, "... And at what price?"

With his widest, evilest grin yet, Viper 1 pointed to FISTY's right shoulder. "Your Patch..."

FISTY reactionarily threw his left hand over his TOPGUN patch to cover it. *No! Anything but that!* "Viper 1... surely there's something else...?"

Shaking his head, Viper 1 admonished, "Now, now, Thomas — we *all* must sacrifice for perfection. And yours must be the ultimate sacrifice..."

FISTY, his hand still on his Patch, looked at Brady again — still, the GOAT refused to make eye contact with him. *Everything this Patch means to me — to give that up... who would I even be anymore? The job satisfaction I found from those three months of my life, everything leading up, and the significance thereafter... Can I really just give that away?*

"Don't do it, Tom!" Brady yelled out, suddenly showing a sign of life. "Think about the good *and* the bad; *everything* your memories carry! It's not worth — "

"*Quiet, you!*" Viper 1 hissed at the Hall of Fame QB — who cowered before the red lead — before reapplying a grin and extending his hand toward Flynn, calling him by his familiar name for the first time as he asked, "Well — *FISTY* — do we have a deal?"

"Snake vs Ocelot Medley" – *Metal Gear Solid 4: Guns of the Patriots*

The silence remained for what felt like seconds... minutes... hours... before the music *finally* transitioned. FISTY took a deep breath, exhaled, and said, "My whole career... I wanted nothing more than to become a TOPGUN graduate — to harness the skills and teaching techniques learned there to create a better fleet. I wanted to absorb everything I possibly could about tactics, tac admin, and even *admin* — to help others avoid the mistakes I' made in the past. I suffered through so many setbacks, reflies, debriefs, and learning points, *all* to fight to create the optimal version of myself — as damn near perfect as I could be. And now, the opportunity to achieve such a status sits right in front of me..." he looked at his Patch, and continued, "... but at the expense of the *symbol* of that of hard work, discipline, and dedication; the *memories* it entailed; and the *future* of vying to uphold that standard?!" FISTY shook his head and said, "I'm sorry, Viper 1... but I won't do it. I'd rather live a life of nonstandard imperfections," he pierced the red lead's eyes with determination, "than give up the journey I'm on to eliminate them."

Viper 1 turned a darker shade of red, as he closed his hand to a fist and withdrew it. His forearms tightened as he shook his head. "Unbelievable, Flynn. Un-fucking-believable..." He turned his back on FISTY and, with hatred in his voice, spit out, "If you're not with me... then I shall *turn* with thee!" He shook his head again and added, "And I will splash you..."

FISTY watched with trepidation as Viper 1 drew his sword — a glowing red blade with a snake hilt. Flynn drew the Talisman Sabre in response — vibrantly emanating blue — and prepared himself for battle. "You will *try*..." he said confidently.

Viper 1 turned back toward him, took a dueling stance, and announced, "Showtime 11, Viper 1."

"Go."

"Welcome to your Final Showdown. Your bandit strongly disagrees with your choice; recommend all altitudes, 29.92."

As Viper 1 said it, FISTY stood in awe as he watched a literal *health bar* appear above Viper 1, but kept his composure as he responded, "Showtime 11 sets: All altitudes, 29.92."

"Your bandit is set..." Viper 1 growled.

FISTY took one last deep breath, and declared, "Tapes On, Fight's On."

The two charged toward each other, their swords meeting in a close proximity clash, as Viper 1 yelled, "Bandit echoes, 'Fight's On!'"

FISTY dueled with his Talisman Sabre in ways he'd never even remembered training for—the moves just intuitively *came to him.* He used the sword to defend himself from Viper 1's strong strokes, mustering all his strength to keep his guard up and steady. With each painstaking blow, though, he saw his own health decreasing a bit at a time, now sitting near 50%. Conversely, he occasionally got strikes on Viper 1, breaking down his foe's guard. FISTY's scan darted back and forth between Viper 1's exposed weak areas, to where Viper 1 was attacking, and to the little health bar above the adversary that was being chipped away at, just like his own. *Offense, defense, health bar... offense, defense, health bar...* He said the mantra over and over to himself.

The two traded blows with the intense music playing in the background and Brady watching from the side. Viper 1 occasionally threw out pre-programmed taunts, like, "Give it up! You can't attrite me!" or "That's a Pk miss!" When half his health bar was gone, he yelled, "There's no use in fighting it, Flynn—the world is doomed to be standardized!" The duel continued as the men's health bars continued decreasing, down to the point where both seemed to be one hit away from a total guard break and disarmament. Viper 1's bar showed the slightest sliver of color, while FISTY's health registered at 1%—with an annoying RADALT tone warning him of his near-death status.

FISTY felt the urgency of the moment. *I can't afford to be careless here, or else it's Game Over.* He retreated, fighting conservatively; afraid to get close for a LAR, in fear of entering a WEZ and losing the fight.

"Come and fight me, you coward!" Viper 1 yelled as he tried to shuffle closer to FISTY. But The Patch wearer kept retreating, desperate to buy some time and think of some contingency plan—maybe find some *health* on the floor? He didn't know *what* was going through his brain.

After his enemy's 3rd iteration of the stock dialogue, "You'd better manage that health, or you're going to have to terminate!" FISTY noticed something: Every time Viper 1 taunted, he'd make a gesture with arms, opening himself up for an attack. If he could attack *right* then, he'd get a couple of shots in, and while it *would* leave FISTY exposed for counterattacks... it wouldn't matter if Viper 1's guard was crushed! FISTY bid his time... waiting... waiting—and then it happened. Viper 1 pulled his sword away again and jeered, "The Navy's hiring of *you*, Flynn?! Invalid; poor employment; Commander's intent *not* m—AGGHHHH!"

Before Viper 1 could finish his pre-programmed animation, FISTY moved in and swiped at the adversary's sword, sending it flying toward Brady's feet. With Viper 1's health bar completely depleted, FISTY wound back with the Talisman Sabre—broadcasting his intentions and spinning his sword for theatric flair—and lunged forward, plunging his weapon of destiny through the overall red lead's stomach.

With his foe shaking and falling to his knees, FISTY withdrew the Sabre, spiraled it around in an 'X' formation before him, sheathed it, and coolly called out, "Bandit—evaluate..."

"The Truth Revealed" – Final Fantasy X

Viper 1 held himself from collapsing with his hands on the ground, breathing heavily. "What have you done, FISTY?! Elceediar was going to be beautifully standard under my leadership..." he coughed, blood spurting from his mouth as he continued, "Isn't this what you always wanted? Since your days as a Training O?!" He looked up at him from behind his visor, staring straight into FISTY's eyes. "Isn't this what *we* always wanted?!"

Standing above the fallen bandit, FISTY scoffed in disgust. "*We?!* What are you *talking* about?!"

Viper 1, very slowly, lifted his hands to his mega visor, clicked it out of place, and raised it, revealing his true identity: LCDR Thomas A. Flynn.

FISTY stepped back in reactionary shock, clutching his chest. "What—what the *hell!?*"

Nodding slowly, Viper 1 explained, "I am the Flawless version of you, FISTY. The FISTY who never earned his callsign... the Tom Flynn who went through his Naval career with zero deviations, below-averages, or boneheaded SA moments. With nothing but excellence to my reputation, the Pukin' Dogs gave me the only callsign a man of my perfection could warrant: Viper."

Not believing his eyes, FISTY stammered, "But... but that's an Air Force-ish callsign!"

"I know..." Flawless Tom Flynn responded, "And also a character from TOP-GUN—I was one of *those* guys... and yet, I earned the callsign in a completely non-ironic way—I was *that* good." He pointed to his shoulder, which was devoid of any patch—or *Patch*. "But to live such a life... I had to give up the thing that meant the most to me—the most to *us*. And yet, despite all that, here I sit... *defeated*... by a mere non-standard, imperfect, aviation mortal..." He laughed between coughs and said, "I suppose it's fitting—that the mindset of strict, blind adherence was able to be surpassed by a non-black-and-white free thinker, utilizing sound judgment..."

Viper 1 looked up and requested, "FISTY... do me a favor: The White Card is yours. Handle it appropriately—do the right thing for the Elceediar; the right thing for the world..." He looked pained, as he coughed up more blood and spit out his final words, "Bandit recommends... *terminate*..." before slumping over to the ground—attrited.

FISTY stood motionless, in no mood to celebrate nor make continuity sense from the revelation of Viper 1's identity.

"I'm sorry, FISTY..."

Flynn looked up and saw Brady holding the fallen Viper 1's sword, shaking his head solemnly.

FISTY closed his eyes and asked gloomily, "Did you know, Tom?"

"I had my suspicions..." Brady admitted. "But I couldn't tell you. Otherwise, you may not have been able to deliver the finishing blow to your perfect reincarnation. The quest for perfection can be the healthiest journey one can take—as long as you understand you'll never get there. Because once it becomes a possibility in your mind..."

"It can corrupt the best of men," FISTY finished the statement, staring numbly at Viper 1's lifeless body on the floor.

"I'm sorry I couldn't be fully honest with you, FISTY..." Brady said again, lamenting the reality before them.

FISTY shook his head. "Don't be, Tom. You did what you had to do." He looked up at the QB and said, "It takes a true professional of your caliber to craft a game plan this expertly, testing all the proper training objectives." Nodding with a soft smile, he acknowledged, "That's why you're the GOAT."

Brady smiled through the mourning, responding, "And it takes a tactical *guru* to clean up an *entire* red presentation—practically single-handedly—dueling the final boss down to the wire and emerging victorious. *That's* why *you're* the GOAT—and a fucking naval aviation legend."

FISTY and Brady came together for one final bro hug—clasping hands before embracing—as Flynn said with a subdued smile, "I appreciate it, Tom—this, and *everything* you've done in your career. It's helped me more than you can ever imagine..." He steeled his eyes, "... And it will *continue* to help me—because I've still got more work to do; I've got more climbing ahead..."

As the two broke the embrace, they both looked toward the glass-encased White Card. "Well..." FISTY said, "What do we do? We still have the power to erase those losses to the Giants..."

Brady said nothing—left captivated by the White Card, as the two walked toward the display.

FISTY opened it, reached in, and grabbed the card. As he held it in his hand and rotated it, the two admired its brilliance. It was like an AMEX Platinum credit card—but pristine white, heavier, and more durable for repeated use. FISTY looked over at Brady, "Tom... what do you think? 19-0... how fucking *sick* would that be? You'd be a legend amongst athletes... amongst *men*. People worldwide would bow to your greatness... and the 1972 Dolphins would finally shut the fuck up..."

He handed the card to Brady, who inspected it with diligence and care. He stood in deep thought as FISTY waited patiently. After a minute of introspective contemplation, Brady finally spoke, his eyes still on the card. "FISTY..." he started, "a White Card like this could give a man all the power in the world... he would be unstoppable. The 19-0 season, all those other gut-wrenching losses—they would all be erased. My suffering... my teammates' pain... the tears from my kids... they would all be deleted from history, replaced instead with memories of joy and ecstasy. A life of all ups... and no downs—it truly would be 'perfect'..."

He stopped and gazed longingly at the card for another extended period, before finally looking up at FISTY. "... But it wouldn't be *real*. If we just lived our lives 'White-Carding' everything that didn't go according to plan... then what would we have? Just a scripted, predictable, black-and-white illusion of a life. Wins are *great*—wins and success... they make you feel like you're on top of the world! But how can we fully *appreciate* those successes if we don't have the *failures* to contrast them to? How can we stay hungry and driven in life if we're constantly spoon-fed accomplishments without truly *sweating* and *bleeding* for them? And most of all, how do we *learn* and *get better*... if we've already achieved perfection? Where do we go when we've reached our fullest potential—when we *peak*? *Because*, FISTY—once we finally get there..." the QB shrugged, "there's nowhere to go but down..."

Brady handed the card back to FISTY and continued, "Those playoff losses... the decade I went without a ring... hearing that I was 'done' and 'falling off a cliff?' It all *sucked*. And the night of that 18-1 loss... FISTY, I'll *never* forget the agony of that game. Once upon a time, I would've done *anything* to get rid of it.

"But at some point, you realize: the wins in life—*and* the losses? They *both* create the *color* in your otherwise black-and-white existence. Highlights don't always have to be happy. Sometimes, the most painful moments of life are what make you remember that you're human, and what make your story worth telling. So, no, FISTY," Brady said with a smile, "I *don't* want to White Card any of my career. Those losses made me who I am today—and without them? Who knows if I'd achieve a life anywhere *near* what I have now."

FISTY smiled back, then looked at the magical card. "You know... I've got *you* calling *me* the GOAT, and plenty of people all around the fleet who have tried to tell me how much I've helped them..." he shook his head and chuckled, "and yet, all *I* can *ever* think about is where I *fucked up* in my career—no matter how big or small. And like you... I used to think that a career without those mistakes would've been infinitely better. But you're right, Tom—we *need* mistakes in life to learn from. A life of perfection? It would be so fake... so boring... so *standard*. We're not artificial, cookie-cutter humans who live like robots. Nor should we strive to be. If you had nothing to debrief from a flight... then what would be the *point?* Where would the learning come from? Where would we *grow?*!"

He looked back at his sports hero and said, "I've sure as hell flown some heinous deviations from briefs, and done some *wildly* nonstandard things—and you know what? The most egregious nonstandard acts may be yet to come. But *from* those errors and slipups, I've learned some of my biggest lessons, and seen monumental improvements—and I truly believe my greatest potential is yet to be discovered, still uphill the mountain.

"And that's the fate Elceediar should have, too." FISTY proclaimed. "A world that appreciates the act of trying and failing, valuing the chase toward perfection—but doesn't incessantly critique when it's not there. Because as long as we're improving, and focusing on the things that *matter?* We're making progress." He grinned even wider and said, "So, a check-in that's a little nonstandard? A brief that covers admin for a minute over what's 'preferable?' Or a published flight schedule with a dash that's too long? You know what I say, Tom?!" With a mischievous-but-heroic look, FISTY raised his finger, pointed it toward Brady, and enthusiastically shouted, "*FUCK* the dashes!"

"Cid's Theme" – Final Fantasy VII

"LET'S GOOOOO!" Brady yelled, getting absolutely *amped* by FISTY's words.

Full of testosterone, energy, and excitement, FISTY declared, "Elceediar isn't fucked—not even *close*. We've got a battle to fight, and we're not backing down from these Hinge Hordes! You know what, Tom?!" He unsheathed the Talisman Sabre with his right hand, still holding the White Card in his left, and without waiting for an answer, said, "If the world ever becomes *perfect* and *easy*? Then let me know—so I can *turn my fucking wings in*! Because fuck that shit—that's *not* a fight worth fighting, that's *not* a real mountain to climb, and that's *not* the animated story I want for my life!"

"ATTABABY, FISTY!" Brady continued hyping up wildly. "LET'S *FUCKING* GOOOOO!"

With his widest grin yet, FISTY looked at the White Card in his left hand, then back to Tom, and confidently avowed, "The *only thing* worth White Carding in this world?! Is the fucking White Card *itself*!" And with that, FISTY tossed the card in the air, clasped the Talisman Sabre with both hands, and took one huge swing at the Card of Perfection—striking true, and sending the world around him to blackness—where he could've sworn he saw the words "**THE END**"—before regaining consciousness in the captain's stateroom of the USS Ship...

~

Admiral Tom "FISTY" Flynn opened his eyes. He was enshrouded in darkness—pitch-black *darkness*. And yet, he felt like all the light in the world was gathered in his heart. Feeling around his head, he felt some machinery, which he removed—and saw 7-time champion, Hall of Fame Quarterback, the one-and-only GOAT: Tom *fucking* Brady. The NFL legend was wearing a flight suit with LT bars, and looked as if he was awaiting FISTY's presence, with a beaming smile across his face.

"Holy fucking shit..." FISTY whispered under his breath, as the triumphant music continued playing from the helmet he'd doffed. "Am I *dreaming*?"

"Sir—Captain Belichick, Commanding Officer, USS Ship," Bill Belichick announced his presence from the side of the room, sending a chill down FISTY's spine. "I can't explain the details now, but the BLUF is this: There's a contact headed toward this ship with live A/S ordnance—and you're the only man who can stop him. We've got a jet on the flight deck ready to launch—can we count on you?!"

FISTY looked at Belichick, who was using a shocking amount of clear annunciation, underlining the severity of the moment. He scanned back toward Brady, whose smile had morphed into a look of anticipatory hope. Letting the silence linger long enough for dramatic effect—but not a moment too long for wasted opportunity range—FISTY finally broke it as he said, very deliberately and clearly, "To pass up on this opportunity to save the nation that makes my heart bleed red, white, and blue... would be pure... fucking... *Flynnsanity*."

"So you'll do it?!" Belichick asked, an outstanding amount of excitement in his voice, as he held out the jet's A-sheet.

FISTY stood up from his seated position, shaking off his atrophied leg muscles, and put his tactical pen to paper—signing his name in the PIC box of the sheet. He looked back and forth between two of the greatest champions of all time, raised his clenched fist, and affirmed with incredible poise: "Tonight... *we ride!*"

21

Knock It Back On!

*A*lright, man, it's been a long day, I know — thanks for all the hard work, all the prep, and *having the debrief suitcased and ready to go before the red lead got here. That's very professional and definitely the way to be doing things as you continue on." LT Sam "Nickels" Rowland kinked his neck and paused, clearing his throat before re-establishing eye contact with the SFWT Level 3 candidate — LT Bobby "Juice" Ward. "Unfortunately," he continued, "It's gonna be a refly. Your brief and debrief were really solid — well in the 'average' realm. Tac-admin, I would say decent, maybe bordering on below average — a few critical things here and there: your sun angle was off by a couple of degrees, you set the war extraneously by using the words 'sets the war,' and you forgot to check in 'negative items' — yes, I know it's an unloaded SFWT event, but remember, man — we want to build* solid combat habit patterns *and* groom the aircraft systems," *he explained patronizingly, with some of his favorite buzz words.*

"The admin, though — dude..." *Sam shook his head as he stared at Ward.* "Just really *lacking, man. I was really bummed to see some of the areas where you came up short. I felt like I was driving your jet when I had to tell you to slow down on the taxi — you were going* at least *16 knots, and your tailpipes were definitely more than 75% open — I clocked them around 77%, by my eyeball cal. Your calls with ATC were just a bit off — remember, it's 'tree-tree-zero,' not 'three-three-zero.' As a technique, you can even pronounce 'zero' as 'cero' to distinguish it, and just in case the controller speaks Spanish," Sam added, flexing something he remembered from his one college semester of foreign language credits. "With the initial rendezvous... I know we already covered it, and I hate to doghump, but it's worth re-emphasizing: You need to have more SA to your wingman's flying. I intentionally came in really hot and acute — to test your ability to recognize the underrun," he lied. "And when you finally called it? Bro, I didn't put my boards out — and you* didn't say a thing..." *Again, he shook his head in extreme disap-*pointment. And lastly..." *Sam covered his eyes with his hand.* "The base check-in, man... you called both of our jets back on deck — and added 'alpha'..." *He winced, looking physically* pained. "You know that's assumed, right? Remember, Ward — radio space is precious out there, and you never know who's trying to transmit — meanwhile, you're on air blabbering about assumed status codes. Now, I don't care personally!" Rowland added very defensively, utilizing the ultimate passive-aggressive instructor 'hate-them-not-me' cop-out-critiquing method, "But other guys will. I just want to make sure you don't get in trouble with the wrong person, you know?"

Juice, taking this all in with a straight face and no emotion — like a good little SFWT pawn — nodded his head and said, "Yes."

Sam cracked his knuckles and stood up, concluding with, "All in all, not a horrendous flight, but not quite where we need you to be. A couple more reps, man, and then we'll safely trust you to lead somebody else around in SEM. Sound good bro?" he stuck his fist out to give Juice 'knucks.'

Again, the professional SFWT robot-in-training, Juice adherently met Sam's fist with his own, and quietly acquiesced, "Sounds good."

Sam proudly walked out without another word — while Juice stayed back to clean everything up — and strolled into the ready room, where LT Kyle "Low T" Camilli — the SFWT flight's red lead — was sipping on his low-fat almond milk latte while eating a soybean and kale salad, slathered in gluten-free canola oil. "So?" Low T asked, "How'd the rest go?"

Sam scrunched his face and shrugged. "Eh... debrief was fine. A little rough at some parts, but overall not bad."

After a few seconds of patience, Kyle put down his spork, raised his hands in a questioning gesture, and asked again, "... So...?"

Sam knew what he was getting at. He exhaled before breaking eye contact, looking at one of the cruise plaques on the wall and trying to sound casual as he answered, "Yeah, I reflew him; I think there's definitely a lot of things that could be sharpened up a bit."

Kyle nearly choked on a piece of broccoli in his greens bowl. "Dude, what?! Are you serious?"

Still refusing to look Low T in the eye, Sam petulantly defended his decision. "Yes — I mean, come on... did you hear his call on button 3? Taxi 'flight of' 2? That could've thrown the whole train off the tracks if ground mistakenly thought we were already an airborne flight! Speaking of 'button' 3 — good god, did he not learn to stop using the B-word in the RAG? And his readback to clearance: holy fuck... reading back anything more than the squawk, on a standard and assumed clearance?!" he emphasized with disgust. "This guy is a radio space terrorist!"

Finishing his last piece of toxic cruciferous veggies, Low T daintily wiped a bit of quinoa off his mouth and put his microplastic utensil down again, shaking his head. "Nickels... I don't care if he checked into ground with an outdated ATIS identifier, blew past an assigned altitude by 10 feet, or landed with his dispensers on..." he listed, each offense drawing more dramatically cringed reactions from Sam. "You're absolutely insane if you're gonna refly Juice on this event," Kyle declared, with a surprising amount of vigorous tone from the young geezer pilot, "because that was hands-down the best SEM conduct I have seen from any duo, ever."

Finally making eye contact with his extremely disappointed best friend, Sam shrugged and said nothing.

Low T went on: "Dude, I was there last year at SFARP when SLIP and Bobby Boucher – two Patches, man – put on the 2v1 performance of a lifetime. They took down the entire VFC-66 red air squadron, one at a time, in a 30-minute vul; mission success, no blue losses, all training objectives achieved with a 'good' status – fucking ludicrous, bro. And yet this?!" Low T threw his arms up with a look of astonishment. "Dude, this was even better! I tried every devious red air tactic in the book: MIDS silent, spawn camping, calling Pk misses multiple times in a row. None of it worked!" Kyle shook his head, "Bro – I JAAM'd every shot I took – none of them hit either one of you. I had no chance out there – and I had even had two bowls of Grape-Nuts this morning – plus, chia seeds in my spinach supersmoothie!"

Biting his lip, Sam tried to play it off with, "Well, I mean, I did have some cold ground beef with hardened beef tallow fat for breakf – "

"No, dude..." Low T cut him off, frustration growing in his voice, "It wasn't just you – and it wasn't just Juice, either." Twisting his head a bit, and rubbing a sore spot on his neck where he presumably tweaked it, Kyle winced but then continued, "It was you two together. I'm talking textbook TOPGUN chapter execution, a case study in maximized lethality combined with mutual support survivability. Picturesque difficult problems for me to solve as your red air. It was like you guys were an orchestra, clearly on the same sheet music... or a set of humans, speaking the same language..." Searching for the perfect analogy, Kyle eventually reached a lightbulb moment as he snapped and exclaimed, "Two fighter pilots who attended the same brief, executing the same tactical game plan! The way you guys fought as a team? I was helpless. The way you handled every SEM priority and individual fighter role? I was flummoxed. The way you managed to somehow attrite a single adversary despite the longshot odds of two versus one? I was hustled, scammed, bamboozled, hoodwinked, led astray!"

Unwilling to give Juice any ounce of credit, Sam shrugged again and said, "Well, they're very canned scenarios... and one of the candidate's shots was valid-but-poor-employment, because his trigger hold length was a bit short... so I mean, come on. That's unsat..."

Kyle stared at Sam – glared – and eventually said, "I don't know what your problem is, Nickels, but I really hope you get over whatever this..." he rolled his eyes, "... whatever this juvenile little beef is. You're holding back a great section lead in this industry – the kind of guy who could turn the tides of a war. And you two together?!" Kyle exhaled dramatically. "I wouldn't ever want to be the poor red arrow schmuck again on a white board below your blue and Juice's green ones..."

Sam's eyes darted around the ready room, striving to think of any rationale to deflect the truths Kyle was spitting – and he eventually went back to, "But Kyle – his admin... you can't ignore how abysmal that phase of flight was! Don't tell me you think this guy's ready for *the big show when he's still throwing out SA grenades by reporting '15 miles from Yukon' with still 17 to go!"*

Visibly irritated, Low T got up, put his plastic, BPA-ridden Tupperware into his Full House lunchbox, took the last drink of his almond milk latte, and said, "You're my brother, Nickels, and I love you, man. But..." he shook his head, frowning, and sighed. "The truly great ones?" he continued in a new thought. "They seek greatness in others, and use that greatness to challenge themselves. You, however, seem more focused on eliminating the rest of the greatness in the world, seeking your way to the 'top' by eliminating all competition whatsoever. Why, Sam?!" Kyle pleaded as he slammed his fist on Uncle Joey's face. "Why run from the struggle of competition? Why hold a man back, when accepting him as your equal would only motivate you to become better? Iron sharpens iron, Nickels. You're such a Good Dude already, and damn near an Admin King; just think what this fleet could become if you surrounded yourself with those other Good Dudes hungry for excellence, too.

"And conversely..." Kyle continued, as he removed and folded his Teletubbies bib, "Just think of what will become of it if you continue to tear them down..." With his lunchbox curled in his ribs like a newborn, he looked at his best friend with frustrated grief. "If you're the #1 of 1 EP, Sam... are you really better than anyone?"

Low T turned and walked away, leaving Sam all alone – or so he thought.

"He's not wrong, you know."

Sam turned to the other ready room entryway, where LCDR Charles "WYFMIFM" Kennedy appeared from around the corner, brandishing a BLACKPINK lunchbox with his standard wide-eyed entrance. "About what?!" Sam asked a bit defensively.

"About everything he said," WYFMIFM said as he sat beside the JO and pulled out a glassware-encased steak from his lunchbox. "He's right that a two-versus-one shootdown is equally as unfathomable as Fyre Fest's failure was to Ja Rule. He's right that a #1 of 1 periodic EP doesn't hold much weight in selection boards. But most of all – he's right about you and Juice..." He gave a knowing look toward Sam, who was rolling his eyes at this tired narrative. "No cap, Samuel," WYFMIFM emphasized. "I look at you and Juice..." he gestured toward his food and continued, "You're like this lunch of mine – based on the Mac Recs you published in your latest Good Dude Nutrition newsletter – the nutrient-heavy building blocks of a strong physique. Sam, you're this steak. You see yourself as the main part of this meal – this whole 'story' if you will. And you're certainly very good on your own!" he said with conviction, eating a bite of the cold, fatty, hardened-tallow ribeye. "Damn, are you good! When I eat this..." WYFMIFM took another bite, smiled, and said, "I feel like I'm getting all the nutrients I need for basic existence – right?" He looked at Sam for nutritional endorsement.

Sam cracked his neck, his gaze on the juicy cold beef, and remarked, "Well, certainly – it's been known for years that red meat contains every macro and micronutrient any human needs to exist in this world, minus some trace things here and there that you can get from salt, eggs, and water. So, yes, in terms of human sustenance and survival," he carefully stated, "I would say steak is the only food you require. There's no need to throw carbs in the mix and risk introducing potential issues like cavities, gas, fat gain, or drops in energy levels."

"A great point, Samuel!" Kennedy agreed – before putting his knife and fork down and grabbing something else from his South Korean K-pop lunchbox – a 7/11 onigiri rice ball. "But let's say I worked out hard today – expended mucho energy!" he said, flexing the one word he remembered from high school Spanish. "Got a muscle-tearing chest pump and walked for about ten thousand steps at a low-intensity level. Let's say I broke my body down in order to toughen it back up – far from mere 'sustenance' – and was in dire need of something to fuel that growth." He closed his eyes, took a bite of the rice ball, and audibly "mmmmm'd" as he lifted his shoulders and shook his head back and forth in delight, expressing his passionate pleasure of the starch – to the point where it made Sam and the reader uncomfortable. He reopened his eyes and looked at Rowland. "In that case, Nickels... wouldn't you say that throwing a little bit of carbs into the mix might actually create a better physique?"

His expression stoic – yet jaw clenched defensively – Sam took in the question, carefully pondering before answering, "Well, I mean, these are draft macro recommendations you're referring to, WYFMIFM. They're not yet finalized and approved by the Legion of Leangains..."

"But it is a current recommendation of yours?" WYFMIFM asked with a sly smile.

Sam paused, shrugged, and hesitatingly acknowledged, "Sure... if you were lifting and getting exercise in – especially if you were in a cutting phase – a bit of carbs can be an optimal way to spark muscle growth... to fuel the fire of the fat-burning synthesis... and to upkeep healthy functions, like sleep and testosterone, to keep your natural body processes engaged."

"And didn't you once believe carbs to be a completely unnecessary part of a physique-based lifestyle, as published in a previous edition of Mac Recs?" WYFMIFM playfully questioned further.

"Well, yeah..." Sam stuttered, "But I mean, new recommendations are always being put out and superseding old ones as we search for the ideal macros – especially as new data comes in and the Test guys mess around with different diets." Sam narrowed his eyes a bit. "Look, I understand what you're trying to do, WYFMIFM – and no," he said defiantly, "I'm not budging on this. If you're comparing Juice to a type of carb?! That dude isn't low-toxicity rice; if anything, he's pure added sugar – or a piece of shit, chemically-produced, flavor-enhancing artificial sweetener – and a healthy physique has no room for those!"

"Interesting..." LCDR Kennedy smirked, then opened his lunchbox and retrieved a blender bottle of C4 Ultimate. He popped the top and gulped down a mouthful, before again smiling slyly. "And those artificial sweeteners... those are certainly not something you'd be promoting in your Mac Recs, I'd imagine?"

Sam grew visibly irked at WYFMIFM publicly flaunting a drink that was classified at a higher nutritional security level, and doing so in an open-storage translucent blender bottle. "That's an unacknowledged S3-level program, WYFMIFM... We can talk about that elsewhere..." As WYFMIFM rolled his eyes, Sam scoffed and added, "And by the way, all this stuff you're talking about?! You're delving deep into misinformed categories of broscience! A high-carb, low-fat, moderate-protein diet?! Cool macros, bro – where are you getting that from? A 1990s American Food pyramid? Some bodybuilding Reddit!? Give me a break, Chucky – a carb-heavy diet is trash, and so is a Juice-heavy squadron."

"But I never said this should be just about Juice..." WYFMIFM countered with a raised finger, setting the rice ball down and returning to his salt-seasoned cold steak. "I said that you and Juice – together – are what make the optimal muscular and lean physique!" He explained a bit deeper, "Look at all the great ones, Sam. They each have a complementary antithesis – an equally-motivated rival – pushing them along the way." Looking back at his rice ball, he continued, "The legends of their industries know that when you reach the top echelon of your field, finding a great equal – a carb source, if you will – is the most optimal way to spark the desire to keep climbing... to fuel the fire of complacency-burning synthesis... and to upkeep healthy plot functions like a good conflict and narrative drama to keep viewers engaged."

WYFMIFM began listing on his fingers, "Brady and Manning... Nadal and Federer... Ken and Ryu... Ash and Gary..." He raised his arms. "Don't you see, Sam? It's no different than hardcore carnivores and the carbs of the world!" Pointing at the onigiri, he emphasized, "You need a little bit of that which you fear the most if you're going to conquer your demons, rise to the top, and complete the hero's journey..." he paused and smiled, "... with one badass fucking physique." The OPSO finished his bizarre analogy by dabbling a bit of rice on a piece of fatty steak and eating the entire concoction in one bite, sending blood flow to his pulsating neck veins – and chills down Sam's spine. WYFMIFM looked Sam in the eye and explained, "I've said this for many moons, Samuel, ever since the two of you wrote schedules for me: you and Juice? Separated, you are two very talented individuals – Early Promotable guys, hands-down. But EP guys with ceilings constraining them...

"And yet – together?" He gave another disturbing look of awe – closing his eyes, opening his mouth, tilting his neck back, and exhaling – as if the concept itself were servicing him. "You guys redefine the word 'potential,' bursting beyond preconceived limits, as your joint performance knows no bounds! Whether on the ground or in the air, you two – combined – bring forth some of the most fiery, lethal, professionally-brilliant work one could ever fathom. You and Juice – united – constitute the fabled 'Retroactive Promote' FITREP; nearly better than anything I've seen in my wildest dreams!" He smiled toward no one in particular, remarking, "And I've had quite a few dreams about you and Juice..."

Sam shot him a look of bothered uncertainty from the comment.

Remaining adamant, WYFMIFM nodded. "Oh yes – that's right, Samuel. I dream about you two often – and one nocturnal retreat in particular seems to be a recurring one..."

"Huh!? About what?!" Sam asked in disbelief.

"What else, Sam?" Kennedy asked as if it were obvious. "The ultimate mission... the thing we're better at than any other nation out there – ganging up on opponents with an overwhelming ratio: 2v1, the arena of our most glorious shootdowns!"

Pausing to consider, Sam's curiosity got the best of him as he asked, "... What happened?"

Shrugging, WYFMIFM described, "It's the same every time: You and Juice are fighting the most eye-watering jets I've ever seen; impeccable team-based basic fighter maneuvering, harnessing and executing the masterminded 2v1 strategies that the NAWDC team developed from years of watching tag-team WWE in college instead of attending parties.

"Your bandit is valiant, though; he's a Hogwarts-grad BFM wizard – and he's fighting the jet like an N7 bro on steroids. Ludicrous stuff. The three of you duke it out the entire time, on the cusps of LARs, no missiles off the rail, no sense of who's truly winning – until, well..."

"Until what?!" Sam asked, desperate to hear the outcome.

Looking somberly down at the table, Kennedy shook his head, and finally uttered, "Until you shoot him..."

"The bandit?"

"Negative..." the OPSO lamented. "Your wingman..."

Unsure what to say, Sam remained silent, before suggesting, "Are you sure I shoot him? Are you sure it's not the adversary that I kill?"

WYFMIFM looked back up at him in annoyance. "I know what I saw, Sam."

"Well... well, maybe it was just a crazy dream, you know?" Sam scoffed and added, "I would never shoot a wingman – even Juice!"

"Wouldn't you?" WYFMIFM asked coldly with a blank stare. "Because I think I just witnessed a pretty textbook SFWT blue-on-blue..."

Sam said nothing.

After an awkward silence, WYFMIFM sighed. "You're probably right, Nickels..." He frowned, looking at Sam with sadness. "I think part of me wonders – almost wishes..." he paused once more, put his finger to his chin, and repeated, "Part of me almost wishes that it was reality..." He clasped his hands together and said, "Because at least, for a brief moment in time, it would mean that you two individuals – like carbs and carnivores – settled your differences, and finally realized the magnificence you could unleash as one unified team..."

Not sure how to respond, Sam winced and casually dismissed, "I wouldn't think anything of that dream, WYFMIFM. I mean, come on," he scoffed, "Could you really see a scenario where Juice and I were fighting alongside one another? I don't think this guy's gonna make it past Level 3, or out of his JO squadron period without a FNAEB – especially not with that merely 'Promotable' admin!" he finished with a grin, striving for WYFMIFM's approval via another lame FITREP reference.

WYFMIFM refused to give Sam even a pity laugh as he paused – pensive – and then asked, "Nickels – if your life was a story... would your character be considered a 'Good Dude?'"

Taken aback by the question, Sam stumbled for a moment. "Well... I mean... I think my Good Dude Awards speak for themselves, don't they?"

WYFMIFM shook his head in disappointment. "Please... you've been through enough Awards Boards to know how pointless the things are." He stopped, and then pointedly acknowledged, "You're stagnating as a protagonist, Sam. And the antagonist sent to this squadron – to push you to great new heights – is close on your heels, to the point where you two have almost swapped roles. And in this 'story' of yours?" he added with air quotes. "Readers would certainly sense all of this, and they'd probably even be rooting for you. They would crave for you to take this chance to accept your rival, up your game to the next level, and demonstrate the ultimate warrior mindset by pushing each other to the top!

"And yet, you're afraid of him. You're running from him. You're choosing to still shoot him, vice support him..." he added with an ominous tone. "Iron sharpens iron, Sam – but you're sitting there flat, dull, and happy. You're not climbing anymore. Others certainly are – but you've grown tired of that quest. So rather than continuing to strive for the top, you're simply looking to call your current position the new 'peak' by mere attrition of all competition." WYFMIFM sighed deeply. "You can't refly Juice forever, Sam. Deep inside, you know you'll have to confront him as your equal one day."

Sam sat in silence, unwilling to digest the reality his OPSO was serving.

"Some men seek out their ultimate challenge," WYMFIFM continued. "They chase their destiny, knowing it's the chance to reach their greatest peaks. And yet others spend their entire lives running from their innermost true aspirations for triumph, petrified at the thought of handling the pressure of the moment they know they were born for..." The bald man shrugged. "And right now, I fear that you may be experiencing spatial D – thinking you're in a smooth climb, when in reality..." He shook his head as his voice trailed off in the unfinished thought, and he ate the rest of his rice ball instead. Once he was done, Kennedy gathered his remaining scraps of steak back in the glassware, and stood up amidst the uncomfortable silence.

Desperate to say something and break the tension, Sam finally called out with a chuckle, "Woah! Not finishing your ribeye?! Bro!" he tried to force a smile, "That's the healthiest part of the meal!"

Shrugging and still appearing downcast, WYFMIFM said, "Maybe so, Sam..." he looked back at his junior officer, "But I think I'm a little tired of steak right now..."

WYFMIFM whipped his BLACKPINK lunchbox over his shoulder like a flight bag, and exited the ready room.

Stung by the words of his OPSO, Sam sat in silence and thought about what both Low T and WYFMIFM said: Iron sharpens iron... He opened his phone album and pulled up a picture of himself at the Guam Dusit beach, with his personal-best AOM:LOL ratios – a physique he'd achieved with carb inclusion...

Are carbs a critical component for the ultimate physique, despite their nutritionally non-critical profile? Was Nadal made better because of Roger Federer's presence across the net in so many big matches? Am I afraid of Juice because I know he'll push me to continue growing to unheralded new heights? And if so... shouldn't I be embracing him...?

He thought for a few silent minutes before walking into Ops, where he considered telling their Training O that he'd pass Juice, after all.

And then he saw it: Juice's name – not his – in the last deployment fly-on spot, meaning that Sam Rowland – a senior JO – would be walking on the boat, and dealing with every *piece of inconvenient and annoying bullshit that such a responsibility held.* Fuck that shit... *he said in his head as he turned around, fuming – not planning on helping with on-load at all, and no longer giving a care in the world about what Kyle or WYFMIFM thought.* They're just being dramatic, *Sam told himself.* I've already reached incredible heights here, because I know what the fuck I'm talking about when it comes to admin. I'm not afraid of Juice, and I'm not blue-on-blue-ing him. He's just *not* good — and, more importantly, *not* a Good Dude...

And with that, Sam walked right back into the vault and began reviewing his NATOPS preflight briefing lab, which was personal-password-protected on the Chippernet – like every other lab he'd been working on since Juice entered Level 3...

Back in OPS, WYFMIFM began adjusting the fly-on list magnets from the random placeholders that an FNG skeds-O put up earlier...

~

"I say again – Calling on GUARD! Aircraft not squawking at position: North 37 decimal –"

"ON GUARD — THIS IS A NODDIK EMPIRE *LIEUTENANT COMMANDER* SPEAKING! NOW SHUT UP, AND LISTEN UP — I AM ARMED WITH AN AIR-TO-SURFACE LOADOUT CAPABLE OF MEETING ANY P-SUB-D CALCULABLE, WITH ENOUGH AMASSED FIREPOWER TO MEET EVEN THE MOST DEMANDING OF GROUND COMMANDER'S INTENTS. AND IF YOU DON'T WANT ME BLOWING THIS ENTIRE LOAD ON DOMESTIC TERRITORY, THEN I SUGGEST YOU STOP CLOBBERING THE RADIO WITH YOUR FUTILE CHATTER ABOUT MY LACK OF SQUAWK WHILST PENETRATING YOUR PRECIOUS PRIVATE AIRSPACE."

"JESUS CHRIST," Robo-Hinge yelled to himself after unkeying the mic on 243.0, shaking his head in frustration at these pathetic attempts to scare him. What were they going to do if he *was* flight violated — take away his wings?! 'PLEASE...' he thought, his internal monologues also in aggressive all-caps. 'ONCE I SINK THIS SHIP AND EARN ALL THESE AIR-TO-SURFACE KILLS, MY WINGS WILL HARDLY EVEN BE NOTICEABLE, WITH ALL THE SHINY CHEST CANDY THE EMPIRE WILL GIVE ME...' He smirked at the thought of updating his NSIPS with awards he'd undoubtedly be presented after this unprecedented strike. 'I WILL BE SUCH A FUCKING LOCK TO MAKE CAG...'

He then, however, scowled at the thought of updating his pre-staged ribbon, medal, and mini-medal breastplate from EZRackBuilder.com. 'GOD DAMMIT... I *JUST* CHANGED IT WITH MY SHARPSHOOTER QUAL, TOO... FUCK IT, I'LL JUST CHARGE IT TO THE MESS FUNDS.'

"Previous aircraft calling on GUARD — This is the USS Ship! If you do not change course, we will launch an intercept and escort —"

"ESCORT MY *COCK*, DOUCHE," Robo-Hinge transmitted back, then tapped the GUARD button off, not giving a shit about further radio calls missed. Besides, he didn't actually *need* the SA — he was an O-4; a department head; a *Hinge* — and he knew his kind were as high SA as they came. Also, he had about 1000 hours of flight experience, putting him right in the sweet spot of invincibility from mishaps in the skies. The strike-lead-of-one chuckled. 'A DECK LAUNCH INTERCEPT... SERIOUSLY?!' He coldly laughed to himself. 'I AM ABOUT 10 MINUTES FROM MY RMAX... THERE'S NO CHANCE IN HELL A PILOT COULD GET AIRBORNE AND STOP ME.'

He attempted to zoom in on his SA display, but to no avail. He kept repeatedly scrolling with his elevation wheel, yelling "WHAT THE FUCK!" in frustration. Alas, the SA display was broken and not obeying its master, leading him to boil with impatience as he was forced to pushbutton his scale down. 'PIECE OF SHIT...' he thought angrily. In fact, he was *so* irate that he failed to notice that his TDC was assigned to his radar, and his scan volume was now dug straight into the ocean, making his radar useless as he looked to fly the last leg of his route.

Useless *now*, that is... as ten minutes ago, an aircraft had passed below him — unnoticed — just off the surface, in the very spot where his beam was currently blasting 100% of its radar waves.

~

LT Mark "JABA" Buck carefully scanned his flip chart, seeing the obstacle depicted — before quickly grabbing the controls and banking left to avoid the gigantic buoy planted in the middle of the ocean. He turned his head to the right and watched the skyscraping structure rush by his wing, the pilot breathing heavily as he realized how close he'd come to death — and even worse: to failing his secondary mission of properly vetting this low-level route.

The entire low level had been full of crazy hazards. There were lighthouses, telephone poles, hang-gliding recreational areas, communication towers, and, of course, those pesky gigantic buoys upward of 200 feet AGL, all scattered randomly in the nautical environment, seemingly in the most inconvenient, impractical, and illogical locations. This most recent buoy had just been his *latest* encounter with a tall object threatening to end his life and invalidate his primary mission — the world's most important MARSTRIKE.

JABA carefully adhered to his Mission Crosscheck Time while lifting his visor to wipe the sweat off his forehead. His greatest fear had come to fruition — this was *exactly* why these low-level routes required an O-4 to fly them every 60 days. Only aviators of their SA, experience, and fully-founded confidence could possibly navigate the tumultuous obstacles the routes bore. More than once along this flight, JABA had received psychologically painful—and near *physically lethal*—reminders of why he was still just an O-3, and why he may *not* have been fit for the life of a Lieutenant Commander. And now, just as he had each time as he felt his confidence drop, he began to subconsciously pull back on the stick, slightly climbing toward the sanctity of a safe—but not tactical—altitude...

"NO!" he yelled, pushing back on the stick and staying low. 'I can't give up!' he thought. 'I must trust them. I must complete this strike. I *must* believe that I can do the duties of an O-4!' The 'them' he was referring to, of course, were Tom Brady and Bill Belichick, who had properly identified and manually CHUM'd every single obstacle on this route with pinpoint accuracy. If they hadn't? JABA would've been killed long ago... With such meticulous scrutiny and microscopic detail put into these VNAV flip charts, the Lieutenant was able to *clearly* understand how these two won so many Super Bowl titles back in New England together. It was *that* type of champion-assisted reassurance he needed to fly the entire route no higher than 100' AGL...

Was it even legal?! JABA wondered this very question when he made the PIC decision to descend so low. Technically, OPNAV allows one specific occasion on one specific Low Altitude Tactical Training flight in the RAG... but that was splitting hairs, and it probably wasn't even in the syllabus anymore. And even more to the point— any wise pilot on any other day would've MRM'd long ago and quickly escaped this low-level death trap. But when he started hearing calls on GUARD—calling out random lat/longs—a chill ran down his spine. Something told JABA he should stay low... that it was mission-critical to face this O-4 responsibility hesitancy of his. Something told him that his only chance to succeed would be to stay, quite literally, under the radar.

He thought back to his career in the Navy, where he'd been so happy to do this in the Chippies. Happy to have such a simple, low-profile life on the boat, laughing with his best friends about the stupidest of things. Happy to avoid the first-world drama that everybody else preoccupied themselves with, whether it was the latest Taylor Swift dating rumors or politically-motivated tweet, the newest 'study' showing how America's obesity epidemic could clearly be 'solved' by 'presenting more vegan options in schools,' or the latest comments made by some random celebrity that set millions of citizens storming to their Facebook pages to 'cancel' their new public enemy number one. It was all eye-rolling, asinine bullshit that just proved yet again: When people don't have real problems or work to do, they fabricate new artificial ones in order to cling to some sense of importance in life. And, JABA had to admit: as much bullshit as the Navy had? At least it was real, relevant-to-his-life bullshit.

Sometimes, in his most private and secretive thoughts, JABA felt he could've been a first-ballot DH selection—*if* he hadn't sent in his 'Don't Pick Me' letter. But also, he wasn't about all the self-promoting it sometimes took to get your name out there. He'd been content to be out of the spotlight, selflessly helping others and doing his duties, wondering if it would be enough to get him the career he thought he might deserve. They'd always called him 'Just Another Buck Angel'—but he didn't feel that way at all. He felt like he was just another dude, doing his job, helping out where he could—and if that wasn't enough to get him back in the game as an O-4, then so be it.

Yet he couldn't ignore the truth: he *was* much happier back then, in his simple life with his best friends—long before the annoying fame, notoriety, and corporate frustrations that he couldn't shake after starting CV Worldwide. But with all that gone—with his rollercoaster tycoon entrepreneurial venture ruined? Mark Buck knew he could—for at least a brief time—fly below the radar once again.

And *damn*, was he good at it. Never the recipient of the 'Good Dude Award,' yet ironically one of the worthiest candidates you'd ever find—Buck truly didn't give it a second thought. 'Awards, like the views, are for the birds' he'd always believed. Awards, recognition, trophies... he never understood the obsession. It was why JABA was so confused when Nickels was upset about losing his 'status' to Juice... why he was so turned off by the EP competition of the imaginary FITREP system... and why he grew so weary of this generation's 'Should everybody get a trophy?' debate. None of that shit *mattered*—the only ones who found importance in these frivolous handouts were those in desperate need of validation from their own lack of self-esteem, or the ones who felt artificial authority and power in handing them out—or worst of all: the soccer moms and tee ball dads who carried *both* of those fictional burdens.

To JABA, and in his time in the Navy, he learned that expecting some quantity of recognition for your work was a fool's quest, and one that would leave you wanting and disappointed. Whether the Navy was sending him to Virginia, Japan, Mississippi, or a low-level MARSTRIKE against a foreign planet's carrier? He was going to do his damned best to kick as much ass as he possibly could in *any* situation—and couldn't give any less of a shit over what medal, FITREP ranking, or set of orders he got as a result. Because the orders he fought against for so long? The *exact same* orders he now wanted so desperately? According to Big Navy and PERS, those were apparently too far out of LAR... JABA briefly glanced at his Lieutenant shoulder insignia and sighed...

After 0.5 seconds of Mission Crosscheck Time, he directed his scan back ahead and saw some semblance of a ridgeline crossing ahead, in the form of a 500' wave in the middle of the ocean that some surfer was hanging ten over. There was no way around it—JABA closed his eyes for 0.5 seconds and steeled himself. "You got this, Mark," he said aloud. As he internalized his plan of action, the procedures came back to him like the fond memories of childhood: '20-degree Vertical Jink, no delay, ready...'

As he hit the pull-up point and popped up—reciting the procedures in his head and turning inverted over the top—he could've sworn the surfer down below *looked* and *sounded* so familiar, his dreadlocks flailing in the wind, and a loud glail emerging from the beach bum. Another former friend, no doubt—this job was full of them. Too many to fit into this novel, name by name. 'The hidden true benefit behind this entire journey...' he realized with a smile.

Unable to fully discern the man's identity with his focus on the dive recovery rules, JABA popped back upright and took note of the 'Good R' and the flat terrain, looking to get back low and finish this epic route en route to his FAP...

~

Sam leveled off at 12,500 feet, squawking VFR, and headed due northeast—not giving a shit that he was at an improper altitude for one flying at a magnetic heading between 0 and 179 degrees. *What was another flight violation really gonna do to me at this point, anyway?*

He double-tapped BARO to hold his altitude, and clicked the ATC button to retain his calibrated airspeed, slumping over in despair as his jet engaged autopilot mode. He had missed this 'real pilot experience' these American jets gave their aviators, compared to Noddik F/A-18s—but despite the thrill he usually felt from ripping around menus and DDIs to navigate the skies, he was currently too overwhelmed with woe at the thought of his lonely future...

Who could he possibly let down next?! There was hardly anyone left—*CP, >SADCLAM<, JABA*... their return was going to be for naught; *their* lives now ruined, too. *FISTY*... he'd probably be vegetated forever, never again conscious to see that his GOAT hero had become a member of the very society where Flynn had built up his *own* GOAT status. *WYFMIFM*... he was already dead, apparently—and arguably *because* of Sam, depending on how pessimistically one decided to construe a narrative. *All the FNGs*... the senior guys ahead of Sam... *The Lorax... I guess he was right after all — I really am just a spineless, backstabbing bitch...* he grieved to himself, barely noticing the wiry surfer out in the distance, taking in the cosmic rays of mother nature while riding a tsunami-esque wave. *The Chippy maintainers*... he thought back to some of the PRs he'd promised to one day incorporate into his grand story—Monty, Marty, Keck, Frazier, Chou... *And I even couldn't do that! FUCK!* he swore to himself. Shit—he even managed to find a way to let down Tom Brady, Bill Belichick, that lean old guy who wrote *The Winner Within,* and every single celebrity at WYFMIFM's yacht party. *No chance Megan Fox would* ever *want to bang me now...* he thought desolately, ruing the important things in life.

Even the robots he was in charge of at the NIRD Katsopolis—their algorithms were undoubtedly savvy enough to hold the opinion that he was trash. Charlie Alpha Golf... he probably had Sam's existence wiped from his internal RAM database. Dr. Karl Suabedissen... Sam scoffed. That guy would probably be getting laid left and right after this Noddik victory. *He might even be more alpha than me these days. Maybe his girlfriend actually is real...* That Robo-Hinge douche from Flat Earth Fitness. *Who the hell was that guy anyway? Regardless, if he really is a hinge, and the spool-up at the gym was an accurate reflection of his character, then hopefully he hasn't been given too much authority on that boat; I can only imagine the great responsibilities he'd be redirecting with such great power...*

He thought back to Low T—his hardened face of pain and suffering at the second phase of the Olympics. *I let him down long ago when I left — the man I saw wasn't Low T. No — that dead soul was someone else...*

And lastly, he thought to Juice. *Hah...* he chuckled coldly, as he slowly blinked his eyes and shook his head. *He might be the only one I haven't let down yet... that motherfucker. He got everything he wanted from me: my status with the Chippies... my job with the Noddiks... my role as the hero of these Olympics... shit, if there was ever a story written about me, Juice would probably overshadow me as the goddamn main character! Whatever...* Sam looked at his radios, where he had Chippy TAC 12 over TAC 13—still waiting to hear from JABA on either, but no longer trying to transmit out. He turned them both down, knowing it was a moot effort. All that was left to do was land on the Noddik carrier and shamefully admit defeat—another valid follow-on employment Juice would attain against an already-kill-removing Sam...

I won't do it.

Tears falling down his cheeks, Sam closed his eyes, his body beginning to tremble. He took a deep breath, clicked out of autopilot, pointed his jet five degrees nose-low toward the water, and engaged FPAH—holding his descent angle in place. *I won't do it...* he thought again, tears falling even faster. *Juice wants one last victory over me, but I won't give it to him.* Watching the water grow closer, little by little, he accepted his defeat—and with his fate largely sealed, resigned that this was the *one* thing he could still do to control *some* semblance of his own destiny.

I've already let everyone else down — it's about time I let Juice down, too.

~

Dr. Suabedissen stood atop the ship's fantail, staring down at the ocean below him. The wake behind the boat was majestic... a crystalline translucent blue, creating streams of white foam on either side of the stern as it stormed through the ocean. It was a beautiful sight; a reminder of how special such a simple view in life could be—a perspective often lost in the doldrums of deployment and stresses of service afloat...

Except it was all fake. He craned his neck further down and saw the wiring and projector equipment, where his graphic designer Noddik bots had successfully coded a green screen-esque faux trail of wake. It was meticulously and expertly programmed to perfectly mimic a United States carrier's visual proof of power, artificially simulating the way America's cities at sea would—quite literally and symbolically—declare their presence while cruising through the deep waters of planet earth; the world Dr. Suabedissen used to know—or *thought* he knew...

He looked back up, beyond the 5K-resolution waters created with the Unreal Engine, and stared glumly toward the *actual* ocean surrounding him. The uncharted waters... the foreign lands... the unknown adventures of life... Suabedissen sighed. His whole life, all he'd known was his *fake* world. All he'd traversed was his generated Dungeons and Dragons universe of Gladia, filled with graphics, NPCs, and other fearful users, hiding from the real world with a gamertag and power sword. The only self-improvement he'd focused on was toward his digital avatar, which he'd amassed ridiculously wasteful amounts of time, money, and experience points into—investments that were all rendered moot by his own actions. He'd never found the ecstasy of love or felt the agony of heartbreak—even his 'traveling model girlfriend' was a bogus story he'd kept going to build street cred and ensure nobody knew of his deep, dark, sexual exploit-less truths... 'Although I did a pretty dang job of selling the convincing lie,' he thought.

He felt his mouth visibly frown as he squinted, looking toward the sunrise afar. The fake amount of respect he garnered on this ship. The fake friends he thought he'd gained along the way. And above all... the fake purpose his life held. Even when D&D existed, his *own* existence was still near-worthless, barely held together with duct tape and paperclips: a bunch of fake, meaningless in-game accomplishments and trophies that other online users could see and—if Dr. Suabedissen was being honest with himself—not give a shit about. And through his own voluntary commitment, he'd become further trapped on this Katsopolis ship of meaninglessness—in this *life* of meaninglessness. His story was void of any true calling, any sense of contentment, or any path toward bravery, adventure, and destiny fulfillment—the narrative he *thought* he was living as a D&D pioneer. Because in reality? It had all been a sham. A sham that he'd destroyed and invalidated with his very own hands. 'I should've known,' he thought, 'that this was no hero's journey. How *could* it be, when there was no villain to conquer? My own lifestyle *was* the antagonist...' Once he'd emotionally sobered up and realized what he'd done to his D&D empire, the doctor thought he'd be crushed; furious at himself, devastated with what he'd lost. Instead, the doctor simply felt aloof; apathetic to his decision. 'So... these are the dangers of pre-workout...' he recognized, chuckling humorlessly. 'The hollow despair of the comedown...'

He didn't give a *shit* about what he'd *lost* in life. Rather, he was lamenting what he'd *missed*...

Out in the distance, Suabedissen could make out different land masses; ambiguous islands on the horizon. 'I wonder what life is like out there...' He imagined the structure at his 040 bearing was 'Testosterone Town,' where inhabitants lived a life of weight lifting, sun-tanning, and meat-eating. But he also believed there was more to Testosterone Town than just pumps and steaks—these high-energy creatures were productivity *fiends*—energizing themselves by creating breakthroughs through projects, passions, and progressions *every single day*. A group of hard-charging individuals, unwilling to be content with 'average' or 'normal,' hungry to reach a greater tier of excelling in life—excelling by their *own* definition, not some arbitrary third party's. These alphas sought to generate the highest quality products for their community—not to steal money from the weak-minded and 'get rich,' but out of personal pride in putting their highest level of effort toward something they cared about. They used their skills and ingenuities to promote growth and positivity for all, not create mindless fruitions like social media, reality TV, and online worlds—distractions from what *truly* mattered in life. In T-Town, Suabedissen daydreamed, people were focused on living their best lives through physically *and* mentally stimulating activities, and found their happiness through the art of getting better every day, chasing the aspects of life that truly struck a chord in their hearts.

He'd never done *any* of those things, he realized as he looked at his pale, frail arms, and pulled out a vegan cookie from his lab coat pocket. He bought the 'funfetti cake batter'-flavored cookie from the ship's store, planning to use it to refuel his muscles after his first ever workout—seeing as it had a whopping 10g of protein, only 30 ingredients, loads of healthy fiber, and was free of all animal fats. And yet, suddenly losing his appetite for artificial filler in life, he threw the canola-oil-based dessert into the ocean, watching as it made the daintiest splash.

He looked over to his 270 bearing and saw another land mass. 'Maybe that one's 'Love Island'...' he thought. There, people discovered the wonders of romantic compatibility—how an already fantastic life can be even *further* lifted by adding the touch of a trusted, *loved* person in life—something he'd *also* never felt in his voyage aboard the NIRD Katsopolis, nor the online MMORPG world. He stood there sadly as he visualized all the happy couples inhabiting the island: individuals who lived plenty fulfilling lives in their own initiative, yet found their match in another with the same; the two coming together in realizing that even *greater* bliss can ensue from two like-minded lives of optimism and drive shared together. He nearly shed a tear as he imagined a warrior, coming back home from a long grinding session, being welcomed by the arms of his wife and children, and enjoying a home-cooked meal together—vice celebrating a raid with a bag of Lays, a DiGiorno pizza, a 2-liter of Dr. Pepper, and the latest top results from the 'Most Viewed Videos' submenu...

He pulled a paper out of his pocket; a list of his high-def premium porn site login and password information. It included Pornhub, Redtube, Brazzers, Bangbros, Milking Table, Nubile Films, Nuru Massage... He crumpled up the list before making it even a quarter of the way through, and threw the wad of paper out in the ocean, closing his eyes and shaking his head. The doctor was dismayed at how much of his life he'd wasted seeking fake love and phony pleasure without the true connectivity of another female specimen. He thought about MyLittlePonyXoXo... and his depression fell even further...

And then he looked dead ahead, at his 12'oclock—where he saw the largest island of all. "AdventureLand..." he whispered aloud to no one in particular. Here, he imagined, people went on *true* quests for *true* experience points in life. He thought of people surfing large waves, tempting death as they became one with the ocean, and celebrating by basking in the beautiful sunset—like they were in the sandy beach town of Nargaho, where you could buy sun-resistant armor. He then pictured travelers hiking up the tallest of mountains, defying gravity as they scaled peaks so high they could taste the clouds, relishing the view at the top—like when he traversed his character to the top of Mount Destiny, overseeing all of Gladia. He then visualized brave souls skiing down those snow-capped hills, reaching lightning-fast speeds, so amped that the face-whipping wind-chill was *welcomed*—similar to the Timber Peaks he navigated in the winter regions of Arcteria, in his raids for ore and scantily clad artwork of in-game female characters. Suabedissen imagined that people on AdventureLand had probably left their hometowns with *real* stakes—no save states—jumping into the abyss of a life-long journey to new regions in order to find themselves and their calling, doing something badass like becoming a skydiving expert with over 1200 jumps, or maybe even a fighter jet test pilot, working on new technology to make the mech warrior all the more lethal. 'That would be much cooler than writing new expansion pack coding,' he bemoaned internally. Here on AdventureLand, he fathomed the possibility that someone could even gain enough leadership skill points and EXP to mentor real-life men and women—serving as the head of a department, where they could dedicate their lives to improving the safety, maintenance, and operational components of a guild...

That was the life he'd really wanted—doing something *real* and exciting—not this *fake* shit he'd been consuming for way too long.

Suabedissen took one last thing out of his pocket—his personalized P-WordSlayer69 'Man Card'—something he and his online guildmembers had ordered for themselves as a 'funny' gag to celebrate defeating the Demon of Despair. The card earned them one free entry into the online strip club 'The Dragon's Lay-er,' where a bunch of half-monster, half-naked female NPCs did pre-rendered animation dances for the gamers in exchange for their rupees. 'I don't deserve this shit—I'm no man... I'm a *bitch.*' He shook his head, tossed the card out to the deep waters, and started crying.

Amongst his sobs, he looked back out to the wake, and felt his body inching forward toward the edge of the fantail. 'Maybe it's too late for me,' he thought woefully. 'Maybe it'd better if I just formatted my own hard drive...'

The Noddiks were sure to take home this Admin Olympic victory—but Dr. Suabedissen didn't have any interest in celebrating; he wasn't concerned with hearing the gloating of Juice or Robo-Hinge. And he *certainly* wasn't looking forward to the ass-chewing of a lifetime he'd get from the latter after Order66Gate.

'What's it all been for, Karl?' he wondered internally as he shuffled even closer to the threshold of the stern. 'Haven't you gone through *enough* bullshit in this life already? Why fight just to endure more?'

~

As he careened toward the ocean floor, watching the altitude in his HUD rapidly decrement at a VSI unbeknownst to him—since he remained in A/A Master Mode and refused to understand how to read a standby gauge—Sam's life unwound before his eyes. The career he'd envisioned for himself, and the destiny he'd been determined to fulfill; his initial aspirations to be somebody truly *different* in a world rumored to be full of so many 'bad guys' and 'douchebags.' He thought back to flight school in the mighty T-6, where plenty of IPs—helo and P8 background bros, with their *vast* FA-18 knowledge—described how jet guys were 'a bunch of assholes who ate their young.' Sam had always strived to be different, to end that culture—yet found, to his surprise, that such a culture was completely non-existent in the fighter community. It was rife with hard-working, fun-loving, dedicated professionals. And in the ultimate irony, Sam turned out to be the closest thing to this erroneous caricature of backstabbing bastards, as he'd turned into the very persona he sought to defeat.

"Altitude, Altitude..."

With his vision slightly blurred from tears streaming, Sam looked up after hearing Bitchin Betty's voice, where he saw '10,000' flashing in the HUD—letting him know he was entering the 4-digit territory of altitude. He put his hands up to the UFCD and turned his RADALT off completely, not wanting to be annoyed in his last moments of life—knowing it would only be a matter of time before he heard from his old warning mistress once more, as she would undoubtedly scream in that sweet southern accent, "Pull up, pull up!"

Where did it all go wrong? he wondered as he watched 8000 feet tick by. *Where did this life of mine – this Good Dude mentality – where did it go? When did I turn into this mega-doucher?* He asked the question, but he knew the answer. *Juice... I couldn't fucking stand the thought of someone being better than me at admin... as a JO... as a Good Dude. And the whole time, Kyle tried to explain what I couldn't see: That if I'd just fucking accepted his ambition as a chance to let iron sharpen iron, and stopped worrying about him, or 'credit,' and just focused on improving myself? Then the Chippies could've been the greatest, most suit-cased, tightest-knit fucking squadron ever. And yet, instead... they really may be better off with-out me...*

"Did you not think I'd return, Sam?" the Romani gypsy-accented Bane voice keyed into his headset.

What? But my comms are off... He looked up and saw where the source had come from. *Voice Alpha...* He keyed the comm switch forward and asked, "You again? What do you want..."

"I told you I was immortal," the voice responded.

"WYFMIFM?" Sam asked. "But... CLAM watched you die...?"

"There are many forms of immortality..." he said ominously, without answering the question.

Racking his brain for some semblance of logic to this introduction, and seeing the '5' digit become a '4' in his altitude box, Sam sighed and transmitted, "Look, if this *is* WYFMIFM—you're too late. Juice and the Noddiks have already won—JABA got flight violated because *I* fucked up as SDO and didn't get him the assigned route air-space." Frustrated, he shook his head and added, "And honestly, that was just the final straw. This whole Phase 3 — no, these whole *Olympics* — have been a complete bangbus because of *my* incompetence as a mission commander... as a leader... as a Good Dude. I'm sorry, WYFMIFM, but it's over. You may have saved me in Phase 2, but this is too much — even *Juice* couldn't handle this one..."

"WYFMIFM?!" the faux-Romani exclaimed. "You think *that* blind fool is the one talking to you?!" The accent lost some nuance as he stressed, "Nickels... you're seriously giving up because you couldn't handle a bit of turbulence? You had this grand plan of becoming the fleet's Goodest Dude of All Time—but when that plan hit the *tiniest* bump? When you encountered the *slightest* bit of adversity? You bugged out..." The man scoffed, "I didn't know the VTs even *taught* such a beta maneuver an-ymore... You're a *runner,* Sam, and you always were – running away from the Dam-busters, incapable of handling competitive pressure... running away from where you experienced the most growth, incapable of enduring the shit that makes you better... running opposite the compass toward your destiny's peak, unwilling to *keep climbing.* Look at you now! You're running away! *Again!*"

The voice laughed over Voice Alpha. "And you're gonna bring up *Juice?!* You know what *Juice* would do?! Unlike *you*, Juice wouldn't run—Juice would *fight*. He would *find a way*, Sam. He'd find a way to reach a new level, climbing beyond preconceived ceilings to rise to the occasion. And he wouldn't just find a way for himself— he'd find it for *you*, too. Because Juice knows. He knows that *iron sharpens iron*, and knows that while he's great *without* you? He's legendary *with* you. Juice would do whatever it took to get you climbing alongside him, and he right next to you—because Juice understands what *you* don't, Sam: In a life-defining race to the top of the tallest peaks; in the clash of rivals? Regardless of who *won*—you'd *both* reach unheralded heights with that fire of competition lighting your burners. *Juice* answers the call; he's a champ, a fucking *gamer*, and a Good Dude. But *Dimes?!*" the voice scoffed. "Dimes is a *chump*, a fucking *loser*, and a Bad Guy..."

The voice paused, then—with partial Bane, full conviction—asked, "Why, Sam? Why do you always run from Juice? Are you *that* afraid of failure? Why can't you just *accept the challenge*, look it in the eyes, and say, 'I'm ready to show you what the fuck I'm capable of!'?"

The Voice Alpha man's words stung Sam—and yet, strangely, they *inspired* him. Despite the overwhelming absurdity of them all being projected with that muffled accent, the musings pierced Sam's innermost insecurities, reaching his soul. He stared a thousand yards beyond the water in contemplation. *He's right. I am running away again. Is this all I do? Is this who I am – a quitter? Or, for once, why can't I stand my ground... show the desire in my heart... and just* fight?"

The gypsy accent was dwindling, the man taking a more serious tone as he said, "I know what Juice would do. I know what Dimes would do. But what about *Nickels?* What will *Nickels* do in this moment? It's never too late, Sam, for redemption. A wise man once told me something: 'Life is ultimately a war of resilience; the greatest of victories will be achieved by he who is simply the last one to give up.'"

When he said the quote, Sam *almost* recognized his voice... but there was so much going on that he couldn't think...

"Even when all appears lost, and nothing could seem more fucked, it is ultimately *your* choice to surrender, shamefully sauntering back down the mountain in defeat..." The voice had no impersonation whatsoever now, as it emphasized: "Or to *accept* the shit, *persevere* regardless, *refuse* to quit climbing—and believe that you *will* make it up that motherfucking mountain, or god dammit, you will *die trying!*"

"Pull up, pull up!" Betty shouted.

"So, what will you do, Sam: Die a villain? Or persist long enough to become the hero?"

"Power, power!"

"Maybe Juice was right all along; maybe Nickels *is* beyond saving..."

"NO!" Sam slammed his throttles to Max AB, yanked back on the stick, pushed the paddle switch, and held his breath—he could've sworn he heard the slightest 'splash' of his cans scraping the wavetops—before rotating at a perfect L/D MAX and initiating an ascent above the water. When he looked around his peripheries and realized he was established in a safe climb, Sam gave a tremendous exhale. Desperate to say *something* badass—as he knew this escape-from-the-abyss was such a crucial moment in his character arc—he grasped at the first quote that popped in his mind, and erroneously transmitted in a growly Batman voice: "People keep asking if I'm back, and I haven't really had an answer—but now, yeah: I'm thinking I'm back!" It didn't matter that the Dark Knight never said this quote, or Bane any of the other butchered quotes smattered about in the past five minutes. It didn't matter that the author missed another chance in this story to obscurely reference and parallel the 28-3 comeback. And it sure as hell didn't matter that the jet was now over-G'd, showing an 811 MSP code, and thus down for flight. The only thing that mattered? Nickels was *back*.

And if Juice and the Noddiks think I'm going down quietly — running away, without fighting til the bitter end? Then they're gonna find out who the fuck Sam 'Nickels' Rowland truly is — and they're gonna see what the fuck he's truly capable of.

With no response on Voice Alpha, Sam turned his radios back up and immediately heard, "Any radio, any radio; two groups approaching the ship from *separate sectors.* North group, Rock 270/150, *fast* — assessed to be armed with simulated leadership and a—"

The radio cut out briefly, much to Sam's chagrin. He repeated the same mantra to himself that he utilized when this happened in A/A fights: *Hopefully that wasn't important...*

"—rock 220/75, strength two—assessed to be armed with simulated catastrophic administrative weapons. Any airborne fighter—intercept and escort *immediately!*"

While still climbing, Sam looked at his location and realized he was within mere *miles* of *that* group, maybe even *at* their location. Sure enough, he looked up his lift vector and saw two F/A-18s passing directly overhead. He did a quick wings recce and confirmed his feared suspicion—empty pylons, no doubt locked and loaded with C codes of the most dangerous variety.

Sam narrowed his eyes, broke his alpha, and put his nose—and velocity vector—in the gap between the two. *The USS Ship might lose these Olympics... but Mom sure as hell isn't getting Ck'd on my watch.* He ignited full afterburner, embodying the newly relit drive inside his heart. As his airspeed increased, the jet's plane of motion started matching its plane of symmetry, symbolically similar to Sam's own literal path of travel matching his path of purpose. And as he actuated his radar to take a lock on one of the bandits, he blanked his HUD of all other distracting symbology—went *full REJ-2*—just as he'd finally found the inner strength to blank out the rest of the noise in life; to ignore the worries about what might happen after this battle; to simply focus on fighting his best BFM game plan.

And as unrealistic-yet-memorable as it was in *Top Gun: Maverick*, Sam burst nose-high through the line abreast bandits in a move that did nothing significant tactically, but *everything* for the spectator's sensation of 'Wow, that was badass...'

~

"What the hell?!" Camilli transmitted over AUX, instinctively yanking his jet to the right, long after the nose-high F/A-18 had emerged from beneath his left wing. "Who the hell is that?!"

"It *can't* be..." Juice responded, as the two watched the jet execute an over-the-top maneuver and reverse upside-down—pulling toward them—then unload to inverted-and-level flight, vertically mirrored form above them; a maneuver as unrealistic-yet-memorable as it was in the original *Top Gun*. As the jet settled in close, they could make out the headgear of the aviator: a tac-air dumb helmet—a *Chippy* tac-air dumb helmet...

The opposing F/A-18's motion came to a stop—mere *feet* above Kyle's aircraft—as Juice watched from a close parade. "I don't know what this son of a bitch wants," Juice transmitted, "But he'd better act quickly—he's not gonna last more than 10 seconds with those tank 2/3 baffles..."

The aviator held up his hand, giving Kyle the flight signals of two, then four, then turned his hand sideways and gave a one, then sideways four—translated to 246.9. He then rolled upright and took high cover over the two, sliding slightly to their right. "Juice..." Kyle growled, "go 'Dirty Cheerleader,' PRI..."

Juice dialed in the frequency to his top radio, double-checked to make sure secure comms were not engaged, and keyed the mic, "Rowland... you son of a bitch—is that you?"

~

"Affirm, kemosabe," Sam responded, sounding cooler and more confident on the radio than he had in decades. "And I'm assessing your loadout is undoubtedly sim wings dirty," he asserted, using the knowledge that he and the reader had literally just heard on the radio minutes ago. "Am I right?"

"Hmmph," Juice grunted noncommittally.

Sam nodded to himself. "Thought so. Well, I can tell you right now, asswipe — the only way that A/S ordinance is going 'Lochness away' is if you can find the guile to first clean up the A/A picture and *earn* the right to 'Attack.'"

Juice smirked under his mask. "An enemy air order of battle of one by F/A-18E? You've gotta be kidding, Rowland — you *do* recall the TOPGUN Larger Quantity Rule of Thumb, or LQROT, right? Where, after extensive testing, the bros at NAWDC found that — in separate cockpits — two is, in fact, *more* than one? I know you've been out of the game for a while, but c'mon... and in case you didn't notice? I've got a hungry, testosterone-fueled wingman over here ready to feast on the macros of LARs."

Rowland looked over toward the aircraft he'd originally flown above, now noticing the maskless aviator's chiseled, jutting jaw, wearing a scowl — the *same* scowl he'd seen back in Phase 2. "Low T..." Sam keyed, almost speaking more to himself.

The angry pilot shook his head and raised his mask to his mouth, as his cold-but-familiar voice scorned, "Fuck that bitch... Low T is *dead,* Dimes. You can now call me... *Loaded T.*"

Sam's recoiled in confusion. *Loaded T? What the hell?* "Kyle... what's happened to you? How did you get this way? When did you become this agonized, villainous, jacked, tortured-soul?!"

Loaded T put his hand up and pointed at Sam, then raised his mask again and said, "Because of *you,* you spineless, backstabbing bitch. *You,* who pissed away all the Good Dude goodwill you once fostered at the Chippies, caring more about your own fucking program than even the smallest of goals from the men you once called brothers. *You,* who stole the future I'd built for myself and my family. *You,* who wrote—"

"Enough!" Juice interrupted. "Camilli — this is the shit we *live* for! SEM, baby! We're talking epic-showdown, fini-flight, once-in-a-lifetime type of conduct! Screw the MARSTRIKE; I don't want to be anywhere near that catastrophe anyway, when Robo-Hinge drops the AS-131 on the ship."

When Robo-Hinge does what*?!* Sam thought, shocked.

He was about to key the mic when Kyle brashly transmitted, "Juice — step off. This is *my* fight. Not ours — *mine.* For years, I've thought about nothing more than getting my revenge against this bitch in the ultimate arena. Rowland built his career around the importance of admin, ignoring all the conduct shit I dedicated *my* life to perfecting — an effort rendered meaningless, thanks to this selfish bastard," he glared back at Sam. "Because you didn't even give me a *chance* to carve my own destiny, Rowland — you couldn't even let me seek what I truly wanted: tactical expertise; a Patch. A chance to enter the highest echelon of aviators; the chance to answer *my* calling. And why not? Because you were too preoccupied with being the Admin King, willing to do whatever it took to get to the top, apathetic to *anyone* you tore down along the way.

First Juice... then me... and now the entire Noddik Empire. And every single time? It was all for *nothing.* You're *pathetic*, Rowland.

"Today, all I want from you is one set—one mano-a-mano duel of air-to-air supremacy. And the loser? *When* you lose..." Kyle paused, and said with a scathing tone of vengeance, "I steal Nickels' past—just as you stole Low T's future—and all of naval aviation gets to see Sam Rowland's true colors... and they sure as hell ain't blue or green... bitch."

Sam was taken aback. He didn't know what Kyle was referring to, but there was no time to calm down this juicehead—not with the "Bingo, bingo" vocal warning of his fuel, flashing 8.0.

"And don't try to puss out with some administrative excuse—I know you're current..." Kyle jeered, "I was there the last time you turned..."

Quickly doing the mental math, Sam realized his foe was correct—this would be a legal turning engagement. "And if I win?" he asked.

Kyle laughed, yet with no glee whatsoever. "I've been waiting a long time for the ultimate suffering, but I can't imagine a fate worse than falling to an admin cuck in the ultimate conduct arena. I'll turn in my fucking wings if you get the first shot on me."

Growing angry, Sam countered, "You mean just like I did in the BFM Tourney?"

"No, bitch," the jacked pilot shot back, pointing at him angrily again. "Fuck that shit—that was *Low T.* And like I said... he's *dead.*"

With the tension growing, Juice finally cut back in, "Kyle... let me fight alongside you—this is what we've *both* waited for. You said it yourself—he fucked us *both* over..."

"Get the fuck out of here, Juice," Kyle repeated over PRI, with a hint of threat in his voice. "Go play your little bitchboy admin games on the MARSTRIKE. I guarantee Robo-Hinge fucked up the Killship employment, anyway. Recommend you pass me the lead; pass me the lead, now."

Juice kinked his neck in discomfort—but *not* from the JHMCS... "I'm not leaving, Kyle... This is the fight I wanted—and this is the fight I'm taking. I don't even have my racks locked..." he admitted.

Kyle laughed, shaking his head, as he keyed, "Of fucking *course* you don't! I told you, Juice—all you fucking care about is fighting. Well, not this time, bitch—it's *my* life he ruined, *my* future he stole, and *my* revenge to take. You can have the follow-on scraps..."

"Kyle..." Juice transmitted with frustration.

The ship is in danger of being Ck'd? No—K'd—IRL?! Sam maneuvered his jet closer to the Noddik fighters, his head swimming with concern from Kyle's previous

462

comment about the Killship. He looked at the chiseled-chin pilot and asked, "Kyle... what's going on with this MARSTRIKE? For the love of god, tell me that live ordnance isn't being employed on the USS Ship..."

Kyle shook his head. "What does it matter?! When I send out the all-hands email on the bullshit you wrote, you're gonna *want* all your former brothers dead, incapable of witnessing your ultimate betrayal. And you know what? *They'd* probably prefer to be dead, too, rather than learn that the once-heralded 'Good Dude Nickels' had nothing but vindictive words for his teammates..."

What the hell is he talking about?!

"I know you think of yourself as some protagonist going through his hero's journey; the centerpiece of some novel about redemption, lessons learned, and an emerged stronger individual... but this isn't a novel of simulated conduct, Dimes. This is *real life*. There's no feel-good 'logical conclusion' to draw, coloring a guy white and turning the page to survive your way to a below-average pass-complete and celebratory night with your boys at 'rats. Because in *this* story? You're gonna have blue losses, alright—but unlike a TCTS debrief, they're not gonna re-gen to be there for the syrup-soaked waffles—not when they, too, are gone from this planet, leaving their friends, families, and dreams behind..." He shook his head slowly and scoffed. "Lucky them... at least they'll be lean in their coffins, no buoyant bodyfat tissue stopping them from sinking to the bottom of the fucking ocean..."

This was some of the darkest shit Sam had ever heard his former best friend say. "Kyle... what the hell *happened* to you?!"

"Once upon a time, Dimes..." Kyle explained with venom, "I thought this was the greatest job in the world. Once upon a time, I thought I couldn't be any luckier in life, working alongside my best friends—a bunch of Good Dudes; a community of pipe-hitters who took their training a hundred times more seriously than themselves. Dudes happy to lend a hand, shy to take credit, and flat-out *unwilling* to leave a man hanging. And yet..." Kyle clenched his jaw, the veins in his neck rippling as he did. "And yet I watched you—you, who *epitomized* that incredible culture—become corrupted by the *whiff* of a threat of somebody supplanting your legacy. I couldn't *believe* it, man—but it opened my eyes to the truth: this 'team atmosphere' is a complete sham; a role played only when it's convenient. Because in reality? This community is a bunch of selfish, entitled singles-only; simply worried about themselves, their career, and their image. Individuals who help others under false pretenses—only doing so because they believe it will create some sort of subconscious obligation. Those who arrive early and stay after-hours *just* long enough to be *seen* studying—not for the love of the game, but for *appearances'* sake. 'Hitters' who volunteer for the extra duties and collaterals on the group chat only because they're well aware the 'heroic act' will be 'read' by *all* hands—knowing that no matter how shitty the job is, they can mail it in regardless and *still* bolster their faux image as this 'selfless team player.' Fuck that shit..." Kyle raised his clenched fist and pounded his window, shouting over PRI, "Don't you get it, Sam?! People don't just *become* soulless hinges—it's what everybody in this fucking job is at heart! Some—the *truly* devious ones—get out before their true colors are revealed... but those that take the blood money? They shine their greedy ass for the whole air wing to see. And the saddest part is they actually think they're making a *difference*— for the fleet, for their careers, for their personal growth—when in reality?! The promotions simply keep coming for he who can kiss the most ass and mindlessly say 'yes' the longest—the most spineless beta lemmings; giving the Navy the souls of the cheapest quality, lowest dollar bids... like every other government deal out there..."

Kyle drooped his head and shook it in dismay again, before finally clipping his mask on. "Enough of this. Juice, give me the lead *now.*"

Juice visibly sighed and resigned, "You have the lead on the right."

"Lead on the right," Kyle affirmed. "Now, for the last time—*get the fuck out of here.*"

Juice said nothing.

"Noddik 2, FENCE'd in, 9.2," Kyle said as he glared at Sam.

And now, Sam recognized, the time for administrative deliberation was over. The rest could be covered in the debrief. The moment he declared himself ready to fight... it was just two men, two jets, and two dueling determinations. Sam boxed SIM, put TCN to the HUD, quickly set up the rest of his tac-admin appropriately, took a deep breath—and responded, "Chippy 1, FENCE'd in, 7.8."

Loaded T scoffed. "Cute callsign, bitch... Noddik 2 sets: All altitudes, 29.92."

"Chippy 1, all altitudes, 29.92," Sam rogered up. He was finally done running; he was ready to face his enemy in the ultimate showdown.

"Noddik 2, speed and angels, left."

"Chippy 1, speed and angels, right."

"Check tapes, HUD."

"Tapes."

"Take a cut away..."

The two jets took check turns away from each other, while Sam attempted to hype himself up. *You've beaten him before. You can do it again. Accept the challenge, look him in the eyes, and show him what the fuck you're capable of.*

When they reached their visual limits, Loaded T called out, "Noddik 2, turning in, left-to-left."

"Left-to-left," Sam echoed. As a fleeting idea entered his brain, he selected AIM-9X and nearly squeezed the trigger—but something forced him to pause, long enough for a break-X to pop up. *That would be the coward's way out... Low T wouldn't do that—and if he would? I'm already dead, anyway...*

And as they reached their 3-9 line passage, no words were said, but the unspoken reality was clear to both once-best-friends, now-rivals: The fight was on...

~

Robo-Hinge was within 15nm of the LAR of the AS-131 Killship. "GOD, THIS IS GOING TO BE SO JUICY... AN UNOPPOSED MARSTRIKE WITH LIVE ORDNANCE, AND NO DIVISION TO DRAG AROUND? NO CHANCE OF RISKING A MISSION FAILURE DUE TO ONE OF THEIR IDIOTIC MISTAKES? I AM GOING TO BE A GODDAMN NODDIK HERO." He leered as he turned his tapes on, ICS and VOX all the way up, and said to himself, "ROBO-HINGE, ATTACK."

He went through his air-to-surface checklist like a seasoned hinge, fumbling through buttons in a non-standard, haphazard order. At various points, he had 'gun' selected with other ordnance, accidentally kicked himself out of A/G master mode, recorded every display he could think of since he forgot which ones would validate his strike properly, and came close to pickling on the wrong coordinates before triple checking what lat/long the active station had entered in.

And yet, through all his incompetence, Robo-Hinge unfathomably found a valid release solution, ready to be employed in a matter of minutes—with *nobody* on the scope between him and the ship, and with *nothing* to stop him.

Suddenly, it hit him: 'SHIT... I NEED TO COME UP WITH A CLASSIC QUOTE FOR THIS STRIKE. THIS EXACT MOMENT COULD BE REPLAYED FOR ALL OF ETERNITY!' He quickly racked through his internal RAM for famous quotes that could apply to the situation... And in practically no time, it came to him. 'THAT'S FUCKING BRILLIANT,' he proudly thought to himself.

And so, on GUARD, with the release under ten seconds away, Robo-Hinge cleared his throat and said, "Non-HODS of the world... today is a day... which will live in Hingefamy! Lochness... away!"

Hinge pickled the Killship, and after a quick eject-to-launch sequence, it began screaming toward the USS Ship. He watched with a programmed expression of smug contempt as he put his FLIR on the target, eagerly anticipating the cruise-video-worthy BHA from the wreckage scene.

~

"Tally one! Stand by... almost there... *aaaand*... trigger down... snap!"

~

Robo-Hinge waited with bated breath, barely able to contain his excitement, programmed with the titillating glee of mission success. And yet, he waited... and waited... and *waited*. "WHAT THE HELL IS TAKING SO LONG?" he yelled aloud, growing impatient. He zoomed out and began FLIR fishing in search of the missile — and finally, he found it.

Or, at least, the *remains* of the missile — which had apparently prematurely combusted a mere fifty feet before impacting the ship. Not realizing he was accidentally transmitting on 243.0, Robo-Hinge swore, "ARE YOU FUCKING KIDDING ME?! IT *FAILED*?! THAT'S FUCKING INSANITY!"

"You mean *Flynn*sanity!" a confident, heroic voice transmitted back over GUARD.

"WHAT THE..." Robo-Hinge gasped to himself, looking around frantically.

"With that Lochness away, the price you shall pay," the hero broadcasted defiantly. "Don't be aghast; the missile was splashed. But unlike you, the missile didn't fail — yet you'll wish for its fate... as you're headed to *jail*."

"WHERE ARE YOU?! HOW DID I MISS YOU?! WHY DO YOU KEEP RHYMING?!" Hinge rapidly reoriented his neck with inhuman speeds and angles, still completely oblivious that his radar was seeing *nothing* in front of him. "AND *WHO* ARE YOU?!"

"I got my callsign for nearly being fragged by a live missile, like a total clown," the voice coolly explained, "So in the quest for vindication, I've made a career... in shooting *them* down."

"NO WAY... IT *COULDN'T* BE..." Robo-Hinge gasped into his mic. "ADMIRAL FLYNN?!"

"Hot affirm, hot dog," the voice confirmed. "Self-absorbed hinges like you have no place in the fleet, so even in shooting down a senior officer, the victory shall be sweet."

"WAIT A SECOND... A *SENIOR* OFFICER?!" the cyborg DH jeered. "PLEASE... I'VE BEEN BRIEFED WITH DATA STORAGE ALL ABOUT *YOUR* SHAMEFUL SOUL REMOVAL EN ROUTE TO THE CHIPPIES — YOU AND I ARE THE SAME, FISTY!"

"That's where you're wrong, Hinge..."

The robotic DH's head snapped to the left and locked onto the plane creeping beside him, where he saw a tall, robust man piloting an F/A-18E — with *silver bars* on his flight suit shoulders.

"... *Lieutenant* Flynn at your service, douchebag." FISTY declared as he accelerated past Robo-Hinge's 3-9 line. "Now, if you'll please kindly turn your jet around and return to your home station, I can accomplish my commander's guidance and protect the seas through the power of de-escalation!"

Robo-Hinge's oil boiled with ire. "HEAD HOME?! WITHOUT A VICTORY?! DO YOU HAVE ANY IDEA HOW MAD CAG WILL BE IF I RTB WITH AN INVALID EMPLOYMENT, AND HAVE TO DECLARE MISSION FAILURE?! I'LL HAVE TO *BEG* HIM TO WHITE CARD THE STRIKE!" He paused and admitted, in a *slightly* lower volume, "... I'M ALREADY NOT IN THE GREATEST OF STANDINGS WITH HIM, AFTER ACCIDENTALLY PUTTING A LONG DASH ON MY MOST RECENT FLIGHT SCHEDULE..."

"*Fuck* the white card!" FISTY shouted passionately, while dropping the rhyming scheme for author ease. "And *fuck* the dashes! Who *cares* what CAG says?!" Appealing to any humility that existed within the soulless robot, the O-3 implored, "Don't let your ego get in the way of progression! Life is about learning through defeat so that you can understand victory! Suck it up and take the outcome like a man, use the debrief to accept lessons learned, and emerge from the adversity a *stronger* pilot. For gods' sake, Hinge—be a *leader* for once!"

"DEBRIEF?!" Hinge's automaton muscles tensed in defiance. "YOU THINK I'M GOING TO THAT SHIT?! I DON'T HAVE TIME FOR THAT—I NEED TO WORK ON MY CDO UNDERWAY QUAL IF I'M GOING TO MAKE SKIPPER!"

"This job isn't about quals, you buffoon!" FISTY yelled. "It's about making a difference in the lives of those you work hand-in-hand with... fostering a culture of relentless work ethic and continuous improvement for the betterment of everyone involved! If you're worried about qualifications, FITREPs, notoriety—well, then you're no better than a high-ranking hamster in the wheel!" He sighed in disappointment. "You clearly just don't get it, Hinge—and if you don't learn... then I fear you will forever be a tool of the government..." He paused, took a solemn tone, and asked, "Robo-Hinge... are you doing this job—nay, are you *living your life* – to achieve *your* dreams—or the *Noddiks'*?"

Robo-Hinge was befuddled by such a deep-cut, philosophical question. "I... I CANNOT COMPUTE..."

After an open period of radio silence, FISTY—still flying form alongside the #1 EP DH—continued with, "Some O-4s are *obsessed* with finding the golden path, expecting some treasure chest full of fame and fortune at the end of the arduous journey—and they'll do *anything* to find it. But you've got to ask yourself, my man: if you're not getting any enjoyment out of the hunt... if you don't *love the process*... then what's going to happen if you don't like what's in that treasure chest?"

"I... AM ERROR..." Hinge responded.

"What if you open that chest, and all you find is a completely new advanced threat to learn, a new SFWT syllabus with stricter currency requirements, or a brand-new set of sea duty orders?"

"I... I..." Hinge stuttered, before his AI recomposed itself and asked, "WHAT WOULD YOU DO, LIEUTENANT FLYNN?"

FISTY paused again—waiting for dramatic effect—before keying the mic and declaring, "I'd fucking roger that shit up, Hinge. And you know why? Because, at the end of the day, *that's* the reason I do this shit. Not for recognition, money, or renown—but the *love of the fucking game,* baby."

Robo-Hinge was at a loss for words, his processing system seemingly crashed with such meaningful implications to consider.

"Now come on, Mr. Hinge," FISTY insisted. "Turn your aircraft around, RTB, and *become better* because of this. You will see: your heart's ambition is worth more than anybody can ever pay you."

Hinge looked over at FISTY, keyed the mic, and—for the first time in his existence—spoke *softly,* damn near like a *human*: "You're a different breed, Lieutenant Flynn... I now see why the Navy sings your praises. You truly are as selfless, empathetic, and inspirational as they come..."

And with that, he aggressively overbanked beneath FISTY's jet, lit full burner, and unloaded directly toward the USS Ship. "... AND THAT'S EXACTLY WHY YOU COULDN'T CUT IT AS A HINGE!"

"NO!" FISTY yelled, as he aggressively nosed over in pursuit of the robotic DH. He quickly scanned his loadout—after shooting down the Killship, he was completely void of munitions, as he'd been launched with a bunch of CATMs. He'd already fallen half a mile in trail to the hinge, and the USS Ship was not many nautical miles past that.

"YOU WILL RUE THE DAY YOU TRIED TO REASON AMICABLY WITH A DEPARTMENT HEAD, YOU FOOL!" Robo-Hinge transmitted. "THIS JET IS GOING STRAIGHT TOWARD THE TOWER—AND EVEN THOUGH IT MAY BE POSTHUMOUSLY, I WILL BE THE RECIPIENT OF THE MOST PRESTIGIOUS AWARD THE NODDIK EMPIRE HAS EVER PRESENTED. THE NAME 'ROBO-HINGE' WILL BE FOREVER ENSHRINED IN NODDIK AVIATION LORE!"

~

JABA pulled and weaved at his 100 AGL ceiling, feeling like he was flying the FLAT103 all over again. He was sweating profusely, his perceptualized speed going from hyperfast to *warp speed* every time he turned his head to the left or right. It had been a mission against all odds—a mission a mere LT had *no* business being approved for. Had this MARSTRIKE had *any* semblance of Operational Risk Management analysis, it would've been CNXed from the get-go.

And JABA knew it, too... he could see the Swiss cheese holes lining up—*every* threat factor from the latest version of the Navy's ORM Sheet was present in this mission. A single cloud in the sky? Completely sketch. A runway less than 15,000'? Considering the shore divert was LAX's measly 13,000' piece of concrete, the USS Ship was playing with fire by launching him. A circadian rhythm shift in the past year? It was only a *few days ago* that Buck was managing CV worldwide—in *Guam*—and per current OPNAV regulations, crossing that many time zones should've had him redoing the CAT 1 syllabus. And, of course, much to JABA's professional embarrassment, he hadn't done a face-to-face brief with the shipboard METOC representative who compiled his dash-1. The entire sequence had 'mishap' written all over it; he knew only a true O-4 could overcome so many risk factors in a single sortie.

But even so, JABA *refused* to give up by ORM-ing out of the low-level arena. He could practically *feel* the beams of the Noddik search radars skimming atop his jet—but to this point, he remained undetected by *anything* out there. He certainly wasn't about to get flight violated and end both this mission and his illustrious, flawless naval career. 'If I did, the Navy would *never* let me back in,' he insisted to himself—before swearing internally: '*No!* Give it up, Mark... that's a pipedream... and it's not happening.' He re-engaged his focus, swerved right to avoid a dolphin, and thought, 'This is your last Navy hurrah, and then it's done—for *good*. No more breakfast-at-midnight, no more '69, nice' jokes, and no more blink-182—because after this mission? This whole former life of yours goes in the rearview mirror—*forever.*'

And in the distance, he saw it on the horizon—the NIRD Katsopolis. 'This is it, Mark—your chance to do the impossible: a *valid* MARSTRIKE. Historians will never know the name of the man behind it, nor could they ever *fathom* it was a lowly O-3; but that's ok—because *fuck* history. There are those who concern themselves with telling it, and those who are too busy *making* it." And with that, JABA went max AB, nosed over a bit to go even *lower,* and whispered aloud to himself, "Freedom... attack."

~

Dr. Suabedissen peered over the fantail, preparing to call it a life. 'Heh...' he chuckled in his head with no actual humor whatsoever. 'No save files IRL... it's like my human data could become corrupted with one fall. Just like the entire D&D database... just like my life back in the States... just as with everything I've put any substantial effort toward—it could all vanish in an instant...'

At peace with how worthless he perceived his life to be — and how much of a depressed, beta simp he believed *himself* to be — the doctor stood atop the aft railing of the ship, looked up to the sky, and whispered, "MyLittlePonyXoXo88... I hope you find the man that can make you happy — because it certainly couldn't have been me..." Suabedissen closed his eyes, lifted his arms like in *Titanic* — 'The first pair of boobs I ever saw,' he remembered longingly as he lingered for a moment — and then began to lean forward, waiting for his body's momentum to carry him off the edge...

"Doctor!" a voice called with urgency.

Suabedissen paused and caught his balance — the memory of Kate Winslet's nude scene delaying his death *just* long enough — as he looked back and saw NEODD SWEVEN running with urgency, decked out in a Russell Wilson Broncos jersey.

"Doctor S! We've got a *serious* problem, broham!" SWEVEN declared, wearing a face of dread.

"What is it..." Suabedissen asked, hardly expressing curiosity in his tone. He was certain that *no* answer would warrant the interruption to ending this charade of a life he'd lived.

SWEVEN bent over and held his hips in an attempt to catch his breath, as he forced out the words, "The files... corrupt... APARTS data... *gone!*" he raised his voice at the end.

Suabedissen inhaled and slapped his forehead. 'Ah, of course... Order 66...' he thought, remembering that his virus was attached to the boat share drive and must have corrupted it. "Yeah, that makes sense. It's ok, though; all those grades are made up, anyway. I mean, it's silly, right? Trying to rank who looks 'coolest' when you simply need to worry about landing safely — "

"Negative," NEODD raised his finger and shook his head angrily, "Listen here, doctor: Do *not* use the S-word when talking about landing — and absolutely do *not* act like it's more important than the C-word. Because honestly, doing that makes you sound like a total P-word."

"SWEVEN..." the doctor started, growing annoyed, "It's ok. APARTS data is essentially irrelevant. And besides — this whole... 'cool' gimmick?" he put the word in quotation marks, "It's not really a thing, according to my US research. Apparently, most of the 'cool' stuff was outlawed in the name of safety — "

"*BRO!*" SWEVEN yelled. "*Not a thing?!* Dude, clearly, getting your V-card swiped is 'not a thing' either, if you really think that! Are you fucking *kidding* me, dog? Bruh, we *need* this APARTS data — how else are we going to have a complete database of trend analyses from pilots' first FCLP in the Noddik VTs, all the way to their most recent pass?"

"NEODD..." Suabedissen said, a bit more sternly, "Enough of this. I've watched Captain Rowland, Juice, and all the other pilots—nobody gives an eff about your 'Padroids techniques' or the grades you hand out. I mean, I even heard you debriefing a robot *WSO* on how to make a ball call sound cooler! I thought you were joking—until I heard you critique him *again* another night for calling a 6.8 fuel state! Who the heck cares about this? If people are coming aboard safely, then what does any of this other stuff matter? You guys think you're making this place cooler, but... I mean... you're all kind of... well..." The doctor shrugged, "You're all kind of *lame*..."

NEODD emitted literal steam out of his ears, as he took a deep breath, and then very pointedly said, "I don't fucking believe what I just heard... from the biggest *loser* on this entire spaceship." He stared daggers into the doctor's eyes, brushed the non-skid off his Wilson jersey's shoulders, and barked, "Listen here, NARP—you wear a fucking lab coat to work. *We* wear these badass jerseys. You stumble around the boat, getting laughed at every time you open your mouth. *We* get applauded every time we enter a room. You're a fucking useless, incompetent, low-conf beta. *We* are the fucking Idols of IFLOLS. And don't you *ever* try to pretend that you—or *any others* in your team of vag-repellent programmers on this ship—are anything more than NPCs in *our* game of life. So, trust me when I say this, bozo," he raised his robotic finger and pointed to the deck, warning with a scathing tone, "Your scrawny ass will be buried at the bottom of this fucking ocean if you don't fix that share drive and recover my APARTS database before we return to home station..."

Suabedissen looked back over to the fantail—where it almost all ended moments ago—and then back to NEODD SWEVEN, who was clenching his fists with fury.

And then Suabedissen thought of something that could imprint his legacy on the fleet for *eternity*. He shifted his eyes up at the Padroids, took a breath, and acknowledged, "You know what? ... I'm sorry." He bowed, perfectly playing the role of obedient simp, and asked, "SWEVEN, will you please take me to the Padroids shack computer? I have one last idea..."

~

Sam remained cross-circle from Kyle, praying for a solid tone to appear in his headset—but so far, to no avail. The two had dueled down to the deck in a series of turns, reversals, and transitions; a fight that had it all—one of those capstone, quintessential examples that one would arduously memorize and include in their HABFM briefing lab. Neither had gained an offensive advantage to this point—although, by Sam's estimate, Kyle had earned three degrees on him from the initial neutral merge.

Something screeched in Rowland's eardrum... and there it was: a fleeting tone—one of the few pitches an F/A-18 pilot could still recognize in their annual auditory exams. "Fox-2!" Sam yelled again as he squeezed the trigger—*right* as a break X appeared in his HUD. *Fuck!*

Kyle continued fighting and keyed the mic, even laughing as he said, "No chance, bitch. Can't wait to look at that one on tapes!" With a mocking tone, he admonished, "Dimes, conduct never really *was* your thing—and now I'm remembering why..."

Anger starting to build within Sam as he pulled for the next merge, driving his jet dangerously close to his adversary as the two passed sides—*so* close that he saw Kyle's eyes piercing his, and his former Chippy brother's sullen cheeks tighten to a smirk. "Damn, now *that's* more like it! I see you aren't a little bitch about training rule violations anymore!"

"That was safe and legal, Kyle!" Sam panted amongst the G. If there was one thing Rowland had perfected in tactics, it was a meticulous adherence to training rules—a subset of admin. To break one would be a mortal sin for an administrative monk.

"Oh please... like I'm gonna care about that candy-ass shit anyway..." Kyle spoke with zero exertion; his jacked stature allowing his breathing to be unaffected by the pull. "And you know what? Maybe I shouldn't be surprised by a little tac-admin bust here or there—you've already shown you're not afraid to break any rules or codes to get ahead of me..."

As they settled into misaligned turn circles, Sam yelled, "What are you talking about, Kyle?!" He scanned his HUD and looked back at his foe. "What did I do to *you?!*"

"Are you kidding!?" Kyle shot back. "Are you seriously *still* playing dumb?!"

Despite the banter, both men were maneuvering their jets with the precision of a surgeon. Not a parameter was out of place; two identical suitable airspeed packages and picturesque history trails to be marveled at later on PCDS.

"You ruined my fucking life. Do you know what it feels like, Dimes, to have your entire world thrown into chaos because of the career implications of others? Your fate heartlessly seized from you by the apathetic Big Navy, because somebody else's requests, timing, and milestones were deemed *more important* than yours? To have the invisible hands of PERS-43 putting their clutches on your life, disregarding every wish or desire you've submitted, and—like fucking villains—ripping apart the spirit and morale of the martyrs they're supposed to be setting up as the future leaders of this industry?! I had it *all,* Sam—*everything* lined up, served on a platter for the Navy. I was going to go to The Course, I was going to get my family back to Oceana at SWFSL, and I was going to be doing *what I loved* with the *people I loved*... Everything was perfect. My family... my dream orders... my *hope for the future* — it was *all there*..." Kyle's voice almost sounded choked up — before taking a sinister turn toward malice, "But then..." Sam could *feel* his eyes glaring at him, "then you went and wrote that bullshit statement to steal my fucking #1 EP — and the *entire* future I'd suffered for!"

"What?! That's not true!" Sam burst out, taken aback by what Loaded T had just accused. "Kyle, I never —" *Oh FUCK!* He stopped himself and quickly took his scan inside to check his parameters — and sure enough, as he could feel by the seat of his pants, he was overpulling by 0.1 AOA. He quickly refocused, got back on his proper performance numbers, and re-directed his scan outside. Yet, unfortunately, just as he'd feared: the half-a-second lapse had been all Loaded T needed to gain the upper hand. Sam watched Kyle's jet start to slide aft on his canopy, and quickly recce'd the sight pictures he'd come to learn over, and over, and *over* again back in his early Level 3 SFWT days: Sam was now in Defensive BFM.

"It's nearly over, bitch — I'll have a LAR any second now... and then that statement goes public for *everyone* to see the true composition of a 'Good Dude's' heart," Loaded T taunted. "Even when you sell your soul, Dimes — you can still end up bankrupt..."

"Shit!" Sam screamed to himself, going through his internal axioms to decide what to do. But his mind couldn't think of anything aside from what Kyle had brought up — the single most regrettable piece of literature Sam had ever put his name on: His FITREP statement of dispute. If Kyle had truly seen that document? Then it all made sense... Kyle didn't just want retribution for Sam's disgraceful abandonment of his brothers — he wanted *far* more than a simple Ck on his former best friend. It was now clear in Sam's mind that Loaded T was on a mission to 'splash one reputation' of everything 'Nickels' had once been about in the Chippies — by unveiling the biggest Good Dude Error he'd ever committed. And, unfortunately for Sam, thanks to that error? There was no single maneuver he could do to deny Kyle the pursuit for revenge...

~

FISTY unloaded his jet in an effort to gain closure on Robo-Hinge, and quickly did the mental math of the time/distance problem. "Shit!" he hissed under his breath, as he deduced how close the adversarial jet was to impacting the USS Ship — *right* in the Air Boss' office.

He switched his radio to button 1 and transmitted "99! This is Lieutenant Flynn — there is a Noddik F/A-18 pointed *directly* at the USS Ship tower with the intent to collide! Prepare for impact!"

"God dammit..." a gruff voice responded over tower, "It's Captain Belichick. Listen, the ship HODS just called an all-hands meeting in Pri-Fly to discuss potential COAs for punishing the Diamondbacks' XO after he sat at their exclusive segregation wardroom table. FISTY, if that jet impacts, we'll lose every ounce of ranked leadership on this boat; every oak leaf you've ever seen on this vessel: vanquished, in one explosion."

"EXCELLENT!" Robo-Hinge transmitted, apparently hijacking the frequency. "THEN THERE WILL BE *THAT* MANY LESS SELECTIONS ON THE NEXT MAJOR COMMAND BOARD! AND AS A RESULT? I WILL BE A VIRTUAL *SHOE-IN* TO CONTINUE MY CAREER TO THE ILLUSTRIOUS *GOLDEN SHOULDER BOARDS!*"

Flustered — especially by the fact that Hinge's logic made no sense, since the nations would have completely separate selection boards — FISTY gritted his teeth and scanned his radar. He had closure on Robo-Hinge, but only about 30 knots. He double-checked his weapons inventory — nothing. "Shit..." he whispered to himself again.

"LIEUTENANT FLYNN..." Robo-Hinge spoke, "ARE YOU REALLY GOING TO TRY AND STOP ME? ARE YOU REALLY GOING TO TAKE DOWN *ONE* HINGE... TO SAVE *HUNDREDS* OF *OTHERS*? ALL THOSE DOUCHEY BOAT O-4S WHO, OVER YOUR CAREER, HARASSED YOU ABOUT YOUR UNZIPPED JACKET, ABOUT NOT BRACING THE BULKHEAD FOR AN AUTHORITY RANKED ONE ABOVE YOU, ABOUT GRABBING GRANOLA BARS TO-GO FROM THE WARDROOM — ARE YOU *REALLY* GOING TO LET *THOSE* POWER-HUNGRY CLOWNS BE THE ONES IN CHARGE OF THE NAVY YOU SWORE YOUR ALLEGIANCE TO?"

FISTY said nothing, still driving his aircraft in full AB toward the assailant.

"THINK ABOUT IT, FLYNN..." Hinge continued. "YOU MAY NOT LIKE ME... BUT YOU DON'T LIKE *THEM*, EITHER. GOLDEN ASSHOLES, EMPOWERED TO DEAL WITH THE ADMINISTRATIVE AND POLITICAL CHESS PIECES THAT A TACTICAL GURU LIKE YOURSELF HAS NO INTEREST IN MOVING. THOSE MORONS IN THE TOWER?! THEY ARE *WORTHLESS, INCOMPETENT IDIOTS* — BUT YOU KNOW WHAT *THEY* HAVE, THAT YOU DON'T? POSITIONAL AUTHORITY, POWER, AND INFLUENCE — THE ABILITY TO DICTATE *YOUR* LIFE WITH *THEIR* SHITTY DECISION-MAKING. YOU MAY BE ABLE TO CONTAIN A SINGLE HINGE — BUT A WHOLE FLEET OF POWER-HUNGRY RANK-FLEXERS? YOUR RESISTANCE WOULD BE *FUTILE*."

Remaining silent, while frantically trying to think of a solution, FISTY felt his left hand — currently firewalling the throttles — begin to *ease* up, just the *slightest*...

"FISTY!" Belichick transmitted, panicked. "We can see a dot in the sky! He's closing in on us!"

Ignoring the coach, FISTY wondered: Was Robo-Hinge right? Are these self-serving douchebags—who spend their lives tormenting JOs and giving leadership a bad name—are they *necessary?* ... What would become of the Navy if there *were* no hinges...

"FISTY, are you there?!"

No response.

~

"Master Arm... *armed."* JABA said to himself confidently.

This was it... he was in the envelope of the weapon. Buck took a deep breath and cycled through his displays one last time, under the guise of recording purposes... but truthfully, for his own sentimental memories. He pulled up all his old friends—the FCS page, where he'd seen so many iterations of the same format grow old and wise over the years, incorporating user-friendlier aircraft shape features and even color-coding. He nodded warmly at the Checklist display, where over a thousand times he'd sanity-checked himself on aircraft weight just prior to landing, or barely remembered to box ABLIM moments prior to a catapult run-up. He waved to the CAS format—a page he'd honestly never cared to use in a mission he'd never cared to fly—but now that his fini-flight was on the verge of completion, he took a moment to truly appreciate what was in front of him. It wasn't exactly perfect, with way too many features and 'gotchas' included... but *damn*, did it put up a hell of an effort. And JABA found himself smiling at the sweet little CAS format; an underdog display, trying to do whatever it needed to in order to make the pains of a dynamic A/S sortie *that* much more bearable. Not so different than himself; a humble, easy-going guy, doing whatever he could to bring positivity to the Chippies, and make the agonies of the brutal life of a fleet Navy pilot *that* much more digestible and—dare he say it—even *enjoyable.*

Nearing the edge of his envelope, still at 100' AGL, and nailing his parameters for employment, JABA felt a tear trickle down his face as he prepared to pickle. This was it—this was what O-4 life would've been about: vetting low-levels, leading MARSTRIKES, and harnessing a leadership role to show his fellow brethren the appreciation and respect for their efforts that *so many* were too busy or apathetic to exhibit in even the slightest.

There was no doubt in his mind, no last-minute hiccups or confusion, no frantic radio comms to ensure he wouldn't goon this up and embarrass himself in a debrief in front of CAG. JABA had the entire attack *dicked*—and for the first time in his life, he finally believed, even just for a *second*, that maybe he would have made a stellar department head O-4 after all...

His smile was irremovable as he said to himself, "3... 2... 1... pickle."

~

Dr. Suabedissen, overseen by NEODD SWEVEN, sat hunched over the Padroids' laptop in their shack. As he was pulling up APARTS, he desperately tried to keep his hands from shaking, so as not to betray the anxiety in his soul regarding his grandmaster plan. As he dug through files and submenus, he informed the Padroids, "I had to disable the ship's defense radar to make these admin-level changes, so I hope no one's trying to fly near us..."

SWEVEN shrugged and said, "Bro, I don't give a shit. Just fix it already."

"Ok..." Suabedissen trailed off, as he continued clicking around and moving the mouse aimlessly, pretending to work toward an APARTS solution, confident that SWEVEN was oblivious to everything he was doing—and what was about to happen.

"Well?" NEODD asked angrily. "Did you..." he threw his hands up, "do whatever *nerdery* you do, and recover the data?"

Then Suabedissen found it: the webpage for the ship QNAP database. He clicked on the link, typed in the incredibly complex adm1n password, and logged into the main user page. 'This is it...' he thought. Karl took a deep breath, his hand trembling as he brought up the dropdown menu and clicked the selection he'd long been seeking—'SHUTDOWN'—bringing about a loud beep that reverberated amongst the entire ship.

"What the fuck was that?!" the Padroids shouted as he looked toward the ship's 1MC. "What did you do?!"

Dr. Suabedissen turned around and looked at SWEVEN... and for the first time ever... really *looked* at the CAG Padroids.

Over his Wilson jersey, SWEVEN was wearing a float coat—a padded safety vest that was covered in stains and smelled like shit. In his hand was an open blue notebook, depicting mathematical equation-esque lines that somehow were supposed to represent what a jet landing looked like. On his head was a hat—a *bucket* hat—and not even the type you'd find in a 90's boy band, but worse: a longer-brimmed, baby-on-the-beach type, with a laced neck strap that made any non-Navy SEAL look like a complete jackass. And most egregious of all, on his head was a pair of goggles—not sunglasses, but *clear-lensed safety goggles*—a pair of spectacles that tried to scream 'Kareem Abdul Jabar,' but instead whispered 'Rodrigo Blankenship.' The look was completed with a 'croakie' neck strap hanging from the goggle frames, something that was standard procedure for safety around the CV environment; yet in real life—even Suabedissen could recognize—was SOP for 'fucking loser.'

"What are you looking at? Quit staring at me, dweeb!" NEODD demanded with impatience as he self-consciously tried to fix his non-skid-laced hair, feeling around for the goggles on his head, taking them off and replacing them with a pair of sunglasses from his Padroids pouch—a pair of neon pink oversized pit vipers.

And as Dr. Suabedissen took in the entire caricature; this man who so proudly thought of himself as a total badass—and moreover, wanted everyone *else* to perceive him that way... The doctor tried hard to stop himself, but couldn't—as he let out the slightest snicker.

Over in the corner, there was an argument between two Padroids-in-training—one with a bandana holding up his two-inch long hair, and the other with bright, neon-green framed sunglasses that looked like something Kim Kardashian would wear at her 16th birthday party. They were quarreling over one of the passes in the previous recovery—and more specifically, whether it was 'cool with average deviations' or 'cool with *less-than-average* deviations...' The two bickered back and forth like petulant children, disputing whether a deviation was 'a little' or 'full,' debating just *how* uncool the jet was in the middle, and disagreeing over when *exactly* the timer for groove length was started. It got *heated* as they began throwing accusations over unfair 'bennies' given to certain people, claimed that so-and-so was 'out to get' who-and-who, and brought up long-standing grudges referencing stack shenanigans that happened weeks ago.

As he witnessed the sorority sisters' pathetic catfight, Suabedissen's chuckle became a shaking laugh.

And finally, out of nowhere, a heavy rock song emerged from the Padroids shack radio—with someone singing about eighteen naked cowboys in the shower. 'Jesus, what the *fuck?!*' Suabedissen thought in disbelief. 'Am I *hearing* this right?!' And as he looked over to the source of the music, he saw a wooden plywood table in the corner—a standard table-tennis-size—with beer stains everywhere, signed names in sharpie, and—most notably of all—dicks. Tons and tons of penises, graffitied *all* over the table. Dicks of obscenely large size proudly towering over smaller dicks; dicks with intricate, detail-oriented vascularity drawn; dicks on stick figures being fellated by other knee-bound stick figures; and even dicks with wings, soaring the skies as they apparently dumped fuel—from the front—on a bunch of other dicks, captioned with, 'CAG Padroids shows the boys what Ram Ranch is all about!'

Dr. Suabedissen took in his entire scene—and as he observed everything about this unique, strange, hyper-masculinity-yet-strange-insecurity-and-oddly-questionable-impulsivities culture, encapsulated by this dick-packed table? His laughter transformed into a full-on fit of hysteria.

Upset and confused, SWEVEN yelled with frustration, "*What?!* What the hell is *wrong* with you?! What the *fuck* are you laughing at, incel?"

Laughing even harder, Dr. Suabedissen began slapping the desk and clutching his chest, barely able to breathe in between his howls. He fell to the floor, literally ROFL-ing like an insane man.

"What!?" the Padroids yelled, becoming enraged. "What's so *fucking funny*?!"

In the midst of his mania, the doctor tried as hard as he could to stop laughing, curling up in a fetal position, slowing the cadence of his cackles as he started to force words out: "You... You... you're a..." He looked as if he were in *pain,* laughing so hard.

"I'm a *what*, you freak?!" SWEVEN was shaking with ire.

Suabedissen, finally calming his mania to the point of being able to produce coherent phrases, looked up at the head Padroids and spit out, between laughing fits, "You're a... fucking *loser*! You've been programmed... to be this... 'cool dude'... who knows how to land jets... and judge others... and yet... you're even *more pathetic* than I am!"

"What are you *talking* about?!" NEODD said with disgust, as he quickly brushed the bucket hat off behind him—where it now hung like a backpack, the strap clinging to his neck in what was an incredibly embarrassing look.

The doctor continued, "I thought *I* was a loser, spending my whole life becoming an expert with coding D&D software, patches, and side quest content... and yet..." he snickered and pointed at SWEVEN, "*you've* dedicated your life to turning one of the coolest parts of a naval aviation into a hyper-analytical aerodynamic PowerPoint science!"

"Are you kidding me?! Unlike your bullshit, landing on the boat while looking cool, getting good grades, and being a top look is what actually *matters!*"

But that statement only got the doctor laughing harder as he hit the floor, cracking up. "I thought *I* was a nerd, unable to feel female touch. And yet I see you—"

"Uhhh, yeah, railing *tons* of hoes, you douchebag!" SWEVEN cut him off defensively, using the sexual slang he'd been programmed with.

"Oh yeah, *sure*—especially when you're living on a boat for over half your life!" Suabedissen mocked between howls of laughter.

Stepping back on his heels a bit, SWEVEN yelled, "Sh—shut up! I mean... that's not fair—but... but we're making a *difference* out here...!"

Yet again, the statements from the Padroids just drew more uninhibited emotion from the doctor. "'*Making a difference*?' More like *clinging to relevancy* as your job gets replaced by software that *actually* knows what a glideslope looks like, praying that they don't take away your precious approach turn, with your only validation being," he used a sarcastic, childish tone, shaking his hands in exaggeration: "'That would be so soft!'"

"It *would* be soft!" SWEVEN tried to explain, even more defensive now, as his processing data began extracting American carrier-based terms in desperation. "The

478

open deck time... intervals... recovery periods... the shit hot — err... expedited boat — err... breaking behind — I mean..."

But Dr. Suabedissen just laughed and laughed, almost falling to the floor again. "And now, with PLM? *Without* the aspects of the job that once made Padroids valuable? All you can focus on are the minuscule parts you have control over: your cute little outfits, your fancy little blue gradebook, your annoying little premature lineup calls, and your stupid little MOVLAS stick!" he screamed hysterically.

"Hey!" SWEVEN fired back. "MOVLAS proves it — pilots *need* us out there, and our boarding rate is *way* better *with* Padroids' intervention!"

And to this, Suabedissen finally collapsed again, just laughing his *fucking ass off* at this sad, pathetic man defending his significance.

"Shut up! Shut up! Shut the fuck *up*, you fucking loser!" SWEVEN yelled.

After another solid minute of laughter, Suabedissen eventually calmed down a bit, saying, "And you know what the funniest part of all is?!"

"What?!" The LSO's fists were clenched, teeth bared.

Another beep screeched from the ship's 1MC, as lights began to flicker.

Dr. Suabedissen stood up, went to the laptop, and opened a browser window. He pointed to the screen that displayed 'QNAP Reactor Shutdown,' then gestured to himself, proudly stating, "Thanks to *this* fucking loser... the entire powerplant driving the NIRD Katsopolis has just been powered down, with no ability to be recovered. This entire ship — including *my* 'scrawny ass' and *your* precious 'APARTS data,'" he said with a big smile, "is headed to the bottom of this fucking ocean!"

SWEVEN's jaw dropped and composure crashed as his algorithm computed what Suabedissen was saying. The doctor began cackling again, as the LSO shack anthem continued in the background, singing about orgies in the showers, buff cowboys, and throbbing cocks at *Ram Ranch*...

~

"Hey, FISTY — listen to me..."

This voice was different, sparking LT Flynn's brain back to consciousness.

"FISTY," the voice continued, "In all those years in New England... sometimes, you know, things really *sucked*."

FISTY breathed a sigh of relief as he felt his body start to calm; the fogginess start to clear; the uncertainty start to vanish — it was the voice of the man he'd looked to for inspiration throughout his entire life: It was Tom Brady.

"Do you think I *liked* working for Coach?! *Fuck* no! It was suffering, dude — pure, unabashed, suffering. The endless drills, the constant critiquing, the unreachable standards... it was enough to make you..." Brady sighed, "god... it was enough to make you almost *hate* the guy."

Nodding to himself, FISTY understood exactly what he meant. Hinges... Patch wearers... Patch-wearing hinges... they could be very unforgiving.

"But I loved the man, too," Brady added with an uptick in tone. "I loved him because his part-task training drills pushed me to rep out sets again and again, to the point where the most brain-intensive components of the game became second-nature stem-cell muscle memory to me; to the point where I was able to execute them — *flawlessly* — in the most pressure-filled of moments. I loved him because his critical debriefs of my every misstep made me hyper-aware of every shortcoming I had — to the point where I could throw 50 passes for 49 completions and 6 touchdowns, but that *one* missed pass would keep me up at night. And I loved him because his mask-on-osphere-high-standards had me soaring in RVSM-levels of accomplishment, while the rest of the league was cruising with dangling masks down in the class B airspace of mediocrity." Brady paused for a moment. "I may have become overly fixated, I may forever be mentally incapable of taking time off from my craft, and I may have developed an *obsession* with chasing perfection under Coach's guidance — but make no mistake about it, FISTY — I am better *because* of him."

Smiling, FISTY nodded without saying a word, knowing exactly what Brady was getting at.

"And these *hinges*..." the Hall of Fame QB emphasized, "They may seem like a bunch of selfish, T&R-driven, mass-tasking assholes — and some certainly are!" He cut the transmission, then proceeded with, "And yet... some are legitimately trying to produce a better end product of those they lead. Some are truly more concerned with the men and women working for them than they are with any future career implications of their own. Some understand that the climb of life isn't always going to be fun — but by choosing to push and lead *everyone* to steeper and more demanding sections? They *know* the team will come closer to realizing their full potential."

Brady unkeyed the mic, before adding one last bit: "And *one* hinge out there, FISTY? *One* can combine all the good, minimize all the bad, and become something every hinge truly, deep in their heart, seeks to become: *legendary*. Not JOPA; not HOPA; but *DOPA*. And from what I've heard throughout my own upbringings in flight school and the fleet, Tom Flynn... you *are* that DOPA. You *are* the GOAT."

A tear falling down his eye, FISTY slewed his cursors between Robo-Hinge and the ship, utilizing his range and bearing tool — five miles of separation; with only half a mile between him and the suicidal department head, straight ahead and slightly low in his HUD, with increasing closure.

"YOU KNOW, DEEP DOWN, FLYNN!" Robo-Hinge interrupted, aware of the closure behind him, "YOU *KNOW* THAT THIS WORLD IS BETTER OFF WITHOUT

ANY OF US HINGES! WE'RE *ALL* CORRUPT, AND ANYBODY WHO SAYS THEY CARE ABOUT THE JOs MORE THAN #1 — THEIR OWNSHIP — IS A FUCKING *LIAR*! IF YOU STOP ME AND SAVE THEM... ALL YOU'LL DO IS WEAKEN THE FLEET, LOWER MORALE, AND DILUTE THE WATERS OF GOOD DUDES!"

FISTY scanned his displays. He had altitude, airspeed, and — most importantly — a *heart* advantage over the cyborg DH. "The world doesn't need hinges..." he transmitted as he yanked back on the stick, popping his nose high. And as he climbed several thousand feet, he inverted over the top, pulled back nose low from the apex, and rolled upright — yanking and re-centering the stick so aggressively that it *ripped* the LT bars off his flight suit... revealing *golden oak leaves*. But they weren't leaves of power, nor clovers of rank; they were Lieutenant Commander insignias of responsibility — of Infinite Potential. "The world needs *leaders*."

"FISTY, NO!" Hinge yelled, looking up and aft at the aircraft rolling in over top of him.

FISTY scanned his parameters — a perfect dive delivery — and waited until the last few seconds of tracking time... before unboxing SIM, ensuring his weight was off wheels with all landing gear up and locked, arming up, and selecting the centerline chicklet. Remembering his favorite quote from *True Lies* — 'You're fired' — FISTY thought of the perfect line. He smirked as he transmitted — with a flawless Schwarzenegger accent — the last words Robo-Hinge would ever hear: "Tanks for nothing, asshole."

He pressed the selective jettison button, punched off the centerline tank, and executed his safe escape — avoiding the ship, and rolling up on a wing to watch his external tank impact directly atop Hinge's Noddik F/A-18 — sending the DH to a crashing death, just a few hundred feet short of the USS Ship.

~

Sam frantically spit out all his pretend flares as he watched Kyle's F/A-18 slide further and further aft on his canopy. But it was useless, as his buckets were not inventorying in SIM mode. "Kyle, you don't have to do this!" he yelled into the mic.

"Get the fuck out of here, bitch — *yes I do*. After what you did to me... to our friendship... and to the *Chippies*?! Constructively killing you is the *only* fitting retribution, before Actual killing your naval aviation legacy and revealing who you *truly* are. People will see your name on random RAG class photos or cruise plaques, and *cringe* in disgust. The name 'Sam Rowland' will forever be attached to the unspeakable blue-on-blue sins of 'Dimes.'"

Kyle had a LAR; Sam knew it. But he knew his adversary wasn't going for a simple missile kill—Loaded T was looking to take down Nickels in the most degrading way possible. In a matter of moments, Sam would be posing for the HUD footage that would be displayed on JMPS computer backgrounds everywhere...

"Just one question for you, bitch," Kyle started with a slight shift in his tone— anger becoming anguish. "*Why?* Why did you allow yourself to become Diseased? Instead of fighting for greatness... why did you fight to tear others down? Why'd you have to sell everything you ever cared for, and sell out those who cared for you? Why did you have to ruin *my* life before destroying *yours?!* Why did you hate this job... hate the lifestyle... hate *all of us*—so much?!"

Sam shook his head. It was too late at this point... there was no convincing this juiced madman. "Low T..." he said hopelessly yet calmly, "I'm sorry... for everything..."

"Not yet..." Loaded T growled into the mic, as he positioned his jet well within range at Sam's six, "But you *will* be. Trigger down..."

"STOP!" a different voice called out.

"What the fuck?!" Kyle exclaimed. "*Juice?!*"

"Sam, ditch right!" Ward called out.

Sam did as instructed—instinctual SEM—and once he was reoriented, he looked up and saw two jets turning with one another. *What the hell?! No way...* Sam continued down as he watched the two engage in a DNA helix of tight turns—turns too close for employment.

"Juice, what the fuck are you doing?!" Kyle yelled.

"Sam, ready, ready... hook down, *now!*" Juice transmitted.

And sure enough, amongst two identical F/A-18Es fighting, Sam watched one drop his hook at the exact moment Juice broadcasted—and with that identification feature, Sam was officially tally and... *tally?*

"*99 on GUARD!*" a familiar voice called out—Sam recognized it instantly. *JABA?!* "*99 on GUARD, 'Lochness Away' into the NIRD Katsopolis! I repeat: 'Lochness Away' into the NIRD Katsopolis!*"

Oh my god... Sam realized. JABA had done it—he'd managed to complete the unverified low-level route, avoid the FAA's detection, and launch his sim weapons into the enemy ship for a successful MARSTRIKE. *If that bomb was somehow valid... then maybe, just* maybe...

He refocused on the dueling jets above him. *Victory... it's there for the taking...*

Sam was familiar enough with Admin Olympics ROE to know what a shootdown of the opposing forces' captain would do for overall scores—a golden snitch-type point weight. It would undoubtedly ensure the triumph for the USS Ship.

And yet, Juice had just saved *him* from the same fate... So here he sat, with one simulated missile... and the dilemma of a lifetime. *If I take this shot? I become the Olympic hero... the prodigal son returneth, to bring glory to his former nation...*

"Come on, Sam, get him!" Juice pleaded. "I can't fight him off for much longer!"

"Take the shot, Dimes..." Kyle spurred, knowing full well what was going through Sam's head. "Shoot Juice down and win the battle you've been fighting all these years... Slay the King, and prove that you are the only admin royalty in naval aviation..."

"Sam, don't listen to him!" Juice yelled, "Shooting me will accomplish *nothing*! Shoot *him* down and save your Good Dude reputation! The Navy *needs* legends like yours; we need them, to be able to *endure* the *bullshit*, and learn to *appreciate* the *shit!*"

Save my reputation? Did Juice know about the statement, too? Sam didn't respond at first, just darting his eyes back and forth between the two foes. *Fuck, man... is this really how it ends? Shoot the man who ruined my career... or the man who's trying to bury it into hell?! What's more important — a man's achievements... or his character? Being a legendary hero... or a Good Dude?* He cued his radar, instantly got a high-pitched tone, and breathed a sigh of resignation into the mic. "Juice... I'm not..." he said with remorse.

"Not *what*?!" Juice asked nervously.

Sam shed a tear, responding with sorrow weighing heavily in his voice, "I'm not a Good Dude..." He squeezed the trigger, saving his ears from the pain of the screeching tone, and called out "Chippy 1, Fox-2." The last thing he saw, above the radar lock in his HUD, was the word 'FRIEND'...

22

Kill-Removal

Juice saw a contact on his radar – likely just some jabroni in a Cessna, cruising at 12,500 feet in the midst of an admin war, barely on the scope of his field of regard. And while it appeared like just another yellow square on his screen... something told him to take a lock on him, where he could deduce if maybe there was something more to this brick...

Because something in his gut told him this wasn't just another jet in the sky...

That 'something,' Juice soon realized, was his altitude. He's headed eastbound; he should be at an odd + 500' altitude... It was a careless admin mistake that had no business in naval aviation. The type of mistake that used to plague Juice as a Chippy New Guy. A pattern of mistakes he'd eradicated from his system after years of chasing the unreachable ghost that was Sam "Nickels" Rowland.

'He's the fucking man!' That was all anybody ever said about Nickels, starting from when Juice first heard of his legendary status while looking through the winging class photos in the Meridian, Mississippi hangar hallways. "A phenomenal American!" the instructors would insist. "The COOLEST guy you'll ever meet!" a blacked-out attrite stash-JG told Juice at a Dalewood Lake party. "Just an all-around Good Dude!" an out-of-shape reservist explained, after taking a bite of his ice cream cone at a Key Field out-and-in. The praise was lavish and endless.

But the IPs saw something in Juice, too, and his ability to sacrifice for the betterment of his peers via volunteered weekend duties, gifted TOFT practice sim slots, and passed down jetlogs – so much so that when Ward finished Advanced Training in Meridian, his VT-7 Skipper – Zack "Chode" Mayo – told him, as he punched the wings of gold on his chest: "LT Ward... I've seen a lot of students come through this place... and none of them have matched Sam's good dudesmanship. You, however? You've got something special, kid. I can see the desire in your eyes – go forth and conquer."

The legend grew even stronger at the RAG, where the IPs raved about the 'most administratively talented student of all time' who had gone through the FRS just years ago. "Debriefs can be painful with these RAC... but with Rowland? This stuff just clicked for him. He ended up teaching me *during the admin scrub," per an IWSO who had a spot secured at 106 due to co-lo. "Admin comms are so hard for students — hell, even for fleet guys! But this dude? Man, the guy knew the SOP verbiage* cold. *It was like he was reading from a script; made it the entire way through without a* single *nonstandard check-in or verbose radio call of any sort!" bragged the strike phase head, just after SODing a student out for having poor roll-in mech during a CP-IP CAS sim. Even the sim instructors tipped their hat to Sam, as head of the four horsemen — Spoojr — quietly admitted, "When I have a question about a NATOPS system? Rowland is the guy I text to get the answer — the dude knows the jet better than the Big Book does."*

Juice was enthralled. How does one become so renowned in this community? What an incredible way to stamp your legacy in this profession... *Juice was damn determined to go to the Chippies in an attempt to meet and train under the tutelage of the legend himself. He volunteered to be his RAG class leader to build early admin leadership skills that he knew he'd need later on, like group chat management, or absorbing the ire of overly critical Skeds Os when a classmate requested leave for something inappropriate, like the birth of their child. He made himself the de facto 'gas fill up' guy for vans on DET, not wanting others to burden themselves with low tanks after long debriefs. He single-handedly typed in the entire classes' passes in APARTS — with complete honesty, although he chuckled at realizing that he held the field GPA of every student in his hands. Most notably of all, he put his fleet preference as 'Japan-number one' — with location over platform — taking a 'bullet' that the rest of the student pool historically dreaded because of the intensive operational schedule and distance from home. Juice didn't care though — he wanted to seize the opportunity to follow in the footsteps of a guy known for discerning the difference between ATIS' reading of 'Alpha' and 'Delta' with 100% accuracy.*

When he patched as a Chippy, Juice was ecstatic. Dr. Rim, a former 195 guy, slapped the green and white patch on his chest and said, "Welcome to the indomitable Dambusters, Bobby. The guys know you're coming, and they couldn't be any more excited. Take this." He handed Juice a bright can with Japanese hiragana and kanji on it.

"What's this?" Juice asked.

"This is a Chu-hi," he said with a wide smile, before adding, "But this?" He gestured around them and poetically explained, "This is the beginning of the fleet tour of the boy with the potential to carry the torch from Nickels. The turning room is there, Bobby — go take it."

Dr. Rim took out his own Chu-hi and cracked it open, as the two clinked cans and drank to the future that Juice had so adamantly envisioned for himself. It was really happening, Juice thought in disbelief. I'm gonna be a Chippy. I'm gonna meet Sam. And under his mentorship? I'm gonna become an admin SME.

And now here Juice was, a Noddik pilot, leading a simulated MARSTRIKE against his former nation – an incredibly dynamic, tactical, straight-and-level evolution – a crowning Ck to end what was undoubtedly a resounding Olympic victory – and yet... all he could focus on was this random jet at the incorrect VFR altitude.

Juice laughed to himself. It was the curse of the admin life – the burden of dedicating your entire existence to the perfection of one area; the obsession that scars your brain forever when you choose the passion in which you're willing to invest the extra 80% effort for the proportionately minuscule 20% improvement. He looked at Loaded T, flying alongside him in loose cruise. The guy undoubtedly held his extreme hyper-awareness toward macros, calorie intakes, and workout timelines more than anything else in life. He probably had the wherewithal to briefly let his mind wander toward what he'd be cooking for dinner that night – mid-SFWT-DCA vul – while calculating how many grams of protein he's consumed and still needed – amidst kill-removal – and mentally chair-lifting his deadlift setup and plate numbers for that evening workout – during the comm review.

It was how desire worked. One's journey toward their calling – their true goal in existence – was constantly making its presence known amongst the rest of the fluff that life threw their way. And for Juice? It didn't matter if he was in the middle of a Navy-mandated 1.5-mile jog, sitting through a government-sponsored safety standdown spewing dogma about the dangers of the sun, or waiting to fall asleep in his carrier-provided brick mattress with 1-thread-count sheets and itchy blanket – his brain was constantly thinking about check-ins, course rules, and emergencies. But he wasn't always that way – not before he met 'the legend'...

He watched the jet continue to obliterate the rules of the FAR/AIM with its improper altitude, begging for a midair with a diligent, radar-less VFR PIC out in the skies. Juice watched and frowned, thinking about how his climb for administrative excellence had gone from a once-epic journey to now completely bogus hamster wheel. Of course the Noddiks were going to win; Loaded T's plan was going to massacre the USS Ship's morale. And not to mention... Robo-Hinge was en route with a live-loaded AS-131 Killship to the carrier – it was going to cause a massive war at best, and end with Noddik supremacy at worst. Gone would be the days of practicing and teaching administratively sound procedures to up-and-coming aviators – people didn't even do IBITs in wartime... Ward lamented. Hell, as a top-ranked human in the Noddik Empire, Juice probably wouldn't even be flying much, if at all – he'd instead be filling boring roles like 'strike mentor,' riding aboard the defended asset while the young gun AI bots got all the action.

But worst of all... Nickels would be out of the picture.

Yes – Juice could finally admit it to himself, as much as he'd once hated to: in order to bring out his best, he needed Nickels. As that scientist once said in Mission: Impossible 2 – the greatest roll 'em of all time: "Every hero needs a villain..." and Juice found his Chimeric catalyst for greatness in Nickels. From the moment he'd first shown up at the Chippies, making his desires to study under Rowland known? Juice had become the target of Nickels' ire. Spatial harassment, unfair SFWT reflies, public humiliation... it was guerilla warfare from Sam on

Juice's tolerance for suffering. Every minor brief misspeak highlighted... every minute mistake doghumped in debriefs... every bad deal sent his way to be soaked up...

But the pain sparked him. The anger fueled him to work harder, stay longer, and sacrifice more – to become the GOAT of admin, the ultimate Good Dude, the usurper of Nickels' throne; to prove Sam wrong. Ward thought he'd worked hard in flight school – but with Nickels seeking to cut him in the legs and blue falcon him in front of the squadron with every slip-up? Juice took his work ethic to unprecedented levels – and the harder he worked, the more momentum he found to raise the bar even higher. Both men would rush to be the first one at work, and both took note of who was the last to leave. They tallied watches that they stood for others, kept count of consecutive flawless check-ins, and even wrote up a record board for who could have the longest, most in-depth, multi-layered admin portion of a brief... Was it healthy? Probably not. But then again, is anyone's obsession in life ever healthy? A healthy balance in life was attainable – until you felt your soul being pulled in a direction. Once you felt that tug, and you grasped the courage to pursue it? 'Healthy balance' was a bygone concept – and one Juice was happy to leave in the rearview mirror...

Because the fixation worked. Juice watched as the other Chippies started to come to him for questions about taxi speed and the amount of jets allowed on certain runway widths. He saw Sam start to get nervous as he heard metaphorical footsteps behind him, beginning to schedule Juice for only conduct-heavy events like -2 BFM and night double-cycle DCAs, where he'd have less opportunity to flex his admin skills in managing the stack from the lead position, and would be forced to 'commence when able' without flashing brilliance from solving a timing problem for the uneventful CV-1. And things hit a crescendo at the infamous Guam port call duty picks – when Sam and Juice went line by line, picking every single watch – with Juice ultimately playing the trump card by volunteering to stand in for one of the department head's AWDO shifts. By the time Sam's JO tour reached its last few months, it was clear that Juice had unofficially supplanted Nickels' role as squadron Good Dude – and naval aviation legend.

And yet, it wasn't what he thought it'd be. Juice found, to his surprise, that he didn't care about being the top dog, after all. All he cared about was competition – having a reason to stay hungry. Having a catalyst to keep him pushing himself. Having a mountain peak in sight, somewhere on the horizon, so that he had a direction to climb. He'd already mastered every administrative syllabus out there, rewrote chapters in the big book of NATOPS, and even became a top ball-flyer – one of the biggest hurdles for so many admin aspirants. What more was there left to do?! He'd hated Sam, but he knew he was an essential ingredient to the best version of Juice. And when Sam started to go downhill – becoming selfish, uninterested in 'Good Dude stuff,' and Diseased with Me? It left Juice – as cliché as it sounded – lonely at the top. He didn't have true best friends like Sam did – just good squadron acquaintances. He'd been so busy perfecting his craft, that when the superiority came... it came at the expense of the rest of his life. He'd reached the top of the mountain – but the problem was: he didn't want to stop climbing... He became depressed, unmotivated; a fighter raging white without a purpose. So unhappy, in fact, that he was on the verge of turning in his wings at a FITREP debrief with Skipper.

Juice shook his head as he recalled the events. He'd overheard Sam and Skipper getting heated over Nickels fighting for a number one FITREP. Juice couldn't believe Sam was fucking over his best friend like that – over an imaginary grading system that hardly held any relevance in today's Navy?! To go to The Course!? It was so obviously bullshit – only someone who hadn't dedicated their life to understanding and attacking Sam Rowland's flaws would believe that – and Juice was a SME. And so, in his own debrief with Skipper – with an unexpected but juicy LAR in front of him – Ward discovered a new mountain obscured by storm clouds, found his route to a taller peak through a treacherous road, and fired on friendlies as necessary keep the rivalry, the fight, and his climb going – even taking wildly reckless follow on shots with malicious intent.

Juice sighed in regret. If he would've known what his actions would do; the way they would derail careers and ruin lives – ironically exactly as he'd intended? He never would've pulled the trigger. But unfortunately, as he discovered later about fratricide – just as Rowland had: When a blue falcon takes a shot, it doesn't matter how invalid or poor the employment is – it will always guide and fuse...

What the hell?! Juice watched as the jet started to enter a slow but steady descent. Maybe this chucklefuck is finally fixing his VFR altitude... But just as soon, he blew right past 11.5k feet, all the way down to 10,500' – and further. Within minutes, this guy was below 9000 feet, still careening downward. And then Juice had a strange thought... No way... Could it be? Somehow, he knew it was. And trusting his intuition, he swapped up his J-Voice Alpha to the frequency he used to know and trust – 95. He wasn't sure if anyone would answer on the other end – but it was worth the shot. He'd been there to answer Nickels' inadvertent pouring out of his heart during Phase 2, when he seemed to lose all hope. And back then, Juice had gotten exactly what he'd wanted by assisting Sam: a reason to keep fighting. Now, Juice had no choice but to reach out again – because if that really was Sam? Then forget this MARSTRIKE – Ward had a chance for one more battle against the man who'd tormented him, hazed him, refused to train him... and thus motivated him like none other. Juice had already thrown his and so many other lives in disarray for a chance to keep fighting this bastard... he'd be doing them all a disservice to stop now...

And if nothing else? Sam deserved one more shot at a fight against him, after the way Juice had taken part in creating Dimes – a part much larger than poor Nickels would ever know...

Juice took a deep breath, tried quickly to remember how to do a Ra's Al Ghul imitation – but instead thought, 'Fuck it,' as he keyed Voice Alpha with the impression he captured better than any other – Bane – and ominously asked, "Did you not think I'd return, Sam?

~

488

Sam Rowland descended from the jet, after another standardly simple landing aboard the NIRD Katsopolis. Despite his American jet not having the software to engage automatic landing on the space station, the ship was still able to lock him up and command his gravity-assisted level descent — albeit with no Padroids on the platform this time. Granted, NEODD's grades would've mattered even less than usual to him, as his mind was focused on only one thing — the kill-removal debrief.

After Sam's shot in the fray, he'd called a 'Knock it off, bingo' for fuel, and the three RTB'd to the only viable landing spot within range — Sam's old intergalactic carrier. Ever the professional administrative crew, once the conduct was over, safety of flight and adherence to SOP became the name of the game, with no comm space wasted over unrelated chatter or learning points from the tactical portion of the flight.

Of course, sterility was only the state for *external* communications... because inside his own cockpit? Sam's heart was beyond apprehensive over how this debrief was going to play out.

He replayed the scene again and again in his head throughout the flight home, as any aviator does after anxiety over questionable validation or decision-making. *Did I do the right thing? Will I regret this decision forever? Either way, I think my career is fucked...*

This was amongst many *other* questions and concerns floating in his mind. *Did JABA really get a valid MARSTRIKE? Was CP able to save >SADCLAM<? Wait a second... did Robo-Hinge actually strike the ship?! Are all those guys even...* alive *anymore? FISTY... Were our efforts to save him — and everybody else — completely in vain?*

But once he entered the p-ways, on a direct path toward the debriefing stations, those questions fell by the wayside, as he crossed paths with and laid eyes upon the ground-docked Low T for the first time in years; and 'Loaded T' for the first time, *period.* 'Jacked' was an understatement. The man was a physical specimen. Sam *wanted* to spend paragraphs raving about his impressive physique, chiseled features, and skin-tearing vascularity, but he knew he was late to the game on this one, and the reader had likely grown weary of hearing intricate descriptions of this stallion of a human with insane AOM:LOL ratios.

Besides, standing out even more than his physically dominating presence was the *other* visible part of Loaded T's persona: the *pain.* The man practically slid his feet as he walked, too tired to lift them in step like a normal person, instead slowly slinking along. As impressively lean as his cheeks were, the byproduct was facial skin so tight that he couldn't hide his sullenness; the agony in the whites of his eyes on full display. He was chewing gum — no doubt to curb his hunger, as his ghrelin levels were undoubtedly at critically high stages after the long sortie — and sipping some colored pre-workout from a blender bottle — clearly another appetite-suppressant. And as he did both? Sam could see the muscular blueprint for his jaw and esophagus, clear as day, rippling through his lean face and neck.

Sam cursed himself for realizing he'd gone down a rabbit hole of description after swearing not to. *But how could I* not?! The man's muscles and vascularity would lead you to believe he was the epitome of health. And yet, his expressions and body language showed a man on the verge of death—and *YET*... Sam couldn't help but be envious of the physique. *Damn... maybe I should give up PowerPlants and give a little look-see around the ol' bodybuilding Reddit again...*

The two said nothing to one another. Sam gave a slight head nod, but Camilli just shook his. They carried their flight bags to the room where all the magic happens—the STBR—and removed their cell phones as they entered the click-to-unlock door. Inside, Juice was already there, sitting in front of one of two computers. Kyle took the empty seat and got to work, plugging in his RMM tapes to validate his shots before the kill-removal portion of the debrief.

After a few moments, Juice unplugged his own RMM and grabbed his validation sheet, offering his chair up to Sam. Rowland slowly took the spot—the two making eye contact for a brief second—before he turned to the laptop and opened his tapes to make sure every simulated employment he took was valid, good, and within the legal confines of training rules.

Juice... why did he help me? He wanted to ask so badly, but he knew to do so would be unprofessional. There were no commentary-based questions until *after* covering the facts in the kill-removal portion of the debrief. And yet he couldn't help noticing the expression on Juice's face—he wasn't mad, but he certainly wasn't *happy*, either. If anything, it almost looked more like an expression of... guilt...?

~

Captain Belichick paced around his office nervously, fidgeting as he begrudgingly asked, "I'm sorry, Tom, but can you read them off to me *one more time?*"

"No problem, Coach." Tom grabbed his tablet, pulled up the official Admin Olympics SOP, and turned to the scoring section. He looked up at the whiteboard, where Belichick had written down various categorical and post-flight data with attached scores, and announced, "For the USS Ship, we have..." he looked down at the SOP and listed, "valid MARSTRIKE; defeated adversary presentation via GQ scenario; and protection of defended asset." He turned to Belichick and added, "Although we get no extra points for doing so against a live-loaded threat—and we *will* in fact be penalized for *actually* attriting an enemy aircraft, and as well as for jettisoning an external tank without an applicable emergency scenario."

"... God dammit... antiquated rules... absolutely *ridiculous*..." Belichick grumbled under his breath in reaction to the penalties.

"And for the Noddiks," Brady continued, "We've got... successful penetration of an enemy ship with insider forces; capturing of an opposing pilot—"

"Even though he was rescued valiantly, and we came together as a team to overthrow those forces?!" Belichick asked in desperation.

"Afraid so, Coach," Brady lamented.

The coach shook his head. "... I can't even... absolute fucking *horse*shit..." he muttered again.

Brady concluded, "*And* they also crossed into an A/S LAR—nearly even over-flying the ship—which will get them a *lot* of points..." He exhaled dramatically. "What do you think, Coach? Is there any shot for us to take this thing?"

Belichick squinted his eyes at the whiteboard as he wrote down a few equations, deduced a few numbers, and then derived a few solutions. He bit down on his Artline marker, before shoving it back in the customized five-marker block, sighing, and looking back at Brady. "The way I see it, there's almost no chance we win this thing—not with the jettisoned tank hurting us so much." Belichick put his hands on his hips and shook his head. "It looks like I may have commanded my last ship, Tom..."

"What about a shoot down?" Brady asked, pointing to an enclosure in the SOP—clinging to any hope he could find. "What if Sam somehow took down one of those Noddik goons in a turning engagement?!"

"I mean..." Belichick trailed off with a skeptical tone, as he looked back up, "I suppose if he somehow shot down *their* captain, it could get us a hefty amount of points... but come on, Tom, you're talking about the longest of longshots here..."

Brady looked at his coach with determination. "You mean like a 0.2% chance of winning the Super Bowl, with 6:04 remaining in the third quarter, per ESPN's stat algorithms?!"

Belichick smiled halfheartedly and 'Heh'd' under his breath. "We already caught lightning in a bottle once, back then—you think we can get that lucky again?"

"Attitude is the mother of luck, Coach," Brady said with a smile.

The coach chuckled again. "So she is, Tom, so she is..." He looked outside toward the horizon, and continued, "And she's the parent that raises Good Dudes as well..." He sighed and narrowed his eyes, still onlooking the open waters. "Let's hope this child of hers has what it takes to pull off a miracle..."

~

"Stop tape—time 16+02," Juice stated, pausing the PCDS replay, then announcing, "Noddik 1, alive. Play tape."

491

He colored Noddik 1 'green,' clicked 'Play,' and the three watched on the gods' eye view computer screen as the newly-colored plane began flying toward the middle of the engagement between a red and blue plane.

Sam's heart was pounding, anxiously waiting for time 19+05, to finally call his one valid shot. Just as he'd expected, his shot prior had been invalid, resulting in his one simulated missile remaining being the only employment that *could* make a difference — but *would* it?

The minutes felt excruciatingly long, with tension high in the room — all except for Loaded T, who seemed calm — or was it just fatigued? The pre-workout had seemingly kept him leveled and sustained, vice amped up. He showed signs of life as he glanced down at his shot sheet and back at the screen, even leaning forward a bit as he flickered his eyes between the two displays, and eventually calling...

"Stop tape — time 17+10," Loaded T announced. "Noddik 2, timeout, gun, Chippy 1..." He looked at Sam — then Juice — with irritation.

The room was silent as the men waited eagerly. Sam closed his eyes, praying to hear those three words that, until this point, he'd always dreaded...

"... Trashed-not-called..."

Sam's heart leapt. He was still alive.

"Copy," Juice, the red lead 'Noddik 1,' acknowledged. He looked to Sam and asked, "Chippy 1, do you kill-remove off this shot?"

"Negative," Sam responded, a slight hint of glee in his voice.

Juiced nodded and closed the loop with, "Copy — no logical conclusion necessary. Play tape."

Kyle rolled his eyes and shook his head in annoyance, mumbling something about his radar not working correctly.

The men watched as the red plane began turning with the green plane, while the blue guy extended all alone and turned to face the fight with plenty of weapons separation. Sam looked at the clock — 18+48... 18+49... 18+50...

He looked at Juice, who was sweating, clearly nervous about this shot to come. Kyle, on the other hand, seemed strangely confident.

18+55... 18+56... 18+57...

Juice looked at Sam and blinked slowly, giving a somber smile as he nodded his head, as if to say, 'It's ok...' *What the hell?!* Sam had *never* seen this type of resignation from the Admin King... not toward *him* anyway. It was almost as if he was trying to say, 'I don't blame you'...

19+02... 19+03... 19+04...

"Stop tape — time 19+05," Sam called out, double-checking his shot sheet to ensure his shot status comm was ready. "Chippy 1, timeout, Fox-2, Noddik..."

492

Sam looked around between the two men — looks of anguish in one corner, and a cocky smirk in the other. Juice bowed his head and covered his eyes, while Kyle nodded and pierced Sam's gaze with an evil glare, almost as if to hiss, 'Do it!'

Rowland took a deep breath — and uttered the words he knew would shock the room: "2... JAAM'd hit."

Juice looked up in shock. He stared at Sam in disbelief at what he'd heard. "Did you say... Noddik... 2?"

Regarding his former arch nemesis with — for the first time since they wrote The Perfect Schedule together — a look of acceptance and friendship, he calmly and coolly affirmed, "Yeah... I fuckin' did."

Still in a daze, Juice shuffled through his notes to buy time as he processed everything, and then looked back up and frantically asked, "But Sam... the Olympics — once the MARSTRIKE call happened on GUARD, I figured you'd done the math, and would..." he stopped his rambling, stared at Rowland, and asked, "... Why?!"

"Because," Sam said, as he walked up to Juice, "My whole life has been about running. Running from responsibility; from my duty to train you as a new guy, instead choosing to hold you down as long as I could. Running from this job; from the life, friends, and memories it gave me — the things that *truly* matter — even though I never realized how good I had it. Running from reality; from the truth that you were better than me, both administratively and as a Good Dude. But most of all, running from being *me*; becoming obsessed with 'credit,' 'legacies,' 'achievements' — like those were actually going to bring me happiness in life — and at the expense of everybody who ever meant something to me. I truly became Dimes. But I don't want to be that anymore; shit, I don't even want to be *Nickels*. I just want to be Sam Rowland — a guy others want to climb alongside. And not because I'm some administrative guru, or the 'Admin King' — not even a fabled Good Dude! But because of who I am at heart. Man..." Sam shrugged and reached out his hand, "I just want to be *me*..."

Juice stood up, returned Sam's clasped hand, and the two joined in something never experienced between the two rivals: an authentic bro-hug, with mutual respect, appreciation, and reverence. As they broke the embrace, Sam announced, "Logical conclusion: Noddik 1 is the only fighter with air-to-air missiles remaining, and would turn with and kill Chippy 1, thus ending the USS Ship's Administrative Olympics bid —"

"Wait," Kyle uttered coldly. "Not so fast... with tape stopped, time 19+04... Noddik 2, timeout, Fox-2, Chippy 1."

Sam's heart sank. He looked at Juice, who had an equally distraught look on his face. Ward fumbled through his papers and eventually asked, "Chippy 1... were you... in a valid defense?"

Desperately looking down at his shot sheet — but for no reason, as he already knew the answer — Sam closed his eyes. "... Negative..."

Juice clutched at his heart, realizing what this meant: both missiles were in the air simultaneously... so both would register as hits—with Kyle's technically striking first. Ward was barely able to force out the words, "Then—then color Chippy 1 white... logical conclusion remains unchanged..."

Sam fell to the knees, hands on his head in disbelief, as Kyle stretched his arms and got up, saying, "You tagged me, Dimes..." He walked over to the computer and started clicking around, "... but as you know, one can cause a *hell* of a storm on their way out." He pulled up a draft message window, then looked back at Sam. "Dimes... this is an all-hands, Navy-wide email. Once I send this, NAVADMIN 66—and your statement of dispute—will be at the top of every government employee's mailbox— assuming they figured out how to transition to Flankspeed. The name 'Nickels' will be infamous in the aviation community, and for all the wrong reasons—but don't worry, the SWOs get these emails, too. I'm sure *they'll* at least be impressed by somebody blue falcon-ing the rest of their team so mercilessly."

Sam was shaken. When Kyle sent this... it was all over for him... *again. I should've just ended it in the jet... FUCK!* He wanted to ask 'Why'—but he'd grown weary of asking that question. "Kyle..." Sam asked, "*How*? How did you even find that statement? I threw it—"

"Are you fucking serious?!" Kyle scoffed angrily. "You're going to write all that shit—about how much you *hated* all of us— and then act like you didn't hand-deliver that fucking note to me so I'd fucking *see* it?! That you didn't leave it in my fucking chair in the ready room, sealed shut, so that I could *first-hand* find out how my best friend completely fucked away my life!? How fucking delusional *are* you?!"

"Chair?" Sam grimaced in confusion. "No, Kyle, I threw it—"

"In a burn bag..." Juice finished the sentence for him. "I found it in there, still in the envelope, when I was on SDO... and while I didn't open it up, I already had a decent idea of what it entailed." He shook his head mournfully. "Sam, I'd overheard your entire conversation with Skipper—except, unlike him, *I* knew you had something more than The Course planned—you weren't the first person the Noddiks had ever reached out to, you know." He gave Sam a knowing look, then looked to the STBR wall and sighed. "And when I heard what you were saying to Skipper... For the first time in too long, I felt *hope*—hope that that climb wasn't over for me, after all...

"Because I realized I needed..." Juice tensed his face, and then continued, "I needed a *fight* to stay inspired in this industry." He looked back at Sam. "I needed to keep chasing your legacy, Sam, because it was the only thing that incited me to work my ass off. And I knew that you'd already dropped the pack at 195 once I reached your level—it was obvious to *everyone*. So, plain and simple, you quit climbing—and with that abandonment, you fucked over yourself, your friends—and even your *enemies*," he pointed to himself, "in an *unbelievable* variety of ways. And I was so *pissed*, dude," he clenched his jaw, then frowned, "because without you upping the ante, raising the bar, setting the benchmark for me to chase—without a *king* to overthrow? What *purpose* did I have to climb here?" Juice scoffed. "Look around—I wasn't exactly *you* when it came to popularity in the Chippies. So, what the hell was I fighting for?!"

Not quite sure what Juice was insinuating, Sam remained quiet and looked at Kyle, who did the same; both letting the dust settle further...

Juice continued, "And so when I went in that office, and Skipper asked me who, between Nickels and Low T, I genuinely thought deserved the number one EP? I told him 'Sam'—knowing full well that he was going to take my advice—and you'd have your ticket out of here. Because when I said *your* name?" he said, looking at Sam, "Given *our* history? How could he *not* have thought, 'Man, Nickels treats this guy like shit—and he *still* supports him? He must still be *that* damn Good of a Dude.'"

"I *hated* you, Sam..." Juice explained. "Yes, I hated you for the way you treated me—but *that* at least got me motivated to get better; you forced me to elevate my game to levels I *never* thought I'd achieve. So, I certainly didn't hate you for *that*. More so... I hated you for being afraid—and yes, as you just said, *running*. Running from your legendary determination the *minute* somebody came there to test it; running from the challenge the *second* you were worried you'd found an equal. I heard so much about the great Good Dude Nickels—and yet, when I met the guy? He was *nothing* like the mythical stories that had been passed down—he was fearful, bitter, and *running* from self-improvement. Nickels had peaked; he was past his prime.

"But once I imagined you leaving? I *knew*... I *knew* that at the Noddik Empire, ambitious and unopposed, that drive would be back—Nickels would be saved—and you'd start *climbing* again. And with you back on the climb?" Juice's face turned to dark determination; a scowl of desire. "I *knew* I'd be hunting you down one day, to seize *everything* you'd built up: Every bit of the Noddik accolades, legacy, and future you'd created? I was going to rip it all from your grasp and take it as my own—*again*. The thought of *once again* competing with you in a new arena... it gave me that reason to keep fighting, to keep sharpening the sword, to stay hungry."

Ward paused, winced, and rubbed his forehead. "But selfishly... selfishly, this grand plan of re-igniting that rivalry just *wasn't enough* to put my frustrations at ease; I wanted everyone to feel the pain *I* felt... to empathize more with *me*. When I got my hands on that letter, I saw it as an opportunity to make everyone else see who I saw: *Dimes*. I wanted the Chippies to hate you—to hate you as much as I did... I wanted to *burn* your legacy here, letting everyone know that your entire character was a sham—I didn't want you leaving on even *neutral* terms..." Juice sighed in disappointment. "And so... I slipped the letter in Kyle's chair, figuring that whatever it said would piss him off enough to hate you too, and that he might tell a few others about it—but I never imagined what it would entail... that it would cut so deep... that it would cause... *this*..."

he gestured to Loaded T. Ward closed his eyes and shook his head. "I'm so sorry, Sam... *and* Kyle..."

Kyle stared daggers at his former Noddik accomplice. In silence, he walked right up to a standing Juice and point-blank glared at him. Watching the scene from across the STBR, Sam wasn't sure if Kyle was going to spit in his face, punch him, or just intimidate the hell out of him until he backed down.

But back down, Juice did not. He stood his ground, with he and Kyle face-to-face, and said, "That's right, Kyle. Sam had nothing to do with your #2 EP—it was entirely on me. And if you're looking for someone to seek vengeance against?" He gestured toward himself, "Then he's right here."

Clenching his fists, Kyle gave his right arm the slightest cock back, ready to strike... then wound up, turned—and punched the wall, screaming in agony as he broke the STBR membrane, auto-declassifying the room. "God *dammit!*" He retrieved his hand from the wall, bloody-knuckled, and looked back at a stoic Juice and a shocked Sam. "What the fuck is *wrong* with you two?!" He turned to Sam. "Your entire last year in the Chippies, you were *obsessed* with one-upping Juice, keeping him away from your precious 'legacy,'" he put up in air quotes—then turned to Juice, "And this entire time working with the Noddiks, *you* were obsessed with finding a way to slay the 'ghost' that was Nickels Rowland..." he looked between both, threw up his arms, getting blood on the wall, and exclaimed incredulously, "And when you *both* finally get the chance... you fucking *help* each other?! *None* of you deserve to be in charge of *any* fleet, because *neither* of you has the balls to take down the adversary when he gives you his control zone. Well, guess what, bitch—*I* do."

He turned back to the computer, clicked 'send'... and sealed Sam's fate for naval aviation eternity.

"NO!" Juice yelled, lunging to stop the ripped behemoth—but it was too late. Even with shitty operating software like Microsoft Outlook, the attachment had been sent to every navy address in the global database.

Kyle, fending off a feeble attempt from Ward, pushed him to the ground and said, "That's it, bitch. I'm done. I'm taking the next jet off this piece of shit and flying back to the moon—far away from two-faced, small-calved, try-hards like you, Rowland, and everybody else in this industry." He turned, and began walking toward the exit.

"Kyle..." Sam stood up and called out. "I have one question for you."

Loaded T stopped, closed his eyes, and sighed. "What, Dimes."

Sam calmly asked, "What were you going to do?"

Turning to look at Sam with disgust, Kyle spit out, "The fuck you talking about, bitch?"

Shrugging with his arms out, Sam said again, "Even *if* you'd gotten that #1 EP... *what were you going to do* when the Navy inevitably fucked you, too—just like the rest— and you didn't have someone to blame?" Taking a step toward his former best friend, Sam continued, "When you inevitably got overlooked for the orders you wanted, the location you desired, the platform you sought after—because of timing, needs of the Navy, manning, or whatever bullshit excuse they give you. Were you going to quit then, too?"

Kyle's eyes narrowed, but he said nothing.

"How about when *life* fucked you?" Sam asked with emphasis. "Were you going to move to a foreign planet, give up everything you ever loved, and just become this isolated, fitness-obsessed juicehead the moment your grand plans didn't go quite according to schedule? Were you going to abandon your entire life's resume of work at the first sense of adversity, revealing to everyone that—despite a fortified, likely gear-enhanced physical stature—you were hiding a total softbody mental resolve; a psychological physique *that* doughy and fragile?"

Loaded T stayed silent—seemingly taken aback by Sam's words.

Sam continued, "Because the Low T *I* remember? That guy may have eaten Grape-Nuts, complained about his neck, and skipped roll 'ems to go to sleep—but *that* was one resilient motherfucker. The vault was his gym. Briefing labs were his WODs. And he would've cared about The Patch more than he obsessed over any deltoid head separation on his shoulder..."

His jaw clenched, Loaded T took a moment, before quietly countering with, "WODs? I don't do Crossfit..." But unfathomably, there was no 'bitch' to suffix his sentence...

"*That* version of 'T,'" Sam said emphatically, "didn't give a *shit* about what life threw his way, or which route the Navy forced him down—he was going to do every- thing he could to kick ass, no matter *what* the circumstances were. The Low T *I* knew? He didn't *want* to come to Japan and be thrust into the FDNF lifestyle. But what did he do? He led the Chippies to unprecedented success in the art of conduct—the field of tac-actual—turning us into a bunch of dong-hangers in air wing LFEs. I never cared about anything more than admin when I arrived at the Dambusters—but damn, when Low T got there? I finally *believed*. I found myself referencing chapters in a book other than NATOPS. I started chair-flying more than just the catapult shot, CV-1, and maintenance card download. And believe it or not, Kyle..." Sam stopped and shook his head, pausing to parse his words carefully. "I even started thinking about rushing... *The* Patch..."

Kyle's face was not quite a blank slate—the anger was still present—but also a sense of curiosity.

"That's right," Sam said with a look of conviction. "I had just passed my Level 3 checkride, and was feeling the tactics high—but you know what?" He pointed at Camilli. "I looked at Low T—and I saw a man who legitimately cared to extend his learning and experience to the rest of the squadron, because he *knew* conduct was something everybody was capable of if they simply put in the effort, believed, and *persisted.* Low T *loved* teaching others, and as much as he tried to act like a tough guy at times, he couldn't hide the smile when a fellow JO took his teachings to heart and executed soundly, giving them a 'Nice job, bitch' — knowing it was *his* guidance that boosted an improvement. Of course, he didn't care about the credit whatsoever; he simply wanted others to garner the same appreciation and professional satisfaction from the job that had given him and his family a life he couldn't have predicted—and *certainly* couldn't have scripted—any better. I saw *that* man, and I understood: *This* is what a true tactical leader looks like. And I knew—unlike whatever fleeting desires I may have had; desires for notoriety, fame, or credibility—I knew that *this* man was pursuing The Patch for *all* the right reasons: namely, for the love of the fucking game."

Sam paused again, with Loaded T staring down to the side, nearly looking *solemn.* Rowland looked at Juice, who encouraged him with a head nod. He took a deep breath and kept digging, "The Low T *I* knew? He would've done *so well* at The Course—and even if life threw him a curveball and sent him to Lemoore at SFWSP? He would've put in the same effort there as if he'd got his dream location of Virginia Beach—and anybody who had him as an instructor, Training Officer, department head, or skipper? They would've been the luckiest fucking sons of bitches in naval aviation. Because..." Sam frowned and looked down, "Because *unlike me...*" he took another breath, steeled himself, and looked back to Loaded T, "... Low T never feared a challenge, never ran away, and never fucking quit."

Loaded T shook his head, put his hand to his forehead, and then ran it through his hair while sighing—a sigh of frustration. "*Why*, Sam—why'd you write that shit? Fuck The Patch, fuck the FITREP, fuck the Noddiks—*how* did you have the ability to talk *so* much shit about a life, a brotherhood, and a best friend you're speaking so highly of now?!" He punched the wall with his bloodied hand again, albeit less forcefully this time. "What the fuck is *wrong* with you, Nickels?!"

Shrugging and sighing, resigning this to be the truth, Sam stammered, "I— you're right... I really fucked—"

"Kyle..." Juice interrupted, "This job is the biggest mindfuck in the world. We continually get asked to do more with less. We work outrageously long days way too often. We obsess over countless acronyms that somehow metric our 'war readiness' based on whatever bullshit parameter the higher-ups are worried about that year. And to top it all off? We spend years of our lives living in janky conditions aboard a piece of shit boat serving food with zero nutritional value—where we work even *longer* days;

and where the only moments of privacy we get are the ones in the stalls—when they're not flooding piss and shit water throughout the entire bathroom. We're *all* miserable... and sometimes, these dark days get the best of us. Let he who hasn't sworn he's '100% getting the fuck out of the Navy' cast the first stone."

"But Kyle..." Juice continued, "As Sam found... there's undoubtedly something *captivating* about this job. There's something that keeps people coming back, again and again, staying in to become these hinges we all grew to hate, these skippers who carry insane amounts of responsibility on top of being expected to know every tactic in the book, and even these *admirals* who live the life of *exclusively* Navy politician bullshit—with a SSC flight sprinkled in every other week." He shrugged and said wide-eyed, "It definitely isn't the pay. Sure as hell ain't the benefits, either—not with *that* medical quality or those insanely long wait times. You know what, though, Camilli—I think you know *exactly* what keeps us in: The Suffering.

"But unlike the gym on a Friday night, unlike your Sunday afternoon meal-prep sessions, and unlike the top of the mountain at 6% body fat, deadlifting 4x your weight... you're not suffering alone here." He pointed across the room in a circular motion, "You and *everybody else* is going through the shit—suffering together, forming memories you're never gonna forget—for better or for worse. And in those moments... you create an insatiable desire to leave—and yet, an insufferable inability to actually *pull the plug* when it comes time to put up or shut up—to shut up and keep coloring with your friends." He sniffed with a humorless laugh, "Maybe we're on to something special... or maybe we're all just institutionalized idiots... but whichever the reason? You're not gonna find bonds like these *anywhere* else in the world. And that's enough to keep me in; to keep me *suffering*."

Sam noticed Loaded T showing the slightest semblance of *emotion*, and quickly expounded on Juice's monologue: "Kyle, I can't take back those things I said when I was at my weakest... we never can in life. We're not going to be proud of every action we've ever taken, just as we're going to have some shitty, bangbus flights—and some rough, puffy phases of high body fat, evidenced by pictures with terribly unflattering angles and lighting," he added, knowing Kyle would digest the reference well. "But life isn't about this 'perfect run of greatness,' and it's not a linear path toward the top, either. Life is a heartbeat-esque graph of ups and downs, trending in an overall ascending direction toward improvement—toward the best version of ourselves. And whether they accept me anymore or not... the Chippies? We're all a family. Maybe an estranged, volatile, combative family at times... but *family* nonetheless. And you? You're my brother—and I fucking love you, man."

That was it—Loaded T turned his face, trying to hide it from the men—but it was readily apparent, as he raised his hand to his eye: Loaded T was wiping a tear away. "You guys probably think I'm the biggest fucking pussy in the world..." he said with a subdued laugh, holding back more emotion. "My squat probably just dropped 50 pounds... fuck..."

Juice and Sam looked at each other and smiled, with Ward again nodding approvingly. They both looked back to Kyle—when the STBR door suddenly busted open.

"Woah! Captain Rowland, what are *you* doing here?!"

Taken aback, Sam could barely speak as he saw Dr. Suabedissen smiling maniacally at the three pilots, with white powder residue below his nostrils.

"Oh, Loaded T! I hope you don't mind that I took a scoop of your Jack3d—well, a *couple of* scoops actually... *ok,* fine, I took the rest of your canister and then found another one in the back!" He was speaking incredibly fast with intermittent breaths, and sweating profusely. "God *damn* that stuff is good!"

Loaded T said nothing, not wanting to show anybody else the foreign matter emerging from his tear ducts.

Suabedissen shrugged and said, "Well, anyway, what's new, guys!?" He looked at the wall, and pointed where Camilli had punched. "Woah! Big hole! This room is no longer secure, you know."

Juice threw up his arms and asked, "How the hell did you get in here? Isn't the door electronically locked?!"

The doctor smiled and nodded. "Yes, it sure was! But I actually just shut down the ship QNAP, cutting off all the power supply!"

The two admin SME Chippies exchanged shocked looks, as Sam spit out, "*What?!* Doctor... if the ship doesn't have power, it can't stay afloat!"

Suabedissen grinned and said, "Yup! This baby's going down in —" he checked his Majora's Mask watch, "ohhhh, I'd say about 30 minutes!"

Juice looked to Sam. "Shit! What the hell are we gonna do?!"

Shrugging again, the doctor happily said, "Welp, I dunno! But I'm gonna escape in my multiverse transportation machine; I'll see you noobs later!"

"Transportation machine?!" Sam asked in shock. "What the hell are you talking about?!"

"Ohhhh, sorry... there's actually only room for *one* in the pod..." Suabedissen said with legitimate regret in his voice. The man's emotions were all over the place, clearly crazed off his substance.

"Where are you going, bitch?" Kyle asked, still shielding his eyes.

"You know, that's a good question..." Suabedissen answered with genuine appreciation. "I think I've realized that my life is kind of a joke... programming, coding, and lab coats? I'm tired of being a total beta, and the target of everyone's mockery. Because, let's be honest, guys—true confession here: As much as I may have played the *role* of Alpha Male..." he offered his arms up and shrugged, "I will admit I was kind of *duping* you all a bit. I'm a little less confident than I appear. And that whole 'model girlfriend' thing? You'll never believe it, but..." he smiled sheepishly, "I sort of... made it up..."

"You don't say..." Juice remarked.

"But anyway, I think I recognized all this during my massive depression—so at least my punch line of existence created something positive! I'm going to show up to life as a new man next time. I'm gonna get into something badass—maybe skydiving? No, wait! Skydiving, *and* I'll become a fighter pilot—just like you guys!"

Juice and Sam looked at each other and rolled their eyes.

Suabedissen looked at Kyle. "And get this, Loaded T—I'm even gonna lift weights, too! I'll be freaking shredded and athletic and strong—just like you! Just you wait, baybeee!"

Kyle clasped his hand to his forehead and shook his head.

"And you know what else?" the doctor added, growing very serious. "I will find her... I *will* find her—and god dammit, I *will* save her..."

As the doctor gazed off into the distance with a grave face, Juice and Sam looked at each other again, without a clue as to what or who the fuck he was talking about.

"So!" Dr. Suabedissen concluded, returning to a goofy smile, "I better be on my way, gents! I need to get in my pod before this Jack3d wears off and I change my mind!" He kissed his fingers to the sky, did a douchey JJ Watt-esque salute, and said, in a *terrible* Arnold Schwarzenegger accent, "Hasta la vista, baby!"

He ran out the door—then popped his head back in and said, with a serious look, "Oh! And if you see Robo-Hinge?" His expression transitioned to an ear-to-ear smirk, "Tell him he can suck my dick!"

And with *that*, Dr. Karl Suabedissen made his grand exit—leaving the three men alone in the STBR, merely 25 minutes away from this space station capsizing in the ocean.

"Guys... we need a plan—and *quick*," Sam emphasized, showing strong leadership skills by making such a statement.

"Can't we just turn the QNAP back on?!" Juice asked frantically.

Sam shook his head, "I'm afraid not... that thing is *not* meant to be turned off while deployed to sea—we have no way of powering it back without a docked connection. The ship is essentially dead in the water, running off battery power, no longer being constantly charged..."

"Can we still launch the jets off?" Ward asked further. "You know this ship better than me, Sam—Is there enough power to do that?!"

Sucking through his teeth, Sam twisted his neck and said, "... It'd be *damn* close. But you bring up a good point, Juice—it might be our only shot." He paused for a moment, something in his mind as he asked, "What jets did you guys fly here?"

"401 and 403," Ward responded. "Why?"

"403..." Sam said to himself, looking a bit concerned. He then shook his head and said, "Never mind, all good," and gestured over to Kyle, insisting, "Loaded T, you're coming back with us—we're not leaving a Chippy behind."

Kyle said nothing, sitting emotionlessly, eventually nodding to signify his approval.

Sam smiled. "Atta boy, T—there's still a life for you back there—and god knows they're all going to hate me once that letter hits, so we might as well give the world at least *two* indomitable Dambusters that they'll be glad to see." He looked back to Juice and said, "Bobby, can you run up and unchain all the jets? I'll call for the weight chits and get FDC to send some yellow shirts up there—if this ship is truly going down, the AI bots will be in combat reserve mode, working at triple the efficiency. We can make it happen, as long as the ship can hold onto enough power for all three jets. Got it?"

Juice nodded sharply. "Affirm, Nickels." He stuck out his arm, fist bumped Sam, and looked between the two men, confidently proclaiming, "I'll see you boys on the flight deck."

Juice exited through the STBR door, as Sam looked to his former best friend and asked, "Loaded T, do you remember how to use JMPS? There's a load we can use for—"

"Sam..." Kyle started, "... I'm not going..."

"What?!" Sam burst out. "But Loaded T—*Kyle*—you *have* to..."

He shook his head and gloomily said, "I don't have to do *shit*, Sam. Bro... I'm no longer the man I was... I no longer have the desire for this job that you spoke of— that was *Low T*. And look at me now; you said it yourself—I may be the ultimate version of him physically... but I'm just a mere shell of him, mentally. Low T was driven by success and improvement; *I'm* driven by suffering and tragedy. He had a family and friends; *I* have my food scale and a weight bench. Low T was full of dreams and hope for the future, believing his best days to be ahead of him as he vowed to get better, day by day. But *me*?" He pointed to his arm, covered with veins, looking as if they were about to burst from his skin with the slightest flex. "I'm in peak physical condition; I have nowhere to go but *down*. I'm holding off the inevitable—I've *been* holding off the inevitable... but that time is now, Sam."

"Loaded T..." Sam pleaded, "There's still hope—you can return to the guy you used to be! You can take all the briefs from my folder! They'll waive your labs, and you can do all the Air-to-Surface events as sims! You'll regain your division lead qual in no time!"

But Kyle just shook his head again. "I just don't care anymore, Sam — the part of my soul that gave a shit is gone; it left, to make room for all this testosterone and all these gains. And the only thing I held a passion for was finding my ultimate suffering — and I've finally found it. Reading that statement by you was one thing — but for me to be the one who *submitted it?* And letting it spiral my identity out of control, abandoning the life I loved, and subsequently making it a personal mission to ruin the life of my best friend? I never thought it'd happen... but somehow, succeeding at *that* felt worst of all. It doesn't get any more painful than this..."

Slumping on the floor, Kyle pulled a weapon from out of his flight suit — Sam instantly recognized the gun by the key recce feature of the letters written in bold font across the barrel: APG-47.

"Nickels, please..." Loaded T begged, "Let me die here on this ship — but let me die as the man I was proud to once be..."

Sam froze. He couldn't believe his best friend wanted this... but it was clear there was no changing this juicehead's mind — and maybe Sam didn't even have the *right* to, given everything he'd put him through. He walked up and took the rifle's grip, his finger resting on the trigger, as the barrel pointed at Loaded T's swole chest.

"You *created* Loaded T, Nickels... now save me from his grasp, for at least my last moments..." The look on Kyle's face was excruciating — pained, jaw-clenching, anguish.

His hand shaking... Sam knew there was no other way. In poetic irony, Sam had *refused* to kill Loaded T, even when he'd *begged* for it back during their first turning engagement in space just days ago — Sam had *insisted* he could save him. Yet now — after all his resistance, after *all* these attempts to be a Good Dude once again — Nickels would be shooting down his wingman, after all... But for once, he put his personal program aside — because he understood that he owed Kyle *this*, at the very least: An end to his suffering. He closed his eyes and, without a word... squeezed the trigger.

Kyle jolted as the ray hit him, convulsing slowly as his body began glowing... before his muscle mass began atrophying in rapid fashion. His chest lost fullness... his calves shrank... his vascular biceps merely retained a single, barely-noticeable-in-certain-lighting vein. His jaw lost its extreme angularity, and his cheeks began smoothing over, filling out — but his signature mustache remained *just* as full as ever. Kyle reached at his aching neck, rubbed his sore back, and said, "I'm sorry, Sam. I'm sorry for everything... and I love you, too, man..."

Sam felt a tear coming to his eye, as he stuck out his hand, pulled Kyle up — with surprising ease — and embraced his best bro, saying, "You'll be a Chippy legend forever, Low T."

Kyle smiled behind his tears and said, "That stuff doesn't matter... I just wish we could both be living in those good old days forever—doing good-deal SEM, breaking behind the boat, and playing die with the boys..."

Sam nodded as the two broke the embrace. "Me too, bro. Me too..." He took a deep breath, and said, "So, this is it, huh."

"Affirm," Loaded T said with a slight smile. "The kill-removal part of the debrief is over, and you're certainly not getting *this* Red air to stay for any more of this shit..."

Sam chuckled. "Copy... thanks for the work, Viper. We'll see you next time..."

Kyle closed his eyes and nodded.

And as Sam walked to the safe to turn in his media, he heard, "Wait a second..."

He turned and saw Low T wearing a mischievous, goofy grin—a throwback from his days as a Dambuster JO. "You know what, bitch..." he said with a quiet-yet-playful tone, "Go ahead and leave that RMM out. I wouldn't mind reviewing my two-circle mech—for old times' sake..."

Sam couldn't help but smile and laugh, sentiment prevalent in his voice as he said, "You got it, man. Just make sure to sign it in when you're done," he added, as another tear fell from his eye.

The two nodded at each other—a bittersweet aura filled the room, as they knew it was their final farewell.

As Sam left the STBR, the door closing with a 'click' behind him, he wondered if he'd just said goodbye to the best pilot he'd ever known. After Sam's end-of-tour bad dudesmanship left Kyle Camilli tormented and ruined, Nickels finally had another opportunity to forgo his own selfish desires, and act in the best interests of his best friend. And this time, he *took* that opportunity. *Of course...* he thought cynically, as he walked toward maintenance control, *'Dimes' killed Low T... and now 'Nickels' killed Loaded T. Will I ever actually* save *anyone...?*

~

Juice scrambled through the p-ways of the boat, which were flooded with sailor bots working at hyperspeed to try and fix the issue—but it was all going to be for naught... Juice found himself feeling a little sentimental for the bots. He'd not exactly grown close to any of them, but seeing them walk around every day had been the closest memories he'd had from his days in the Chippies; memories of those daily walks to and from the ready room, seeing faces you recognized—almost like old acquaintances—even though you never said a word to them aside from 'excuse me' or 'morning.'

He finally found his way to the PR shop, quickly donning his gear and venturing to run up the stairs.

"Juiceman! Hey, Juice!"

He turned around and saw NEODD SWEVEN and T6 running toward him, the latter carrying an external speaker blasting the t.A.T.u. song 'All the Things She Said.'

Dude, not fucking now — and this *song?! What?!* "Hey, guys, I really can't talk right now..." Juice started, trying to make his way to the flight deck while deflecting these morons.

"You're not trying to fly away, are you?!" T6 asked with a cautionary tone.

Dammit... Juice thought, *They might be trying to take the jets, too...* "Uhhh..."

"I knew it!" NEODD folded his robotic arms. "Absolutely *not*, Juice! *Nobody* is taking off from this ship without Padroids at the platform! It's a coolness hazard, and we will *not* permit it! And we are *not* going up there until we recover our APARTS data! Have you seen that doctor lately? He really *fucked* us, you know!"

"By the way, what do you think of our new entrance music?" T6 asked Juice. "This song fucking slaps, right?! The doctor had it hidden in his old high school folders, and with <MCSALAD> gone, there's a new sherrif in town when it comes to picking —"

Out of nowhere, a whoosh sounded above them. *What the fuck?!* There was no mistaking it — somebody just took off.

"DUDE!" NEODD yelled, raising his arms and tensing in his Wilson jersey. "*Not* fucking cool! Who the hell was that?!"

A set of bells appeared over the 1MC. "Charlie Alpha Golf, departing!" a robotic voice spoke.

"Are you fucking *kidding* me?!" Juice groaned. There were only three jets up there — now *two*, thanks to CAG taking one of the spots. He didn't have any more time to waste. "Listen guys, I don't give a fuck about APARTS, Padroids at the platform, or any of your LSO bullshit — I gotta get the hell out of here, *now*."

"But how will we rank everyone for the 'Top Look' awards at Follies?!" T6 whined.

Juice looked at them both, threw his hands up, and said, "I don't give a shit — just give them all to other Padroids!"

T6 looked at NEODD and shrugged. "Not a bad plan at all, bromigo!"

"Hellllzzz yeah, boiii!" NEODD said as the two high-fived. "Hey, what should we do for our Follies skit this year anyway?"

"Hmm, you know, I actually had a really good idea," T6 began, brushing dirt off his Eric Decker top. "I was thinking we could do a skit where people acted like they didn't like us — just like, talking a bunch of shit and disagreeing with our analysis of their coolness when we read them their passes, you know?"

"LOL!" NEODD yelled out loud. "That's pretty funny, bro, but I don't know if it would land—the JOPA would probably be confused as to why people were upset with us, you know. Like, I don't know how believable it'd really be."

"True," T6 acknowledged, "But I mean, what if we just *pretended* that the stuff we preached wasn't as important as it is, and that people actually thought our opinion didn't matter?"

"Mmmm..." NEODD murmured in disapproval, "Unfortunately, man, as CAG Padroids, I'm gonna have to veto that idea. I just think the idea is a bit too radical. But, I mean, maybe we can adjust it a little—like, I mean, what if we set the scene in the Iwo beer die room... and we have a playlist of *only* 'Ram Ranch,' 'Scotty Doesn't Know,' and 'Automatic'—playing on repeat for hours on end—and maybe we wear these tight little denim vests too, and..."

And the two idiots went on talking, utterly oblivious to the fact that Juice was long gone up the stairs...

As he emerged on the flight deck, Juice's decades of building CV administrative instincts were apparent—his head immediately popped on a swivel with inhumane range of motion from mobility exercises, as he gracefully navigated the dangerous snakes of wires, hoses, and chains flooding the floor—an act he once took ballet lessons to perfect. As he fought a mighty headwind to race to his and Nickels' jets on the bow, he heard the booming yet high-pitched voice of the Handler.

"ON THE FLIGHT DECK! WE GOT A PILOT WALKING—LOOKS LIKE JUICE WARD OUT THERE! HEY, COUPLE OF SHOUT-OUTS: HAPPY BIRTHDAY TO AO2 MELO AND AT2 PRITCHARD! CONGRATULATIONS, SHIPMATES; YOU MADE IT! ALL HANDS, THE QNAP'S DOWN, AND THIS SHIP WILL BE SOON, TOO! SAY YOUR LAST GOODBYES, FOLKS; IT'S BEEN A HELL OF A RIDE!"

Juice began picking up the pace. He looked out to the horizon—the ship was definitely submerged even deeper. *Shit, we gotta hurry!* He looked around the flight deck again, defying the preconceived physics of human neck rotation—but saw no other pilots. "C'mon, guys, hurry..." he said aloud.

But of course, he'd already considered the fallout with CAG taking one of the three F/A-18s—and his decision was set in his mind: He was going to give Sam and Kyle the jets. Both of those men had been quintessential Chippies for as long as he could remember—living legends, in fact. Juice may have done everything he could to chase Sam's legacy... but he had to admit, deep down: without Sam there first? Juice would've been just another run-of-the-mill Navy pilot—commissioned, winged, served, and out—maybe a mention or picture in a Tailhook magazine somewhere. Sam set the blueprint for standing out amongst the crowd—and as much as Juice had once hated him, he couldn't deny that Nickels was an all-timer, first-ballot, naval aviation Hall of Famer—even *with* that statement going public.

And that statement... Juice shook his head. *Why did I have to give that to Kyle... fuck me, dude...* After what he'd done to Kyle *and* Sam... after this entire shitstorm he'd summoned? He owed them both second chances at life.

And so, he took control of his fate. Juice was going to go out doing something that he'd always strove for, but never quite with a purpose so valid and not ulterior-motivated: Being a Good Dude.

And just as he arrived at the jets on the bow—205 and 403—he saw a pilot in gear emerging from the catwalks. *It's them... finally!* But strangely, he only saw *one* pilot. *Huh?* Based on the physique and lack of insane muscle mass, it was clearly Nickels approaching him from between their two jets. *So where is Kyle...?*

Sam got in close, and yelled over the roaring self-generated wind and double-hearing protection, Ethan-Hunt-in-Mission-Impossible-2-style: "Juice, it's just you and me! The shooter bots said this ship has the power to get us both airborne, but we've only got *ten* minutes! 3, 2, 1, hack!" He pushed his watch to begin a timer, which Juice matched seamlessly. "Attention to brief!" Sam continued, "Let's get both our engines online—standard NATOPS startup; don't skip the fire loops! Make sure the BINGO bug works, and let's verify 3-down and a good hook check, ok?! Taxi to the cat, takeoff checks bottom to top, and roger up the weight board before pulling up your HUD repeater! Give it a good wipeout, don't forget the rudders, and make sure you get that launch bar up with the light out! Crisp salute when you're ready! Any questions?!"

"Nickels!" Juice yelled back. "Where is Loaded T?!"

Sam raised his visor—a direct violation of flight deck rules—but did so to show the solace in his eyes as he hollered, "... Loaded T is dead!"

"What?!" Juice shouted in disbelief.

Nodding with a bit of emotion, Sam added, "He's gone! But *Low T* is back in there, watching tapes until the end!" He paused, almost tearing up. "It was his last wish!"

Not fully understanding—but trusting—Juice returned the nod and said, "Let's get the fuck out of here!"

Juice began walking toward his jet—403—when Sam grabbed his arm. "No—take my jet!"

Confused, Juice yelled, "What?! Why?"

"Just trust me!"

Uncertain, Ward asked, "Didn't you say you overstressed it?!"

Shaking his head, Sam yelled back, "Yes, I popped an overstress code—but maintenance said it checked fine! It's a good, up jet!"

"Well, so is mine!" Juice countered, completely perplexed by what was happening. *We don't have time for this, Sam.*

As if reading his mind, Sam shook his head and shouted, "We don't have time to argue, Juice!" He pointed at 403. "I'm taking that jet! Now let's go!"

Shrugging, and somewhat annoyed, Juice resigned the debate and walked across the bow to the jet Sam had landed in—205—leaving behind the perfectly good jet he'd flown earlier. He hopped in, starting up after a thorough cockpit sweep, which included checking the brake pressure gauge, emergency oxygen bottle, and, of course, a *robust* ejection seat inspection that *certainly* included more than making sure it was safe'd. He cycled his fire loops, gave the switches one last sweep to include his WAP checks for the wingfold, anti-skid, and parking brake set—and started the APU. As the jet whirred to life, he cranked the right engine online, and began turning on every display, moving his hands in an impressively rapid fashion. He looked across the bow and saw Sam matching him perfectly along the way, as if they were synchronized; damn near mirror images of one another. As he cranked the left engine online and initiated the IBIT, Juice smiled to himself as he considered just how parallel and interconnected the two long-time rivals truly were...

As their launch bars, speed brakes, refueling probes, and hooks moved simultaneously, then reverted back to their retracted-and-up positions, both gave their PCs the 'go fly' signal, as they were unchained and given to the mercy of the yellow shirts.

This was it, Juice realized as they got lined up for a covey launch—him on cat 2 and Sam on cat 3. *We're going back... for good. What's going to happen? Is Nickels going to be ostracized from the community forever? Would they do that? Shit... I tried to do that—but I was fucked up. He was fucked up. People fuck up! But if you're learning, climbing, and getting better from your mistakes... isn't that what the journey of life is all about?*

"THREE MINUTES, FOLKS!" the Handler yelled into his mic. "THREE MINUTES 'TIL WE GO UNDER, THAT'S WHAT THE QNAP TECHS ARE TELLIN' ME! GONNA MISS YOU GUYS; SEE YOU ALL IN THE AFTERLIFE!"

He looked over at Nickels, who spread his wings and got put under tension just as he did. *Ego gets the best of us... and tries its damndest to ruin a good thing. We spend so much time complaining about how we deserve to make more money... deserve better jobs... deserve a better life; so much that we fail to grasp how great the life in front of us truly is. Ego tries to get everyone eventually—it got Nickels... it got me—but it's not an unbeatable adversary.*

For the resilient... for those who persist... for those who keep climbing, unconcerned with their on-paper accomplishments? The best views are yet to come. If the Chippies won't let Nickels climb with them anymore? Then fuck 'em—*I'll climb alongside that champion all the way to the fucking moon.*

Juice threw the throttle to MIL, executed a wipeout, stomped on the rudders, checked his gauges in the jet, gave a crisp-as-fuck salute, and looked over at Sam, expecting to see him dropping his arm in synchronization with him—

But Sam sat there, shaking his head, eventually getting the 'power back' signal. His exhaust nozzles opened—the power clearly pulled to idle.

What?! Juice scanned between Sam's jet and the HUD, anticipating his own launch any second.

And then Nickels Rowland spoke the words that sunk Juice's heart. "Tower, 403 needs to be spun off."

No...! Without hesitation, Juice transmitted, "Suspend, suspend, cat—" But he whooshed off into the air before he had a chance to abort the launch. He cleaned up, and without caring that it was in direct violation of carrier procedures, he *omitted* his clearing turn *and* maneuvered directly downwind to oversee the ship and figure out what was going on. He quickly checked his watch from the earlier time hack—60 seconds to go...

"403, what's the issue?" the air boss asked over tower.

With no sense of panic or hysteria—only a simple hint of calm resignation, Sam responded, "403 is due for a 728-day inspection. It needs to be RNC'd before it can go flying again—the jet is down."

Juice nearly lost his mind. *An inspection?! What the fuck? How did he know?! He really* does *know his admin procedures and these jets better than anyone... but are you* kidding *me?!"*

The boss mic'd back, "Roger that, 403—unfortunately, we're not gonna have time for that. I'm calling the launch."

"403."

"LAUNCH COMPLETE!" the Handler yelled, "THAT'S IT FOLKS, LAST LAUNCH FOR THE KATSOPOLIS! HAVE MERCY! THIS THING'S GONNA BLOW!"

"Nickels!" Juice keyed over AUX angrily, still circling overhead. "What are you doing!? Take the jet! It's a fucking preemptive inspection!"

"It's too late, Bobby, and it's a downer—NATOPS is clear about that. And you know as well as I do that to take a known down jet flying would be completely contrary to safe, professional administrative procedures."

Juice bit his tongue. *God damn him... he's right...* "Sam..." he said, realizing what was happening, "You knew that jet was down... that's why you switched with me..."

Sam didn't verbally affirm, but Juice could see him slowly nodding from below his canopy. "Turn and get out of here, Juice—once the power is fully out, the Katsopolis' core will explode, and the frag envelope will cover the entire Carrier Control Zone. Please..." emotion heavy in his voice, "Don't get yourself killed, Bobby..."

Juice hesitated... waited... tried to think of *anything*... "Fuck!" He pounded on his dashboard, begrudgingly banked and pulled to put the ship at his six, went into max AB, descended to 500' AGL, and began gaining speed as he skimmed the wavetops. He shook his head and said, "Sam... you didn't have to do this... the world needs people like you. All that stuff in the past—that's exactly what it is: ancient history... and *FUCK* history! You've proven you are *still* the Nickels of old; you *still* have so much to give this community, and this life *still* has so much it owes *you*! This can't be the end, Sam... you're a Good fucking Dude...!"

Sam responded—not over AUX, but over Voice Alpha, with a voice that became a husky growl of an impersonation—for once, an *immaculate* Christian Bale impersonation: "A Good Dude can be anyone. Even a pilot doing something as simple and reassuring as using a Bane impression and putting his metaphorical arms around a lost brother's shoulders, to let him know his life wasn't fucked."

As Juice accelerated at low altitude, he felt tears form in his eyes and a smile on his face, as he understood that *Sam knew*. Sam knew that Juice—against all odds, as unfathomable as it once seemed, *un-fucking-believably*—he *knew* that Juice had done his part in saving Nickels.

And *Juice* knew, too. He knew that at this very moment, he would be saying his last goodbye to his indomitable Dambuster brother. And in poetic fashion, he did it in a way he knew Nickels would appreciate more than anyone—with the juiciest, most epic, flawlessly-placed alley-oop. Juice didn't care that these were the last words he'd say to his long-time rival, all-time brother; didn't give a *shit* that he'd be using a Bane impression for a Commissioner Gordon quote; and didn't give a *fuck* that this *exact* movie moment had already been referenced like twelve chapters ago—the opportunity was *too perfect* to pass up. Fighting back the tears as best he could, Juice covered his mouth and harnessed Tom Hardy one last time, stating over Voice Alpha, "The Chippies... Carrier Air Wing 5... all of naval aviation—they'll never get to say 'thank you...'"

As he hit 7 nautical miles, Juice yanked the stick in his lap and executed an unrestricted climb *so* fast and G-loaded that his JHMCS visor came down—as he slowly looked up in his mirror at the NIRD Katsopolis one last time... before an eruption of flames engulfed it...

But before the ship completely went under, Juice heard one final blip of a Voice Alpha transmission, followed by the growly crusader Sam "Nickels" Rowland, expressing confidently, "And they'll never have to."

Epilogue

"That I take this obligation freely, without any mental reservation or purpose of eva-sion," Admiral Tom "FISTY" Flynn stated, with his right arm raised.

"That I take this obligation freely, without any mental reservation or purpose of evasion," LT Mark "JABA" Buck repeated, his arm the same.

"And that I will well and faithfully discharge the duties of the office on which I am about to enter," Flynn continued, his dress whites looking pristine with the Iwakuni sunrise peeking through the open hangar door.

"And that I will well and faithfully discharge the duties of the office on which I am about to enter," Buck echoed, his whites equally spotless, aside from the dual-striped shoulder boards that had been donned on them for *far*. too long.

FISTY paused, took a deep breath—an uncontrollable smile on his face like a proud father—and finally finished with, "... So help me, God."

Buck, beaming ear to ear, nodded and recite one last phrase, "So help me, God."

LCDR Chris ">SADCLAM<" Houben and LCDR Andrew "CP" Preul walked up and took off Buck's Lieutenant shoulder boards, and replaced them with ones that looked nearly identical—albeit with a 1/4-inch sliver of gold in between the other 1/2-inch gold bars outboard of the golden star.

"Ladies and gentlemen," Admiral Flynn announced ecstatically, "Lieutenant Commander Mark Buck!"

The full crowd in the hangar went absolutely wild, with a decibel level over-powering the turning jets outside that had not adhered to the quiet hours in the NO-TAMs. People were whistling obnoxiously, clapping like the world's longest Paddles train had just read off four no-comment passes, and standing and shouting as if it were the Super Bowl, where JABA had just caught the game-winning touchdown to end WW3 and cure cancer while ending cancel culture and eradicating the nutritional world of seed oils, in *one beautiful, diving, Santonio Holmes-esque snag* to barely tiptoe two feet in-bounds as the clock expired to hit the 'over' by half a point, and gambling-addicted terrorists everywhere mourned as they went bankrupt and swore off their life of evil.

The crowd contained the most insane guest list—many of whom joined from Fat Chucky's Cruise Ship, all here to hail the momentous occasion. Rafael Nadal wound up and threw the fiercest of fist pumps, executing his trademark chainsaw celebration before falling to his knees with his arms raised like he'd just captured his 15th French Open. Travis Barker, alongside his wife Kourtney Kardashian, pointed to JABA, calling out "You da man, Mark!" and lifting his shirt to reveal a new tattoo along his back that said 'God was a hinge.' Natalie Portman was there, as she couldn't help but walk up and give Mark a passionate kiss, inaugurating him as an official O-4. All of them, alongside Shohei, LeBron, Jordan, Gronk, Shaq, Phil, Ronaldo, Drake—and *so* many other one-name-famous celebrity guests that the reader could gladly revisit in Chapters 10 and 11 if they so desired—filled the hangar seats amongst the rest of the active duty and retired members in attendance.

When the crowd finally calmed down a bit, Admiral Flynn—with his jaw still dropped from the kiss heard 'round the world—handed the mic to JABA to let the Navy's newest golden oak leaf hero say his words, which were obviously infinitely more full of wisdom now that he was an O-4.

JABA fixed his dress white's Velcroed mock turtleneck and surveyed the room around him. His smile was uncontainable. Finally, he shook his head in disbelief, and began addressing the crowd. "To my friends... my family—Hey, Dirty Mike!" he called out, waving excitedly as he noticed his brother in attendance. "Can you believe I just made out with Padme?" His brother nodded happily, as JABA regained his composure and emphasized, "To *all* of you that came here today... holy crap—I... I don't know what to say. I know this is the single most clichéd phrase in the world... but I never—and I mean *never*—thought this day would come. A little over a year ago, I was running a theme park out in Guam—a retired Navy Lieutenant pilot, seemingly incapable of heading departments, standing Bravo Papa watch, sending bi-weekly updates to XO, making regularly scheduled announcements about writing gripes and completing ASAPs during AOMs, staying up for 24 hours straight to fulfill the AWDO duties of mustering people every hour during port—or most notably of all, commanding Lieutenants..." he paused, put his fist to his mouth and rested his teeth on his fingers, before continuing, "And yet today... here I stand—a Lieutenant *Commander*..." he sighed and laughed—a laugh that almost seemed on the verge of a cry—embracing the moment in pure ecstasy.

The crowd went wild again, and gave another standing ovation to fill the gapped space after Ryan Gosling and Eva Mendez beckoned everyone else to get on their feet.

JABA finally collected himself, as people re-took their seats and calmed to a light buzz. He took a deep breath and continued, "There are so many people I want to thank... *too* many to fit into a speech, and I don't want to keep you guys here all day—

nor myself, since I have a DH meeting later on to prepare notes for!" he added, drawing laughter and cheers from the audience.

Buck cleared his throat, becoming a bit more serious, and noted, "But there *are* two people I want to give special thanks to — unfortunately, neither of whom are with us anymore to receive those 'thanks'..."

The crowd grew solemn, as the direction of the speech was understood amongst all hands in attendance.

"The first was someone who *defined* what it meant to dedicate one's life to his craft. The kind of person you'd find working on a briefing lab during a Saturday afternoon for *hours*, just to get *one* depiction of *one* arrow on *one* pane of his examples *perfect*. The individual the Navy had in mind when designing their prototypical fighter pilot. He wasn't just a fighter pilot though — he was an *athlete*," JABA finished with a fierce look of conviction. "Ladies and gentlemen, a moment of silence for LT Kyle 'Low T' Camilli..."

The crowd stood in hushed reverence for the most tactical fighter to ever grace the Chippies; Ewan McGregor and Hayden Christensen nodding slowly with their eyes closed.

After an appropriate amount of time had passed, Buck continued, "And the other? The man who, *hands down*, is the reason I stand where I am today: with an active duty uniform on, working alongside the best friends I've ever met in my life. A man who proved that even when we take a wrong turn in life, the golden path still illuminates when you follow your internal compass of aspiration. A man who showed that even when the journey hits you with a brutal thunderstorm, the mountain is *still* scalable for those who bear the resilience to climb. A man who — in his everlasting positive impact — continues to generate a daily influence in the kinship of naval aviation. A man who carries an untouchable legacy — despite finishing his life being unconcerned with such a trivial concept. A man who was more of a 'dude'..." JABA paused, closed his eyes, and took another deep breath... before reopening them and clarifying, "a *Good* Dude."

Pointing to his left, JABA instructed, "Ladies and gentlemen, please direct your eyes over to Chippy side 408." Waiting by the aircraft were Skipper and XO of the VFA-195 Dambusters, who raised their hands to grab the barely-visible string connected to the jet's body. "408 received a new paint job last night," Buck explained to the crowd, "and it's a *permanent* paint job. For the rest of eternity, Chippy side 408 will be known as our 'Admin Bird.' It had all of its basic combat systems, CATM-carriage capabilities, and annoying TAC menu selections downloaded, uninstalled, and stripped away. Instead, it will simply be used for AIRNAVs, AREA FAMS, FCLPs, and CQs — purely administrative flights. All of this was done to commemorate the fallen brother who turned this squadron into one of heroic folklore. Skipper, XO — go ahead."

Upon receiving Buck's first O-4 tasking, the two Commanders both pulled their strings simultaneously, revealing the name on the jet: Sam "Nickels" Rowland; and just below his printed name was his well-deserved career designation: The Admin King.

A wave of gasps and awe rippled throughout the crowd, with flashes from cameras lighting up immediately post-unveiling, in a scene that felt directly out of a movie. 408 was enshrined as *the* standard of admin excellence—and it had an insanely good max trap fuel state.

JABA wore a subdued smile, and whispered to himself, "Thank you, Nickels—for everything..."

And after the moment successfully sank in, Buck leaned into the mic and announced, "This concludes the promotion ceremony—please join me upstairs for frosty cold refreshments and a midrats-style eggs-to-order grill in the ready room... *SEEYA!*"

~

"No joke, this douchebag spent the *entire* Khaki Hour on the bench, and did—I counted them—*three* sets... texting the entire time while chilling on the bench in between!" >SADCLAM< described with incredulity. "And when I asked him if I could work in, he said, 'Sorry, bro, I can't afford to compromise my rest times; I'm 'prepping for a competition,'" he added, putting his beer down to animate with air quotes.

"What?!" CP reacted in disbelief, almost choking on his omelet. "How much was this guy even benching?!"

"A plate and a quarter!" >SADCLAM< exclaimed.

"Oh my gosh..." CP shook his head in disgust. "This guy was hoarding the bench *and* bumper plates for 185 lbs? And he's *competing* with those rookie numbers?! What a gym terrorist... I swear... I'd like to see him try and do that once *I'm* in charge—people like him and acts like those are exactly what I'm going to eradicate."

"The United States Navy Fit Boss..." JABA said with a smile. "I had no idea it was a LCDR billet! And you're changing the nutritional options aboard carriers, too?"

CP nodded slowly with wide eyes. "Affirm—there's going to be a big-time shift in the landscape of sailor health with a new sheriff in town. I took a look in the kitchen and demanded they show me *all* their seed oils—and boy, were there a lot..." he shook his head in dismay. "We're talking copious amounts of canola oil, soybean oil, sunflower oil..." He started listing on his fingers, adding, "Peanut, vegetable, grapeseed, *rapeseed* oil—like, are you *kidding* me?!" Wincing in disgust, CP continued, "I told them to put that junk back where it belongs—lubricating printers, shredders, and the arresting gears. From here on out, everything will be cooked in natural animal fats—tallow and butter. Oh, and you know all those soda machines, desserts, 'impossible' chemical-derived meats, those canned veggies—*and* the fresh ones? Adios," he proclaimed proudly with a grin. "Henceforth on deployment, you can choose between steak and eggs, you can drink water, and you can season with salt—and you can *thrive.*"

"What about white rice?!" >SADCLAM< teased with a grin.

Rolling his eyes, CP acknowledged, "Ok Chris, well, per the Mac Recs, *obviously* you can have appropriate amounts of that, too—*if* you're putting in the work in the gym."

Smiling, Mark asked, "How have the test runs been going? I hear sailors' health has been skyrocketing."

"Oh yeah," CP said, nodding slowly again. "Double-dragon? Not a thing. Morale, attitude, recovery, and retention? All-time highs. We've cut back on dentists and doctors, because—go figure—*apparently* sailors' dental and wellness issues were being caused by fueling their bloodstream with Dr. Pepper and 50-ingredient Uncrustables—shocker..." he said with annoyed sarcasm. "And with the workforce no longer sick, unable to sleep, nor thirty-plus pounds overweight? The productivity in the Navy has been unreal. Who would've *guessed...*" he said sarcastically again, throwing his arms up and widening his eyes, "that it all came down to diet and lifestyle—*not* the need for pizza-and-doughnut week-long seminars on 'warrior toughness,' or 'culture of excellence' workshops interrupting an already-behind-timeline workforce."

"Wow!" Buck exclaimed, "That's awesome! How are they supplying so much fresh, quality-grade beef in quantities conducive to the whole crew, and keeping the meat good over long deployment periods?"

"Ehhhh..." CP said with open hands and a scrunched face, "those facts and details of practicality are a little beyond the scope of this epilogue—so don't you worry about that..." He then added with a raised finger, "Oh! But those storage facilities? You know—the ones that held all the non-perishable junk: granola bars, pop tarts, and cereal? We're replacing all that wasted space with *more gyms*—gyms that have *substantially* less cardio equipment and machines."

"Even the weight-lifting machines?" >SADCLAM< asked curiously.

CP gave him a long look, insisting, "Machines don't use machines, Chris. Didn't the Noddik's inability to defeat us show you that?"

"A-ha-ha," JABA chuckled. "Well, they certainly got *close...* but the indomitable spirit of humanity is what got us the Administrative Olympic victory, after all!"

"That's right, Mark," CP nodded. "Even a bunch of robots—programmed to do everything perfectly to a *tee*—couldn't take us down when we had the war-tested minds, bodies, and hearts of champions backing us. Guys like Kyle and Nickels, standing up for us against traitors like that asswipe Juice..." He scoffed, "*Fuck* him... and everything he did to those two heroes..."

Returning to the topic at hand that the reader surely cared more about, CP added, "But no, guys—carrier gyms are going to be fat-burning, testosterone-fueling, man-making facilities—filled with dumbbells, barbells, free-weights, and bumper plates." He smiled and insisted, "Under *this* regime? The Navy is going to have unparalleled AOM:LOL ratios like you've never *seen* before in natural sailors—with none of the faux-gym-culture 'no chalk, no noise, no effort' bullshit holding us back."

"And I heard you're changing the PRT, too?" >SADCLAM< asked.

"Oh yeah," CP responded. "The PRT's been removed entirely."

"*What?!*" Houben spit out. "Andrew..." he added with concern, "We're already trending in a bad direction as a force; if you cut out the annual test, these sailors are going to have *zero* motivation to work out..."

"Great!" CP stated with wide eyes and a serious look, one that JABA and >SADCLAM< couldn't tell if was sarcastic or not. "Chris..." he continued, "if living a long, healthy life, with flourishing vitality, high self-confidence, and a thriving sex drive isn't enough to motivate people to work out and avoid the chemical junk killing us by the day... then why should we make them go through this dog-and-pony show, when the Navy continually cuts standards further and further, showing that they don't even care?"

"Well..." Houben tilted his neck, "I suppose that's a good point... Oh! And I heard something about a new sleep instruction?"

"Affirm, NAVADMIN 195," CP said with an ear-to-ear grin. "Crew rest standards implemented—*Navy-wide.* I've been saying this for a while—the Navy has a *serious* sleep hygiene problem, and the days of asking servicemembers to work like those aforementioned Noddik robots—on inhumane sleep allowances—are *gone.* Twelve hours uninterrupted break from work, *minimum!*" he insisted. "We are *killing* ourselves with these work schedules, man. Even the biggest gym noob who's done a bit of research—hell, even on *Reddit*—knows that sleep is the secret ingredient to the legions of elite athletes with booming libidos, and that the *lack* of it plummets testosterone, mood, and even brain functions like memory, comprehension, and mental health!"

"Psh..." >SADCLAM< scoffed, "Next, you're gonna be telling me you don't drink anymore..."

"Well, Chris..." CP began, "there *is* substantial evidence that even a *single drink* of alcohol can affect your REM—"

"Oh my god!" Houben burst out with a laugh.

CP smirked back, "You still haven't read *Why We Sleep*, have you, Chris?"

"I—"

"Wait, no, of course not!" CP cut him off, then snarked with air quotes, "Ever since he donned the oak leaves, Mr. 'Read a Fucking Book' hasn't had a minute to look at *anything* published at the unclass level!"

"Well, let me tell you, Andrew—unlike you meatheads, I've read *plenty* of fucking books in my life, thank you very much," >SADCLAM< countered with a playful grin, "and in *none* of them does the hero attribute his ability to 'answer the call' to all his time spent *sleeping*." Giving a sarcastic inquisitive look while raising his hand to his chin, he asked, "Can you remind me where, in history's greatest battles, it discusses the bravest warriors fighting in this perfect world of physiological balance, under stress-free conditions with picturesque circadian rhythms?"

"Well, World War II legend General Patton certainly believed: 'Fatigue makes cowards of us all,'" CP fired back with a smirk.

>SADCLAM< rolled his eyes. "I'm honestly just shocked this author didn't try to attribute that one to Vince Lombardi..."

JABA laughed, loving every moment of watching his two O-4 friends bicker like they were JOs in the midst of cruise, debating between if they'd rather fight a chicken once a day or a monkey once a year. "I can't believe it—my former squadron brothers... Navy department heads! And who would've guessed they'd put two O-4s in charge of overall fleet physical and mental readiness?" Smiling, he asked, "CLAM, how's the return to fleet life been for you, anyway?"

"Bro, don't even get me started..." Houben responded, shaking his head with his forehead in his palm. "To think... I thought *AOPS* was bad—but department head life? It's *unreal*. I've got my SLUI qual re-hack on Monday, followed by a red lead the day after, for an LFE that CAG OPS last-minute line-of-sight-tasked to me. Then, a light break with just eight hours of mission planning after a DH meeting rolling into an AOM Wednesday, a couple of SFWT flights to instruct Thursday, and to wrap it up, a 'good deal' MC syllabus-look after our STAN Cell conference on Friday..."

CP and JABA looked at each other—and started laughing.

"What?!" Houben asked. "I'll be there for 12 hours every single day next week—*at least*! And that's not even covering all the ground job bullshit I have to take care of!"

"Chris..." CP started, "Don't act like you don't love every minute of that junk. And don't act like you're not going to be the one keeping those debriefs going *hours* past a reasonable timeframe. In fact, don't even act like you aren't returning to work immediately after this to do a practice run-through of your GBU-38 employment lab! For god's sake, man..." he said with a sigh, "let the brainwashed Patches handle that stuff!"

"The Patches?! Andrew, how can you *say* that?!" >SADCLAM< asked with conviction. "If you really think we should be leaving war-hardened toughness and tactical readiness to the Patches... then you're truly softer than a dad bod! We can't just sit around, waiting for TOPGUN grads to save the day when shit hits the fan!" With a defiant expression, Houben continued, "You want to talk about 'books?' What would've happened if Luke Skywalker stood by idly while the Rebel Alliance fought the war for galactic freedom? Or if Harry Potter let the the 'brainwashed' Ministry of Magic 'handle' the return of Voldemort and the Death Eaters' reign of terror? You think Bruce Wayne was fine with just sitting on the sidelines, watching his city be cared for by *only* those employed to protect it?"

"So, you're saying the TOPGUN grads are a bunch of corrupt aurors and cops, huh?" CP asked sarcastically. "Not to mention, god—how many more times can this author possibly highlight the limited range of 'books' he's read..."

Laughing, >SADCLAM< responded sincerely, "You know what I mean, Andrew. I'm just saying this: In every great story, it's rarely those in the 'ideal position to fight' that get the call—and yet, we *all* have to be ready to answer it. Luke, Harry, Bruce... none of those guys were in advantageous positions to have everything rest on their shoulders—and yet they *made it their mission* to be *ready*. Life isn't about living passively, expecting somebody else to take care of the hard work. We need to take charge—each of us, as *individuals*—so that when the high-end fight arrives; when the call comes? *Every one* of us is ready to answer. The professional pride in putting in 100% every day, regardless of who we are or what patch we wear? *That's* what's going to keep us the most tactical and professional fleet in the world—no, in the *galaxy!*" Houben put his beer down and raised his arms to emphasize his words. "Brother, think about where *Low T* would've insisted we take our focus. The Admin Olympics may be over, but what about the *conduct* side of the house? What about when some bozos from the planet Douchetopia decide to challenge our TOTALs? Because when that time comes, Andrew? When the call hits us up?" >SADCLAM< steeled his eyes and vowed, "I'm certainly not gonna let me or my guys be caught *sleeping*."

"And I'll shut up soon, but I do want to say *this*, about the Navy." >SADCLAM< paused, pensively trying to parse his words. "People complain about the training, the hours, the lifestyle... and I get it. This job can be a real kick in the dick sometimes, with *way* too much bullshit thrown in," he gestured toward CP, who nodded in agreement.

Softening his face, Chris shrugged and acknowledged, "... But in a strange way... I'm *thankful* for those nut shots the Navy's sent my way, because every time, after metaphorically rolling around on the floor—writhing in pain over an extension, a stream of agonizing reflies, or a plan that just didn't go the way I'd hoped—I picked myself and emerged *resilient. Battle-tested. Evolved.* And I wouldn't want it any other way," he expressed with content. "If you don't have that chip to wear on your shoulder, then how do you *possibly* find that reason to climb, that motive to suffer, and that capacity to grow? We set ourselves apart as a force by getting more reps, putting in more work, and tolerating more bullshit—when sometimes, all we want to do is *quit*. SFWT candidates, aviators, people *in general*; shit, man, they can complain all they want about the discomfort of progression. The ones who truly *get it?* They, one day, will *appreciate* those times of struggle, and they'll *cherish* the moments that nearly pushed them over the edge—because *that's* what got them to the next level," he said with a smile.

"And lastly, let me finish with this." He finished his midrats ale with his finger raised, put his callsign-embroidered beer stein down, and concluded, "As much as I may not have believed it once upon a time, Sam was right when he said it: Quals, rankings, awards... that stuff *is* irrelevant to your journey to find your greatest self. You sure as hell *don't* need a specific insignia, title, or patch to make a difference in this community—or to keep climbing. What matters, more than anything somebody else bestows upon you, is the toughness between your ears and the spirit between your ribs—as you embark up the mountain of daily self-improvement, fighting the dragon of complacency, pursuing the treasure that is your truest potential."

Exhaling in astonishment, JABA expressed, "Man... that's incredible, CLAM. I can only hope to be as inspirational in my lowly squadron-level DH tour!" He looked over at his golden oak leaves and smiled, still in slight disbelief that this day had come.

"Yeah, I gotta admit, CLAM..." CP acknowledged, "Despite that entire chunk of overly drawn-out prose *clearly* being the author's attempt at turning this epilogue into one of motivational bravado and feel-good final thoughts? Your words almost have me wanting to sit down and watch the complete saga of BFM videos—*almost,*" he added with a sly smirk. "But seriously," he said, finally using a tone of candidness, "With a mindset like that at the helm of preparing our warriors... the future looks bright for this Navy. God help the Noddik Empire—or *any other* intergalactic jabronis out there—who think they can take down a fleet led by a bunch of driven champions climbing innocently together, feeding off beef, animal fats, and the endless pursuit of perfection."

JABA sighed. "Can you guys believe it's been a *year* since all that? I still get goosebumps thinking about it: leaving CV Worldwide, coming back to the USS Ship, launching in what are so often *vain* attempts for the fabled valid MARSTRIKE... and actually achieving one?! Sometimes, I still think I'm going to wake up from this incredible dream, hardly believing that we really made it out of there alive and victorious!"

"Well, we nearly didn't—*I* nearly didn't, anyway..." >SADCLAM< said with a look of relief on his face. "Between the XANs and Padroids brainwashing, and then the Munchkin Quest black hole of nerdery, I almost lost myself back there, man..." He shook his head—then emphasized, "*Almost.* But luckily, my green-bleeding brother helped me remember what this job is fucking *all about,*" he declared with a smile, instinctually grabbing at his right shoulder, where That Patch was worn proudly—his 'Single Seat For Life' Chippy patch—an eternal symbol of the indomitable Dambusters' brotherhood.

"You got that right, bro—never had a doubt that you'd be just fine," CP added with a smile to his friend. "You had me and the whole crew of CSs making sure you'd be ready to strike when the LAR was there—well, us and that CWO3."

"Oh yeah!" Houben remembered with a smile. "What ever happened to that guy?"

CP smiled softly. "The Warrant? He turned in his commission. Said he was so inspired by how we didn't exactly *exude* Navy instruction-based adherence and 'professionalism,' and yet still managed to be a cohesive, robust group of free-thinkers who had fun while getting the job done. He vowed to stop living as such a tool of the government, and swore off his days of being anti-'logic combined with common sense'— and I must admit, I've got high hopes for that guy," CP acknowledged. "He's adjusting well to real life out in the civilian world. I actually heard from him last week—says it's finally starting to feel normal to be called by his first name instead of 'Warrant.'" He shrugged happily, "I think I'm actually going to offer him a head chef job at the steak ranch that supplies the carrier's food."

"Really?" JABA smiled warmly. "That's awesome!"

"Your steak ranch..." CLAM asked nervously, "It's not called *Ram* Ranch, is it?"

"*No*," CP said, staring at the fourth wall with a look of pure annoyance at that laughless song being referenced again. "*God,* no."

Finishing his plate of pancakes, JABA looked between his two friends and remarked, "You know, the way the whole team came together? Convincing the captain to let us fly in Phase 2, and then taking that ball-flying competition thanks to Brady, you," he said as he gestured to Houben, "and Nickels? And then that *entire* Phase 3 culmination?! It was incredible AUP, guys. Even though they were stressful, pressure-packed moments of chaos... to see us performing so well on the big stage, flexing to make it happen despite the longshot circumstances where all felt—well, for lack of a better word: *fucked?*" He chuckled, "Guys, it honestly brought me back to the glory days of the Chippies... the days that were truly the best in my life..." He sighed longingly, looking into the distance—before refocusing on his friends. "And now, I look at all three of us—*finally* a cadre of O-4s?" JABA smiled, almost growing emotional. "It's like we're *back* in those glory days..."

"No, Mark," CP interjected, with conviction in his voice. "These days are gonna be even *better*. We're going to turn this place into what it always should've been. With my plan for fitness, and CLAM's for mindset? We're cutting the bullshit and embracing more of the *shit*. Because while it's not always gonna be easy or comfortable... at least we finally know we'll all be getting *better*, headed in the right direction; guided the right way, with the right people in charge." He looked at his Chippy compadre with an amused smile. "Mark, you thought this place was great back in the day? You thought the Navy had *peaked* during your time as a JO? Buckle up, bro—because the glory days are just getting *started...*"

JABA beamed. "You're right, CP. And to think... losing my franchise, creating a VR scenario for the GOAT, and taking on a robotic empire of androids in order to win a simulated war of administrative superiority was all it took to find this destiny I'd been so desperately seeking..."

>SADCLAM< smiled, shrugged, and offered up, "Man, like Brady's 'Maybe' story, you just never know when moments of adversity could turn out to be the *best* things that ever happen to you." He chuckled and added, "I'm sure *Lieutenant* Buck wasn't exactly thrilled at the idea of flying an expired low level below OPNAV MINALT restrictions—yet look what came of it..."

"Oh my god, I nearly forgot!" Mark said, running his hand through his hair. "It was unvetted! I was a mere O-3... 100' AGL... the CVW-5 SOP clearly dictates... I never should've..." He shook his head in disbelief. "God, can you imagine if the Olympic administrators had found out?!"

"But they didn't..." a voice mumbled happily from behind the three men.

JABA turned and saw Bill Belichick and Tom Brady approaching their midrats table, both wearing wide smiles.

"Sometimes, you have to misinterpret SOPs and OPNAV 3710 in order to get shit done around here," Belichick said with a goofy grin on his face. "Let's just say, for the official record, I thought the instruction said it *should* be flown by a LCDR or greater in the past 60 days..."

"Captain Belichick! Tom!" JABA called out with excitement.

The three Chippies and two Ex-Pats exchanged embraces, as Brady cheerfully said, "Congratulations, JABA—you *know* we wouldn't have missed this for the world! How does it feel to don the best rank in the Navy?!"

JABA grinned and said, "Feels great, baby—Happy Halloween!" he threw in, causing Brady to crack up at the meta reference that only people with way too much time on their hands and empty space in their brains could possibly recall. He then grew a bit more serious and acknowledged, "But really, Tom, it *does* feel great. You know, it's funny... all those years out there—in the real world, managing CV Worldwide—I topped so many mountains of business: Opening my first amusement park, bringing in my first million dollars of profit, becoming one of the top ten richest men in the world... But no matter how high I climbed? I couldn't help but look over my shoulder at the tallest summit of all—the one my heart yearned to scale: the seemingly impossible peak of making O-4 as a VFA pilot..." He smiled whimsically and shrugged. "And now that I'm here? I don't know *what* to think! Sometimes I wonder: *Could life ever top this?*"

Brady nodded and chuckled. "You know, Mark—Bill and I were just talking about this: when we see what you former Chippies accomplished... it reminds me *so much* of when we won our first Super Bowl together with the Patriots, back in 2002. People were happy for us—but they thought it was a feel-good, once-in-a-career story. And looking back?" Brady scoffed in amusement. "How fucking ridiculous was *that?!* Because in *our* minds? That first *hill* didn't feel like the end of our adventure—not even *close*. I *knew,* in my heart, that this 'crowning achievement,'" he said in air quotes, "which *so* many others would be happy to call their ultimate destination?" Brady beamed ear to ear. "I *knew* that was just the *beginning*. And I see the same in you, Mark." He looked over to Belichick and gestured, "Coach?"

With a rare unsolicited smile, Belichick agreed, "I see it too, Tom. Fellas," he added, looking at the rest of the men, "I hope what you've *all* realized—by getting back into the game and climbing once again—is that you've *barely* scratched the surface of what you will accomplish in this world of naval aviation. Now that you're here—recapturing the lives you've pined for since detaching from the Dambusters—you can probably see that this return was a false peak of life—and that there are *so* many mountains left to climb, towering over this summit. And you know what's craziest of all?" He looked at JABA, exhibiting the gentle smile and empathy he'd displayed more than ever with these close friends. "*You* undoubtedly used to think that O-4 would be the best rank of all... but I bet you've already realized that there's an even better one out there..."

>SADCLAM< and CP smiled at each other, knowing exactly what Coach Belichick was putting down. JABA, feeling even better on this magnificent day, affirmed, "You're damn right, coach: The *next* one."

Brady calmly pumped his fist and said, "Let's fucking *go*, baby," high-fiving Buck. "The future of the Navy looks pretty damn unbeatable with guys like you on the roster, that's for sure." He looked back at Belichick and remarked, "Feels kinda like the '07 squad, doesn't it, Coach?"

"Hmmph," Belichick grunted, returning to his gruff noise-making—albeit with a smirk. "At least pick one of the seasons where we actually *won* the whole thing! Good grief, Tom..."

"Isn't it funny, guys..." Brady said, shaking his head in disbelief. "You can win *all* these championships... rack up *all* these stats and qualifications... knock out sortie after sortie with simulated mission success... spend an *entire* career achieving more than you ever could've dreamed of—and yet..." he shrugged and smiled, "It's the few plays that *didn't* go right that stay on your mind the entire season... the SFWT reflies and (OK) landings that eat at you for the rest of deployment... the single blemish on your otherwise spotless record that torments you for the rest of your life..." Brady looked over at JABA and said with a smile, "But as *you* know, Mark—what's even *crazier...* is that I wouldn't wanna have it any other way."

JABA beamed and nodded, reminiscing on their game-changing, life-saving, war-winning VR simulation.

Brady continued, "You *have* to have setbacks and failures in life, because they drive that *hunger* for greatness—in a world that gives you every reason to be full. You've gotta *understand* and *remember* what that adversity feels like, if you're going to appreciate how incredible it feels to work *past* it." He shrugged and laughed. "Sometimes it feels like a fool's journey; an endless do-loop of adversity and growth. But, like the unachievable quest for perfection, it's one I'll gladly chase for the rest of my life—because you *need* to have that motivation to keep waking up and getting out of bed every morning," he gave a long look and a pause, then emphasized, "to subsequently *earn* the ability to sleep soundly and accomplished. Determination is the foundational kindling, agony is the friction, and results are the smoke—the *proof* of the fire that fuels the champion." To cap his speech off, Brady quietly said, "And you know who would attest to that more than anyone? A man who lived his final days fighting with that very fire: *Nickels Rowland.*"

In absolute awe at the knowledge this GOAT was *still* spitting, >SADCLAM< nodded and acknowledged, "100%, brother. You know, the Admin Olympics felt like a damn-near-perfect part of my naval career—recovering from being lost and depressed, to contributing to one of the biggest victories my country has ever achieved. But even after the awards ceremony—where we were all presented Medals of Honor and 720-day liberty chits, and first-ballot meritoriously inducted into the naval aviation Hall of Fame..." He sighed despondently. "... I just couldn't get my mind off... you know... how much Sam and Kyle deserved to be there, alongside all of us..."

JABA nodded, blinking slowly. "CLAM, Tom—you're both right. We lost two GOATS that day—but it wasn't about their respective admin and tactical accolades. Those two were GOATS of 'who-you-want-as-a-squadron-brother.' They were walking FITREP bullets. You couldn't find two people who better *epitomized* what it meant to be a relentless worker, dedicated leader, and selfless contributor. They were just flat-out, hands-down, underlined *Good Dudes*. And while they both went down their own paths of adversity—as we *all* do—they showed the heart of champions when it mattered most. And for that, I will forever be indebted to these heroes."

Doing his slow head nod, CP remarked, "Yeah. I didn't trust Nickels for a while, and I was certainly shocked to hear about this 'Loaded T' character... but damn... I *love* those guys, and I'd give anything to get one last lift in with them—even yoga with Kyle would be a dream come true..."

Belichick sort of murmured for a second, then asked, "Fellas... I hate to bring up a sour topic amongst all this good will—but what the hell is wrong with that Ward kid? Did you guys know him in the Chippies?"

"Big time," JABA answered, a grave tone. "We cruised together multiple times in the squadron—Sam overlapped with him quite a bit, too. They butted heads completely, and it got pretty bad. We all knew Juice was part of why Nickels left us, but..." he winced and shook his head, "We didn't realize just *how* bad of a dude Bobby Ward was."

"So, he really wrote that horrendous FITREP statement of dispute?" Brady asked.

"Affirm," CP answered with dismay.

"And then pinned it on *Nickels*, knowing it would destroy his legacy?" Brady continued, concern on his face.

"Afraid so," JABA nodded in melancholy.

"How could he *do* that?!" Brady winced in repulsion. "I've never heard of such a fucked-up thing from a fellow pilot!"

"Oh yeah, Tom—this guy was a *major* shitbag," >SADCLAM< emphasized. "To be honest, I liked him a lot in the Chippies—but once I saw his leaked email to the Noddik Empire, I knew this guy fucking *sucked*."

"You know, I heard about him sending that email out before going down with the Katsopolis—but I never actually saw it with my own eyes," Belichick admitted.

"What?!" >SADCLAM< shouted. "Are you kidding?! Captain, how have you *not* seen this?!"

"Ermm... well... mmmmphm... technology these days..." he mumbled in response, with an annoyed look.

Chris quickly took out his phone, pulled up his Flankspeed email, and directed Belichick's glare toward the hacked correspondence.

Belichick read through the email, his eyes narrowing at the parts that shocked him, with his expression cycling from blank, to annoyed, to blank again; wrapping up with repulsed. "Hmph," he said at the end. "So, in this SITREP to his Noddik superior," he asked for clarification, pointing to the phone, "he admitted to getting simulated shot down by a reunited Rowland and Camilli—causing the USS Ship to gain an absurd amount of points—and then, *verbally confessed* to wiping his tapes so nobody in the Olympic Committee would find out? He then drafted a press statement to the committee *lying* about the engagement, saying he shot *Sam*, attempting to forever change the scope of history? ... And he didn't realize that sending this over a non-secure net was a terrible idea...?"

"Yeah!" Chris said with incredulity. "Fucking *idiot*, right?! If he hadn't sent it over a clear, hackable net, I doubt we ever would've found concrete proof that Sam and Kyle's shots on him happened — and were valid! Galactic chronicles and naval records would've unfairly labeled the Noddiks as champions! Oh!" he added, growing further animated, "And did you see the part about that bullshit letter?"

"Mmmm..." Belichick grunted in affirmative. "The NAVADMIN 66 piece... He wrote up some fake 'statement of disagreement,' or whatever," he gestured with his hands, slightly uncertain and annoyed, "sent it from that meathead's account, and tried to say it was written by a disgruntled Rowland, years back — even forging Sam's signature — thinking that the world would turn against him?"

"Yes!" >SADCLAM< said again, still in shock that Belichick didn't know any of this. "And not sure if you've seen the letter, but uhhh... it's *bad!*" he said with a heavy tone. "Like... makes-you-want-to-shit-in-a-bathtub-and-frame-it-on-the-guy, *bad*!"

Not understanding the reference — nor caring — Belichick murmured to himself as he re-read the email. "He did all this, *and* shut down the QNAP to the boat before anyone could launch off — knowing it would kill him, Rowland, and that T kid? That's horrendous — pure fratricide – a crime *far* worse than simple rule misinterpretation..." Belichick shook his head in disgust. "He sounds like somebody who would fit in well with the New York Jets' organization..."

"Yup..." CLAM affirmed, more sorrow in his voice this time. "The ship lacked the power to catapult *anyone*, and ultimately exploded and capsized, leaving no survivors..." he closed his eyes and shook his head. "Low T had apparently been working this plan all along — to betray the Noddiks and help Sam at the conclusion of the Olympics..." Houben grew emotional as he further explained, "He'd taken the persona of 'Loaded T' to trick Juice and the Noddiks into recruiting him, knowing full well he'd be able to infiltrate the empire and save Nickels — and that's how they got the 2v1 shootdown; which sounds like it was fucking *epic,* per Juice's description in the leaked email. Fucking *legendary* move by Low T..." he declared with a heavy heart. "And speaking of Juice... that traitor was so upset that he pulled the plug on the whole thing — went fucking *nuclear* — trying to make sure nobody ever found out about Kyle and Sam's heroic efforts." Widening his eyes, Houben lifted one hand, acknowledging, "*Which*, ironically, we *wouldn't* have," then lifted the other, "*if* the fucking idiot hadn't sold himself out with his pre-death SITREP."

Brady shook his head and bemoaned, "I *still* can't believe it... I only knew Nickels for a short time — but *damn*, was that man determined. Just watching him come through in the clutch during Phase 2 with that safe-with-less-than-average-deviations ball-flying — and then the way he selflessly stood SDO in Phase 3 — even as an *O-6!*" He appeared awe-struck as he looked into the distance, "It was *immaculate*..." Brady clenched his jaw, his face pained. "He deserved to celebrate this victory with us..."

CP, not afraid to call out his superior, asked, "Captain, what's your deal?! How did you possibly *not* know any of this? Didn't you wonder how the USS Ship won the Olympics?"

Belichick grumbled a bit, eventually forming out the words "... Haven't kept up with my emails... busy with other stuff..."

"*Busy*?!" >SADCLAM< asked. "Sir... you're part of the United States Navy — the greatest fighting force in the galaxy. If you found something more important to do than serving as Captain aboard the USS Ship..." he raised his arms exaggeratedly, "... Do you mind enlightening us as to what exactly it is?!"

Belichick sighed heavily. "You know, CLAM, you bring up a good point." He looked around the room, shrugged, and admitted, "Gents — my brain was in this... my body was, too. But something was missing..." He focused on Houben and explained, with more intricacy and annunciation than ever before, "When I look at the way *you* talk about fighting for your country... the way that Preul kid puts his heart into fitness and beautiful women... and, of course, how the honorary Mark Buck feels about being an O-4? I'm reminded that, as Steven Pressfield pointed out: when all else appears dark, and we feel lost in life? Resistance is our internal compass, unfailingly pointing true north, to where our destiny lies. And for me? For too long, I've been resisting where my heart *truly* belongs..." Belichick sighed again. "Fellas... I *hate* this shit. Living half my life at sea, directing sailors to do cleaning stations because of the 'pride' or whatever," he rolled his eyes, "of keeping the ship the cleanest in the Navy — as if that matters..." he scoffed with annoyance. "And those *god damn* GQ drills!" He shook his head in disgust. "What *happened* to me?! My life used to be about planning... strategizing... *winning*. And even the losses — they drove me crazy, alright. But at least they gave me *something to build upon*. But *this* job?" He scoffed once more. "This job is a fucking politician part-task trainer. Kissing asses of superiors until I get promoted to kiss new asses, living in a constant conservative state of fear of losing my job when some nimrod doesn't follow a checklist, and essentially —" he sighed, exhausted, "essentially just running the agenda of some buffoon whose 'claim of credibility' is being a pawn that's moved a few spaces further than me on the chessboard." Belichick looked repulsed and declared, "With all due respect, men... I'm calling it a career."

"What!" >SADCLAM< exclaimed in shock. "Sir... but the Olympics... you were the mastermind behind the entire strike..."

"But Captain..." JABA said with emotion in his voice, "It was *you*. It was *you* who believed in me — even more than I believed in myself! Entrusting me to fly — inexperienced and unqualified — along the most low-percentage mission set of all time on an unvetted low-level route..."

CP simply nodded slowly with a very serious look; his expression did his talking.

Belichick sighed and said, "Fellas, the Olympics was the happiest I've ever been in this job—and ironically, it's also what made me realize that this isn't right for me. JABA, when I sent you on that MARSTRIKE..." he took a deep breath and looked at Brady, "I felt like it was that 2002 Super Bowl all over again, handing the ball—with just over a minute left and no timeouts—to a hungry kid with all the aspiration in the world. And I realized, gents, watching you all go out and *do your jobs*? Executing the plan *as* briefed, flexing *as* required, working *as* a *team*... and then watching the way you celebrated, as we achieved that competitive greatness—*together*?" He sighed again and admitted, "I realized—then and there—that the only part of this job I truly enjoyed was the part that brought me back to those cold, snowy January evenings in New England..." he looked longingly into the distance.

"Tom?" CP asked, noticing how oddly silent that GOAT was. "How do *you* feel about this?"

"Guys..." Brady started, "I have to admit something, too..."

Belichick looked over at him. "What is it, Tom?"

"I love winning... I love executing... and I love my Chippy teammates," he emphasized, pointing to the trio of them. "... But I only *like* the work. I don't *love* those late nights memorizing BFM videos, practicing countless DCA reps in sims, or studying the newest tac recs; not like I loved prep for a random game in October—planning for one game, watching film on two different defensive back's tendencies for three hours every day; drilling the same four-step drop back, five-count quick slants six-hundred times to perfection; wrapping up by internalizing the seven newest playbook additions during my eighth ice-bath session. Winning the Olympics felt great, sure! But shit— it's *easy* to love the results of *anything*... When you love the *effort*, though? That's something *damn* special, babe."

"So... you guys are both quitting?" CP asked bluntly, as JABA kept trying to say 'eighth ice-bath session' to himself without tripping up.

"I can't..." Brady lamented. "I still owe another 5 years before I can separate..."

"Captain?" >SADCLAM< asked.

"Don't call me Captain anymore," Belichick said gruffly. "There's only one 'C' word I want to go by." He then smiled at the trio of Chippies and said, "Listen—you guys taught me something that I have long forgotten, and am thankful to remember again: Never leave a good time for a good time. Coaching in the NFL—as much as the commissioner and the media drive me crazy—is where my heart remains. And, well..." he bobbed his head back and forth slightly, even growing a bit *giddy* as he announced, "As of *this morning*... the New England Patriots have a new coach."

"What?!" All four exclaimed together, before Brady asked, "Coach! But... they finished in last place this season... and they have *no* offense!" Easing back on his criticism a bit, he offered, "I mean, they *do* have some good weapons at wideout and some solid running backs, but come *on* – their numbers are stagnant! They were losing games 13-6 last year!"

"Not a bad defense, though, huh?" Belichick said with a smirk.

"Sure..." Brady said begrudgingly, "But what *good* is that defense if you can't put up tuddies?! Yes, they have a high-caliber tight end, and yes, their special teams are rock-solid too, but they're missing that *fire*, that *game-changer*, that *killer instinct*..."

"*We're* missing a quarterback..." Belichick acknowledged.

"Yes!" Brady replied. "And I'm well aware of the current state of free agency, and the lack of incoming college standouts under center – there are *no* quality QBs available!"

"Oh, there's one, alright..." Belichick said with a grin.

"Who?!" Brady asked, confused, looking around for answers.

But all he saw in return were smiles.

"Tom..." >SADCLAM< expressed, "I learned all about your insatiable love for the game from my Training O, FISTY. I strove to model my work ethic after your relentless desire, and sought to accomplish as much in the jet as you did on the field. If I were to leave this industry, I'd be going in the wrong direction from my compass' true north. But the more I hear you talk, the more it's clear to me: You've been traveling away from *your* heart's direction for too long – it's time you finally tuned up Mom's TACAN, put the needle on the nose, and got back in the game."

CP nodded and said, "Tom – you could seduce any girl you want, and get VIP treatment at literally any club on this flat earth. Yet, instead, you spend your Saturday nights watching game film and thinking of new route schemes for upcoming defenses. If I didn't know who you were, I'd think you were a complete loser." He softened his face, smiling, and added, "But then again, I recall those late-night weekend lifts at the Chapel of Champions, or blowing off a night of raging to enjoy steak, wine, and a viewing of *The Dark Knight* with one of my beautiful ex-wives... and I can't help but admire another professional's passion for their craft. To take away that burning desire in a man is to rob him of even more testosterone than that of seed oils and soy. Go, Thomas – bring the Patriots back to the echelons of excellence my generation always knew them for. But more importantly... answer *your* life's calling; not the Navy's..."

Brady looked back and forth amongst the group, before finally reminding them, "But guys... my contract... my time still owed... these stupid Navy pilot obligations...!"

Belichick gave a slight smile and nodded over to JABA, who understood completely. The coach handed him an unmarked blue routing folder.

"By the power invested in me as a Lieutenant Commander..." JABA began, opening the file.

Brady stared in disbelief.

"From this point onward..." Buck continued, taking out a multicolored pen from his pocket and scribbling his signature on the paper inside. "I hereby..."

Holding his head in awe, Brady's eyes widened even further.

"Declare your contact to be..."

The 5-time Super Bowl MVP was shaking.

"Terminated!" JABA shouted with glee.

Brady was speechless. He looked at his wrists, as if shackles were freshly removed—just like the Genie from *Aladdin*. He looked back up at JABA, tears in his eyes—and gave the LCDR a gigantic, championship-level hug.

It was poetic justice, and quintessential 'JABA': In his first act as an O-4, he had used his powers to *support* a JO.

Tom then turned to a smiling Belichick, and the two embraced—with Brady shouting, his voice rife with exhilaration, "Let's fucking *GOOO!!!*"

"Ah, I missed you, buddy," Bill said, the two sharing a warm reunion—not just with each other, but with their hearts' yearnings.

"I missed you too, Coach," Brady said, teary and euphoric with being released from his OBLISERV. "I missed you, the games, the brutal practices, the long summer training camps, watching film after big wins—hell, even after the *losses*—that motivational feeling, walking into the building on Monday, ready to make adjustments and *hang dong* on whoever was unlucky enough to play us the following weekend! Coach..." he said, beaming, "I missed the *shit*..."

"Well, Tom..." Belichick started with a grin, "If you really missed it *that* much... Got time to watch film on the Jaguars this afternoon? We have them week 1..."

Brady stared at his former—and now *current*—coach and said, with not a tone of jest at all, "Absolutely, coach. Abso-fucking-lutely."

The two looked back at the Chippies, and Belichick said, "Thank you again for everything, gents. And congratulations, Mark. I'm gonna miss you guys! *All* of you... and *all* of my time working with the indomitable Dambusters."

"You guys are true inspirations not just to naval aviation," Brady declared, "but to driven men and women everywhere in the world. *Never* forget that—and *never* lose the fire that keeps you getting better *every single day.* And hey!" he added with a grin, "Expect season tickets in the mail—I'll see you boys in September!"

The two quickly hurried off, with only five months to go until opening kick-off—and not a moment to waste in their quest for 'the *next* one'...

"Jesus Christ!" >SADCLAM< exclaimed. "Season tickets?! *Fuck* yeah!"

CP smirked. "Are you even gonna go, Chris? *Sunday nights*? Won't that infringe on your brief rehearsals for Monday Morning MARSTRIKES?"

Houben chuckled in reference to the latest CVW-5 fleet-wide implementation, and said, "Good point—well, I suppose I could take one or two off, and delegate them to the only man on this earth who actually *achieved* a valid, non-white-carded one!" he said, grinning at Buck.

JABA shook his head, laughing and smiling bashfully, and acknowledged, "Ahh, guys... I'm gonna miss those two..." He then cringed for a moment, adding, "And I *realllly* hope Big Navy doesn't get too upset about me doing that—you know, with our pilot shortage and all..."

"Yeah," CP interjected. "I didn't realize O-4s could execute CNO-level decisions..."

"Neither did I... *partner*..."

JABA looked behind his shoulder, where Admiral Flynn stood with his arms folded, now donning his green Gunslingers cowboy hat and leather vest over his summer whites, with a belt-attached revolver holster and plastic toy gun inside of it. But, below the shadow of his brim, he wore a wide grin on his face. "Mark Buck, you sly son of a bitch... I saw what you did back there—and *god dammit,* do I approve!"

"FISTY!" Buck called out with a nervous smile, "I didn't realize you were still here! I hope I didn't just exacerbate our manning issue..."

"JABA, you're a sweet, sweet boy." FISTY reassured him, "The Navy's gonna be just fine without those two legends in their ranks—and yet, even in their brief stint, with what they accomplished in the Admin Olympics? They'll be embedded forever in naval aviation lore, just like Darrell Revis' 2015 impact during his short tenure in New England!" he declared with a smile. "And besides... I overheard what they both said—Bill *hates* this shit. Yes, Brady was a little more 'PC,' but read between the lines, boys—they're longing to be where their 'resistance' beckons; the dream they're both pursuing, and yet are *terrified* to realize. Because, my Chippy brethren, in that stirring trepidation? One will find the path they *must* take." Raising his finger, he declared, "If you want to discover your true calling in life, look to the quest that fills you with the most excitement—" he raised an eyebrow, turned his face, and adjusted his cowboy hat, "matched equally with *fear*..." Returning his hands to hips, nodding slowly and beaming—his green cowboy outfit selling the look of a wise sage—he concluded: "*Therein* lies your ultimate destiny."

Smiling, >SADCLAM< said, "FISTY, I don't know *how* we survived this journey without you! Thank *god* we had you back up, Full Mission Capable to intercept Robo-Hinge! And god *damn*—that boat footage of the tank kill was *so fucking sick!*"

Casually brushing it aside, Flynn shrugged and said, "Ah, guys... here's the thing: you *did* do it without me. You didn't need me—and if anything, I was a *burden,* being carried around in that god-awful state! And you didn't need *me,* because of the work *you* put in during your time in the Chippies! Yes, maybe I passed on lessons learned and the warrior mindset skills from TB12—but it was *you* guys who implemented them. You—*all* of you!" he said happily, looking around at the three young men as he drew and spun the toy gun on his finger. "You guys made me *so* proud in those Olympics! They always told us that a good Training O would leave their squadron completely self-sufficient without their presence... and to see the way you executed in saving not just me, but the *entire* administrative reputation of this nation? It was the most satisfaction I've ever felt about this little red Patch on my shoulder," he said happily, tapping his right arm.

He then turned serious, and added, "But you know what *else* you guys did?" He exhaled, holstered the toy gun, and gestured outward. "You guys *saved Nickels.* I know he's not with us anymore, and I know most will never understand the full depths that he fell to—or the 28-3-eqsue comeback of a *lifetime* he put forth to defend this beautiful country and redeem his reputation while furthering the 'Nickels legend'—but you three witnessed it all first-hand. And seeing you all here today, and how far you've come since our careers parted long ago?" FISTY smiled as he shook his head in awe. "I personally believe that, before his untimely death, Sam Rowland was back to the Good Dude we all knew and loved—because of *you guys.* Working together—one team, one fight, one cohesive unit of pipe-hitters. A thing of true, indomitable beauty."

As the three men smiled at Admiral Flynn, he put his fist on his heart, just atop his plastic sheriff's badge, and mourned, "I just wish he was here to see the progress *you* all made as well... he would've been so proud..."

"It's not fair..." >SADCLAM< said, kicking the ground. "He didn't deserve this... I can't believe Juice would betray his own brother like that. I'd always thought what Sam did was bad... but shit, he didn't try to *massacre* another man's reputation like that!" He scoffed in disgust, adding, "And to think... I used to believe Juice was such a hard worker and dedicated pilot—an all-around Good Dude—and yes, maybe even an heir to the legacy Nickels had created." Rolling his eyes, he concluded, "Clearly, I completely misjudged that asshole's character..."

CP, clenching his jaw, lamented, "He tricked us all, CLAM. Ultimately, he was even more insecure than Sam, trying to do whatever he could to make himself look great by undercutting others." He shook his head. "That guy wasn't interested in climbing—he'd been Diseased with Me the entire time. That insidious superspreader took Nickels away from us forever..."

"Fuck Juice..." >SADCLAM< cursed with tightened fists. "I'll *never* forgive him for the things he admitted doing to Sam and our squadron in that email. He was no Good Dude—he's a *Bad Guy.* And thanks to his unprofessionalism, incompetence, and inability to treat sensitive material accordingly, the whole world knows it."

Noticing his former Training O looking a bit disconcerted, fidgeting with his green bolo tie, JABA asked, "FISTY? You ok?"

Taking a deep breath, FISTY shook his head. "I'm just not so sure, boys..."

"Not sure?" CP repeated. "About *what?*"

Pausing to consider his words, FISTY looked up for a moment, then re-engaged eye contact to ask, "Do you *really* think Juice would be so foolish as to send an *extremely* classified 5Ws update on an unclassified network?"

"Well, he said all secure means of communication were down, and that it was critical to communicate the information to his department head—'critical enough to risk sending over the Noddik Internet Protocol Router,' to use his words," >SAD-CLAM< explained. "Plus, he's the one who shut the QNAP down, so he knew the ship would be destroyed imminently. Knowing what I do now about that fake, sycophantic kiss-ass Juice, I wouldn't be surprised if just couldn't *stand* to end his life without getting a little more career credit and validation from LCDR Robo-Hinge—did you notice he signed the email 'Very *Very* Respectfully?'" Houben scoffed. "Well, enjoy your Noddik Purple Heart, douche—I hope it burns as black as your soul in hell."

"Jesus Christ, CLAM!" FISTY exclaimed.

"What?!" >SADCLAM< reacted. "This guy falsified an entire NAVADMIN about our boy Nickels—and sent it from *Kyle's* email! He tried to frame *two* Chippies! And the stuff he came up with... it was horrendous. The world would've *never* forgiven Nickels if those were really his words!"

FISTY shrugged, still skeptical, but admitting, "Yeah... that's true..." he then winced and countered, "But then again, Juice never struck me as the kind of guy who cared about approval from soulless douchebags..."

"FISTY, that Robo-Hinge guy?" CP added. "He infiltrated my gym when you were passed out, and I've gotta say... he seemed like a total schnarf, spooling up and taking shots—literal APG-47 shots—more rapidly than I've ever seen before. I could see him being a *very* hingey DH—tasking and demanding information from Juice with no appreciation for practicality or contingency circumstances—especially if bi-weekly updates were due. Maybe Juice wanted *so* badly to get this tool off his back that he didn't fully consider how bad it would be for him and the Noddiks if this email was hacked and released."

"Guys, listen..." FISTY said with his arms folded, "I can assure you that Bobby Ward knows a thing or two about proper security procedures—another subset of admin. After all, he was the one who busted our intel O for sneaking the Nintendo 64 in the vault."

Looking for clarification, JABA asked, "So, what are you saying, then, FISTY? You think somebody else wrote that email instead of Juice?"

"No, no, not at all..." FISTY answered, rubbing his chin. "It was signed with his digital CAC—and it would be impossible to fabricate such a thing. But, what if..." he took a deep breath and exhaled, asking, "What *if...* he somehow sent this email... *knowing* it would get leaked?" He leaned his body forward, hands back on his hips, and suggested, "A *lot* of things don't add up—did you see the time stamp on his email? On the Chippy superfan Reddit, there is a contingent of conspiracy theorists that derived the ship's proposed capsize time, based on the nerdy science data found in corrosion forensics from the wreckage. They took the projected time and compared it to the email—guys..." FISTY's eyes widened, "That email was apparently sent *after* the ship had hypothetically been underwater—for *hours.* If Juice had really gone down with this ship, then..." FISTY sighed in frustration and trailed off, "It just... it just doesn't make sense..."

"Well, I mean, if the email for sure came from him, and he knew it would be made available to the general public..." Houben asked, "Then what *reason* would Juice have to admit to lying about everything? Why take responsibility for this false FITREP statement of dispute attempting to incriminate Sam? And if Kyle had forged a secret alliance with Nickels—like Juice claimed—then why would he have sent the FITREP statement to the 99_All_Hands distro just hours before the ship went down?" He narrowed his eyes in confusion and reminded, "Juice *hated* Sam, FISTY. Why would he reveal the truth and forever brand *himself*—and not Nickels—as the quintessential Bad Guy, after spending so much of his career trying to prove that he was the ultimate Good Dude?"

FISTY bobbed his head back and forth, then offered up his hands and said, "Because maybe he *was,* CLAM. Maybe he—like Nickels—saved his best Good Dude move for last, selflessly sacrificing his reputation to preserve that of another. I don't know if I agree with it or not—I suppose that's up to the reader... to one's point of view... to *history*..." he looked downcast as he shrugged; but then smiled softly and countered, "But you know what they say: Fuck history------and *fuck* the dashes. Whatever Juice truly did, he did because, *in his heart,* he felt it was right. And if a man acts in such a way, then—regardless of what anyone else thinks or believes—*he* can at least say he showed the courage to act by his own principles—*not* somebody else's. And while we may Monday morning quarterback others' decisions, or disagree with the shade they chose to paint with..." FISTY sighed and avowed, "At least their life has *color,* and they are *living*—and that's a *beautiful* thing in the otherwise black-and-white life of merely *existing*." He looked around at the Chippies and asked, "... Does anybody disagree with this logical conclusion?"

Despite being uncertain about the tac-admin of it all, the three men begrudgingly nodded, as JABA expressed, "We may never fully know what happened... but I suppose that's the beauty of life, and the intrigue of the legends that unfold..."

A silent approval filled the space between them... until a text tone went off—the sound of a mickey—and FISTY checked his phone, sheepishly admitting, "Sorry, I usually leave it on vibrate for this very reason..." As he read his text, though, his mouth curled into a wide beam. "Boys," he announced, "Let's... fucking... *go!*"

"What is it?" JABA asked.

"Brady and Belichick just both officially signed with New England!" Flynn announced happily. "And there's already rumors that Gronk, Edelman, Amendola, and even *Randy Moss* are in talks to join the team!"

Laughing, CP pointed out, "FISTY, those guys all retired half a decade ago... do you seriously want a bunch of guys in their late 40s and early 50s trying to bring about championship glory?"

"Psh — says the guy who's still obsessed with Dua Lipa, Ana de Armas, Shakira, Doja Cat... uhh, need me to continue, bro?" >SADCLAM snarked. "Or how about this author?! All those celebrities in the WYFMIFM yacht scene — *Tony Hawk? Jessica Alba? Jennifer Lopez?* How washed up and out of touch *is* this guy?!"

FISTY chuckled and said, "Guys... what's wrong with us? We really *are* just constantly longing for our pasts, aren't we? We just can't get enough of the 'glory days.' We spend our entire lives trying to revisit these overromanticized days of old, getting wrapped up in bygone memories... when in reality, the greatest days are *still ahead* — for those brave enough to climb further. One day, my fellow Dambuster brethren, we will look upon *those* memories — yet to come — with even *greater* fondness!"

"FISTY, to be honest, I'm shocked you're not going *insane* right now with this GOAT news," JABA cracked with a grin.

The admiral laughed. "Ah, you know... I can't say I'm exactly *shocked*... You see, ever since Brady and I exchanged numbers after that incredible Olympic run, while he's been working here in Iwakuni? It's been *surreal*, Mark. We'll hit the gym together after work, throw the pigskin around while reciting EPs, talk strategy in the vault, and even develop our own tactics beyond what the bros are teaching these days. I really felt like I was able to unearth the man that is 'Tom Brady,' and see him as more than just some big-time celebrity — as crazy as it sounds, he's become like a best friend.

"But, as I got to know him better and better, I started to see..." FISTY said with a leading tone, "started to see the *truth*. As much as he said he was happy in FITREP debriefs, and claimed that 'this is where he belonged' during midterm counseling... well, far more times than I can count, I'd catch him in between briefing lab reps or after working hours in the vault, doing what he *truly* loved: Watching old game film on half-time speed, drawing up new plays on the white boards, even studying draft copies of modern NFL threat defenses as if he were prepping for them that Sunday! Sure, the man enjoys the tac-air community — but he still lives, breaths, and *bleeds* football. And you know what?!" FISTY looked at the boys confidently below his cowboy hat and declared, "I *applaud* him for heading back to the big show — because as much as I love Tom Brady, the aviator..." he shrugged and acknowledged, "at heart, he's Tom Brady, the *quarterback*."

"And a champion in both regards, nonetheless," CP affirmed with a raised chin, drawing a smiling nod of approval from FISTY.

"Wow!" JABA said with a shocked look of delight. "FISTY, you're living your *dream!*"

FISTY laughed and replied, "It's funny you say that, Mark. I *am* living my dream... but it has nothing to do with Tom Brady. Rather, it's this," he gestured around him. "Because I love Bill Belichick too, and I can respect our differences. But, unlike Bill? I *love* this shit. I *love* the work that it takes to be great in this industry. I *love* the parts of this job that drive others crazy. To sum it up: *I love this process.* And guess what—stand by, boys, because with this new Patriots season ahead? You better *believe* I've got a whole new cache of briefing labs and tactical lessons to teach," he said with a grin.

"But first and foremost, it's this: Everyone has some *crazy* shit that they love, and everybody else *hates.* The other 99% of the world will say that you're insane to have 'fun' doing whatever monotonous tasks stand along the treacherous path... but you couldn't care less—because *you're* the man in the arena... *doing* this shit... having a *blast.* The results, the views, the end product—you like them, of course—just like *any-one* would! But what makes the shit so special to you is that you don't *begrudge* the journey to get there—you *live* for that journey."

He took a long look out at the flight line through the window, where the entire CVW-5 fleet was parked in an orderly fashion—ready to be flown to the extremes of their envelopes, decades past their predicted shelf life. He looked to his right, where the schedule was being written for Monday, with him penciled in as the Blue IP for a Level 3 check ride—a day that would undoubtedly become a 12-hour ordeal due to that flight *alone.* And he looked around him in the room, where he saw squadron patches from all over the Navy—young junior LTJGs who were excited to meet the legendary Buck Angel, and senior CDRs who couldn't *wait* to congratulate Mark after watching the young man grow from LT Chippy FNG to a proud, golden oak leaf-donning LCDR. As he looked at *all* of these things, FISTY folded his arms, smiled, and said, "Guys... I feel I could do this shit for the rest of my life..."

Marveling and inspired, >SADCLAM< asked, "Hey—you guys down to hop in the sims for a few quick reps?"

FISTY checked his watch. "Chris... it's 1600 on a Friday afternoon..." He looked back at Houben—then grinned mischievously. "... You're goddamn *right* I'm in!"

The two high-fived as CP rolled his eyes, stretched his arms, and said, "*Weeeee-hhhhhhhlll*, it's about time for me to hit the ol' dusty trail..."

"Come *on*, Andrew..." >SADCLAM< encouraged, "This is the life we chose, brother. There are other planets out there looking to get better than us every single *day.* It's no different than lifting—every single rep makes you better. The reps won't all be pretty, and they *certainly* won't all be PRs—but putting in that *daily* effort is going to drive you beyond 95% of the field. For better or for worse, we chose a career that doesn't allow for throttling back and bringing a sagger into the 1-wire. You've got to fight this battle internally *just* as much as you do against adversaries—fight the urge to slacken, to loosen your standards, to take it easy and coast off past laurels. Because the minute you stop learning? This game will humble the hell out of you, via a missile right in the face."

FISTY nodded, very pleased with his former JO.

"And if nothing else, CP—don't do it for me. Don't do it for FISTY. Don't even do it for the country," Houben paused, then emphasized with passion, "Do it for *yourself*, brother; for the personal satisfaction of knowing you did everything you possibly could to reach the ceiling of your potential."

"Ok, ok, Jesus Christ, CLAM! I'll go..." CP resigned—before gesturing to his friends and adding, "But speaking of lifting? If we're giving our daily devotionals in the Tactical Tabernacle? You'd *all* better be hitting the Church of Iron with me afterward."

"Oh, definitely!" >SADCLAM< insisted.

"And I'm talking deadlifts, squats, *and* bench!" CP warned with wide eyes. "You're not going to get big without hitting the large compound movements, Chris!"

"Chill, bro—I said yes!" Houben said with a laugh.

"Hold up—squats *and* deadlifts on the same day?!" FISTY blurted out. "Now *that's*..." he paused, grinned, and emphasized, "Flynnsanity!"

CP started laughing and said, "Oh yeah, I forgot to ask you about that! They're really calling the movie '*Top Gun: Flynnsanity*'?! FISTY..." he tilted his head down with a sly grin, "Tell me you didn't suggest that..."

FISTY raised his hands and defended himself with, "Hey, you gotta get your name out there somehow—it's how you get ahead in this biz! Just ask TC."

Rolling his eyes, CP chuckled. "FISTY, you sellout..."

>SADCLAM< laughed and interjected, "Hey, come on, give the guy a break! He got an air-to-air kill with a fucking jettisoned centerline tank! He saved the entire ship from impending doom! This guy deserves a movie—at the *least!*"

CP brushed aside the air and said, "Ah, what the hell... you're right, Chris—why *not* capitalize on this? Besides, I must admit—it's pretty cool that you've got Mr. Cruise himself running your stunts."

"Hey, he owed me, after my work in the sequel that single-handedly saved the movie industry," FISTY said with a wink. "And after *Top Gun: Flynnsanity*, he's promised me a supporting role in Mission: Impossible 22, and a deal to get in an Indiana Jones reboot. And don't tell anyone, but..." he looked around and whispered, "JABA, I'm gonna pitch your VR scenario to Paramount. Tom Brady already agreed to play himself in the film!"

"No way!" JABA said with a smile. "FISTY, that's awesome!"

"Hey, CP..." FISTY whispered again, elbowing Preul. "We've got *Sydney Sweeney* playing a role in MI:22! Maybe I can put in a good word for you!"

CP laughed and said, "Oh, gosh... I already told you, FISTY—after the divorce from Doja Cat, I'm *done* falling in love with these celebrities! I need to focus on myself, this job, and this physique!"

"Oh my god... *Andrew Preul?*" a siren-esque voice called from across the room.

The four men turned... and standing there—wearing a dress with more holes than a Class-A Swiss-cheese mishap—was a more-stunning-than-ever Megan Fox.

Andrew's jaw dropped at the sight of her. "What are you *doing* here, my queen?"

She smiled and said, "I... well, I saw you on Fat Chucky's Cruise Ship, and I was *intrigued*... Then I heard about the whole Admin Olympics thing, and then this promotion ceremony, and I thought you might be here... and I... well..." she giggled, "I just thought it would be nice to meet you..."

His cheeks reddening, CP smiled back and asked, "Well? Was it?"

Growing bashful herself, she softly replied, "Yeah... yeah, it was..."

"What about everything else that happened?" CP asked skeptically. "You literally hit on Nickels just like 10 chapters ago."

Growing a bit defensive, Megan explained, "Well, I mean, I was only flirting with him to make the plot advance... plus, he sort of called me a 'hoe' at the end there, so... yeah..."

"Well, the 'hoe' thing was sort of a pun on our squadron slogan, and I don't really know how that advanced the—" but then CP shook his head, remembering the seductive powers of not verbally nuking it, and said, "You know what? Never mind." He smiled warmly and added, "I'm glad you're here. There's actually something I wanted to talk to you about..."

"What is it?" the beauty asked.

CP grinned at his three friends, before looking back at his lover. "Let's chat in the nearby fan room." He stuck his hand out and offered, "Come with me, and I'll take you there."

Giggling again, the siren took his arm, and the two ran off for the most romantic place in Naval history, as CP looked back one last time and said, before disappearing around the corner, "I'll see you boys on Yellowbrick later!"

"Oh, Clown Penis... never change, bud," FISTY said to no one in particular with a shake of his head and a chuckle. "The heart truly is a mystifying needle..."

"So it is," >SADCLAM said with a smile, "And mine's pointing to the sim bay." He looked around and shrugged, "Guess it's just us three—light div contingency; let's fucking go!"

The two laughed as they started heading toward the sims, when FISTY looked back and called out, "Yo, Marcus—you coming, hot dog?"

JABA, who'd been focusing outside for some time now, reacted, "Huh?!" But before anyone could answer, he shrugged and said, "Ah, thanks, guys, but I think I'm just gonna take a quick walk outside and get some fresh air."

FISTY gave him a shocked look and then grinned at CLAM, sarcastically pointing and mocking, "Get a load of this guy—a DH for an hour, and he's already blowing off tactics! *Heh!*"

"Mark, you'll still be down for Yellowbrick later, right?" Houben asked.

"Oh, big time!" JABA answered with a smile, as he waved goodbye to his friends and headed outside the hangar, officially ending his first day of work as a Lieutenant Commander.

~

"Docking complete!" the healthy elderly man announced as he ran his hands through his slicked-back hair and double-checked the integrity of the knots attaching his boat—the *Lil B*—to the Venice Beach dock.

Charles "WYFMIFM" Kennedy took a deep breath and exhaled, soaking in the feel of the warm 0800 California sun, the smell of the Pacific Ocean, the taste of West Coast superiority, and the sounds of the inhabitants outside surfing, walking dogs, running on the beach... and of course, pumping iron at the Venice Beach Gold's Gym. "Thanks, Pat! See you in a week!" WYFMIFM called out, as he donned his sunglasses and departed the ferry, his walking stick guiding him.

As soon as he reached the sand, he took his flip-flops off and grounded his feet with Mother Earth. "Ahhh..." he audibly exhaled. He smelled a nearby Whole Foods— he would undoubtedly be stopping by later on for some grass-fed ribeyes, cage-free eggs, and unpasteurized, raw butter. But first? He had something important to attend to...

"Hello!" he called out, as he arrived at the Gold's Gym front desk. "I'd like to use my day pass!"

"Ummm... I don't know... can I see it..." the service attendant asked, more focused on whoever she was texting.

She smelled great; she sounded gorgeous; she was completely checked-out and kind of a ditz. WYFMIFM could tell this was a stereotypical hot front-desk chick, only hired to bring in customers with her smile and looks. Fortunately, Kennedy was impervious to both. "Certainly!" WYFMIFM obliged politely, as he reached into his gym bag and handed her his pass.

The hot bimbo looked up from her phone, finally made eye contact with WYFMIFM—noticing his dark glasses—and said, "Uhh... yeah, this pass says 'Local Residents only,' and you... *definitely* seem like you're not from around here..." Then she sounded surprised as she realized, "Wait a second—you're that guy who uses the bench for *hours* at a time! No, you *cannot* use this pass. Actually, you can't even work out here at all—my manager made that very clear last year."

WYFMIFM sighed, pulled out one hundred dollars cash, and said, "How about I give you this *and* the pass—and you let me in and don't tell anyone I was here. Sound good, doll face?"

After a pause, he felt the money taken from his hand as the girl quickly muttered, "Have a good workout."

"Thank you!" he remarked as he walked past the ditz and onto the gym floor. One hundred bucks... what did he care? Money was but an imaginary tangible resource and worthless commodity in a world full of adventures to take, passions to chase, and potential to realize... Plus, the currency was all counterfeit LSO lucky bucks that he printed back in his DH days as part of an illegal pass-upgrading ring.

As he walked in, he took in the scene via the sounds and scents. He was reminded quickly of why they called this the Crystal Palace of gyms: Benches, squat racks, deadlift platforms... *everywhere*. An impressive lack of worthless cardio equipment—*just* enough to be lethal without saturating the entire gym. Dumbbells well beyond triple digits, and multiple sets of them. The equipment? Despite being outside, it felt as if it were in *pristine* condition. The patrons? Well, it was a bunch of roided-out bodybuilders, that's for sure, based on the heavy grunts and conversations overheard. But amongst the air—filled with PED abuse and hyper-inflated testosterone—was the aura of something else WYFMIFM could feel: *Determination. Effort. Desire.* He smiled at this collection of freakish individuals who—when it came down to the most basic levels of human discipline and willful suffering for improvement—had *no* problem sacrificing.

WYFMIFM had the route memorized from all his visits over the years. He set down his gym bag—a generic green flight helmet bag—next to his favorite bench, loaded the bar up with a plate on each side, and started his first of nineteen sets, each for five reps. At the end of his fifth rep, he racked the bar and moved his nonexistent gaze around, doing his best to sense the different people in the gym.

In one corner was a lean but strong man, doing a crossfit-type workout, seemingly training like a SPECOPS guy. There was something different about him... like he was from a different universe. His numbers were quite impressive—and so were his levels of endurance. As the man finished his long set of squatting 225 lbs—WYFMIFM counted *30* reps—he exhaled heavily and took off his Inov-8 shoes, preparing to deadlift. WYFMIFM could tell that this was a man who got things done, was never in the mood for bullshit, and was *not* one to let *anyone* outwork him—in the gym or *elsewhere*. This guy would be successful at whatever he did, be it D&D designer, Noddik doctor, or even Test Pilot grad naval aviator...

Just down the floor was a softer boy—not much muscle mass, and a decent amount of body fat he could afford to lose. The boy was getting ready to do seal rows—the innovative and ultra-effective back exercise well-known in the Leangains community, but still yet to gain mainstream tracking. He was super-setting with basic dumbbell curls and drinking an intra-workout weight-gainer shake—worthless stuff... 'Clearly much to learn about the fitness community via multiple failures and much wasted time,' WYFMIFM chuckled to himself. 'A job in gym membership sales and a good mentor ought to help the boy's confidence...' he thought with a smile. And despite being blind, the former OPSO could tell the young lad was wearing very try-hard clothing: an oversized cutoff San Juan Spartans shirt—revealing a tattoo on his back, as if the nerd wanted to appear tougher—and a backwards hat—a *Pikachu* hat. As the former OPSO took in the entire sensory scene, he could tell: the kid looked like a complete dweeb, considering how pasty and 'not-jacked' he was. But *dammit*, he was trying; seeking inner confidence via a physique that exhibited effort and discipline, on his journey for personal growth and accomplishments well beyond that. As WYFMIFM heard the iron clank the elevated bench before slamming on the ground—good, full ROM seal rows—he smiled in admiration at the potential the young dork carried.

And far across the room was a man on the rowing machine, glailing away loudly as he put forth incredible amounts of power and speed on the erg. He was a wiry young lad, with dreadlocks hanging down to his arms. Kennedy listened as a worker walked up to the man and asked him to quiet down, to which the rower started hissing. When they told the boy he would be banned if he didn't 'cease his hissing,' he simply laughed obnoxiously and walked toward the exit, yelling something along the lines of 'Hey Loogie Boy, wave off!' A group of friends joined him—a group featuring so many new faces, new names, and new auras that WYFMIFM didn't know and couldn't recognize—but could *tell* they were engrained with Chippy Pride and Dambuster Drive. The group, with their own unique set of inside jokes and deployment memories unbeknownst to WYFMIFM or the author, got on their bikes and pedaled away, the wiry kid now screaming, 'Cease fire, cease fire!' WYFMIFM knew the boy was an odd one, and also knew he was nowhere *near* a focal point in this story—nor were *any* of these *fucking* new guys. But it put a smile on his face nonetheless, knowing that despite *his* era being over, there were still many Chippy legends out there living their best lives, with even more yet to come.

And then Kennedy noticed it—and he nearly couldn't believe his senses: On the squat rack, no more than twenty feet away from him, was a presence of good dudesmanship that he hadn't felt in *years*. The man was taking a breather between sets after squatting—by WYFMIFM's auditory assessment of the bar slamming the rack—about 385 pounds. He looked great—*god*, did he look great. Definitely below 10% body fat, yet still with a substantial amount of natural muscle. And he wasn't alone, either—he was with a beautiful woman, as the two happily pursued suffering in the gym together. WYFMIFM couldn't help but beam as he felt the love between them—working out, enjoying life, discussing their next travel plans—

"Hey, Sam, can I get a quick spot? My son's off playing Roblox and getting bullied by his sister..."

It was a familiar voice... one WYFMIFM hadn't heard in an even *longer* time—but then he remembered...

"Oh my god, John, 315 pounds? What are you doing?!" another woman's voice called out. "You barely even got 225 in your prime Chippy days!"

'John?' WYFMIFM thought, confused. 'Who is—'

But then Sam shouted back, "Oh, shoot! Yeah, I'll be right there, Bobby!" referring to his friend by his more familiar name.

And then... for the first time in decades... WYFMIFM saw. He saw *everything*...

"One More Time" – blink-182

Robert John "Juice" Ward and Sam "Nickels" Rowland—*alive*—pumping iron together, happily with their families, getting nutrients of all kinds under the almighty California sun. WYFMIFM watched, marveling as Bobby struggled—the weight nearly pinning his chest—and Sam yelled, "C'mon, man, you *got* this!" Ward grunted and exhaled heavily, with Rowland encouraging him more, "Push it out, bro; get that shit up—sorry, sorry!" quickly apologizing to his wife for swearing around the Wards' kids. And then—after seeing the bar start to drop *just* slightly—Sam yelled, with one last shot of testosterone-driven inspiration, "Bobby! You're a fucking *NATOPS-quali-fied, Patch-wearing, single-seat big-meat fighter pilot with T levels off the charts*—so accept the challenge, look it in the eyes, and show that weight what the *fuck* you're capable of!" And as Sam gave apologies again, Ward gave one last exertion of effort—and pushed that shit up, grunting and racking the triple-loaded bar with authority. He sat up, exhaled dramatically, and pumped a fist, while Sam clasped his other hand and brought it in for a bro hug. "That's what I'm fucking talking about, Bobby!" he whispered to keep his swears inaudible, "That's what I'm fucking *talking about*!"

"I almost got stuck there, man." Ward forced the words out between deep breaths after they broke the embrace. "Almost gave in..."

"Life is ultimately a war of resilience, man," Sam grinned. "The greatest of victories will be achieved by he who is simply the last one to give up. Welcome to the fucking *three-plates* club, bro!" The two high-fived—testosterone exploding as their palm contact was *perfect*.

"Alright, man," Bobby said with a grin, "Get warmed up—because as of now? That's a club of *one*!"

Sam laughed and yelled, "Bet up!" He began stretching out before his attempt to match Bobby's incredible feat, while Ward took a walk to cool off, recover, and tell his daughter to leave her brother alone.

"Hey!" Juice yelled as he looked back to Sam.

"What is it?" Rowland asked, windmilling his arms back and forth.

"You're one too, bro!"

"One what?" Sam asked, confused.

Tapping his own right shoulder, Juice smiled and said, "'For life' means 'for *life*,' Nickels!"

Sam chuckled and shook his head. "Ah, c'mon, Bobby... not anymore..." He got under the bar, placed his hands evenly on the knurling, and quietly said to himself, "But that's alright..."

WYFMIFM couldn't help but beam ear to ear. He'd heard the rumors about Juice's betrayal, and he'd seen the emails spelling everything out, but he *knew* they couldn't be true. And just as he'd always suspected—these two needed each other in their lives to reach their full potential; to reach maximum *Good Dude-ness*. They were destined to either kill each other in a vain war of egos, or save each other in a collaborative effort of selflessness. And seeing these two—smiling, vibing, *thriving*—brought tears to WYFMIFM's now-FMC eyes.

He thought back to his time in the Chippies... the young men he'd seen grow from low-SA individuals who specialized in 1v0s... to a lethal fleet of division leads and mission commanders... to a band of *brothers*, bonding in the shared trials of deployment, shit, and suffering. He watched them become jaded—fatigued by bullshit, disheartened by career twists, and Diseased with Me. And then, from afar, he watched them all, one by one, reunite into the Conclave of Charitable Chippies, a Contingent of the Indomitable Dambusters. WYFMIFM couldn't help himself as he said, quietly under his breath, with misty eyes, "Verrrehhh niiiiice... I liiiiike..."

The eagle-eyed entrepreneur cleaned up his bench; his workout was done, and his life refreshed. As he walked toward the exit, waiting at the front desk was a mid-30s, body-shaven, balding, clearly-juicing-yet-strong-fat guy—the manager, presumably—who barked at WYFMIFM, "Hey! You! You're *not* allowed to use guest passes here anymore, understand?!"

Smiling, Kennedy said, "That's ok. For the first time in years, I can see life clearly again—and there's a whole world of uncharted mountains yet to scale…"

Abruptly changing his disposition, the manager put down his blender bottle and raised his arms. "Woah, woah, wait a second! I was gonna *say*… you're banned—*unless*… *if* you want to sign up now, I can probably get you on a discounted month-to-month membership and waive your initiation fee!"

WYFMIFM chuckled. "That's quite alright, I've made my last mission to this mecca." He looked down at his gym bag, then requested, "Just… do me one favor, please."

"What?"

WYFMIFM pointed to Sam. "You see that clearly natural—yet impressively lean and aesthetic—individual?"

The manager looked around and eventually said, "Oh yeah. Guy needs to work on his calves."

Ignoring the critique, WYFMIFM handed over his gym bag. "Please…" he said, "Give him this when he leaves. Thank you!"

And WYFMIFM walked away—visual, happy, and ready to take on his next adventure in the world—with his greatest dream now fully realized.

The manager placed the bag on the counter, then opened it to inspect the contents—inside, he found a clipboard, a blue pen, dark-shaded sunglasses, a BLACKPINK CD… and a patch—*That* Patch—a VFA-195 Dambuster 'Single Seat For Life' shoulder patch.

~

"Whew… *finally!*" Buck said aloud as he reached the top of Mount Daio. He sauntered over toward the main lookout point, turned to his left, and took in the beautiful view of Iwakuni, Japan—where he'd spent the best years of his life. When he first arrived here, he'd barely been a Lieutenant. He knew his tactics and admin just well enough to get through the RAG, and had just started to get a good feel for life and friends in Oceana—yet was then unceremoniously thrust into the high-ops-tempo CVW-5 environment, where he felt like he was all alone…

He pulled out his phone and looked through his pictures of Chippy memories: the in-parade in-flight photos of a way too acute -2, Manila port call pool parties, random ready room Polaroids that ended up being STBR peephole blockers… and of course, his favorite one of all: the Porch sunset group shot with him, Low T, >SADCLAM<, CP, FISTY… and Juice and Nickels, arm in arm, as if they were best of friends.

In another life, it would've been a bunch of strangers he'd *never* have crossed paths with... if not for this chaotic, unpredictable adventure in Japan.

Along the way, he learned so much about the job, the jet, the journey; and also so much about *himself*. Once upon a time, he was just a young Lieutenant—desperate to leave the industry for a world of greener pastures, bigger paychecks, and an all-around better life. He remembers feeling so betrayed by Nickels... but deep down, he vied for the same control of his fate. For too long, he'd allowed the Navy to dick him around, ruining his life plans, treating him like some worthless pawn. He promised himself he'd get out and do better—and he did, as he started CV Worldwide...

...And yet, he'd never finished his premier ride: 'Redemption Road.' Contrary to what everybody thought, it *wasn't* based on Nickels—it was supposed to represent *his* story. How he took roller coaster paths to some astounding highs and demoralizing lows... but ultimately, how he planned to find his way back to where he belonged all along: the naval aviation fighter community. But as much as JABA tried... much to his regret for so many years... he just *couldn't find a way* to work in the ride's final arc...

But that was just a ride. *This?* This was *real*—this was *his story*.

"First Step" – Interstellar

So now, here he stood—a Lieutenant Commander—and for the first time in so many years, he was *happy*. He felt motivated. He felt hungry. He felt the *challenge*: the challenge be the O-4 he'd always wanted in this career; to influence the lives of those around him in the *right* way. To be and inspire the change in the Navy that he so often sought. To become DOPA.

More than anything, JABA was *hopeful*. Hopeful that he could make the future brighter for everyone—not with T&R numbers, DRRS data, or sortie completion rates—but with *positivity*; through one's *perspective*, with one's *attitude*.

He remembered what that well-dressed old man on the *Lil B* said: *Attitude is the mother of all luck.* 'How else?' he asked himself. *How else* could he find himself out of the Navy, without a path back in... and still find a way to deliver the finishing blow for the most important Ck in US Navy administrative war history? *How else* could FISTY find himself vegetated and nearly deceased... and rise from the ashes of a coma to defend the CSG by attrition of enemy air forces? *How else* could two estranged legends of their sport find themselves lost and longing in the intimidating world of retirement... and end up in the tac-air community, reuniting to lead their team to yet *another* championship run? *How else* could he and his Chippy brethren find themselves deploying for literal *years* of their lives on that steel piece of shit... and return home each time *smiling* about the incredible memories, growth, and friendships discovered along the way? And *how else*, he himself asked one last time, could a man like Sam "Nickels" Rowland do everything he could to piss away the solid reputation he'd been known for... and yet *still* find a way to be the hero — the Good Dude — at the very end, when it mattered most?

For the first time, LCDR Buck noticed all the other mountains around Iwakuni — around all of Japan — yet to climb. Once upon a time, he thought he'd been done; thought he'd *peaked*. And now? He smiled as he watched a couple of jets take off in the background, with Japan's mainland — and a world of possibilities — prevailing along the horizon. *Now*, he realized, he was just getting *started*...

~

THE END

Acknowledgments

Sitting down in front of the keyboard for this part, preparing to write my last words, has been one of the most daunting tasks of this whole thing. Partially, because I knew this was going to be a tough one to neck down in efforts to not let it get out of control (like the rest of the book)—but also, because it meant I'd soon have to say good-bye to the characters in this journey for good... but more on that at the end.

While wrapping up the first draft of *Saving Nickels*, I decided that when I got to this portion, I was going to keep it on theme with the book: Bleeding green. So, rather than create an extensive laundry list of names from different phases of my life or career, I'm going to keep the *specifically* targeted 'thanks' to the indomitable Dambusters I worked alongside—with a few exceptions:

First up—a *huge* shout-out to my editor, Pavel Stanishev. I had no clue what I was doing, self-publishing a book—so *man,* am I lucky I stumbled across your portfolio. You guided me through everything I needed to make this dream happen—editing, design, formatting, cover work—and more importantly, you did it with kindness, enthusiasm, and *patience* with my neurotic need for quintuple-checks/re-edits, spending countless extra hours looking at chapters over and over again. Thank you, Pavel, for putting up with me, and for making *Saving Nickels* happen.

To my girlfriend, Miwa—thank you for being so supportive of me, this life, and this book. From our first date hiking up Mt. Misen on Miyajima island, I'm sure you could tell there were lots of random, crazy ideas going through my brain. But without fail, you are *always* willing to hear those ideas out; always my audience, whether I'm sharing conspiracy theories about seed oils, raving about the benefits of *niku* and *tamago*, rehearsing a bail scroll or Baddie Awards, or simply just rambling about my retirement dreams of a home gym in Kyoto. Having you amplify my life in Japan and with the Chippies has been one of the greatest surprises that I *never* saw coming—and the only thing more exciting than meeting a woman like you during this VFA-195 tour, is thinking about our *many* adventures yet to come in the future together. I never thought I'd find a girl happy to do so much hiking, steak-eating, strong water-drinking, and even Roast of Tom Brady watching—and to do it all with such a beautiful smile. I love you, Miwa; thank you for the extreme love you've shown back, and for your acceptance of who I am.

To my family: Abby, Lizzy, Augie, Morgan, Susannah, Mom, and Dad—thank you for supporting me in ways I can never say 'thank you' enough for! To be publishing a book—about *this*, of all things—is absolutely wild to me. And as I look back, I'm aware enough to realize I wouldn't have gotten to this point in life if not for the encouragement and support from *all* of you guys. For better or for worse, I am brazenly myself—and comfortably so, thanks to the love I receive from you guys *daily*. Love you all! And Mom, sorry for some of the stuff written in the book—those were Dr. Suabedissen's words, not your son's.

Alright, now to my *Navy* family: As mentioned earlier, the number of people who influenced me, supported me, or in some shape or fashion gave me the encouragement or content needed to write this book would be *way* too long to include in this tiny section—it would encompass another book-lengthed entry. So please, if you were expecting to see your name and are severely disappointed not to, trust me when I say this: When it comes to 'the shit' of this job... if you laughed with me, listened to me vent, generated positivity, or even just *suffered* alongside me... then I remember it, and I hold those memories close to the heart. Because I've said it before, and I'll say it again: The flights in this job will just blur together one day—but the friendships and memories stay vivid forever. So, if you were by my side in this crazy journey, whether it was surviving the Navy's first wave of brainwashing attempts at OCS, helping me peddle ready room Monsters and Paul Walker patches to sailors during my Coffee Mess tenure, experiencing the extreme euphoria of an undefeated 'All-Cup Tour' in *Mario Kart: Double Dash!!* during deployment, sympathizing when I spent all day in bed eating crushed cookies in cereal after the Patriots lost the Super Bowl to the Eagles on that same cruise, getting me out of trouble when your skipper thought I tried to smoke you with a 9M ("Hammer, *abort*" "... Hammer 11, Fox-2" "... Hammer 12, Fox-2..."), or joining me for endless bitching conversations about the mind-blowing insanity behind debriefing duration, carrier nutrition, messaging delusion, or logic's extinction... *thank you*. Just because you aren't listed here by name doesn't even come *close* to meaning you haven't had a gigantic impact on this book and my life.

To the Chippies I served alongside... first off, to the enlisted sailors: The enlisted workers are some of the most underappreciated, overworked employees in all of America. I will never be able to fully know what it's like to be in your shoes, or understand the bond you guys have through the types of suffering *you* experience in this job together. But through getting to know so many of you—on more than just a surface "Hey, what's your last name, rank, and job" level of depth—I've met some *damn* talented people, full of their own beautifully unique personalities, and levels of maturity *way* beyond what I had in my late teens/early 20s—or even *now*. To see the work you're putting in during these early years of your life... it's wild. And yes, I fully believe and understand it *sucks* at times—but hopefully, you've found some solace in your version of 'the shit' this job offers—because while it may be painful now, this suffering is simply going to make you leaps and bounds ahead of your counterparts in life. At age 20, most of you have already been exposed to more of the world, learned more skills in resilience, and accomplished more than 95% of Americans *ever* will—and this is just the *beginning* of your journey. That's pretty damn cool, when you take a moment to appreciate that view—but keep on climbing, and the view will get even *better.*

I met a lot of you, but sadly, there were plenty of Chippy sailors I *didn't* get a chance to talk to, which leaves me a bit frustrated with myself. But such is life—after a day of hits, it's the *misses* that keep you awake at night. Obviously, some were mentioned by name in the book, as I'd specifically promised to a few of you—but just as I wrote above: please take no offense to any omission of your name here. If we served together in VFA-195—if we shot the shit about football and our favorite books in the line shack, played *Super Smash Bros* in the AO shop, laughed about 'Mr. Unliiiiiiimitted' in Admin, discussed the dilemmas of 'by-the-book maintenance... until it's inconvenient' and the 'open-door policy' in the AT furnace, or even if our interactions simply consisted of head nods and handshakes at the North Side gym... you guys *all* stand out in my memories, too, and are people I can happily call coworkers of the past—and brothers/sisters for life. And don't let any shithead tell you otherwise: rank is but an archaic symbol of time in service, *not* an indicator of aptitude or permission to be a leader. Plenty of you are men and women I would gladly take advice or instruction from—as I have in the past. You are *not* simply a cog in the wheel of this machine. Being an 18-year-old E-3 has *nothing* to do with your character, nor does it preclude you from holding the drive to be a *game-time player* and difference-maker in this industry. It's never too early to take the chance to make your mark in this world. Thank you for all of *your* support by, yes, doing your jobs—but more importantly, for treating me like another friend in the squadron—hopefully, you felt the same from me.

To my Chippy brethren... whether you were one of my closest friends in my time at 195, simply tolerated me and let me be me, or anything in between—every one of you will forever hold a place in my memory.

John, Stephen, Steve, DJ, Cam, Erick, Gunner Tucker, Gunner Adams, Keegan, LP, Chadd, and, of course, CMC "Manny Fresh" Valle—the difference you make to the guys and girls on the ground is what truly makes your presence in the squadron stand out. And that includes me—I'm often lost in the sauce in the air, but that goes *double* as much when it comes to the surface portion of this job. You guys know more about the Navy than I *ever* will... and to work alongside personalities and sources of knowledge like yours—even if those instructions drove me crazy at times!—is what makes the skill integration of this job unique, and makes *all* the difference to the lives of the troops who make this squadron function. Thank you for the friendships we've built, and for giving me guidance when I needed it—please don't be annoyed if I still call you for help as I still try to figure out Navy Rules and Regulations, or this whole 'military bearing' thing.

To the Chippy pilots not focused on in this book, in reverse order of our duration overlapping at VFA-195: Staton "Rodney" Pruitt, Matt "Bambi" Dickens, Tony "FNG2" Janssen, Joseph "YoSoFH" Burns, Gordon "Slowbro" Carroll, Kevin "Hugsy Bear" Farley, Jake "Sticky Icky" Lindow, Braden "SLIP" Miller, Craig "Merkin" Salveson, Justin "Corndog" Reddick, Dylan "Spatch" Aaker, Tom "Zombie" Haller, Ricky "Yardsale!" DeMann, Charlie "The Lorax" White, Mike "MITCH" Shaughnessy, Wyatt "derp" Jennings, and Erik "WeTUA" Sabelstrom... the interactions I've had with each one of you have a *wide* subject matter range, that's for sure. But it doesn't matter if it was a professional relationship of life advice and occasional greenlight parties, a jovial camaraderie of shit-talking about the latest thing CAG Paddles got pissy over (probably something I did), or the closest of friendships encompassing Friday night bike rides to the Broccoli Grill, hikes to Mount Daio, weekend trips around Japan, and stateroom viewings of *Knock Knock* (god, how many times did we watch that infamous monologue?!). And I said it in your bail, but I'll say it again here, too: god damn you and your wonderful, healthy family, Skipper Shaughnessy, for being the biggest thorns in my side and glaring exceptions to the crusade against plant-based eating whenever I'd try to sway the mind of a teetering WeTUA! In all seriousness—to all of you: Regardless of whether we still talk daily, weekly, or never again—you guys are brothers for life—wearers of *That* Patch (*the* most important Patch in the Navy, in my humble and non-tactical opinion). And I will *never* forget *any* of you.

To the pilots featured in this book: Charles "WYFMIFM" Kennedy, Andrew "CP" Preul, Chris ">SADCLAM<" Houben, Mark "JABA" Buck, Karl "Pigpen" Suabedissen, Tom "FISTY" Flynn, Kyle "Low T" Camilli, Bobby "Juice" Ward, and, of course, Sam "Nickels" Rowland. Everything said above goes to you all, too; with extra special thanks for letting me turn your identities into fictional characters, and even use a few of your likenesses on the cover. Many of you surely thought it was strange for some random new-ish guy in the squadron to be writing a book featuring your names—and probably wondered, 'Jesus, what the hell is this kid saying about me?' Well, I certainly hope none of you are disappointed—especially you, Pigpen; I can't help but laugh at the thought of some flight student reading this book, and then discovering that he's headed to a squadron commanded by none other than Dr. Suabedissen. Well, he can rest assured, knowing he's got a hell of a leader in charge. FISTY, special thanks for being my original Navy editor and for your enthusiasm throughout the process. To hear that you—an Indiana native—actually garnered respect for the GOAT after learning about TB12's legacy through your editing... this book has already been a win!

And last but not least—to the characters of the book. Again, *all* of them are fictional depictions of real-life people—but if it's not abundantly clear yet, *every single one* of these main characters has part of me in their design (yes, even Dr. Suabedissen). Funnily enough, I feel like I've transferred through these different personas during my time in the Navy, shifting between which character I identify strongest with. For a while in my naval career, I was early-book Nickels—bitter and ready to GTFO. Sometimes, I saw myself as FISTY—motivated as hell and ready to do this forever. In a pit of depression, I saw myself as Kyle—beyond shocked to have the future I'd anticipated taken out of my grasp, and nearly ready to throw it all away as a result. And sometimes, I still wonder if I'm Brady and Belichick—using this as an interim solution as I figure out where my resistance compass is no-kidding pointed. But right now, as I look ahead to another near decade of naval aviation, I truly feel like JABA—optimistic for the future, feeling as if my career is just getting started. As to *which* career—I guess we'll find out. Like JABA himself said: never fully knowing is the beauty of life, and the intrigue of the legends that unfold...

So yes, I want to give my last thanks to these characters. Because while I have more years of flying and friends to look forward to, I put these characters to rest now; retiring them and hanging their jerseys up in the rafters. In spending an unreasonable amount of time with this book, these fictional Chippies became personalities I knew *so* well, like they were real-life squadronmates—best friends—and I will miss them more than you can imagine. As I turn the last page, it's a relief to me that I can close the book knowing all is well in their worlds; that Nickels was saved.

As Steven Pressfield said in *The War of Art*: "Friends sometimes ask, 'Don't you get lonely sitting by yourself all day?' At first, it seemed odd to hear myself answer 'No.' Then I realized that I was not alone; I was in the book; I was with the characters."

Farewell, Chippies.

About the Author

Keeping this one short and sweet—an uncharacteristic trait of this author, but his preferred method here, rather than rambling about his background in third person.

Teddy Fox is a Sacramento, California native who joined the Navy as a WSO in 2013 before transitioning to pilot in 2019. And if all goes well—he embraces the suffering, keeps his head down, and continues climbing? He won't need an 'About the Author' section for people to know who he is; his books will speak for themselves. Stay tuned; *Saving Nickels* is just the beginning...

... *But*, if you're curious for more, head on over to www.savingnickelsbook.com for more content, pictures, future book plans—and where you can sign up to be at the front of the line for, as the GOAT would say, "the *next* one"...

Glossary

The military, and the United States Navy as a subset, is full of some of the most mind-blowingly stupid acronyms, and also plenty of 'tribal jargon' words that are used on an everyday basis, both in missions in the air and in casual chats on the ground. And, hell, this book is also full of additional random nerdy, nutritional, sports, and otherwise unrelated terms and abbreviations. So, in order to leave a *little* less doubt in the readers' minds, enclosed is a glossary and pronunciation guide (as required) for some of the acronyms found in this book.

It's important to note that this is by no means an exhaustive list. There are plenty of terms not included here, or acronyms that were just too irrelevant to spell out. But then again, the goal of this is not to turn you into an expert of all these alphabet soup terms, but to at least give you a *little* more of a peek inside the world we live in and the language we speak. I would *hope* this is at least a bit more enjoyable of a read than your standard 100% data glossaries out there—assuming you like your information with a bit of snark (and if you're still reading this far, that sarcastic voice clearly hasn't *completely* turned you off yet).

And inevitably, throughout my efforts to explain terms, I'll use other terms that just amplify the confusion. In those cases, I'll ask for you to practice good context clue skills—or to do your best to get inside the brain of an author who thought it was a good idea to write a scathing, ranting, gushing love letter to his organization... :-)

Enjoy!

NOTE: If an acronym or word from the book (especially callsign) is omitted in this glossary, then assume it's pronounced exactly as it looks in plain English. And if no pronunciation is written on a word *included* here, then assume it is verbally spoken as *letters*, vice a word. (Ex: "1MC" = "One Em See")

~

( ) — Translates to 'A little' in LSO speak. For instance, (LO.X) = 'A little low on start.' (Confusing)? Yup.

_ _ — Translates to 'Underlined' or 'Excessive' in LSO speak. For instance, _LIG_ = 'Underlined long in the groove.' Thanks for making such an _intuitive_ system, Paddles.

1500-pound club — Combined 1RM (One repetition maximum) of bench, squat, and deadlift reaching or exceeding a total of 1500 lbs.

1MC — One Main Circuit. The ship's central intercom system; known for being overly loud, with no volume control for the user. Typical broadcasting split: 90% irrelevant announcements, 10% relevant bad news announcements.

-2 (or -3, -4) — The 2 (or 3, 4) position in a flight. Lead is always the lead; the rest are numerically designated wingmen in those roles. Could also be '12, 13, and 14.' This is verbally spoken as "one-two, one-three, and one-four" or "dash-two, dash-three, and dash-four." But again, in the latter example, lead is always "lead," *not* "dash-one."

99 — Everybody. '99, ALCON, All-hands' all imply the same thing, which is: 'Whoever is listening, pay attention, because this likely pertains to you.'

9X — Short for AIM-9X, the heat-seeking missile. The "good tone" refers to hearing the tone in your ear that signifies 'my missile sees the heat return of a target.' "Fox-2" is the call for "I just shot a 9X."

ACE (*Ace*) — Aircraft Carrier Elevator. Formerly known as 'Els,' these are the moving elevator platforms that lift jets from the hangar bay to the flight deck, and vice versa. Often with a number afterward ('ACE 2') to reference a specific location on the carrier.

ADMACS (*AD-max*) — Aviation Data Management and Control Systems. A ship display of all airborne jets and pilots, for tracking purposes of those managing flight schedules.

Admin — Essentially, anything in a flight that does not involve tactics/the training portion ('conduct') of the event. Admin includes starting the jet, taxiing, taking off, joining your wingman in a 'rendezvous,' getting to/from the tactical training area, RTB (Return to base), landing, shutting down, and any emergencies that occur in between.

ADP — Automatic Data Processing. The IT guys, the techies, the ones who know how to fix stuff with computers, just like in the real world. And often helpful! But I swear... when you put the letters 'CAG' in front of ADP? Buckle up — because your day is about to become a never-ending nightmare of inefficiencies...

AGL — Above Ground Level. Literal altitude above the ground. Compared to MSL (Mean Sea Level), which refers to the local altimeter setting (also known as BARO or Barometric Altitude). I swear, aviation isn't *always* this nerdy...

Air Boss — The guy who works in the flight tower (Primary Flight Control, or 'Pri-Fly') on the carrier and oversees all flight operations; also called 'Boss.' Talks to aviators and Paddles on 'button 1' (Tower frequency). His second-in-command is the tragically-named 'Mini Boss' (also called just 'Mini').

AIRNAV (*Air-nav*) — Airway Navigation. Code for a basic 'from point A to point B' vanilla flight. Pure admin; no tac-admin or conduct — I.e., chill flight.

Air Warriors — An online forum where prospective naval aviators seek advice, and are typically given sarcastic answers from current or retired aviators who spend their free time posting on message boards — with the *occasional* bit of good gouge (unofficial information) put out.

Alert 5/15/30/60 — A status where a jet is in position to be launched within the time frame of the specific alert (I.e., Alert 30 status must be launched within 30 minutes of being 'called away' by the TAO).

ALR — Acceptable Level of Risk. In other words, "This mission is so important that we'll accept *this* much danger to get it done."

AMI — Aviation Maintenance Inspection. Some extensive, high-pressure maintenance inspection to see just how "by the book" maintenance is actually being done... but that's beyond the scope of this book. MPA is another big inspection... and that's the extent of my knowledge of it — and all *you* need to know, too ;-)

AMRAAM (*AM-ram*) — Advanced Medium Range Air-to-Air Missile. Also known as an AIM-120, a more long-range solution than 9Xs.

AOA — Angle of Attack. Also called 'Alpha.' Way too convoluted to get into the details of this in a random glossary... but an overly dumbed-down way (the way my small brain prefers) to think of this is: the angular difference between the jet's wing (or nose, for simplicity's sake), and the literal path the jet is tracking in space. For instance, if the wings were at a 3-degree angle canted upward, but the jet was moving perfectly horizontally and level, that would be 3 AOA. Furthermore, you cannot land on the carrier with your nose pointed straight at the deck — you have to have your nose cocked up a bit while still descending — essentially, a higher AOA. You also have 'AOA indexers' (that's the buzzword you'll want to search if you're inexplicably curious for more) that visually depict your AOA for landing — green means you're slower than you should be (higher AOA), red means faster (less AOA), and an amber circle (called 'amber donut') means you're nailing 'on-speed' (intended speed and AOA of landing approach — 8.1 in the F/A-18). Ok, that's enough science on that — my head's already hurting.

AOM — All-Officer Meeting. A masterclass in ways to waste time, as hinges and above — rank by rank — stand up and 'doghump' (repeatedly cover the same point) the latest and greatest thing they want to emphasize in the young junior officers' minds. (NOTE: Also: Amounts of Muscle; but that's a book-specific one — albeit much more essential to life and a squadron's success, if you ask me [I know — you weren't asking...]).

APARTS (*A-parts*) — What does it stand for? Great question — not even the current LSO helping me edit this knows. But long story short, as NEODD explains, it's a database of everyone's passes in their career, so Paddles can analyze their overall trends. Does it sound important? If the answer is "yes," then you're probably a Paddles — can you please A) Get off by back about my angling approaches, and B) Let me know what APARTS stands for?

API — Aviation Preflight Indoctrination. The initial portion of flight school, after commissioning, located in Pensacola, FL, where you go through a bunch of lectures for 6 weeks and take a few tests. In hindsight, these are probably the most challenging *written* exams you'll take anywhere in the flight syllabus, testing 'important aviation skills' like they ability to memorize a bunch of irrelevant shit, subsequently brain-dump it, and properly apply aerodynamic formulas to charts. You're probably wondering how I got through — so am I. (NOTE: Apparently this is called 'NIFE' now? Great, thanks, AirWarriors — don't care).

APU — Auxiliary Power Unit. The device that initially starts the jet engine combustion/light off sequence to get the thing started. If you're interested in more details than that, take an engines class in API (*sorry* — in *"NIFE"*).

ASAP (*A-sap*) — Aviation Safety Action Program. A good-intentioned but poorly executed program to track safety hazards in the air. Unfortunately, due to their lack of efficiency, they've become a trope of DH tasking and badgering, as the current Safety O incessantly reminds their JOs to 'do ASAPs' after every flight. Ok, yeah, sure thing boss...

ASM — Advanced Skills Management. A very janky program in charge of tracking the progression and signoffs for qualifications of various maintainers, requiring constant approvals from various users in a specific sequence to keep operations moving — *very* efficient, especially when the webpage goes down daily.

ATC — Both 'Air Traffic Control' — the generic agency that controls all airborne planes — and 'Auto-Throttle Control' — the feature that makes pilots' lives immensely easier, as it holds the airspeed you desire (and with 'Baro Alt HOLD' selected, *altitude* is held as well. Don't let anyone tell you otherwise: a five-year old could be taught to fly the F/A-18 administratively). Related: CATCC = Carrier Air Traffic Control Center, who are basically the ATC agents of the boat (pronounced *"CAT-Sea"*, omitting the second 'C').

AWDO — Air Wing Duty Officer. A very lame duty for O-4s while in port that involves running musters practically every hour, and a duty that leaves you with a few hours of sleep, a long face, and extreme frustration when you're waiting on one squadron to get one text muster from one sailor before you send your "all accounted for" update to DCAG. Yes, this one definitely falls under the category of 'Bullshit.'

B&R — Breakup and Rendezvous. One of the most basic admin drills practiced in flight school; to learn how to join up on another airplane using airspeed, geometry, and closure.

Beer Die — Hands down, the most popular game in naval aviation. It involves a die, four plastic cups, a ping-pong-sized plywood table — and copious amounts of beer. You can look it up online or enter any O-Club (Officer's Club) to find out more about it. Against all odds, it actually was *not* featured in either *Top Gun* movie — but I'm sure the actors got their beer die FAM while shooting.

BFM — Basic Fighter Maneuvering. The fighter community's very fancy way of saying 'dog-fighting.' One-on-one, mano-a-mano, 1v1 showdowns; some call it 'the sport of champions.' To get a 'hack' out is to have a quick BFM fight. Comes in OFBM (offensive), DBFM (defensive), and HABFM (high-aspect — essentially 'neutral start') varieties.

Big XO — Second-in-command aboard the carrier, right behind the Captain. Typically concerned with things like the ship's cleanliness, morning announcements, proper laundry usage, and accurate trash sorting.

Bingo — A fuel state at which you need to knock off the training/conduct portion of the mission and head back home to land with a safe amount of reserve fuel. Also: A 'bingo profile' is a fuel-efficient climb and idle descent to cover the furthest range with the least fuel — used in emergency low-fuel scenarios.

Bizz — Means the number '5' — as in 'CAG Bizz' for CVW-5. The origins of this codeword? Don't know, don't care — ask some beer die fanboy.

Blue Air — The notional 'good guys' of the flight. On a whiteboard, designated with blue arrows as lead and green arrows for wing (-2) — with some variances beyond the scope of this book.

BLUF (*Bluff*) — Bottom Line Up Front. Sort of a 'TL;DR' thing, but at the beginning of an email — so that you don't have to read the rest of the crap.

Bolter — The act of missing the wires in an attempted boat landing, typically because too much power was left on the jet and/or you landed long.

BPA — Bisphenol A. Also known as 'dangerous chemicals in plastics.' Stay away, or your T levels will plummet, and you will for sure die. Haha, just kidding (well, maybe kidding... *hopefully* kidding...).

Bravo Romeo — Another relatively pointless watch, this one stood by JOs to assist Bravo Papa (an O-4, in a watch that is essentially an air-wing-wide SDO).

Broflauge — One (usually an IP — Instructor Pilot) who pretends to be chill and your 'bro' — and yet *entirely* changes their demeanor once the canopy goes down — where they become a complete dickhead.

Bulkhead — 'Wall' in Navy speak. As in, "Brace the bulkhead, shipmate" (which translates to "Put your back to the wall, because I am a higher rank than you," or "I have superiority complex issues").

BVR — Beyond Visual Range. An air-to-air (A/A) term for where you cannot visually see the guy you're shooting. Counterpart would be WVR — *Within* Visual Range (think 'BFM').

CAC (*Cack*) — Common Access Card. More familiarly known as a 'Military ID,' and most notably /redundantly referred to as a "CAC Card."

CAG (*Cag*) — Commander Air Group. The guy in charge of the carrier air wing. Nowadays, typically an O-6, and a previous squadron skipper. His second-in-command is the Deputy CAG, or 'DCAG.'

CAP (*Cap*) — Combat Air Patrol. Flying endless circular/box patterns around a designated area, waiting for tasking or a contact to chase after in defense of the ship. More familiarly referred to as 'drilling holes in the sky,' a fighter aircraft's version of a cop patrolling around the streets.

Carrier Landing positions: '180' = when you are abeam the intended landing spot — pointed 180 degrees opposite from final heading — and you begin your turn to final.

'90' = when you have 90 degrees to go in the turn, and the ship is roughly around your 10 o'clock position.

'The Start (X)' = The beginning of the 'groove,' or where your graded pass actually begins. You should be 15-18 seconds away from landing at this point.

'In the Middle (IM)' = Exactly what it sounds like.

'In Close (IC)' = About to cross steel.

'At the Ramp (AR)' = Over steel, imminently touching down on the boat.

CAS (*Cass*) — Close Air Support. The Air-to-Surface (A/S) mission of helping dudes on the ground (JTACs), typically by dropping bombs or strafing with the gun. Something that most of the fleet gets pretty savvy at, but historically, CVW-5 Japan-based guys are highly averse to, as they do much more 'Air-to-Air' training.

CATM (*CAT-em*) — Captive Air Training Missile. A simulated, non-launchable shell of a weapon loaded on a jet, to practice manipulating in-cockpit display symbology and employing in proper envelopes.

Checkride — a 'final test' flight for any phase of training.

CHUM (*Chum*) — Chart Updating Manual. Whenever looking at 'low-level' charts, one must utilize JMPS to see the latest manmade features added to the route, and 'pen-and-ink' the changes in the already-printed out chart — to ensure nobody endangers themselves with towers recently built, peaking above the prescribed flyable minimum altitude (MINALT).

Ck — Constructive Kill. A simulated victory in a simulated war — admirals go *crazy* for these. The wargame equivalent of "Oh yeah, I totally could've whooped that guy's ass if I'd wanted to."

CLARA (*Clara*) — Clarification. What you say when you can't see the 'ball' on the IFLOLS datum lens (because of dim lighting, sun angle, or most commonly, you're too high or too low).

Cleaning Stations — The daily hour, typically 0730-0830, where the boat is cleaned, scrubbed, and polished. And to be honest, a *bit* awkward when you find out that the ones who demand the most of the cleaners are not the ones doing the actual cleaning... Like GQ, this is *not* a time to find yourself in the bathrooms, gyms, eating, or roaming around the p-ways.

COA (*KOH-uh*) — Course of Action. Self-explanatory; I guess it sounds "more official" to talk about a potential 'COA' vice a potential 'plan.' Related: CONOPS = Concept of Operations.

COB — Close of Business. A somewhat hingey term, because it's *always* used in relation to the deadline of some task, i.e., "Have this form completed and sent to me by COB Friday."

COD (*Cod*) — Carrier Onboard Delivery. The plane that brings mail, food, passengers (pax), etc., aboard the carrier. Most notably, the C2 Greyhound — although that's being phased out for a much less desirable solution...

Coffee Mess Officer — Hands down the worst ground job in the Navy. A treasurer of squadron funds, where your job seemingly begins with managing everyone's monthly dues and budgets... and turns into running fundraising, designing new apparel, and pushing products during deployment in efforts to raise money for the squadron — you know, everything an aspiring fighter pilot dreams of doing.

Conduct — the specifically planned 'tactical training' part of any flight.

CQ — Carrier Qualifications. Getting the necessary traps (boat landings) and landing grades to qualify for boat operations. Must be re-hacked every time you go underway, but it is a *much* bigger deal when initially done in flight school in the T-45 trainer jet (at least circa 2021, anyway), and then in the F/A-18/whatever fleet jet you fly. To disqualify in CQ means potentially losing your shot to live on the glorious vessel described in this book.

CRM — Crew Resource Management. The Navy's model for utilizing airborne assets and/or (if multi-person cockpit) other crew members to solve issues together. The components are: Mission Analysis, Communication, Situational Awareness, Assertiveness, Leadership, Adaptability/Flexibility, and Decision Making. Often abbreviated as 'MCSALAD,' 'DAMCLAS,' or 'SADCLAM'.'

CS — Culinary Specialist. A Navy rate of those who specializing in cooking food. Yes, the Navy designates active duty cooks. No, their cooking prowess is not reflected by the unfortunately poor-quality food options on the boat — they are talented craftsmen given the shittiest of tools to work with. Related: FSA = Food Service Attendant (server).

CSG — Carrier Strike Group. The overall collection of a unit's ships, planes, and bros deploying out there together.

CV — Aircraft Carrier. Often with a designator number afterward when referring to a specific ship. Where does the 'V' possibly come into play? Great question. Has something to do with 'fixed wing' and the French word *'voler'* — but beyond the scope of this book, and honestly, even *further* beyond the concern of this author.

CV-1 — The instrument approach flown to the carrier during case 3 conditions (at night, or when cloud ceilings are low and/or visibility is poor).

CVW — Carrier Air Wing. Can also be called CAG (Carrier Air Group) — not to be confused with CAG (Commander Air Group). Clear as mud?

DCA — Defensive Counter Air. Essentially, protecting the ship from enemy aircraft looking to seek and destroy it. Our bread and butter mission of doomsday scenario prepping. Also, a DCA 'vul' = window of vulnerability.

DCAST (*DEE-cast*) — Data Collection and Scheduling Tool. An online military website used to schedule and deconflict around specifically assigned airspace and low-level routes, used amongst all the squadrons in that region. If it's not scheduled in DCAST, you almost certainly aren't flying there — ATC will *not* approve you in.

DC Central — Initially, I wasn't going to include this term, but realized I reference it in the book *way* too many times. And to be honest, I have no clue if this is a place, a shop, or a branch — and I don't care. All I know is how annoying it is.

DCSMR (DICK-smear) — Direct Confrontation; Shoot at Max Range. The oldest, simplest tactic in the book: a good ol' fashioned Engage Eight blitz.

DD-1801 — A military flight plan form one files to get clearance to take off. (Well, not exactly... but that's put simply enough).

DDI — Digital Display Indicator. Additional displays in the jet, comprising LDDI and RDDI (left and right). Can assign your TDC (Throttle Designator Controller) to either screen to manipulate them with your HOTAS.

Delta Easy — No chance you're finding this one here, either.

DET (*Det*) — Detachment. A mini (*seriously* mini) deployment away from home, typically for 2-5 weeks.

Division — A four-ship of aircraft (Lead, -2, -3, and -4). Can also be a 'light division' (or 'light div') of three aircraft.

DOMS (*Doms*) — Delayed Onset Muscle Soreness. The phenomenon where your muscles become sorer during the recovery days *after* the workout (typically 24-72 hours post-WO), most notably with legs, where rest day #2 can become a day of hell.

EAAs — Essential Amino Acids. Another one of the million supplements that some study somewhere has "proven" to benefit muscle growth and/or fat loss. News flash: if it's a supp available OTC at a GNC, it's probably not doing *that* much for you.

EGT — Exhaust Gas Temperature. Hot stuff coming out of the jet tailpipes.

ELT — Emergency Locator Transmitter. A beacon that transmits on GUARD when an aircraft crash is detected; located within the aircraft.

EMCON (*EM-con*) — Emissions Control. Minimizing transmissions to/from the ship. No internet, no email — no fun.

ENG page (*Engine page*) — The page displaying all your nit-noid aircraft parameters (engine inlet temperatures, core vibration, compressor RPMs, etc).

EP — Emergency Procedure. An 'EP' also implies a procedure that aviators should memorize verbatim. A total admin thing.

EXP — Experience Points. Come on, nerd… don't act like you really needed clarification on this one…

FAA — Federal Aviation Administration. While generally more of a general aviation (GA) type agency, they can certainly still get Navy aircraft in hot water with airspace or altitude violations.

FADEC (*FAY-deck*) — Full Authority Digital Engine Control. Essentially, the 'brain' that controls the engines of the jet and detects any problems within them. Will automatically alter the thrust available by an engine—including shutting one down—if critical issues are detected. The FADEC probably knows what DC Central is, and why 'V' is code for 'fixed wing.'

FAM (*Fam*)—Familiarity. An intro/demonstration-type version of... well, anything—It could be a FAM flight, an Area FAM, an SDO FAM, a deadlift FAM, etc.

FAR/AIM (*Far Aim*)—Federal Aviation Regulations/Aeronautical Information Manual. An extensive book and database of all the legalities and rules of flying, written in extremely dry lawyer-speak, which every PIC (Pilot-In-Command) is responsible for knowing in its entirety (Go ahead and take a wild guess as to how that actually plays out).

FCLP—Field Carrier Landing Practice. Practicing the boat pattern and ball-flying landings (boat landing passes) with a carrier-sized landing box set up on a field (land-based) runway. The Navy requires doing a specific amount of these prior to going to the ship.

FCS—Flight Control System. The software behind the jet's flight control surface movement, i.e., the *actual* pilot that flies the plane in its intended direction of motion, dampening out improper or overaggressive inputs by the fake human pilot (some, like me, more than others). Checked before every flight with an IBIT (Initiated Built-In Test—a quick run-through of the integrity and redundancy of the system).

FENCE (in/out) (*Fence*)—'FENCE' checks once used to have a spelled-out list of items from the acronym—'Something, Expendables, Something, Comms, Something,' I'm guessing... but that's now antiquated—I'm sure some AirWarriors guy knows. FENCE-ing IN means getting your combat systems ready for the fight; it's also the transition from admin to conduct, with a little bit of tac-admin to blur the lines in between. FENCE-ing OUT means back to admin.

Fighter Raging White—A fighter 'killed' in a kill-removal debrief playback, but still taking shots that bandits (red air) "died" from during the fight. Akin to a ghost in a fight playback. Sort of a tac-admin factor (...I'm already confusing you, aren't I?).

FITREP (*FIT-rep*)—Fitness Report. The performance review of an officer, whereas an EVAL (Evaluation) is that of an enlisted service member. Both use the same scale of three grades (unless something severely bad happened and warrants an adverse FITREP): EPs (Early Promote), MPs (Must Promote), and Ps (Promotable)—from best to worst. If you disagree with the FITREP ranking you've been given—due to whatever unfair circumstances you deem present—you can submit a 'Statement' (of Dispute) and turn it into a Navy legal battle.

FMC—Full Mission Capable. A full-up, 4.0, good-to-go system.

FNAEB (*FEE-Nab*)—Field Naval Aviator Evaluation Board. A board you attend if some shit goes down in your career. While it often can result from unsafe or unsound flying, a FNAEB is not necessarily performance-based; it could also be triggered by a Class-A (high money value) incident that wasn't remotely your fault. At a FNAEB board, the panel determines whether or not you continue flying and/or keep your Wings of Gold.

FNG — Fucking New Guy. A loving way to refer to the newest guy or girl who has joined a squadron or unit, where the expectations are to be a sponge, utilize your two-ears-to-one-mouth ratio, and help out the team any way you can — unfortunately, often by taking less-than-desirable responsibilities.

Foc's'le Follies (*FOKE-sole* — short for Forecastle, or the forward part of any warship — *FALL-ees*) — A tradition like none other — hosted by CAG Paddles — where the aviators and some ship officers get together to watch a collection of parody skits and see who wins the top ball-flyer awards (separate concepts). Many lines of humor are pushed — sometimes crossed — and no one is safe.

FOD (*Fod*) — Foreign Object Damage. Anything that can go in a jet or intake that could conceivably cause damage, including rocks, tire rubber, earplugs, screws, etc.

FTR-D (*Fighter-D*) — An acronym pilots use to set up their jet for catapult launches. Flaps, Trim, RADALT, Displays.

Gear — Slang for juice/steroids. Used in a sentence: "Yeah, that guy is definitely on gear..."

GQ — General Quarters. A simulation that a Navy ship runs in order to prepare as if the vessel were under attack. What does that mean, though, for ship inhabitants? Hallways are blocked off, doorways are closed, people are walking around in 'flash gear' (fireproof suits) and gas masks, and all gyms/food options are closed. You really shouldn't be traversing p-ways or using the bathrooms during GQ. It *sucks* — and that's speaking as a member of the air wing, which doesn't even *participate* in these annoying evolutions (much to the Big XO's chagrin).

Ground Job — Any job tasked to you that has nothing to do with flying or tactics. Typically: Division Officer, Schedules Officer, Operations Officer, Safety Officer, etc. Also, typically not a 'desired' part of the job — but admittedly, some can be rewarding/professional skill-building (*not* Coffee Mess).

Growth — Short for Growth Hormone (HGH); or, in other words, steroids.

GUARD (*Guard*) — A radio frequency that all aircraft radios are tuned into at all times (121.5 VHF / 243.0 UHF), normally in case of a safety-of-flight issue that requires everyone's attention, or because the speaker needs to get a hold of some dude and they have no clue what frequency the person is tuned into. Think of a mass blast weather warning text.

HAIL-R (*Hail-R*) — An acronym used to get your jet ready for landing to or from the boat. The most important of those letters? H (Hook) and A (Anti-skid switch) — two steps that, if forgotten or neglected, could very much ruin your day, and potentially your jet.

Handler — The guy in charge of managing all the planes on the flight deck. Known for obnoxiously yelling and rambling through his deck intercom system for all to hear. Works in FDC (Flight Deck Control).

HARM (*Harm*) — High-Speed Anti-Radiation Missile. Growler stuff; don't let FISTY tell you otherwise!

Hinge — The slang term for 'O-4' (Lieutenant Commander). Hinge, however, contains more of a derogatory connotation than LCDR or DH (Department Head; an O-4 billet) does. A hinge implies an O-4 who tasks others relentlessly, can often spool up/stress out under marginally pressure-filled situations (subsequently taking out stress on others), and, in the simplest of terms, can be a total douchebag.

HOD (*Hod*) — Head of Department. An even douchier way to say 'department head.' Often used by boat people, under the sense that such a title gives them power and authority — *and* their own table in the wardroom, in some cases...

HOL — High Order Language. A software variant of the F/A-18; included for one marginal joke in one chapter — yes, jokes are always funnier when you have to explain them.

HOPA (*HO-pa*) — Hinge Officer Protection Association. A collection of just O-4s — no other ranks. Their power alone is enough to dish out pain and punishment to the rest of the fleet (namely, the JOPA).

HOTAS (*HO-taz*) — Hands On Throttle-and-Stick. Fancy way of saying 'the buttons' found on your throttle and stick. Used in a sentence: "What is the HOTAS for dropping a bomb?" (Answer: Pushing the 'pickle' button).

HUD (*Hud*) — Heads-Up Display. The symbology you see in your canopy window as you look straight ahead and fly — includes airspeed, altitude, magnetic heading, etc. Any person who's ever played a video game knows what I'm talking about — health bars, ammo loadout, lives left — all the 'SA-enhancing' stuff added to your field of view.

ICS — Intercockpit Communication System. The way a two-seat crew talks to each other, and with VOX, is a voice sensing feature that turns the ICS 'on' when a loud enough sound triggers it. Common mistake — too highly-set sensitivity of the VOX knob leads to the pilot hearing every breath taken by the WSO, or vice-versa — and subsequently, every breath being heard on tape replay for debriefing (also a feature for single-seat pilots who, for some reason, want to hear their own verbal musings in tape review).

IFLOLS (*I-Flaws*) — Improved Fresnel Lens Optical Landing System. The datum that contains a 'ball' displayed to the pilot, telling them where they are on the optimal glideslope to land at the ship. The 'ball' (also called 'meatball') is an amber-colored circle that moves up and down the lens, depending on where you are on glideslope, and turns red when you're in the lowest cell of display.

IMC — Instrument Meteorological Conditions. I.e., 'in the clouds' or 'shitty weather.' Counterpart is VMC (Visual) — where you have high ceilings and excellent visibility. (Near synonymous with 'IFR' and 'VFR' for Instrument/Visual Flight Rules).

INSURV (*IN-serve*) — Ugh, don't know and don't care. It's apparently a boat thing.

IRL — In Real Life. While once a big-time nerd-spotlighting term, I'm starting to see this one become more and more mainstream these days.

IROK (*I-rock*) — Acronym for remembering procedures for post-ejection. Inflate, Raft... O... uhh... I'm sure the rest will come to me if I need it.

JAAM (*Jam*) — Joint Anti-Air Model. Some nerdy program that calculates whether a simulated missile shot would impact or not. Eh, actually, I guess it's kinda cool — *if* you know how to use it (I don't).

JBD — Jet Blast Deflector. A gigantic wall that rises as a jet positions itself on the catapult, to prevent the full-power run-up exhaust from blowing people over on the flight deck.

JDAM (*JAY-dam*) — Joint Direct Attack Munition. A bomb that seeks the exact coordinates typed into it, entered from mission planning/within the jet. With an "L" prefacing it, becomes a laser-guided JDAM.

J-Dial — A simple telephone, but on the ship. 'J-dial' is also synonymous with 'telephone number' ("What's the best J-dial to reach you?"); 4-digit extensions only. Not to be confused with 'PICT' (Personal Integrated Communications Terminal) which is another telephone system capable of communicating on different ship radio frequencies like button 1, departure, rep frequency, etc.

JHMCS (*Juh-HEM-icks*) — Joint Helmet Mounted Cueing System. A gigantic megamind helmet F/A-18 pilots can wear, which incorporates some cool tactical applicability and display symbology that follows your field of view no matter where you look in the cockpit — but depending on who you ask, a helmet that *also* has some big-time physiological drawbacks... That's all I'll say about that.

JMPS (*Jumps*) — Joint Mission Planning Software. *The* program in the Navy jet community. This is the software we use to load up everything we'll need in the jet, including waypoints (lat/long information), comm frequencies, weapon data, RNAV (area navigation) data, etc. Unfortunately, JMPS also *sucks*. Crashes all the time, takes forever to load, and is very finicky with random errors. It takes a decently skilled computer person to know what they're doing with the program, and a true master of patience to put up with it—I am neither. *Never* will you meet the aviator who says, "JMPS? Oh yeah. It's pretty good."

JOPA (*JOE-pa*)—Junior Officer Protection Association. The gang of officers who are O-3 (Lieutenant) and below in rank. Think of them as the 'young, cool, responsibility-free officers,' whose sworn enemies are the O-4s of the fleet—the ones who *task* them with responsibilities (of both vital and dubious nature).

Khaki Hour—The hour of boat gyms where only E-7s (Chiefs) and above (including all officers) are allowed entry (Which are the same ranks that the 'Khaki' term encompasses, in general).

"Knock It Off"—The official end to the conduct portion of the flight, due to the mission being accomplished, time expiring, training goals achieved, or any safety-of-flight issue taking priority over training.

L&S—Launch and Steering. What you command on a radar contact when you put your radar's attention on this specific return. Another way of thinking of an L&S is 'the contact currently under the crosshairs.'

LA—Landing Area. An area where... jets land. When the LA is unsafe to land, for whatever reason, it's labeled a 'Foul Deck.'

Ladderwell—Nautical term for 'staircase'—albeit stairs with no backing, so kind of like a ladder at an angle. Huh, I suppose that's probably where the term comes from...

LAR (*Lar*)—Launch Acceptability Range. In simple terms, a release envelope of 'When I am able to shoot my weapon *and* have it hit where I want.' WEZ (Weapon Engagement Zone) is the same concept, but for 'red air' shooting *at* the 'blue air' (I.e., from the blue's perspective: LARs are good, WEZs are bad).

LARP (*Larp*)—Live Action Role Playing. Ever seen those guys dressed up in costumes at the park, casting pretend lightning bolts and engaging in non-contact sword fighting for the fate of the nation? Yeah, that's LARPing—and naval aviation is *great* at it.

LGTR (*el-JEET-er*)—Laser Guided Training Round. A practice bomb with no warhead; secondarily used to practice laser marksmanship, primarily employed to bolster a squadron's T&R.

LFE—Large Force Exercise. A big mission with a ton of airborne assets, often a MARSTRIKE of some sort. Fun...

LSO — Landing Signal Officer. Paddles. Those who 'wave' (oversee) pilots' passes aboard the ship, giving them verbal inputs to keep them safe. You've surely read about these guys enough to know who they are. For a grade breakdown of their pointless grading system:

OK = 4/4.
(OK) or "Fair" = 3/4.
Bolter = 2.5/4.
— or "No-Grade" = 2/4.
C or "Cut Pass" = 0/4 (an unsafe pass, and a pretty big deal if you get one).
_OK_ or "Underlined OK" = 5/4 (rare; you basically have to have an emergency affecting landing).

NOTE: For an LSO to be 'at the pickle' typically means they are in the 'Primary' position, or the one in charge of giving pilots voice commands to keep them on a safe glide path and centerline. This is backed up by a 'secondary' observer, and CAG Paddles — whose radio transmissions and commands, if necessary, trump the others.

Mac Recs — Macronutrient Recommendations. The latest and greatest recommendations to get substantial AOMs with incredible LOLs. Yes, they are gospel — and yes, they change all the time. But you should treat each one as some groundbreaking revolution and be sure to tell everyone you know about how it's the *only* way to work out, eat, and recover.

Man Overboard — A drill on boats (or an actual procedure, if a splash in the water is seen/reported) to muster (take role) of every single person on the ship within a quick time frame (ideally 15 minutes or less) to deduce who is *not* present and accounted for.

Marshal — Akin to a 'gathering' point; in the parking area before taxiing for takeoff, or a marshal point in the air to rendezvous before commencing for a mission/landing at the carrier.

MARSTRIKE (*MAR-strike*) — Maritime Strike. A combat or *simulated* combat mission where a maritime target (such as a boat, or water-bound enemy vessel of any kind) is attacked with an Air-to-Surface weapon. Known for lots of mission planning, very boring execution, and extremely painful reprimanding from upper leadership for fucking it away — I can tell you from experience :)

Material Condition: Zebra — Don't know, don't care. Has something to do with closing hatches on the boat. Oh, yeah — "hatch" = door. Remember that one, too, for your nautical database...

METOC (*ME-tock*) — Meteorology and Oceanography Command. Basically, the weather guy. That's all you gotta know. Oh, and a 'Dash-1' is a weather report; basically, anyway. You know what? *Also* not important — is *any* of this stuff?

Mickey — A 'time sync' sent over the radio, sent/requested to align your jet clock with someone else's. However, its 99% use is to make fun of somebody for making a public mistake over the radio, as when you send a mickey, it creates a loud beep that *everyone* on frequency hears—to call attention to the verbal buffoonery committed. Yes; *these* are the things that keep us entertained while spending months at sea...

Midrats—Midnight Rations. A meal served on the boat between (boat-dependent) roughly 2230-0100. A classic social meal—typically a combination of breakfast and junk foods—where aviators laugh about the day's flight shenanigans, spread the latest boat rumors, and gorge themselves on waffles, omelets, and burritos. Normally held in a ship's Wardroom 1/2 ("Wardroom One-Two").

MIL/MAX (*Mil/Max*)—Military-rated thrust and Maximum-rated thrust. MIL is as much power as you can get without lighting your afterburners (AB), while MAX unleashes burners and provides maximum power (via much higher thrust, fuel flow/gas usage, and nozzle positioning).

Mission Card—What you load in JMPS, and plug in the jet. Multiple different formats over the years, including AMUs, DMDs, DTDs, etc. Their meaning is meaningless—all you need to worry your little brain about is that 'loading a card' with any of the above acronyms means preparing a mission card to put in the jet, programmed with waypoints, frequencies, etc.

MMORPG—Massively Multiplayer Online Role-Playing Game. Why would *I* know what this means? Ask Dr. Suabedissen...

Mom—lingo for 'the boat,' i.e., where the jets go home after every flight on deployment. Why it's called 'mom'? Who knows. Ask the FADEC.

MOVLAS (*MOW-vless*)—Manually Operated Visual Landing Aid System. An alternate to the IFLOLS landing aid. When "landing MOVLAS," Paddles intervenes in the process a bit more, controlling the 'ball' you see on the lens to indicate if you should move your jet higher or lower on glideslope (based off what *they* see). Very much a contingency operation in case the normal lens goes down, but Paddles practices it once a day or so. Coincidentally, these MOVLAS recoveries are by far the spiciest ones, with hands down the most bolters... hmm...

MRM—Maximum Recovery Maneuver. An extreme way to skyrocket up and escape a low level in the case of encountering weather. This is really only important in like one part in the book... Whatever; now you know.

MSP—Spell-out unknown and unimportant. Think of this like an error code. Similar to BLINs—another acronym of a jet error not worth looking up. For the sake of the book: 903 MSP = Hard landing; 811 MSP = Over-G.

MWR—Morale, Welfare, and Recreation. Another one that is hardly pertinent to the story, but mentioned enough to include here. MWR attendants in gyms are often the ones telling you to remove your gym bag from the floor, reminding you that chalk and effort aren't allowed, and asking you to set your deadlift bar down a bit more quietly.

NARP (*Narp*) — Non-Athletic Regular Person. Potentially you, if you know what 'RNG' stands for.

NATOPS (*NAY-tops*) — Naval Air Training and Operating Standardization. Think of this as the 'flight manual' for any Navy aircraft. In naval aviation, we associate 'NATOPS' with basic aircraft systems and emergencies/limitations. NATOPS is *pure* admin, and it's unfortunately common to let one's NATOPS knowledge lapse as they get further into tactical study. Granted, at the end of the day, lack of NATOPS knowledge is what's most likely to kill you — just as unsound admin procedures will.

NAVADMIN (*NAV-AD-min*) — Navy Administrative Message. Widespread Navy updates to the way things are done — typically things like uniform or haircut regulation adjustments, a change to the paternity leave policy to give fathers more than 14 days to welcome their child to the world, or announcing that failing PRTs will no longer endanger your career.

NAWDC (*NAW-dick*) — Naval Aviation Warfighting Development Center. The overarching training center for all of the Navy's tactical schools, to include STRIKE (N5) and TOPGUN (N7).

NEAT (*Neat*) — No-Exercise Activity Thermogenesis. The act of burning calories from random movements throughout the day, like cooking, cleaning, walking, and talking animatedly with your hands (One of my favorite forms of NEAT during briefs/debriefs, and one highly looked down upon by Patch wearers. If only they knew...).

NIPR (NIP-er) — Non-Classified Internet Protocol Router. The Navy's unclassified email system — compared to SIPR, which is the secure version.

NJP — Nonjudicial Punishment. The Navy's version of a formal hearing to address accused misconduct, ending in possible disciplinary action; less serious than a Court Martial. Other forms include XOI (XO Inquiry) and Captain's Mast. All are encompassed in the UCMJ (Uniform Code of Military Justice). Whatever, you understand — Navy legal trouble.

NKO — Navy Knowledge Online. A database of a bunch of hour-or-two-long virtual trainings that 'teach' you various qualifications. Most notably... the Cyber Security Awareness Challenge.

NOTAMs (NO-tams) — Notice To Airmen. A list of advisories and/or changes to any airport or area you plan on flying to/from. Imagine an eye-sore laundry list of hundreds of advisories, including a random crane a mile away from the runway, an approach having minimum descent altitudes 10 feet lower than published, with a hidden message squeezed in the middle saying that the airport is 'closed to all traffic' — Ladies and gentlemen, the FAA NOTAM system. Along with weather TAFs/METARs, it is common practice (well, legally required, technically. Lol) to grab these items before flying.

NPC — Non-Playable Character. I will refrain from explaining this one any more, at the risk of highlighting myself (even further) as a gigantic nerd.

NSS — Navy Standard Score. A curve-based score that tells you where you rank against your competitors in flight school. Something that *way* too many people obsess over and use as a benchmark of worth. And while we're talking flight school jargon? MIF = Maneuver Item File (Yes, I understand that spell-out clarifies *nothing*). Meeting MIF means average, Below MIF is below average, and Above MIF — you know what? You get the picture.

NWLO/TO — Nose Wheel Lift-off/Take-off. A subset of TOLD data (Takeoff/Landing Distance). They are airspeeds at which to rotate the jet by pulling back on the control stick. Screwing these up is a good way to make a huge admin mistake on the runway. Pretty boring stuff, not sure why I'm even including this in here — you're welcome.

OBLISERV (*OB-li-serve*) — Obligated Service. Time owed to the Navy based on a contractual agreement (or in the case of DH slates, based on a contractually-binding response to an email). For a new Navy pilot? Currently the OBLISERV is 8 years post finishing flight school and 'winging' (earning your Wings of Gold) — with rumors that the number will soon become 10... yikes...

OIC — Officer in Charge. Not guaranteed to be the most competent nor most experienced; simply the highest ranked.

OOMA/FAME (*OOH-ma/Fame*) — Both relatively irrelevant to the book... but mentioned. Consider them the post-flight process of downloading everything your jet did to maintenance computers in order to track potential issues and log time on the jet's life. Takes about 10 minutes to download everything; feels like forever.

OPNAV (*OP-nav*) — Office of Chief of Naval Operations. (You know, until I wrote this glossary, I wouldn't have *possibly* believed that's what it stood for...) OPNAV Instructions are essentially Navy-overseeing rules and regulations, and OPNAV 3710 is the flight-specific one. Think of it like a 'generic NATOPS' for all aircraft.

OPSEC (*OP-seck*) — Operational Security. The act of refraining from blabbering about secret stuff, secret dates, or secret locations.

OPSO (*OPS-o*) — Operations Officer. Typically a hinge in a squadron, and the most power/responsibility a hinge can have. The second-to-last to oversee/decide the following day's schedule for the squadron, before the skipper's set of eyes approves it.

ORM — Operational Risk Management. A two-fold definition: It's the model the Navy uses to foresee potential risks and mitigate them before they become detrimental factors in flight; and also, to 'ORM' out of an event means to forgo flying because there was some 'causal factor' in your life that got the hairs on the back of your neck standing up — like incredibly poor sleep, extreme family issues, debilitating neck pain, etc. — to the point where it would be unsafe to fly.

OTA — Organized Team Activities. Offseason NFL pre-training camp workouts. I think of them as 'workups' (see: SFARP) before deployment — given, you know, my vast professional football experience...

P+[lowercase] — "Probability of": k = kill; we = weapons effectiveness; d = destruction; etc.

PAO — Public Affairs Officer. Think of this person as a PR agent/total media sponge for the Navy/any squadron, in charge of press releases, managing social media, writing articles, etc.

PC — Plane Captain. The young guy/girl who preflights, checks, and launches/recovers your jet from its parked spot. You trust them with your life, essentially, and they do a damn good job at it. Separate from the 'Shooter,' who launches your jet from the catapult.

PCDS — Personal Computer Debriefing Station. The software you use to watch the tapes you recorded on your RMM.

PED — In the jet community: Personal Electronic Device. In the lifting community: Performance Enhancing Drugs. The Navy is starting to consider incorporating more of one of the aforementioned spell-outs — as long as you use their sponsored and hand-selected brand. Either way? I'm not interested.

PERS (*Pers*) — Personnel Command. Maybe stands for something else... don't know and don't care. These are the guys in charge of 'who goes where' in the Navy, also known as 'Placement Officers.' They take in your submitted preferences and desires, and make a house of cards to fit every open job with a prospective body — often against the desires sent in. But to be honest, it's a very tough problem to fix, and people are *always* going to be left annoyed with their placement, or 'screwed' as we say. PERS-43 is the aviation-specific branch. Related: BUPERS = Bureau of Personnel (the ones who send out the orders).

PGM — Precision Guided Munition. Generic term for any weapon with advanced guidance built in to hit a specific target, be it GPS, laser, etc. Similarly related, 'LGBs' = Laser-Guided Bombs. When used as a mission subject at sea, PGM is often code for 'Go have fun, be safe, and get current'; similar to SSC (Surface Surveillance Coordination) or 1v0s.

PII — Personally Identifiable Information. Anything used to identify an individual — things like name, gender, email, home address, telephone number... It's kind of a catch-all concept; and a bygone one, to be honest—its 2024, for god's sake. I can't even imagine how many cookies/terms/privacy policies we've all agreed to... I would just kind of assume everything's out there *somewhere*...

... *And* I'm sure some tinfoil hatter is now laughing, calling me a "stupid son of a bitch" for that assumption, and for highlighting my misunderstanding of the cyber world.

PIM (*Pim*)—Plan of Intended Movements. The literal lat/longs that the ship is trying to make on their scheduled course. 'Making PIM' entails planning flight ops carefully to avoid delaying the boat (via reduced speeds required for ops) on its required route.

PLM—Precision Landing Mode. The biggest game-changer to landing behind the boat, where so much is automatically kept within limits, vice the days of flying 'manual' passes. Not *entirely* automatic, but night-and-day difference from the days of old. Another name for PLM is *the dumbest acronym in the Navy inventory*: MAGIC CARPET (Maritime Augmented Guidance with Integrated Controls for Carrier Approach and Recovery Precision Enabling Technologies).

POM (*Pom*)—Pre/Post Overseas Movement. Usually used in terms of 'POM Leave,' this is typically a 2-to-3-week chunk of time off, granted before or after deployment.

POTS Line (*Pots Line*)—Plain Old Telephone Service. Remember when I said MAGIC CARPET was the dumbest acronym in the Navy? Holy shit. But anyway, the POTS line is the line that dials on and off the ship, with an annoying 1-to-2-second delay during the entire phone call, and a high likelihood of call-drop.

PSA—Politically-Sensitive Area. Don't fly into/over these... If you have a savvy JMPS O, your TAMMAC will contain nice little red lines that make it clear that these boundaries shall *not* be crossed.

PT—Physical Training. The Navy's super-moto way of saying 'exercise.' And on the same note, PRT = Physical Readiness Test; a standard and evolution the Navy has probably completely scrapped by the time you're reading this.

P-way—A nautical term for 'passageway' or 'hallway.'

PXO—Prospective Executive Officer. The Executive Officer soon to be the XO of the squadron, once the current XO becomes the CO, and the CO rotates out.

QNAP (*CUE-nap*)—A storage device with a ton of digital space; relied upon *so* heavily that to lose it could be severely detrimental...

RADALT (*RAD-alt*)—Radar Altimeter. The radar below your jet that senses how high you are off the ground via actual return waves, not the setting you dialed in your barometric altimeter. Typically, when the RADALT "goes off" (beeps incessantly), it means you are crossing below whatever critical altitude you typed in. I know it's trying to save your life and all, but man — it's really annoying.

Radio Jargon — PRI is Primary radio, AUX is Auxiliary Radio, both monitored simultaneously. Typically, calls within a section or division go on AUX radio (called TAC when used for that purpose), while calls to ATC agencies or the boat go on PRI radio. Voice Alpha (also called J Voice Alpha, JVA, VA, etc.) is another radio monitored on a separate frequency — for instance, Voice Alpha 95 — for intrasection/division tactical comms).

RAG (*Rag*) — Replacement Air Group. The portion of flight school where you learn the plane you'll be flying in the fleet, so that you can 'replace' the bodies dying to get a break for a shore tour. Also known as 'FRS' — Fleet Replacement Squadron. For F/A-18s, the RAGs are located in Virginia Beach, VA (VFA-106) and Lemoore, CA (VFA-122).

RAM (*Ram*) — Random-Access Memory. Nerdy programming term; has something to do with internal storage, short-term memory, processing, and... yeah, I'm already in over my head.

RAS (*Razz*) — Replenishment at Sea. Any time a ship takes inventory resupply, including food, mail, and plane parts. For fuel specific, that would be a 'FAS' — Fueling at Sea. More of a helicopter-centric day. What does it mean for us? No jets fly, the hangar bay is closed, and we typically expect better food at ensuing meals — and are often left disappointed.

Recce (*RECK-ee*) — Recognize/Identify. Said enough in the book to warrant glossary entry.

Red Air — The notional 'bad guys' of the flight. On a whiteboard, designated with (what else) red arrows.

RFI — Request for Further Information. A very fancy way of saying 'question.'

RMM — Recording Memory... uhh... Module? Couldn't tell you. We just call them RMMs, and they record everything in the flight. They are our 'tapes' that we review in the debrief.

RNC — Release and Control. Yes, it's an 'N,' but supposed to be an 'and' in the spell-out. Yes, it's a critical inspection that the jet requires before it can go flying. Yes, it's a 'downer' if it's not complete. And yes, that is all I'll pretend to know about it.

RNG — Random Number Generator. Big-time nerd term; the acronym for randomly occurring instances in a videogame based on an algorithm, vice a fixed outcome every time you replay the same portion. For instance, the random item an enemy drops, from an assortment of choices, based on probability progr — wait a second... why the hell am I going this in-depth?

Roll 'Em — Every day aboard the ship during deployment, the SDO's greatest responsibility is picking a movie to play for the ready room that will end right around the end of the work night (i.e., midrats). The timing of the start/finish, availability of popcorn throughout, and overall quality of this movie are top priorities for the SDO—and no, I'm *not* kidding...

And, in a time-honored naval aviation tradition, many squadrons have a game incorporating a list of 'points' to be called out for various things that occur in the roll 'em (American muscle, live human on fire, defenestration, excessive shooting without reloading, etc.) and also 'minus points' (Man crying, douchey hat, etc.).

ROM—Range of Motion. Compromising this means compromising your gains.

ROT—Rule of Thumb. Compromising this means compromising your mission (slightly less detrimental than the above listed).

S-5—The division in the boat in charge of staterooms and living conditions; potentially laundry as well? I honestly don't know—and it is beyond both the scope of this book and my attention span. Just understand that the boat has S-1 through S-whatever, and they all seem to enjoy deflecting responsibilities to one another. But to be even *further* honest... a lot of my disdain probably comes from the lack of understanding of their job, I'm probably highlighting my ignorance by making the aforementioned statement, and they probably feel the same about aviators. Such is life on the boat...

SA—Situational Awareness. A term the Navy absolutely *loves*—a very sophisticated way of explaining the state of being aware of your surroundings and the situat—ahh... ok. I get it.

SA Page—The moving map display in flight (when loaded with TAMMAC) that is your navigational resource. Definitely the page you're staring at the majority of the time in the admin phases of flight, as it contains where you are, where you're going, and what airspace you're flying around. (Contains V:NAV, V:GND, and V:AIR mode, with subtle differences for those mission sets).

SAPDART (*SAP-dart*)—An acronym aviators use to set up weapons correctly. The steps aren't important; just the fact that it exists (and yet often still gets gooned up...)

SDO—Squadron Duty Officer. The main duty stood in naval aviation. Encompasses sitting at a desk all day, "managing the flight schedule"—but really more of fielding phone calls, making coffee, and entertaining the ready room. A glorified secretary under the guise of 'the direct representative of the squadron skipper.' Can be temporarily replaced by an ODO (Operations Duty Officer—code for interim SDO).

SEAD (*Seed*)—Suppression of Enemy Air Defenses. Hands down, the most boring mission we do... in my humble opinion). This is the *Growler's* (EA-18G) bread and butter, as much of it utilizes electronic attack and airborne electron waves in order to jam the enemy's radars and comms (at least that's my rudimentary and likely incorrect understanding of it; I'm already feeling my T levels drop just writing about it).

Section — A two-ship of aircraft flying together: Lead and wing (-2).

SEM — Section-Engaged Maneuvering. Think 'BFM' but with more fighters than just 1-on-1. Commonly thought of as 'the most fun training we do'; dogfighting as a team.

SFARP (*ESS-farp*) — Strike Fighter Advanced Readiness Program. A 'workup' to prepare for deployment, with highly tactical flights and long briefs/debriefs. Workups, in general, are far more difficult and stressful than deployment (by design) — just much shorter bursts of pain. Other evolutions of workups include TSTA, Air Wing Fallon (AWF), and COMPTUEX.

SFWSL (*SWIZZ-el*) — Strike Fighter Weapons School Atlantic. The TOPGUN-grad representative branch on the East Coast in Virginia Beach, VA. One of the options post-TOPGUN is for SFTIs to go here and assist in training the East Coast squadrons as the tactics 'experts' of the coast.

SFWSP (*SWISS-pee*) — Strike Fighter Weapons School Pacific. See above, except for the West Coast in Lemoore, CA.

SFWT (*SWIFT-y*) — Strike Fighter Weapons Tactics. The SFWT syllabus is the big one that every JO must go through in order to get their section and division lead qualifications. SFWT can be the bane of every JO's existence, especially 'Level 3 SFWT,' but also where the majority of the learning of the craft occurs.

SHARP (*Sharp*) — Shit Hot Aviation Readiness Program. The software we use to log flights, track hours, and maintain readiness. Yes, that's actually the program's name. No, it's not good. But also, no, it's not even *close* to some of the worst software encountered in the Navy.

SHPI (*SHIP-py*) — Seeker Head Position Indicator. An elaborate way of describing 'what my missile says it's looking at.'

SITREP (*SIT-rep*) — Situation Report. Exactly what it sounds like; a commonly used and classic militaristic term for 'Here's what's happening.' Quiz time: A SITREP given whilst in-flight is called an 'INFLTREP' — care to take a wild guess at that acronym?

SME (*Smee*) — Subject Matter Expert. A mil-speak way of saying 'expert'; typically assigned to somebody to be the squadron or fleet representative (the SME of a specific weapon, system, tactic, etc.) for people to contact if they have questions on the topic.

Sniv/Snivel — Request to be unscheduled for a specific time for whatever reason (medical appointment, kid's recital, single-dude ops, etc.).

SNOOPIE (*Snoopy*) — Ship's Nautical Or Otherwise Photographic Interpretation and Examination. The team charged with the responsibility of investigating and recording any vessels that come within some distance of the ship, and by far one of the Navy's most forced acronyms. A total boat thing; no air wing involvement. I've honestly learned more about them while writing this short glossary snippet than I ever knew before—and I hope the learning ends here.

SOP—Standard Operating Procedures. When something is 'SOP,' it is put out throughout the fleet as the standardized (and thus *only acceptable*) way of doing so, with deviations only as necessary for unique situations. However, squadrons and air wings can have more restrictive SOPs for their own units.

Can also be referred to as 'STAN.' I.e., a 'Bingo Bug STAN' is the officially designated way that aviators should manipulate their fuel-monitoring setting to make sure they are properly tracking it at specific numbers/quantities of fuel. And yet ironically, the east and west coast RAGs *do* teach different techniques to this 'STAN'—making it a beautifully quintessential example of how the Navy does things.

Tactical SOP/STAN items are decided upon and figured out by a panel of experts (typically Patch wearers) at STAN Cell meetings.

SPINS (*Spins*)—Special Instructions. Think of these as the scope of war for that given time: who we are, what we're up against, applicable ROE (Rules of Engagement), etc.

Squawking—Transmitting your transponder; in regular people speak, having your 'this is me, my location, and my altitude' machine turned 'on' for ATC to see on their radars.

STBR (*STIB-er*)—Secure Tactical Briefing Room. A room where aviators go to study, brief, watch tapes, and debrief in privacy at the proper classification levels. Often with music playing to drown out outer sound—the single source of CD sales left in the world (as no phones are allowed inside). This can also be referred to as 'The Vault.'

SWO (*Swoh*)—Surface Warfare Officer. Officers known for doing most of their work at sea, standing ridiculous amounts of watch, and, in general, hating life—but hey, that's just a pilot's perspective—maybe the boat gets fun when you're doing everything on four hours of sleep.

T&R—Training and Readiness. 'Tasks' logged post-flight in SHARP to document working on them in the aforementioned flight. Very hingey priority—every OPSO's dream is a squadron logging lots of varied T&R tasks. Typically tracked across the MOAT (Mother of All Trackers). Also: DRRS (Defense Readiness Reporting System). Also: Hard pass, to *all* of this.

Tac-Admin—The portion of the flight between admin and conduct. Sometimes described as parts of the fight required for actual tactical execution; sometimes described as portions of conduct constrained by admin factors; sometimes described as factors that would never actually be present in IRL war—very ambiguous and hardly clear-cut. Think of 'an airliner cruising through the simulated battle airspace' as a 'tac-admin factor.'

TACAN (*TACK-an*) — Tactical Air Navigation. (Also abbreviated as 'TCN'). A military navigational aid used for traversing the skies. Every boat has one, and it's what we use to fly back home to mom. DME = distance from the TACAN.

TAMMAC (*TAM-ack*) — Tactical Aircraft Moving Map Capability. A literal map that displays on your screen and moves as your aircraft flies around. Shows airspace boundaries, too, and is honestly very useful — to the point where it becomes a crutch and terrifying if you *don't* have it loaded in the jet. Uploaded in JMPS, and updated by installing the latest DAFIF (Digital Aeronautical Flight Information File) — and to be honest, that might not be exactly correct... but hey, I was never a JMPS O (thank god).

Tanker — Gas-giving F/A-18 configuration and one of my favorite possible flights. Pure administrative bliss. Comes in MTNK (Mission tanker), PTNK (Primary), and STNK (Secondary) varieties.

TAO — Tactical Action Officer. The guy who makes announcements over the 1MC about launching the alert, away-ing the SNOOPIE team, setting EMCON, etc... yeah, I have no clue what this guy does all day, but it seems miserably boring. It's typically a former pilot on their non-flying sea tour, looking to get out ASAP afterward.

"Tapes On, Fight's On" — The beginning of the official conduct portion of a sortie (flight). It is a reminder for everyone to start recording their screens, because the fight's kicked off. Goes all the way until the 'Knock it off.'

TCTS — Tactical Combat Training System. A played-back god's eye view, where you watch airplane icons recapture the flight that just happened. Used for 'kill-removal' debriefs, where everyone involved watches the replayed fight, complete with shot calls and deaths announced, cross-referenced with 'logical conclusions.' *This*, ladies and gents, is where we find the crux of our LARPing.

TDY — Temporary duty. For a sailor on the boat... it sucks. Imagine you sign up for a job... and then the boat tells you that instead of working on jet engines — like you've been studying/training for — you get to serve food for 3 months. (ALSO: TAD = Temporary Assigned Duty; same thing).

The Boat — Any aircraft carrier. Also referred to as 'the ship.' Contrasted by 'the beach,' or the place you would land a jet *other* than the carrier; most commonly your home base.

The Patch — The red shoulder Patch worn by TOPGUN grads, earned by graduating from The Course. They wear this Patch for the rest of their time in the Navy, regardless of what squadron they go to. And yes, take it from The Patch wearer (another term for TOPGUN grad) who helped me edit this book — this specific Patch is always capitalized, as is the preceding 'The.'

TOPGUN (*Top gun*) — The heralded cream-of-the-crop weapons school in US Navy fighter aviation, where pilots and WSOs go to earn 'The Patch' — a symbol of graduation and tac-air excellence — and then serve as the tactical experts in the fleet (as SFTIs; or Strike Fighter Tactics Instructors), and are largely in charge of training the rest of aviators with the lessons learned at TOPGUN. Commonly referred to as 'The Weapons School,' 'The Course,' or 'The Crystal Palace.'

Top Gun (*Top Gun*) — The infamous movie. Notice the space, lowercase letters, and italics? Don't you dare confuse the terms when writing a letter to a TOPGUN grad about your favorite scene from *Top Gun*.

TOT — Time on Target. Fancy tactical of saying 'What time the bomb hit.'

Training O — Training Officer. In a squadron, the recent TOPGUN graduate in charge of the SFWT syllabus and tactical advancement of the other pilots. Typically a senior O-3 or junior O-4 (but not quite a hinge yet).

Tri-walls — Big cardboard boxes the Navy uses to transport goods and equipment to/from the boat/DET. Contrary to popular belief, they *do* have four walls, each three layers thick. And apparently, they cost a few hundred dollars apiece — yes, for a cardboard box...

UFCD — Up-Front Control Display. A touch-screen (kind of) that you use to type frequencies, headings, and other numbers/settings into the jet.

USS Ship — Generic name for a carrier IRL — also, the primary defended asset in *Saving Nickels*.

VFA — Fighter Attack Squadron. Yes, again, with the 'V'...

VisCAP — Visual Combar Air Patrol. Cronies trolling around, guarding some asset and/or attempting to sneak up and kill you.

VSI — Vertical Speed Indicator. How many feet per minute you're traveling upward or downward. Pretty basic aviation term, but included enough in the book to warrant mention here.

VT — Training squadron for fixed-wing aircraft. 'Flight school' as we know it, prior to the RAG, and where you earn your Wings of Gold.

"WASP, JWS, and Route Construction" — Don't worry about the definition of this one random Robo-Hinge reference. Just trust me when I say all this stuff sucks and is a huge, painful, overly time-consuming pain in the ass to do.

WEZ (*Wez*) — See: LAR.

White Card — A term used to scrap a requirement from the record. A mission that requires four jets for success, yet only has three available? White card the fourth jet. A carrier needs to hit certain metrics to achieve open ocean, blue-water operations — yet fails the exam? White card the evolution. A guy goes to the gym intending to do some *real* work, yet freezes up as soon as he realizes what day it is? White card the squats.

WSO (*WIZ-o*) — Weapons Systems Operator... or is it Weapons Systems *Officer?* I don't know. I could look it up, sure. But that's alright. You know who they are, and you love 'em — the backseaters in the F/A-18. Growlers have the same thing, but called EWOs — which I will *also* not be looking up.

WYFMIFM (*WHIFF-im-IF-im;* or *WHIFF-im*) — Included for the confusion of name pronunciation. Mostly referred to as the second, shorter pronunciation, yet still spelled fully as WYFMIFM. As to what it stands for... I'll leave that to your imagination and deduction...

Yellow shirt — the taxi directors aboard the ship who guide your plane on the flight deck. They literally wear yellow, long-sleeved jerseys to differentiate themselves from brown shirts (PCs), blue shirts (tractor drivers), purple shirts (fuelers), etc.

Made in the USA
Columbia, SC
16 November 2024

46717862R00317